REAGAN

Other Books by Lou Cannon

Ronnie and Jesse: A Political Odyssey

The McCloskey Challenge

Reporting: An Inside View

REAGAN

LOU CANNON

A PERIGEE BOOK

Perigee Books
are published by
The Putnam Publishing Group
200 Madison Avenue
New York, New York 10016

The author gratefully acknowledges permission from Hawthorn Properties (Elsevier-Dutton Publishing Co., Inc.) for selections from *Where's the Rest of Me?* by Ronald Reagan and Richard G. Hubler, copyright © 1965 by Ronald Reagan and Richard G. Hubler.

Library of Congress Cataloging in Publication Data

Cannon, Lou.
  Reagan.

  Reprint. Originally published: New York : Putnam, c1982.
  Bibliography: p.
  Includes index.
  1. Reagan, Ronald.   2. Presidents—United States—Biography.   3. California—Governors—Biography.   I. Title.
E877.C36   1984   973.927′092′4   [B]   84-7628
ISBN 0-399-12756-9
ISBN 0-399-51077-X (pbk.)

First Perigee printing, 1984

Printed in the United States of America

1 2 3 4 5 6 7 8 9 10

Dedication

For my friends
   and colleagues
at the *Washington Post,*
And for
   Jim and Sarah Brady

Contents

Acknowledgments

All biographies are in large measure dependent on the assistance, kindness and cooperation of others, and that is especially true about *Reagan.* Many people made this book possible. Foremost among them was Robin Gradison of the *Washington Post,* who started out checking some stray facts and became full-time researcher, assistant, interviewer, editor, critic and friend. She was present at the creation of many of these pages and worked steadfastly to improve all of them. Without her help, this book would not have come into existence.

Nor would it have been written without the time and encouragement provided by Benjamin Bradlee, the executive editor of the *Post.* Ben and my other editors—Bill Greider, Richard Harwood and Howard Simons—were patient and understanding when extra months were needed to complete the biography, and I thank them.

Two present colleagues, David S. Broder and Joel Garreau, and a former one, Al Eisele, read every chapter and offered guidance that was both considerate and critical. These three friends and accomplished authors share in the book's felicities; they bear no responsibility for its shortcomings. Other *Post* colleagues made valuable contributions. John M. Berry contributed his considerable expertise to the economics chapter and read the manuscript of that chapter. Historian Allen Weinstein, editor of the *Washington Quarterly,* and formerly of the *Post's* editorial staff, read and improved the chapter dealing with Reagan's involvement with the anti-Communist investigations of Hollywood. Katharine Macdonald of the *Post's* bureau in Los Angeles assisted in many ways. She compiled my own files during the 1980 campaign, read several early chapters of the book, obtained photographs of Reagan's Hollywood and Sacramento days and researched the correspondence between Reagan and Jack Warner. Lee Lescaze, my colleague in covering the Reagan White House during 1981, kept me well informed while I was writing and was consistently encouraging.

President Reagan, whom I have interviewed more than a score of times since 1965, gave a responsive interview specifically for this biography. Members of his White House staff were helpful and informative, especially Michael K. Deaver, William P. Clark, Edwin Meese III and James A. Baker III. Clark, who was Governor Reagan's executive secretary in California and is his national security adviser now, was kind enough to make available to me the minutes of Reagan's cabinet meetings during the first years of the governorship. Meese provided access to his private papers on the California welfare reform bill, which are stored in the Reagan collection at the Hoover Institution on War, Revolution and Peace at Stanford University. Molly Sturges Tuthill, of the Hoover Institution, provided timely and well-informed assistance on this legislation and other matters. George F. Will made some useful suggestions and caught some mistakes.

Two chapters dealing with Reagan's 1966 campaign and with his first year in the California governorship stand on the shoulders of my 1969 book, *Ronnie and Jesse: A Political Odyssey*. My wife, Virginia Cannon, splendidly researched that book. My friend Jud Clark, now of California Research Associates in Sacramento, read every page of that work, performing a service that many shared for *Reagan*.

Bill Roberts, the California campaign consultant who managed Reagan's first campaign in 1966, was interviewed extensively by me in 1968 for *Ronnie and Jesse*. I have drawn upon these interviews in the California campaign chapter. His partner at the time, Stuart Spencer, became the guiding light of the Reagan presidential campaign in 1980. Interviews with Spencer, speechwriter Kenneth Khachigian, pollster Richard B. Wirthlin and James S. Brady, one of the persons to whom this book is dedicated, were particularly useful in reconstructing the 1980 general election campaign.

The account of Reagan's governorship in California owes much to many people, especially Bill Hauck of California Research Associates, former Assembly Speaker Bob Moretti, and George Steffes, who served as legislative liaison for Governor Reagan.

Thomas Kizzia, a free-lance writer with a background in environmental reporting, did most of the reporting and interviewing for the Interior Department section of "The Westerners" chapter. He produced enough good material to write a book of his own, and he also reviewed the chapter. The conclusions and form of the presentation are my own, and I take full responsibility for the information. Secretary of Interior James G. Watt was helpful and cooperative, as were a number of his principal critics.

Myron (Mike) Waldman of *Newsday,* whose examination of Reagan's roots during the 1980 campaign was the most exhaustive and detailed of any reporter's, made his files and interviews available. Nearly all of the interviews on Reagan's Des Moines days were conducted either by Waldman or by Robin Gradison.

Martin Salditch, who covered Reagan in Sacramento for the *Riverside*

Press-Enterprise while I was doing the same for the *San Jose Mercury News,* kindly turned over to me his copious file of the Reagan years in Sacramento. They were used extensively.

David Hoffman, now a reporter for the *Washington Post,* kept a day-by-day record of the 1980 Reagan presidential campaign, which he capably covered Knight-Ridder newspapers. I am thankful for use of his files and for suggestions which improved the final version of the chapter on this campaign.

Michele Davis typed this manuscript, transcribed the majority of the interviews and remained consistently cheerful from beginning to end. Of how many people can that be said?

The staffs of various private institutions helped on large points and small. Special thanks to the national, library, financial and photo staffs of the *Washington Post,* to the staffs of the motion pictures room and the loan division of the Library of Congress, to the staff of the *Los Angeles Times* Washington bureau, to the press office and photo office of the White House. Joseph Walega and the staff of Copy World generously duplicated copies of the manuscript.

I also appreciate the assistance of Cecil Andrus, Ellen Ash, Lee Atwater, Eric Barnau, Doug Baldwin, Phil Battaglia, Peter Behr, Deidra Berger, John Berthlesen, Jeanne Burington, Malcolm Byrne, Richard Cheney, Marlene Cimons, Donna Crouch, Ed Dale, Richard Darman, William Dickinson, Fred Dutton, Michael Evans, Judy Cannon Fitzgerald, Les Francis, Mrs. B. J. Frazer, Alex Gallup, David Gergen, Connie Gerrard, David Gerson, James Gerstenzang, Michael Getler, Vera Glaser, Barry Goldwater, Bill Gradison, Robin Gray, H. R. Gross, Peter Hannaford, Suzanne Hanney, Mark Harroff, Celeste Heritage, Jackie Hill, Kim Hoggard, Annie Hughes, E. Pendleton James, Jeane Kirkpatrick, Denison Kitchel, Cheryl Klein, Jim Lake, Ed Langley, Lois Lanham, Laurence Laurent, Paul Laxalt, Frank Levy, Mildred Lilly, Norman Livermore, Bob Markin, Guy Martin, Charles McDowell, Sally McElroy, Ralph McKinzie, Peter Milius, Robert Monagan, Shirley Moore, Lyn Nofziger, Pat O'Brien, James Perry, William Perry, Bill Plante, Diane Powers, Olwen Price, David Prosperi, Florence Randolph, Gary Raymond, Maureen Reagan, Neil Reagan, Tom Reed, T. R. Reid, Nancy Reynolds, Wilson Riles, Harold Rissler, John Roberts, Maralee Schwartz, Doug Scott, Joe Scott, Robert Shogan, Susanna Shuster, Nancy Skelton, William French Smith, Larry Speakes, Potter Stewart, David Stockman, Betsy Strong, Flo Taussig, Peter Teeley, Robert Teeter, Valarie Thomas, Robert Toth, Charles Townes, Margaret Tutwiler, Morris Udall, John Walker, Jude Wanniski, Mark Weinberg, Caspar Weinberger, Myrtle Moon Williams, Jeanne Winnick, Lucila Woodard, and Bernard Witkin. I also wish to thank several persons whose names do not appear on this list because of the sensitivity of their positions. Their anonymity does not lessen my gratitude for their assistance.

And finally, my special thanks to two persons who made this entire project a reality—my agent Richard Kahlenberg and my editor at Putnam's, Diane Reverand. I appreciate their confidence and support.

Lou Cannon
January 21, 1982

Foreword

On October 27, 1964, a washed-up fifty-three-year-old movie actor named Ronald Reagan made a speech on national television on behalf of a Republican presidential candidate who had no chance to be elected. Nearly everyone in the country knew that on the following Tuesday Lyndon Johnson would defeat Barry Goldwater and earn in his own right the presidency he had inherited by assassination the previous November. Reagan knew his speech had no chance to change the outcome, and an examination of his text would not have altered any expectations. Most of Reagan's address was standard, antigovernment boilerplate larded with emotional denunciations of communism and a celebration of individual freedom. His statistics were sweeping and in some cases dubious. His best lines were cribbed from Franklin Roosevelt, and he quoted from nearly everybody else as well— Plutarch, Alexander Hamilton, James Madison, Sumner Schlicter, Karl Marx, Joseph Clark, Harry Byrd, John Ramsey McCulloch and Howard K. Smith, to name a few. Goldwater's closest advisers were opposed to the speech. The audience, as Reagan remembers it, was over-conscious of being on television and was at first unresponsive.

But this last-ditch oratorical effort turned out to be the one big hit of the Goldwater campaign. It brought in $1 million for Republican candidates, more money than had been raised by any political speech up to that time. Washington columnist David S. Broder called it "the most successful political debut since William Jennings Bryan electrified the 1896 Democratic convention with his 'Cross of Gold' speech." In a half hour of national television, Ronald Reagan had transformed himself from a fading celebrity into the nation's most important conservative politician. With the wisdom of historical hindsight, we now see that special half hour as both the culmination of a long political evolution and the beginning of a remarkable career which has done much to transform the nature of American government.

Like the U.S. cavalry he so much admired, Reagan had arrived on the scene at precisely the right moment. Millions of Americans in 1964 already

shared with Goldwater a conviction that something was out of kilter with
the American dream. They were middle class Americans, mostly, and they
were frustrated by the signs of decline in the automatic progress which they
had taken for granted since the end of World War II. And there were dis-
turbing little signs on the horizon that the time of troubles was just beginning. The Vietnam War, from an American point of view, was in its infancy.
(Within a year, conservatives would say, with gallows humor: "They said if I
voted for Goldwater we'd wind up in a war, and I voted for Goldwater and
we did.") The student demonstrations which would become a springboard
for Reagan's political career lay ahead. Watergate was far in the future,
along with the energy crisis, the gold boom and double-digit inflation. But
the omens of national frustration were already present.

Goldwater had appealed to this frustration with the directness of an Old
Testament prophet and the integrity of a frontier banker who finds the town
is living beyond its means. Unfortunately for Goldwater and the movement
he represented, his lip-shooting frightened ordinary Americans and diverted
attention from the message to the messenger. He had expended his best energies in waging a holy war to win control of the Republican Party, and most
of the people around him lacked either the inclination or the skill to put together the political party they had just torn apart. Even if Goldwater and his
strategists had possessed these qualities, it is unlikely that the electorate
would have turned out the Democratic successor to a martyred President
while memories of the assassination—and of the slain President—remained
so fresh.

Reagan, speaking to the future of America with a vision of the past, gave
hope of things to come. To those who shared the gospel of a better life with
less government, he offered the promise of Goldwaterism without Goldwater. But even those who did not share this vision were apt to be stirred by
Reagan. He spoke in the language of past American leaders, and he spoke to
all Americans. His metaphors were derived from the New Deal or from
those days of World War II when the struggle between freedom and slavery
seemed anything but an abstraction. Like the great wartime speakers, Reagan offered tangible reassurance along with his dire warnings. Even when
making a stump speech, he was not a shouter. Rather, he came into a family's living room, on television, like the nice neighbor next door who was
armed with simple and plausible answers to great and complex questions.

A few members of the conservative political community saw that Reagan was their coming superstar, really the first successful television communicator of conservative political concerns. But many of Reagan's future
followers just liked to hear him talk. They were attracted by Reagan's patriotism, resolute anticommunism and enormous idealism. Pointing out that
this idealism was matched with a monumental naiveté, as Reagan's critics
did, only made him seem the more sincere. He spoke, as Alistair Cooke
would observe about his presidential speeches, in "gutsy, simple, well-

cadenced sentences" which effectively conveyed his meaning. From beginning to end, Reagan had a vision of America, a vision that is with him still
and which has affected all of us.

This is a book about the man and his vision. It is a book intended to be
something more than "the first rough draft of history," as Philip Graham
once defined journalism, and something less than the last word on a subject
who is more complex and enigmatic than he appears. As a journalist I have
been covering Ronald Reagan ever since his first campaign for governor of
California in 1966. I viewed him at close hand in the early years of his governorship—1967 through 1969—and returned from the Washington bureau
of Ridder Publications (now Knight-Ridder) to report on his 1970 reelection
campaign. I also covered what might best be described as his two and one-
half presidential campaigns—his abortive and belated effort in 1968, his
near run against Gerald Ford in 1976 and his successful campaign against
all Republican comers and Jimmy Carter in 1980. I report on him still, in
my capacity as White House correspondent for the *Washington Post*. And I
find that after all these years and many interviews Reagan has yet to be fully
defined by either his advocates or his opponents.

The unwritten strictures of truth in journalistic advertising require me to
state publicly what my friends already know—that I like and respect Ronald
Reagan while remaining skeptical that his actions will achieve the results he
intends. When he became President, I was uncertain about his ability to deal
with foreign policy, sympathetic to his basic domestic goals and skeptical
about whether his economic theories would translate easily into practice.
Readers of my earlier book (*Ronnie and Jesse: A Political Odyssey*), which
centered on California politics, know that I had mixed views about Reagan's
record as governor. In general, I found that he started ineptly but soon
evolved into a competent governor who was willing to sacrifice ideology for
political achievement.

All of the foregoing and everything in this book except this paragraph, the
postscript to "The Delegated Presidency" chapter and the epilogue were
written during the first year of the Reagan presidency. In the intervening
years Reagan has won victories in the Congress, suffered some foreign policy
reversals, watched the nation emerge from a long recession, and decided to
seek a second term. Any judgment of his presidency must of necessity await
the outcome of the election and, if Reagan wins, the results of what promises
to be a difficult congressional session in 1985. Can he sustain economic recovery and begin to address the structural deficit? Will he use the military budget
increases he sought and obtained as leverage for a strategic nuclear arms
agreement with the Soviets? Will his energy flag during a second term in
which he would be nearly 78 years old at its completion? As Reagan might
have put it in his announcing days, stay tuned.

Lou Cannon
Oakton, Virginia, April 15, 1984

1

The Worlds of Ronald Reagan

H E kept waiting for the excitement to come to him, that special excitement that told him he was about to become the fortieth President of the United States. The vast powers and the life-and-death responsibilities of the presidency were soon to pass into his hands, but Ronald Wilson Reagan could not summon up the feelings he had assumed would come to him naturally that day. Embarking on his great adventure, he was the same person he had been all his life. When trusted aide Michael K. Deaver had roused him in Blair House that morning to dress for the inauguration, Reagan had not even wanted to get out of bed. "It's time to get up, Governor," Deaver had said. "Why do I have to get up?" said Reagan, not opening his eyes.[1] Both men laughed. It was the way they talked to each other, and the way Reagan talked to those who were close to him, in running one-liners. Still, Reagan would acknowledge later, there was "a sense of unreality" that he felt no differently on this particular morning. It was a special time for the United States of America, as well as for Reagan. While Reagan slept, President Carter had spent a sleepless night at the White House, in a final effort to secure release of the 52 Americans held hostage for 444 days in Iran. The task would become Reagan's if the hostages were not freed, but the President-elect had not lost sleep worrying about it. He was not one to borrow trouble before it faced him. And on this morning, the report from Deaver was that the hostages would indeed be coming home even as Reagan was inaugurated. The weather report was good, too. A warm front had moved in from the South, raising the temperature by twenty degrees and bringing a fine, false spring day in the midst of an icy Washington winter. Everything was falling into place, and still there was no special feeling. Reagan had talked to his wife Nancy about this, as he always talked to her about what was most important to him. "Both of us kept thinking there was going to come a moment when all of a sudden it hits us, but things kept happening and there you were making a speech, and the crowd, and you still did not have that thing that you thought would happen, that moment of awesomeness," Reagan said.[2]

17

Perhaps this was the old performer talking, the professional actor who holds himself in check lest he give way to his emotions at the wrong moment and appear too sentimental or theatrical. And perhaps Reagan had already expended more emotion than he knew. Both of the Reagans had fought back the tears the Saturday night before, when the Mormon Tabernacle Choir sang "God Bless America" and "The Battle Hymn of the Republic" at the inaugural opening ceremonies. As fireworks streaked the sky against the gleaming marble backdrop of the Lincoln Memorial, a crowd of 15,000 cheered their President-to-be and chanted, "We Love Ronnie." Reagan did not speak, but he stepped forward to the front of a huge blue-and-white podium built in the shape of an eagle to acknowledge the cheers. The next day at Blair House, meeting with speech-writer Ken Khachigian to put the finishing touches on his inaugural speech, Reagan discussed his emotions of the moment. Khachigian, all business about the speech, thought that Reagan displayed "a sensitivity and tenderness" he had rarely seen in any man.[3]

"Ken, did you have a chance to get to that ceremony at the Lincoln Memorial last night?" Reagan asked.

"No, sir, I was at the office," Khachigian said.

"I don't think I've been to anything quite like it," Reagan said. "That Lincoln Memorial, and in those columns . . . it's such a beautiful place. I've never been filled with such a surge of patriotism. It was so hard not to cry during the whole thing. That choir, the Mormon Tabernacle Choir, singing 'God Bless America.' Well, it was cold, but it was so moving, I was crying frozen tears."

And as Reagan told Khachigian this story, his eyes filled up again with tears and he looked at his speech-writer and said, "It's going to be hard to keep my eyes dry."[4]

His heroes had always been heroes.

"I'm a sucker for hero worship," Reagan wrote in 1977, listing the books which had made a deep impression on his life as a young man.[5] His heroes were soldiers, Presidents, athletes and achievers who started with nothing and became captains of industry or public servants. Born three years before the Great War, as Americans then knew World War I, Reagan grew up in an Illinois town where the arch on Main Street celebrated the deeds of those who had fought and died in Europe for what he was taught had been the cause of lasting peace. That arch touched older memories in a state which had given so much of its human treasure to preserve the Union. The Civil War was a living memory in Illinois when Ronald Reagan was a boy. Veterans of the Grand Army of the Republic survived in every town and hamlet. As a young child, Reagan fought hours of solitary battles with lead Civil War soldiers, shutting out the outside world while his brother played games with other boys. Heroes, dead and alive, were all around him.

Despite these martial heroes, or perhaps because of them, the United States of America to which Reagan was born in 1911 was more peaceful and protected than the nation he was to become President of seventy years later. It was not a safer land. The homicide rate was less than a third of what it is today, but infant mortality was thirty times higher. Diseases such as diphtheria, whooping cough, strep throat and measles frequently were fatal. Reagan's mother nearly died of influenza when he was seven years old. But the disasters and the diseases and the myriad human tragedies seemed part of a natural order that was at once accepted and comprehensible. It was a world which men were to look back at with sentiment and a sense of loss, the kind of world that George Orwell's middle class heroes inhabited in England before the Great War. "It isn't that life was softer then than now," recalls one of these heroes. "Actually, it was harsher. People on the whole worked harder, lived less comfortably and died more painfully. . . . You saw ghastly things happening sometimes. . . . And yet what was it that people had in those days? A feeling of security, even when they weren't secure. More exactly, it was a feeling of continuity."[6]

Reagan belonged to such a world. It was a world of heroes and a world of continuity and a world in which an American boy, if not an English one, could think that he could grow up to be whatever he wanted. Reagan wanted to tell stories and to draw. One of his favorite books was a now forgotten novel called *That Printer of Udell's* by Harold Bell Wright, with a hero modeled after those in the success stories of Horatio Alger. The hero, Dick Falkner, works by days as a printer and attends night school. He marries not the boss's daughter, as would a proper Alger hero, but a beautiful socialite whom he saves from a life of prostitution. Falkner blends Christian and business principles to uplift a midwestern town, caring more for the principles than he does for either the church or the business community. At the end, he is off to Congress. "All in all, as I look back I realize that my reading left an abiding belief in the triumph of good over evil," Reagan wrote about books like these when he was sixty-six years old. "There were heroes who lived by standards of morality and fair play."[7]

He lived in a world defined by such stories, a make-believe world in which heroic deeds had the capacity to transform reality. His father had an Irish love of storytelling, favoring the tall tales and the ribald stories told in males-only company. His mother, whom Reagan much resembles in temperament, believed in the magic of the stage. Reagan united these perceptions. As a child he read Edgar Rice Burroughs, preferring to the popular Tarzan books the even more improbable exploits of Martian warlord John Carter. As a college athlete, he made up mythical football games which he broadcast to his friends through a broomstick microphone. As a parent, he invented for his children stories of previous lives. Maureen Reagan's favorite was her father's past life as a cold germ, enjoying himself by infecting everyone with coughs and sneezes. The germ's life comes to an end when he dives into a dish of green mold. In his next existence, he finds out that this event was part of the discovery of penicillin. It was, like so many stories Reagan would tell in public life, a mythic variation of a real event. In this case, Reagan's mother had been saved from the influenza by her doctor's prescription of a diet of green, moldy cheese.

The capital of Reagan's make-believe world became Hollywood. The stories which he loved so well possessed a special power on the screen. The myths which Hollywood promulgated as history became actual explanations of the past. When Reagan first ran for public office in 1966 and was asked what kind of governor he would be, he quipped, "I don't know, I've never played a governor." And in 1975, campaigning for President, Reagan gave a cinematic version of how segregation had ended in the armed services: "When the first bombs were dropped on Pearl Harbor, there was great segregation in the military forces. In World War II, this was corrected. It was corrected largely under the leadership of generals like MacArthur and Eisenhower. . . . One great story that I think of at the time, that reveals a change was occurring, was when the Japanese dropped the bomb on Pearl Harbor there was a Negro sailor whose total duties involved kitchen-type duties. . . . He cradled a machine gun in his arms, which is not an easy thing to do, and stood on the end of a pier blazing away at Japanese airplanes that were coming down and strafing him and that [segregation] was all changed." When a reporter pointed out that segregation in the armed services actually had ended when President Truman signed an executive order in 1948 three years after the war, Reagan stood his ground. "I remember the scene," Reagan told me on the campaign plane later. "It was very powerful."[8]

The heroic world of make-believe and the real world coalesced. The man who lived in both of them could not always distinguish one from the other, and he came to believe in many things that weren't true. He believed that budgets could be balanced, and taxes lowered, by the simple elimination of waste, fraud and abuse. With equal simplicity, he believed that the nuclear waste problem could be solved for all time by compressing the waste into particles the size of baseballs and dropping them into the ocean. He believed that the Shah of Iran had presided over "a progressive regime." He believed, and believes, that the United States is more popular abroad than it used to be. But he also believes, or understands, that men and women are moved by grand visions and by a sense of obligation and duty to their country. His text for inaugural day was heroism, and his example was of an Army private who had given his life in France during World War I. The example sounded too heroic, too make-believe to be true, but it was real. The soldier, Marvin Treptow, had been killed by artillery fire. He left behind a diary with the words "My Pledge" written on the flyleaf. Underneath he had written: "America must win the war. Therefore, I will work, I will save, I will sacrifice, I will endure, I will fight cheerfully and do my utmost, as if the issue of the whole struggle depended on me alone."

Across the street from Blair House, in the real world of the Oval Office, Jimmy Carter was doing his utmost to free the hostages during his last hours as President. Reagan aides had cooperated, joining the defeated President during the transition to send a single message to Iran which said, in effect, "Don't expect a better deal from Ronald Reagan." The negotiations had nonetheless dragged on, to the consternation both of Carter and the Reagan team. "The best thing that could happen to us would be to have the hostages free when we took office," Reagan's counsellor Edwin Meese had said privately three days before the inauguration. It almost happened. At one point during the long night before the inauguration the release seemed so assured that Carter and his aides drank a champagne toast to the captured Americans. But it was a premature celebration. By dawn, Carter had recognized that he would no longer be in office by the time the hostages left Iran.

At Blair House, Deaver awakened Reagan and told him of the delay. When Carter called soon afterward, at 8:31 A.M., Reagan asked the President if he would be willing to meet the freed Americans whenever they arrived in Germany. "He liked the idea," Reagan said, after the hostages were safely home, knowing that the gesture had proved useful to both of them and to their country. In the awkward ride with Carter to the Capitol for the inaugural ceremony, Reagan agreed he would say nothing about the hostages unless the planes bearing them to freedom had cleared Iranian airspace by the time of the inaugural address. Shortly before Reagan moved forward to the podium to take the oath of office from Chief Justice Warren Burger, he looked over at Carter. "Not yet," Carter said. Reagan nodded, and said nothing.

And then, just before noon on January 20, 1981, Ronald Reagan became President of the United States. Standing before the nation on the west front of the Capitol, Reagan could see before him a panoramic view of official Washington and its most celebrated memorials. To his left, beyond the haze of the Potomac, rose the Jefferson Memorial and the hills of Arlington Cemetery. Before him, across the mall and the reflecting pool, stretched the spired elegance of the Washington Monument and, far beyond, the Lincoln Memorial. It was a mighty moment in history for this man who had come so far and lived so long, and yet he still did not feel that excitement he had expected to come over him. And then, this new President, who had given so many speeches and knew so well in his heart what he wanted to say, was speaking anyway, and he did not need the magic. Now he was the practiced, evocative performer, doing what he does best as he invited the thousands clustered on the grounds below and the millions watching on television to share his vision of America. "Standing here, we face a magnificent vista, opening up this city's special beauty and history," Reagan said. "At the end of this open mall are those shrines to the giants on whose shoulders we stand." To Reagan, these giants were an inspiration and a reminder that every American could be a hero. "Let us renew our determination, our courage and our strength," he said. "And let us renew our faith and hope. We have every right to dream heroic dreams."

2

The Optimist

THE obligatory mythology for modern Republican Presidents requires that they be of humble origin, preferably born in a small town, and that they share a vision of an America redeemed by the values of hard work and upward striving. Ronald Wilson Reagan qualifies. Throughout his adult life he has celebrated his midwestern boyhood, relishing sentimental journeys with old friends from Illinois and Iowa and undertaking dutiful pilgrimages to the shrine of his alma mater, Eureka College. He spent his childhood in a succession of small Illinois towns, with a brief early interlude in Chicago. His family, never prosperous, came close to being crushed by the Depression. There is much to commend Reagan's description that "we didn't live on the wrong side of the tracks, but we lived so close to them we could hear the whistle real loud."[1] Nevertheless, Reagan's memories of his growing up, including his memories of the Depression, are largely happy ones. "We were poor, but we didn't know we were poor," he has said in looking back on his boyhood.[2]

In his rose-tinted autobiography Reagan describes this boyhood as "a rare Huck Finn idyll" in which he discovered butterflies and birds' nests, explored the dark mysteries of woods and waterland in the gently rolling hill country of northwestern Illinois and enjoyed a series of friendships and escapades in a sheltered and happy land.[3] Like Voltaire's Professor Pangloss, Reagan believes he inhabited "the best of all possible worlds." But Pangloss would seem a sourpuss compared to "Dutch" Reagan, whose sunny nature and optimistic attitude have been dominant characteristics of his personal life and political career. When times were bleak for the Republican Party, in the aftermath of the Watergate-influenced midterm election of 1974, Reagan began many of his political speeches with the story of the two little boys, one a dour pessimist and the other very optimistic, who were taken by their parents to a psychiatrist. The parents want to make the pessimist more cheerful and the optimist more conscious of the obstacles of life. To accomplish this, the pessimist is locked in a room with shiny new toys

22

and the optimist in a room with piles of horse manure. When the parents return, the pessimistic child is crying, refusing to play with any of the toys out of fear that they might break. The optimistic child is happily shoveling the manure. He tells his parents, "With this much manure around, I know there's a pony in here someplace."

Ronald Reagan was always the boy who hoped to find the pony, the child who believed that success was there for the finding and that it would surely come his way. His older and only brother, Neil, who also has been successful, has other memories of their shared boyhood. He remembers, better than his brother, the family itinerancy and poverty and uncertainty, inflicted by their father's alcoholism. He remembers sharing a cramped bed with Ronald which both boys wet. Here is the way that Neil describes his Saturday morning chore in Chicago when he was seven years old and Ronald only four and a half: "I was given a dime and sent down to the meat market on Cottage Grove Avenue and Sixty-Third Street to buy a ten-cent soup bone. In those days the medical profession hadn't gotten to the point where they felt there was much value to liver. When I went down to buy the ten-cent soup bone, I was also told to ask the butcher for liver for the cat. We didn't have a cat. Our big meal on Sunday was always fried liver. We ate on the soup bone all the rest of the week. My mother would put it in the pot and keep on adding potatoes and slices of carrots and more water, and we ate on the soup bone until it was Saturday again."[4]

Neil Reagan had been expecting a baby sister when Ronald was born on February 6, 1911, in the front bedroom of a five-room flat above the general store where his father worked. The store was on Main Street, the one business street in Tampico, Illinois. With a population of only 849 people, the town was too small to have a doctor. Nelle Reagan was in need of one. The midwife had told her that her delivery would be so difficult that a doctor was required. By luck, the midwife found one who had been stranded in Tampico by an unexpected blizzard the day before. The doctor, Harry Terry, performed a delivery which took such a toll on Nelle Wilson Reagan that he advised her not to have more children.[5] So Ronald, whose brother wouldn't look at him because he was a boy, became the second and last of the Reagan children.

He was, from the beginning, the joy of his soft-voiced, religious mother, who gave him her maternal name and a contented childhood. His father was John Edward Reagan, a muscular, handsome Irish-American known to everyone as Jack. He was so proud of his new baby that a week after Ronald was born, he was giving customers at the Pitney Store thirty-seven inches for a yard and seventeen ounces for a pound on their purchases. Jack was a premier shoe salesman who had learned his trade at something called the American School of Proctipedics, and who always believed that he would one day own a fancy shoe store and strike it rich. But his progress was impeded by what townspeople of the day sometimes referred to as "a powerful thirst."

Though the Tampico flat where the Reagans lived was large enough by city standards, it seemed small to his parents after Ronald was born. And Tampico was never large enough for Jack and his ambition. When Ronald was two, the family moved to Chicago where Jack took a job as a clerk in Marshall Field's department store. Most of his salary went for rent. The combination of low pay and Jack's drinking took its toll on the family. Jack's search for "the big break" led the Reagans on a nomadic procession through Illinois towns: Galesburg, Monmouth, Tampico again and, finally, Dixon, when Ronald was nine years old.

Reagan considers Dixon his home town. "Dixon is part of me," he says,[6] and it is true. Many of the attitudes which Reagan brought to the presidency—on welfare, conspicuously, but also on women's rights and race— were those he formed in Dixon more than a half-century ago. The volunteer impulse was especially strong. Nelle Reagan, who strove to help the sick, needy and unfortunate, taught her sons that it was also their obligation to help others. The dominant attitude of the family and the neighborhoods in which they lived, an attitude often encountered in small towns in those days, was that people were supposed to look after one another. There was a presumption of goodwill, the kind of presumption that makes it possible for Reagan, or for Gerald R. Ford before him, to take a negative position on government welfare spending without ever feeling that he is abandoning people in the process. Each assumes that there will be people like Nelle Reagan to look after other people.

The Reagans moved to Dixon in 1920, the same year that Warren G. Harding, another midwestern small-town boy, was elected President, and the year that the Sinclair Lewis novel, *Main Street,* appeared. "Main Street is the climax of civilization," Lewis wrote. "That this Ford car might stand in front of the Bon Ton Store, Hannibal invaded Rome and Erasmus wrote in Oxford cloisters." It was a sneer that would have gone right by Jack Reagan, and that his son Ronald might later have accepted as a literal truth. "Main Street" represented values to be defended, not derided. In 1980, presidential candidate Reagan toyed with the idea of describing himself as "a Main Street Republican," a phrase intended to show that he was a grassroots candidate in contrast to the favorite of the board rooms, John B. Connally.

Though Reagan left Dixon as soon as he could, the small town never left him. In his best acting roles he was an unsophisticated small-towner, playing himself with the winsome "aw shucks" quality that provided a devastating campaign counterpoint to the pieties of Jimmy Carter in the 1980 presidential debate. A small-town aura clung to Reagan even when he assayed larger roles. In his most acclaimed film, *King's Row,* based on Henry Bellaman's novel of a small southern town with a darker side than Dixon, he was cast as playboy Drake McHugh. With plots and subplots of sadism, lust, incest and insanity, the book and movie together accomplish about as much for the good name of small towns as the *Titanic* did for ocean voyages. But Reagan would have accepted at face value the words which Bellaman wrote sardonically of King's Row as being an accurate description of Dixon: "A good town, everyone said. A good clean town. A good town to live in, and a good place to raise your children."

In 1920 the town of Dixon had a population of 8,191. Lee County, of which it is the county seat, had a population of 28,004. The business of this northwestern Illinois county was farming, and the principal business of Dixon was servicing these farmers, especially the dairymen. Dixon boasted a large milk-condensing plant, owned by Borden's. One of the community's oldest firms was the Grand Detour Plow Company, established in 1837. There was also a train depot, a public library, a teacher's college ("Normal School," in those days), lots of churches and a YMCA. In 1922 a new theater for vaudeville and silent movies opened its doors. The nomadic Reagans lived in five different houses in Dixon in a decade and a half. Ronald Reagan went to high school there, and played football, and fell in love with the daughter of a preacher. He was an ordinary football player, but a powerful swimmer, who for seven summers worked as a lifeguard at Lowell Park, a recreation area on the Rock River three miles north of town. As a lifeguard, Reagan claims to have saved seventy-seven people from drowning. He says that a number of them were ungrateful when he pulled them from the water. After Reagan made it to Hollywood, a legend grew up that he had come to the rescue of pretty girls when they were in no danger of drowning. Reagan says this story is not true, adding, "I never got my suit wet unless there was a need for it."[7]

The younger Reagan much more resembled his mother in personality than he did his father. When I first asked Reagan some fifteen years ago about his family, he talked nonstop about his mother for several minutes without even mentioning his father. To her sons, Nelle Reagan was a remarkable, energetic and extraordinarily kind woman who was considered a do-gooder in her day and would be considered one now. Ronald Reagan used to tell the story about the time he was a banquet speaker and the waiter offered him a steak instead of the "rubber chicken" everyone else was eating. The waiter was a fan—of his mother. He turned out to be a former tuberculosis patient whom Nelle Reagan had regularly visited while he was convalescing.[8]

Nelle was a lifelong member of the Christian church (Disciples of Christ), and she succeeded in making Ronald a member, too. Neil had been baptized a Catholic like his father. The sons say that in a home where there wasn't any excess of food or clothing, their mother was always helping unfortunates. At times she had ex-convicts paroled into her custody. In his autobiography, Reagan says of his mother that "she had the conviction everyone loved her just because she loved them. My father's cynicism never made the slightest impression on her, while I suspect her sweetness often undermined his practical view of the world. Neither she nor my father had ever graduated from any school but the elementary grades. No diploma was needed for kindness, in her opinion, just as my father believed energy and hard work were the only ingredients needed for success."

Alcoholism blighted the life of Jack Reagan. His older son Neil says bluntly that it prevented him from becoming a business success. Ronald, more diplomatically, blames the twin curses of drink and the Depression. But the Reagan boys escaped much of the bitterness which can afflict the children of alcoholics because their mother, as both boys remember it, counseled them that their father's drinking was "a sickness" which deserved their compassion.[9] "She told us repeatedly that he had no control over those periods when he was drinking," Ronald Reagan said in a 1968 interview. "And she asked us to help him and love him."

However, even the relentless cheerfulness of the Reagan autobiography cannot conceal the younger son's abhorrence of his father's drinking. Reagan relates how he came home one day to find his father flat on his back on the front porch, "drunk, dead to the world." The boy was eleven years old, and he was alone. Somehow, the scrawny child dragged his muscular father inside the house, smelling "the sharp odor of whiskey from the speakeasy" on his breath, and got him to bed.[10] The experience left Reagan with an aversion to hard drinking. Years later, when he was recovering from an illness, Reagan accepted a doctor's suggestion that he take a glass or two of wine with dinner. Once he explained to me how "wine has food value, even though they aren't allowed to advertise it that way." Though he will occasionally down a vodka martini, Reagan's drinking is largely limited to that glass or two of wine.

In many ways the Reagans were avant-garde for Dixon. Not only were they Democrats and Jack a Catholic in a time and place devotedly Republican and Protestant, but both the Reagans supported the rights of working men. This was a controversial subject in Illinois, where striking coal-miners had been massacred in Herrin in 1922. At home the boys called their parents by their first names and their parents called them "Moon" and "Dutch," a name the younger son then preferred to the "sissy" Ronald. Neil's nickname derived from the comic strip character "Moon Mullins." Ronald got his from his father, who thought that his youngest son in infancy looked "like a fat little Dutchman." Both parents, and especially Nelle, were determined that their sons go to college, even though they had never been to high school.

Despite his drinking, Jack Reagan did well in Dixon. Ronald thought his father "the best raconteur I ever heard." He could talk for hours about shoes, which he had sold for years, and he had an ear for the off-color story, which Ronald Reagan also learned to tell skillfully—but never in mixed company. Jack Reagan was proud of his Irish ancestry. The Reagans now trace his roots back to Brian Boru, an eleventh-century king who was the first Irish national hero and whose ancestry is presumed by droves of Irish-

Americans. Research by Debrett's of London and Hibernian Research of Dublin has established that Jack Reagan's great-grandfather, Michael O'Regan, left County Tipperary during the famine of the 1840s and settled in England.[11] He was believed to be the only member of the family who could read or write, but he evidently didn't write very well. When he married another Irish refugee, Katherine Mulcahy, in the St. George's Cathedral in the London borough of Southwark on October 31, 1852, he signed his name "Reagan," dropping the "O" and inserting an "a."

Jack Reagan was born in Illinois in 1883 and brought up by an English-born aunt after his parents died. He and Nelle were married in a Catholic church in Fulton, Illinois, in 1904, and Nelle acceded to her husband's wishes to have their first son baptized a Catholic, which Neil has remained throughout his life. But the church tie had weakened when Ronald was growing up, and Neil remembers his father as "more Elks" than Catholic.

Still, Catholicism was a sign of separateness in middle America in those days. In the early 1920s, the Ku Klux Klan was active in Illinois and anti-Catholic "nativist" prejudice was commonplace, often linked to anti-Semitism. Jack Reagan would not permit his sons to see the film classic *Birth of a Nation* because it celebrated the white southern repression of what he called "the colored." Ronald Reagan's proudest story of his father is of the time when he traveled as a salesman to the only hotel in a small town and was told by the desk clerk that he would like the place because it wouldn't accept Jews. Jack Reagan stormed out, after telling the clerk that he soon would be rejecting Catholics, too, and spent a cold winter's night in the car.

Nelle Reagan had married a Catholic, and she shared her husband's distaste for racial and religious prejudice. She encouraged her sons to judge people as individuals, not by their color or their creed. And she encouraged her youngest son to take a broad and happy view of life. His early reading, his attempts at writing, his fondness for drawing caricatures which has persisted into adult life—all these received the stamp of maternal approval. She did not leave either boy with the feeling that she favored one of them over the other, but she was the exemplar for Ronald Reagan. She was proud that he could read before he went to school and that he could memorize anything that was given to him. She let him know that she was proud of him.

In her quiet way, Nelle Reagan dominated the household and pushed both sons in the direction of education and a better life. She was a determined improver, dragging her husband and her children to lectures, recitals and plays. Jack Reagan shared a fondness for music, and both Reagan parents participated enthusiastically in theatricals, inculcating their children with a love of the stage which has never left them. Neil, believed to be the better actor of the two boys, did most of the performing at the benefits staged by the Elks at the vaudeville theater that was the pride of Dixon. Ronald was more subdued when he was very young. Speaking about his brother as a small child, Neil said: "He was sort of a quiet boy, not one you would suspect would wind up as an actor or a politician, even. He was very quiet and he could go for hours all by himself playing with lead soldiers. He was a great collector of lead soldiers in those days."[12]

Despite his martial play, he had no taste for blood. In Dixon, he was captured by a fantasy of spending life as a trapper in the woods along the Rock River, which harbored muskrats, rabbits and a variety of birds. But the would-be trapper subsequently withdrew from a scheme of Neil's to sell poultry and rabbits for meat because he had helped raise the rabbits and did not want to kill them. Young Ronald was a reader, not a trapper. He had begun to read when only five and seemed a prodigy to his mother, who showed off his prowess to neighbors. Reagan recalls reading aloud an account of a bombing in San Francisco on July 22, 1916, which occurred at "Preparedness Day" ceremonies sponsored by advocates of America's entry into World War I. Young Reagan's reading performances brought him such approval that he took to reading the newspapers regularly, beginning with the comics and the sports page. The habit has persisted into adult life.*

Reagan's solitary pursuits were encouraged by the family's frequent moves in his early childhood. Neil remembers that his brother made friends wherever he went, but did not seek them out. Already, he was developing that combination of easy manner and reserve which would as an adult attract other people to him but keep them from becoming intimate. "He had a wide circle of friends at the tail end of grade school and in high school, but he also was quiet and a lot of his activities were partly by himself," remembers Neil Reagan. "I always sort of ran with gangs. He didn't."[13]

Ronald was thirteen years old when he entered Dixon's Northside High School in the spring of 1924. He was short and slight of build and wore thick, horn-rimmed glasses to compensate for his extreme nearsightedness. This myopia precluded him from playing baseball, but it didn't keep him out of football games. The Reagan home at this time was on an embankment above the high school football field, and while still in elementary school Ronald developed the habit of wandering down to the field and watching the Dixon high school team practice. "I just had to wear one of those purple-and-white jerseys," Reagan said in a 1981 interview. "In high school then there was a lightweight team with a limit of 135 pounds, and I was the captain and tackle. About midseason of my junior year, I replaced a 180-pound guard on the varsity. I think I was put in to get something going, to motivate him. I stayed in his spot."[14]

In his senior year, Reagan shot up to his present height of nearly six feet. He gained 30 pounds and weighed in at 165. As a small child, he had played

* One of Reagan's favorite strips during the 1980 campaign was "Doonesbury," which did an extended satire on "Reagan's brain." In the pressure-cooker atmosphere of the campaign's final weeks, "Doonesbury" was often Reagan's first reading of the day.

rough-and-tumble football games with his brother and other older boys, referring to them in his autobiography as "the happiest times in my life." Now, he was able to play on an equal size and footing. For Reagan, football deeply touched some atavistic need for combat and competition with his brother and the world. In 1981 he gave this view of the sport to columnist Mark Shields: "It is the last thing left in civilization where two men can literally fling themselves bodily at one another in combat and not be at war. It's a kind of clean hatred. . . . I know of no other game that gave me the same feeling football did. That's why you can look at the bench when the TV camera comes over and see the fellows there crying. I've sat there crying."[15]

Dixon High fielded a single football team in the days Dutch Reagan played, but the school had separate Northside and Southside campuses. The Reagan family moved from a rented house on the south side of town to a rented house on the north side the year Dutch started high school. Moon continued attending the south campus, while his brother went to classes at Northside. Dutch thought this fortuitous for he had a crush on Margaret (Mugs) Cleaver, the pretty daughter of a local minister and the brightest girl at Northside. Despite the mythology of classlessness which imbued little Dixon, there was no doubt that Northside was supposed to be the "better" school. The Northside crowd, especially the boys, was too genteel for Southside tastes, where the meeting place for high school young men was Red Vail's pool hall. It was a favorite hangout of Moon Reagan, though not of his brother. Appropriately, the chosen meeting ground for the Northsiders, boys and girls alike, was an ice cream store—Fulf's Confectionary. The Southsiders looked forward to work after finishing high school. At Northside, there were those who talked of college.[16]

In retrospect, it may have been fortunate that Dutch went to a different campus. The scholastic separation gave the younger brother running room, allowing him time to develop his own friends and personality. Dutch was no introvert, but his style was less exhibitionist than Moon's. The older brother liked to draw attention to himself, was considered a leader of his crowd and excelled in elaborate pranks, such as the time he disassembled a manure spreader and reassembled it on the roof of Southside High School. Dutch's method of attracting attention was to try out for and win the lead role in the Philip Barry play, *You and I,* where the female lead was uncoincidentally the desirable Mugs Cleaver.

In his pleasant, cheerful way Dutch was now blossoming and becoming a big man on the Northside campus. He was helped by his height and handsomeness and also by the acceptance which achievement at athletics gives boys in high school. Reagan wasn't all that good a player, but he was a courageous one on a team that probably had less overall prowess than he did. In 1926, Moon's last year, the Dixon team went undefeated, winning eight games and tying one. Moon was an end on that team. But in 1928, when

Dutch was the best but also the lightest tackle on the Dixon squad, the team's record fell to two wins and seven losses.

By this time Dutch had won an important victory—he had emerged in Mugs Cleaver's affections as her steady boyfriend, winning out over a friend, Dick McNicol, the quarterback of the football team. Dutch delicately describes this triumph in his autobiography, mixing it with praise for McNicol. In his senior year, Dutch Reagan was elected student body president at Northside. The class photo shows a good-looking young man in a bow tie, the hint of a smile on his face, and both his given name and his nickname under the photograph. It was the custom of school yearbooks in those days to include a motto, usually written by the student, that was supposed to describe his attributes or his outlook. The motto beneath Reagan's nickname reads: "Life is just one grand sweet song, so start the music." Those words were almost surely written by Dutch, the art editor of the yearbook, for they are taken from a poem Reagan wrote in high school. The poem, entitled "Life," is a ballad of youthful optimism.

> I wonder what it's all about, and why
> We suffer so, when little things go wrong?
> We make our life a struggle,
> When life should be a song.
>
> Our troubles break and drench us.
> Like spray on the cleaving prow
> Of some trim Gloucester schooner,
> As it dips in a graceful bow . . .
>
> But why does sorrow drench us
> When our fellow passes on?
> He's just exchanged life's dreary dirge
> For an eternal life of song[17]

There is more, in the same vein, from which the reader will be spared. None of it menaces the reputation of Robert Frost, but all of it expresses the growing credo of Ronald Reagan that the world was his oyster. "Small-town Illinois tends to give people that sense of optimism," says Dan Balz of the *Washington Post,* who grew up in Freeport, within forty miles of Dixon. "It's insulating in all the ways that were observed in *Main Street.* You end up being somewhat naive. But the schools are good, the churches are supportive, the people are friendly. Growing up the way he did isn't especially challenging, but it's very pleasant. It leaves you with the feeling that people are basically good and will treat you right if you're good to them. Ronald Reagan exudes that."[18]

Those who shared Reagan's boyhood in Dixon found him to be a little on the goody-goody side, in the manner of the Northsiders. A little, but not too much. One such boyhood friend, John Crabtree, says he never saw Reagan swear, "and the only time I knew him to take a drink was the time this family out at the park gave us each a bottle of homemade wine for helping teach their kids to swim. Well, we finished off the wine and took a stroll through town. In those days, the stoplights were on top of short cement posts right in the middle of the intersections. Dutch just climbed up on one of those stoplights and sat there. The police chief came along in his Model T and asked Dutch what he was doing. 'Twinkle, twinkle, little star. Who do you think you are?' said Dutch. And the chief took him in, and he was fined a buck."[19]

What ended the Reagan idyll, as it did so many others, was the Depression. When I asked Reagan during the 1980 campaign to name the single most important influence on his life, he replied without hesitation, "the Depression." The Depression cost Jack Reagan his dream—a partnership in a shoe store, "Reagan's Fashion Boot Shop," which he had opened with borrowed money. It sent his mother to work in a dress shop for $14 a week. It made Reagan, then at Eureka College, go to work on the side so he could send his mother $50—without Jack's knowledge—to enable the Reagans to continue getting credit at a local grocery store.

The occasion which prompted that filial contribution has been related by Reagan on hundreds of occasions, including the November 13, 1979, speech in which he announced his presidential candidacy. The two Reagan brothers were back from Eureka on Christmas Eve, 1931, when a special delivery letter arrived for Jack, who was again working as a traveling salesman. Jack had been hoping for a bonus. Instead, the letter contained a blue slip informing him that he had been fired.

Ronald Reagan is nearly always in tears when he tells this story, which he used to great effect while campaigning for working class votes in 1980. But his upbeat autobiography, *Where's the Rest of Me?*, written in 1965 by Richard G. Hubler from stories related to him by Reagan, treats Jack Reagan's firing as an event that was all too common during the Depression. Part of the difference in emphasis may be because Reagan in 1965 was a relatively new Republican who was trying to emphasize his conversion rather than his New Deal roots. Fifteen years later, the story of Jack's firing became a useful way to relate his own life to the lives of unemployed auto and steel workers.

Reagan succeeded in this political effort, and he is doubtless right in saying that the Depression made a deep impression on him. What it did not do, however, was impose a sense of personal limitation. The Depression-era stories Reagan tells in his own book are stories of achievements—of athletic positions or dramatic prizes captured, of a student strike won, of glorious dates and of collegiate good times. The firing of Jack Reagan, however much it may have dampened the family's 1931 Christmas, did not even make a dent in the younger son's optimism. And this may have been partly because Jack Reagan had plenty of optimism of his own. Even though the

Depression forever ended his dream of owning a shoe store, the senior Reagan fared better than many of his contemporaries. Instead of cursing his luck, he plunged into politics, working in the campaign of Franklin D. Roosevelt as one of the most conspicuous Democrats in Dixon. When Roosevelt won, Jack was put in charge of the local welfare office—helping those who were less fortunate than himself, including some who had been well off before the Depression. Hearing the stories of others who were having harder times than his father helped Dutch Reagan keep what was happening in perspective. Since his own family was employed and eating regularly, Reagan was able to see the Depression as a national tragedy rather than as a personal one. It was a calamity to be sure, and young Reagan hoped that Franklin Roosevelt would make everything right, but there was no need to abandon the basic small town values that had been learned in Dixon.

The Depression did affect Reagan's economic and political attitudes, as it did almost everyone else who lived through this era. Like many other young adults of his generation, Reagan emerged from the period with a desire for material success and for an economic cushion that would provide security for himself and his family should another Depression strike. He would ever afterward tend toward frugality in his personal habits and would become known, in the old phrase, as someone who "respects the value of a dollar." But the Depression's most immediate effect upon Reagan was to spur his political interests along the same path as his father's. The youngest Reagan thrilled to the buoyant optimism he heard from Roosevelt, who became his first political hero.[20] He listened to all the "fireside chats" on radio and developed an accomplished imitation of Roosevelt, complete with imaginary cigarette holder.

When Roosevelt was first inaugurated on March 4, 1933, Reagan was twenty-two years old. He memorized passages of the inaugural address, including the famous line in which the new President declared, "My firm belief is that the only thing we have to fear is fear itself." These words, to quote an expression of the day, were right down Reagan's alley. Though Reagan's politics ultimately would evolve into opposition to some of the most enduring legacies of the New Deal, his style has remained frankly and fervently Rooseveltian throughout his life. His cadences are Roosevelt cadences, his metaphors the offspring of FDR's. Reagan responded especially to the dramatic quality of Roosevelt, to the flair for the grand gesture that was an essential element of the Roosevelt style. For Reagan and for millions of his fellow Americans, Roosevelt's message in the darkest days of the Depression was less an economic one than a call for renewed self-confidence and courage. On this score, young Reagan proved a willing disciple.

3

The Shape of Things to Come

THE happiest night Ronald Reagan spent during the presidential campaign was the night he came home to Eureka College. It was October 17, 1980, and I have never seen Reagan more joyous—not even the night three months earlier when he had accepted the Republican presidential nomination, nor the night three weeks later when he won the election. Amidst shouts of "Dutch" and "Teke" and "We Want Reagan," the star graduate of the class of '32 returned to a pep rally so unabashedly sentimental that it might have been created in the Hollywood which gave us Reagan on film as the glorious, doomed Notre Dame football hero George Gipp.

Certainly, Hollywood would have delighted in the Reagan homecoming. Hollywood would have wanted sixty-nine-year-old Ronnie Reagan to walk on stage with a tear in his eye and a broad smile on his face and accept the gift of a red-and-white football jersey from his eighty-six-year-old former football coach Ralph (Mac) McKinzie. In Hollywood, as on that night at Eureka, Reagan would have pulled the jersey, number "80," over his head without mussing his hair and found that it fit perfectly. And Coach McKinzie would have turned to the Eureka football team and exhorted the players to "win one for the Gipper" against Concordia the following day. Hollywood would have liked the style with which Reagan lit the bonfire outside the gymnasium after the pep rally. And Hollywood would have loved the way Ronnie held Nancy's hand as he joined with the student throng in the full-voiced chorus of the old school song, " 'Neath the Elms." It was that kind of night.

The presidential candidate gave a speech which had nothing to do with the campaign. He told about McKinzie as Eureka's fullback, and player-coach, scoring all of his team's 52 points in a rout of old-rival Bradley. He told about playing on the ungraded Eureka football field of his day, where the slope was so great that the safety man had to wait for a punt to come over the hill. He seemed to be reliving the old stories as he told them. The signs of greetings from Tau Kappa Epsilon, his old fraternity, and from the

33

girls' dormitory still named Lyda's Wood had stirred memories which Reagan wanted to share. These memories produced a curious little speech about the joys and trials of attending college in the Depression. Times were so hard that some of the faculty members worked without pay and were extended credit by the townspeople, Reagan said. He recalled that he had worked "at one of the better jobs I've ever had," which was washing dishes at Lyda's Wood.

"I have since had the opportunity by the way of the office I held in California to serve on the board of regents of a great university system of nine campuses and a giant state college system. . . ." Reagan said. "And if I had to do it all over again, I'd come right back here and start where I was before." Quieting the applause which filled the gymnasium, Reagan continued: "Let me tell you, please believe me when I tell you, they [the big universities] may look attractive and they may look glamorous on a Saturday with the stadium full and everything. . . . Those big assembly-line diploma mills may teach, but with all due respect to them, you will have memories, you will have friendships that are impossible on those great campuses and that are just peculiar to this place. As far as I am concerned, everything good that has happened to me—everything—started here on this campus in those four years that still are such a part of my life."[1]

The statement was true. In the four years he attended little Eureka College, twenty-one miles east of Peoria, Ronald Reagan's activities would foreshadow his life's work—sports announcing, acting, public speaking, political achievement. It was at Eureka that Reagan learned how much he enjoyed the plaudits of a crowd. And it was at Eureka, also, that Reagan first demonstrated a talent for rousing oratory and directed this oratory toward a political result.

None of this was on Dutch Reagan's mind when he arrived at the Eureka campus in 1928 with a steamer trunk and $400 accumulated from his summers of work at Lowell Park. What seems most to have preoccupied him was football and Margaret Cleaver, not necessarily in that order. Dutch and Mugs, whose father was a Disciples of Christ minister and whose sisters had attended Eureka, often had talked of going to the college together—and so they did. They were two of 220 students that year at Eureka, a teacher's school turned liberal arts college that had been chartered in 1855 and was the first college in Illinois to admit men and women students on an equal basis.

Eureka, also the motto of the state which Reagan would one day govern for eight years, is Greek for "I have found it." In Reagan's case, the words fit. His autobiography gives a striking and detailed account of his love-at-first-sight relationship with the college, where he had been accepted in advance as a pledge by Tau Kappa Epsilon. Reagan quickly negotiated an athletic scholarship, based as much on his swimming prowess as his football record, which paid half of his $180-a-year tuition and his board. He worked to pay his room charges, first washing dishes at the fraternity and subsequently moving to the better job, complete with dishwasher, at Lyda's Wood. His scholarship was the maximum allowed at Eureka, an underendowed school which Reagan has correctly described as "perpetually broke."[2] In the best of times, Eureka needed repeated fund drives and aid from its supporting church to stay afloat. When Reagan started as a freshman, the stock market crash was still a year away; but the Depression had arrived in the farm belt before it came to Wall Street, and Eureka was beginning to feel the pinch. While Dutch Reagan was looking forward to four glorious years playing football for the Eureka Golden Tornadoes, there was serious talk among the trustees that the college might have to close its doors.

Into this drama came Ronald Reagan's first political opponent, new Eureka president Bert Wilson. Believing as much in a balanced budget as Reagan would later, Wilson proposed to put the college into the black by eliminating courses he considered marginal and laying off the faculty members who were teaching them. The plan had budgetary appeal for the trustees, but it would have done away with courses which juniors and seniors needed to graduate. Because of this, the Wilson plan immediately provoked opposition from upperclassmen and from faculty members concerned both with their jobs and with Eureka's academic rating. Students and faculty made common cause and agreed to strike unless the trustees kept the threatened courses.

Even today, after two terms as California governor and half a term as President of the United States, Reagan can recount the saga of the strike committee's daily maneuvers with a detail that eludes him on many presidential issues. Most likely that's because it was this strike which first thrust Reagan into the limelight and made him a hero to his peers. He was the freshman representative on the strike committee, which gathered in the Eureka chapel at midnight on the eve of Thanksgiving vacation in that autumn of 1928. The same evening the trustees had met and agreed, reluctantly, to endorse Wilson's plan for eliminating the classes. As Reagan remembers it, the plan was to be put into effect during the vacation period, confronting students and faculty with a fait accompli when they returned.[3]

By his own account, Reagan had been a mere member of the strike committee until the midnight meeting. He was chosen to be a spokesman that night because he was a freshman and did not have a vested interest in the courses that were to be eliminated. Reagan sprang to his feet at the appointed moment, reviewed the history of the negotiations and emotionally accused Wilson and the trustees of bad faith in their dealings with faculty and students. "I discovered that night that an audience has a feel to it and, in the parlance of the theater, that audience and I were together," Reagan wrote in his autobiography. "When I came to actually presenting the motion there was no need for parliamentary procedure: they came to their feet with a roar—even the faculty members present voted by acclamation. It was heady wine. Hell, with two more lines I could have had them riding through 'every Middlesex village and farm'—without horses yet."[4] Within a week Wilson had resigned and the classes which had been done away with were restored. It was a sweet victory and one for which freshman leader Reagan accepted his full share of credit.

The strike was Reagan's first venture into politics, and it is notable that he measured his success by theatrical metaphor, in this case the "feel" of an audience. Always, for Reagan, politics and the stage would be closely linked. Always, and it is no small measure of his effectiveness in public life, Reagan would think of speechmaking as a way of binding himself and the audience together. Since a speech was a theatrical event, Reagan felt free to take dramatic liberties with its content. Later, when he began his public speaking career in Des Moines as a lecturer to civic and youth groups, Reagan would use dramatic stories with himself as hero to establish a bond with the audience. One frequently repeated story concerned a time when he supposedly admitted an infraction of the rules, which cost Dixon High School a football game.* Over the years this fable showed up in other forms, attributed to other football players. Sometimes Reagan told a version in which a player admitted dropping a touchdown catch in the end zone even though the official hadn't seen it. The story was impossible to verify. But it made a dramatic point.

Soon after the strike was over, Dutch and Mugs were taken by the Cleavers to see a touring London play, *Journey's End.* Reagan identified with the major character, Captain Stanhope, saying that "in some strange way, I was also on stage." When I asked him in 1968 whether this marked the birth of his ambition to become an actor, he replied: "I knew then that I wanted to be an actor, but it wasn't considered a way to make a living."[5]

From then on Reagan missed few opportunities to go on stage. He joined Alpha Epsilon Sigma, the student dramatic society. He played in a comedy loosely based on *Pygmalion* called *The Brat.* And he excelled in Edna St. Vincent Millay's play *Aria da Capo,* in which he played a shepherd who is strangled to death. The Eureka drama department took the play, which also featured Margaret Cleaver, to a prestigious one-act competition at Northwestern University where the play finished second and Reagan won an indi-

---

* Reagan's account, as reported by the now defunct *Rockford Morning Star,* was this: "I'll never forget one game with Mendota. The Mendota team yelled for a penalty against Dixon at a crucial point. I'd been the culprit and I knew they were right. The official hadn't seen the play, however, so he asked me. I was in an awful spot. But truth-telling had been whaled into me, also a lot of sports ethics which, from the storm that incident raised, evidently weren't exactly practical for fatheads. I told the truth, the penalty was ruled, and Dixon lost the game. I finally wrote a story about it and sold it to a national boys magazine. That sale just about turned the tide for me away from professional sports and coaching on the one hand and acting on the other." There are no contemporary accounts of any incident of this sort, and Dixon High lost to Mendota only once when Reagan was a member of the varsity team. In that game, when Reagan was a senior in 1927, Mendota won 24–0.

vidual acting award. *Aria da Capo,* an antiwar play, comported with Reagan's pacifism of the time, an outlook unsurprising in the Middle West, which would become the "isolationist" heartland of resistance to U.S. entry into World War II. "I went through a period in college, in the aftermath of World War I, where I became a pacifist and thought the whole thing was a frame-up. . . ."[6] Reagan said many years later. He does not discuss this in his autobiography or dwell on the politics of his college years. But he always held opinions on world and national issues. While football and drama and Mugs Cleaver dominated his life, Reagan was even then a political person.

He was not the instant success on the college gridiron that he was as an actor or strike leader. He remembers spending most of his freshman season on the bench and sulking because of it, developing an opinion that Coach McKinzie was prejudiced against him. McKinzie is the official living legend at Eureka. He was the team captain in three sports, and the students petitioned successfully to have him named football coach while he was still a student.[7] He spread his senior year classes over several years so he could both coach and attend class, eventually graduating in 1923 after eight years at Eureka. McKinzie's analysis of Reagan as a freshman player was that he lacked speed and was too self-impressed by his high school football credentials. But he could block and tackle, and McKinzie was impressed by his spunk. The coach called Reagan "a plugger" and made him a starting guard midway through his sophomore season. Reagan remains appreciative of that decision until this day. He played his heart out for McKinzie during the next two and one-half years. Neither he nor the team were all that good. Competing in a small-school conference called the Little 19, Eureka never had a winning season during Reagan's playing years. The Golden Tornadoes came close with a 3–3–2 record in 1929, Reagan's sophomore season, but had 2–6 and 3–4–1 records in the seasons after that. Reagan's teammates, like his coach, remember him more for his personality and his pluck than for his ability. He was as spirited as he was slow, and a tonic to his teammates. On the way back to the gym after practice, recalls former teammate Garrard Camp, Reagan would sometimes pretend he was a sports announcer, and relate entire imaginary football games. "He was pretty good at it," Camp remembers.[8]

One of Reagan's teammates at Eureka was the late William Franklin Burghardt, known to his teammates as "Burgie." He was a center on the Eureka team in Reagan's senior year, playing next to Reagan in the line, and captain of the team two years after Dutch had graduated. Reagan had helped recruit him from Greenfield, Illinois, where Burghardt's father, grandfather and uncle worked as barbers. Burgie was black, and blacks in those days were routinely segregated in the Middle West. Reagan had been taught by his parents that racial prejudice was abhorrent, but his first-hand experience with segregation was limited.

In 1931 the Eureka team, en route to play undefeated Elmhurst, tried to check into a hotel. McKinzie left the bus and went inside to make the arrangements. It took such a long time that Reagan left the bus to find out what was happening. What was happening was that the hotel manager was telling McKinzie that the hotel wouldn't take Burghardt and the team's other "colored" player—and that neither would any other hotel in town. McKinzie didn't know what to do. Reagan remembers that the coach was angry and thought the entire team should sleep in the bus, but Reagan said that would embarrass the black players because everyone would be discomforted. He had a better idea. Dixon was fifteen miles away, Reagan told McKinzie, and Burghardt and Jim Rattan, the other black player, could come home with him. "Are you sure?" McKinzie asked. Reagan firmly insisted that the players would be welcome at his home and McKinzie provided cab fare to Dixon.*

It is a measure of Reagan's naiveté that he believed for years that the cover story he and McKinzie quickly devised had fooled Burghardt and Rattan. They simply told the black players that the hotel didn't have enough room and that Reagan was taking them to his house in Dixon, where Jack and Nelle warmly welcomed their youngest son and his friends. "I just don't think he was conscious of race at all," Burghardt said in 1981. "If you listened to the Carter debate during the campaign, Reagan said that when he was growing up they didn't know they had a race problem. It was the dumbest thing a grown person could say, but he'd never seen it. I believe that hotel was his first experience of that sort."[9] Burghardt and Reagan became fast friends and remained so until Burghardt's death. He voted for Reagan in 1980, saying afterward that he and the President "seem to have a mutual respect and admiration."†

Burghardt's memory of Reagan during his Eureka days was that he had "a personality that would sweep you off your feet." He also recalled Reagan as being a practical joker who once electronically wired the front row of seats at the college chapel. That would have made him just right for the Tekes, who supposedly honored in the breach the school taboos on gambling, drinking, smoking, sex and dancing. The most popular pastime was "kegging," which meant taking a girl, a blanket and a picnic basket to a nearby graveyard used by Eureka as a lovers lane. When the picnic basket was omitted, students referred to the occasion as simply "blankets."

---

* There is no dispute about the essentials of this story, but there is some discrepancy about how Reagan and the black players actually reached Dixon. McKinzie recalls that the incident occurred in Aurora, sixty-eight miles away from Dixon, and that Reagan and the players went home by bus. The account given by Reagan in his autobiography, and subsequently by Burghardt in an interview with the *Washington Post,* was that the incident took place in a town which they did not name, ten to fifteen miles from Dixon, and that McKinzie gave them cab fare.

† After graduating, Burghardt played semipro baseball and basketball, earned his masters and doctorate degrees and became head of the Physical Education departments at Morgan State and Bowie State before he retired in 1979. He died on August 8, 1981.

A leading participant in the hijinks was Neil Reagan, who to the dismay of his mother had spent three years working in a cement plant after graduating from Dixon High. Nelle did everything she could to convince her oldest son that he ought to go to college, and Dutch made it possible by landing his older brother a job in the Teke house and a partial scholarship, then convincing the college to defer its tuition until after graduation. With the help of Mugs, Dutch had already made the same deal for himself. Though Reagan is modest about it in his autobiography, both brothers have acknowledged that Dutch's intervention made it possible for Neil to enroll at Eureka, where his superior speed enabled him to outshine Dutch on the football field.

No memories of scholarship intrude on the Reagan recollections. Dutch Reagan's photographic mind let him drift through Eureka as he had drifted through Dixon, finding satisfaction on the football field and the stage and in the friendly graveyard without ever having to come to grips with book learning. In Reagan's entire autobiography, with all its wonderful tales of college life, there isn't a single story from the classroom. There aren't any in my interviews with him, either. Neil remembers a professor complaining that Dutch, an economics and sociology major, never opened a book. "And yet when the test comes, I just have to give him his grade," the professor told Neil. "He has it all cold."[10] This is the way Dutch studied, according to Neil: "He would take a book the night before the test and in about a quick hour he would thumb through it and photograph those pages and write a good test."[11]

The professor Neil was quoting was Archibald E. Gray, Eureka's only professor of economics and sociology. Gray was popular because he did not work his students hard. But his lectures, according to Barrus Dickenson, who later became president of Eureka, were canted toward social justice. "He taught economics with a special viewpoint," said Dickenson, now publisher of the weekly *Woodford County Journal.* "The viewpoint was that what was needed was social reform. He talked about the strikes at the coal mines of southern Illinois, the violence there. He made you realize that we had to pay a price for the automobile. He would talk about Henry Ford's assembly line method and what it did to workers to do the same thing, pushing the pieces around, day after day."[12]

So it may have been that Reagan had a point, after all, about the value of this little college. There may have been a useful purpose to a place that treated coed students equally, a place where faculty and students struck together to save classes and academic standing and where Dutch Reagan could win approval for opposing racial discrimination. There may even be a point to Eureka's present-day boast: "One hundred and twenty-five years of serving central Illinois, the nation and the world." There is something appealing about Eureka's claim that one-third of all graduates have become doctors, lawyers or clergymen. And something compelling about its list of distinguished graduates, which in addition to Reagan, includes two other governors, twenty-six college and university presidents, thirty-three foreign missionaries and such individuals as Durward Sandifer, coauthor of the United Nations declaration of human rights, Paul Cramer, a developer of antiknock gasoline and Joyce Funk, the first woman elected student body president at Yale Divinity School.

Reagan kept coming back to Eureka, at least ten times after graduation. He returned for the first time on September 16, 1941, when he was a movie star, attending a pep rally and taking his place at guard during a practice of the Eureka football team, which by then had changed its nickname to the Red Devils. Photos of the occasion show Reagan dining at the Teke house and signing his name to a guest book at the new Christian Church. Reagan came back again in 1947 to crown the queen of the Pumpkin Festival and begin the first of his terms on the Eureka College Board of Trustees, on which he still serves. That same year he received an honorary doctorate of humane letters for "understanding and exposing Communists and their influence as president of the Screen Actors Guild." In 1967 Reagan was the principal speaker for the library dedication, advising the students to look beyond the generational conflict of the day to the contributions which their parents had made. Burghardt saw him riding astride the radiator of his old car on the drive into the campus and reflected that Reagan hadn't changed a bit. Reagan was back again three years later, swapping sports stories with other old grads at the dedication of the Reagan Physical Education Center named for himself and his brother.

Because of his fame, his outspoken support of the Vietnam War and his antistudent rhetoric as governor of California, Reagan in these later visits lost some of the aura of home-town hero which had clung to him in his acting days. The *Peoria Journal-Star* commented on the change in an editorial the night Reagan returned in the 1980 campaign:

> Ronald Reagan returns to Eureka tonight to visit the college from which he graduated so long ago, a place where he would have won election to almost anything by a landslide.
>
> The late Stansfield Major of Eureka, a classmate, once said of Reagan's popularity as a student at Eureka College: "I can't think of anyone who disliked him," then adding: "which to me, personally, is a black mark."
>
> Stan Major, who believed that one measure of a man is the enemies he makes, would probably be pleased to know that Reagan no longer is non-controversial. Indeed, he has stirred up enough enmity around the country that, while he leads in the polls, there is still doubt that he can defeat the incumbent president at a time when the economy is sick and foreign policy is in disarray. . . .
>
> Reagan was into almost everything as a student. Two weeks after arriving on campus. . . . he was a sub on the varsity football team and a reporter for the school paper. By the time he graduated in 1932, Reagan had served three years

as president of the Booster Club, three years as a first-string guard on the football team, three years as the principal basketball cheerleader, three years as the school's Number One swimmer and one year as its swimming coach, two years as feature editor of the yearbook and two years as a member of the student senate, including one as its president.

He left behind a body of goodwill as a man whose company was enjoyable, whose integrity was strong—a hard worker and a person of courage. Today, even his detractors find little to fault in his personal traits. It's his politics, his economics, his social concerns, his overall stature, and yes, his age that give some people pause although many—a majority, say the polls—find him preferable to the alternative.[13]

I doubt Reagan thought of Jimmy Carter the night he came home to Eureka in 1980. He was too busy being a boy again, too busy celebrating the excitement and the sentiment and the "clean kind of hatred" of football he loves so much. "Everything good that has happened to me—everything—started here on this campus. . . ," Reagan said, and he meant it. But as is usual for him on such occasions, Reagan couldn't stop there. Carried away with the emotions of the moment, Reagan capped his nostalgic speech by turning to the football team and delivering a bromide beloved of the late Vincent J. Lombardi: "A team that can't be beaten won't be beaten." The crowd went wild. The players yelled and cheered, vowing to win one for their Gipper the following afternoon. Reagan took off for a day of hard campaigning in southern Illinois. Alas, for real life stories that do not follow scripts. Either the Eureka players didn't get Reagan's message or Lombardi's maxim was suddenly adopted by lightly regarded Concordia, which had won but a single game all season. It won its second game the day after the Reagan pep rally, defeating Eureka 14–7.

4

The Announcer

Rᴏɴᴀʟᴅ Reagan graduated from Eureka College on June 7, 1932, during the bottom of the Depression. Along with the millions of others, he had dreams but no prospects. Nearly one of four Americans was out of work.[1] In Chicago, the center of little Dixon's universe, the percentage of unemployed was one in two and Mayor Anton Cermak pleaded for $150 million in federal relief funds. The alternative, he warned, would be the sending of federal troops later.[2] But the troops were kept in Washington where the Hoover administration was braced for the arrival of an Army from the last war. World War I veterans were marching on the nation's Capitol demanding a bonus payment for military service. Some of the veterans sported empty sardine cans hooked to belts which had once held shiny mess kits. The Senate voted down the bonus after the House had approved it, and the marchers were routed by troops under the command of Douglas MacArthur. The story was big news in Dixon, and there was other news that hit even closer to home. Dixon was dairy farming country, and milk prices had fallen so low that cows were not worth milking. In neighboring Iowa farmers who were receiving two cents a quart for milk that distributors were selling for eight cents embargoed all deliveries except those going to hospitals.[3] It was a time of fear and disillusionment and class division.

The Depression also had engulfed Dixon by that late warm spring of 1932. The cement plant where Neil had worked closed down. The Fashion Boot Shop, Jack's dream, had closed, too. Jack worked at what odd jobs he could get and later threw himself full time into the presidential campaign of Franklin Roosevelt. Most of the Reagan family's income came that year from Nelle, who continued working as a seamstress at the Marilyn Shop in Dixon. The Reagans subleased most of their rented home at 226 Lincoln Way to supplement their meager income. They lived in one room and cooked on a hotplate. The next door neighbor, Helen Kennedy Lawton, remembers that her grandmother at times cooked for the Reagans and handed the meals through the window.[4]

Everyone worked as best he could. Jack Reagan had heard of a sales job in the sporting goods section of Montgomery Ward, and Dutch Reagan applied for it. The job paid $12.50 a week for six days and two or three nights a week. Reagan lost out to another young Eureka graduate. He went back for a seventh summer of lifeguarding and odd jobs at Lowell Park. One day at the river resort he talked to his former high school drama teacher, B. J. Frazer, who encouraged him to broaden his horizons. "Aren't you going to have a shot at communications, the field in which you have so much talent?"[5] Frazer asked. This was what Reagan wanted to do, but he did not know how to go about it. He talked it over with Sid Altschuler, a wealthy Kansas City businessman who had married a Dixon girl and returned each summer for vacation. Reagan had taught Altschuler's two daughters to swim, and the businessman reciprocated by counseling the young lifeguard. However, Altschuler had no connections in the broadcasting industry. He advised Reagan to take the most menial job he could find at any studio, anything to get his foot in the door.[6]

Reagan tried. After discussing his plans with his mother, he hitchhiked to Chicago, then the regional radio center of the Middle West. At night he bunked in the fraternity house of a former Eureka classmate who was attending medical school. By day he made a painful round of the studios, hoping to demonstrate his ability as a sportscaster. No one was interested. He was an inexperienced small-town college graduate looking for a job at a time when hundreds of experienced applicants also were looking for work. At WMAQ, the NBC station in Chicago, a secretary took a fancy to him and said that Reagan was making a mistake to try for a job in Chicago. Go find a small station in the "sticks," she told him. Reagan hitchhiked back home.[7]

Reagan told me in 1968 that he was "pretty down and discouraged at this time." He was also so determined to land an announcing job that he let his romance with Margaret Cleaver go on the rocks. In his autobiography Reagan makes only a fleeting reference to the breakup, saying that "our lovely and wholesome relationship did not survive growing up." He does not mention that Margaret was his fiancée, and that their families and their friends expected them to be married. The relationship was so close that the president of Eureka College broke tradition at their graduation, where seniors carried strands of ivy between them that were cut in symbolic recognition of their parting. The president smiled at Dutch and Mugs and refused to cut their ivy strand. But real-life bonds didn't last.

"As soon as he was out of school he was so imbued with the idea of getting a job that he ignored everything," Neil said. "Everything else was put on the shelf temporarily. She went her own direction."[8] Margaret went home to teach in a small high school in Cropsley, Illinois, while her fiancé made the rounds of the radio stations. He hitchhiked to see her once before heading for his unsuccessful interviews in Chicago. "She wanted to be a homebody; he was going for the bright lights," said a reporter who interviewed several persons who knew Margaret Cleaver well at the time.[9] The following year, Margaret traveled to Europe with her older sister who had majored in French. She met a handsome foreign service officer, James Gordon, who was an attorney and a member of a well-to-do Virginia family. They fell in love and he proposed. Mugs sent Dutch back his engagement ring.

With Lowell Park closing down late in the summer of '32 and no job to be had in Dixon, Dutch Reagan borrowed his father's well-worn Oldsmobile and set out on a one-day swing of nearby small-town radio stations. His first stop was Davenport, Iowa, seventy-five miles west across the Mississippi River, the home of WOC, or "World of Chiropractic," a station founded by B. J. Palmer and housed in the same building as his chiropractic school. WOC had been advertising for an announcer for a month before Reagan arrived, and had just hired the most promising of the tryouts. There were no other jobs, station manager Peter MacArthur told him. Angered at himself that he hadn't known about the tryouts, Reagan burst out, "How in the hell does a guy ever get to be a sports announcer if he can't get inside a station?" Impressed with Reagan's spunk, MacArthur gave him a tryout. Reagan improvised an account of a football game based on a Eureka victory over Western Illinois the previous year, crediting himself with making a block which he had missed in the game. MacArthur liked what he heard. He offered Reagan five dollars and round-trip bus fare from Dixon the following Saturday to broadcast a University of Iowa football game. MacArthur said Reagan could announce the other three home games if he did well on the first one. Reagan did so well that MacArthur hired him immediately and raised his salary to ten dollars for the other games. It was the necessary foot in the door.[10]

Reagan spent two anxious months in Dixon after the football season, waiting for a staff announcer's job to open up. MacArthur, whose memory Reagan reveres, kept in touch with his young prospect, calling him at Christmas time and telling him not to get discouraged. Early in 1933 he made another call, this time telling Reagan that an announcer's job was open. Reagan jumped at it. It paid $100 a month, which for the time and circumstances was a lot of money. A machinist in Iowa made 63 cents an hour in 1933, a telephone company technician $16.36 a week, a farm laborer $16.50 a month. Reagan paid $18 a month for his rooms at the Vale Apartments at the corner of East Fourth and Perry streets in Davenport, a short walk from the WOC studio. He bought a meal ticket at the Palmer School cafeteria entitling him to 18 meals a week for $3.63. He had enough money left over to help his parents and sent $10 a month to Moon to help him finish college at Eureka.

Reagan was twenty-two years old when he began as a rookie announcer at WOC. He knew next to nothing about announcing, but he had a pleasant manner and a remarkable voice which projected warmth, excitement, earnestness. His voice was his great gift. It is a voice, wrote a subsequent observer, that "recedes at the right moments, turning mellow at points of intensity. When it wishes to be most persuasive, it hovers barely above a whisper so as to win you over by intimacy, if not by substance. . . . He likes his voice, treats it like a guest. He makes you part of the hospitality. It was that voice that carried him out of Dixon and away from the Depression. . . ."[11] Certainly, it was the voice which caught MacArthur's attention and suggested to him that here was a great announcer of the future. And Reagan had a commanding presence, both before the microphone and away from it. "As a speaker and as a personality, you were always aware when he came into a room that someone was in the room," recalls Myrtle Moon, then Myrtle Williams and the program director of WOC's big sister station WHO in Des Moines.[12]

Despite his talent, Reagan struggled in the beginning. He had no formal training as a broadcaster, and it showed when he was reading material that didn't come as naturally to him as ad-libbing a football game. In particular, he couldn't get the hang of reading commercials during station breaks. "The secret of announcing is to make reading sound like talking," he wrote years later. "I still am not good at a first reading of a script. At that time I was plain awful. I knew it, and so did the listeners. What was worse, so did the sponsors. I couldn't give it that easy conversational persuasive sell."[13] Reagan developed the ability he lacked by rehearsing his delivery, as he would learn in politics to rehearse his important speeches. He found that if he memorized a passage and repeated it out loud before he had to deliver it, the words would sound spontaneous. Soon, Reagan's weak point became a strength, and he has been a persuasive salesman ever since. If the voice is a gift, the delivery which sounds so natural is the result of hard work and careful preparation.

But Reagan almost had his career cut short at WOC because of his naiveté about the broadcasting business. One of the evening programs at the station was a program of organ music furnished by a local mortuary. The exchange for the organ music was supposed to be a "free" plug for the mortuary. Reagan didn't understand that the plug was part of a business arrangement between the station and the mortuary and said his "dramatic instinct rebelled at mentioning a mortuary in connection with 'Drink To Me Only With Thine Eyes.' " The sponsor complained, and Reagan was told that he would be replaced by a teacher who already had been interviewed for the job. He was assigned to break in his replacement. The story which Reagan tells is that the teacher, not wanting to give up a secure job during those hard times for a position at a station which fired announcers so capriciously, demanded a contract. When he didn't get one, he went back to teaching, and Reagan was rehired for the job he already had.[14]

At this time, WOC's sister station, WHO in Des Moines, was building a new, 50,000-watt clear channel transmitter which could be heard throughout the region. The WHO and WOC operations were being consolidated, and the WHO executives brought Reagan to Des Moines, where he scored immediately as a sports announcer. Reagan announced football games, swim meets and track events. But what he did best was recreate Chicago Cubs baseball games in the broadcasting booth. The art of telegraphic recreation in which an announcer constructs a game out of a laconic pitch-by-pitch wire account was at its height in these pretelevision days. With his gift for invented detail, Reagan gave the listeners the feeling they were at the ball park. "You just couldn't believe that you were not actually there," said Myrtle Williams. "Of course, he knew baseball and that helped."[15]

Reagan's own favorite story, from the more than six hundred games he recreated, is the oft-told one of the time the wire went dead and Reagan faked the game until the wire returned to operation. There are some constants in the story, as Reagan tells it, and some variables. Dizzy Dean is always pitching, and it usually is the ninth inning. The batter varies. Sometimes, as in the autobiography, it is Augie Galan, and at other times it is Billy Jurges. Here is the version in which Jurges was the batter, which Reagan gave to a Baseball Hall of Fame lunch in the White House on March 27, 1981:*

"When the slip came through, it said, 'The wire's gone dead.' Well, I had the ball on the way to the plate. And I figured real quick, I could say we'll tell them what happened and then play transcribed music, but in those days there were at least seven or eight other fellows that were doing the same game. I didn't want to lose the audience. So I thought real quick, 'there's one thing that doesn't get in the scorebook,' so I had Billy foul one off . . . and I had him foul one back at third base and described the fight between the two kids that were trying to get the ball. Then I had him foul one that just missed being a home run, about a foot and a half. And I did set a world record for successive fouls, or for someone standing there, except that no one keeps records of that kind. I was beginning to sweat when Curley [the monitor in the control booth] sat up straight and started typing . . . and the slip came through the window and I could hardly talk for laughing because it said, 'Jurges popped out on the first ball pitched.' "

Reagan was not confined to sports announcing. He also did interviews, including one with Aimee Semple McPherson, the noted Los Angeles evangelist. The interview concluded ahead of schedule and Reagan signaled for music to fill in the remaining minutes of the hour. As he tells it in his autobiography, "a sleepy engineer in the control room reached out, pulled a record off the stack and nodded to go ahead." Reagan announced there would be "a brief interlude of recorded music" and the station played "Minnie the Moocher's Wedding Day." The announcer, Harold (Red)

---

* I asked Reagan about this discrepancy during a July 31, 1981, interview. He thought a moment, and then said, "It was Jurges."

Rissler, says he wasn't sleepy at all. As Rissler remembers it, the night was excessively hot and Reagan had gone outside after the interview to get some fresh air, a privilege denied engineers. "I thought it would be very good to . . . teach him a lesson," Rissler said, and played the offending record deliberately. His boss, he added, didn't think it was funny, and Rissler nearly lost his job.[16]

Reagan was on his own now, without a steady girlfriend for the first time since early in high school and with money in his pockets. A series of raises boosted his weekly pay to $75—more than twice the highest salary his father had ever made. But he was not a big spender. In his spare time he visited the Teke fraternity house at Drake, which like Eureka was associated with the Disciples of Christ. Sometimes he would date Drake coeds, but he seemed a reserved and even shy figure to many who knew him during this time. Paul McGinn, manager of the Hotel Kirkwood in Des Moines, befriended the young announcer and introduced him to Jeanne Tesdell, a pretty and popular recent Drake graduate. The otherwise reserved Dutch Reagan was to her an outgoing person with a stage presence. "He had a lot of talent and in what direction it would be used I didn't know then," she once said. Reagan dated her for nearly a year, but the relationship ended in what Tesdell described as a "bittersweet" breakup. She married local attorney Don Burington, and Reagan came to the engagement party at McGinn's.[17]

Drought was the accompaniment of Depression in the farm belt during these early years of the thirties. The worst year was 1934, when vast dust storms uprooted millions of acres of land in the central plains and Middle West, searing crops, killing livestock by thirst and starvation and blotting out the midday sun. Des Moines was on the edge of the Dust Bowl, as the catastrophe came to be called, but in the center of the heat wave which created it. Stories about record temperatures, withered crops and heat deaths dominated the *Des Moines Register and Tribune* in July 1934 when the temperature frequently topped 100 and the average temperature was 82.6 degrees. People slept on roofs and fire escapes or, if they had the price of admission, crowded into the Paramount Theater for the blessings of its air conditioning. WHO had an air-conditioning plant, too, one that was prone to frequent leakage. Rissler remembers that people walking by the studio would smell the escaping ammonia fumes and complain. There was no air conditioning in the control room. "The control rooms had no windows and double doors," the retired engineer recalls. "The only air we got was to open the front and back doors, and if we did that we got the smell of the garbage in the alley."[18]

On his nights off, Reagan kept cool at Cy's Moonlight Inn on the west edge of town. It was a big barn of a building with a long bar, a dirt floor, dance records and an air-conditioning system more primitive than WHO's—a huge block of ice in the center of the room over which fans blew to dispel cooled air. Near beer sold for 25 cents a bottle at Cy's and was sometimes spiked with pure alcohol. "Everybody had flat thumbs," McGinn said. "The flat thumbs came from turning the bottle upside down so the alcohol could mix."[19] Reagan liked the club and the girls who came there, but he did not drink much. On those occasions when he visited the nearby Club Belvedere, which had a casino, he did not gamble at all. What Reagan did do was keep in excellent physical shape, swimming almost daily at Camp Dodge and riding with Myrtle Williams and her friends at the Valley Riding Club. Later, he enlisted as a reserve cavalry officer so that he could ride at Fort Des Moines, a decision Reagan later called "one of the smartest things I ever did."[20]

Already Dutch Reagan was a celebrity known throughout the Middle West and much in demand as a banquet speaker. He kept so much to himself that even many of his fellow announcers at the station did not know where he lived. But he was a good friend of Williams, who was several years older. "He's eaten more eggs at my apartment than anyone," she says, also recalling Reagan's fondness for macaroni-and-cheese dinners. Her memories of their friendship are happy ones: selecting records for Reagan when he was a disc jockey, going to lunch together and counting their money beforehand, going for church services to Drake where Williams was a Sunday soloist. When President Roosevelt came to town, Williams dashed to get Reagan in time to see FDR go by. She cared little for politics in those days, but Reagan was thrilled by the glimpse of his idol.[21]

Reagan lived on the east side of Fourth Street within walking distance of the station. Williams remembers the place as a big, pleasant apartment with beautiful woodwork in a rundown section of town where the houses have since been torn down. By now Reagan was the recognized breadwinner of his family. A series of heart attacks had made it impossible for his father to work any longer at the relief assistance job which his political support of Roosevelt had earned for him. Reagan sent money home, enabling Nelle to quit her job at the dress shop. After Moon graduated from Eureka, Dutch found work for him at WHO, where his older brother started out as the Saturday night football scoreboard announcer whenever Dutch was returning home from out-of-town games. Myrtle Williams remembers that Dutch also was generous to a newsboy he liked, known to them only as "Jimmy," who sold papers on a downtown street. Reagan on occasion tipped him as much as five dollars, she recalls. Mostly, though, Reagan saved as much as he could out of a salary which by 1936 had been raised to $90 a week.

Reagan had his heart set on buying a new Nash convertible which he and Williams often had admired in the auto company's showroom. Finally he was able to pay cash for the car. "The young women thought he looked handsome in it—beige car, brown hair, brown tweed, brown pipe," wrote Myron S. Waldman, after interviewing many of Reagan's friends in Des Moines.[22] Reagan drove the Nash to Hollywood in 1937 and kept it for many years, even when he could have afforded another automobile.

Did Reagan in this flush of youthful success have a vision of the larger future in store for him? Certainly not in the sense that he foresaw a career in public life, much less the presidency. But Reagan was restless and interested in the world beyond Des Moines. Once, at Eureka, a French professor with a reputation as a psychic had predicted to Reagan's awed freshman class: "This is a class of destiny."[23] Many years later Reagan recalled this forecast, but it was not on his mind in Des Moines.

However, Reagan's dream of being an actor had never died. In 1936, when Gene Autry signed a hillbilly band which had appeared on WHO to a contract for one of his western movies, Reagan began to think that he could succeed in Hollywood, too. He believed in destiny, in luck, and suddenly it seemed to be working for him. He had never been to the West, but WHO approved his request to go to Catalina in 1937 to cover the spring training of the Chicago Cubs. At a double date one night before he left, McGinn introduced Reagan to Joy Hodges, a Des Moines girl who had worked at WHO before becoming a Hollywood singer and actress. Hodges invited Reagan to look her up when he came to Southern California with the Cubs. When he did, she persuaded Reagan to discard his horned-rimmed glasses, and took the near-sighted sports announcer to her agent, Bill Meiklejohn. His clients included Robert Taylor, Betty Grable and a little known actress named Jane Wyman. Reagan freely lied to Meiklejohn about his experience, converting the Eureka Drama Club into a stock company and telling him that he was making $180 a week. But Meiklejohn liked the pleasant young man who was telling him those things.

With true Hollywood hyperbole, he called Warner Brothers casting director Max Arnow and informed him, "I have another Robert Taylor sitting in my office." Arnow had heard that sort of talk before. Still, Meiklejohn had sent him some good talent, and he agreed to give Reagan a screen test. At that test Arnow picked out a suitable part, that of a clean-cut young man from the Middle West (Johnny Case in *Holiday*). Arnow remembers that Reagan read the part, memorized it and gave a perfect test on camera. Reagan, who subsequently saw the test, said he was "terrible" and claimed to have asked Arnow why he had hired him.[24] But it was good enough for Arnow to offer Reagan a contract at $200 a week. Joy Hodges happily wired back to the *Des Moines Register and Tribune* the news that sportscaster Dutch Reagan had become an actor. Improving on Meiklejohn, she said that Reagan was "the greatest bet since Taylor."

Hollywood is where actors change their given names and sometimes lose their identities. Reagan was known universally as "Dutch" and much preferred his nickname to his given name. Now, however, he was being christened again at a meeting of the Warners brass who were evaluating his screen test. Suddenly Reagan realized that he stood a good chance of losing both of his names, and the prospect was not pleasing. Timidly, as he recalls it, he suggested that he be known on screen as "Ronald Reagan." In a par-

ody of a movie scene the name was tossed around the table with Arnow repeating the words "Ronald Reagan, Ronald Reagan," and finally declaring,
"I like it."[25] So, Ronald Reagan it was. Migrating to the community where
many people lose their names, the young announcer from Iowa had been
given back the name he had been baptized with in Tampico twenty-six years
before.

5

The Actor

IN his early days in politics the quickest way to get a rise out of Ronald Reagan was to suggest that he was a mediocre actor trying for a second career after failing in his first. Criticisms of his acting career, Reagan told me in 1968, "touch an exposed nerve."[1] He said he had been prepared for political criticism but he hadn't expected that his adversaries would make fun of his films. Movie acting was serious business to Reagan. He spent the prime of his life in Hollywood and earned good reviews for the majority of his performances. In public life he spices his speech with stories of the movie days, approaches issues in cinematic terms and uses film analogies to make political points. For thirty years he made his living as an actor, and as a representative of actors. He has been married twice, each time to an actress. His children were born, or adopted, in Hollywood. From the time of his first screen test until he went to Sacramento as governor of California in 1967, Reagan was Hollywood's child, citizen, spokesman and defender.

Reagan's "exposed nerve" was touched especially by a frequent canard of the 1960s that he "never got the girl" in his films. In our 1968 interview he brought up this comment without being asked about it and said it demonstrated that many of those who criticized his films had never seen them. Then he ticked off a list of the movie heroines he had "gotten"—Ann Sheridan in *King's Row* and *Juke Girl*, Priscilla Lane in *Million Dollar Baby*, Shirley Temple in *That Hagen Girl*, Eleanor Parker in *The Voice of the Turtle*, Doris Day in *Winning Team*, Virginia Mayo in *The Girl from Jones Beach*, Barbara Stanwyck in *Cattle Queen of Montana*, Patricia Neal in *John Loves Mary*. After diplomatically remembering to mention that he also was married to his real wife, Nancy Davis, in *Hellcats of the Navy*, Reagan concluded: "I always got the girl."[2]

Before he was a politician, Reagan usually was viewed as an able, durable actor who could rise to the occasion when given an important part. At the beginning of World War II he was on the borderline of becoming a "star." He never quite got there, but he was better than a journeyman actor, and on occasion better than his self-assessment as "the Errol Flynn of the B's." In the low-budget pictures where Reagan learned his trade, he was cast as a radio announcer, a reporter, an insurance adjuster, an attorney, a fruit picker, a pilot, a soldier. Four times he engaged in improbable exploits as Secret Service Agent Brass Bancroft. Many of these early roles were stereotypes in which Reagan played a male lead who was earnest, brave and not too bright. He did indeed, in most cases, get the girl. *New York Times* critic Bosley Crowther suggested one of the reasons. Praising Reagan's performance in *The Girl from Jones Beach* in 1949, Crowther wrote that Reagan had "a cheerful way of looking at dames."

One measure of Reagan's ability as an actor is that he frequently won praise in films panned by the critics. In other films Reagan performed competently but was overshadowed by major future stars making their debuts. This happened in Reagan's first acclaimed film, *Brother Rat,* in 1938, where Eddie Albert was the overshadower, and continued through the years to *The Hasty Heart* (1950), where Reagan was a supporting actor in a cast that featured Richard Todd and Patricia Neal. Todd won an Academy Award nomination for his portrayal of a soldier in a Burmese hospital and went on to a big career. Though Crowther found Todd's portrayal of a dying Scottish officer "eloquent" and "irresistible," he also praised Reagan as "amusingly impatient and blunt" in the role of a wounded American.

By good fortune Reagan came to Hollywood with an approach to acting that was suited to the screen. Years before "method acting" was in vogue, his high school drama teacher B. J. Frazer was instructing students to act out the emotions of the characters they were creating. "I did not have training as a professional drama coach," said Frazer. "I think my ignorance stood me in good stead. I wanted them to be this character. I used to sit the cast down and ask, 'Why, why, why are the characters doing these things?' When they got out on the stage, they *were* the characters. I understand that this became the standard for Hollywood. Reagan was good. He never forgot his lines or his actions. When he got on the stage, he was the character."[3]

Reagan was drawn to his drama teachers. Frazer became a booster and a friend, and the two men were close enough for Reagan to write Frazer that Mugs Cleaver had returned her engagement ring. When he went off to college, Reagan received more encouragement toward an acting career from Marie Ellen Johnson, the respected drama teacher at Eureka. The acting ambition was submerged in the years Reagan was learning to be a radio announcer, but it was never far from the surface. "I'd rather act than anything else," he told the *Des Moines Register and Tribune* after he had signed his contract with Warners. "But I didn't think that anyone would go home and give their husband arsenic after seeing me, so I turned to radio as a second choice."

In Hollywood, Reagan first played a radio announcer in *Love Is on the Air.* It was a crime picture, casting Reagan opposite June Travis as a crusading announcer who is demoted because of pressure from local businessmen in cahoots with the racketeers he is exposing. In the end the racketeers are tricked into confessing before an open microphone and Reagan wins his job back, plus Travis. The film set the pattern for Reagan's predominant "good guy" roles, and also for the casting of him as a high-minded announcer or reporter. It must have been this film, and *Nine Lives Are Not Enough,* which Reagan had in mind when he described his early career. "I always played a jet-propelled newspaperman who solved more crimes than a lie detector," Reagan said. "My one unvarying line which I always snapped into a phone was: 'Give me the city desk; I've got a story that will crack this town wide open.' "[4]

Reagan was fascinated by film-making. He wrote painstakingly of the technical intricacies of making a movie in a series for the *Des Moines Sunday Register* after he completed his first film in 1937.[5] The accounts are spiced with self-deprecatory stories for the homefolks about how it felt to be "a male *Alice in Wonderland.*"* But the focus of the series is on the importance of camera location, scene lighting, film editing and rehearsing. "Picture making continues to amaze me," Reagan wrote with a sense of wonder, after filming a scene a dozen times before the director finally gave his approval.

Reagan's photographic memory and willingness to take direction were well suited to the assembly-line style of production which Jack Warner had developed. The B-picture division of Warner Brothers, a consistent money-maker, turned out films quickly and efficiently, without qualms about artistic quality. An actor who memorized scripts quickly, as Reagan did, was money in the bank. Reagan's easy-going disposition was an additional asset. In the early years he did not agitate for star roles, and he was willing, maybe too willing, to accept a bit role in a big movie after being a hit in a small one. This combination of qualities helped keep Reagan in the second division at Warner's, which was loaded with stars who had Reagan's on-screen wholesomeness but were more difficult to deal with on the set.

In 1938 Reagan made eight films, most of them B's, ending with *Brother Rat,* a movie adaptation of the play in which Eddie Albert had starred on Broadway. Reagan won favorable, though overshadowed, critical comment for his portrayal of Virginia Military Institute cadet Dan Crawford, who romances the daughter of the VMI commandant. The daughter is played by Jane Wyman, who a year and a half later would become Reagan's wife. In 1939 Reagan made another eight films, including *Dark Victory* with Bette

* One story which Reagan told was of how he tried to get a date with June Travis in *Love Is on the Air,* which was shot with the working title of *Inside Story.* The director had instructed Reagan to whisper something in her ear in the next-to-last scene when he "gets the girl" to make it seem more realistic. She whispered back, and Reagan ruined the scene by saying out loud that he couldn't hear her. The stage hands laughed and shot the scene again. "I whispered my question again, this time heard her reply," Reagan wrote. "Her answer was 'No.' "

Davis, Geraldine Fitzgerald and Humphrey Bogart. By the beginning of 1940 he had become typecast as a pleasant, second-line lead actor. He had not fulfilled the prediction of early stardom, but he had learned his trade quickly and well in the factory of B-film production. What Reagan remembers from those days, other than the leading ladies he was paired with, are the techniques of the actor's trade: where to stand, what to wear, how to kiss a girl. He had laid the foundation for a solid career.

Reagan's breakthrough came in 1940, the year he married Wyman and played opposite her in a flat sequel to *Brother Rat* entitled *Brother Rat and a Baby,* which unwisely carried the adventures of the VMI cadets into civilian life. Warner Brothers tried again to capitalize on the Reagan–Wyman marriage by casting them as husband and wife in a comedy called *Angel from Texas.* The movie attracted little attention, and Reagan and Wyman went their separate ways on the screen after that. Reagan then completed the exploits of Secret Agent Bancroft with *Murder in the Air,* a respectable thriller by the standards of the day. But this sort of role had paled for Reagan, who for the first time decided to battle for a part he wanted. By the time Reagan tested for the role of George Gipp in *Knute Rockne—All American,* Warner Brothers had tried out ten other actors for the part. None of them "looked like football players," as Reagan remembers it, adding that few persons of normal build look like football players out of uniform.

Reagan wanted the part in the worst way. He felt he was perfect for the role of Gipp, a talented Notre Dame football player who had died young of pneumonia. He also saw that the part had the potential for rescuing him from the B epics in which he had been typecast. Reagan showed Bryan (Brynie) Foy, who was in charge of B-film production at Warners, pictures of himself in a Eureka College football uniform. Foy was impressed but said that Reagan also had to convince Hal Wallis, who was producing *Rockne.* Reagan then went to Pat O'Brien, who had been the uncontested choice for Rockne. The two actors had appeared together in *Submarine D-1,* where Reagan's role was left on the cutting room floor, and again in a 1938 film, *Cowboy from Brooklyn.* O'Brien, then a star, liked Reagan and knew of his athletic background and interest.

"As far as Jack Warner was concerned, it was just another picture," O'Brien said years later. "I was excited about it, being an athletic buff, but there weren't too many contract players at Warners who were athletically inclined. I asked who was going to play the Gipper. 'Who's the Gipper?' Warner said. I said, 'This is a helluva important role. A lot of the people you have under contract don't know a football from a cantaloupe. This guy does.' I said, 'I'll tell you what I'll do. I'll make the test with him.' Warner said I could do it if I was that excited about it. I made the test with him, and the rest is history. Ronald Reagan breathed life into the Gipper."[6]

Even with a lifeless Gipper the film would have been interesting, because O'Brien is ideal as Rockne, the Norwegian immigrant who became Notre

Dame's football star and its most famous coach before losing his life in a plane crash.* Much of the film has passed before Reagan comes on screen, but his arrival is worth waiting for. The scene is Gipp's first practice at Notre Dame, and Rockne asks him if he can carry the ball. With an insouciance that anticipates candidate Reagan, Gipp looks quizzically at the coach and asks, "How far?"

Forty-one years later O'Brien and Reagan looked back on this film with sentiment as they embraced on the stage of the Notre Dame fieldhouse, where both men were receiving honorary degrees. "Guess they liked the picture," Reagan whispered to O'Brien.[7] It was May 17, 1981, and President Reagan's first trip outside Washington since he had been wounded by a would-be assassin on March 30. Reagan had on this occasion rejected the advice of aides who wanted him to talk about foreign policy, as President Carter had done four years before at a Notre Dame commencement. Reagan had written his own speech. What he wanted to talk about was Knute Rockne.

"Now, I'm going to mention again that movie that Pat and I and Notre Dame were in for it says something about America," Reagan said. "First, Knute Rockne as a boy came to America with his parents from Norway. And in the few years it took him to grow up to college age, he became so American, that here at Notre Dame, he became an All-American in a game that is still to this day uniquely American. As a coach, he did more than teach young men how to play a game. He believed truly that the noblest work of man was building the character of man. And maybe that's why he was a living legend. No man connected with football has ever achieved the stature or occupied the singular niche in the nation that he carved out for himself, not just in sport, but in our entire social structure.

"Now, today I hear very often, 'Win one for the Gipper,' spoken in a humorous vein. Lately, I've been hearing it by congressmen who are supportive of the [economic] program that I've introduced. But let's look at the significance of that story. Rockne could have used Gipp's dying words to win a game any time. But eight years went by following the death of George Gipp before Rock revealed those dying words, his deathbed wish.

"And then he told the story at halftime to a team that was losing and one of the only teams he had ever coached that was torn by dissension and jealousy and factionalism. The seniors on that team were about to close out their football careers without learning or experiencing any of the real values that a game has to impart. None of them had known George Gipp. They were children when he played for Notre Dame. It was to this team that Rockne told the story and so inspired them that they rose above their per-

* The film, made at Loyola University in Los Angeles instead of Notre Dame, won praise for its faithfulness to Rockne's actual life. The script by Robert Buckner had the advantages of materials provided by Rockne's widow and the private Rockne files at Notre Dame.

sonal animosities. For someone they had never known they joined together in a common cause and attained the unattainable.

"We were told when we were making the picture of one line that was spoken by a player during that game. We were actually afraid to put it in the picture. The man who carried the ball over for the winning touchdown was injured on the play. We were told that as he was lifted on the stretcher and carried off the field he was heard to say: 'That's the last one I can get for you, Gipper.'

"Now, it's only a game. And maybe to hear it now afterward—and this is what we feared might sound maudlin and not the way it was intended—but is there anything wrong with young people having an experience, feeling something so deeply, thinking of someone else to the point that they can give so completely of themselves? There will come times in the lives of all of us when we'll be faced with causes bigger than ourselves, and they won't be on a playing field."[8]

The Rockne film led to major roles for Reagan in *Sante Fe Trail* and *The Bad Man,* a melodrama dominated by accomplished scene-stealers Wallace Beery and Lionel Barrymore. Reagan's best stories on the campaign trail have come from the latter film, in which he tells of being simultaneously upstaged by Beery and bruised by a wheelchair operated by Barrymore in his role as a crippled rancher. *Sante Fe Trail* is a historical disgrace in which Errol Flynn has the lead role as Confederate cavalryman J.E.B. Stuart and Reagan the second lead as General George Armstrong Custer, supposedly Stuart's friend and a fellow 1854 graduate of West Point. Actually, Custer was fifteen years old when Stuart graduated that year, and the two men never met at any time in their lives. It was as if Hollywood were making up for its rare excursion into historical accuracy with *Knute Rockne* by a particularly goofy rewrite of Civil War history. Oswald Garrison Villard wrote *The Saturday Review of Literature* in protest against the film's historical inaccuracies. "It was Jefferson Davis, according to this Hollywood version, who was the real champion of the union," declared *The Christian Century.* But Reagan looked good on a horse and performed well enough as Flynn's mythical best friend to give his career another boost.

Three other Reagan films were released in 1941, all to good, though not exceptional, reviews. Reagan was a young pianist in *Million Dollar Baby,* a young newspaperman in *Nine Lives Are Not Enough,* and an American stunt pilot in *International Squadron.* By now, Reagan was knocking on the door of stardom and making $1,000 a week. He was rewarded with what most critics consider his best role, that of Drake McHugh, a rake from the wrong side of the tracks who has his legs amputated by mad surgeon Henry Gordon (Charles Coburn) because he is making out with Gordon's daughter Louise (Nancy Coleman). "Where's the rest of me?", McHugh's cry when he discovers he is legless, became the title for Reagan's autobiography. The star-studded cast, as they used to say, also featured Ann Sheridan, Claude Rains, Robert Cummings and Betty Fields.

Reagan shares the critics' view that this film, *King's Row,* was his finest film. In his early days in politics he was stopped frequently by admirers who remembered the movie, and obviously enjoyed being complimented for his performance. "It was my best picture," Reagan said, and he has used the McHugh role to illustrate the precepts of acting he first learned from B. J. Frazer in Dixon. "I always ask myself how do I, Ronald Reagan, feel about it," he says. "How much is Ronald Reagan with his legs cut off and how much is Drake McHugh? If I divorce myself and say, 'How does Drake McHugh feel?' it's not a good job. But if I scream in horror, 'Where's the rest of me?' and I feel it, that's me, and it's right."[9]

King's Row caught the fancy of many reviewers, although there were some who thought that too much had been lost in transferring Ballaman's portentous novel, with its taboo subject of incest, to the screen. Hollywood substituted "insanity" for "incest," and tacked on a happy ending by allowing McHugh, who dies in the book, to live. *Time* reviewer James Agee, no easy mark, called director Sam Wood's interpretation of the novel, "powerful, artful cinema," and *The New Yorker* said the film will "give you that rare glow which comes from seeing a job crisply done, competently and with confidence." *Commonweal* praised Reagan for "a splendid performance." But not everyone was equally gaga about the film or Reagan's role in it. Crowther in the *New York Times,* a frequent booster of Reagan in lesser roles, thought that he and Sheridan "make only casual acquaintances" with the characters they portray.

Crowther was in the minority, but it is hard to see in looking back at Reagan's excellent acting in half a dozen other films, starting with Gipp, how *King's Row* can so assuredly be classified as his best performance. What it was, for certain, was Reagan's most celebrated role and one that finally brought him to the brink of stardom. Unfortunately for Reagan, *King's Row* was filmed in 1941. By the time it was released the following year, the Japanese had attacked Pearl Harbor and the United States was at war. So was Reagan, in a manner of speaking.

He had kept his commission in the cavalry reserve, which he had joined in Des Moines to ride horses, and he was called to active duty in April 1942, although disqualified from combat because of his nearsightedness. After brief service at Fort Mason in San Francisco, Reagan was transferred to the First Motion Picture Unit of the Army Air Corps, which had taken over the Hal Roach studios only a few miles from the Warner Brothers studio. It was easy service for Reagan, who was able to live at home and participate in some of the memorable training films made by "Ft. Roach," which also earned and enjoyed a reputation for unmilitary wackiness. Reagan played in three training films—*Mr. Gardenia Jones, Rear Gunner* and *For God and Country,* in which he portrayed a Catholic chaplain. In 1943 he was detached from his unit for a role in *This Is the Army,* a successful wartime musical written by Irving Berlin, who appeared on screen to sing, "Oh, How I Hate to Get Up in the Morning."

From the point of view of a combat serviceman, Reagan's role during the war could hardly have been cushier. But he was paying a professional price for the timing of *King's Row,* as he came to realize during the filming of *This Is the Army.* As Reagan recalls it, Berlin came to him after the filming of a segment to praise his acting and suggest that he go into show business after the war. Reagan thanked him but says he never knew whether Berlin was unaware that he was a movie actor or had forgotten him because he hadn't been on screen for so long.[10] It was a distant early warning of what would happen to the budding star while he was away making training films.

6

The First Time Around

Describing himself to his fans in August 1942, Ronald Reagan said he was "a plain guy with a set of homespun features and no frills" whose tastes and preferences were those of the average man. "I like to swim, hike and sleep (eight hours a night)," Reagan said. "I'm fairly good at every sport except tennis, which I just don't like. My favorite menu is steak smothered with onions and strawberry shortcake. Mr. Norm is my alias. I play bridge adequately, collect guns, always carry a penny as a good-luck charm and knock wood when I make a boast or express a wish. I have a so-so convertible coupe which I drive myself. I'm interested in politics and governmental problems. My favorite books are *Turnabout* by Thorne Smith, *Babbitt, The Adventures of Tom Sawyer* and the works of Pearl Buck, H. G. Wells, Damon Runyon and Erich Remarque. I'm a fan of Bing Crosby. My favorite actress is my wife. I like things colored green and my favorite flower is the Eastern lilac. I love my wife, baby and home. I've just built a new one—home, I mean. Nothing about me to make me stand out on the midway."[1]

Reagan's celebration of his supposed averageness, in a *Photoplay* article called "How to Make Yourself Important," was a message to the fans he left behind when he was called to military service. Implicitly, it reflected Reagan's liberal outlook of the time, stressing equality over exceptionalism and crediting his film success to the shared average values of his fellow citizens. "Average will do it," Reagan wrote, expressing a credo that would survive throughout his various political incarnations. Reagan's ranking of himself as an average man carried with it a power to speak for "the people," permitting him to identify with whatever audience he was facing. The actor's key advice to the fans he left behind was "(a) love what you are doing with all your heart and soul and (b) believe what you are doing is important—even if you are only grubbing for worms in the back yard."[2]

Mr. Norm was made to order for Hollywood, then the undisputed mass culture capital of the United States. In the salad days of silent films, Hollywood had boasted a carnival atmosphere and was known to staid Los Angelenos as "the movie colony," where loose morals had replaced good manners. Carey McWilliams counted the other side of the coin, crediting Hollywood with liberating the manners and morals of Los Angeles "from the sillier rituals of middle-class life."[3] But a series of morals scandals after World War I, coming when filmmaking was emerging as one of the nation's most profitable industries, jolted Hollywood and led to formation of a trade association, a code of conduct and a censor (the Hays office) empowered to police the themes, messages and morals of every movie. A morals clause became a standard part of an actor's contract, and press agents were hired by the studios to sell and sanitize the private lives of stars and starlets. Actors, particularly young actors, were supposed to be clean-cut and wholesome. And the studios were always on the lookout for "ideal couples" and "perfect marriages" that could be paraded before American movie-goers as symbols of happy Hollywood home life.

Enter Ronald Reagan and Jane Wyman, made to order candidates for exploitation of their private lives. They were young, attractive, naive and untainted by scandal. In a community where divorce was supposed to be commonplace, Reagan had never been married. The blonde and fiery Wyman had been married once, briefly, to apparel manufacturer Myron Futterman. She met Reagan while on the rebound and dated him during the filming of *Brother Rat.* Their relationship was encouraged by Hollywood gossip columnist Louella O. Parsons, whose initial bond with Reagan was based on the coincidence that Parsons also came from Dixon, Illinois.

Gossip columnists, particularly Parsons and her rival Hedda Hopper, were powerful forces in the movie community in those days. Words of praise from a gossip columnist could signal a producer or an agent to the presence of a rising star. Parsons gave a boost to Wyman, who was trying to escape typecasting in chorus girl roles and boxing pictures. The columnist included both Reagan and Wyman on a nine-week "stars of tomorrow" vaudeville tour in 1939. With Wyman taking the initiative, the romance blossomed.

"Long before Ronald was aware of Janie's existence, she knew *he was there,* breathlessly reported *Photoplay.* "But Ronnie had had his heart bashed in once and wouldn't look Janie's way for a long time. When he did, it was all over but the wedding."[4] Parsons, of course, announced it. "Life was very much the way Jane wanted it on a certain day our vaudeville tour took us to Philadelphia," Parsons said long afterwards. "Her brown eyes were sparkling and her voice was bubbling with happiness as she told me: 'Have I got a scoop for you! Ronnie and I are engaged!' I had known that Janie worshipped Ronnie, but I hadn't realized he was falling seriously in love with her. I announced the engagement that night from the stage and in the newspapers."[5]

Even before Reagan and Wyman were wed, studio publicists, gossip columnists and fan magazine writers competed in their haste to proclaim the Perfect Marriage. One publication offered the couple an expense-paid trip to

Hawaii if they would take a cameraman along to record their marriage ceremony and honeymoon. Instead, Reagan and Wyman were married in Glendale on January 26, 1940. They attended a reception given by Parsons at her home, honeymooned in Palm Springs and moved into the Beverly Hills apartment where Wyman had lived before the marriage. On January 4, 1941, Wyman's 27th birthday, a baby daughter they named Maureen Elizabeth was born to the Reagans. The publicists cooed, celebrating a marriage they believed was made both in Hollywood and heaven.

A release from Warner Brothers publicity department on June 2, 1941, was headed, "THE HOPEFUL REAGANS. They Are Looking Forward to More of Everything Good—Including Children." Much of it is in banal dialogue between Ron and Jane that would have been more suitable for Jane and Tarzan. The Reagans, with their baby, "show signs of becoming one of the important first families of the film colony, a new dynasty, one might say, which will bear watching. It is a busy little family what with both papa and mama working in Warner Brothers pictures and little Maureen Elizabeth about to cut her first tooth—in advance of all predictions, too." The rest of the release is even gooier. Both parents rave on about the baby, and Jane confesses that, unlike Ronald, she was "terribly disappointed" when she learned her baby was a girl. Ronald, ever the average man, is quoted as saying: "The Reagans' home life is probably just like yours, or yours, or yours. We do the same foolish things that other couples do, have the same scraps, about as much fun, typical problems and the most wonderful baby in the world." The only negative note comes when Jane explains how they are using old furniture and want to buy new when they move into the eight-room house they are building on a hill overlooking Hollywood. Ronald interrupts before Jane can finish. "Depends on conditions and prices and war and things," he says. "We don't intend to get out on a limb."

By August, with her husband filming *King's Row,* Jane is bragging about the marriage in *Silver Screen* in an article entitled "Making a Double Go of It." Mary Jane Manners quotes "Janie" as saying: "Neither Ronnie nor I were stars. We were both featured players, making $500 a week. I wasn't a glamor queen, and he wasn't a matinee idol. We were just two kids trying to get the breaks in pictures. But look at Ronnie now. He's taken a scooter and gone leaps and bounds ahead of me. But I'm terribly proud of him—all the same." There is more, too much more, about how Ronnie converted her from nightclubbing to swimming, golf and other sports, and about how they spent their time looking at model houses before finally spotting the one they wanted in a movie. There is another published appeal for new furniture. There is a confession from Wyman that she had "always been the kind of girl that if there was anything I wanted, I'd go and buy it and think about whether I could really afford it afterward but Ronnie won't go in debt." Finally, there is a glimpse of how they get along together. "Ronnie and I are perfect counterparts for each other," she said. "I blow up and Ronnie just laughs at me. We've never had a quarrel because he's just too good-natured. I pop off and am over it in a minute. Then he makes me ashamed of myself because he's so understanding."[6]

It might have been called the Goldfish Bowl Marriage. The expectations were so high and the claims made for the marriage by the studio so extravagant that the first signs of normal marital discord were treated by columnists and magazine writers as a national tragedy. Reagan, according to the accounts of friends and what he was quoted as saying at the time, appears to have accepted the studio propaganda as literally true. He publicly celebrated the marriage and the sterling qualities of Wyman. He was unprepared for the snide realities of a breakup, which the columnists covered as avidly, albeit sympathetically, as the public romance. Reagan's pride would have been damaged in any case, but he was embarrassed by the repeated references to marital trouble and lashed out in criticism of the columnists for invading his private life. Never again would he allow them to come so close.

With the unfair advantage of historical hindsight, it is easy to see that there were plenty of potential difficulties in the Reagan–Wyman marriage which the columnists initially overlooked. Apart from their acting, and they never clicked on the screen after *Brother Rat*, Reagan and Wyman had different interests. He was interested in sports, both as a participant and a spectator, and she was not. Despite her *Silver Screen* disclaimer, she still liked nightclubbing, and he did not. Reagan was soon heavily involved in union and political activities, which did not interest Wyman. And there were differences in personality, too. Reagan was optimistic and open, she more anxious and introverted. "He was such a sunny person, I never felt free to talk to anyone until I met Ronnie," she was quoted as saying early in their marriage.[7] But they were in love and tried to have more children. When they were unable to, they adopted a boy, Michael Edward, in March 1945, nine months before Reagan was discharged from the army. Then in 1947, Jane became pregnant again. When Jane was five months pregnant, Reagan contracted viral pneumonia, the disease which had killed George Gipp. It almost finished off Reagan, too. He believes he would have died at Cedars of Lebanon Hospital except for the efforts of an unnamed nurse who kept coaxing him to take another breath. Reagan says he "kept breathing out of courtesy"[8] and slowly regained his will to live. While Reagan was fighting for his life, Jane gave birth on June 26, 1947, to a baby girl that was four months premature and died the following day. Parsons said afterward that the baby had come early because Jane was "distraught" and "almost out of her mind with worry" over the illness of her husband.[9] Parsons, whose own husband was in Cedars of Lebanon recuperating from an illness, dropped in to see Reagan frequently. "When Jane was stricken, it was Ronald's turn to worry and he was almost desperate," Parsons said. "He was so miserable because he was unable to be with her during her ordeal. He tossed and fretted in his hospital bed, telling me how magnificent Jane had been and how fearful he was of her health. Little did he realize that this illness of hers might bring about their separation within a few months."[10]

While Reagan had been off to his peaceful war, Wyman's career had taken an upward turn through her compelling performance as an alcoholic writer's wife in *The Lost Weekend* (1945). It gave her an opportunity to escape from the comedienne roles in which she had previously been typed. In 1947, she was acclaimed for her performance in *The Yearling*. After recovering from the death of her premature child, she started work on the role that would in 1948 earn her an Academy Award—the deaf mute in *Johnny Belinda*. By the time the award was announced, the Reagans were separated. She attended the Oscar ceremony in the company of Lew Ayres, who in *Johnny Belinda* plays the role of Wyman's sympathetic doctor. Reagan went alone and was left to tell Hedda Hopper his most oft-quoted comment of the breakup: "I think I'll name *Johnny Belinda* as the co-respondent."[11]

He was kidding on the square. Reagan's career was declining, and Wyman was quoted in 1946 as saying he was "restless" about it, and frustrated that his poor eyesight had kept him out of combat. Her own career was flourishing. But those who were close to the Reagans hinted at personal reasons rather than professional ones for the foundering of the marriage. In the February 1948 issue of *Photoplay*, Gladys Hall quoted Wyman as telling a reporter during a 1947 trip to New York: "We're through. We're finished, and it's all my fault." Was it? Hall's article, entitled "Those Fightin' Reagans," asked more questions than it answered.

"Is there some hangover from a past Ronnie does not share?" she wrote. "Some conflict, still unresolved in Jane's memory? Certain it is, however, that Jane last autumn was visibly unhappy; was nervous; was irritable— many times in public—with Ronnie. But Ronnie was cajoling, always very easy with Jane, and very sweet. Always in there, trying."

Hall's sympathy for Reagan was shared by columnists Parsons and Hopper. According to them, Reagan had been astonished when he read Jane's New York comment in three papers, while Parsons was "genuinely shocked" and Hopper "stunned." It was as if something they themselves had created were being destroyed. Parsons weighed in with one last try in the April 1948 issue of *Photoplay*: "Last Call for Happiness: This is Ronald Reagan's Heart Speaking, With the Frankness that would be Given Only to an Old Friend." When Ronnie got a chance to say what happened, he replied enigmatically, "Nothing—and everything. I think Jane takes her work too seriously. . . . She is very intense—but she's been a wonderful wife and unsure because of that very thing. The trouble is—she hasn't learned to separate her work from her personal life. Right now Jane needs very much to have a fling and I intend to let her have it."

Reagan also told Parsons that Wyman was "sick and nervous and not herself. Jane says she loves me but is no longer 'in love' with me and points out that this is a fine distinction. That I don't believe. I think she is nervous, despondent and because of this feels our life together has become humdrum." He did concede, however, that he may have been spending too much time on union business. "Perhaps I should have let someone else save the world and have saved my own home," he said.

Wyman gave her version in court. She announced in February of 1948 that she was suing for divorce, reconciled briefly in April and filed a complaint in May charging "extreme mental cruelty," then the catchall provision used for most California divorces. "I've never known any divorce to come as such a surprise," wrote Parsons. "Jane and Ronnie have always stood for so much that is right in Hollywood." In the court proceeding which followed, Wyman said the Screen Actors Guild took up much of her husband's time and that she did not share his interest. She said Reagan wanted her around the house for discussion of union issues but that the discussions were "far above me" and that no one was interested in her ideas. "Finally, there was nothing in common between us, nothing to sustain our marriage," she said.

In a divorce decree granted initially on June 28, 1948, and made final on July 18, 1949, Wyman was awarded custody of the two children and $500 a month for their support. Reagan had to maintain $25,000 life insurance policies on both himself and his wife and allow Jane horseback riding privileges on the eight-acre ranch they had bought in Northridge and named "Yearling Row," after Wyman's performance in *The Yearling* and his own in *King's Row.* Subsequently, in 1952, Wyman wed film-studio musical director Freddie Karger, but divorced him two years later. Wyman and Karger married again in 1961, but this marriage also ended in divorce.

In the intervening decades Wyman has refused to be interviewed about her marriage to Reagan. The closest she came to a public comment was relayed through a friend, Father Robert Perrella, in *They Call Me the Showbiz Priest* (1973): "She admits it was exasperating to awake in the middle of the night, prepare for work, and have someone at the breakfast table, newspaper in hand, expounding on the far right, far left, the conservative right, the conservative left, the middle of the road. She harbors no ill feelings toward him."

Whatever Wyman's feelings, Reagan's were shattered. Actress Patricia Neal remembers him at a party soon after the separation was announced, "and it was sad because he did not want a divorce. I remember he went outside. An older woman went with him. He cried."[12] A close friend of Reagan's in those days said that after the divorce he was "despondent, in a way I had never seen, because he usually was such a happy, optimistic man."[13] After a while, Reagan went into a shell—much as he had done when Mugs Cleaver sent him back his ring a decade and a half earlier—and tried not to talk about divorce at all. When he did talk, he agreed with the verdict of the columnists and the fan magazines (even while decrying their repeated incursions into his failed marriage) that he had been a "victim" who would never have initiated a divorce on his own. Because he did not initiate or want the breakup, Reagan acted as if he had not really been divorced at all. He never changed this way of looking at what had happened to him. Thirty-two years later President Reagan told an interviewer: "I was divorced in the sense that the decision was made by somebody else."[14] On the lecture circuit in behalf of the film industry soon after the Wyman divorce, Reagan surprised audiences by invariably including a line or two in his speeches about the high success rate of marriages in Hollywood. The community was divided into two groups by Reagan—the "multiple marriage set," which received all the publicity, and the stable, family people, who Reagan said were in the vast majority in the entertainment industry. Even before he met Nancy Davis, he put himself in the latter category.

Reagan had other troubles after the war besides his marriage. Even though he had the financial cushion of the seven-year $1-million contract which Lew Wasserman had negotiated for him when he was in the Army,* Reagan had far fewer illusions than Warner Brothers about the prospects for postwar success. "They thought I was the hottest thing around and didn't realize that the sixteen-year-olds didn't know who I was,"[15] Reagan said. Reagan's solution was to seek a picture that would be guaranteed box office and in which he could become acquainted with the new audience. The picture, or so he thought, was *Stallion Road,* which was supposed to star Humphrey Bogart and his wife Lauren Bacall. But the Bogarts backed out at the last minute, and the film was changed from a big-budget technicolor production to an inexpensive black-and-white film. It starred Zachary Scott and Alexis Smith in the roles the Bogarts were supposed to play. Reagan was cast as a hero veterinarian who is afflicted with anthrax. He performed competently and attracted reasonably good reviews, but the movie was a financial flop. Even worse, and much worse artistically, was *That Hagen Girl,* starring Shirley Temple in her first grownup role. Reagan suspected that American film-goers of any age weren't ready to accept the childhood sweetheart as an adult, particularly with Reagan as her overage lover. But he was in a weak position to bargain and unwisely accepted the film. It was while making *That Hagen Girl* that Reagan was stricken with pneumonia and that his wife lost their baby.

Reagan's life had lost its harmony. He battled with the studio and spent as much time at the negotiating table on behalf of the Screen Actors Guild as he did on the movie set. In 1949, the year his divorce became final, he spent four months in England filming *The Hasty Heart* and cursing British food and weather and the British law restricting the amount of currency he

---

* The contract reflected Wasserman's negotiating skill, Reagan's success in *King's Row* and Jack Warner's anticipation of Olivia de Havilland's victory in a landmark lawsuit which overturned the long held studio practice of tacking suspensions onto an actor's seven-year contract. Usually, the suspensions were a response to an actor's refusal to play a role he thought unsuited for him. Until the de Havilland ruling, he had the choice of taking bad parts or being bound to the studio in perpetuity.

could take out of the country. This was Reagan's first look at what he believed to be socialism in action, and he claims to this day that his experience was one of the reasons he turned Republican.[16] Patricia Neal remembers that Reagan on one occasion became so disgusted with the food that he sent to "21" in New York for a dozen steaks. The film was splendid, but Reagan's bad luck continued. In 1950, back in the United States, he played in a baseball game between leading men and comedians at old Wrigley Field in Los Angeles and broke his right thigh in six places while trying to slide into first base. Reagan was in traction for two months, in a cast for months more and used crutches for a long time after that. His leg has never totally recovered its flexibility, though this has not stopped him from riding a horse at every opportunity.

By now, Reagan was in a constant personal battle with Warner Brothers, which he felt was misusing him as an actor. Warners may also have resented the leading role he was taking in negotiations for the Screen Actors Guild, of which he was elected president in 1947. Others shared Reagan's view that Warners wasn't up to the mark in its use of him. "He was a good actor, but Warner Brothers didn't always know what to do with its properties," said Pat O'Brien. "Let's face it, Jack Warner wasn't a Phi Beta Kappa thinker. He once bought *Main Street* and changed the title to *I Married a Doctor,* saying, 'Who would want to see a picture about a street?' I was in that picture, and it died before it was born. We were the peasants of the industry. We weren't MGM."[17]

When Reagan returned from *The Hasty Heart,* he expected to star in a Western called *Ghost Mountain,* which he had brought to the studio before he left for England. Instead, he heard that the studio was assigning the role to Errol Flynn because *That Hagen Girl,* which Reagan had opposed from the first, was a flop. Reagan blew his top, and not even Wasserman could calm him down. A story by Bob Thomas in the *Los Angeles Mirror* on January 6, 1950, quoted Reagan as saying: "I'm going to pick my own pictures. I have come to the conclusion that I could do as good a job of picking as the studio has done. . . . At least I could do no worse. . . . With the parts I've had, I could telephone my lines in and it wouldn't make a difference." Later in the story, reflecting on what he had said, Reagan commented, "Well, I can always go back to being a sports announcer."

Reagan's comments irritated Warner, prompting him to write an angry letter to Reagan. The letter said that the implications of Reagan's remarks were "very damaging" to the pictures in which he appeared and added:

> If you are not satisfied with the roles you have portrayed in the past, and undoubtedly you will have the same attitude with respect to future roles, I would greatly appreciate your sending me a letter cancelling our mutual contractual obligation with respect to the two remaining pictures you are to do with this company.

I have always considered you a very good friend and I would rather have you remain as such than to have business matters interfere with such friendship. Recently, when your agent asked me to advance certain moneys on your contract, I was very happy to do so. However, I do not feel that I personally nor our company nor the pictures in which you have appeared for us are deserving of the uncomplimentary and erroneous rap that is reflected in the interview.*

Reagan felt that Warner was using tough language to cover up a broken promise. He conveyed this view directly to studio executives and wrote Warner a letter on May 4, 1950, pretending that he did not know that Flynn already had been assigned *Ghost Mountain*. Reflecting Reagan's hurt feelings, the letter is laden with sarcasm:

I know that you will recall our discussion some time ago with regard to *That Hagen Girl*. You agreed the script and role were very weak but asked me to do the picture as a personal favor which I gladly did. At that time you encouraged me to bring in a suitable outdoor script which you agreed to buy as a starring vehicle for me. I found such a property in *Ghost Mountain* and the studio purchased it with me, through MCA, acting as go between to close the deal with the author.

Of late there have been "gossip items" indicating you plan to star someone else in the story. Naturally I put no stock in these rumors—I know you too well to ever think you'd break your word.

However, I am anxious to know something of production plans—starting date, etc., in order to better schedule my own plans. Frankly I hope it is soon as I have every confidence in this story.

Production was already scheduled—but with Flynn in the starring role and the film retitled *Rocky Mountain*. Wasserman rescued Reagan from trying to carry out this empty threat of becoming a sports announcer again by negotiating a compromise contract with Warner Brothers that committed Reagan to doing one picture a year at half his former salary. One week later, Wasserman negotiated a five-year, five-picture deal for Reagan with Universal Studios. Ironically, Reagan's irritation with Warner Brothers had given him the free-lance status he had long sought just at the time many

* The letter, now in the Warner Brothers Archives Collection at the University of Southern California, is marked "never sent" at the top. But R. J. Obringer, a studio executive, informed Warner in a February 17 memo that he had communicated Warner's concerns to Reagan. Obringer's account of what he said to Reagan is similar to the language of the Warner letter and ends with the same suggestion that Reagan terminate his contract. Reagan gave Obringer no answer but used the occasion to make some more scathing remarks about his treatment at Warner Brothers. "Reagan went into some more alleged abuses," wrote Obringer to Warner, "and particularly the fact that he lay in the hospital for six weeks with a broken leg without anybody from the studio contacting him or ascertaining his condition except at the last minute when *The Girl from Jones Beach* was released."

other postwar feature players were turning to the security of long-term contracts.

Retrospectively, Reagan's work on screen during this troubled period of his life looks better now than it did then. He made fifteen films in the postwar period beginning with *Stallion Road* in 1947 and ending with *The Winning Team* in 1952, the year he married Nancy Davis. Only *That Hagen Girl* and *Night unto Night,* the second film Reagan made after becoming a civilian although it was not released until 1949, were clinkers. Four of his films—*The Voice of the Turtle, The Girl from Jones Beach, John Loves Mary,* and *The Hasty Heart*—gave Reagan a chance to display his flair for light comedy. The best of these is *Voice of the Turtle* (1947), where Reagan has the male lead as an Army sergeant who falls in love with a young actress. In this instance Warner's judgment was better than Reagan's. He had bought the rights of the award-winning play by John Van Druten with Reagan in mind and refused to let his returning would-be star accept a bit part in *Treasure of the Sierra Madre.* The critics liked the performances of Reagan and new star Eleanor Parker in *The Voice of the Turtle.* "Ronald Reagan turns in a pleasingly sensitive performance as the marooned sergeant," wrote *Newsweek* in a typical comment.

Reagan's newfound contractual independence gave him the chance to do what he had always been denied at Warner Brothers—make a genuine western. Starting with *The Last Outpost* for Paramount in 1951, he made four for three different filmmakers, with the best being *Cattle Queen of Montana* with Barbara Stanwyck for RKO. The others are run-of-the-plains westerns where Reagan probably benefits more from his riding ability than from his acting. He also made a 1951 comedy, *Bedtime for Bonzo,* which enjoyed a television revival in the late 1960s after it became the staple of opposition political gags. The gags aside, it's an amusing comedy in which the chimp steals most of the scenes from the human actors. Reagan's best picture of this period, though, was *The Winning Team,* which Reagan enjoyed making because it brought him into touch with professional athletes. The movie is the story of pitcher Grover Cleveland Alexander, whose drinking bouts masked an epileptic condition he never revealed to his teammates. Even though Warner Brothers wouldn't let anyone mention the then taboo word "epilepsy" on screen, Reagan's acting manages to suggest that there is more to Alexander's fainting spells than alcoholism.

By the mid-1950s Reagan's interests had turned to television and politics, and his films became less and less frequent. He made a single movie in 1955 and none the following year. His last feature film, *Hellcats of the Navy,* premiered in San Diego on April 11, 1957. Reagan and his wife Nancy appeared at the Spreckels Theater on behalf of what the approving local newspaper called "the new submarine drama in which they co-star with Arthur Franz." The movie was big in San Diego, with its large naval audience, but is otherwise remembered mostly because Nancy Davis was in it and because it marks the end of Reagan's movie career. It was his fifty-second movie. Purists, of which I am not one, would also list a fifty-third, a made-for-television film that was instead released in movie houses in 1964 because it was judged too violent for the home screen. This movie was called *The Killers* and shares nothing in common with Ernest Hemingway's famous short story except a title. It is of interest chiefly because it is the only time that Reagan, cast as an underworld mobster, plays a villain on the screen. He was uncomfortable in the role and has said on more than one occasion that he wished he never made the picture.[18]

Apart from this historical curiosity, Reagan was a good guy throughout his film career and a reasonably good actor. He had a nice comic touch in his better movies, and his two sports films were among the best of their genre. Many of the movies Reagan made were rushed or uneven, and Reagan is right in saying that "some of the B-pictures turned out to be A-pictures and some of the A's turned out to be B's." He is also accurate in analyzing his postwar career when the contract system was breaking up. "I was under contract when the contract system failed," he said in looking back at it. "I was under contract when I shouldn't have been and wasn't when I should have been. Then, when I went into television, I thought it would help me in the movies. They [the movie-makers] didn't see it that way. They thought that people wouldn't come to see someone in the movie theater when they saw him on the screen."[19]

As it turns out, people still come out to see Reagan in all kinds of settings. In a nation enchanted with celebrities, he remains the world class example of a politician who has parlayed fame in one field into a second career in public life. But Reagan, while acknowledging the head start his movie fame gave him in politics, values his acting career in its own right. His frame of reference continues to be the industry where he spent three decades as a working actor, television host and negotiator for his union. He freely acknowledges that some of his films were flops, but he remains sensitive to criticism about the body of his work on screen, which he considers to be accomplished. Most of the time Reagan conceals this opinion beneath his own one-liners about the movie business, but sometimes he lets his true feelings show.

I remember one particular interview in 1968, late at night on a campaign plane that was returning home to Los Angeles after Reagan had spent several days on the road. We were tired of talking politics, and Reagan turned to stories about the days he had spent in Hollywood and what had happened there. With a sudden burst of emotion he took scornful issue with what he called "this *New York Times* kind of business of referring to me as a B-picture actor."[20] He talked with eloquence of the first-line actors and actresses he had appeared with, often getting better reviews than they did, and said that no one referred to them as B-picture actors. The list was long and included, but wasn't limited to, James Cagney, Eddie Albert, Claude Rains,

Lionel Barrymore, Richard Todd, Humphrey Bogart, Olivia de Havilland, Bette Davis, Barbara Stanwyck, Ann Sheridan and Eleanor Parker. Reagan said he was thankful to have worked with these stars and thankful, too, to have been a part of Hollywood in its heyday. Then he paused for a moment and, almost shyly, added something more. "I'm proud of having been an actor," he said.

7

The Politician

Viewed strictly as a partisan spokesman and candidate, Ronald Reagan is a late political bloomer. He was fifty-three when he made his television speech for Barry Goldwater, fifty-five when he was elected governor of California, nearly seventy when he became President of the United States. His partisan experience prior to his first gubernatorial campaign in 1966 had been limited to making speeches for other candidates. Professionals of both parties put Reagan down as an out-of-work actor trading on his celebrity status to get ahead. Even after he became governor, legislators tended to consider Reagan more of a celebrity than a politician. Reagan contributed to the misapprehension by describing himself as a "citizen-politician" who had answered a call to public duty. He talked as if he were on loan from the entertainment industry and would return to his basic calling after serving, like Cincinnatus, when his country needed him.

First impressions die hard. Though Reagan went on to master the governorship, the impression that he was really not a politician persisted, perhaps because politicians who have come through the ranks are reluctant to say that a former actor is better at their profession than they are. When House Speaker Thomas P. (Tip) O'Neill met with President-elect Reagan on November 18, 1980, less than two weeks after the election, he told Reagan that his California experience was "minor league" and that bills might not move as swiftly for him in Washington as O'Neill thought they had in Sacramento. "This is the big leagues," O'Neill told Reagan, who did not contradict him. Six months and two budget defeats later, O'Neill was asked by a constituent in Boston what was happening. "I'm getting the shit kicked out of me,"[1] the speaker replied.

O'Neill had not been bested by an amateur. Despite his own disclaimers, Reagan has been a political person all his life. He was class president in high school, played a key role in the student strike at Eureka and was much in demand in Hollywood as a campaign speaker. In 1942 he wrote that his interests from college days had been "dramatics, athletics and politics." In

1946 Democrats asked him to run for Congress. In 1948 he campaigned effectively on radio for President Truman and Democratic Senate stars of the future like Hubert H. Humphrey. Friends in the Screen Actors Guild kidded that Reagan was the "boy on the burning deck" because of his proclivity for making speeches at union meetings. But he was good at it. The Guild elected him president for five consecutive years and brought him back in 1959 to lead the first successful strike against the movie producers. Inevitably, Reagan won the propaganda battle for whatever side he was on, whether his opponents were producers, the House Un-American Activities Committee or a political party. He also proved adept at different times in escaping the potentially suffocating clutches of the Communists, the John Birch Society and the Moral Majority. And as a touring spokesman for General Electric from 1954 to 1962, Reagan made the most of a unique opportunity to develop and polish a basic speech before captive audiences. What his opponents did not realize, and what Reagan did not acknowledge, was that he entered public life as a successful, practicing politician.

The Screen Actors Guild won its four-year battle for recognition from the movie producers in 1937, the year Reagan arrived in Hollywood. It took a strike vote supported by the vast majority of working actors to do it. Though a number of the Guild's members, including Reagan, subsequently became rich, the organization was not at the time an association of wealthy Republicans playing at trade unionism. Except for a few stars, actors in 1937 were peons in an industry owned and operated for the most part by primitive, antiunion entrepreneurs. Earlier, when times were better, they had blacklisted actors who had joined in an attempt by Actors Equity Association to organize Hollywood. Then, in 1933, the producers forced contract players to accept a 50 percent cut. The size of that cut, huge even by Depression standards, brought the Guild into being. At the time it was organized, more than half its members made less than two thousand dollars a year, and many of these so-called "day players" worked one day a week for $15. For these lesser-known actors, the Guild was the means of survival in an industry which has never cared well or widely for its own.

Reagan was recruited into the union in 1938 by actress Helen Broderick.[2] Because the Guild was trying to represent every category of player and every level of experience, Reagan soon found himself on the union board of directors with some of the big actors of Hollywood—Robert Montgomery, Edward Arnold, Charles Boyer, James Cagney, Eddie Cantor, Cary Grant, Ralph Morgan, Dick Powell. They were famous men, and Reagan might never have met any of them if he had stuck to his job as a B-player at Warners. At union meetings, they received the young actor as an equal. Reagan was impressed by their commitment because he realized that many of these actors were so highly in demand they could have negotiated favorable contracts for themselves without the help of a union. He saw their participation as the selfless actions of successful men who remembered what it was like to be young and unknown. Reagan related what these well-known actors were doing to the central purpose of his own life. "My education was completed when I walked into the board room," Reagan wrote in his autobiography. "I saw it crammed with the famous men of the business. I knew then that I was beginning to find the rest of me."[3]

Reagan retained his enthusiasm for the actors union during the war years. When he returned to a Hollywood troubled by rising costs, labor disputes, foreign films and the prospective threat of television, he found the Guild to be a prestigious union occupying a strategic position in a divided community. The ostensible basis of the division was a bitter union jurisdictional dispute in which it became difficult for any member of the film community to remain neutral. But the roots went deeper than that. Hollywood had long been a magnet for both materialistic and idealistic impulses in American society. Because of Hollywood's unique role as a center of American culture, the industry was high on the list of Communist priorities for changing the "social consciousness" of Americans, just as it would later be high on the political action agenda of the American Legion and the Legion of Decency, who feared that movie-goers were being subverted or corrupted by Hollywood films. The money to be made in Hollywood and the willingness of some producers to enter into "sweetheart" deals with unsavory union leaders caused the industry to become a target for the underworld. The residue of these materialistic and idealistic forces, more than anything, led to the great Hollywood strikes after the war, strikes which contributed mightily to the political education of Ronald Reagan.

The mob had moved into Hollywood in 1936 in the persons of gangsters Willie Bioff and George Browne, who were backed by the Chicago syndicate and assisted by a $100,000 contribution from producer Joseph Schenck. Bioff and Browne took over a moribund industrial union of stagehands, the International Alliance of Theatrical Stage Employees (IATSE), signed up several producers, and assessed each employee 2 percent of his pay check in union dues. In six years they raked in $6.5 million, which they divided with the Chicago underworld syndicate. After a series of highly publicized investigations, Bioff and Browne were sentenced to federal prison in 1941 for extorting $550,000 from five major studios. Bioff was subsequently murdered by a bomb set off by the starter in his car.* The International Alliance lived on and prospered under the leadership of a tough-talking Nebraskan named Roy Brewer who had been brought in to clean up the union.

The Communists enjoyed two periods of influence in Hollywood. The first occurred during the Popular Front collaboration of Communists and

---

* For an account of the mob takeover of IATSE, see "The Life and Times of Willie Bioff" in *The Education of Carey McWilliams,* Simon and Schuster, page 91. McWilliams was an attorney in Los Angeles at the time and represented some of the union members who were fighting crime control of their local. Of Bioff's murder, McWilliams wrote, "Thus did Willie Bioff depart this life, not with a whimper but with a bang."

liberals which began in 1936 and ended with the Nazi-Soviet pact of 1939. The second came after the German invasion of Russia in June 1941 and ended with the collapse of Nazi Germany in April 1945 when, under Stalin's direction, the Communist parties of the world ended their wartime policy of cooperating with the Western democracies. The Conference of Studio Unions, which contested with the Alliance for labor control of Hollywood, was born in this second Popular Front period. It was the brainchild of Herbert Sorrell, who ultimately would be expelled from the National Executive Board of the Painters Union for having "willfully and knowingly associated with groups subservient to the Communist Party line."*

The Conference, organized in 1941, flourished during the war years. It took liberal positions and capitalized on the film community's distrust of the Alliance and on a lingering belief that the union's new leadership, while not crooked, was in bed with the producers. "The Communist Party was very much interested in the success of the Conference of Studio Unions," said Max Silver, a Los Angeles County Communist leader during this period. "Its interest lay in the main to establish what we called a progressive center in Hollywood instead of the IATSE. . . . The party was interested in establishing a nerve center that would be to some extent influenced by party policy and party people."[4] In 1945 the battle was joined by its 16,000 members and the Conference of Studio Unions and its 10,000—for control of the film industry work force in Hollywood.

Looking back on this period from his later conservative vantage point, Reagan marveled at his own ignorance. "To say that I was naive is putting it mildly," he commented thirteen years later. "I knew about Browne and Bioff, of course, but I wasn't up on the Communists."[5] His naiveté ran smack into economic reality. Studios were cutting back on pictures, and many of the returning actors were, like Reagan, conscious that a brand-new audience had sprung into being while they were away at war. They wanted to work, and the strikes were getting in the way. The actors, whose union was affiliated with the American Federation of Labor, thought they might be in a position to do something because they had taken no side in the dispute and because their support was coveted by both sides. The contesting unions knew that studios would be shut down by any widespread refusal of actors to work. The Guild, on Reagan's motion, decided to investigate the causes of the labor dispute.

Despite its official neutrality, the Guild leadership began its inquiry with sympathy for the liberal CSU and skepticism about the suspect IATSE. In October 1945 the Guild honored CSU picket lines during a brief walkout. But when the Conference of Studio Unions struck again in 1946, the actors

* Sorrell was later identified on the basis of handwriting before HUAC in 1947 as a man who had signed a Communist Party document under the name "Herb Stewart." However, Sorrell told the House Education and Labor Subcommittee in 1948, "I am not now nor have I ever been a member of the Communist Party."

were reluctant to go out. Some of the Guild leadership, Reagan included, had begun to wonder why Sorrell insisted that he had no jurisdictional goals and simply wanted higher wages for set decorators and other manual workers. It was common knowledge in the community that both the Conference and the Alliance wanted to put the rival organization out of business. The conflict between Sorrell's claims and his actions first made the actors suspicious of him. Nonetheless, the Guild tried hard to arrange a truce between Brewer and Sorrell and worked out a brief settlement in July 1946, which the actors grandiloquently called "The Truce of Beverly Hills."

The truce ended a two-day strike but did not last long. A month later an AFL arbitration decision confused the jurisdictional issue and threatened the demise of the Alliance at the hands of the mammoth Carpenters Unions. Sorrell interpreted the decision as a green light to win control of the set decorators. On September 12, the CSU struck again and picket lines were thrown up around Warner Brothers and MGM. The Guild held an emergency meeting and, with Reagan doing most of the talking, decided to send a delegation to the AFL convention in Chicago. The actors, including Reagan, Wyman, Walter Pidgeon, Dick Powell, Alexis Smith, Gene Kelly, Robert Taylor and George Murphy, were shunted from meeting to meeting before being allowed to present a resolution calling for binding arbitration of the Hollywood labor dispute. The resolution passed unanimously, but to the frustration of a group of actors growing less naive by the hour, never was enforced.

Reagan testified later before the House Labor Committee that he had threatened AFL President William Green with a proposal to fly Hollywood stars to every major American city in denunciation of the community's labor violence unless Green agreed to the resolution.[6] Green immediately arranged a meeting between the actors and William Hutcheson, the Carpenters Union president, who crustily agreed to withdraw his designs on the set decorators. But Hutcheson also, according to Reagan, denounced "the Commies," threatening to "run Sorrell out of Hollywood" and to destroy his union.

By now the Guild delegation was no longer starry-eyed about Sorrell, and merely wanted the labor dispute to end. In front of the Warner Brothers studios strikers fought pitched battles with police, who escorted Alliance members across the Conference of Studio Unions' picket lines. Each side blamed the other for the violence, but the weaponry was on the side of the Los Angeles police and fire departments, who brought in tear gas and fire hoses to quell the strikers.

Reagan managed to avoid most of the violence, however, because he was on location in the Sierra Madre, north of Los Angeles, filming *Stallion Road*. Years later, testifying in a civil suit, Reagan said he was called to the telephone at a gas station near the film location. "I was told that if I made the report a squad was ready to take care of me—fix my face so I would never be in pictures again," Reagan said.[7] He took the threat seriously enough to carry a gun, and for a time was also under police protection.

But nothing happened to him, and it was the CSU which got "fixed." The Screen Actors Guild concluded that the Conference of Studio Unions was engaged in a jurisdictional strike. On October 2, 1946, the membership backed up the board by an overwhelming vote, and the Guild took the lead in a proclamation of twenty-five unions denouncing Sorrell and the CSU. The actors, and almost everyone else, crossed the picket lines. The strike collapsed. The Conference of Studio Unions disappeared from the face of the earth.

Reagan's emergence as a union leader in this postwar period coincided with the failure of his marriage and the postwar downturn in his film career. In the years 1946 and 1947, it was union activity rather than filmmaking which frequently was at the center of Reagan's life. Often, it seemed that he was interrupting union activity for a film rather than the other way around. Late in 1946 Warner Brothers suspended work on a Philip Wylie potboiler, *Night unto Night,* so that Reagan could travel with the Screen Actors Guild delegation to the AFL convention. When the film was finally resumed, Reagan found working on the movie a lot less satisfying than labor mediating.

The movie was supposed to be the American film debut of Swedish actress Viveca Lindfors. She and Reagan didn't get along. Lindfors many years later put him down by saying that her agent had warned her that he wasn't good enough.* Lindfors had fallen in love with the movie's director, Don Siegel, with whom Reagan was also having problems. Reagan, cast as an epileptic biochemist, rebelled at the way Siegel wanted him to play the part but never succeeded in putting his own stamp on it. When the film was finally released in 1949, an astute *Time* reviewer spotted the conflict, though he did not know the reason for it. "Reagan plays the role of the epileptic with the abstracted air of a man who has just forgotten an important telephone number," the reviewer wrote. The movie, which also featured Broderick Crawford, was widely panned and quickly forgotten.

Reagan had other challenges outside the studio. Just when labor peace seemed to have been restored in Hollywood, the House Un-American Activities Committee announced an investigation into supposed "Communist infiltration of the motion picture industry." Before the committee was finished, ten screenwriters who refused to cooperate would go to prison and hundreds of others would become unemployable. The reputation of participants on every side of the inquiry would suffer, and Hollywood would be revealed as a repository of cowardice, silliness and ignorance. But in May 1947 when Committee Chairman J. Parnell Thomas of New Jersey and

* Lindfors commented in *People* magazine of August 10, 1981, that what she remembered best from her association with Reagan was his comment that sex was best "in the afternoon, after coming out of the shower."

John McDowell of Pennsylvania, both Republicans, convened a closed session of fourteen friendly, anti-Communist witnesses at the Biltmore Hotel in Los Angeles, the power of the committee to divide and harm was underestimated by its opponents in Hollywood, including the Communists.

The conventional historical wisdom in 1947 lulled the film community into believing that investigating committees were mostly harmless hot air. Two Red-hunting Democrats far better known than Thomas had previously attempted to stir up Red scares and failed. Representative Martin Dies of Texas, the first chairman of the House Un-American Activities Committee, had tried to embarrass Hollywood in 1938 and had ended up embarrassing himself. Jack B. Tenney of Los Angeles, a one-time left-wing legislator who had turned against the Communists and coauthored the bill which removed them from the California ballot, had conducted a state investigation and been laughed out of town in 1943. There were many who believed, until it was too late, that Thomas and his inquisitors would suffer the same fate.

Carey McWilliams observed that Hollywood is a community better defined in industrial rather than geographic terms, "a world within a world" with a strong sense of group identity.[8] Spokesmen for this community tend to react with one voice when it is threatened from the outside. This defense impulse after the scandals of the 1920s led to the promotion of "wholesome Hollywood." Two decades later it led even anti-Communist producers to avoid the Tenney Committee as if it were a plague. But the community's defenses were down in 1947, as both stars and studios looked fearfully at a changing economic structure which promised fewer and more costly pictures. The external fearfulness which Hollywood would display before the Thomas Committee reflected an internal economic insecurity which prompted even liberal producers to throw their radical baggage overboard. When the producers finally capitulated, their fear that continued employment of suspected Communists would hurt box office receipts was the decisive consideration.

The investigations also coincided with a rising domestic fear of Communists and growing hostility between the United States and the Soviet Union. Both the Congress of Industrial Organizations and the United Auto Workers were purging their ranks of Communists, and teachers and other public employees were confronted with a spate of loyalty oaths. The same week Reagan testified before the House Un-American Activities Committee, the Soviet Union was completing its destruction of democracy in Poland, which then seemed irrevocable. Through purges or rigged trials, the Communists already had silenced their opponents in Hungary, Bulgaria and Rumania. While the Soviets consolidated their domination of Eastern Europe, the Communist Parties in Europe and the United States with one voice denounced the Marshall Plan for reconstructing Western Europe as "capitalist imperialistic gangsterism." President Truman had acted to prevent Communist takeovers in Greece and Iran, and Communist pressure mounted weekly on the still democratic government of Czechoslovakia. The Cold War was in full swing.

The changing sentiments of Americans toward the Soviet Union and its defenders were reflected in Hollywood, which had responded with enthusiasm to the patriotic fervor of World War II. There had been rallies, and fund drives, and tributes to "our gallant Russian allies." Hollywood had made propaganda films, as it does in every war, in which Korean-Americans and Chinese-Americans played malevolent Japanese pilots, the Japanese-Americans having been precipitously evacuated from California with little more than the clothes on their backs. The propaganda, encouraged by the Roosevelt administration, included occasional pro-Soviet films, such as *Mission to Moscow* and *Song of Russia,* and several other wartime dramas with a scrap or two of ambiguous dialogue that the Thomas committee would diligently dredge up as dubious evidence that made-in-Moscow sentiments were being subtly implanted in the minds of American moviegoers. Reviewer James Agee, writing in *The Nation* in 1943, suggested that Warner Brothers' "cuddly reverential treatment of President Roosevelt" in *Mission to Moscow* and *This Is the Army* was "subject to charges of indecent exposure and quite possibly of alienation of affections." But Roosevelt was President, after all, and the Soviets really were U.S. allies at the time. In retrospect, it is probably a commentary on the anticommunism of many Hollywood producers that there were so few pro-Soviet films. Servicemen who saw the well-made Army Signal Corps film, *The Battle of Russia,* got a far stiffer dose of pro-Russian sentiment than any civilian moviegoer.

Looking back, even in the context of the Cold War, it is difficult to understand the preoccupation of the Thomas Committee with what now seems such a trivial enterprise. The premise of the investigations can be understood only if one recognizes that congressmen, Communist writers, producers and Ronald Reagan alike shared a delusion that millions of Americans could be swayed by the insertion of a fragment of political sentiment into an otherwise benign movie. Not even the fearful Jack Warner would acknowledge that this had actually happened, but nearly everyone who appeared before the Thomas Committee, including Reagan, agreed that such subversion would be of the utmost significance. They agreed because the House Un-American Activities Committee, which proved a bust at investigating Communist penetration into key industrial unions, accepted Hollywood's premise of its own self-importance.

"In those days one of the greatest influences on American life was the motion picture," says Neil Reagan. "You can't laugh it off."[9] This was the animating, if unproven, notion underlying the inquiry, and it was accepted as an article of faith by all sides. On the right, such vigilant anti-Communists as Lela Rogers, Ginger's mother, said she had turned down one script for her daughter because it contained the Communist sentiment: "Share and share alike—that's democracy." On the left, the Hollywood Communists expressed great satisfaction with the triumph of Alvah Bessie, one of the Hollywood Ten, for slipping into *Action in the North Atlantic* a scene where a Soviet plane dips its wings to an American freighter and a U.S. merchant seaman cries out, "It's ours!"

At the time he left the service in 1945, Reagan doubtless would have agreed with the sentiments expressed by this seaman (actor Dane Clark). Reagan was, he once told me, "not smart about the Communists,"[10] and he was inclined to think, not without reason, that "Red" was a charge which was hurled rather indiscriminately at Democrats and liberals. Neil Reagan, already a staunch Republican conservative, had other ideas, and the two brothers would argue whenever Neil mentioned the word "Communist" to Ronald. "He would say right away quick, 'Oh, you're coming out with the Communist story,' " Neil remembers. "And then the occasion arose as a result of the strike when these people began to hit him over the head, figuratively speaking. And then, while I'm sure he would never admit it to me or to anyone else, some of the things I'd been saying to him began to soak in."[11]

In his autobiography Reagan describes himself as "a near-hopeless hemophiliac liberal" who bled for every cause that came along. Naive about the Communists he certainly was, but this is laying it on a bit thick. Even in his liberal phase, Reagan was no indiscriminate joiner, and most of his political activity in the immediate postwar years was limited to the Screen Actors Guild. He took a brief fling with the World Federalists, but at a time when liberal-sounding Communist front organizations were a dime a dozen in Hollywood, Reagan joined only two—the Hollywood branch of the American Veterans Committee and the Hollywood Independent Citizens Committee of the Arts, Sciences, and Professions (HICCASP). He left both of them as soon as he saw that Communists were running the show.

In the case of the AVC, which Reagan believes to have been a worthy organization that was subverted, he quit when he found a tiny minority trying to launch a studio strike in the name of the membership. At HICCASP, Reagan lasted slightly longer and briefly tried to change the direction of the organization. He joined forces with James Roosevelt and Olivia de Havilland (who first shared with Reagan a mutual suspicion that the other was pro-Communist) in a series of meetings at Roosevelt's home, to draft a resolution which declared, "We reaffirm our belief in free enterprise and the democratic system and repudiate communism as desirable for the United States." The Communists and their allies, led by screenwriter John Howard Lawson, refused to let this resolution come to a vote of the membership. Reagan remembers that Lawson told him that the membership was "not politically sophisticated enough to make the decision." When the HICCASP executive board, with only de Havilland in support, voted down the resolution, Reagan made his own decision and resigned.

His only other brush with the left came later in 1946, just before he issued his formal report to the Screen Actors Guild finding that the Hollywood strikes were jurisdictional in nature. At a meeting at the home of a prominent Hollywood actress, Reagan defended his findings and was booed and called "Fascist" for his pains. He spoke to no more such meetings after that.

I see no evidence that Reagan was scarred by these battles from which he emerged a lifelong anti-Communist. His was not a guilty liberalism which had looked to the Soviet Union as the hope of mankind and felt disillusioned or betrayed by the Russian purge trials, the Stalin-Hitler pact or the postwar Soviet takeover of Eastern Europe. Reagan had never paid the Russians that much attention. While he had a keen interest in domestic, economic and political issues, his view of foreign affairs was patriotic, idealistic and unformed. What interested Reagan at the time was the Hollywood strike and the activities of the Screen Actors Guild, and his political instincts in these union matters were sound. No matter what would have happened in HICCASP, where the Communist faction was arrogant by any standard, Reagan certainly would have broken with the Communists once he had found that they were determined to undermine the Guild's position on the jurisdictional strike. In his retelling of the stories of this period, Reagan seems rather to have enjoyed standing up to the Lawsons and urging them to go along with a denunciation of communism. After a while, Reagan came to believe that his ill-fated resolution, which was rejected by the Hollywood Independent Citizens Committee of the Arts, Sciences, and Professions, actually had caused that organization to expire. He also proudly claimed credit for exposing Communist influence in the Hollywood strikes, and would approvingly quote the testimony of Sterling Hayden, who in 1951 related to the House Un-American Activities Committee how the Communists had attempted to mobilize support among actors for the CSU strike. "The move was very successful," Hayden said. "It ran into the board of directors of the Screen Actors Guild, and particularly into Ronald Reagan, who was a one-man battalion against this thing. He was very vocal and clear-thinking on it."[12]

Actually, the Communists in Hollywood had run aground, like Communists elsewhere, on their own intransigent Stalinist policies. What is missing from Reagan's one-dimensional account of this period is any recognition of what happened to the Communist Party as the wartime alliance came to an end. What happened was that the Communists, under orders from Stalin, changed from a policy of collaboration with liberals to a hard anti-American line. In 1944 U.S. Communist Party leader Earl Browder, with Moscow's approval, dissolved the party and replaced it with the Communist Political Association. In 1945, with the Nazis defeated and the Soviets contesting for power in Europe, "Browderism" became a grievous error and Browder was replaced by the Stalinist William Z. Foster. In 1946 Browder was ejected from the party, and many of his like-minded followers in Los Angeles and Hollywood were similarly expelled.

The Communist opposition to Reagan's "innocuous" anti-Communist resolution in the Hollywood Citizens Committee of the Arts, Sciences, and Professions, which Reagan found so surprising, was the required expression of the party line. And it wasn't the withdrawal of Reagan and James Roosevelt, who no doubt would soon have quit HICCASP anyway, that killed the organization, as Reagan contends in his autobiography. Instead, the Communists killed it themselves by insisting, as a matter of party discipline, that their supporters oppose liberal but anti-Communist U.S. Senate candidate Will Rogers, Jr., in the Democratic primary in favor of a candidate who was willing to accept Communist support.[13] The Communists prevailed on the endorsement, but the organization collapsed. What was left of it was absorbed by the Progressive Citizens of America, which became the launching pad for the left-wing presidential candidacy of Henry Wallace in 1948.

Because of their own dogmatic behavior within organizations such as HICCASP, the Communists had lost most of their liberal allies by the time the investigations of the House Un-American Activities Committee began in 1947. The classic horror story that was told and retold within the liberal community in Hollywood involved screenwriter Albert Maltz, who would become one of the best-known of the Hollywood Ten and was perhaps the most talented. Writing in the *New Masses* of February 12, 1946, Maltz eloquently denounced what he called the "vulgarization" of the Communist idea that "art is a weapon." He also made the additional mistake, from the Communist point of view, of praising the works of James T. Farrell, the author of *Studs Lonigan,* whom Maltz accurately described as "one of the outstanding writers in America." Maltz was answered promptly in *The Daily Worker* by Communist cultural commissar Mike Gold, who called Farrell "a vicious voluble Trotskyite" and said "that Albert Maltz seems to have let the luxury and phony atmosphere of Hollywood at last to poison him." Maltz recanted in an April article in *New Masses* entitled "Moving Forward," heaping criticism upon his own "distorted view of the facts, history and contribution of left-wing culture to American life." Maltz's willingness to chastise himself was another of the periodic eye-openers which Communists gave to liberals in Hollywood. His two articles, and Gold's, read into the record of the House Un-American Activities Committee, constitute a far more impressive indictment of the Communists than anything Parnell Thomas was able to devise.

Reagan's eyes were wide open by this time, and his view of the situation was more balanced than it is in retrospect. He knew what the Communists were about, but also regarded Thomas and his committee as "a pretty venal bunch."* As a result, Reagan was especially wary when the committee's

---

* Reagan's feelings about Thomas were justified. An investigation, launched after columnist Drew Pearson reported that Thomas had padded his congressional payroll in return for salary kickbacks, led to an indictment for fraud and one for receiving kickbacks. He pleaded no contest, was fined $10,000 and was sentenced to Danbury, Connecticut, prison where two members of the Hollywood Ten also were incarcerated. Thomas was paroled on September 9, 1950, after serving nine months.

chief investigator, Robert Stripling, came to his hotel room on the night of October 22, 1947, to quiz Reagan about his testimony the following day. They sparred, with Reagan relating his own anti-Communist experiences in HICCASP and declaring the opposition of the Screen Actors Guild to communism. Reagan told Stripling that he couldn't prove that any particular adversary was a Communist and wouldn't make such an identification on the witness stand. When the issue came up the following day, Reagan handled the issue with a politician's touch:

MR. STRIPLING: As a member of the board of directors, as president of the Screen Actors Guild and as an active member, have you at any time observed or noted within the organization a clique of either Communists or Fascists who were attempting to exert influence or pressure on the Guild?

REAGAN: Well, sir, my testimony must be very similar to that of Mr. [George] Murphy and Mr. [Robert] Montgomery. There has been a small group within the Screen Actors Guild which has consistently opposed the policy of the Guild board and officers of the Guild, as evidenced by the vote on various issues. That small clique referred to has been suspected of more or less following the tactics that we associate with the Communist Party.

STRIPLING: Would you refer to them as a disruptive influence within the Guild?

REAGAN: I would say that at times they have attempted to be a disruptive influence.

STRIPLING: You have no knowledge yourself as to whether or not any of them are members of the Communist Party?

REAGAN: No, sir; I have no investigative force, or anything, and I do not know.[14]

Reagan's testimony did not delight the red-necked, short-fused Thomas, who a week later would smash a gavel to splinters while putting down a hostile witness.

At the time Reagan testified, the committee investigation seemed to be going downhill in a hurry. In May, at the closed hearings in Los Angeles, the word had been leaked to reporters of a supposedly sensational accusation: Robert Taylor was said to have charged that he had made *Song of Russia* under pressure from the Roosevelt administration. In October, the day before Reagan came before the committee, Taylor labored to correct this impression "lest I look a little silly by saying I was ever forced to do the picture. I was not forced because nobody can force you to do any picture." This testimony by a star who wanted to send the Communists "back to Russia or some other unpleasant place" undercut one of the already thin premises of Thomas' investigation and left the chairman in a bad mood. But Thomas was in no position to bully the celebrities he had invited to give luster to his proceedings. As Taylor left the room, according to a contemporary account, "more than half the spectators stamped for the door, clustered happily around him and followed him more than a block down the street to his automobile."[15]

Reagan had never become that "another Robert Taylor" advertised by his agent at the time he was signed to a movie contract. But he was a star, too, and younger than Taylor and Montgomery. The *New York Times* reported that when Reagan entered the room, wearing a tan gabardine suit and blue-knitted tie, "there was a long drawn-out 'ooooh' from the jam-packed, predominantly feminine audience." Many accounts observed that Reagan looked younger than his thirty-six years. His testimony was careful and controlled. Taylor had named Howard Da Silva and Karen Morley, both well-known Hollywood radicals, as two of the "few who seem to sort of disrupt things once in a while." Reagan did not even do that. Instead, he told a story about how he had been asked to lend his name to a hospital fund recital sponsored by the Joint Anti-Fascist Refugee Committee at which Paul Robeson would sing, and how it turned out not to be a benefit for the hospital at all.[16]

Reagan's testimony then turned to the strikes in Hollywood. The Screen Actors Guild, Reagan informed the committee, "is better informed on the situation and on the jurisdictional strike than any other group in the motion-picture industry." When Stripling tried to lead Reagan into saying that Communists were responsible for the labor trouble in Hollywood, the actor surrounded the question without every really answering it. "After all, we must recognize them [the Communists] at present as a political party," Reagan reminded Stripling. "On that basis we have exposed their lies when we came across them, we have opposed their propaganda, and I can certainly testify that in the case of the Screen Actors Guild we have been eminently successful in preventing them from, with the usual tactics, trying to run a majority of an organization with a well-organized minority.

"So that, fundamentally, I would say in opposing those people that the best thing to do is to make democracy work," Reagan continued. "In the Screen Actors Guild we make it work by insuring everyone a vote and by keeping everyone informed. I believe that, as Thomas Jefferson put it, if all the American people know all of the facts they will never make a mistake. Whether that party should be outlawed, I agree with the gentleman that preceded me [George Murphy] that that is a matter for the government to decide. As a citizen I would hesitate, or not like, to see any political party outlawed on the basis of its political ideology."

The Thomas Jefferson reference stung Thomas, who replied, "That is just why this committee was created by the House of Representatives, to acquaint the American people with the facts." But Reagan wasn't through. After Thomas had thanked him, Reagan put what might be called the genteel case against the committee in these words:

"Sir, if I might in regard to that, say that what I was trying to express, and didn't do very well, was also this other fear. I detest, I abhor their philosophy, but I detest more than that their tactics, which are those of a fifth column, and are dishonest, but at the same time I never as a citizen want to see our country become urged, by either fear or resentment of this group, that we ever compromise with any of our democratic principles through that fear or resentment. I still think that democracy can do it."[17]

Reagan, Murphy and Montgomery won praise for their testimony from *Life,* the *New York Times* and other major publications. In retrospect, Reagan's testimony still looks good, and even liberal critics of him like Phillip Dunne have agreed that he made "a fine statement of civil-libertarian principles on the stand."[18] In his testimony Reagan had walked a fine line. While agreeing that Communists sought to control the film industry, he had argued that no measures beyond vigorous democratic trade unionism were needed to combat them. He had named no names and recanted no principles. He had defended his union. Years later he would obscure his own moderate and politically astute conduct by exaggerating the danger of the Communists had posed to the film industry, quoting approvingly from the findings of the committee and denying that a blacklist really existed. But at the time of his testimony, Reagan was both sensible and restrained, paying the minimum homage to the committee and to the fearfulness which it had created in the film industry.

Had the movie producers been similarly inclined, the Thomas committee might have met the fate of its predecessors. When the chairman suspended the hearings after three days of questioning unfriendly witnesses, the widespread view was that the investigation had flopped. Newspaper editors protested Thomas' tactics, and a Gallup Poll showed that the public also had a low opinion of the way the investigation had been conducted. But the hostile writers also had made a damaging public impression in the course of following a prearranged and confusing strategy of refusing to answer questions while insisting that they were answering them in their own way.* What they really were doing was using the hearings as a platform to denounce the committee that was holding them.

Writers were dragged off the stand to the sound of Thomas' gavel-pounding while shouting their attacks on the committee. John Howard Lawson, the premier unfriendly witness, yelled at Thomas: "I am not on trial here, Mr. Chairman. This committee is on trial here before the Ameri-

---

* A Gallup Poll taken November 7–12, 1947, shows that Americans did not have a high opinion of either the writers or the committee. By a margin of 46 to 29 percent, the poll respondents thought that writers who refused to answer questions about their Communist affiliations should be punished. But a question about the way the investigation had been handled produced only a 30 percent approval response, with 36 percent disapproving and 27 percent undecided. This negative response is even more striking when put in the context of American anticommunism at this time. A Gallup Poll taken October 24–29 found Americans by a margin of 62 to 23 percent favoring a law outlawing the Communist Party. In response to other questions, substantial majorities of Americans said they believed the U.S. Communists took orders from Moscow and were loyal to Russia.

can people. Let us get that straight." Maltz called Stripling "Mr. Quisling," using the name of the World War II Norwegian traitor. Only Ring Lardner, Jr., tried a lighter approach, responding to a question about Communist membership, "I could answer it, but if I did I would hate myself in the morning."[19] The performance of the unfriendly witnesses rescued the unfriendly Thomas. The committee voted without dissent to cite the ten uncooperative witnesses for contempt. The full House agreed in a vote that was both an assertion of congressional investigative prerogatives and an expression of militant anticommunism.

When McDowell called for the contempt citation of Maltz, he read a list of countries that had fallen to the Soviet Union and declared that Maltz was "a colonel in the conspiratorial political army of Soviet Russia."

The contempt citations were a signal to the increasingly fearful producers who met at the Waldorf-Astoria Hotel in New York on November 22 and 25, 1947, to decide what to do about the uncooperative writers. Eric Johnston, the head of the Motion Picture Producers Association, warned that boycotts against films written by the Hollywood Ten were already being organized or threatened, including one by the American Legion. Sam Goldwyn argued that this was not sufficient cause to justify a blacklist, but found no backing among his colleagues. The producers agreed to blacklist the Hollywood Ten unless and until they had purged themselves of contempt.

This decision, which was made public in a declaration that became known as "the Waldorf Statement," was not immediately communicated to the outside world. Instead, a committee of the producers headed by Louis B. Mayer met privately with representatives of the three major guilds—the actors, directors, and writers—on November 27 for the purpose of obtaining their cooperation with the producers' blacklist. Reagan, as president of the Screen Actors Guild, represented the actors. He raised the question of how "innocent people" would be protected under the producers' new policy. Sheridan Gibney for the writers and William Wyler for the directors voiced similar concerns. The producers committee met again with the guild leaders on December 3, the day the Waldorf Statement was finally made public, but failed to win their support. Afterward, the directors opposed the declaration as "fundamentally insincere" while neither the writers nor the actors took a stand. The Screen Actors Guild, with Reagan in support, voted in mid-January to require non-Communist affadavits of its own supporters. For all practical purposes, this signaled that the Guild would not oppose the studios for firing actors who refused to say whether or not they were Communists.

Despite his evocation of Thomas Jefferson on the witness stand, Reagan dodged the civil liberties implications of a blacklist. He did this by refusing to acknowledge that a list, as such, existed, and by saying that he would oppose creation of a list of persons unemployable for political reasons. At the same time he acknowledged the right of studios to be cognizant of an actor's outside activities or reputation in employing him. This meant, of course, that no Communist or suspected Communist would be employed. Reagan continued, however, to be concerned about "innocent people" who were vulnerable to the unofficial vigilante blacklists that sprang up in Hollywood in the wake of the congressional investigation. The Guild did its best to help repentant actors who were hauled before the House Un-American Activities Committee. This meant, in effect, helping those who were willing to name the names the committee demanded, and letting the unrepentant fend for themselves. When Gale Sondergaard, wife of the Hollywood Ten's Herbert Biberman, took the Fifth Amendment before the committee in 1953, Reagan as president of the Guild told her that the union would oppose any secret blacklist. "On the other hand, if any actor by his actions outside of union activities has so offended public opinion that he has made himself unsaleable at the box office, the Guild cannot and would not force any employers to hire him," Reagan said.[20]

Reagan's views were centrist and unexceptional for the time, very much in the mainstream of the Truman administration which he supported. He was not hysterical about communism and in his speeches denounced "witch-hunters" as well as Communists. The speeches he gave for Truman and other Democratic candidates in 1948 were aimed at what Reagan then called "Republican inflation" and did not deal with Communists or foreign policy. Reagan supported the Democratic ticket in 1950, which included Democrat Helen Gahagan Douglas for U.S. Senate seat against Republican Richard Nixon, who won. Nixon was a junior member of the House Un-American Activities committee when Reagan testified, and Douglas was one of the few House members to vote against the contempt citations of the Hollywood Ten. Reagan now says that too much has been made of all this, and that he did not campaign for Douglas separately but supported all Democrats. Reagan claims that by the time of the 1950 election, he already thought that Douglas was "awfully naive about the subject of Communists" but wouldn't have "name-called or red-baited" by saying it publicly.[21]

I know of no one, either publicly or privately, whom Reagan has called a Communist other than those who have proclaimed their own communism. He either learned during the Hollywood Red-hunting days or intuitively understood that such personal accusations are diverting, damaging and often rebound against the accuser. His own sense of fairness led him in the direction of scrupulous political dialogue and away from personal vilification. At the same time, he developed a resolute conspiracy theory about Communists which he has never abandoned. More of a talker than a thinker, Reagan loves to talk about phenomena he has figured out for himself, whether it is a crack-back block, a technique of announcing or his new discovery in the postwar era that Communists exploited liberal causes and did the work of Russia. With the enthusiasm of a new convert, Reagan explained his discovery to anyone who would listen in lectures that were at once refreshing and simpleminded. Read today, these lectures on communism seem like the poster during the comic book revival in which Batman points a finger and warns, "It Is Well To Remember That Evil Is A Very Bad Thing." Since Reagan's awakening occurred before the fissioning of the world communist movement into rival Soviet and Chinese camps, his sermons inevitably linked all Communists to Russians. The following, from an article which Reagan wrote for the January 22, 1951, issue of the magazine *Fortnight,* is a fair sample:

> But suppose we quit using the words Communist and Communism. They are a hoax perpetrated by the Russian government, to aid in securing fifth columnists in other countries and to mask Russian aggression aimed at world conquest. Every time we make the issue one of Communism as a political philosophy, we help in this hoax. Substitute "Pro-Russian" for the word Communist and watch the confusion disappear. Then you can say to any American, "You are free to believe any political theory (including Communism) you want," but the so-called "Communist Party" is nothing less than a "Russian-American Bund" owing allegiance to Russia and supporting Russia in its plan to conquer the world. The very constitution behind which these cynical agents hide becomes a weapon to be used against them. They are traitors practicing treason.

In the same article Reagan asserted that "the real fight with this new totalitarianism belongs to the forces of liberal democracy, just as did the battle with Hitler's totalitarianism." He also denounced professional hate groups which "masked their racial and religious bias" behind anticommunism and those "anti-labor forces (that) used 'red-baiting' to fight unions. . . ." But never again would Reagan put up an argument when Neil told him that the Communists were behind something.

What is most remarkable about Reagan's immersion in the anticommunism of his time is that he emerged from it in such good health. Others on both sides with more complex turns of mind and less balance than Reagan were psychologically trapped by what had happened to them in the great Hollywood Red hunt. Some were forever encumbered by the experience, which became the central reference point of their lives. Reagan was not trapped. He became more wary than he had been before, and his views changed, as his views would change on other things, but he rarely became obsessive about his new opinions. Looking back on his experiences, he never apologized and hardly ever explained. In a time of hysteria, he could talk about Communists without raising his voice. What had happened to Reagan had changed his mind. It had not changed his personality.

8

The Conservative

REAGAN was now in transition—between careers, between marriages, between political parties, between ideologies. The 1940s had been a time of awakening and disillusionment for Reagan, as for other Americans. If a decade could be summed up in a single sentence, it would, for Reagan, be contained in the despair of Drake McHugh as he cried out, "Where's the rest of me?" Reagan was still an actor, but acting was not enough for him. He still thought of himself as a family man, but he no longer had a family. He dated and went out to parties, going through the motions of being a bachelor again. Even among his closest friends he was reluctant to talk about what had happened to him.

The 1950s would be another kind of decade for Reagan, a time of renewal and coming together. The one-sentence summary of this decade might be the then popular slogan of General Electric: "Progress Is Our Most Important Product." Thanks to Nancy Davis and GE, the life of Ronald Reagan in the 1950s became stable and rewarding again. While remaining for the time an actor, Reagan discovered a larger purpose in his life.

At the beginning of the transition Reagan was restless and unusually critical of the industry that had nurtured him. He sniped at producers for failing to appreciate the talents of its prewar stars and at the "irresponsible journalism" of the Hollywood press for celebrating scandal and divorce. "A star doesn't slip," Reagan told Hedda Hopper in 1950, "He's ruined by bad stories and worse casting."[1] Even the friendly Hopper demurred, telling Reagan that a theater owner of her acquaintance had told her that "he can't sell the older stars." Reagan kept at the producers, nonetheless, and he took after the press as well. "Certain elements of the press, the kind that are addicted to yellow journalism, certain types of gossip columnists, and so forth decided that they could attract more readers and sell more papers and get more listeners if they always went in for the more flamboyant, the more colorful, the exaggerated side of things, and in most cases the messy side of things," Reagan said while serving as master of ceremonies at the *Photoplay* awards dinner on February 12, 1951.[2] Without mentioning the breakup of his own marriage, Reagan objected to "an invasion of our personal and private lives," partly on political grounds. "I object to it not only from the standpoint of our right not to live in a goldfish bowl, but I also happen to think that it is very bad basic public relations," he said.

Despite greater visibility in political and union activities and increasing choosiness about film roles he would accept, Reagan says he did not at this time envision a public career. Instead, he was preoccupied with making a go of the free agency he had finally achieved. Off screen, the characteristic optimist was uncharacteristically moody. His divorce stung him deeply. Reagan saw his children frequently, as his daughter Maureen remembers it, but his absence from them on a daily basis gnawed at him. At the time of the divorce it was taken for granted that children should be placed in the custody of the mother. Years later, Reagan remarked to a friend that he approved of the joint-custody arrangements then becoming popular and talked of how he had missed the growing-up time with his children. "He really felt guilty that he had not spent the time with Maureen and Michael, that he felt that he owed them," said the friend. This friend viewed Reagan as a person who needed to be married and was "totally unsuited" for bachelorhood. Reagan acknowledges as much. Speaking of the period between his divorce and his introduction to Nancy Davis in 1951, he says "I was footloose and fancy free, and I guess down underneath, miserable."[3]

Nancy Davis changed that. At the time she met Reagan she was an obscure and attractive actress at MGM where she was working in the film *East Side, West Side.* Her mother, Edith Luckett, had been a well-known stage actress. Her mother's husband, Loyal Davis, was a successful Chicago neurosurgeon who had adopted Nancy. After graduating from Smith College in 1943, Nancy had capitalized on her mother's Hollywood connections and she became an actress. On MGM studio records she had listed her birth date as July 6, 1923, two years later than it actually was.* Although not without talent, she had no illusions of being a star and no particular ambition to become one. Supplying biographical information to MGM in 1949, she said her "greatest ambition" was to have a "successful happy marriage." In 1975, for a compilation on the achievements of Smith College alumni, Nancy Reagan said: "I was never really a career woman but [became one] only because I hadn't found the man I wanted to marry. I couldn't sit around and do nothing, so I became an actress."[4]

She did not know Ronald Reagan. He was a good-looking actor and the respected president of the Screen Actors Guild. When the opportunity to meet him presented itself, she demonstrated an inclination for the main chance that is one of her abiding characteristics. The pretext came when the

---

* According to her Smith College records, Nancy Reagan was born on July 6, 1921, two years earlier than she claimed on the MGM biographical questionnaire.

name "Nancy Davis" showed up repeatedly on a Communist mailing list and then on a list of left-wingers published in the *Hollywood Citizen News.* This was in 1951, at the height of the Red scare. On the set of *East Side, West Side,* she complained to director Mervyn LeRoy, who said he would fix matters by calling his friend, the Screen Actors Guild president. "I had never met Ronnie, and certainly Ronnie didn't know me from a hole in the wall, but I told Mervyn it was a fine idea,"[5] Nancy Reagan recalled years later, making no secret that her desire to meet Reagan heavily outweighed her fear of being falsely branded a Communist. By the time Reagan called back and reported that it was a case of mistaken identity, LeRoy realized that Nancy wanted more than political clearance. He insisted that Reagan convey his own messages, and a dinner date was arranged. Reagan, ever cautious, invented an early morning shooting schedule which would enable him to take his date home early if she proved a dud. She responded with an invented film shooting of her own. At their meeting, she was completely smitten by the tall, athletic and courteous actor who arrived at LaRue's on crutches because of the leg he had fractured at a Hollywood charity baseball game. He was tired of bachelorhood and much taken by this young woman who was obviously more interested in Reagan than in her own career.

From the first, Reagan's friends thought of Nancy as a woman who was "good for Ronnie" and would be faithful to him. Soon they were "an item" in the gossip columns, though both of them would always be far more discreet about their own intentions than Reagan and Wyman had been. A Hollywood newspaper account of the time describes "the romance of a couple who have no vices" in these terms: "Not for them the hot-house atmosphere of nightclubs, the smoky little rooms and the smell of Scotch. They eat at Dave Chasen's, they spend their evenings in the homes of friends, they drive along the coast and look at the sea and a lot of time they're quiet. They go as 'steady,' according to one reporter, as any couple in Hollywood and Nancy knits Reagan argyle socks, though she doesn't cook for him."

They were married on March 4, 1952, with Bill Holden as best man and Ardis Holden as matron of honor. Without regrets, Nancy quit her career to become a wife and mother. Patricia Ann Reagan was born by a cesarean section seven and one-half months later, on October 22, 1952.

Contrary to mythology, Nancy did not covert her husband to conservatism. Apart from her disinclination to receive Communist mail, Nancy Davis was almost totally apolitical. But she was keenly aware that he was interested in politics and aware, too, of Wyman's complaints that the Screen Actors Guild activities had bored her. If Nancy was bored by Reagan's stirring accounts of triumphs over greedy producers and treacherous Communists, she kept it to herself. Friends remember Nancy listening avidly to her husband's lectures without offering disagreement or contrary ideas.

Reagan was an active Democrat at the time of the marriage and would remain a registered Democrat for another decade. In 1952, he was one of a group of prominent members of his party who wired Dwight Eisenhower urging him to run as a Democrat. "I wanted him for President," Reagan said. "No one knew what party he belonged to."[6] Reagan at this time was a well-off Democrat who was drifting toward the Republican Party without realizing it. His income increased sharply in the mid-1950s when he signed a contract with General Electric, and he felt the pinch of a steeply graduated income tax which in those preaveraging days disproportionately affected wealthy individual taxpayers who lacked the tax writeoffs available to corporations. Reagan's first conservative issue was a personal one—reduction of the progressive income tax. But he gave it something of a liberal twist, saying that actors and others whose productive earning period was limited should be allowed a personal depreciation allowance just like the oil companies.

The evolutionary process was slow. Reagan was such a dyed-in-the-wool Democrat and so distrustful of Republicans and their corporate backing that his growing personal conservatism at first made only reluctant inroads on his partisanship. He had campaigned strenuously for Democratic national candidates in 1948 and 1950. In a 1948 radio address sponsored by the International Ladies Garment Workers Union, Reagan had delivered a well-conceived appeal for President Truman and Hubert H. Humphrey, the thirty-seven-year-old Minneapolis mayor who was running for the Senate against Senator Joe Ball, a Republican conservative. "While Ball is the banner carrier for Wall Street, Mayor Humphrey is fighting for all the principles advocated by President Truman, for adequate low-cost housing, for civil rights, for prices people can afford to pay and for a labor movement free of the Taft-Hartley law," Reagan said. This was still Reagan's basic philosophy in 1952, though he joined millions of Democrats in crossing over to vote for Eisenhower. In 1953, Reagan was back in the fold as head of the committee to reelect Los Angeles Mayor Fletcher Bowron. The office was nonpartisan, but Bowron had the enthusiastic backing of the city's liberal Democrats and labor unions, most of whom still considered Reagan as one of their own.

The new marriage restored Reagan's happiness but not his career. The recession was a depression in Hollywood, where competition from television had driven the studios into a funk. For the most part, as Reagan accurately observed, the industry responded to the challenge by lowering the quality of its pictures instead of raising them, and the slump grew worse. Reagan, however, displayed a care about his own choice of films he had never felt free to exercise in his contract days at Warners. By his own count, he rejected $500,000 worth of films he thought unsuited to him during one fourteen-month period.

Nancy was sympathetic, choosing to believe that her husband would have been much in demand for choice roles except for his "unselfish" devotion to the Screen Actors Guild. "He was active in industry politics for as long as he was active in Hollywood, and there's no doubt this hurt his acting career," Nancy wrote years later. "When producers are casting pictures, they envision various actors in the roles. When they have spent years at the negotiating table across from an actor or served on industry committees with him, this can influence how they think of him. It's difficult for them to visualize him leading a cavalry charge or heading off the rustlers at Eagle Pass. When Ronnie was trying to talk his way into a Western, he once told Jack Warner that if Jack ever did give him a Western he would probably cast him as the lawyer from the east."[7]

The Reagans lived in Nancy's apartment after their Arizona honeymoon, then bought a small house in Pacific Palisades at a time this presently gilt-edged community was one of the most reasonably priced residential areas in western Los Angeles. They also traded in Yearling Row, Reagan's eight-acre Northridge ranch, on 350 acres in the Malibu mountains, a transaction which ultimately would have made the Reagans millionaires even without other investments.

In the early 1950s, in a typically California way, they were property rich but cash poor. They needed money so badly that Reagan agreed to play Las Vegas with a nightclub act known as The Continentals. Reagan, who neither sang nor danced, performed an opening monologue and an introduction. "I've notified all my comedian friends to be on guard," Reagan quipped when he announced his Las Vegas plans. "If they say anything funny, it might wind up in my act." Reagan was less desperate than he sounded. Acting on his friend George Burns' prescription that "truth is the basis of all good comedy," Reagan managed to draw his share of laughs during two weeks at the Last Frontier with a routine based on the premise that he had to introduce other people because he had no talent himself. The act was popular, and Reagan received offers from nightclubs around the country. He turned them all down, having discovered in two weeks that he and a nightclub life were never made for each other. Nancy was anxious to return to their daughter in Pacific Palisades, and neither she nor her husband had any taste for gambling. They spent most of their off hours in their room. "When we got back home, we thought of it as just so many more weeks we'd bought that we could hold out in our waiting game," Reagan wrote in his autobiography.[8]

The waiting game ended with an offer from the late Taft Schreiber, then the head of Music Corporation of America's Revue Productions, who sounded out Reagan on becoming the host for a new television series that was to be sponsored by General Electric. Schreiber approached Reagan gingerly, for the actor was outspoken in his criticism of television, which he thought was ruining Hollywood. But the price—$125,000 a year, which GE would soon raise to $150,000—was right, and the contract contained an unusual proposal which intrigued Reagan. Not only would Reagan act in some of the weekly dramas and introduce all of them, he also would tour the country for ten weeks a year, plugging GE products and meeting company executives and employees.

The proposal was the brainchild of the brilliant, controversial and corporatively progressive president of General Electric, Ralph J. Cordiner, who had pioneered in decentralization of his vast company and in promoting the role of GE as "corporate citizen." Reagan did not know Cordiner, but he admired what he had heard about him. "He was the man who really was the leader of decentralization of industry and business," says Reagan. "They had 139 plants in 38 states, and he was the one that had the courage as the chief executive officer and chairman of the board to say to the managers of those plants, 'I want you to run them as if they were your plants.' They never had to get a ruling from the board of directors. There'd be a general code of ethics laid down, and this is how the theater came about. Cordiner had the idea that not only would they do this television show but that the spokesman they got to do the theater, which turned out to be me, would a certain number of weeks be put on tour in visiting the plants. The employees, scattered as they were, would realize that the headquarters knew they were there because here's that fellow they saw on Sunday night coming to visit them."[9]

For several years Reagan had been doubling as a spokesman for the movie industry, and this sideline now paid rich dividends. It was Reagan's success as a speaker on what he always called "the mashed potato circuit" which convinced Schreiber that Reagan was the ideal man for the job—he could act, introduce, sell products and make a decent speech. But nothing was said to Reagan about speeches when he signed the contract with GE. During his first tours, his speaking for the company was limited to brief anecdotes. Then in a GE plant one day, Reagan was asked to draw upon his experience with motion picture charity fund-raising and speak in behalf of a United Fund drive. As Reagan remembers it, he did so well that the public relations man accompanying him confided to Reagan that he had been getting requests for speeches and turning them down out of fear he would have to write them. "No, I have spoken on behalf of the industry," Reagan replied to him. "If you want to accept a speaking date for me, I'll take care of it."[10]

Once GE found that Reagan could make a speech, the company would hardly let him stop. By Reagan's own account, he gave as many as fourteen speeches a day and spent a total of two years of the eight he was under contract to General Electric on the road, visiting every one of the company's plants and meeting all of its 250,000 employees. He was afraid to fly, and his contract specified that his travel would be entirely by train. GE took advantage of this clause the first year, keeping Reagan on the road for eight consecutive weeks until he protested. After that, the company agreed on more frequent but shorter tours, none of them more than three weeks at a time. GE is a company which believes—in the words of former company public relations man Edward Langley—in "demanding a Cadillac at Ford prices," and it asked and received more than its money's worth from Reagan. "We drove him to the utmost limits," says Langley. "We saturated him in Middle America."[11]

The experience taught Reagan the economies of campaigning, which would become valuable to him when he became a political candidate. He learned how to conserve his voice and how to fill his martini glass with water until the last reception of the day. Most importantly, for he was already an accomplished radio speaker, he learned how to listen to a live audience. He paid attention to the response of his listeners, making mental notes about which jokes succeeded and which statistics served to make his points. Politicians and performers love to please their audiences by saying what they think those audiences would like to hear, and Reagan is good both at politics and at performing. The audiences on Reagan's GE tours usually were of the service club or corporate variety, and the questions thrown at him often focused on inflation or government regulation. In the process of answering these questions in a manner pleasing to the questioners, Reagan became a defender of corporations and a critic of the government that the corporate leaders thought was strangling them. The process was gradual, but pervasive. Reagan believes in what he says, and he wound up believing what he was saying. More than anything, it is his GE experience that changed Reagan from an adversary of big business into one of its most ardent spokesmen.

Reagan acknowledges that the GE tours were a fine political training ground. He saw his audiences as representing the broad majority of Americans. Langley recalls that after one tour Reagan said to him: "When I went on those tours and shook hands with all of those people, I began to see that they were very different people than the people Hollywood was talking about. I was seeing the same people that I grew up with in Dixon, Illinois. I realized I was living in a tinsel factory. And this exposure brought me back."[12]

Both on the air and in the GE plants, Reagan exceeded even Schreiber's high expectations. *General Electric Theater* presented a wide range of dramatic material, including a memorable Western version of Dickens' *Christmas Carol* with Jimmy Stewart. Until *Bonanza* came along in the early 1960s, *GE Theater* dominated the Sunday night ratings. But the company which had seemed so progressive and decentralized when Reagan took the job guided its television program with a heavy hand. A GE censor vetoed various scripts on the basis of "taste," including several which Reagan and others associated with the program thought quite tasteful. Reagan, however, defended the company in its best-known exercise of censorship, which was directed at a script set in a fogbound airplane where the airplane instruments malfunction. General Electric, which manufactures instruments for airplanes, was "naturally sensitive" about this, said Reagan,[13] and the script was changed.

On the road, Reagan was beginning to stir some sensibilities of his own. He had a habit of affixing brand names to products, and GE executives were annoyed by Reagan's use of the term "Frigidaire," manufactured by a competitor, as a generic name for refrigerators. Worse was to come. Reagan had started out his GE speaking career with a bland and basic speech that combined patriotic exhortations with a one-note defense of Hollywood, where, said Reagan, the crime rate was extremely low and the divorce rate 10 percent below the national average. Responding to the concerns of his audiences, Reagan's speeches evolved into a broadscale assault on wasteful government programs with titles like "Encroaching Control" and "Our Eroding Freedoms." In 1959 Reagan made himself the darling of conservatives by including among his targets the Tennessee Valley Authority, then a revered symbol of New Deal progress to most Democratic liberals, and also a $50-million-a-year customer of GE products. Reagan said he did not have this relationship in mind when he made a speech declaring that "the annual interest on the TVA deal is five times as great as the flood damage it prevents." But it wasn't long before Reagan heard that TVA was pressuring GE to drop him or lose its business with the agency. Reagan had never met Cordiner and considered him "a very distant and austere figure up there on the bridge,"* but he called him to see if the GE president was worried by the TVA complaint.

"Mr. Cordiner, I understand you have a problem that has to do with me," Reagan said.

"Well, I'm sorry you found that out," Cordiner replied. "It's my problem. I've told them we don't tell an employee what he can or can't say, and we're not going to start."[14]

Reagan was unprepared for the response and grateful for it. "I suppose I still had some lingering boyhood ideas from the Great Depression about big business being not that way, and I was overwhelmed . . . ," Reagan told me in a 1981 interview. But his response to Cordiner's apparent graciousness was worthy of an experienced politician. He told Cordiner that he would not like to say anything in his speeches that might cost GE workers their jobs. "This is a chance we have to take," Reagan quotes Cordiner as replying. "It's a matter of principle," Reagan persisted. "Well, Mr. Cordiner, what if I told you I could make the same speech and be just as effective, and I don't have to use that paragraph at all?" The GE president replied, in a warm

---

* As he used this figure of speech, Reagan put his hand up, salute fashion, creating the image of a ship in which Cordiner was the commanding officer and Reagan his earnest second-in-command. Reagan said he had never read any of Cordiner's speeches, much less met him, but Reagan's evolving ideas about the harm caused by government interference in the marketplace paralleled the GE executive's. In a lecture to the Columbia Graduate School of Business in 1956, Cordiner said: "The deepest reason why state planning has failed wherever it has been tried is that centralized bureaucratic control fails to provide either the information or the productivity that is provided by the United States' system of incentives and competition in a substantially free market. . . . Where there is little freedom at the marketplace for people to decide what they want and what they will pay for it, one sees the artificial shortages or surpluses that plague every state-planned economy in the world, including the farm economy of the United States." The words could well have been uttered by Reagan.

voice: "Well, it would make my job easier."[15] The offending paragraph disappeared, only to make a comeback when Reagan emerged as a spokesman for Goldwater.

By now, Reagan was frequently sought as a speaker by groups such as the National Association of Manufacturers. "There appears to be a lessening of certain moral standards and certain principles of honesty and honor in our country, even a lessening of patriotism," he said on a NAM-sponsored radio show in 1957. On the same program he agreed with a former Commissioner of Internal Revenue that "the present income tax law is making us a nation of liars and cheats." Reagan was especially sensitive to the tax law because he had more and more income taxes of his own to pay. He had moved into a larger Pacific Palisades home with Nancy that had been supplied by GE with every electronic gadget imaginable. On May 28, 1958, the Reagans added a son to their family—Ronald Prescott Reagan, who throughout his boyhood would be known as "Skipper." For the Reagans, it was both a happy and a prosperous time.

Increasingly, more and more of Reagan's income came from public speaking. A GE executive late in the decade told him he was more in demand as a public speaker than anyone in the country except President Eisenhower. And, increasingly, Reagan found that his audiences were fervent and approving in response to his denunciations of government. By the time of the 1960 elections Reagan had become well enough known as a conservative spokesman that Republican officials asked him to speak in favor of the presidential candidacy of Richard Nixon. Reagan says he offered to reregister as a Republican but was told that he would be more effective if he spoke for Nixon as a Democrat. By now, however, it was clear that Reagan found himself more comfortable with the views of Republican candidates than with the positions taken by most Democratic leaders.

After the election of John F. Kennedy as President, Reagan became too controversial for GE. His option came up for renewal in 1962, at a time when *Bonanza* had pulled ahead of *General Electric Theater* in the ratings and a new format was being considered for the Reagan show. Before the format could be resolved, Reagan received a call from a GE executive he did not know, telling him that the company wanted him to confine his speeches to the selling of GE products. Reagan got hot about it. He told GE that he was constantly getting requests to speak and would continue to do so on his own time. "There's no way that I could go out now to an audience that is expecting the type of thing I've been doing for the last eight years and suddenly stand up and start selling them electric toasters," Reagan said. "You'd suffer, and so would I. I can't do that." The conversation continued, with the executive saying that GE wanted Reagan to speak, but only on behalf of its products. Finally, Reagan said: "That's it. If it's the speeches, then you only have one choice. Either I don't do the speeches at all for you, or we don't do the program; you get somebody else."[16] Within two days, General Electric had canceled the show.*

By now, Reagan accepted the various published descriptions of himself as "a prominent conservative spokesman," although he always bridled when the word "right-winger" was added to the description. He thought of himself as an orthodox and patriotic American who was drawing attention to a problem of government growth that would destroy the country if it wasn't corrected. While still a registered Democrat, Reagan realized he had become a Republican. Reagan says the recognition came the week of Kennedy's inaugural when he gave his customary GE speech in Bloomington, Illinois, and was immediately denounced in the AFL–CIO paper as "a right-wing extremist." Reagan couldn't see what the labor paper was so upset about. "I'd been making this same speech for years, and no one objected," he said, "and a Democratic President is elected and suddenly they find I'm a right-wing extremist." Years later, Frank Sinatra told him that after years of raising millions of dollars for the Democrats, he had been threatened with a boycott of his shows for the first time in his life because he was helping Reagan. "Frank, let me tell you the facts of life," Reagan said, and related the Bloomington incident.[17] Sinatra's complaint reinforced Reagan's belief that a double standard remains abroad in the land for Democrats and Republicans.

The essential political fact of Reagan's life in 1962 was that he was very much in demand on the Republican right. On the other side, liberal Democrats regarded him as an apostate. Reagan realized this and was in no mood to continue the partisan fiction. When California Republicans approached him in 1962, Reagan expressed his willingness to campaign, but only under his true colors. "I didn't want to be a professional Democrat campaigning for the Republicans," Reagan told them. "I'm going to reregister and become a Republican."[18] He did so, at a subsequent political meeting where he spoke on behalf of the ill-fated Nixon campaign against Governor Edmund G. (Pat) Brown. Reagan didn't know it then, but Brown would be his first Democratic political opponent. The one-time New Deal liberal Democrat from Dixon had become a wealthy, card-carrying conservative Republican with a bright political future.

* Reagan told me that Cordiner was retired when GE canceled the show and that it would not have happened if he were still in charge. According to General Electric officials, however, Cordiner did not retire as chairman of the board and chief executive officer until December 1963, more than a year after *General Electric Theater* went off the air.

9

The Candidate

"You and I have a rendezvous with destiny," Ronald Reagan said, looking into the camera. "We can preserve for our children this, the last best hope of man on earth, or we can sentence them to take the first step into a thousand years of darkness. If we fail, at least let our children, and our children's children, say of us we justified our brief moment here. We did all that could be done."

These were the fatalistic and final words of Reagan's pretaped televised oration for Barry Goldwater on October 27, 1964. When the speech was over, or more precisely, a week later when the American voters had buried the Republican presidential nominee under what was up to that time the greatest landslide in presidential election history, the mantle of conservative political leadership in the United States had passed from Goldwater to Reagan. *Time* called the speech "the one bright spot in a dismal campaign." The day after Reagan's speech a group of conservatives formed "Republicans for Ronald Reagan" in Owosso, Michigan, Thomas E. Dewey's home town. Within months, a well-financed committee, "Friends of Ronald Reagan," had come together in Los Angeles to launch his candidacy for governor of California.

The new leader of the conservatives was a striking stylistic contrast to the fallen hero he had replaced. Goldwater was blunt, impatient, honest and profane, with a proclivity for the self-destructive phrase ("let's lob one into the men's room of the Kremlin") that alarmed even some of his own supporters. In its heavy-handed portrayal of the Arizona senator as "a right-wing extremist," the Democratic opposition found most of its work already accomplished by Goldwater and his more wild-eyed followers. Reagan, however, was a smiler. Though his speech had been more controversial and hyperbolic in content than any which Goldwater had given for himself, Reagan inspired where Goldwater tended to terrify. Reagan's words were radical, but his manner was reassuring, replete with self-deprecating little jokes and that winning smile. His professional training had made him smooth without making him slick, blending the best of both Hollywood and Dixon. In manner and style, he was a small-town boy, but one who had made good in the big city.

Reagan's language added to the impression of reassurance. Culturally, he remained a Democrat who drew his metaphors and inspiration from the New Deal. Other Republican politicians spoke to the majority of the electorate as outsiders, trying to induce Democrats to come over to their side. Reagan spoke as an insider. Though he had left the party of Franklin Roosevelt, he refused to abandon the words and phrases which provided a shared language and a common bond with his fellow citizens. When Reagan spoke, ordinary Americans did not have to make the mental translation usually required for conservative Republican speakers. He undermined the New Deal in its own vernacular. The phrase "rendezvous with destiny" which Reagan liked so much had been borrowed consciously from FDR, who had used it in accepting the Democratic presidential nomination for the second time on June 27, 1936. And Reagan's speeches were peppered with other borrowings from Roosevelt, whose words and memories stoked hidden fires of approval and patriotism among American working men and women. While Reagan's words called for sweeping change, his style and personality promised continuity.

Reagan's own speeches had changed little since the days he had campaigned for Democrats in the forties. It might be said that he continued always to give the same basic speech while directing it to a different result. Invariably, he used extraordinary examples to make points which were also relentlessly undergirded by statistics. Speaking for Truman and Hubert Humphrey in 1948, Reagan went after the problems of "Republican inflation" in this way:

> The profits of corporations have doubled while worker's wages have increased by only one quarter. In other words, profits have gone up four times as much as wages. And the small increase workers did receive was more than eaten up by rising prices, which have also bored into their savings.
>
> For example, here's an Associated Press dispatch I read the other day about Smith L. Carpenter, a craftsman in Union Springs, New York. Seems that Mr. Carpenter retired some years ago thinking he had enough money saved so that he could live out his last years without having to worry. But he didn't figure on this Republican inflation which ate up all his savings and so he's gone back to work. The reason this is news is Mr. Carpenter is 91 years old.
>
> Now, take as a contrast the Standard Oil Company of New Jersey, which reported a net profit of $210 million *after* taxes in the first half of 1948. An increase of 70 percent in one year. In other words, high prices have not been caused by higher wages, but by bigger and bigger profits.

By 1964, and Reagan's Goldwater speech entitled "A Time For Choosing," big government had replaced big business as the enemy, and the statistics came fast and furious. "Since the beginning of the century our gross national product has increased by 33 times," Reagan said. "In the same period the cost of federal government has increased 234 times and while the work force is only one and one-half times greater, federal employees number 9 times as many." As Reagan explained it, workers were no longer menaced by excessive corporate profits but by high taxation and the costly welfare programs these taxes paid for. Some of the examples he gave to demonstrate what had gone wrong were fully equal to the strange case of Smith L. Carpenter:

> Recently, a judge told me of an incident in his court. A fairly young woman with six children, pregnant with her seventh, came to him for a divorce. Under his questioning it became evident that the husband did not share this desire. When the whole story came out, her husband was a laborer earning $250 a month. By divorcing him she could get an $80 raise. She was eligible for $350 a month from the Aid to Dependent Children Program. She had been talked into the divorce by two friends who had already done this very thing.

In 1948 President Truman had succeeded in pinning the blame for inflation and a stagnant economy on the "do-nothing 80th Congress" and had pulled off a stunning political upset. Two decades later, after the Great Society and the Vietnam War, voters turned against the Democrats. With his call for fewer programs, less government and lower taxes, Reagan was on the cutting edge of this reaction. He had the right message at the right time.

He also was in the right place in California, where the once-dominant Republicans had fallen upon sad days. Until 1958, the GOP had lost the California governorship only once in the century and had usually controlled both the congressional and legislative delegations. As late as 1954, California Republicans claimed both U.S. Senate seats, an overwhelming majority in the House delegation, the governorship and control of the legislature. Three-term Republican governor Earl Warren had been elevated by President Eisenhower to the Supreme Court. Another ambitious Californian, Richard Nixon, was Vice-President. Except for Attorney General Edmund G. (Pat) Brown, an amiable San Francisco lawyer, the state's political landscape was unblemished by a well-recognized Democrat.

In 1958, with no effective partisan opposition to contend with, the Republicans committed a bizarre act of political suicide which did for the Democrats what they could never have done for themselves. The proximate cause was U.S. Senator William Knowland, an intractable bull of a man whose lack of diplomacy was exceeded only by his ambition. Knowland wanted to be President. Since governors in those days controlled state delegations at national conventions, he thought that Sacramento was his best route to the White House. His immediate obstacle was Republican Governor Goodwin Knight, who had started out as a conservative but moved steadily toward the center after succeeding Warren. In the Warren tradition, Knight cultivated organized labor and enjoyed good relations with many members of the state's union hierarchy. Knowland's campaign was based on a right-to-work initiative which employers' groups put on the California ballot in 1958. He used the leverage of his conservative contributors and the influence of his newspaper family (the *Oakland Tribune*) to pressure Knight into running for the U.S. Senate instead of another term as governor. This brought Brown, who probably would not have run against Knight, into the race as the champion of the union shop. Knowland's maneuver also provided the usually outgunned California Democrats with union money and precinct workers as the national labor movement made the California initiative a major test. Labor won, the initiative lost, and Brown trounced the previously unbeaten Knowland. Knight's compliance cast him as a weak politician who had allowed Knowland and the party's financial fat cats to roll over him. Knight lost, too, and the Democrats won control of the legislature. In 1962 Brown was reelected with a skillful campaign against Nixon who, after two terms as Vice-President, gave Californians the accurate impression that he had only a passing interest in state government. Then, to complete the Republican Party's self-destruction, the moderate and conservative wings of the GOP cut each other to pieces in the 1964 presidential primary where Goldwater confronted New York Governor Nelson Rockefeller. Goldwater was depicted as a right-wing bomb-thrower who would lead the nation into war. Rockefeller was portrayed as an untrustworthy eastern liberal who had betrayed his party and abandoned his wife. Goldwater won a narrow victory, and the Republican Party wound up the loser.

When the California GOP survivors cleared the littered battlefield of the wounded after the 1964 campaign, they found few leaders of any consequence to do battle against Governor Brown in 1966. Warren, Knowland, Knight and Nixon were out of the picture. Thomas Kuchel, a moderate U.S. Senator, was distrusted by the conservatives for his opposition to Goldwater. The other senator, elected in 1964 over Democrat Pierre Salinger despite President Johnson's one million vote victory in California, was Reagan's old friend from the Screen Actors Guild, George Murphy. His election was timely as far as Reagan was concerned, for it demonstrated that Californians were not reluctant to choose a former actor for high political office.

But did Reagan want political office? Those who came to call upon him were of two minds. Reagan often told members of his family and prospective bankrollers of his campaign that he saw himself as a spokesman rather than a candidate. He brought up potential obstacles to a successful Reagan candidacy, remarking on the division within the party and his own identification with the Goldwater side. Some of his visitors formed an impression that Reagan, even if he did become a candidate, was more interested in the national arena than in a state office.

In 1962 his daughter Maureen, working as a secretary in Washington, D.C., had expressed concern about the liberal direction of the country in a letter to her father and suggested that he could run for governor of California, as a few conservatives were beginning to suggest. "Well, if we're talking

about what I could do, Mermie, I could be President," Reagan wrote back.*[1]
She knew he was kidding, but thought it was a good idea. By late 1964,
Maureen was openly encouraging her father to run for governor. So was
Reagan's brother Neil and the person most influential to the prospective
candidate, Nancy Reagan. When Maureen visited her father soon after the
1964 election, she asked him if he was going to run for governor. He ges-
tured toward Nancy and said with a smile, "Oh, my God, they're closing in
all over."[2]

My guess is that Reagan, usually the reactive man, would never have
sought elective office except for the insistence of those who came to him and
the absence of any other untarnished Republican candidate available to run
against Governor Brown. Certainly he would not have taken the initiative in
seeking office. A long time ago, trying to break into radio, Reagan had
reached out for a job he wanted. Once, in Hollywood, he had created his
own opportunity by pursuing and winning the role of George Gipp. But he
had not asked for anything for a long time. Ever since the war and his divorce from Wyman, the good things in Reagan's life had come to him. That
had been the case with Nancy Davis and with General Electric. When the
opportunities had landed on his doorstep, Reagan had responded. In 1959
the Screen Actors Guild asked him to return for a sixth term as president,
and Reagan led the union in its first successful strike against the movie producers. After *General Electric Theater* folded, Reagan was asked to be the
host and occasional actor on *Death Valley Days*. And in 1964 he was sought
by California Republicans as a speaker on behalf of Goldwater. He responded with the best effort of that ill-conceived campaign.

The 1964 speech became a springboard for Reagan largely because its
sponsors insisted on making it one. They were convinced that Reagan, alone
among any Republicans available at the time, had the qualities to be a successful candidate for governor. The leader of the group was Holmes P. Tuttle, a soft-spoken and highly successful entrepreneur whose Ford Motor
Company dealerships in Los Angeles were the base of a profitable complex
of businesses. Not well known outside his own wealthy circle, Tuttle had
been a Republican fund-raiser since the first Eisenhower campaign. He had
supported Goldwater but thought the bitter Republican national convention
of 1964 "a fiasco" in which the nominee had foolishly passed up a chance to
unify the party by selecting Pennsylvania Governor William Scranton as his
running mate.[3] No zealot, Tuttle wanted a gubernatorial candidate who
would not repeat the Goldwater mistakes. He had been friends with Reagan
since the Wyman marriage and thought the actor could rally the voters and
his divided party. In 1964 Tuttle had organized a $1,000-a-plate dinner in
Los Angeles and invited Reagan as the speaker. The speech electrified the
crowd, and convinced Tuttle and his friends that they should put "A Time

---

* To the best of my knowledge or research, this is the first expression from Reagan,
even in jest, of a specific interest in the presidency.

for Choosing" on national television. But Goldwater campaign manager Denison Kitchel and adviser William Baroody, Sr., objected to a national telecast. The speech seemed to them too controversial, particularly in its references to Social Security. To demonstrate the power of the speech, Tuttle and his friends aired it in California with a trailer asking for contributions. The Californians raised so much money that they were able to tell the Republican National Committee, then hard-pressed for funds, that they could pay for the national telecast.

Kitchel and Baroody still objected.* They convinced Goldwater to telephone Reagan at home the Sunday before the intended broadcast and request that he withdraw the speech. Reagan asked Goldwater whether he had seen the taped film, and the Arizona senator replied that he had not. "Well, it's not really that bad, Senator, and I don't think it will do you any harm," Reagan said. "Please read the script or see the film. If you are then of the opinion that it will hurt your campaign, I'll abide by your decision and cancel the release."[4] Though Baroody and Kitchel continued their opposition, Goldwater did not call back and the speech was shown. The subsequent widespread praise for the Reagan speech convinced the California Republican millionaires that they knew more about what appealed to voters than did the national leadership of the Goldwater movement.

Now, with the Goldwater debacle still a vivid memory, Tuttle and his millionaire friends decided to run Reagan for governor in 1966. They made their decision two months after Goldwater's defeat in a conference of millionaires at Tuttle's home. The other prime movers were the late A. C. (Cy) Rubel, chairman of the board of Union Oil Company, and Henry Salvatori, founder of the Western Geophysical Company. "Reagan is the man who can enunciate our principles to the people," said Rubel, paying homage to the communicative skills of their designated candidate.[5] Tuttle, who had known the prospective candidate longer than any member of the group, carried the message to Reagan, who expressed concerns about the cost and difficulties of conducting a statewide campaign. "I told him I knew it would be a sacrifice but that he was the man we wanted," Tuttle said.[6] Reagan agreed to think it over. Tuttle went home, optimistic that Reagan would give him a commitment if the millionaire backers showed they could put together a campaign.

Tuttle's next stop was at Spencer-Roberts, the Southern California political management firm which had run Rockefeller's near-miss primary campaign in 1964. Stuart Spencer and Bill Roberts had started out as unknown organizers for the Los Angeles County Republicans Central Committee and had parlayed their success in this project into campaign management. Before managing the Rockefeller campaign, they had won 34 of 40 congres-

---

* This is the account given by Stephen Shadegg, who reconstructed the incident soon after the event in *What Happened to Goldwater?*, pages 252–253. Kitchel's personal recollection in a November 2, 1981, interview was that he had objected and that Baroody, now deceased, "thought that the passages were fine. . . ."

sional races with a wide variety of Republican candidates. "We checked with people around the country, and they said Spencer-Roberts was the best," said Tuttle. "We didn't want anything less than the best."[7]

Since they were the best, the partners did not jump at the opportunity to manage a Reagan campaign. "We had reservations about Reagan," Roberts said afterwards. "We had heard that Reagan was a real right-winger and we thought that a right-wing kind of candidacy would not be a successful one. We'd also heard a lot of other things—that Reagan was a martinet, that he was difficult to work with."[8] But Reagan dispelled most of these qualms when he met with Roberts at Cave de Roy, a Los Angeles key club restaurant, to talk about his candidacy. "We found him to be an open and candid person, easy to talk with, and a good listener," said Roberts.[9] The prospective campaign manager was also encouraged by the commitment of Tuttle, Rubel and Salvatori, who pledged to raise whatever money was necessary to make Reagan governor. Soon after this meeting at Cave de Roy, Reagan called Tuttle again and declared he was ready to make the race. Immediately, Reagan began to prod Roberts to make a commitment. On their third meeting, this time at Reagan's home, Reagan said, "Well, what about it? Are you going to do it? You've been asking me questions for three meetings now."[10] Roberts quietly answered that he was ready to manage the campaign.

In no other populous state of the nation at this time could a handful of millionaires and a political consultant so easily have decided on their own to run an aging actor for governor without consulting with party leaders. But in California such consultation wasn't necessary. Statewide campaigns in California have a partyless peculiarity which is the outgrowth of a political system fashioned by early-century Progressive reformer Hiram Johnson. It is the long shadow of this Progressive legacy, as much as anything, which made possible the rapid rise to power of Ronald Reagan. Johnson was contemptuous of political parties because he found them totally controlled by Southern Pacific Railroad's machine and its allied corporate interests. He smashed the machine and brought down the parties with it.* The "direct de-

---

* Southern Pacific, the railroad company which linked California to the nation and dominated the state's economic and political life for four decades, was at the height of its power when Johnson came along in 1906. He was a young attorney and son of a Southern Pacific lobbyist who had served a term in prison and another in the U.S. House of Representatives. Hiram Johnson opposed both his father and the company which owned him, and fate gave him an opportunity to strike back. During the bribery trial of notorious San Francisco political boss Abraham Ruef, the prosecutor was shot and seriously wounded in the courtroom. Young Johnson took over the prosecution, convicted Ruef, and emerged as the leader of the state's growing Progressive movement. In 1910 he won the Republican nomination for governor and was elected after a campaign in which he promised to break the political power of the railroad. In office, he was as good as his word. The Progressives also put California on the track of becoming the modern, social welfare state which Reagan would inherit as governor by enacting workmen's compensation, child labor laws, and women's suffrage long before most other states adopted these reforms.

mocracy" introduced by the Progressives included the primary, the initiative, the referendum and laws which made it illegal for party organizations to endorse candidates. Johnson's crowning achievement was the introduction of a unique cross-filing system which allowed a candidate to seek a nomination of his own party and all others on the ballot. Since candidates were not identified by party, name recognition became a major determinant of election. After the system had operated for several decades, nearly three-fourths of the state legislators were incumbents who had been elected in primaries where they had won both Democratic and Republican nominations. In this nonparty system the political functions that Johnson had stripped from the parties were performed by other institutions and individuals. Since the parties had practically no funds, wealthy entrepreneurs like Tuttle and Salvatori became the financiers. Since the parties were too weak to provide campaign management, this function was performed by outside consultants like Spencer-Roberts. While cross-filing had been repealed by the time Reagan came along,* it had left in its wake a tradition of nonpartisanship which influenced business, labor and newspaper endorsements.

Most importantly, the near destruction of the parties had created a star system of personality politics long before television arrived. At a time when most other states favored candidates who had advanced through the ranks, California selected potential office-holders on the basis of real or supposed charismatic appeal, a condition ideal for Reagan. Candidates who displayed qualities of will or flamboyance—above all, candidates who appealed to the persistent independent streak in the California electorate—could be reelected again and again while the state swayed back and forth politically.

Popular Earl Warren, who started out as a crusading district attorney, was elected governor three times and in 1946 accomplished the unprecedented feat of winning both the Democratic and Republican nominations for governor.† Though Warren was the Republican nominee for Vice-President in 1948, he was so nonpartisan that he once irritated GOP leaders by skipping a party gathering to attend a University of California football game. Like Hiram Johnson, Warren was a progressive who fought for corporate taxes, public power, public health insurance. Republican governors

---

* It was repealed because the Republicans outwitted themselves. In 1952 the GOP tried to head off an initiative abolishing cross-filing with a measure that simply put partisan designations on the ballot. The measures affected the same section of the law, and the one with the most votes would be the one to prevail. But the cross-filing repealer lost, while the GOP measure won. The result was that partisan designations appeared on the ballot starting in 1954, and a lot of Democrats discovered they had been voting for Republican office-holders. Democrats gained steady ground after that and abolished cross-filing in 1959 after taking control of the legislature the previous year.

† What is often overlooked is that Warren, who was said to have moved left after becoming governor, started his career as a nonpartisan seeking approval from all parties. When he was elected attorney general as a Republican in 1938, he cross-filed and won the nominations of the Democratic and Progressive parties.

Johnson, Warren and Knight actively campaigned for Democratic votes in Democratic primaries, further loosening the already thin party ties of California voters. This was a boon to Reagan, who had been a registered Republican for less than three years when he told Tuttle he was willing to run. Such a recent conversion would have been a mark against Reagan in many places, but it mattered little in a state where partisan ballot identification was still a novelty. Few Californians knew and fewer cared that Democratic Governor Brown, who had come to politics by the Warren route of law enforcement, was once a Republican. In California, in the oft-used phrase of the day, it was the man and not the party that counted.

Reagan, for different reasons than Warren, also believed he could win Democratic votes. But he started his efforts knowing that the first task was to repair a Republican Party still shell-shocked by the debacle of 1964. In hiring Spencer-Roberts, which many prominent California Republicans still identified with the Rockefeller campaign of 1964, Reagan took one step toward party unification. He took another step which helped his party and his prospective candidacy at the same time by making himself available to speak to Republican organizations seeking to pull themselves together in the wake of that 1964 election. Reagan's message in these speeches was that the Republicans shared a common goal of replacing the Democratic administrations in Washington and Sacramento. The most important precondition of a successful gubernatorial candidacy, Reagan agreed in conversations with Tuttle and Roberts, was to have a united party behind him.

The vehicle for this unity was "Friends of Ronald Reagan." Created by Roberts and Tuttle and supported by forty-one wealthy donors, the Friends began operation in the late spring of 1965 out of a small office provided by Rubel in the Union Oil Building in downtown Los Angeles. Reagan's decision to run was now widely known, but he left himself an escape hatch in case neither money nor support materialized. "If by August or September, we feel there's overwhelming support from the Republican Party to win an election, not just a primary, I'll do it," Reagan said.[11] By setting down this condition Reagan put his campaign on the opposite tack of Goldwater's 1964 effort, which had been aimed at overthrowing the Republican establishment. Operating in a state where there was almost no establishment to overthrow, Reagan's effort was directed from the outset at winning the general election against the Democrats.

To a Spencer-Roberts list of Republican activists, the Friends of Ronald Reagan sent a letter, written by Roberts and signed by Rubel, which began with the words of Reagan's 1964 speech, "A Time For Choosing," and then declared:

> For several years, Ronald Reagan has spoken, forcefully and eloquently, to the above subject. Again and again, he has called upon the American people to awaken to a decision they must ultimately make. Simply put, the question was,

and still is: Will the people control the government or will the government control the people?

Again the challenge—a time for choosing—but in another way. Today, the question is: Who shall govern this, the largest state in the nation?

Ronald Reagan, out of a deep sense of duty and dedication, is willing to serve his Republican Party as its candidate for governor providing a substantial cross-section of our Party will unite behind his candidacy.

The response, so enthusiastic it surprised even Roberts, became a principal source of the $135,000 spent in the precampaign period by Friends of Ronald Reagan. Tuttle, who contributed $5,000, observed that the original group of wealthy backers could easily have put up the funds themselves, but decided that fund-raising solicitation would give a broader group of people a stake in the success of the Reagan campaign. The enthusiastic letters which accompanied the solicited donations convinced Roberts he had a live-wire candidate.

The absence of any formidable Republican opponent also encouraged Roberts. Senator Thomas Kuchel, an anti-Goldwaterite who never succeeded in mending his fences with the party's conservative troops, briefly considered the race and then decided against it. By fall it was clear that Reagan's only major opponent would be George Christopher, a former San Francisco mayor and dairyman who had twice been defeated in statewide campaigns.

By coincidence, a Christopher backer had approached Roberts within hours after he received the first overtures from the Reagan camp. Even though Roberts was then uncertain about Reagan, his mind was made up against Christopher. "Losing twice had not made his candidacy palatable," said Roberts afterwards.[12] Knowing that Christopher had heavy liabilities in a television age, Roberts welcomed him as Reagan's principal opponent. Swarthy and heavy-set in appearance, Christopher had been uncharitably described as looking and talking "like a losing television wrestler." He saw the campaign as simply a replay of 1964, with Reagan cast in the role of losing right-wing extremist. In a 1966 television speech Christopher said, "The Pat Brown Democrats will concentrate heavily on Reagan's statements that he would have voted against the Civil Rights Act of 1964. They know that a candidate who opposes civil rights is a losing candidate." Christopher also believed that Reagan would be damaged by the acknowledgment in his just published autobiography, *Where's the Rest of Me?*, that he had once joined Communist front organizations. When a reporter at Christopher's opening press conference asked him to name the front groups, Christopher replied, "They're in his book." The ex-mayor's campaign continued ineptly and made it easy for Roberts to follow a strategy of running against Governor Brown and ignoring Christopher. Reagan received timely assistance from Gaylord Parkinson, a San Diego obstetrician who had become the state

GOP chairman. Parkinson's contribution to party unity was the so-called Eleventh Commandment, "Thou shall not speak ill of any fellow Republican," by which Reagan eagerly promised to abide. Twice during the campaign Parkinson rebuked Christopher for supposed violations of this political scripture, further inhibiting a losing candidate who was already on the defensive.

Reagan, meanwhile, was boning up. Spencer and Roberts quickly realized that Reagan was brighter than he had been billed and had tremendous potential as a candidate. But they also recognized that he was uninformed on state issues. The Spencer-Roberts remedy for this was a team of behavioral psychologists, Stanley Plog and Kenneth Holden, who taught at Southern California universities and operated the Behavior Science Corporation in Van Nuys. Spencer-Roberts hired them to work for Reagan. Working from Reagan's speeches and from interviews with him, Plog and Holden isolated seventeen issues, arranging each into a philosophical framework. Eventually, they produced eight black books which contained factual references for Reagan to cite and which ultimately became the partial basis of his first attempts at a legislative program. And they expanded his already wide range of literary allusions to include such names as Tocqueville and Belloc, helping Reagan to employ what David S. Broder subsequently called "a sort of wisdom-by-association technique also used by President Kennedy"[13] in his speeches.

While Plog and Holden deepened Reagan's understanding of issues, their work made little impact on Reagan's basic speech. His message remained as simple and unspecific as the one which had emerged from the GE days and excited the followers of Barry Goldwater. People were too dependent on government, which had become the master instead of the servant. Government must be reduced in size and taxes lowered. Businessmen should not be strangled by government regulations. Ordinary citizens were competent to take charge of their own government and their own affairs. "I am not a politician," Reagan said in several of his speeches. "I am an ordinary citizen with a deep-seated belief that much of what troubles us has been brought about by politicians; and it's high time that more ordinary citizens brought the fresh air of common-sense thinking to bear on these problems."

On the Democratic side of the fence, there was no fear of any "citizen-politicians." Pat Brown had spent a lifetime in real politics and made no secret that he took Reagan lightly. After defeating Knowland and Nixon handily, Brown wasn't worried about what an actor could do to him and made little effort, until it was too late, to assess the impact of a Reagan candidacy. His aides, accustomed to touting Brown's "greatness" to one another and to the press, were also overconfident. They brushed aside occasional press speculation that Brown, whose rotund, jowly face had led to him once being described as "an affable owl," would be at a disadvantage against

Reagan on television. Reagan, they believed, would crack under hard questioning.

Brown also suffered from a regional misperception. He was from San Francisco, which has a style and political culture at odds with the rest of California, and which was then isolated from the conservative revolt flaring up in the suburbs of Los Angeles, San Diego, Orange and Santa Clara counties. San Francisco had been at the center of the state's political life when Brown's career had begun, but its influence had waned and its population had remained static during a period of mass migration and growth in California. When Pat Brown's son set out to make his own political career, he would build a base in Southern California. But Pat Brown was a staunch and loyal San Franciscan, the product of a community which is at once the most cosmopolitan and provincial in California. San Francisco's immigrants tended to be foreigners and Easterners, not the conservative middle-class whites from the Middle West and the South who flooded Southern California. Pat Brown overestimated the importance of San Francisco, the one community in which his support remained secure. He overestimated the political potency of Christopher, who shared many of his views and traits and had been a capable mayor of San Francisco. Brown underestimated the growing conservatism which would make 1966 a Republican year across the nation. He also underestimated Reagan, whom he knew only from his movies. Brown saw Reagan as at best a Hollywood variant of Goldwater who would be unable to attract moderate voters. A variety of public opinion surveys bolstered the view. The most respected of them, Mervin Field's California Poll, in February 1966 gave Reagan a narrow three-point lead over Christopher with 27 percent of the potential Republican voters undecided. In matchups against Brown, however, this same poll showed Christopher leading by seven points and Reagan trailing by four. This finding helped encourage one of the classic misjudgments of American politics—a decision by Brown to help the Republican voters of his state nominate Reagan.

Against the recommendation of his own campaign manager, Don Bradley, the governor gave his stamp of approval to a plan by a pair of political in-fighters, Dick Kline and Harry Lerner, to discredit Christopher. They in turn hired Dick Hyer, a former San Francisco newspaperman, who dredged up a 1939 conviction of Christopher for violating a "fair trade" milk-pricing statute which had been resisted by many California dairymen. The prosecutor in the case had termed the violations technical. The material had been repeatedly aired without success against Christopher in his San Francisco supervisor and mayoralty campaigns. But the charges were news in Southern California, as Kline knew they would be. Bradley leaked the material to columnist Drew Pearson, who in turn made them the basis of an assault on Christopher's honesty which forced him on the defensive and hurt his campaign. But Reagan would have won the Republican primary anyway, and the smear of Christopher was harmful to Brown. Harry Farrell, then political writer for the *San Jose Mercury News,* summed up the damage afterwards: "Some people thought that Pat Brown was indecisive or bumbling but no one denied his sincerity or dedication. After the Christopher smear he was just another politician."[14]

Based on his record, however, Brown was more than just another governor. Elected when the state had exhausted budget surpluses accumulated during the wartime boom years, Brown nonetheless devoted his energies to maintaining and expanding the public works and social programs for which California had long been in the forefront of the states. California had the best freeways, an impressive parks system, the largest program of college construction. Brown's pet project was the gigantic California Water Project, which transferred water hundreds of miles from the water-rich northern section of the state to thirsty and populous Southern California. The governor had helped sell this multibillion dollar project to the legislature and the electorate, and he seemed annoyed, even hurt, that no one stopped to give him credit for it in 1966.

The voters had other issues on their minds. For many middle class and working class voters struggling with inflation and growing families, the costs of state and local government seemed to be exceeding the benefits. These Californians, many of them residents of brand-new suburbs with costly new roads, schools and sewer systems, wanted lower taxes, not more government programs. The social changes of the 1960s also had deepened class, racial and generational differences. The Watts riots of 1965, coming when Brown was vacationing in Greece, shocked Los Angelenos who thought that racial riots were something that happened back East. The "free speech" and "filthy speech" movements at the University of California, forerunners of the antiwar student mobilizations later in the decade, angered middle-aged parents, many of whom felt that something had gone seriously wrong with their institutions of higher learning.

Beyond the voter discontent which signaled the nationwide Republican resurgence of 1966, Brown had problems of his own. He was opposed in the lower house of the legislature by an Assembly speaker of his own party, the capable and ambitious Jesse Unruh, who blocked many of Brown's programs. Politicians of both parties viewed Brown as indecisive. The word in Sacramento was that he listened best to whoever saw him last. Brown was also hurt by his bad luck in being out of the country when the Watts riots occurred. The impression that he was not on top of his job was compounded by his delayed reaction to the student takeover at the University of California's administrative office in Berkeley. Brown had hesitated, then sent in the California Highway Patrol to clear the building. Though he had acted on the advice of law enforcement officers at the scene, including a young Alameda County deputy district attorney named Edwin Meese, Brown was blamed both for acting too slowly and for acting at all. Fairly or not, Brown seemed the embodiment of the unkind description given of him by Unruh—"the tower of Jello."

Racial issues also helped Reagan and hurt Brown. By another stroke of bad luck Brown was in an airliner over Denver, returning to Sacramento from a weekend trip in Washington, when a near-riot broke out in Watts in March 1966. Brown persuaded the pilot to fly directly to Los Angeles, but the news stories of the event reminded voters that the governor had been vacationing abroad during the big Watts riot of 1965, which had claimed thirty-four lives. This new outbreak was quelled after two deaths, but another three-day riot broke out in September in the Hunter's Point area of San Francisco after police shot and killed a fleeing sixteen-year-old auto theft suspect. Racial tensions also were fanned by a decision of the state Supreme Court which struck down Proposition 14, a 1964 ballot measure which had invalidated California's fair housing law, the Rumford Act. Reagan had supported the ballot proposition, which passed by a 2–1 margin, while Brown opposed it. Brown partially retreated from his support in 1966, enhancing his image as a waverer, while Reagan remained staunchly opposed to the fair housing law, which he said, "By infringment on one of our basic individual rights sets a precedent which threatens individual liberty."

Reagan's own worst moment of the campaign came on the racial issue. Appearing before a convention of the National Negro Republican Assembly in Santa Monica on March 6, 1966, Reagan was gently twitted by Christopher for his opposition to the federal Civil Rights Act of 1964. The remark irritated Reagan. Later, near the end of a question-and-answer session which followed speeches from the two candidates, a delegate asked Reagan how he expected to get the votes of Negro Republicans when he had opposed the Civil Rights Act. Christopher, commenting on the answer, said he would have voted for the act and declared that the position taken by Barry Goldwater in opposition "did more harm than anything to the Republican Party, and we're still paying for that defeat. This situation still plagues the Republican Party, and unless we cast out this image, we're going to suffer defeat."

The questioning would have ended there except that Reagan rose to his feet and said he wanted to make a point of personal privilege. "I resent the implication that there is any bigotry in my nature," Reagan yelled at the surprised delegates. "Don't anyone ever imply I lack integrity. I will not stand silent and let anyone imply that—in this or any other group." He then stalked out of the meeting. Some reports of his departure said Reagan had tears in his eyes. One reporter said Reagan had declared, "I'll get that S.O.B." It was an unexpected crack in the carefully prepared Reagan campaign, and his aides were distraught.

Reagan press secretary Franklyn C. (Lyn) Nofziger, a cigar-chewing, wise-cracking Washington political reporter borrowed from Copley News Service, had visions of stories describing Reagan as unbalanced and unable to take criticism. Nofziger and issues specialist Holden persuaded Reagan to return. The press secretary blamed the entire affair on a severe virus infection which had noticeably weakened Reagan at a state Republican gathering a week earlier and was still bothering him. Christopher suggested that the problem was a mental one, extending his "sympathy" to Reagan "in this moment of his emotional disturbance." But Reagan's return to the hall blunted the impact of his walkout. Once back, Reagan was his usual smiling self. He apologized to the delegates for leaving, reinterated his personal abhorrence of discrimination, and declared that his opposition to the Civil Rights Act was based on constitutional grounds. He remained carefully unruffled when reporters asked him what the incident revealed about his emotional state. At a state capitol press conference four days later, he turned aside one such question by quipping, "My wife says I'm very even-tempered."

All in all, Reagan's tantrum cost him very little. This may have been partly because it was a time of reaction against the civil rights movement by white voters, but the larger reason probably was the timing of the incident. Roberts believes that Reagan was fortunate that the walkout occurred in March, three months before the primary, rather than later when voters had begun to focus on the election. In terms of the campaign itself, the incident proved useful to Reagan. It reminded his advisers, who had been casually working Reagan to his limit without protest from the candidate, that he was both inexperienced and needed to be rested. And it encouraged Brown in his original belief that Reagan couldn't take the heat and that everything would be all right if the Republicans could be prevented from nominating Christopher.

The results of the primary, however, provided the first clue that Reagan was a ballot box candidate who runs more strongly on election day than he does in the polls. Reagan received 1,417,623 votes to 675,683 for Christopher and 92,751 for three minor candidates. By winning 65 percent of the total Republican vote Reagan accomplished the party unity which had been his first objective. A narrow victory would have encouraged further party division. Since Reagan was clearly the choice of rank-and-file GOP voters, moderate GOP politicians who might have been tempted to nurse leftover grievances from the 1964 campaign swung quickly into line. Reagan encouraged the newfound GOP harmony by gracious overtures to the loser and his supporters, and Roberts saw to it that letters were sent out the day after the primary offering prominent Christopher backers positions in the Reagan campaign.

The results of the Democratic primary advertised the disarray of a party which came apart at the seams in California two years ahead of its national schedule. Brown had lost support on the left and some of his aura of liberalism by teaming with state Controller Alan Cranston to pressure the volunteer California Democratic Council to kick out its president, Si Casady, a vocal and sometimes intemperate critic of both President Johnson and the Vietnam War. On the right, Brown was bedeviled by the potent candidacy of Los Angeles Mayor Sam Yorty, a much traveled demagogue who sounded Reagan campaign themes in his criticism of Brown's lack of leadership. Yorty's campaign was effective. Though Brown won, he received only 52 percent of the total Democratic vote, polling 1,355,262 to 981,088 for Yorty and 234,046 for four other candidates. Precincts carried by Yorty became immediate targets of the Reagan campaign.

After the March blowup Reagan and his strategists conducted a near flawless campaign. They sidestepped the anticipated "extremism" issue by keeping well-known right-wingers on the sidelines. "Any people we knew who were Birchers or were real Birch sympathizers or even strongly conservative, we deliberately excluded from positions in the campaign," Roberts said. "Later on some of them might have wound up on some little periphery things that didn't matter, but they were not in front." Reagan readily agreed to this strategy, also supported by Tuttle, and to a corollary suggestion of Roberts to put "new fresh faces," undamaged by past battles, in positions of campaign leadership. "I agree with you 100 percent," Reagan told Roberts. "I want a Reagan campaign and I want it to be identified as such. I want it to be mine."[15] Reagan chose as his campaign chairman thirty-one-year-old attorney Philip M. Battaglia. His northern California chairman was engineer Thomas C. Reed, just thirty years old.

With the help of polls taken for Spencer-Roberts and the black books of Plog and Holden, Reagan had developed and held to a few standard themes. First and foremost among them, as would be the case when Reagan won the presidency fourteen years later, was the "failed leadership" of the Democratic incumbent. All of the other issues—the university "mess," high taxes, the growing cost of welfare—in one way or the other were related to Brown's supposed lack of leadership. While making his case against Brown and big government, Reagan was careful to say that he would not support right-to-work legislation or changes in California's generous program of unemployment insurance. He believed, correctly, that working class voters could be attracted to his banner if reassured that their own hard-won benefits would not be taken from them.

Reagan discovered the most potent issue of the campaign long before the Spencer-Roberts surveys did. Late in 1965, under the auspices of Friends of Ronald Reagan, Reagan made a number of speaking trips around the state to give short talks and answer questions. The speeches were Spencer's idea, developed as an advance rebuttal to anticipated criticism that Reagan was simply an actor repeating lines others had written for him. Reagan, who compared these talks to those he had given on the trail in his GE days, fielded the questions skillfully and demonstrated that he was a genuine politician. He showed that he had learned to listen well, observing to an aide after one speech that "this university thing comes up each time I talk."[16] The surveys taken for Reagan at first showed the demonstrations at UC to be a minor issue, but Reagan did not believe them. Eventually, the polls commissioned by Spencer-Roberts caught up with the candidate and found that public concern about demonstrations at the University of California was indeed an animating issue of the campaign. Long before this happened, Reagan was declaring at every opportunity that student dissidents should "observe the rules or get out."

As a campaigner, Reagan proved effective. Because of his professional training, both his managers and the opposition had expected that he would do well in prepared speeches and, especially, in television appearances. But to the surprise of many, Reagan also succeeded in establishing a rapport with the reporters assigned to cover him at a time when it was an article of faith among California conservatives that the press was out to "do in" their candidates. Richard Nixon in 1962 had vehemently denounced the press in private, allowing his true feelings to spill out in his famous "last press conference" after his defeat. Goldwater had engaged in a running battle with the press in 1964, and both Reagan and Nofziger were known to share the view that reporters, as a group, favored liberal causes and candidates. But Reagan neither advertised these views nor patronized the press. Toward reporters he displayed the mixture of reserve and friendliness that was a distinctive feature of his personality.

Many reporters found him monumentally ignorant of state issues, but few, if any, took a dislike to him. Nofziger coached Reagan against over-answering and encouraged him to dodge entirely those questions designed to pull him into the deep water of the many issues about which he was ignorant. Most of the time, this strategy and Reagan's friendliness enabled him to survive. Reagan benefited because the reporters, as a rule, shared the community's low opinion of his capabilities. As a result, he tended to get high grades for average answers. By the time of the general election, Reagan already had confounded the early press predictions by his decisive defeat of Christopher. He was a phenomenon and a celebrity. Governor Brown, known to most reporters simply as "Pat," was old hat.

Reagan took advantage of these perceptions. He realized, after a short time, that reporters had a job to do and that conservatives were hurting their own cause by picking needless quarrels with the press. Sometimes he became angry at stories he considered unfair, but he did not nurse a grudge. And while he didn't completely trust those assigned to cover him, he came to realize that reporters, like all people, respond more favorably to courteous treatment than they to do criticism. His opposition complained, as it would again in 1970 and 1980, that Reagan received a favorable press.

Mindful of what had happened at the Negro Republican Assembly, Roberts and Nofziger tried to keep their friendly candidate fresh and well rested. They knew that Reagan's even temper was apt to be disturbed by overwork and lack of sleep. On most days the campaign schedule included an afternoon rest stop at a motel where Reagan could nap before his evening speech. This practice gave Reagan a reputation for laziness which he never fully overcame by hard work in subsequent campaigns. Nofziger contends that Reagan tired more easily in 1966 than in any other campaign because he never really recovered from the virus infection which had afflicted him in March.[17]

Both candidates had their episodes of political hoof-in-mouth disease. Brown specialized in a south-of-Market-Street syntax which Californians associate with Irish-Americans from San Francisco. He had a gift for mala-prop, and was once widely quoted as having said about the Eel River floods, "This is the greatest disaster since my election." Reporters enjoyed Brown's company, poked fun at him and noticed that he seemed more sensitive and irritable than in previous campaigns. Reagan engaged in hyperbolic decla-rations which seemed a parody of his own position. In a speech to the West-ern Wood Productions Association in San Francisco on March 12, he de-clared: "I think, too, that we've got to recognize that where the preservation of a natural resource like the redwoods is concerned, that there is a common sense limit. I mean, if you've looked at a hundred thousand acres or so of trees—you know, a tree is a tree, how many more do you need to look at?"

Californians like to look at trees, and this was a potentially damaging blunder. But, like Reagan's blowup before the Negro Republican Assembly, his speech to the wood producers occurred before most voters had focused on the campaign. And Brown's campaign staff made the mistake of trying to improve on the quote by claiming that Reagan had said, "If you've seen one redwood, you've seen them all." This paraphrase was picked up in the press and given currency, providing Reagan with an opportunity to say he was misquoted.

What unnerved reporters who spent considerable time with Reagan, however, was not his misstatements but his proclivity for repeating the same memorized answers over and over again in the manner of a man who is say-ing them for the first time. It was as if someone had hit the "play" button on a tape cassette recorder. When asked whether he was receiving John Birch Society support, Reagan invariably replied, "Any members of the society who support me will be buying my philosophy. I won't be buying theirs." Reagan also had a tape cassette reaction to what should have been Brown's most effective issue—Reagan's lack of any administrative experience. "The man who has the job has more experience than anybody," Reagan would say. "That's why I'm running."

While Reagan advanced, Brown floundered. His own campaign leader-ship was divided and less than the sum of its parts. State Finance Director Hale Champion was in charge of Brown while Bradley supposedly was in charge of the campaign. Brown had brought Frederick Dutton, an old friend whom he had appointed to the University of California Board of Regents, back from Washington as a key adviser. "You were here for the takeoff, I want you here for the crash landing," Dutton remembers Brown telling him. But Dutton and Bradley* did not get along, and no one knew who really was directing the campaign. When Bradley was asked about it he replied, "It just depends on whose day off it is." The division added to the impression of Brown's indecisiveness.

Years afterward, Dutton looked back on the 1966 campaign and said it was a mistake for him to have returned, even at Brown's request. "Bradley and Champion worked well together," he said. "I was an outsider."[18] Returning to California after practicing law in Washington, Dutton saw accurately that something had happened to his old friend Pat Brown, who had always prided himself on being "a man of the people." Dutton found a governor who seemed to have lost his approachability and who appeared on camera surrounded by uniformed highway patrolmen, talking about his own past achievements and how little the voters appreciated them. "He kept talking about his record, and it sounded like a broken record to me," said Dutton. "It was too much government, not enough politics. People didn't want to hear what government had done for them. They wanted to know what we were going to do next."[19]

Brown's disappointment at this lack of appreciation showed. So did his desperation. He started out well enough in the campaign by comparing Reagan, the citizen-politician, to a pilot telling his passengers that it was his first flight "but don't worry—I've always had an active interest in aviation." Soon, though, he was regaling voters with achievements "while my opponent was making *Bedtime for Bonzo.*" It never seemed to occur to Brown that actors, particularly in California, are better known and more apt to be admired than politicians. Brown also behaved as if the year were 1964 and his opponent were named Goldwater.

On August 4, 1966, state Democratic Chairman Robert L. Coate issued a twenty-nine-page document, "Ronald Reagan, Extremist Collaborator—an Expose." It was short on documentation and long on accusations that Reagan was a "front man" who "collaborated directly with a score of top leaders of the super-secret John Birch Society." State Controller Cranston, helping Brown because he believed his own reelection secure, tried to draw attention to the accusations by pretending that he had new and persuasive evidence that the John Birch Society was riddled with anti-Semitism. Cranston provided comic relief to Brown's effort to revive the two-year-old Birch issue as he pursued Reagan from airport to airport in an effort to deliver his report. This publicity stunt backfired. When Cranston finally caught his quarry at the Sacramento Airport, Reagan said to him, "All right, you've made your grandstand play. Now why don't you run against your opponent." Afterwards, Reagan referred to the attempt to link him to the Birchers as "guilt by disassociation." Whatever it was, it was a wasted maneuver politically.

* Bradley died on October 2, 1981.

Equally wasted and more ludicrous were the depths of the antiactor campaign. On one occasion actor Jack Palance walked out on a Democratic telethon to protest against the attempt to equate the word "actor" with "know-nothing." "Attack him if you wish for lack of experience," said Palance of Reagan. "But don't go after him just because he's an actor."[20] The bottom of the barrel was exposed during a thirty-minute television "documentary" labeled *Man vs. Actor,* which depicted Brown as the legitimate heir of Hiram Johnson and Earl Warren and then showed the governor telling an integrated class of young school children, "I'm running against an actor, and you know who shot Lincoln, don'tcha?" The Democrats thought this bit of political lunacy so clever they excerpted it for a one-minute spot which was shown several times during the last week of the campaign.

Reagan, meanwhile, stuck to his basic set speech on Brown's purported lack of leadership, the fiscal condition of California and the "mess at Berkeley." He finished each speech with the words "Ya basta," the Mexican equivalent of "Had enough?" Because the October polls showed Reagan winning easily while other Republican statewide candidates either led narrowly or trailed their Democratic opponents, Reagan spent most of these final weeks in joint appearances with his running mates that were aimed at producing a GOP sweep.* He almost succeeded, with only Democratic Attorney General Thomas Lynch surviving the landslide.

Reagan's margin of victory was huge. He polled 3,742,913 votes to 2,749,174 for Brown, a margin of 993,730 votes, and carried traditionally Democratic working class precincts in which Brown had swamped Knowland and Nixon. The Republican candidate did well with middle class voters, particularly in suburban and rural areas which also were strongly Democratic in registration. Reagan ran marginally behind traditional Republicans in silk-stocking GOP areas, though he still carried these areas handily, and substantially ahead of most Republicans in Mexican-American neighborhoods, most of which he nonetheless lost. The Republican voting trends extended to the legislature, where the Democratic margin was reduced to four votes in the Assembly and two in the state Senate. By any reckoning, it was a Reagan landslide.

What produced it? Part of it was the national trend in 1966, when Republicans won ten governorships previously held by Democrats. Part of it was the normal reaction against an incumbent who had been eight years in office. Part of it was the series of campaign blunders by Brown and his divided staff, and the skillful campaign of his underestimated opponent. And

---

* Nixon ally Robert H. Finch, the Republican candidate for lieutenant governor, led the ticket after Reagan's intervention, though surveys a month before the election had shown him only slightly ahead of Democratic Lieutenant Governor Glenn M. Anderson. Among the Democratic losers was the supposedly safe Cranston, who wished afterwards that he had taken Reagan's advice and run against his opponent. The new controller was a moderate young assemblyman named Houston Flournoy, who had entered the campaign after a night of hard drinking when his companions offered to put up his filing fee.

part of it was simply Reagan. Here are three judgments, from those who saw what happened at close hand:

Said Brown, in a 1968 interview with the author: "I think I was tired of the job. I think that manifested itself. Being governor eight years, you lost a little of the zip. You've appointed your friends judges, the people you've grown up with. You've appointed other people to higher office, you've put over a great water plan and a master plan for higher education and you're building three universities. You're seeking out something to do—what do you do now? Now we get down to the tough parts of politics, like a revenue program, and here's where I ran into the stone wall of Jesse Unruh in the Assembly. That's where Ronald Reagan came along."

And Roberts, the Reagan campaign manager, also speaking in 1968: "They always had the feeling until late in the campaign that he was just another movie actor and the movie industry is noted for its feather-brained, irresponsible people. That impression got through to them—why, I don't know, but it did. They felt he was incapable of putting up a good race and that he'd make a boo-boo some afternoon and they'd catch him and ruin him."

And Dutton, the Brown advisor, in 1981: "Reagan was underestimated, and he still is. We tried to make him out a sinister figure, as Jimmy Carter did in 1980. It didn't work for us, and it didn't work in subsequent campaigns. Reagan has no harsh edge to him. Part of what happened is that we took him on as an actor, putting down one of the great industries of the state, but the roots of the mistake go deeper. Reagan is terribly pleasant, highly articulate and has a serious approach about politics. People like him, and we didn't understand that. We missed the human dimension of Ronald Reagan."

10

The Novice

I<small>N</small> the final line of a 1972 movie, *The Candidate,* the newly elected senator turns to his campaign manager and says, "Marvin, what do we do now?" California reporters who had covered the rise and fall of Senator John V. Tunney felt on familiar ground. But the film's tag line would have served with equal measure to describe the plight of Ronald Wilson Reagan in the weeks and months after he became California's thirty-third governor. Reagan had shown during the rough-and-tumble of the campaign that he could stand the gaff of questioning better than his opposition believed. However, he was ignorant about state government, and most of those he brought to Sacramento with him knew little more than he did. Lyn Nofziger said it best, using words nearly identical to the film's fictional candidate, long before the movie was made. "Unlike Goodie Knight or Earl Warren or other political personalities, Ronald Reagan materialized out of thin air with no political background, no political cronies and no political machine," Nofziger said. "He didn't even run his own campaign. His campaign was run by hired people who then walked away and left it. Therefore, when he was elected, the big question was 'My God, what do we do now?' And really, we were so busy running that . . . no one really sat down until after the election and said, 'Where do we get our hired help?' 'What do we do now?' We were so innocent that we tried to run government from Los Angeles during the transition and discovered that we couldn't."[1]

Reagan had goals, but no programs. He had ideas, without a practical conception of how to translate them into reality. He did not know how government functioned or the processes by which it reached its objectives. "We can start a prairie fire that will sweep the nation and prove we are number one in more than size and crime and taxes," Reagan had said in a famous line at his first general election campaign speech on September 9, 1966. "This is a dream, as big and golden as California itself." They were fine words, but in the months immediately after the election Reagan seemed more a man in a trance than one possessed by a great dream. He had campaigned against Brown's supposed profligacy but acted surprised that the state was in debt. Lacking any experience with government budgets, he approved across-the-board reductions which penalized the most efficient departments in state government. He did not have a tax program for he did not then acknowledge that tax increases would be necessary. And he had little knowledge about other programs which bore the administration's stamp of approval. On March 14, two and one-half months after his inauguration, a reporter asked Reagan what his legislative program was and found that the governor didn't know. Looking at his aides for assistance, Reagan said, "I could take some coaching from the sidelines, if anyone can recall my legislative program."[2]

Lacking clues on how to proceed, Reagan made the mistake of turning over transition planning, and later, the day-to-day duties of running the governor's office to his wunderkind, Philip Maher Battaglia, the campaign manager who had become Reagan's executive secretary. Battaglia was overpoweringly bright. He had been admitted to the University of Southern California's law center at twenty after two years of undergraduate work and had obtained his law degree at University of Southern California while also serving as student body president, editor of the *Trojan Bar Quarterly* and director of the USC Law Alumni Association. Battaglia worked as a law clerk for the prestigious Los Angeles firm of Flint & MacKay to help pay his way through law school and joined the firm upon graduation. Four years later he was a full partner. He spent the last month of the campaign at Reagan's side and would, especially in the interim after the election, frequently hand him notes on three-by-five cards. To the astonishment of people who had known Reagan for a long time, the governor-elect dutifully repeated what his young aide told him to say, including a key note reminding Reagan to announce Battaglia's appointment as executive secretary.

Both Reagan and Tuttle were mesmerized by the drive and intelligence of the thirty-two-year-old Pasadena attorney, who proclaimed his total loyalty to the governor's philosophy and goals and said, a month into the new administration, that he and Reagan "have yet to disagree about anything."[3] For his part, Reagan was uncharacteristically gushy about the merits of his top aide and unconcerned with suggestions that he had risen too far too fast. "Phil is my strong right arm," Reagan said,[4] and it was true. "Reagan thought Phil was the greatest thing since sliced bread," said a former associate of both men who once shared the same opinion. Battaglia reinforced his position by paying homage to the authority and wisdom of the millionaire backers, who, in return, sang his praises to the governor. Others in lesser positions of influence saw another side. They found Battaglia furtive, suspicious and conspiratorial in nature, with a wheeler-dealer tendency to cultivate the powerful and ignore everyone else. Rank-and-file legislators distrusted him and so, too, did some of the starry-eyed conservatives who viewed Reagan's election as the big break they had been seeking to push

American government in a new direction. Many of these foot-soldier conservatives were true believers who did not share Reagan's sanguine assumption that Battaglia had political principles. "Ronald Reagan was the man who was going to save the world," said one of these conservatives after he had left the Reagan administration. "He was the man who was going to get rid of Lyndon Johnson, stop the war in Vietnam and do the things that Barry Goldwater wanted to do but wasn't smart enough to figure out how. And he was the only guy in the United States who could go all the way to the presidency to get that done, in the view of the believers. And, lo and behold, the Holy Grail was in custody of a power-hungry kid."

Others also competed for power in the vacuum created by Reagan's lack of knowledge. Next to Battaglia in authority and manipulativeness was Nofziger, who was then totally trusted by Reagan for advice about the press. But Nofziger wanted to be more than a press secretary. He soon took for himself the title "communications director" and brought in as press secretary a *Los Angeles Times* reporter, Paul Beck, who had covered Reagan during the campaign. Another influential aide was Reed, who occupied the key post of appointments secretary and stressed the not always compatible qualities of intelligence and political loyalty. Tuttle and Salvatori remained influential, particularly in the Los Angeles days of the transition. (Rubel, the other founder of Friends of Ronald Reagan, became seriously ill soon after the election and died in June 1967.)

The millionaire backers had become known as the Executive Committee in the 1966 campaign, the Major Appointments Task Force in the transition and the Kitchen Cabinet after that. In addition to Tuttle and Salvatori, this group included Reagan's lawyer, William French Smith, and Taft Schreiber, the MCA executive who had brought Reagan into television. Other original members of the Kitchen Cabinet were Leonard Firestone, president of the tire company which bears his name; wealthy San Francisco industrialists Jaquelin Hume and Arch Monson, Jr.; Leland M. Kaiser, a multimillionaire retired investment banker; and Edward Mills, vice-president of Holmes Tuttle Enterprises. What these men had in common was wealth and a fervent belief in the efficacy of the marketplace in which they had made their millions. In the transition they were keenly interested in their new toy of state government and played a significant role in the appointments process. But their interest waned when Reagan went off to Sacramento, though the mythology of their great influence continued to grow. For the most part, however, these millionaires had little genuine concern about the workings of government and were perfectly willing to let Reagan take the lead. The problem was that the new governor did not know how to go about accomplishing his own goals.

Reagan's most pressing problem was the state budget, which he was constitutionally required to balance. Brown had circumvented this requirement in 1966 and avoided a tax increase in an election year by adopting the recommendation of Finance Director Hale Champion to change the state's accounting system from cash to an accrual basis. As a result, California began counting state revenues when they became collectible instead of when they were actually collected. This changeover was never funded, as good accounting practice would have required, because it really had nothing to do with accounting. Its purpose was the entirely political one of avoiding a tax increase. When Caspar W. Weinberger, assisting the Reagan transition team, asked the finance director what he would have done if Brown had been reelected, Champion replied bluntly, "Raise taxes."[5] Reagan explained the problem accurately in his inaugural message, calling the accounting changeover "a gimmick that solved nothing but only postponed the day of reckoning." But Reagan behaved as if he had uncovered a mysterious plot which Brown had withheld from the public, even though the accounting changeover had been widely criticized by legislators of both parties and legislative analyst A. Alan Post at the time it was made.

Now, with accrual accounting a reality, the Reagan administration was faced with a cash flow shortage the following January and February and a prospective budget deficit of indeterminate amount at the end of the 1967–68 fiscal year. Reagan proposed to solve these two problems with the single solution of severe economies in government and across-the-board budget reductions. "For many years now, you and I have been shushed like children and told there are no simple answers to the complex problems which are beyond our comprehension," he said January 5, 1967, in an inaugural speech he wrote himself. "Well, the truth is, there are simple answers—there just are not easy ones. The time has come for us to decide whether collectively we can afford everything and anything we think of simply because we think of it. The time has come to run a check to see if all the services government provides were in answer to demands or were just goodies dreamed up for our supposed betterment. The time has come for us to match outgo to income, instead of always doing it the other way around." After observing that California's population was increasing and that it would be necessary for the overall cost of government to increase, Reagan said that each individual's share of the tax burden should be lighter. "We are going to squeeze and cut and trim until we reduce the cost of government," he said, in what became the best-known sentence of his inaugural speech. "It won't be easy, nor will it be pleasant, and it will involve every department of government, starting with the governor's office."

In California, the state finance director holds a job second in importance only to the governor himself. Since the governor of California has authority to blue-pencil budget items added by the legislature, what the finance director proposes and the governor agrees to usually becomes the budget of the state. The appointment of a finance director normally has the highest priority with an incoming administration, and this was expected to be especially true with Reagan, whose priority was budget cutting. But it didn't work out that way. Reagan's first choice for the job, respected legislative analyst A. Alan Post, turned him down. So did Richard Krabach, the nationally known and conservative budget director of Ohio. Reagan's aides then sounded out the type of "$100,000 man" whom candidate Reagan had hoped to lure to Sacramento, Lockheed executive Dudley Browne. Again, the administration came up empty-handed. Highly qualified corporate executives were simply unwilling to sacrifice their pay and perquisites for public service, as Reagan had naively expected. Battaglia and Nofziger then proposed naming Weinberger finance director. But conservatives in the Kitchen Cabinet remembered Weinberger's vigorous support of Nelson Rockefeller in 1964. Tuttle sided with the conservatives, and Weinberger was rejected.

Finally, in desperation, the Kitchen Cabinet accepted the bona fides of a man who aggressively sought the job. He was Gordon Paul Smith, a diminutive (5 feet, 5 inches) but combative management consultant from the firm of Booz, Allen and Hamilton. Hired December 16, 1966, Smith knew as little about state government as Reagan and the millionaire bankers and seemed unaware that the California constitution makes the Department of Finance the property of the governor-elect. He was contemptuous of Champion, the best source of budget information available to the incoming administration, and ignored him during the transition. As a result, Smith had only two weeks to prepare a 1,005-page budget which had to be presented January 16. It was this combination of lack of knowledge and deadline pressure which produced Smith's proposal for 10 percent budget cuts in every department, a mindless approach to budget cutting which was eagerly embraced by Reagan.

The new governor and his team had other money-saving proposals, most of them symbolic. The most effective was an immediate freeze on hiring which prevented departments from filling a vacancy when an employee resigned or retired. The least effective, and the silliest, was a Battaglia proposal asking state employees to work voluntarily on Lincoln's and Washington's birthdays. Reagan approved this proposal because he and others in the inner circle shared a conviction that public employees were less zealous than their counterparts in private industry. But public employees regarded the call for unpaid work as an insult, and less than 2 percent of them showed up on the two holidays. Other Reagan economies were more orthodox: a freeze on purchase of state automobiles, a near ban on out-of-state travel, cancellation of a new state office building, sale of the ancient state airplane, the Grizzly. These decisions mingled without distinction some rational attempts at governmental belt-tightening with transparently false economies. In one case the Department of Transportation was prevented by the purchasing freeze from completing the buying of forty trucks even though it had already purchased the cabs. One well-informed study of the transition called such measures "ludicrous diseconomies."[6]

If Reagan was making only small dents in the state budget, he was, as usual, winning the public relations battle. In a report on the first one hundred days of his administration, he collected all the economy measures into one document and declared, in a Nofziger line, "The symbol of our flag is a Golden Bear; it is not a cow to be milked." Despite the skepticism in Sacramento, that was great stuff on evening television, and opposition legislators acknowledged that their mail showed increasing and widespread support for the new governor's efforts to cut the costs of government.

Behind the scenes in his cabinet meetings and also in his weekly meetings with the capitol press corps, Reagan was struggling to match his belief that there are simple answers to almost everything with the complex realities of state government. On the plus side the minutes reveal a novice governor with considerable common sense who on some issues showed a direct political grasp of solutions. But the minutes also show the governor as even more naive than his public statements made him out to be—and less in touch with some of the more sober realities. On February 20, 1967, during a discussion of Medi-Cal budget problems, Reagan said, "I don't mean to seem harsh, but I say a whole lot of misinformation has led to some of these programs. I venture to say that there isn't anyone in the U.S. that was ever let go without medical care." And he said on March 15 of one stand of redwood trees during a discussion of the then pending Redwoods National Park, "I saw them; there is nothing beautiful about them just that they are a little higher than the others."

At other times Reagan could sound both conservationist and innovative. At the February 20 cabinet meeting, during a discussion of a proposed nuclear plant, Reagan and Nofziger both criticized what they saw as the Sierra Club's total unconcern for the rights of private property owners. But the governor then made this comment: "The Sierra Club is telling private land owners that they can't use it [the land] because someday they might want it. Let me ask, what would happen if we would ask the Sierra Club to select sites for construction, since they seem to think of themselves as authorities on wilderness? Why should not they, as concerned citizens, pick out an area that would not be hurt by a development of this type?" When Spencer Williams, who headed the Human Resources Agency, said that the Sierra Club might come up with "something unfeasible," Reagan replied: "Put them on the spot; they are always saying no to everything."

Under discussion at the time was the Pacific Gas and Electric Company's proposal for a nuclear plant in Diablo Canyon. In the following decade Diablo Canyon became a rallying issue for the antinuclear movement in California, but the ostensible question in 1967 was the more directly conservationist issue of whether any plant at all should be built in the scenic wooded canyon in the central coastal area of California. Conservationists were maneuvering to set the canyon aside as a park. When the issue came up for the second week in a row at the February 27 cabinet meeting, Reagan quoted from a *Los Angeles Times* article by Jerry Gilliam, including a passage which said, "There has been no overall planning of the kind necessary to determine future sites for power plants in relation to scenic values, future needs for parks and other requirements." In the indirect way which became his style at cabinet meetings, Reagan said, "I wonder if there is any possibility of finding out on this. I must say, they do make the Diablo Canyon sound very beautiful." When resources director Norman (Ike) Livermore tried to dismiss the article as favoring the Sierra Club, Reagan wasn't convinced. "Even if it is not going to be a park area, the Diablo Canyon seems to lend itself to some other purpose better, for instance a residential area or other private development," he said. After discussion of four other issues, the governor concluded the cabinet meeting by apologizing for talking so long about Diablo Canyon. "I really was hoping that someone would say the canyon is just too beautiful for a plant," Reagan said. "It sounds like a great place for a ranch."

It did not seem to have occurred to Reagan in those early days that he was the "someone" who might have said the canyon was too beautiful for a plant and directed his resources agency to come up with a proposal for preserving it in rustic form. The minutes confirm what reporters were learning in the weekly press conferences, which was that Reagan was heavily dependent upon a few top aides for his policy decisions. For information the governor usually relied on the stylized one-page "mini-memos" devised by his cabinet secretary William P. Clark. Issues, even those of great complexity, were reduced to four paragraphs—one for the statement of the problem, another for the facts, a third for discussion and a fourth for a recommended course of action. Reporters and legislators made fun of the mini-memos, but they served Reagan well. Clark's predecessor as cabinet secretary in the Brown administration, James Alexander, thought they were a useful way of dealing with the tremendous flow of information which passed through the governor's office.[7] The memos filled many of Reagan's information gaps but his lack of knowledge at this time was monumental. Reagan tried to compensate wherever he could, by relating state issues to personal experiences in Hollywood. Sometimes there was no relationship. At a March 15 cabinet meeting, during a serious discussion of mental hospital budget cuts, Reagan said irrelevantly: "Do you know how hard it is to mispronounce 'psychiatric' once you know how to do it right? I had to do it in *King's Row* and at first I couldn't do it. It is like deliberately singing a flat note."

Reagan's deficiencies of knowledge inhibited his ability to "squeeze, cut and trim" the cost of government as he had promised in his inaugural. He received little help from Smith, who had bragged to others about his proposal to cut each department's budget by 10 percent, and then complained that others were taking the credit for his brainstorm. But the cuts were illusions. The "flat and undetailed 10 percent reductions" provided no guidelines for real economies, said legislative analyst Post, who for the first time in his career found himself urging budget increases. The late George Miller,

Jr., then the influential chairman of the Senate Finance Committee, said the governor's budget consisted of nothing but a series of dotted lines, marked, "Cut here."[8] By March 2, a month and a half after he introduced the budget, Smith was forced to acknowledge that the departments were not making the 10 percent reductions he had ordained. On March 28, Smith presented to the legislature a new budget from the governor which totaled $5.06 billion, an increase of $440 million. It cast Reagan as the author of California's first $5 billion budget, a distinction he had hoped to avoid. However, the backdown was overshadowed by a dramatic budget reduction announced by Battaglia on March 14 in the Department of Mental Hygiene, which administrated the state's mental hospitals.

Reagan took office at a time when new drugs, principally tranquilizers, were making it possible to move mental patients out of the large hospital "warehouses" then common in the United States back into their home communities for treatment. California had pioneered in community treatment, and the population of the state mental hospitals had dropped from a high of 33,000 to 19,000, giving Smith and Battaglia what they thought was a splendid opportunity and a statistical case to cut the budget. Neither of them knew anything about the situation in the mental hospitals, always difficult and bordering on desperation. They were deaf to the arguments of doctors, nurses and psychiatric technicians that the hospitals had been left with the hard cases and could ill afford a staff reduction equivalent to the decrease in patient load. Their determination to make a "dramatic" reduction in some department was enhanced by the performance of Dr. James Lowry, the holdover director of the Department of Mental Hygiene, who sought and received an appointment in the Reagan administration. A year before, under Brown, Lowry had argued for budget increases. Now he demonstrated his loyalty to the new administration by embracing its across-the-board formula of budget cuts. In an economy-minded administration infatuated with statistics, Lowry's approach guaranteed that his department would suffer most heavily from the new direction in Sacramento.

Reagan was ill-informed about what his own administration was about to do, which was to lay off 2,800 mental hospital employees and leave unfilled another 900 jobs. The minutes of the March 14 cabinet meeting reveal both Reagan's remoteness from the process and his sensitivity about firing people.

WILLIAMS: We propose to have the Personnel Department make a special effort to place these people in other departments of state government. While we are laying off, others may be hiring.

REAGAN: We have cancelled the freeze?

BATTAGLIA: No, we have not.

REAGAN: These positions are absolutely surpluses?

SMITH: Yes, at the present level of services in Mental Health they are; it's not as crucial as in other departments.

WILLIAMS: The Department of Hygiene has been retaining the same staffing level even though the patient level has dropped. We are trying to achieve the recognized national standards between patient and staff. Thus, if we drop off the attrition and the layoff, we will lose 2,600 positions. However, this will maintain the same staff ratio to patient. We have three alternatives to do so. One, a $19 million saving would be achieved by laying off 600 on July 1 and the balance the first of the year.

SMITH: That would reach the 10 percent. There were an average of 33,000 patients; for the next year we will be close to 20,000. There has been a 40 percent drop of occupancy. We are suggesting a decrease of a little over 10 percent in employees of mental hospitals. . . .

WILLIAMS: They'll say that the increased staff ratio is because they are ending up with tougher cases.

SMITH: If we don't take all of the surpluses, we have two alternatives. In the tax bill we had $55 million that was being restored. The last tally of this is within one or two millions. If we don't reduce all of the $19 million, it will cause a problem. It will diminish the economy program.

REAGAN: You don't realize this is the most dramatic thing you have given me. I'd like to hide. It has nothing to do with the economy but it reminds me of my father who got his slip on Christmas Eve. That was in the Depression days and my imagination is still that of a little kid who gets up and cries. On the other hand, if you fellows tell me that we don't need these employees, I don't see what else we can do. I still like the phasing out better than giving them the slip. And we should help them as much as we can.

BATTAGLIA: We had a long meeting about that last night and decided that the final decision had to be yours. . . .

When Reagan viewed the layoffs in terms of his own origins, state employees were transformed from shirkers who needed to be called in for unpaid work on holidays to human beings with families to feed like those he knew in Dixon. But this personal compassion did not translate readily into public policy. The mental patients remained figures in a ratio that Reagan repeated endlessly in defense of a decision that had been made for him by others. He was impervious to the argument that the patients remaining in the state hospitals were the harder cases and required more care than those who had been released into the community. Nor would Reagan risk seeing for himself what these hospital conditions actually were, as Governor Earl Warren had once done when he was told about a hazardous condition at the Stockton mental hospital. Reagan turned down all invitations to visit the hospitals himself. He was not willing to expose himself either to mental patients or to the facts contained in a memo from Williams to Battaglia which revealed that the California mental hospitals had never met minimum staffing standards promulgated a decade and a half earlier, in 1952. When a reporter asked about a proposed reduction in the $5 for personal articles alloted each mental patient, Reagan said the state was paying $4,800 a year per patient, down from $5,700, and declared: "It seems to me out of $4,800 a year we ought to be able to afford soap and towels."[9]

Such exchanges with the competitive Sacramento press corps were frequent in the early years of the Reagan administration and were a valuable tool of the governor's learning. Reagan takes in information best by verbal confrontation, and the press questioning sharpened him and forced him to acquire detailed knowledge about his proposals. Nofziger thought the press conferences were valuable because they gave Reagan a chance to put his own case, relatively unfiltered, on television. But he cautioned the governor against his tendencies to overexplain and to answer hypothetical questions. Nofziger said reporters might be frustrated if Reagan said, "I don't know," to a question, but would have to accept this answer. On the other hand, he predicted, they would hit Reagan hard if he gave a wrong answer which could be checked. The advice was sound. "I don't know" was a frequent refrain at Reagan's press conferences, but the governor's biggest problems arose when he should have used this response but didn't. At his first press conference as governor in January he incorrectly stated that there would be no cutback in the University of California budget. A few days before, budget reductions were proposed to the university regents. "Yeah, I goofed," Reagan said when he was asked about them at the next press conference. "It's as simple as that." On March 14, Reagan was asked if he would support a public referendum on capital punishment rather than leaving the issue to the legislature. "Oh, we had one, how many times is it that Californians have voted on this?" he replied. "I know it's more than once; several times. I don't see that there's any evidence of a change in people's thinking now that would warrant taking another score on it." California had never voted on a capital punishment referendum.

The Reagan "goof" which had the deepest implications occurred in response to legislation by Senator Anthony C. Beilenson of Beverly Hills to liberalize the state law which then permitted abortion only to save the life of the mother. It was a new topic for Reagan but an old one for Beilenson, who as an assemblyman had twice failed to win changes in a law he denounced as "archaic, barbarous and hypocritical" for purportedly forcing "women and girls to seek out the services of quacks and criminal abortionists."[10] Beilenson estimated that 100,000 illegal abortions were performed in the state every year. This was familiar rhetoric, and few thought that Beilenson's attempt to change the law was likely to succeed when the measure was introduced the third time early in 1967. But Beilenson displayed qualities both of persistence and compromise, and his measure caught the crest of the rising women's movement. After nine San Francisco physicians were charged with performing abortions on women with German measles, a disease which can cause deformity in a child, four suburban women quickly gathered 8,000 signatures on a petition urging that the physicians not be punished and that the law be changed.

After an emotional and exhausting debate, the Senate Judiciary Committee sent a liberalizing bill to the floor, with Republicans providing five of the seven favorable votes. Reagan had expressed general approval of the legislation. His aides, along with most others in the capital, had expected the measure to fail. Now, with the bill headed toward him, Reagan had second thoughts. His legislative liaison in the Senate, former Senator Vern Sturgeon, quietly attempted to sidetrack the Beilenson measure back to committee. When Beilenson tried to take it up for a vote, he was told that the administration was working against him and astutely postponed action, putting the bill on the inactive file.

Downstairs in the corner office, as the governor's office is known in Sacramento, Reagan had been plunged into a state of political indecision worthy of Pat Brown. Usually he could rely on the collective leadership of aides who settled their own differences before they came to cabinet. Now the aides were hopelessly split. Battaglia and Sturgeon opposed the measure, Nofziger favored it and others among the inner circle hoped, with Reagan, that the Beilenson bill would simply go away. At his May 9 press conference Reagan discovered a "loophole" allowing abortion for mothers afflicted with German measles. It was not a loophole at all, but a major purpose of the bill. Reagan left an overwhelming impression that he just didn't want to make a final decision of any kind. Colorado, he said, had just passed a nearly identical bill, giving "a great opportunity for the rest of us to take a look at a laboratory example after awhile and see how it worked." When Earl (Squire) Behrens of the *San Francisco Chronicle,* then the dean of state capitol correspondents, asked Reagan whether he meant "to leave the inference that you are more or less opposed to the bill," the governor replied: "No, I'm trying not to. I'm trying to say that I'm—I'm still, and I've continued to study not just this, but all that I can find on this subject, Squire, and I'm just—this is not in my mind a clear-cut issue and I—I just can't give you a decision."

Reagan told me the following year that the abortion decision was the most difficult one he had ever faced. "Those were awful weeks," he said.[11] His usual support system was disrupted, and his friends were on all sides of the issue. Spencer-Roberts, which had managed the Reagan campaign in 1966, was now employed as a lobbyist against the measure, and Reagan accepted Stu Spencer's invitation to meet privately with Francis Cardinal McIntyre and discuss it. The governor lied to reporters that he had "not had one word" from his old campaign firm about the issue and also denied he had met with McIntyre. The Cardinal's opposition to the bill was matched by support for it from Loyal Davis, the governor's father-in-law. Reagan told me in 1968 he had listened long and carefully to both the Cardinal and the surgeon and added, "I have never done more study on any one thing than the abortion bill."[12] But neither his study nor the influential advocacies which were pressed upon him from all sides could resolve Reagan's indecision. With the decision pending in the Senate, Reagan concluded that allowing abortions for mothers who might, as in the German measles cases, have deformed births was "not different from what Hitler tried to do." Beilenson, disgusted by Reagan's wavering, nonetheless thought the bill was valuable and amended it to remove the offending provision. With this amendment, it passed the Senate with the minimum 21 votes required and an expectation that it would easily clear the less conservative state Assembly and be signed into law by the governor.

The Assembly manager of the Therapeutic Abortion Act of 1967 was Craig Biddle, a young Republican moderate from Riverside and former prosecutor. As the measure reached the Assembly it permitted abortions in cases of rape or incest and also if a physician found that continuation of the pregnancy would endanger the life or health of the mother. McIntyre had warned Reagan that this latter provision was a very big "loophole" which would allow widespread abortions, but Reagan was told by the bill's Republican sponsors and medical authorities that physicians would be careful in their application of this exception. Reagan assured Biddle that he would sign the bill if it reached him. Then on June 13, two hours before the Assembly was to vote, Battaglia and Spencer-Roberts obtained a legal opinion questioning the effect of the Senate changes.

At a press conference Reagan said he was "quite concerned" and had discovered some other "loopholes" he had never mentioned before. "There is a loophole left with regard to the idea of the prospect of a less than perfect child, causing grievous mental suffering to the mother, and there, also, I think, should be a tighter provision with regard to hospitals to prevent just the springing up of abortion-type hospitals, smaller hospitals. I think there should be a minimum size requirement. Then, too, I was assured that there was going to be a residence requirement, so I never made any point of that because I thought that was incorporated." Reagan's invention of a residency requirement, which no legislator involved in the struggle recalls him ever mentioning previously, infuriated assemblymen on both sides of the issue. The legislators believed that the controversial and emotional issue of abortion was politically risky. They wanted the issue resolved, one way or the other, in 1967, not back before them in the election year of 1968. Angrily, Biddle arose in the Assembly and told his colleagues that Reagan would be "breaking a pledge" if he refused to sign the measure. The Assembly passed the Therapeutic Abortion Act 48-30 without further amendments and sent it to the governor's desk. Nofziger, who supported the abortion liberalization, immediately went to the office of his glum and dispirited governor and asked for permission to issue a press release saying that Reagan would sign the bill as passed. Failure to say so, Nofziger warned, would lead to speculative news stories questioning Reagan's credibility as well as a new round of pressure from the antiabortionists directed at the governor's office. Reagan, still unhappy about having to decide, agreed with Nofziger's assessment, and the press release was issued. Most of the stories on the following day focused on the supposed consequences of the legislation and gave scant treatment to Reagan's indecisive performance before the bill was passed.

There are worse maladies than indecision. Reagan really wanted to veto the abortion bill. He agreed with Cardinal McIntyre that abortion was murder. Later in his political career he would become an ardent supporter of the Human Life Amendment advocated by antiabortionists. In 1968, when the consequences of the Beilenson bill were still uncertain, Reagan told me with some pride that he had been right in insisting upon the amendment not allowing abortion for mothers who might have deformed babies. "You can't allow an abortion on grounds the child won't be born perfect," Reagan said. "Where do you stop? What is the degree of deformity [required] that a person shouldn't be born?[13] Crippled persons have contributed greatly to our society." He sounded the same theme in a 1970, "Dear Citizen" letter when he opposed further liberalizations of the law. "Those who summarily advocated a *blanket population control* [Reagan's emphasis] should think carefully. Who might they be doing away with? Another Lincoln, or Beethoven, an Einstein or an Edison? Who shall play God?" On July 27, 1979, Reagan stated his support for the Human Life Amendment in a letter to Representative Henry Hyde in these terms: "I personally believe that interrupting a pregnancy is the taking of a human life and can only be justified in self-defense, that is, if the mother's own life is in danger."

The novice governor realized too late what the Beilenson bill would accomplish. Later in his governorship, he would have given early signals of a veto, making legislators more reluctant to pass such a controversial measure. But Reagan had not reflected on the abortion issue until long after he had made his commitment to Biddle. At this point he faced divided counsel within his own administration. For the first time on an important measure, Reagan had to make the decision himself. Left to his own devices, he didn't know where to turn. He was caught between his political commitment and his personal opposition to abortion. Rationalizing that he had already improved the measure enough to honor his political pledge, Reagan signed the bill.

Afterward, when abortions increased exponentially, Reagan would say that physicians, especially psychiatrists, took advantage of a loophole in the bill of which he was not aware when he signed the measure. This contention is hollow. Cardinal McIntyre warned Reagan exactly of what would happen, and Reagan displayed his own knowledge of it in a press conference on June 13, 1967, the day the measure was sent to him and signed. "The prognosis of mental health would be easier to exaggerate than the diagnosis of physical health, and this of course could allow certain leeway for a doctor who wanted to do this [perform an abortion], to make a statement that he believed that this grievous suffering or this mental health deterioration would result," Reagan said.

The results of keeping the mental health provision in the bill were what the antiabortionists had feared and what Reagan had been told. For all practical purposes the measure which Reagan signed permitted the "abortion on demand" he has ever since denounced. In 1967, the year the measure was enacted, there were 518 legal abortions in California. In 1980, the last full year for which figures are available, there were 199,089 abortions in California hospitals and clinics. The total number of abortions performed from 1968 to 1980 was 1,444,778.[14]

Reagan faced other tests on social issues during that difficult first year of his governorship. The most troublesome of these began with recurrent rumors in the early spring of 1967 about a homosexual clique which supposedly existed on his own staff. Supposedly, the center of this group's activities was a cabin in Lake Tahoe where the clique had engaged in an "orgy" while Reagan and Paul Laxalt, then governor of Nevada, were meeting to discuss the troubled future of that environmentally threatened alpine lake, which is bisected by the boundary of the two states. Like so much else that went on in those days, the rumors did not reach Reagan. But they were picked up by Nofziger, who was most protective of his insulated, novice governor. Nofziger took them seriously.

In his attitudes toward homosexuality, Reagan is a product of his generation and his work experience. Homosexuals were regarded with fear and loathing in the pastoral, small-town world of Reagan's boyhood. There was more tolerance of divergent life styles in Hollywood during the 1930s, but the studios were image-conscious, and whispered rumors of homosexuality could harm an actor's career. Reagan, who was heterosexual and athletic, was not himself a victim, but he was sensitive to the undercurrents in a community which increasingly prided itself on being a reflection of American ideals.

Reagan's personal views on the subject were conventional and tolerant for his community at the time, and they have changed little over the years. He considers homosexuality a sickness. He is also respectful of the privacy of others and is not the sort of person who bothers about what people do in their own bedrooms. On occasion, he would tell jokes about homosexuals, whom he referred to as people who were "that way." As a young actor with a small part in Dark Victory—a movie which starred Bette Davis, Humphrey Bogart and George Brent—Reagan resisted the efforts of a director who wanted him to play his role in an effeminate manner. "I had no trouble seeing him in that role," Reagan wrote of the director, "but for myself I want to think if I stroll through where the girls are short of clothes, there will be a great scurrying about and taking to cover."[15] In 1980, when his talented youngest son Ronald Prescott Wilson wanted to become a ballet dancer, the then presidential nominee was worried about him entering into an occupation he thought might be dominated by homosexuals. In 1981, after his election, Reagan told me he had no concern about his son, whom he knew to be "all boy."[16] But Reagan was concerned enough about the business that his son was getting into to call his old friend, dancer Gene Kelly, and ask his advice. Kelly, not surprisingly, reassured Reagan about dancers, and Reagan gave his blessing to the career in which his son has since flourished.

Reagan's political record on civil liberties of homosexuals is much better than that of many liberal politicians. He was repelled by the aggressive public crusades against homosexual life styles which became a staple of the right-wing politics of the late 1970s. In 1978, at a time he was preparing to run for President, Reagan openly opposed an initiative that would have removed homosexual teachers from the classrooms and established procedures inviting witch-hunts of those suspected of advocating homosexuality. The sponsors of the initiative, which was resoundingly rejected by California voters, blamed Reagan for its defeat. Reagan, well aware that there were those who wanted him to duck the issue, chose to state his convictions. He carefully opposed the advocacy of homosexuality in the classroom but said that existing laws were sufficient to deal with any such problem if it arose. Working from a draft presented him by Nofziger and Ed Meese, Reagan assailed the civil liberties implications of the initiative and summed up its deficiencies: "Innocent lives could be ruined."

Meese was legal affairs secretary to Reagan and Nofziger was the governor's communications director during the investigation of the homosexual clique in 1967. Originally, the rumor involved two aides, with the suspicion that there might be others. Nofziger discussed the issue first with a close friend, Arthur F. Van Court, who had been Barry Goldwater's bodyguard in the 1964 presidential campaign and who had moved on to perform a similar service, with the title of travel secretary, for Governor Reagan. Van Court, a former Los Angeles police officer, agreed to sound out friends in the department. He also called a private investigator of his acquaintance. Soon, this informal background checking had blossomed into a full-fledged and never officially authorized investigation which implicated another administration official, a former aide, two sons of a state legislator and a member of a California campaign management firm.

Nofziger soon became convinced that the allegations were true. Efforts to entrap the suspects and to photograph or record them in the act were unsuccessful, serving only to put the supposed homosexual aides on their guard. The clumsiness of the investigation soon became a joke even to some of those who were conducting it. On one occasion the suspects realized that they were being followed and eluded their pursuers in a high-speed chase.

Nofziger was in a difficult spot. He was out of favor with Nancy Reagan, who disliked his slovenly dress and his irreverent sense of humor from which even the governor was not spared. But Nofziger was no clown. His ready wit and constant puns masked an extraordinary capacity for hard work and a devotion to Reagan unmatched by any aide. Nofziger wanted Reagan to run for President in 1968. He recognized that any scandal involving homosexuality would damage his candidacy, perhaps fatally. He also realized that the longer Reagan took to remove the suspect aides, the more likely he was to be politically tainted. Nofziger took others into his confidence. He went to former appointments secretary Tom Reed, who also ardently supported a Reagan presidential candidacy. He sought out Meese and William P. Clark, a low-key lawyer who was Reagan's cabinet secretary. Stuart Spencer, of the Spencer-Roberts team which had managed Reagan's campaign, was also informed. But Reagan was not. Nofziger and other aides thought that Reagan was better off not knowing what was happening. Some of the aides said afterward that they were concerned that Reagan, with his Hollywood background, would be overly tolerant. Others, aware of the gravity of the accusations, simply wanted to be sure of the facts before they presented them to the governor. The unofficial investigators agreed to prepare a documented report on the activities of the homosexual clique with the dates and places of their suspected get-togethers.

On September 7, a hot late summer day in Sacramento, conspirators Nofziger, Reed, Clark, Meese, Van Court and others on the Reagan staff held a secret meeting. Reagan was in San Diego, 513 miles away, and the conspirators decided to present the evidence to him without warning the following day. One by one, they slipped out of Sacramento on a variety of pretexts and assembled at the Coronado Hotel in San Diego. Reagan had not been expecting any staff, and he was in pajamas and bathrobe when the eleven aides made their way into his suite. Wordlessly, they handed him the report. Reagan read it, his face slowly turning white. "My God, has government failed?" he said to one aide, and then remarked that the action he must take was obvious. The staff members left, some of them wondering what Reagan would do. They didn't have to wonder long. The next day, operating through an aide, Reagan informed the chief suspect that he was demanding his resignation and the resignations of anyone else who was involved. The aide was told that if he resigned immediately no announcement would be made of the reasons he was leaving. The resignation was announced quietly without advance notice. The press, then without clues as to what had really happened, speculated that the aides were victims of a right-wing coup sponsored by the millionaire backers of the governor.

The ten-week period which intervened between the firings of the suspected homosexuals and the public revelation of Reagan's action was a period of intense and damaging pressure within the governor's office. The surviving aides, unable to discuss their story with outsiders, lived in constant worry that the truth would become known. Many of them were distracted in their daily work. "It was a heart transplant where one wasn't replaced and where the operation was performed with a dull knife," said one who participated in the investigation. "The trauma was so severe that the patient—the governor's office—went into a state of shock for four months. And the governor cut himself off from a lot of things that he shouldn't. The governorship went into receivership."[17]

Shaken, Reagan turned to Tuttle and the Kitchen Cabinet, who provided sympathy but not much else. The millionaires agreed among themselves that Reagan had over-delegated, but they were delegators themselves and tended to see their friend and governor as an unfortunate victim of circumstances he could not control. Many in the Kitchen Cabinet wanted Reagan as a presidential candidate and were more concerned about suppressing the scandal than correcting the conditions which led to it. None of them grasped that the central problem was not an aide's purported homosexuality, but a governor's unwillingness or inability to make himself informed. Even if he had no suspicions, an involved governor would certainly have learned about the investigation. Reagan was as surprised as if he had been living on Mars.

Beyond the stray remarks he made to friends and aides, Reagan's inner feelings about what happened are not known. Aides found him more distraught than he had ever been in the first nine months of his governorship, but he showed no inclination to change his method of operation and directly administer the governor's office. What Reagan seemed to want was harmony, an interval of quiet and assurances that no one would any longer take decisions in his name. Top members of the staff, drawn together by a mutual secret which they could not share with outsiders, were agreeable with these goals. The new collective leadership was headed by Clark, a quiet, gentlemanly attorney who had been hired as cabinet secretary after serving as Reagan's Ventura County campaign manager in 1966. His courtly ways made him a favorite with Nancy Reagan and the millionaire backers, and his sense of fairness endeared him to subordinates. Some who dealt with Clark thought him too shy and introverted for the position he held. But in this period of emotional convalescence, Clark was the right man for the job.

Late in September the first hint of the coverup's failure appeared in the Periscope column in *Newsweek,* which Reagan insiders attributed to the well-informed Karl Fleming. The item did not mention Reagan but said a "top GOP presidential prospect has a potentially sordid scandal on his hands. Private investigators he hired found evidence that two of his aides had committed homosexual acts. The men are no longer working for the GOP leader but the whole story may surface any day." Within the Reagan administration high aides and even Nancy Reagan urged Nofziger to "do something" to discourage further circulation of the story. Nofziger went to three well-known California reporters—Carl Greenberg of the *Los Angeles Times,* Jack McDowell of the *San Francisco Examiner* and Bill Eames of CBS News—and told them what had happened. Subsequently, at the national governors conference aboard the USS *Independence* late in October, Nofziger also passed along the story to David S. Broder of the *Washington Post,* Paul Hope of the *Washington Star* and Fleming. By now the story had achieved such general circulation that reporters were no longer dependent on Nofziger for their information. At the time I was a reporter for the *San Jose Mercury News,* and I found out about the incident from separate sources. When Nofziger learned of this, it confirmed his view (with which I concur) that the story would have come out even without his active efforts to circulate it.

The storm broke in a Drew Pearson column on October 31. "The most interesting speculation among political leaders in this key state of California is whether the magic charm of Governor Ronald Reagan can survive the discovery that a homosexual ring has been operating in his office," Pearson wrote from Los Angeles. The column then compared Reagan's response to that of President Johnson in 1964 when he learned that an aide had been involved in homosexual activity. "Johnson acted immediately," Pearson wrote. "Reagan, on the other hand, waited for about six months."

The comparison was misplaced. The Johnson aide, Walter Jenkins, had been apprehended in a YMCA washroom, and the incident recorded in a public police record. The Reagan homosexual hunters had searched for such a record without success. Their effort to make a taped record of their own had failed, and the result would not in any case have been admissible in court. Reagan's choice was therefore much more difficult than Johnson's, for he had to decide on his own whether to make the names public. It was an agonizing decision. When an aide said to him that such disclosure could have a harmful effect on the families of the accused, Reagan snapped: "You don't have to give me a lecture. I'm well aware of it." Reagan took out his frustrations on Pearson, whom he had disliked since his GE days when the columnist had attacked him for opposing compulsory medical insurance. Pearson's account of the homosexual ring contained a number of factual errors, the most serious of which was the allegation that Reagan had "waited six months" before he acted. Reagan chose to believe that these errors were deliberate, and he counterattacked by saying that Pearson was "lying."

At a press conference the day the column appeared, Reagan said Pearson was "stooping to destroy human beings, innocent people." When the governor was asked about a report that appeared the same day in the *New York Post,* claiming that Nofziger had leaked the story aboard the USS *Independence,* Reagan said, "I am prepared to say that nothing like that ever happened. . . . I've even heard rumors also that behind closed doors I gave statements to the press and this is just absolutely not true. Want to confirm it, Lyn?" Without hesitation Nofziger said, "Confirmed." Inadvertently, Reagan had forced his communications director to lie in public. Though the governor himself had been consciously lying about the homosexual ring, he had not known that Nofziger had widely leaked the story. When I asked Reagan about this more than a year later, he still rued his reply. "The thing I always regretted was that I should never have put Lyn on the spot. You know, I should never have turned to him. I should have waited until I could have talked to him and said, 'Lyn, why did they ask that question? Was there an indiscretion?' "[18]

Pearson responded to the Reagan counterattack with some sharp jabs of his own, saying that "the facts in this case are incontrovertible." Said Pearson of Reagan: "He has been posing as Mr. Clean and yet tolerated homosexuals for approximately six months and did not act regarding them until he was pressured." Reagan again called Pearson "a liar" and said he better "not spit on the sidewalk" if he came to California. When reporters picked up the issue again at a November 14 press conference, Reagan exploded and said he would not answer further questions on the subject. The transcript shows this exchange:

> REAGAN: Look, let me ask you something. I just can't believe you fellows want to continue to pursue this thing. Now I told you a few days ago that I had made my last statement on this subject. I have never had and do not have any evidence that would warrant an accusation. No accusation or any charge has been made. Now, if there is a credibility gap, and I'm responsible, it is because I refuse to participate in trying to destroy human beings with no factual evidence. And I'm not going to do that, and if that means there is a credibility gap, so be it. There is a credibility gap.
>
> PRESS: Mr. Nofziger has been accused by six newsmen of now owning up to telling them confidentially that people left the administration because of immoral behavior.
>
> REAGAN: Yes, I don't know that this is true, and I told you on this subject, as far as I'm concerned, is closed. Now do we want to have a press conference or do we want to just stand here with me refusing to talk?"

By now, Reagan did know that Nofziger had leaked the stories; the governor was lying, almost defiantly, for what he believed were defensible reasons. The press, unable to get more from Reagan and unwilling because of the lack of formal accusation to print what it knew, went on to other things. So, after a time, did the administration, though there was much finger-pointing at Nofziger either for the inexpert way he had leaked the story or for the fact that he had leaked it at all. Campaign consultant Stu Spencer and Nancy Reagan urged that Nofziger be fired, with Spencer arguing that the communications director had put the governor in the position of publicly appearing to be a liar. But Reagan wanted no more firings, and he did not make Nofziger the scapegoat for a story which almost certainly would have emerged no matter what the communications director had told the six reporters. Nofziger offered his resignation, but it was not accepted until a year later, after Reagan's abortive presidential campaign. Never again, however, was Nofziger the totally trusted Reagan insider he had been before the homosexual affair.

Reagan remains convinced that he did the right thing in protecting those involved in the purported homosexual ring. The affair did him short-range damage, by encouraging him to withdraw from detail at the very time he needed to become more involved, and by making his then prospective presidential campaign less palatable in other regions of the country. At the same time, it produced the kind of collective staff leadership which in subsequent years worked efficiently for Reagan in California and set the pattern for the President's White House staff. While it didn't seem that way to many who were involved or who wrote about it at the time, Reagan's stubborn refusal to name names and his defense of his own conduct eventually won public approval and ceased to be an issue. The chrome of Reagan's reputation for truthfulness was dented, but the vehicle itself was undamaged and continued to run smoothly.

Art Hoppe of the *San Francisco Chronicle* caught Reagan's shaky triumph best in one of his fine columns about Sir Ronald of Holyrood, a mythical knight who with his faithful squire Sancho Nofziger was always plunging into the Tangled Thicket crying, "For Decency, for Purity and for Just Plain Goodness." In this episode Sir Ronald met the Pearson-Person, nose to the ground and moustache quavering, who uttered an identical cry and, as the challenged party, chose to joust with words. The Pearson-Person scored first, charging that Sir Ronald had "sought the help of a secret Faerie Ring in your quest for the glittering White House." Sir Ronald, sorely wounded, sought help from Sancho, who muttered "confirmed" and ducked behind a nearby tree.

"It was then [wrote Hoppe], when all seemed lost, that Sir Ronald rose to the most brilliant play the Tangled Thicket has ever seen.

"I never lie," he said, his words darting this way and that. "And if I lied, I lied to protect those who lied and later didn't lie. But they didn't lie and if they lied, I didn't lie, because if I'd lied, would I lie to you and. . . .

"I yield!" cried the Pearson-Person, lying flat on his back and looking dazed. "Verily, I have jousted with the greatest of knights, but never have I seen such mastery of this weapon."[19]

11

The Reagans

On screen and off, Ronald Reagan is a role player. He learns by trial and error, acting in ways which worked before and trying to find out what is expected of him. While he has a passive nature, he persists toward the goals he has set for himself. He has the ability to focus, and an inclination to succeed. As a radio announcer, he was fired because he couldn't read commercials properly but persevered and became one of the best sportscasters in his region. In Hollywood, he needed a score of pictures and four years of hard work to land a first-rate role. He stumbled badly at the onset of his gubernatorial campaign of 1966 and again in the early stages of his 1976 and 1980 presidential campaigns. On two of these three occasions he recovered and won a decisive victory.

When Reagan went to Sacramento in 1967, he did not know what was expected of him as governor of California. The Reagan of that day was not the accomplished politician who arrived in Washington in 1981 determined to forge a working majority in a divided Congress. Governor Reagan was a mystery to California's sophisticated and well-staffed legislators, many of whom thought him as standoffish as he was uninformed. Despite the prodding of his own legislative aides, Reagan was reluctant to mix with the legislators, who had been accustomed to dropping in on Goodie Knight and Pat Brown whenever they needed to see them. Reagan remained aloof, a celebrity within his own administration. Never a workaholic, he frequently left the capitol by 5 P.M. for a chauffeured ten-minute drive to a stately Tudor residence in a choice Sacramento neighborhood.* At home Reagan rested, swam in the pool, lectured old friends about the evils of government growth,

* The governor's mansion, since replaced, was a recognized firetrap on a busy one-way street near the capitol carrying Reno-bound traffic through Sacramento. Nancy took one look at the place and refused to live there. The Reagans then rented the house on 45th Street from a Sacramento councilman. Attempts by Reagan's millionaire backers to raise $500,000 in a subscription drive for a Reagan residence failed. When the councilman wanted to sell the home in 1969, the millionaire backers purchased it for $150,000, then leased it to the Reagans for the $1,250 monthly rent they had been paying.

and spent quiet evenings with Nancy and their nine-year-old son, whom they called "Skipper." Dinner was simple fare of meat and potatoes or macaroni and cheese. After dinner there was television, which Reagan had installed in his bedroom so he could watch his programs lying down. The favorite of favorites was *Mission Impossible,* though Reagan also liked *Mannix,* Carol Burnett, Dean Martin and the weekly professional football games. Sacramento was San Francisco '49ers and Oakland Raiders territory, but Reagan remained a loyal Los Angeles Rams fan throughout the eight years of his governorship. Southern Californians to the core, the Reagans usually spent their weekends at their real home in Pacific Palisades.

To those whose lives and existences were centered in the state capital, Reagan was an unlikely Sacramentan and a less likely governor. His life in politics seemed so unreal he might have been the star of a successful soap opera called *Citizen Governor.* In a letter to William Meiklejohn on July 31, 1967, Reagan joked with his former agent that he was sorry he couldn't pay him a commission for "this new part" of governor. "Of course I could complain that the contract makes little provision for time off and no provision for overtime, and while I'm trying to play the 'Good guy,' the script is written so that most of the time I feel out-numbered," wrote Reagan.

Perhaps it was this sense of humor, this ability to see himself as others saw him which eventually rescued Reagan in Sacramento. Offstage, he had a decent respect for the opinions of others and a gentle perceptiveness which made him responsive to criticism. During one period he allowed himself to become involved in a series of public recriminations with defeated Governor Brown. When young legislative aide George Steffes said to Reagan that such criticism should be "beneath" the governor of California, Reagan looked up at him quietly and said, "You're right, and I won't do it anymore." On another occasion, at a lobbyist's reception where Reagan had uncharacteristically imbibed an extra pair of vodka martinis, he was drawn into verbal sparring with a volatile Republican critic, Assemblyman William T. Bagley, a bright and flamboyant legislator who made no secret of the fact that he considered the governor a know-nothing. Reagan had no use for Bagley, whom he regarded as a Democrat in Republican clothing. On the ride home after the reception, he thought about what had happened and said to an aide, "You know, all Bill really wants is attention, and we're going to give it to him. Find some bills we can work together on and have him be the author."

In these ways, Reagan learned bit by bit how to be a governor. What he had to overcome, as much as lack of knowledge about state government, was a misconception about politics derived from his own antipolitical rhetoric. Reagan came to public life believing that the legislators were venal connivers intent on feathering their own nests and perpetuating themselves eternally in office. There was a grain of truth to this notion, but it was, like so many of Reagan's perceptions, a parody of the real world in Sacramento.

Over time Reagan learned that legislators really were not that much different from other people. He learned that the approaches which had worked for him in Dixon, Des Moines and Hollywood would also prevail in Sacramento. Over time Reagan's personality triumphed over his ignorance.

Nancy Reagan's adjustment to Sacramento was more difficult than her husband's. He was nearly fifty-seven when he arrived in the state capital, in the midst of his second marriage and his third career. She was ten years younger, with two children and a private marriage that had been abruptly transformed into a public one. Unlike her husband, Nancy Reagan was not a political person, and she did not enjoy the company of ordinary people. Diminutive and pretty, Nancy's interests were in fashion and money and the gossip of the wealthy, socialite circle she had left in Southern California. Above all, however, she saw her role as protecting the privacy of "Ronnie" and the life they enjoyed together. "My life began when I got married," she used to say. "My life began with Ronnie."[1] In Sacramento, and afterward, protecting Ronnie became a full-time job.

It wasn't easy. For all her wealth and poise, Nancy Reagan's world was less secure and optimistic than the one inhabited by her husband, the governor. She lacked the advantage of growing up in Dixon, Illinois, and the even greater advantage of a stable family situation when she was a young child. When Nancy was born Anne Frances Robbins at a Manhattan hospital in 1921, her father, a car salesman, did not bother to show up. That same year he left her mother. Nancy last saw him when she was thirteen. He locked her in a bathroom for objecting to a remark she made in defense of her mother. To this day Nancy dislikes small rooms and locked doors.[2] But Nancy was, in a very real sense, also abandoned by her mother, stage actress Edith Luckett, who didn't want to take her young child with her on the road. When Nancy was only two, her mother deposited her with an aunt and uncle in Bethesda, Maryland, where she lived for the next five years. Nancy's memories of this period are of loneliness and missing her mother. Nancy saw her only when Edith Luckett was performing in New York, when her aunt would take her there by train. On one occasion, Nancy relates in her autobiography, she saw a play starring her mother "where her part called for being treated unkindly by the other characters, and it upset me terribly."[3] The actual account which Nancy Reagan has given to friends is more vivid. What she saw, as a young girl, was her mother being killed on stage. Nancy believed that her mother was dead and could not be consoled even by the sight of her alive, backstage. Some of the actors laughed while the little girl wept. Nancy Reagan has never forgotten it. "Her early childhood was very unhappy, insecure and lonely," says a close friend. She had to be strong to survive it.

The first man who rescued Nancy Robbins from an unhappy life was Loyal Davis, a famous Chicago neurosurgeon who married Luckett when Nancy was seven years old. A man of great personal charm, Davis was

known in Chicago medical circles as a tough taskmaster and strict discipli-
narian. A California physician who interned under him remembers his fellow interns chafing under Davis' strictness. Interns were in those days frequently called upon to deliver babies in the city's black wards, and they
would sometimes be asked to suggest a name for the baby. Davis was not
fond of blacks, and the interns revenged themselves by naming various
black children after the surgeon. This practice was brought to the attention
of Davis, and a bulletin board edict appeared directing that interns would
under no circumstances suggest names for the children they had assisted
into the world.[4] Whatever he was to his interns, Davis was the man who
saved Nancy Robbins. "She wanted a father so desperately," says a friend,
"someone who was there every day, could be strong, give her guidance, give
her everything—and give her status."

Davis did all of this and more. He gave her back her mother, who quit
the stage and moved with Dr. Davis to Chicago's North Shore and the exclusive address of 209 Lake Shore Drive. She lived in an elite world. Nancy
was enrolled at the prestigious Girl's Latin School. Afterward, she was sent
to Smith College. She had good clothes and rich boyfriends and a debu-
tante's coming out party. She also learned formal rules of conduct, for Davis
was a rigorous as well as a loving father. She admired him and respected his
ways and his habits. To this day, she chews each morsel of food thirty-two
times, just as he told her to do. When she was fourteen, Nancy took the
name of her stepfather and legally became "Nancy Davis." In her official
biography, when her husband was governor of California, Nancy insisted on
listing Dr. Davis as her father. When a magazine writer pointed out that
Who's Who said Nancy was adopted, she dismissed the information with a
wave of her hand. "I don't care what the book says," Nancy told an aide.
"He is my father. In my mind, he is my father. I have no father except Loyal
Davis." The aide shrugged, and gave up. If anyone asked, Loyal Davis was
Nancy Reagan's father.

Because of the conviction that she could impose her own view of the
world on reality, Nancy was an easy target for the press. Her husband could
mangle statistics, distort facts and forget his legislative program and yet
somehow emerge as a big, likeable lug of a citizen-politician who was striving to do his best for all the citizens of California. She could turn on all the
charm and say all the right things and come out as brittle, suspicious and
shallow. Reporters mocked "the Gaze," which was Nancy's transfixed way
of looking at her husband whenever he appeared in public.* In mid-1968,
just about the time the national press was for the first time beginning to real-

---

* I was one of the mockers. In a passage in *Ronnie and Jesse: A Political Odyssey,*
published in 1969, I referred to her gaze as "a kind of transfixed adoration more appropriate to a witness of the Virgin Birth." Nancy was understandably furious, and two friends
told me she had ripped the offending page out of the book. I lacked the guts to verify this
with Nancy.

ize that Reagan might possibly have something other than tinsel between his ears, Nancy was the subject of a savage portrait in the *Saturday Evening Post* by Joan Didion, who described Nancy's famous smile as a study in frozen insincerity. "Nancy Reagan says almost everything with spirit," Didion wrote, "perhaps because she was an actress for a couple of years and has the beginning actress's habit of investing even the most casual lines with a good deal more dramatic expression than is ordinarily called for on a Tuesday morning on 45th Street in Sacramento."[5]

Nancy Reagan was crushed by this piece. Nancy Skelton, one of the most observant writers about Nancy Reagan, interviewed her for the *Sacramento Bee* a couple of days after the Didion piece appeared and found her "moved almost to the point of tears of anger that she had taken Didion into her house and down to the capitol and had spent a lot of time with her."[6] In her story for the *Bee,* Skelton quoted Mrs. Reagan as saying of Didion: "I thought we were getting along fine together. Maybe it would have been better if I snarled a bit." Six years later, after a similar interview in Nancy's sunroom, Skelton would make the same point as Didion in a piece that was more balanced, but no more gentle in its judgment. "The hour comes to a close," concluded the Skelton story. "And still nothing has happened in the sunroom by accident."[7]

One reason for Nancy's bad press is that many of the most penetrating stories about her—Skelton's interview, Didion's piece, a two-part series by Wanda McDaniel in the *Los Angeles Herald-Examiner,* a Sally Quinn piece in the *Washington Post* in 1976—were written by women. In most cases, Nancy Reagan does not relate well to women, viewing them as competitors for her husband's attention. The McDaniel series quotes socialite Cheryll Clarke about an incident in 1975 when she boarded an elevator with actress Ruta Lee at a Republican fund-raising luncheon. "The doors were standing open with Nancy already inside, so we just walked in," Clarke was quoted as saying. "Then all of a sudden she [Nancy] was saying, 'Oh no, you can't come in here.' Well, we got off, but just then Ronnie showed up and said, 'Sure, they can ride with us.' I couldn't figure out what had happened until a friend of theirs later told me that Nancy simply didn't want two good-looking women in the same elevator with her husband. Honestly, I couldn't believe it."[8]

Nancy was a good protector, as good as there ever has been. She called Reagan "Ronnie," and he called her "Mommy," and she made sure that he took his galoshes with him on bad-weather days. In political campaigns she guarded her husband from advisers who wanted to take advantage of his communicative talents by working him beyond his limits. She never complained about being worked beyond her own. "I can get Nancy up at 6 A.M. and put her on television as we did at Miami," said Nancy Reynolds, then her press secretary after the 1968 Republican convention. "She had sixty-eight interviews in Miami. I had her going morning, noon and night and she was fine. If she heard that I was going to have Ronald Reagan up at 6 A.M. on a television show, she'd scream bloody murder, but that's because she wants him to get his rest. She has a genuine concern for him. . . . I can drag her through the mud, but if it means Ronald Reagan's going to get a cold, forget it, baby."[9]

Except for Reynolds and Michael K. Deaver, whose wife, Carolyn, is also a Smith College alumna, most Reagan aides gave Nancy a wide berth.* Some were afraid of her and others were appalled by the example of Nofziger, whom Nancy would not speak to for five months after the homosexual scandal was publicly exposed to her husband's detriment. Behind her back, aides called Nancy "the Iron Maiden," and worse. But there was another side to this story. Aides who stuck it out in the governor's office eventually learned that if Nancy could be a hindrance, she also could be a tremendous help when she approved of someone's activities. Reporters who needed interviews, especially during Nofziger's period of coventry, learned that Nancy's favor did them no harm. For most members of the state capitol press corps, such approval was a case of relative disfavor, since Nancy could have done without any reporters at any time. When the Reagans held a press party at the Executive Residence, as the rented home on 45th Street came to be known officially, Nancy looked frequently at her watch as the appointed hour for the end of the event drew near, and finally said to an aide, "C'mon, it's time to get rid of them." Reagan, oblivious to this concern, was telling old movie stories to reporters in the garden.

In this period, when Reagan was still learning the ropes, the myth of Governor Nancy developed. It was a myth with a core of plausibility, for Nancy has always had more push than Ronnie. A case can be made that she pushed him towards the presidency when he was not certain that he wanted it for himself. It is also true that Nancy may have been influential in one policy area which did her husband no good, leading him to oppose the Equal Rights Amendment he had once endorsed. But the notion that it was Nancy who ran the state of California was hooey. This myth grew to gigantic proportions essentially because Reagan is a gentleman who will always take his wife's calls, even in cabinet meetings. During one memorable moment in California, an aide heard Nancy call with complaints about foul-mouthed militant Eldridge Cleaver, who had just delivered a number of unprintable

---

* Reynolds, a former San Francisco television reporter who was brought to the Reagan staff by Nofziger, was one of the few aides who had a genuine affection for Nancy Reagan and worked well with her. The attractive and vivacious Reynolds was popular with the press and improved Nancy Reagan's always shaky press relations during her Sacramento years. When Reynolds left, Nancy Reagan no longer had a buffer. Deaver, the aide who is closest to Mrs. Reagan and understands her best, thinks that a stereotype developed of her being "uncaring" and "more interested in fashion and the beautiful people" than anything else. "We spent so much time on doing a good job for him," said Deaver of the President's public image in 1981, "that we really haven't paid attention to that as far as she's concerned. . . . That may be part of the problem."

opinions about Reagan. "But, honey, I can't have him arrested just because he says those things," Reagan replied.

When I asked Reagan about this, he was philosophical. "She bleeds pretty good," he said with a laugh in 1968. "Sometimes I come home and find she's pretty sore about something I laugh off. It's much harder on them [women] than it is on us—there's no way for them to fight back."[10] Reagan then explained with some self-satisfaction about how he could, on occasion, mollify Nancy while continuing to do his work. In the first term of Reagan's administration, the governor's most unrelenting journalistic critic was the *Sacramento Bee,* the newspaper which also provided the most in-depth coverage of state capital affairs. Nancy was so incensed at *Bee* editorial comments about her husband that she refused to subscribe to the paper or have it in the house. Reagan, who read the *Bee* daily and sometimes clipped from it as he did from many papers, was not about to give it up. He allowed Nancy to cancel the subscription at home, while he took it at the office. Reagan explained this solution to me as if it were worthy of Solomon, so happy was he at the result. He had been able to please Nancy and also keep abreast of the news.[11]

So it was that Reagan groped toward mastery of the governorship while his wife served as the lightning rod that deflected from him as much of the inevitable criticism, interviews, outside attention and gossip as she could. She made a pleasant home for him, took care of their children, monitored the telephone calls, and made sure that Ronnie had rest and support and the food he liked to eat and time for his favorite television programs. During the presidential campaign of 1968 and the gubernatorial reelection campaign of 1970, she gave ground grudgingly, admitting a few influential aides and legislators and even some requisite members of the press to the inner sanctum of their home on 45th Street. But she kept most of the intruders at arm's length and always made certain that her husband had a peaceful haven to which he could retreat.

No one doubted that the Reagans were very much in love. The reason that "the Gaze," now much more restrained than it was then, bothered people was that it was unnecessary. "She loves him so much that she could look natural," said a friend of Nancy's in the only criticism I ever heard her make of Mrs. Reagan. "She doesn't have to act, when she cares so much about a man, yet she always does. But she's such a good actress she probably doesn't even know she's acting." Tears would come to Reagan's eyes when he was asked about what kind of a wife she was. "How do you describe coming into a warm room from out of the cold? Never waking up bored? The only thing wrong is, she's made a coward out of me. Whenever she's out of sight, I'm a worrier about her."[12] In 1974 Nancy Skelton asked Nancy Reagan if she had ever thought of divorcing her husband and received this reply: "Never! Oh! The thought of it would terrify me, the thought of being without Ronnie. It would kill me. You see—he's a rare man. When we first came up here, there were comments that he was kind of snobby because he didn't hobnob with the rest of the fellows after work. Well, it was the same way in the picture business, after a day's shooting, he'd never stopped for a drink in the dressing room, he always wanted to come home. And I don't go off by myself, either."[13]

He was the protected one and she was the protector. He was the beneficiary of his upbringing, which taught him that all men were created equal. She was the product of hers, which taught her that the economically and socially privileged are a special class deserving of all good things which come to them. He had been inspired by a father who chose to sleep in a car in wintertime rather than patronize a hotel which discriminated against Jews. She had been raised in an elite environment by a father who was intolerant of minorities. He was the social democrat, who seemed at ease with everyone, and she was the snob who enjoyed the company of a rich, fashion-conscious social circle and kept others in their place.

And yet, those who knew the Reagans best, even those who had no use for Nancy, realized that she was absolutely critical to his success and indispensable to his well-being. Eschewing the modern, political role played by women who see themselves as advisers and celebrating a traditionalism which enraged feminists, Nancy Reagan was the spark and drive in her husband's life at the same time that she was his comforter. Passive and pleasant, Ronald Reagan was married to a woman who was neither, but who realized that the husband she had married required a private and secure retreat from which to sally forth with his mythical battle cry of "For Decency, for Purity and for Just Plain Goodness." Nancy Reagan provided such a fortress, and she permitted none to breach its walls. She was not the governor of California, and she had no interest in being the President of the United States, but Reagan would not have held those offices without her support and guidance. "Nancy Reagan spent a good deal of her time in life making a good life for Ronald Reagan," said Deaver, the aide who knows her best. "Making sure he was comfortable. Making sure things were done right. . . . I don't think she's gotten credit for that, but she is as much responsible for his success as he is."[14]

12

The Governor

"ELSEWHERE, the tempo of development was slow at first and gradually accelerated," wrote historian Carey McWilliams in 1949. "But in California the lights went on all at once, in a blaze, and they have never been dimmed."[1] Tracing California's development from the 1849 gold rush to its surge of new subdivisions a century later, McWilliams saw California possessed of "peculiar and highly exceptional dynamics" which sped social change and foreshortened economic processes. In the two decades after he wrote these words, California became the great microcosmic nation state of North America, again and again establishing patterns which were copied by the rest of the nation. Its population doubled, exceeding 20 million. In 1964, two years before Reagan was elected governor, California passed New York and became the nation's most populous state. Its geography was the most diverse of any state, its resources the most enormous. California's gross national product was greater than all but five nations in the world—the United States, the Soviet Union, West Germany, Japan and France. Its per capita income exceeded every nation's. Classified as a nation, California would have been among the world leaders in agriculture and exports. It was first in freeways and aerospace technology, in swimming pools and backyard barbecues, in mobile homes and motorcycles, in mass culture and junk food. The hula hoop was born in California, along with high technology. And California led the way in fads and trends and cults and drugs and political movements of every conceivable kind. Alan Cranston once said that California was supposed to be the state where the fruit and nuts were on the ground and the people in the trees. But the state also produced some of the most significant political movements of our time.

Many of the first campus rallies in favor of civil rights and against the Vietnam War which typified the 1960s took place in California. The state also was a spawning ground for the conservationist and antinuclear movements and the United Farm Workers, and a major recruiting area for the John Birch Society. In California, celebrities like Reagan and George

Murphy could become politicians, and politicians like Jerry Brown could become celebrities. In California, an unknown and overweight Texas share-cropper's son like Jesse Unruh became the power-wielding speaker of the state Assembly. For all its people and problems and urban sprawl, Califor-nia remained an outpost of the western frontier where nothing seemed im-possible and everything could be achieved. California was the wave of the future.

Reagan saw the coming wave and rode the edge of the conservative counterrevolution which swept across the nation. The movement had eco-nomic reasons for being, as Americans became disenchanted with govern-ment growth, runaway inflation and rising taxes. But its deeper causes were social. In the 1960s middle class Americans looked around them at urban disorders, rising black militancy and antidraft protests spurred by the Viet-nam War and did not like what they saw. Middle class parents who had striven to put their children through college particularly did not like what they thought was happening at the University of California's best-known campus at Berkeley. In 1965, a part-time student named Mario Savio led the Free Speech Movement into protesting a ban on distribution of political ma-terial at the university's Sather Gate entrance. When the university persisted in its restrictions, the protests grew, degenerated into a "filthy speech" movement, and were finally and reluctantly put down by force on orders of Governor Pat Brown. Later, as violence rocked campuses across the coun-try, including California, the UC demonstrations of 1965 would seem quite tame. But Americans at the time of the first Berkeley demonstrations were accustomed to quiet, orderly campuses and angry at those who disrupted this order.

Reagan's audience roared with approval when he promised to "clean up the mess at Berkeley" where, he said, had occurred "sexual orgies so vile I cannot describe them to you." After being rebuffed by the chairman of the state Senate Subcommittee on Un-American Activities in his demand for an investigation, Reagan promised in his campaign to name a commission headed by former Central Intelligence Agency Director John J. McCone to "investigate the charges of communism and blatant sexual misbehavior on the Berkeley campus."[2] Nothing came of the investigation, but it set the tone for a running battle between Reagan and the state's higher education estab-lishment which continued during most of Reagan's first term. On December 3, 1966, a month after his election, Reagan issued a warning to dissidents, "Observe the rules or get out." An unknown admirer made a bronze-and-walnut plaque of these words and sent it to Reagan. The governor liked his own admonition so much that he hung the plaque on the cloth-upholstered wall above the entrance to his office.

From the first day of his governorship, Reagan and higher education saw each other as the enemy. On inauguration day, Reagan's inept finance director, Gordon Smith, prematurely disclosed the governor's plan to impose a $400-a-year tuition at the university and a $200-a-year tuition at state colleges in addition to the 10 percent budget cuts. The higher education establishment, overcome by suspicion and hostility, interpreted these proposals as punitive and reacted with denunciations nearly as extreme as Reagan's had been of the UC demonstrators. In the meantime, reports circulated within both administration and academic circles that UC President Clark Kerr would soon be fired. Kerr, a former professor and labor mediator of distinction whose administrative skills had been questioned even by some of his supporters, was at the center of the Berkeley controversies. One of his favorite sayings was, "The university is not engaged in making ideas safe for students; it is engaged in making students safe for ideas."[3] Kerr was assailed on the right by such foes of "permissiveness" as state Superintendent of Public Instruction Max Rafferty, a member, as was the governor, of the university Board of Regents, and on the left by radicals like Savio, who blamed Kerr for the impersonality of what he called "the multiversity." Several of the regents had been critics of Kerr since 1964, and others considered him too politically damaged to negotiate with Reagan over the university budget. A majority wanted his resignation.

Kerr talked it over with the chairman of the regents, Theodore Meyer, and the vice-chairman, Dorothy B. Chandler, both of whom asked him to resign. Kerr refused and instead sought a vote from the full Board of Regents. The action surprised Reagan, who was so preoccupied with his budget problems that he wanted to postpone any decision on the university presidency. Reagan told me in 1968 that he thought Kerr had "outlived his usefulness," but that he didn't want to instigate a move to fire him. Kerr did that himself, by asking for what was in effect a vote of confidence. On the motion of Laurence J. Kennedy, Jr., an appointee of Governor Brown, the regents voted 14–8 to dismiss Kerr with Reagan supporting the majority. "We had tuition and the budget on our hands, and I would have preferred to wait until June or so," said Reagan afterwards. "But you can't turn around and give a man a vote of confidence in January and then fire him five months later."[4] *

Kerr's dismissal occurred on January 21, 18 days after Reagan took office. Reagan's low-key maneuvering on this issue and his unwillingness to take the lead in firing Kerr was one of the first clues that he would be a governor more restrained in his practice than he had been in his rhetoric. An-

---

* Kerr blamed Reagan for engineering the firing, as did a number of the governor's critics. Determining precisely what had happened was complicated by the conflicting stories of board chairman Meyer, who said the day of the firing that "certain regents" had initiated the vote, and subsequently said that the issue was precipitated by Kerr himself. Reagan insisted to me in a July 1968 discussion and again in October of that year that he knew nothing about a vote on Kerr until Meyer talked to him about it. "Who said what to whom I'll never know," said Reagan. "But Chairman Meyer told us that Kerr had said he wanted a settlement of the affaire Clark Kerr. That was a bombshell and most of all to me."

other clue came a month later when Reagan offered only token resistance to the regents' decision to postpone consideration of the tuition. In his dealings with the university and state colleges, Reagan from the outset looked for ways in which he could prevail by compromise. He cultivated those willing to defer to the administration, notably the flexible Glenn Dumke, chancellor of the state colleges. Secure in his public support for a firm stand against campus dissidents, Reagan believed he could afford a strategy of delay and compromise. Usually his more militant, or thoughtless, adversaries played into his hands with some disorderly protest that made Reagan a sure winner on television. Even as a novice governor, Reagan understood that rational objections tended to be drowned out by irrational ones on the nightly news.

On February 9, 1967, a quiet and orderly group of University of California demonstrators marched on the state capitol protesting tuition and the budget cuts. Reagan spoke to them and was politely applauded when he defended his own program, but the students reserved their cheers for Unruh, who called tuition "a tax of the worst kind—a tax on education." Outside of Sacramento the entire demonstration received only mild attention. Two days later, a band of wild-eyed demonstrators organized by the American Federation of Teachers descended on the capitol, sporting beards and signs proclaiming "Tax the Rich." Seen on television, they might have been a band of anarchists assembled by Central Casting who were marching on Sacramento to overthrow the government. Nofziger was overjoyed. "Did you see me with the mask on behind the tree there yelling names at the governor?" he quipped to a reporter. But neither Nofziger nor any of the governor's other aides saw the public relations potential of the march as clearly as Reagan did.

Brushing aside the advice of his aides, who pointed out to him that he was overdue to leave town for a political speech in Portland, Reagan made a surprise appearance before the demonstrators. They greeted him with boos. "Ladies and gentlemen, if there are any," responded Reagan on cue. He was drowned out by more boos. Again, Reagan tried to speak. "The people do have some right to have a voice in the principles and basic philosophy that will go along with the education they provide," Reagan said above the din. "As governor, I am going to represent the people of the state. . . ." Again he was drowned out, this time by a chant of, "We are people." Reagan left to catch his plane but paused in the capitol rotunda to comment, "If they represent the majority of the student body of California, then God help the university and the college system." On television it was another triumph for the Great Communicator.

The university establishment was as emotionally committed to "free tuition" as Reagan was to halting the demonstrations. This commitment ignored the realities of rising costs which had made "free tuition" something of a misnomer. While university students who graduated from California high schools were not charged tuition as such, they faced a fee schedule which could amount to several hundred dollars a semester, equivalent to what students paid in other states where there was no pretense of providing a free higher education. Before Reagan was elected, Governor Brown's director of finance, Hale Champion, had pointed out the conflict between the slogan of "free tuition" and the reality of rising fees in a speech which received little attention from either educators or the press. Reagan's tuition proposal frightened the university and its supporters, however, because it seemed as much an attempt to punish the system for its toleration of student dissidents as it did a legitimate budget-balancing device.

California educators tended to regard Reagan as a primitive who had attended a tiny liberal arts school and knew nothing about the purposes and practices of a great university system. Reagan resented this attitude, and responded with equal contempt. Once he accused universities of "subsidizing intellectual curiosity." He chose as his education adviser Alex C. Sheriffs, a one-time liberal Democrat who interpreted all campus disorders not as real responses to real events or grievances, but as the fruition of a parental permissiveness which had produced students who were "immobilized in relation to their own feelings" and incapable of dealing with a militant minority.[5] *

Sheriffs told Reagan that many students, though unwilling to risk group disapproval by speaking out, preferred parents and political leaders who were willing to assert authority. Reagan accepted this explanation and was willing to assert authority when the occasion arose. On January 5, 1969, a day before classes reopened at violence-torn San Francisco State College, Reagan proclaimed his willingness to keep the college open by force. "Those who want to get an education, those who want to teach, should be protected in that at the point of bayonet if necessary," Reagan said at an airport interview in Sacramento.

A month later, when the issue was again Berkeley, Reagan showed that he meant what he had said. Students entering Sather Gate to attend classes during a proclaimed student strike were mauled by pickets claiming to represent the "Third World Liberation Front." This was too much for Reagan. Throughout the morning of February 5, he waited impatiently in his office while his staff assembled reports of the incident from the chancellor's office.

---

* Sheriffs was one of the University of California administrators who denied the Free Speech Movement permission to distribute off-campus political material on campus. He was fired when he tried to pursue a hard-line approach, which was overruled by Kerr. At the time Sheriffs was a Democrat and considered liberal. He subsequently reregistered Republican. There were those at Berkeley who felt that Sheriffs was "getting even," an accusation he denied. Whatever his motivations, Sheriffs was influential in convincing Reagan that "permissiveness" had much to do with campus unrest. "These youngsters," said Sheriffs of the campus protesters, "are the first children raised by parents who were unsure of their role as parents—even of their rights as parents, the first parents who instead of depending on their common sense and human traditions and personal feelings had to look it up in a book by Spock or Gesell."[6]

Then he prepared a statement, called a press conference a day ahead of schedule, and told hastily assembled reporters he was proclaiming a state of emergency and calling out the California Highway Patrol to protect the university from "criminal anarchists" and "off-campus revolutionaries." "Students have been assaulted and beaten as they attempted to attend classes," Reagan said. "Streets and sidewalks providing access to the campus have been physically blocked. Classes have been disrupted. Arsons and fire-bombings have occurred and university property has been destroyed." Reagan was happy about what he had done, saying to his press secretary, Paul Beck, on the way back to his office, "I'll sleep well tonight."[7]

But Reagan's action did not bring peace to the campus or the surrounding community. Riots and fire-bombings continued to plague Berkeley, both on and off campus. In May a group of radicals and "street people" occupied university-owned land they had designated as "People's Park" and stoned police who tried to eject them. The police summoned help from the California Highway Patrol and the Alameda County Sheriff's deputies. On May 15 a bloody riot ensued in which marchers hurled tear gas canisters back into police ranks and deputies finally resorted to firearms. James Rector, a 25-year-old San Josean, was killed by wounds suffered from a shotgun fired by one of the deputies, scores of other persons were injured, and hundreds were arrested. The outnumbered law enforcement agencies declared they could no longer guarantee the safety of the city and asked Reagan to send in the National Guard. Without hesitation, the governor complied, and the Guard enforced an unofficial martial law in Berkeley for seventeen days.

Reagan privately expressed his distress about the killing of Rector, but he was convinced that Berkeley police had exercised restraint and pointed out that they had not fired their revolvers even when hit repeatedly by rocks. On June 13, reviewing what had happened, Reagan said that only the arrival of the sheriff's deputies and their shotguns had prevented isolated police officers from being stoned to death. And he believed, and still does, that sending in the National Guard had saved lives. "No one can take pleasure from seeing bayonets in an American community or on a college campus," Reagan said. "But the arrival of the Guard with bayonets brought almost total de-escalation of hand-to-hand fighting and violence." The Guard had used tear gas to quell the rioters, and Reagan acknowledged that some innocent people had suffered distress. "There also can be no question that the alternative to the gas—hand-to-hand combat between the mob and the Guardsmen—could have produced real tragedy," he said.[8]

Reagan won all his individual battles with the university system, but the war ended, like so many in the twentieth century, without a clear-cut victory for either side. He fought hard through the summer of 1967 to obtain agreement from the university regents to implement a tuition charge in 1968. The regents, perceiving that Reagan had no intention of backing down, began searching for a compromise. Reagan took them to the brink at the dramatic regents meeting at UCLA on August 31, 1967. By now he had grasped some of the complex political dynamics of the Board of Regents. He understood that the face-saving slogan of "free tuition" was important to some regents who were otherwise willing to concede Reagan's point that students and their parents should pay a greater share of an education which in most cases vastly increased their earning power. Once the regents acknowledged this, Reagan was able to insist on an up-or-down vote on the issue as he had presented it. "I, for one, have no intention of discussing anything except tuition," Reagan said. "Tuition, yes or no." Spurred by regents Vice-Chairman Dorothy Chandler, who wanted the board to move on to the pressing issue of naming a replacement for Clark Kerr, the regents voted down Reagan's proposal 14–7. When the vote was announced, a tight-lipped Reagan immediately proposed a luncheon recess and said to Nofziger, "You never leave the stadium at the half."

Half-time was a closed-door luncheon in the cafeteria where Reagan turned on the personal charm. He was aware that a number of the regents were acutely discomforted by having had to vote openly against him. He was aware, too, that others among the regents cared less about tuition than about the university budget the following year and wanted to make some concession if they could. Reagan was gracious. He listened, rather than talked. Host Chancellor Franklin Murphy explained to Reagan that educators feared that tuition would be increased rapidly once any was imposed. Regent Ed Pauley, a conservative oilman, agreed with Murphy and explained to Reagan that he had not wanted to vote against him but felt he had no choice. "What's the alternative?" Reagan asked. The other regents, with the help of a draft prepared by Murphy, showed him. Reagan allowed himself to be persuaded that a new "charge" would accomplish the same purpose as "tuition." He was smiling when he returned to the meeting room. Reagan made a motion for a $250 charge, then allowed Pauley to amend it to $200. When regent Frederick G. Dutton offered additional amendments that could have tied up the board for hours, Reagan calmly agreed to delete the figure from the resolution. He had won, and he knew it. The final version called for a "charge . . . to be paid by all students, other than nonresidents, to finance a program of student aid, faculty enrichment and/or other uses to be determined by the regents." The nonresidents were exempted because they already paid a hefty tuition, further acknowledgment that the "charge" was tuition by another name. "If it walks like a duck and quacks like a duck, it must be a duck," Reagan said to Nofziger.* [9]

---

* Unruh was so furious with the regents' indecision and change of heart that he charged that they were "no longer competent or able to give leadership to the university," an accusation that carried little sting because Unruh seldom came to the meetings. But it took the regents so long to specify a fee that the governor, too, became impatient with the board. Discussing his compromise action with me in November 1968, Reagan said scornfully, "That was like throwing a fish to a seal."

The episode demonstrated the growing skill of the novice governor, always at his best in situations where he could employ the authority of his compelling personality. One aspect of that personality, demonstrated at the regents' private luncheon, was that the combination of Reagan's determination and pleasantness made him a person whom others wanted to please. Confronting cameras or a mob, Reagan spoke with passionate rhetoric. But in private he could be a quiet listener, displaying the negotiating skills he had learned in the Screen Actors Guild. Always, he realized, the other side has to offer something. "It pays to listen to what they're offering," he told me in 1968, displaying insight into a basic principle of negotiation. More than anything, it was this skill which would eventually make of the Great Communicator a competent governor of California.

The university profited from the regents' face-saving compliance. After the tuition confrontation, some of the tension faded from the university's relationship with the Reagan administration, though it never entirely disappeared. The new university president, Charles Hitch, proved a moderate who maintained the truce and managed to win back much of what had been denied in the first Reagan budget. When Reagan ordered out the Highway Patrol in the crisis of '69, Hitch joined in the request for a state of emergency. Reagan never entirely lost his distrust of "Berkeley," but he did not revenge himself on the university's educational programs. Over the eight years of his governorship, budgets for both the university and the state college system steadily increased. State spending on higher education during the Reagan years rose 136 percent, compared to a 100 percent increase in overall state spending. The mass exodus of faculty talent which had been widely predicted when Reagan took over did not occur, perhaps because the crises on the campuses spread to other states and no longer seemed a phenomenon specifically related to the Reagan administration. When Reagan left office, the respected Dean McHenry, chancellor emeritus at the University of California at Santa Cruz, summed up what by then had become a widespread feeling about Reagan even in the educational community: "His bark proved worse than his bite."

The Reagan proclivity for doing what was necessary at the expense of his rhetoric emerged again during the first year of his governorship on the critical issue of the tax bill. In principle, Reagan was against any tax increase and had created the impression in his campaign that one could be avoided. His initial public statements after becoming governor were based entirely on the "squeeze, cut and trim" idea of balancing the budget. He never publicly acknowledged that this was an unrealistic notion. Nor did he ever, during that first year, accurately determine the size of the prospective deficit, which changed with each new set of figures from his finance department. But Reagan did grasp, right from the start, the political realities of the situation confronting him. The day after his inauguration he said he did not want to wait "until everyone forgets that we did not cause the problem—we only inherited it." His aides interpreted this comment as a mandate to negotiate tax increases with the legislature, no matter what Smith was saying for public consumption. When Reagan met with Unruh early in his term, the only discussion between these two competing politicians was the form the tax increase should take.

Good politicians are those who see issues coming down the trail, and Unruh foresaw the property tax restlessness which would finally culminate in 1978 in the excessive antitax revolution of Proposition 13. Reagan, in his first campaign for office, picked up the issue intuitively and immediately. Like Unruh, he was committed to property tax reform. If the governor and speaker had not shared this mutual insight and commitment, it is altogether likely that the Proposition 13 revolt would have engulfed California years earlier.

If Reagan more than equaled Unruh when it came to political intuition, he knew next to nothing about the state tax system. Unruh knew a lot. An Assembly committee under his encouragement had prepared a masterful study which showed that the property tax levied by local governments and school districts was far more regressive than the state sales tax, which in California is not levied on food or prescription medicines. Property taxes were getting out of hand because of the rapid increase in the cost of local government services and the vast number of new subdivisions, roads, sewers and schools then being built in California. Unruh's solution was to rebate some of these property taxes from the state, giving himself and the legislature the credit. Brown had failed to realize that a governor, far more visible than any legislator, would gain even greater political credit from such a maneuver. Reagan realized it right away. Without much discussion, the governor and his aides accepted the Unruh solution of paying for property tax relief and balancing the budget by raising state income taxes, then among the lowest of any major state, and also boosting sales, liquor, cigarette and bank-and-corporation taxes. The one serious difference between the governor and the Assembly speaker was over Unruh's advocacy of state income tax withholding, which Reagan opposed with the slogan "taxes should hurt" and the accurate contention that it would be easier for future legislatures to raise income taxes if these taxes were taken out of weekly pay checks rather than paid in a lump sum. Most of the press attention given the tax bill was preoccupied with this sideshow issue instead of the fundamental agreement between Reagan and Unruh over the content of the revenue measure. In a sense, the Reagan tax bill of 1967 worked for exactly the same reasons that his omnibus tax cutting bill was approved by Congress in 1981. In 1967, when governments were still trying to raise taxes to meet anticipated deficits, the net of the Reagan tax bill was widely cast to embrace every legislator's favorite revenue-raising scheme. And lobbyists, traditionally opposed to tax increases, went along, too. "The state needed so much money that every interest group knew it would have to share some of the load," said a big lobbyist of the time.[10]

Reagan was helped, as he had been so many times in his political career, by the division between his principal Democratic opponents. On the tax issue the Senate Democrats were led by George Miller, Jr., a skillful and bitter foe of Unruh. Miller, the finance chairman, refused to accept property tax relief, which made the tax bill more of a contest between the two Democratic-controlled houses than between the legislature and the Reagan administration. Reagan's tax package, contained in a bill by state Senator George Deukmejïan of Long Beach, passed the conservative Senate but languished in the Assembly. Unruh knew he couldn't get his own bill, which contained income tax withholding, out of the Senate over Reagan's opposition. Reagan needed Unruh's help to get anything out of the Assembly. The two men negotiated through their aides, with Reagan circles playing on the hostility between Unruh and Miller. Finally, Unruh agreed to postpone withholding and to accept the Reagan bill in a form amended by Unruh. This measure was sent back to the Senate for concurrence. Unruh then used his considerable political muscle to force the Senate to act. For weeks, he allowed Senate bills to accumulate in the Assembly. The Reagan administration meanwhile kept the pressure on the Senate, going so far as to trade two judgeships with Democratic Senator Alfred E. Alquist. This combination of Reagan administration carrot and Unruh stick finally produced a $1 billion tax bill, by far the largest ever passed in California up to that time.

What had happened is that a combination of Reagan shrewdness and ignorance, Unruh pressure and miscalculation, and a real and perceived need for property tax relief had come together to produce a tax bill which is one of the great ironies of the Reagan administration. It is ironic because the man who said "taxes should hurt" and who had campaigned against the profligacy of the Brown administration had sponsored a tax increase far beyond anything the state needed to balance its books. It is doubly ironic because much of these added taxes came either from corporations or from the upper middle class, both of which overwhelmingly supported Reagan in his two races for governor. Partly this was because Reagan lacked an accurate estimate of the deficit from his own director of finance. Partly it was because the committees in which the bill was written were dominated by bright young staff aides, many of them recruited by Unruh, who were as sophisticated about government as Reagan was unknowledgeable. And partly it was because Reagan, even while still in the learning stage as a politician, realized that the time to win approval of a tax bill was while he was riding the crest of his popularity.

What the tax bill did was to change the state revenue-raising system from a regressive one which took little account of ability to pay to one that had many progressive features. During the Reagan administration corporation taxes nearly doubled, from 5.5 percent to 9 percent. The tax on banks went from 9.5 to 13 percent. The state's share of the sales tax rose from 3 to 4.75 percent. The maximum on personal income taxes rose from 7 percent to

11 percent, and brackets were narrowed to put more persons in a higher tax bracket.*

Reagan's approval of the mammoth tax increases brought with it an unexpected bonus of opposition from the far right and a softening of Reagan's image as a doctrinaire conservative. Most Republicans supported the Reagan tax bill, but the legislature's best known right-winger, state Senator John G. Schmitz of Santa Ana, refused to go along. He resisted all the pressure to vote for the tax bill and instead promoted a book, *Here's the Rest of Him,* written by Kent H. Steffgen with the help of Schmitz's administrative assistant, Warren H. Carroll, which depicted Reagan as a turncoat. "From a governor who campaigned on promises to economize and relieve the tax burden on productive citizens, so that their energies might be released in a 'Creative Society' this kind of tax increase is utterly indefensible," Steffgen wrote. "It hurts most those he promised to help most."[11]

Reagan took this attack from his right wing in stride, aware that it made him seem a "responsible" governor who would not let his ideology get in the way of running the state. Reagan did not view his pragmatism as a retreat from conservative principles, but simply as a practical action which preserved his ability to govern in future years. "Schmitz strikes me as a guy who jumps off the cliff with flags flying," Reagan told me when recalling the episode a year later. "I'm willing to take what I can get."[12] What he got was a government that was fully funded for the first time in four years and a state surplus that opened up new political opportunity. It was more than the vaunted Earl Warren was able to achieve in his first term and more than most California governors had attempted. After the tax bill, Reagan had room to maneuver.

Reagan might have achieved the gubernatorial competence of his second term late in his first except for the homosexual scandal and the 1968 presidential campaign. The bad publicity of the scandal prompted Reagan's personal withdrawal from gubernatorial affairs late in 1967; the presidential campaign preoccupied him for much of 1968 and diverted his attention from pressing state business. Reagan approached the 1968 elections in a contradictory frame of mind which reflected the different opinions among his own advisers about whether he should run for President. During the 1966 campaign Reagan had conveyed the impression that he intended to serve out a full term as governor. But in the spring of 1967, before the country had turned against President Johnson and the Vietnam War, the Republican presidential field appeared to be largely limited to two nonconservatives, George Romney of Michigan and Nelson Rockefeller of New York. Richard Nixon, nine months away from demonstrating his strength in GOP primaries, was widely regarded as having been too damaged by his successive

---

* The figures used here are for the Reagan administration as a whole and include some adjustments made in later tax bills. Most of the basic changes, however, came in the 1967 legislation.

defeats of 1960 and 1962 to be a winner. Reagan had scattered support and Nofziger and Tom Reed argued to the California governor that he should, in a phrase always highly favored by Unruh, "preserve his options." Nofziger had wanted to make Reagan President from the time he first laid eyes on him. Reed's interest was in the national arena. By the time Reed completed the appointments process and left the administration on April 11, he was determined to spent most of 1968 stirring up "spontaneous" support for Reagan around the country. An oil millionaire with both business and political ties, Reed had the time and money to indulge his fancy. He also had the unofficial blessing of Tuttle and Salvatori, both of whom liked the idea of having their favorite communicator in the White House. Salvatori, the most politically conservative of the millionaire backers, carried his zeal for Reagan so far that he tried to talk Rafferty out of running against incumbent Republican Senator Thomas Kuchel in the 1968 primary. Even though Salvatori preferred Rafferty's ultraconservatism to what he regarded as the liberalism of Senator Kuchel, he was concerned that a Rafferty race would revive disunity within the Republican Party and prove harmful to Reagan.* Secure in the knowledge that Tuttle and Salvatori thought he was doing the Lord's work, Reed set to work to create an unauthorized political groundswell for Reagan.

Nofziger did his part. Reagan insisted in private meetings as well as public ones that he was not a candidate, but Nofziger talked him out of making a "Sherman-like" statement which disavowed a presidential candidacy under any circumstances. "Nobody else ever made this statement except Sherman and it wasn't a particularly good idea for him," Reagan said. Nofziger believed that the press, particularly the television press, would assume that Reagan was just being coy and concentrate on his presumed presidential ambitions rather than on what he was as governor. The press obliged, with an enthusiasm which surprised even the press-wise Nofziger.

Reed, meanwhile, was banking on Reagan's desire to please. He knew the governor, out of politeness, if nothing else, was unlikely to close the door completely to visiting supporters who urged him to run for President. So a presidential candidacy was born in Sacramento even though Reagan repeatedly said he was not a candidate and, in fact, did not want to become one. In private conversations with his wife Nancy, his executive secretary William P. Clark and his millionaire backers, Reagan repeatedly disavowed interest in the presidency, even on one occasion when Tuttle said to him, "There's a lot of support for you out there, Ron."[13]

---

* Leland Kaiser, a member of the Kitchen Cabinet, followed up on Salvatori's appeal by warning Rafferty he would have a hard time raising money if he persisted in running. Rafferty ran anyway, ending Kuchel's career by beating him in the 1968 Republican primary and salvaging Alan Cranston's by losing to this veteran Democrat in the general election. Rafferty returned to his nonpartisan post of state superintendent of public instruction after the election, but he was never again close to Reagan or the Kitchen Cabinet.

But the Reagan Presidentialists, as I called them in those days, were initially willing to settle for Reagan's acquiescence because they were convinced that the governor would become more interested as he went along. By mid-1967 Reed had booked Reagan into strategic speaking events throughout the country, with emphasis on presumed Reagan strongholds in the Mountain states, the Plains states and the Deep South. One correspondent, after a southern swing, said that in Dixie the California governor was "the greatest thing to come along since corn pone and hog jowls."[14] Nofziger, meanwhile, strategically distributed airplane schedules showing reporters the best ways to reach out-of-the-way cities in the South and West. Nixon had yet to demonstrate his strength in the 1968 primaries, and the presidential entourage hoped that a showing of interest from the grassroots, however contrived, would convince Reagan to change his mind. Their view was expressed in an October 2, 1967, confidential five-page memo from Jack B. Lindsey, a food-specialty-firm executive who had served as Reagan's liaison with other Republican nominees during the 1966 campaign. The memo recapitulated what had become the conventional wisdom among the Reagan Presidentialists: Nixon was a loser, Nelson Rockefeller couldn't get the nomination, and George Romney had failed to catch fire. "Most politicians do not believe the non-candidate stories being put out by the Reagan camp," Lindsey wrote in the memo, which was addressed to the governor, with copies to Reed, Nofziger and Clark. While many thought that Reagan was playing a "smart non-candidate role *at this time* [emphasis Lindsey's] . . . they all expect to see evidence soon of some national organizing effort." The memo concluded with an exhortation: "Overriding conclusion: the top spot is available for REAGAN, but it will not fall automatically, nor is it the result of a deadlock. It is available by pursuit, and a well-conceived effort can capture the prize."

Reagan failed to approve any all-out effort. Reed and Nofziger, with the help of $440,000 from the millionaire backers, were able to provide the trappings of a national campaign for their favorite son candidate, but they couldn't convince Reagan to openly seek the nomination. "I thought the whole thing was bad chemistry," said Reagan. "My feeling was that to go straight from Hollywood to governor and one year after you were there to be in a position of saying, 'I want to be President of the United States,' there was no way I could do that and be credible."[15]

He was encouraged in his reluctance by Executive Secretary Clark, who thought the presidential campaign diverted Reagan from the governorship at a time he needed to give the job his full attention. Reagan assured Clark, who told everyone who asked and some who didn't, that Reagan would not be a candidate unless he was actually drafted as the nominee. Few in the press believed this, but the *Washington Post*'s David S. Broder accurately conveyed the mood both of Reagan and his Presidentialist entourage in a January 14, 1968, article. "The decision—though compelled by homestate troubles—fits comfortably with Reagan's disposition," Broder wrote. "He is described by his associates as fatalistic almost to the point of naiveté in his belief that events will order themselves. 'Ron honestly believes that God will arrange things for the best,' says one Republican colleague. 'But some of the people who made him governor are willing to give God a hand in making him President, and they're not too happy with the slowdown.' "

To give the Lord a lift, the Presidentialist entourage hired F. Clifton White, who had been the leading light of Goldwater's drive to the nomination and now, according to a friend, wanted to win "by playing exactly the opposite game—nominating a real dark horse who starts out far behind the rest of the field." White tried to circumvent the heavy liability of having a Hamlet as his candidate by encouraging the assumption that Reagan would enter the race at the strategic moment. That time never came, thanks first of all to George Romney and secondly to Nixon. On August 31, 1967, on a Detroit television show, Romney was trying to extricate himself from the image of having a fuzzy position on the Vietnam War, and said: "Well, you know when I came back from Vietnam, I just had the greatest brainwashing that anybody can get when you go over to Vietnam. Not only by the generals, but also by the diplomatic corps over there, and they do a very thorough job." Romney went on to say, long before most people in his party were saying it, that the United States should not be involved in the Vietnam War, but it was the admission of having been successfully brainwashed that stuck. When a Republican poll showed him trailing hopelessly during the New Hampshire primary, Romney withdrew and Nixon rolled to a series of primary victories in which he was largely unopposed. After taking New Hampshire on March 12, Nixon won primaries in Wisconsin, Indiana, Nebraska and West Virginia and approached the free-for-all Oregon primary on May 28 in a position to virtually nail down the nomination.

Reagan, true to his pledge of non-candidacy, had not allowed his name to be placed in nomination anywhere. But in Oregon he was automatically on the ballot unless he filed an affidavit declaring he was not a candidate. Nofziger argued against such an action, saying that it would damage Reagan's credibility the following week when he was a favorite-son candidate in the California primary, which Nixon was not contesting. Reagan bought the argument and said unconvincingly to reporters that he would be "almost committing perjury" if he filed the Oregon affidavit. The absence of such a declaration permitted Bob Hazen, a Portland savings-and-loan executive, to run the first presidential primary campaign of Reagan's career, using the theme that Reagan was "the WINNING candidate for President," and issuing an eight-page supplement on the California governor's supposed accomplishments that proclaimed, "No Problem Is Too Big for Reagan."[16] This ability at problem solving did not include winning the Oregon primary as a non-candidate. Reagan polled a dismal 23 percent of the vote. Nixon had 73 percent.

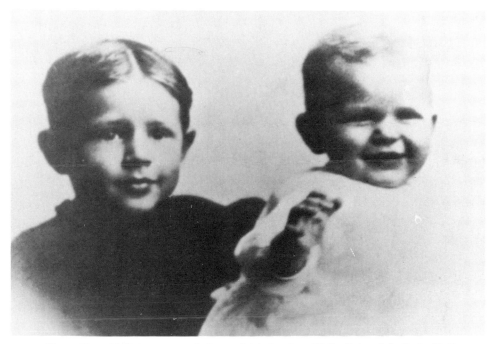

Above, Ronald Reagan as a baby and his brother Neil. *Below left,* Jack, Neil, Ronald and Nelle Reagan. *Below right,* Young Ronald Reagan in Illinois. (*White House photos*)

Above, lifeguard Reagan at Lowell Park in 1931. (*White House photo*)

Above right, Reagan as a football player at Eureka College. (*White House photo*)

Right, Reagan as sportscaster at WHO, Des Moines. (*White House photo*)

Above, with Jane Wyman, Priscilla Lane and Wayne Morris in *Brother Rat* (1938). Reagan and Wyman were engaged soon after completion of this film. *(Copyright © 1938 by Warner Bros. Pictures, Inc. Renewed 1966 by United Artists Television, Inc.)*

Right, Pat O'Brien as Knute Rockne and Reagan as George Gipp in *Knute Rockne, All American* (1940). *(Copyright © 1940 by Warner Bros. Pictures, Inc. Renewed 1966 by United Artists Television, Inc.)*

With Ann Sheridan in *King's Row* (1942), Reagan's most famous picture. In this scene, after his legs have been amputated, Reagan as Drake McHugh was actually sitting down in a hollowed-out section of the fake bed. The bandages were wrapped too tightly, causing Reagan's legs to grow numb and adding, he said afterward, to the sense of realism. (*Copyright © 1942 by Warner Bros. Pictures, Inc. Renewed 1969 by United Artists Television, Inc.*)

Ronald and Nancy Reagan on their wedding day, March 4, 1952, with best man William Holden and matron of honor Ardis Holden. (*White House photo*)

Ronald Reagan takes the oath of office as governor of California on January 3, 1967, with Nancy Reagan looking on. (*United Press International telephoto*)

The Reagans, son Ron and daughter Patti in 1967 (*White House photo*)

With Dwight Eisenhower at the medical center named after him at Palm Springs on March 13, 1967. (*United Press International photo*)

A grim-faced Ronald Reagan announces state of emergency at University of California's Berkeley campus on March 2, 1969. Ed Meese, his executive secretary, is at left, and Alameda County Sheriff Frank Madigan and California Highway Patrol Commissioner H. W. Sullivan at right. (Sacramento Bee *photo by Ward Sharrer*)

Ronald Reagan takes on the protesting students at University of California Regents meeting, February 12, 1967. (*Sacramento Bee photo by Ward Sharrer*)

Anxious aide Lyn Nofziger watches the first ballot voting at Republican convention in Kansas City in 1976, which nominated Gerald Ford. (*Dennis Warren photo*)

The Michael Evans photo of Ronald Reagan that became his official "Reagan Country" campaign poster in 1980. (*Michael Evans/Sygma*)

Despite the magnitude of this defeat, Reagan was comfortably frozen into his rationalization that he was not a presidential candidate as long as he did not call himself one. Since he was not a candidate in his own mind, he did not have to withdraw. He won the favorite-son primary easily in California the following Tuesday, against an underfunded independent delegation with no status in the party, but 52 percent of the voters who participated in the Republican primary skipped the presidential race. All of the interest in that primary was on the Democratic side, where Robert F. Kennedy, Eugene McCarthy and a slate favoring Hubert Humphrey competed for the nomination which had been abandoned by President Johnson. Kennedy won, but lost his life. In the aftermath of this tragedy, Nixon looked like a winner in the November election, even with George Wallace in the race.

Conservatives who wanted to avoid a divisive intraparty struggle now began to pressure Reagan for an endorsement of Nixon. Goldwater, who had discussed the situation with Reagan during Easter week, on June 19 wrote the California governor a blunt letter which declared: "The middle of June has come and I would hasten a very strong guess that Nixon can well win on the first ballot. This, of course, would be guaranteed if a large state such as yours or Texas moved in his direction. I told you at the time [Easter week] that California, which means you, could become the leading power in the Republican Party if Nixon were assured of victory because of a decision on your part to release your delegates together with a statement that your vote would go to Dick. I fully respect and understand why you have refrained from doing this, but the outward reasons for this plan and for this action no longer exist, so a new area of decision now faces you."

Goldwater was referring to an earlier concern expressed by Reagan that his withdrawal would leave the path clear to nomination of a nonconservative. The Arizona senator was none too gently reminding Reagan that the shoe was now on the other foot, and that it was Reagan who had the capacity to split the conservative forces and make it possible for that hated moderate Nelson Rockefeller to win the nomination. Though Goldwater's appeal was well conceived, the letter did not, for a variety of reasons, accomplish its purpose. One reason was that some of Reagan's own staunch supporters did not really regard Nixon as a conservative, even though they approved of most of what he was saying in 1968. Another was that Nixon was more politically tarnished in California than in other states as a result of his defeat by Governor Brown in 1962. Apart from Reagan's own self-interest, there were many in the governor's entourage, including Nofziger and several of the millionaire backers, who doubted whether Nixon would be a successful candidate in November. After all this is weighed, I am convinced—although Reagan remembers it otherwise—that the California governor had now been smitten unawares by the romance of running for President. He did not ever actively seek the nomination. But he allowed himself to be persuaded that he would lose all bargaining power at the convention as California's favorite son if he took himself out of the race beforehand. This argument was too weak to convince anyone who did not have at least a remote interest in becoming President. It convinced Reagan.

In his new role as a non-candidate candidate, Reagan cultivated southern support by refusing to criticize the segregationist advocacies of Alabama Governor George Wallace, who was then launching his own campaign for President. On the advice of Clif White, who pointed out that a frontal attack on Wallace would not sit well with southern Republicans, Reagan acted as if Wallace's views on race were a mystery and not a particularly important one at that. On July 16, three days before he launched a southern speaking tour, reporters finally pinned Reagan down on his differences with Wallace and were told: "On his past record and as a governor he showed no opposition particularly to great programs of federal aid and spending programs and so forth. Right at the moment he's dwelling mainly on law and order, patriotism, and so forth, and these are attractive subjects, and I'm sure that there are very few people in disagreement and I think this perhaps is responsible for some of the gains he's made."

On the flight through the South, I asked Reagan whether he was actively seeking the racist vote. "We don't get the racist vote," he replied. "We don't want it. Neither party wants it." But he did not share this sentiment with audiences of Republican national convention delegates he addressed in Amarillo, Little Rock, Charlottesville (Va.), Frankfort (Ky.) and Birmingham, with a stopover at the National Governors Conference in Cincinnati. Reed quipped that the trip was "more of a southern solicitation than a southern strategy," and he was kidding on the square. Delegates in every state left me with the impression that Reagan was their emotional first choice but that the California governor's official non-candidacy had persisted for so long that Nixon had become their intellectual commitment. The Nixon operatives had done their work well, locking up most of the important politicians in the South and making a suggestive argument that a vote for Reagan would in reality end up as a vote for Rockefeller. Everywhere Reagan spoke he roused audiences to the fervor they had felt when they heard "A Time For Choosing" in 1964. But he came out of the South without having improved his chance for the nomination.

Reagan now was urged to follow an alternative course, which might have made him the Republican hero of 1968, if not the nominee. It was urged most persuasively, with Clark's encouragement, by Rus Walton, the Reagan program development specialist who had painful memories of the Goldwater campaign.* In a July 31 six-page memo, Walton warned of the danger of Reagan being caught up in a campaign that would "split the

---

* Walton was an ardent supporter of Goldwater in 1964, and the producer of a controversial campaign documentary, *Choice,* which was withdrawn after a press preview because of objections to the way the film portrayed President Johnson.

conservative forces" and allow "wrecker" Rockefeller to become the Republican nominee. Walton proposed a hard count on the eve of the convention. If this showed Nixon a first-ballot winner, then Reagan should allow himself to be nominated, arise to a point of personal privilege and "with the eyes of the nation upon him . . . decline the nomination and urge his people to vote for Nixon."

But Reagan had been persuaded by White that he had hidden strength in the southern delegations bound to Nixon under the unit rule. Had the delegates not cheered him? Had they not asked him to be an active candidate? What would happen if he became one? The California favorite-son delegation which Reagan headed had been carefully balanced between Nixon and anti-Nixon forces. Would even his own Californians follow him unanimously if Reagan told them in his convention speech to the delegation that he actively was a candidate for the Republican presidential nomination? Reagan did not know the answers to these questions. Though he is a splendid politician by instinct, the mechanics of politics have always bored him, and he did not have an accurate appreciation of the delegate strength which Nixon had accumulated. At the moment Reagan was considering his course, big Bill Knowland,* the former U.S. senator, came to him with a political judgment which had not improved since he elbowed Goodwin Knight aside and made possible the California Democratic landslide of 1958. Knowland had just visited Ohio Governor James Rhodes, also a favorite son, who was trying to figure out a way to keep the convention open. If Reagan became an active candidate, Knowland said, then Rhodes' own favorite-son candidacy would be more credible. By all inside accounts of which I am aware, including Reagan's, the Knowland advocacy tipped the scale toward the course which Reagan had been emotionally favoring. "I felt I was running the risk of becoming a Stassen joke," Reagan told me two months after the convention. "I was keeping my fingers crossed because I was afraid of a battle inside our delegation if I did [announce my candidacy]. When I got the word that it was unanimous for me, it did make it easier. I was getting edgy in having to address all these delegations and tell them that I would be a candidate when my name was placed in nomination and they could so consider me at that time."[17]

So, Reagan told the California delegation that he was, in fact, a candidate for the Republican presidential nomination. It was an announcement which angered the Nixon forces in the delegation, led by Lieutenant Governor Robert H. Finch, and disappointed Reagan supporters back in California who by then favored a united effort for Nixon. The belated declaration of candidacy bewildered Nancy Reagan, who for perhaps the only time in her married life was not well clued in on what her husband was doing. She heard the announcement over the radio as she was preparing to give an in-

---

* Knowland died on February 23, 1974.

terview. "I was the most surprised person in the world when it happened," she said afterward.[18]

Viewed in cold political terms, Reagan's romantic non-candidacy of 1968 seemed a mistake at the time. His last-minute plunge at the convention was clearly a mistake, for despite White's will-o'-the-wisp claim that eight votes would have unlocked the unit rule in three southern states and opened the door for Reagan, Nixon had the nomination nailed down by the time the Miami Beach convention opened. Reagan was able to salvage only a shred of Walton's bold strategy by striding to the podium shortly after 2 A.M. on August 8 to urge that the convention "declare itself unanimously and unitedly behind the candidate Richard Nixon as the next President of the United States." To those who wondered why Reagan had not done this earlier, on prime time, and spared himself the agony of being counted out, Reagan's friend, columnist William F. Buckley, had a ready answer. "It was projected by Republican conservatives in the summer of 1967 that steps should be taken to guard against the possibility of a collapse by Nixon in the primaries," Buckley wrote. "Accordingly, friends of Ronald Reagan asked him to stand by, and contrived the favorite-son facade to spare him the embarrassment of an unbecomingly precipitate ambitiousness. What then happened is what so often happens in politics. Contingent operations become vested interests. The royalist passions of the entourage take over, and before long the principal is carried along into the vortex without the rationale he had been promised to hang on to."[19]

This was a large part of the answer, but not all of it. At times during the summer of 1968, the "royalist passions" also seized Reagan and rushed him to a brink which his best instincts told him to avoid. But these instincts had been sufficiently strong most of the time to prevent the kind of active candidacy which might have split the party and damaged Reagan for future seasons. Often Reagan knows more about his limitations than he lets on to others. Years later he told me that he felt a "sense of relief" when Nixon was nominated. Late that summer he confided to Michael Deaver an even more fundamental feeling. "I wasn't ready to be President," he said. What he was ready for was a long rest. Borrowing a yacht from some of his millionaire friends, Reagan and Nancy cruised the Florida Keys for a long weekend after the convention. "I averaged sleeping 14 hours at night and then I would take a nap in the afternoon," said Reagan. "We both felt the same way."[20]

In retrospect, it is not so clear that the 1968 presidential campaign, "bad chemistry" and all, was really a mistake for Reagan. In fact, it is possible to argue that he would have not have wound up President without it. Jimmy Carter excepted, most modern politicians who have traveled the path to the presidency arrive there after cultivating a long familiarity with the electorate. Frequently this effort is a precondition for later success, and often it involves an unsuccessful attempt to secure a place on the national ticket. John

F. Kennedy's well-organized try for the vice-presidency at the 1956 Democratic convention failed but helped establish him as a logical contender for 1960. Goldwater's stirring speech for Nixon at the 1960 convention, in which he directed his own following to loyally support the nominee, gave the Arizonan a running start for 1964. Many of those whom Reagan roused in 1968 remembered him eight years later, and followed his banner to Kansas City and beyond. Reagan came out of Miami Beach a loser. But his losing had helped prepare him for the victories which lay ahead.

13

The Reformer

ON August 4, 1970, Governor Reagan sent a confidential memo to his cabinet and senior staff which revealed his true feelings about those who depended on the state of California for their well-being. Announcing a study of the state's public assistance and education programs, Reagan wrote: "This study will place heavy emphasis on the tax-payer as opposed to the tax-taker; on the truly needy as opposed to the lazy unemployable; on the student as opposed to educational frills; on basic needs as opposed to unmanageable enrichment programs; on measurable results as opposed to blind faith that an educator can do no wrong."[1] The memo, drafted for Reagan by Edwin Meese, was the governor's call to action for the welfare reform legislation that would become the dominant issue of his second term. Looking beyond the coming election, it called for recommendations by January 1971 that would propose administrative remedies, suggest a long-range legislative program, pinpoint problems with the federal government and make local government more accountable. "I am determined to reduce these programs to essential services at a cost the tax-payers can afford to pay," Reagan concluded the memo. "This is our NUMBER ONE priority. We must bring all our resources to bear on this endeavor. Therefore, I am asking you to make available your best employees including directors for this all-out war on the tax-taker. If we fail, no one ever again will be able to try. We must succeed."[2]

Such apocalyptic rhetoric might have been suited for a commando raid or, at best, a meeting of the Young Republicans; its presence in a cabinet memorandum reflected Reagan's growing realization in the final year of his first term that he was a long way from accomplishing the bold goals of his inaugural message. As the memo recognized, the Reagan administration had braked the growth of government in some areas but had failed to do anything about welfare and educational costs, "which are virtually out of our realm of authority because of outmoded constitutional and statutory requirements and federal laws and regulations." By any standard, after nearly four years in office, Reagan's achievements were modest ones. After his initial fling at across-the-board budget cutting, he had become a fairly orthodox governor who had restored funds for higher education and provided money for a community mental health treatment program. A year into his administration, he had rid himself of Gordon Smith and brought in knowledgeable Caspar W. Weinberger as his finance director, this time with no protest from the Kitchen Cabinet. He had replaced Battaglia with William P. Clark, who turned out to be an able executive secretary, and after Clark's departure to a judgeship, had brought in Meese. The top appointments in the Reagan administration were faulted by some critics for a probusiness bias, but generally accorded high marks for competence. The administration's environmental record had in many aspects pleasantly surprised conservationists, thanks largely to the abilities of Reagan's natural resources administrator, Norman (Ike) Livermore, and his parks and recreation director, William Penn Mott, Jr. Reagan had blocked an environmentally damaging high dam at Dos Rios on grounds that it would have violated a treaty with the Indians who lived there. He had approved some mild prison reforms, including a program which permitted conjugal visits in some instances. He had allowed the creation of a Department of Consumer Protection. Except for the "homosexual scandal," there was not the suggestion of taint in any aspect of the administration. Even Reagan's stern law-and-order rhetoric had been tempered by reality: he had refused to stay the execution of one murderer who appealed to him for clemency, but he had spared another on grounds that the killer may have suffered from brain damage.* All in all, Reagan's record as governor had been moderate and responsible but undistinguished. He had failed, after the 1967 tax bill, to get his most cherished programs through the legislature. He was running for reelection as much on the record of not having done the terrible things predicted by his opponents as on the record of what he had actually accomplished.

Nevertheless, Reagan had definite reasons for satisfaction as he contemplated the future in the late summer of 1970. His cabinet and staff, under a

---

* Aaron Mitchell, 37, was executed on April 12, 1967, for the killing of a Sacramento policeman during an armed robbery. Governor Brown, a foe of capital punishment, earlier had refused to grant clemency to Mitchell, but the state Supreme Court had granted him a new trial at which he again was sentenced to death. After accepting the recommendation of legal affairs secretary Edwin Meese and refusing to grant clemency, Reagan told reporters: "In this particular instance the man, the father of two children, who was killed was a policeman. I think that if we are going to ask men to engage in an occupation in which they protect us at the risk of their life, we . . . have an obligation to let them know that society will do whatever it can to minimize the danger of their occupation. I think any policeman is entitled to that. There are no bands playing or flags flying when he shoots it out with a criminal on our behalf." Subsequently, Reagan spared the life of Calvin Thomas, who had killed the baby of his girl friend by hurling a fire bomb into her home. Those were the only capital punishment decisions which came before Reagan because the state Supreme Court on December 7, 1976, struck down California's capital punishment statute. To the disappointment of Reagan, the opinion was written by Chief Justice Donald Wright, whom Reagan had appointed to the Supreme Court.

reorganization engineered by Meese, were finally functioning as a team. Unlike many governors, he had a blueprint for action in his second term, one born both of his ideology and of his recognition that the state faced a new spending crunch in 1971. By 1970 the dividends of the overly generous 1967 tax bill had been expanded, and the legislature passed what was actually a deficit budget in which the shortfall was made up by transfers from other funds. "Welfare and its voracious accomplice—Medi-Cal—have dragged California to the brink of fiscal disaster," said Reagan's human resources secretary, Lucian B. Vandergrift, an aide who lacked the gift of understatement.[3] Reagan's tax bill was turned down by the 1970 legislature, and a variety of conflicting educational financing measures were also rejected. Though the mood was less desperate than it had been in 1967, fiscal management, Reagan's favorite issue, was once again dominant in Sacramento.

Few truly difficult political decisions were made in the shadow of an election, and the do-little legislature of 1970 reflected this political axiom. One of the many ironies of the eight Reagan years in Sacramento was that the governor was in most respects least successful during the only two years—1969 and 1970—that he enjoyed a Republican majority in both houses. Much of this was Reagan's own fault. Though he had discarded some of his initial stereotypes about legislators, he didn't enjoy spending his social time with people whose talk was apt to be about politics, power and sexual prowess. Furthermore, he lacked a close relationship with Assembly Speaker Robert T. Monagan, the able Republican who had become Assembly speaker after Jesse Unruh stepped down in 1969. Monagan had been a Christopher supporter in 1966, quipping that "Ireland lies closest to Greece." He considered Reagan more of a citizen than a politician and thought that the men around him were even less political than the governor.* Reflecting a court-ordered reapportionment, the state Senate was also changing in ways not especially helpful to Reagan programs. The reapportionment had ended the traditional "cow county" domination of the upper house, making the Senate slightly more liberal even as it became more Republican. But it was still a more cautious legislative body than the Assembly, and it was especially cautious in that election year of 1970 when Sacramento awaited the outcome of the confrontation between citizen-politician Reagan and master-legislator Unruh.

There are no boyhood photographs of Jesse Marvin Unruh, the most important state legislator of this century. He grew up poor in Kansas and Texas, and his family was too busy finding food and clothes and schooling for the children to have a camera. Unlovely to look at and crude and pro-

---

* Reagan and Monagan shared an Irish temper and a distrust of one another. Once, at the governor's house, Reagan asked Monagan why a Republican assemblyman critical of Reagan was "acting like a prick." "You can't call my friend a prick," responded Monagan. "Then he should stop acting like one," Reagan said.

fane in many of his ways, Unruh was nonetheless as remarkable an American success story as Ronald Reagan. As a child, Unruh was overweight, undernourished, out of place. He spoke with a lisp, which to all but the best teachers concealed a restless, inquiring intelligence that was matched by a driving ambition to better himself. Overcoming his speech handicap, he migrated to California in 1940 and talked his way past Navy recruiters despite flat feet and low blood pressure. After the war he enrolled at the University of Southern California on the GI Bill, studying journalism and political science. Classwork bored him, but he was smart, was good with figures, and had a passion for politics. At twenty-four he won an election representing veterans on the campus, presenting himself as a rank-and-filer opposing a privileged candidate who favored fraternities. Out of school, he drifted between odd jobs. Always, he worked in Democratic political campaigns, helping himself by helping others.

At thirty-two Unruh won a state Assembly seat. In Sacramento he was assigned an out-of-the-way office next to the cafeteria and left to learn. He was brash, inquisitive, fun-loving and eager for the hard-drinking, free-wheeling legislative life. He liked liquor and good clothes and women, and these were available in Sacramento as they had never been in his earlier life. He was also a valuable legislator. Though he frequently would lose his temper when he lost a bill and could be a bully as a committee chairman, he remembered his origins. In his early years he put his name and stamp on a civil rights bill and on a measure to curb loan sharks. Always, however, he sought the levers of power. He cultivated the rich and powerful in the legislature and the lobbyists, known as the Third House, who supported them. He was a keen observer, and he found that the legislature was far less organized than it looked from the outside. At election time each assemblyman would cut his own deal with the lobbyists for campaign funds.

Unruh found the system demeaning and wasteful. When his good friend, oil lobbyist Charles R. Stevens, talked to him about a campaign contribution in 1956, Unruh suggested that he give the money to "good guys" in neighboring districts and tell them where it came from. This arrangement was the start of Unruh's power, and the source of it. He guided contributions to candidates when they were starting out and most in need of money, and he had an eye for the candidate who was likely to win. Soon a formidable coterie of Unruh-assisted legislators inhabited the state Assembly. They knew that Unruh spoke literally when he uttered the words which became his trademark and his albatross, "Money is the mother's milk of politics." Fondly, they named their leader "Big Daddy" after a supposed resemblance to the domineering father in *Cat On A Hot Tin Roof.* In 1961, at the age of thirty-nine, Unruh was elected speaker of the Assembly by these grateful legislators. By now Unruh had struck myriad bargains with the Third House, and many of the lobbyists followed his instructions on contributions. It was heady power for the poor boy from Texas, but his personal sense of security did not match his influence. "I'm still not sure I'm not going to wake up someday and be on a small farm out there in Texas,"[4] he told an old friend at a time when newspapers and other politicians were describing Unruh as the most powerful politician in the state.

When Unruh reached the top, he remembered what it was like on the bottom and tried to change the system. Traditionally, legislators had been dependent on lobbyists for their information. Unruh changed that, providing his colleagues with a well-funded research and staffing operation that became a model for state legislatures. He pushed through a constitutional revision which ignored most of the thorniest problems of the unwieldy state constitution but gave legislators the power to raise their own salaries. Taken as a whole, Unruh's reforms brought the California legislature into the twentieth century and encouraged this trend in many other states. For all his wheeling and dealing with lobbyists, Unruh did more than any legislator to free colleagues from dependence on the Third House. It is an enduring achievement.

But as a candidate for governor against Reagan, Unruh was afflicted with enormous political liabilities. Though eleven years younger than Reagan, Unruh had been in partisan politics longer, and his name was synonymous to many people with political manipulation. Unruh's public image had been forged in 1963, when at the height of his power he imperiously locked up Republicans in the Assembly chambers because they refused to vote on the state budget unless Unruh would first let them see a pending education bill. The tactic backfired, in full view of the voters. Republican assemblymen sent out for sandwiches and took turns denouncing Unruh as power-mad "Big Daddy" whose authority had gone to his head. The refrain was taken up in the press. Unruh backed down, but he never lived down the public impression he had created. Trying to change his image after the lock-up, Unruh dieted strenuously, reducing from more than 280 pounds to less than 200. It helped him physically, but not politically. When Reagan ran for reelection in 1970, he ran not against Jesse Unruh but against "Big Daddy."

Unlike Reagan, Unruh had to wage a primary campaign. His one serious opponent was Samuel Yorty, who four years earlier had ruined Pat Brown's chances. By 1970, however, the Los Angeles mayor had climbed into too many rings and taken too many political punches. He was an ideal opponent for Unruh, who was out of favor with organization Democrats except in comparison with the party-baiting Yorty. Relying on anti-Yorty sentiment and the knowledge that regular Democrats preferred Unruh to the mayor, Unruh won without spending a dime on billboards or television advertising. When the votes in the Democratic primary were counted, Unruh had 64 percent of them compared to 26 percent for Yorty and 10 percent for eight other candidates.

Unruh's strategy for running against Reagan was to portray him as a rich man's governor who was the tool of the "half-hidden millionaires" who had financed Reagan's gubernatorial and presidential campaigns. Running against "the interests" has been a well-worn theme in California ever since the initial success of Hiram Johnson. Unruh believed that a campaign waged on the theme of "Reagan, Tool of the Rich," would attract some of the blue-collar voters who had deserted the Democratic Party in 1966. As a strategy, this idea was not without promise. The 1970 property tax relief bill, which Unruh's Democrats had blocked in the Assembly, did offer substantially larger tax breaks to wealthy and upper middle class Californians than it did to those in lower tax brackets. But since the bill had failed to become law, the issue was not a burning one with the voters. Polls taken for Reagan showed that most voters had only a dim idea of the specific provisions of the legislation.

Unruh's other principal campaign goal was to force Reagan into a debate. He believed that in any face-to-face confrontation he could show up the governor despite Reagan's demonstrated skills on television. Reagan's aides thought so, too. No one in the Reagan camp, including the governor, entertained the slightest notion of getting into a debate with the knowledgeable Unruh. Reagan started from a position of strength, and was a cautious candidate much of the way. Tom Reed, running the campaign from a secret office called "the Bomb Shelter" five blocks from the official Reagan headquarters on Western Avenue in Los Angeles, hyped up the Reagan record while simultaneously trying to revive the memories of "Big Daddy" in the minds of the voters. No one knows how successful he would have been on his own. As it turned out, he had significant help from Unruh himself.

California campaigns traditionally begin on Labor Day, which on September 7, 1970, dawned bright and sunny in Los Angeles. Up early, Unruh stood outside the Bel-Air mansion of Henry Salvatori, a principal Reagan contributor, explaining to two busloads of reporters who filled the narrow street that Salvatori stood to receive $4,113 in property tax relief from the governor's tax bill. Salvatori's house was valued at $700,000, Unruh said, and every renter in the state with an annual income of $8,000 or less would be paying $25 to the "Henry Salvatori tax relief fund." The trip to Salvatori's home was intended to demonstrate how Reagan's friends did well for themselves by doing good for the governor. The Salvatori mansion was supposed to be a vacant backdrop that would provide a useful television prop. Unfortunately for Unruh, his advance men had failed to discover that the Salvatoris were not away for the day as Unruh believed. Tipped off by a neighbor, an angry Grace Salvatori was standing behind a closed iron gate awaiting Unruh's arrival. Soon she was joined by her husband, in tennis garb, who refused Unruh's proffered hand through the gate and said, "Is this the way you have to get your publicity? You have to get it at a private home? It's the most ridiculous campaign trick." Then the Salvatoris came outside the gate while Unruh, with charts and easel, delivered his pitch in the driveway. When Unruh brought up the $4,113 "tax break," Salvatori interrupted, "Oh, you ass you, stop being so silly." When Unruh mentioned the "Henry Salvatori tax relief fund," the industrialist looked squarely at him and said scornfully, "You're a liar, Mr. Unruh." Grace Salvatori joined the fray, outshouting either of the men. "We worked for the money to pay for it," she said of the house. "We pay taxes, and we support every university in this state, practically." In response to Unruh's charge that he benefited from tax loopholes, Salvatori told reporters: "I have no tax loopholes. I earned my money. If he's trying to imply that I supported Reagan to get a $4,000 tax relief, he's stupid."

Unruh finally retreated, to begin a four-day campaign swing. That night his staff members were excited because, as one young aide said, "We had made the national news."[5] Unruh had indeed done that. His invasion of the Salvatoris' privacy was the lead story in the *Los Angeles Times* and in most other papers of the state. It was big on television, too. And Unruh never recovered from the impact. In a single stroke Unruh had revived the image of "Big Daddy," the domineering political bully who had no respect for the rights of others. When Hiram Johnson and his imitators had campaigned against the special interests, they had done so by depersonalizing the corporation and by depicting their adversaries as monsters or machines. Unwittingly, Unruh had done the opposite. Instead of campaigning against anonymous "half-hidden millionaires" who were supposed to be pulling Reagan's strings, Unruh had personalized the forces he was supposed to be depersonalizing. Californians value both their holidays and their privacy, and they identified with the nice-looking elderly couple whose castle had been invaded on a holiday by the dread Unruh. Rarely has a self-inflicted wound so thoroughly undermined what might have been a promising campaign.

Jesse Unruh has many virtues, but one of them is not the ability to readily acknowledge mistakes. The day after his disastrous campaign opening he launched an undignified pursuit of Reagan, determined to force him into a debate. He missed the governor, however, at the San Jose Airport, and the following day changed his schedule so he could picket the Reagan residence in Sacramento. Again Reagan was away, though the governor told reporters who were with him in Southern California that he had an opponent who "paid house calls." Unruh was rapidly becoming a laughing stock. Late in the week he blundered again, saying that an appointee of Reagan's was being rewarded for work his father had done in the 1968 Reagan presidential campaign. This time Unruh had to acknowledge he was wrong and issue an apology. The Reagan appointee's father had been dead for ten years.

At this point Reagan could be excused for being overconfident, which he was. Speaking to reporters at the San Jose airport where Unruh had unsuccessfully tried to find him, Reagan said that his opponent's visit to Salvatori's home had been "very unseemly." When Unruh compounded his problems by picketing the governor's residence in Sacramento two days later, Reagan saw his opportunity and used it as an excuse to avoid a debate he had already rejected. "One thing my opponent has done is make it clear I was right in refusing to debate him," Reagan told reporters in Santa Rosa on September 9. "His idea of debate obviously is cheap demagoguery." Reagan also refused to disclose his assets, as Unruh had done, saying that this would be "an invasion of privacy" and adding, "I have no conflict of interest whatsoever."

In the early weeks of his campaign Reagan appeared to be a safe, front-running candidate, defending his record before safe, friendly crowds with safe, defensible statements. The complacency of the Reagan campaign bothered Reed and his loyal cadre in the Bomb Shelter. Reed was worried that the lagging economy would push blue-collar workers into the Democratic column even if Unruh wasn't able to get them there on his own. The strategy of the Reagan campaign was to direct the dissatisfaction of these potential Democratic voters to some other target than the governor—in this case the "welfare cheats" Reagan liked to denounce.

Always most comfortable in the role of citizen-politician, Reagan campaigned as if he were going to Sacramento to clean up a mess someone else had left behind. "Welfare," said Reagan repeatedly, "is the greatest domestic problem facing the nation today and the reason for the high cost of government."

Unruh, heavily outspent and shaken by the reaction to his blundering beginning, did not give up. He stuck to his campaign theme throughout, repeatedly trying to provoke the governor into a personal exchange. During a Watts speech Unruh said that Reagan's millionaire backers "don't need a governor because they can buy the governor's house and probably even the governor."[6] Unruh's television commercials, what he had of them, were well made and sounded the same theme less shrilly than the candidate. His young campaign management team, inexperienced in a state-wide race, started weakly but improved as the campaign went along. The Unruh advance operation, however, remained a source of embarrassment to the candidate from beginning to end. "We were thinking of having Jesse kidnapped to create some sympathy," quipped an Unruh aide during the final week of the campaign. "But we canceled the plan because we were afraid the advance men would go to the wrong house and kidnap the wrong man."[7]

Reagan and Reed, meanwhile, capitalized on the lingering resentments of the Pat Brown wing of the Democratic Party. Elements of organized labor had never forgiven Unruh for what they regarded as his sabotage of Brown programs in the legislature. These labor leaders, including the then influential Joseph T. DeSilva, head of the 25,000-member Retail Clerks 770 in Los Angeles, were persuaded to organize a labor committee for Reagan. The Reagan fund-raising operation also stroked former business contributors to Brown, convincing some of them to donate to the Reagan campaign. Reagan didn't need the money, but Reed saw to it that stories about defections were given to the papers, fostering the impression that a bipartisan consensus was building for the governor.

Reagan took it easy, his managers and Nancy Reagan mindful of what had happened to him when he became overtired in 1966. But reporters who had covered Reagan in both campaigns found him a more polished performer the second time around. When pickets showed up in Modesto bearing a sign, "Get Lost Ronnie," Reagan gave a good account of himself. "In 1966 the novice Reagan would have given them a dirty look, waved shyly to his supporters and then hustled into his car to get away from it all," wrote Bill Boyarsky in the *Los Angeles Times.* "Not the 1970 model Ronald Reagan. He walked directly to the fence, shook a few friendly hands and when the unfriendly people began to heckle them, he heckled them back." Along with this new polish came occasional hints that the citizen-politician had learned something about politics. When a South Gate worker yelled at him, "When are you going to clean up politics?" Reagan answered, "Politics is far more honest than you may think."

This was a new perception for Reagan. It showed that the citizen-politician, despite his strategy of running as if he were outside government, recognized that he was, in fact, governor of the nation's most populous state. And Reagan also recognized, as Pat Brown had failed to do four years earlier, that voters wanted to hear what their governor was going to do for them, not what he had done. Reagan told them. As he had promised in 1966 to clean up "the mess in Berkeley," Reagan now pledged to clean up "the welfare mess," about which he had done little for four years. "Public assistance should go to the needy and not the greedy," Reagan said, as he exploited a popular issue and built support for the welfare reform plan he would present to the legislature. Reagan also emerged in the campaign as the optimistic defender of his own generation against youthful critics of American materialism. Speaking to 750 business and agricultural leaders in Sacramento, Reagan said, "We have never been more prosperous, or more generous with our prosperity, never more truly concerned with the welfare of the less fortunate, with education and equality of opportunity, never more determined to bring decency and order to the world. It is time we ended our obsession with what is wrong and realize how much is right, how great is our power and how little we really have to fear."

At the end, as happens in California political campaigns, there were the inevitable wild charges and strained appeals to the worst instincts of the electorate. Unruh, posing for a picture with a girl on either side, recalled the homosexual scandal and said with a smile: "We used to have a saying in Sacramento in those days. Prove you're straight and take a girl to lunch."[8] Reagan, employing a preplanned tactic designed to look spontaneous, attacked Unruh by name in the final week of the campaign. Instead of replying to his challenger, however, he brought up an old charge of his own, claiming that Unruh had misrepresented his interest in a Long Beach apartment building. Stung by the repeated attacks on his millionaire friends, Reagan also called Unruh "a demagogue," "a hypocrite," "dishonest" and "a man who has no regard for the truth."[9]

Back in the Bomb Shelter, the Reagan polls showed Unruh closing ground in the final weeks as Democratic voters returned to the fold. Reading these polls and hearing the reports from the field, Reed was thankful that Unruh had stumbled badly at the start and didn't have more money for commercials.* In the final week of the campaign, Reed couldn't wait for election day.

For different reasons, millions of Americans probably shared Reed's feelings. Even by the most rough-and-tumble standards of Nixon-era politics, the election of 1970 was raw. It featured Vice-President Spiro T. Agnew on the stump for "law and order" and the defeat of "radiclibs" in a strident attempt to change the composition of the Senate. President Nixon added a strident note of his own after his motorcade was bombarded with rocks and bottles following a speech in San Jose the Thursday night before the election. Going on the attack before a Republican rally in Phoenix, Nixon proclaimed that Americans had "appeased aggression here at home" and created further violence. "The time has come for the great silent majority of Americans of all ages and of every political persuasion, to stand up and be counted against appeasement of the rock throwers and the obscenity shouters," Nixon said. Reagan's friend Senator George Murphy, running for reelection and present with Nixon in San Jose, was confident the stoning had helped his reelection chances. Reagan, also at the San Jose rally, wasn't so sure. "Violence never helps anyone," he said afterward, before issuing his own denunciation of the rock throwers.

The elections of 1970 were a setback for the Nixon administration and the Republican Party, but a ratification for Reagan. The governor won a second term with 3,439,664 votes and 52.9 percent of the total to Unruh's 2,938,607 votes and 45.1 percent. Candidates for the left-wing Peace and Freedom Party and the right-wing American Independent Party almost evenly divided the other 2 percent of the vote. But Reagan's reelection, along with Rockefeller's unprecedented fourth-term victory in New York, was one of the few big races that Republicans could cheer about. Agnew's purge attempt had failed, with Republicans gaining only two Senate seats and losing nine in the House. Except for California and New York, the gubernatorial races were even more disastrous for the Republicans than they

---

* Primary and general election expenditures filed with the California secretary of state, as reported by *California Journal* of December 1970, showed that Reagan spent $3,550,549 in the primary and general elections and Unruh $1,207,684. It worked out to $1.05 a vote for Reagan and 42 cents a vote for Unruh. The actual discrepancy was even greater than these figures showed, since Reagan did not have a primary opponent and also, in his position as governor, received more "free television" from coverage of legitimate news events than Unruh did.

had been for the Democrats four years earlier. The GOP lost eleven state houses. In California, John V. Tunney defeated Senator Murphy by a margin exceeding Reagan's. And Reed's fears about a Democratic comeback in blue-collar districts proved justified. Democrats picked up three seats in the Assembly and two in the state Senate, winning control of both houses. The Democratic gains were most conspicuous in working class precincts, where Reagan ran ahead of the GOP ticket but less strongly than in 1966. There had been a Reagan victory but not a Republican one.

Reagan's mandate was reduced, but his sense of purpose was keener and his goals more focused in his second term. Instead of waging a vague war on government programs of all kinds, Reagan now proposed a focused battle for what he saw as welfare reform. This time he had reliable information from the Department of Finance where Verne Orr had replaced Caspar Weinberger, who went on to become Nixon's budget director. Since August, a fifteen-member task force of state officials and private citizens headed by Ned Hutchinson, the governor's appointments secretary, had been reviewing federal, state and county problem areas in welfare. A primary focus of the review was the much maligned program of Aid to Families with Dependent Children (AFDC). Unless this program was curbed, Orr warned the governor and Meese, a huge tax increase would be necessary in fiscal 1972.

AFDC began its existence as a minor section of the Social Security Act of 1935. It was designed to strengthen "mothers' pensions," state programs to support children whose fathers were disabled or had abandoned their families. The federal government shared the costs, indirectly encouraging benefit increases by the states, but Congress left the determination of benefits to the states themselves. In California, this determination had not been beneficial to AFDC recipients under either Democratic or Republican administrations. Despite the Democratic ruckus about Reagan's supposed lack of compassion, AFDC grants had not been raised a penny in Pat Brown's eight years, during six of which the Democrats controlled the legislature. The grants hadn't been raised in Reagan's first four years, either. The result was that AFDC recipients had suffered a considerable decline in real income since their last increase in 1957. According to the state Department of Welfare, the minimum monthly income required for a subsistence existence by a family of three in San Francisco was $271 in 1971. The maximum such an AFDC family could be paid was $172.

These were not the figures which concerned Reagan, though he did take them into account in designing his welfare plan. What alarmed the governor and his top aides was the soaring increase in AFDC caseload. In 1963, there had been 375,000 AFDC recipients. By 1967, when Reagan took office, that number had doubled to 769,000. By December 1969 the AFDC rolls totaled 1,150,687. A year later, a month after Reagan's reelection, the total had reached 1,566,000. AFDC caseload was increasing by 40,000 a month, and Orr warned that a continued increase of this magnitude would bust the budget in 1972. Reagan conceded after the election that a deepening recession had contributed to the problem. "But the big villain . . . that has kept all of our savings from being returned to the people in reduced cost of government is the thirty-five-year heritage of welfare programs that are out of control . . . ," Reagan said in a December 16, 1970, interview with *California Journal*. "And we find ourselves in a position of cutting back on the type of things people should ask of government—parks and everything else—to feed this welfare monster."

The "monster" grew throughout the first two months of 1971 as the task force completed its recommendations. Robert B. Carleson, a former small-town city manager who would ultimately become the state welfare director and then U.S. commissioner of welfare, assumed a leading role. So did Meese, who was emerging as the leading Reagan policy formulator. However, for the first time in a detailed and substantive way Reagan played a major role in the fiscal proceedings of his own administration. During the first term he had intervened with political skill on the tuition issue and had realistically accepted the need of a tax increase. But on most issues of public policy his contribution had been strictly rhetorical. This changed with the proposal which became the California Welfare Reform act of 1971.

Reagan's reforms were presented in a lengthy report to the legislature containing seventy specific proposals for changes, basically the work of the task force put into political form.* Reagan called his proposal the "lengthiest, most detailed and specific legislative proposal ever originated by a California governor." The governor made his usual condemnation of the welfare system, but for the first time matched his criticism with an acknowledgment that welfare recipients were underpaid. Reagan said:

> The crisis in Welfare and Medi-Cal presents a challenge to all Californians. We simply cannot sit idly by and do nothing to prevent an uncontrolled upward spiraling of the welfare caseload, as most other states and the federal government appear resigned to do. The whole system itself is about to collapse, nationwide, from the burden it is placing on the taxpayer each year. . . .
>
> Additionally, the system does not adequately provide for the truly needy. Virtually everywhere in California the truly needy are barely subsisting, many below the poverty line, while thousands of the less needy with other sources of income and various exemptions and disregards are getting a disproportionate share of the available money.

The four goals of the Reagan program were to "increase assistance to the truly needy who have nowhere else to turn to meet their basic needs," re-

* The Democratic leadership, believing that Reagan would score rhetorical triumph without following up with any solid legislative proposals, took the unprecedented step of denying the governor's request to present his message to a joint session of the legislature. Some newspapers and television stations responded unfavorably to this tactic. Meese is probably right when he says that Reagan wound up getting more coverage from his Town Hall speech than he would have received by making a speech to the legislature.

quire those who were able to work to seek a job or job training, place Medi-Cal benefits on the same footing as health benefits received by persons not on the program and "strengthen family responsibility as the basic element in our society." Reagan's welfare plan elicited letters of praise from the public and criticism from the legislature. The legislative leadership accepted the alarming data about the staggering increase in the welfare caseload and its potential consequences for the state budget, but many legislators blamed the caseload increase on the recession rather than on welfare cheaters. The favored legislative solution to the welfare fiscal problem was a federal take-over of the system, as envisioned by President Nixon's Family Assistance Plan then pending in Congress.

Whether recession born or not, the welfare problem certainly extended beyond California's borders. Some states were taking draconian measures to curb the rising caseload. In neighboring Nevada, a Democratic governor permitted house-to-house searches for nonsupporting fathers; in Kansas, 20 percent across-the-board cuts were made in benefits; in New Jersey, grants were eliminated for families with unemployed fathers. Other states postponed changes, awaiting what they believed and hoped would be congressional approval for the Family Assistance Plan, which would have raised federal costs but reduced the burden on the states.[10] Reagan, almost alone among prominent Republican office-holders, was an ardent foe of the Nixon proposal. In retrospect, he believes that his opposition helped rally congressional conservatives against it and discouraged Nixon from advancing the plan a third time after two defeats. But in 1971 Reagan was under pressure from the federal government and needed help from the Nixon administration. For two years the Department of Health, Education and Welfare (HEW) had been pressuring California to increase its maximum payments to reflect cost-of-living changes. The state had one of the highest AFDC payment schedules in the country, and Reagan thought that the federal government was picking on his administration. In Reagan's mind, HEW's insistence that the state comply with the law was a retaliation for his consistent opposition to the Family Assistance Plan and its variants. The villains from Reagan's point of view were HEW Secretary Elliot Richardson and his undersecretary, John G. Veneman, a former Republican assemblyman from California who had clashed with Reagan and carried Unruh's tax bill. But the courts also found that the Reagan administration was not complying with the law. On September 10, 1970, a federal judge ruled in a lawsuit filed by the San Francisco Neighborhood Legal Assistance Foundation that the state must increase its payment schedule or lose the more than $400 million a year it received in federal funds for the AFDC program. The Department of Health, Education and Welfare then announced that these funds would be cut off on April 1, 1971, unless California complied.

Having lost in the courts, Reagan sought a political solution. He called Vice-President Spiro Agnew, who promised to help. A few days later, after conversations between Agnew and HEW officials, the details of which have never been publicly divulged, the department backed down from its deadline. But Reagan knew that his administration faced additional lawsuits unless the payments were increased. In March he met with President Nixon in San Clemente and, according to information provided by both White House and Reagan administration sources, reached a broad agreement with the President. What Nixon wanted, and got, was Reagan's agreement to bring California into compliance with federal regulations and to soften his public denunciations of the Family Assistance Plan. What Reagan wanted, and also got, was an assurance that HEW would cooperate with a pilot program in California requiring able-bodied AFDC recipients to work for their welfare checks. On July 1, California increased its maximum payments, and a federal court ruled that retroactive payments were not required.

Nothing of any consequence, beyond rhetoric, was happening in the legislature. Reagan's proposed budget was unbalanced, and he intended to balance it by eliminating the traditional open-ended welfare appropriation. Democrats accused Reagan of conducting government by press release and television broadcast, and Republicans accused Democrats of being obstructionists who had no plan of their own to solve the state's impending budget crisis. Because Democrats held legislative control, Reagan needed their cooperation. At the time the Democrats had no hope of passing anything over a gubernatorial veto, and Reagan had demonstrated his willingness to use the California governor's extraordinary power of vetoing line items in the budget. By June the legislative session looked like most of the others which had preceded it under the Reagan administration: much talk, little action, plenty of mutual recriminations. Then leadership was displayed unexpectedly by the new Assembly speaker, Bob Moretti, a brash, energetic Democrat who was only thirty-four years old. Moretti seemed an unlikely initiator of a compromise. He had a reputation as a partisan. Elected to the legislature as an Unruh protégé when only twenty-eight, Moretti had parted company with his mentor while following Unruh's practice of striking mutually rewarding alliances with key lobbyists. Moretti was a tough-talking Italian-American from Detroit, who had graduated from Notre Dame with a major in accounting. He represented a middle class district in the San Fernando Valley, where there was much resentment of runaway welfare costs. Bright and ambitious to run for governor, Moretti saw that Californians were becoming increasingly disgusted with the nonperformance of their state government. He had a low opinion of Reagan and believed that the governor felt the same way about him. "I shared an image of him as a pitch man who was a good communicator, who was more interested in selling himself and his administration than he was in accomplishment," Moretti said. "We knew how powerful he was when he was on the media, that he did have a good way of persuading people. We thought that he either exaggerated or stressed unimportant points to get something across. But he was the governor, and it was get together or do nothing."[11]

Actually, it was Moretti's top aide, William Hauck, who first suggested an initiative to break the impasse. "This blasting back and forth has become debilitating to both of you," Hauck said to Moretti one day in June when the prospects for any action looked particularly hopeless.[12] On June 28, 1971, Hauck wrote and Moretti signed a letter which proposed "that we set aside our personal and philosophical disagreements and work to assure the people that our state will prosper.* As we have both said publicly on a number of occasions this year, if we do not act positively on at least a few of our major state issues the people of California will properly hold us all accountable." Moretti proposed, "in the spirit of reasonable compromise and agreement," a meeting with Reagan. He called for the meeting on the same day because Hauck knew that there were those in the governor's office who would oppose such a meeting if its existence became widely known.

Downstairs in the corner office of the governor, Hauck's friend, Reagan legislative liaison George Steffes, had been waiting to hear from Moretti. Steffes, too, thought that the time had come for cooperation between the governor and the speaker. While Hauck believed that Reagan was becoming tired of his own rhetoric and felt the need to accomplish something, Steffes thought that Moretti needed a record on which to run for governor. Both aides were right. Soon after Steffes received the letter, he called Hauck and asked when Moretti would release it to the press. "We're not," Hauck told him. "He wants to get something started and the condition for starting it is that the two of them meet alone with no one there."[13] Steffes said he would let Hauck know.

A decade later, there are conflicting memories of what happened in the governor's office. Everyone was willing for Reagan to meet with Moretti, but several aides questioned whether he should do so alone. Steffes pressed for the meeting. Meese considered both sides of the issue, convinced that Moretti's letter was a useful signal but also uncertain about a private meeting. What everyone recalls is that Reagan was favorable to the proposal. The governor was confident of his ability in personal negotiation and impatient to find some break in the wall of legislative resistance to his programs. Late on the same day, Steffes called back Hauck and asked if Moretti could come down within an hour.

Moretti still vividly recalls this first private meeting with Reagan, whom he had previously seen only on ceremonial and social occasions. "I remember he was sitting at his desk and there was a chair right off to the right where I sat and he said, 'Yeah, what do you want to talk to me about?' And I said, 'Look, governor, I don't like you particularly and I know you don't like me but we don't have to be in love to work together. If you're serious about doing some things, then let's sit down and start doing it.'"[14]

Reagan does not remember the meeting with such clarity, perhaps because he has presented it on the campaign trail as an occasion when a Dem-

---

* This letter is preserved in the Reagan archives at Stanford. The words "work to assure the people that our state will prosper" are underlined by pen in the copy, apparently by Meese.

ocratic leader (he does not mention Moretti's name) came to him and said, "Stop these cards and letters from coming" on the welfare bill. But Reagan recognized immediately that Moretti's proposal was genuine, pointing out afterward that the speaker would have gone to the press with his proposal if he were simply trying to make points. Within a few minutes, he had agreed with Moretti to hold a series of meetings with aides and key legislators in an effort to compromise on welfare and the budget. This meeting was the turning point that marked Reagan's transformation from communicator to governor. Until this time Reagan had been limited to what a strong-minded governor with access to television can accomplish by rhetoric alone. He had done well in situations which put a premium on political instinct rather than knowledge, as in his meeting with the university regents. Beyond the 1967 tax bill, however, he had no important legislative accomplishment to his credit, and he did not even seem to regard legislative success as an important measure of his governorship. From Reagan's initial meeting with Moretti came a series of detailed and often acrimonious encounters in which the governor and the speaker negotiated, compromised, swore and questioned each other's motivation. That first meeting also generated the processes which led to passage of the California Welfare Reform Act, a major improvement of school financing and property-tax relief. And from these meetings emerged a strange, mutual respect between Reagan and Moretti, who are as little alike as any public officials I have known. Reagan came to regard Moretti as tough and principled and to compare his conduct with that of a good negotiator who might have faced him across the bargaining table in his old Screen Actors Guild negotiating days. Once, when an aide expressed doubt that Moretti would do something he promised to do, Reagan said simply, "He gave me his word."[15] Moretti also changed his opinion of Reagan. "Both he and I developed a grudging respect for each other," Moretti said. "We came from different kinds of worlds. I don't think that socially we'd ever have mixed, but when the governor gave a commitment he kept it, and when I gave a commitment, I kept it. So that working on the development of legislation with him was relatively easy because we always knew where the other guy stood."[16]

The agreements did not come overnight, and Reagan and Moretti were not the only players. The process required a week of intense negotiations at meetings presided over by Reagan and Moretti, and another ten days of even longer negotiations where details were hammered out by the staffs who ultimately produced a compromise welfare bill and budget. More negotiations were required later on the school finance and property-tax-relief issues.* On the campaign stump in 1976 and 1980, Reagan would boast that, when he couldn't "make the legislators see the light, he made them feel the

---

* On the legislative side, other key negotiators included state Senator Anthony Beilenson of Los Angeles, whose abortion measure had given Reagan so much trouble, and Assemblymen John Burton and Leo McCarthy. Carleson played an important role in the welfare negotiations for Reagan's office, but the man who took charge was Meese.

heat." But Meese's painstaking notes of the meetings show that what really happened was that the Reagan administration came of age politically on the welfare bill. On one detailed Meese note about a myriad of details on the welfare bill are jotted the words, "RR: quid pro quo for welf reform out of Senate committee."[17] Following are the names of three Democratic senators notorious for their special-interest horse-trading and a reminder of what it took to get their votes for the bill in a Senate committee. One of the notes is the name of a judge wanted by a Democratic senator. After the name of another judge-swapping senator, less particular in his preferences, is written the word "anyone."[18] It was through such careful attention to political tradeoffs that the Reagan program finally prevailed in a Senate more accustomed to political payoffs than idealism.

The process in the governor's office was painstaking and on several occasions came near to collapse. The Reagan team basically trusted Moretti, but not Democratic Assemblyman John Burton. Recognizing this, Moretti would sometimes arrange to have Burton feign an angry outburst and pronounce some provision unacceptable. On the Republican side, Carleson played the heavy. Moretti complained that Carleson "would drive the Pope to drink in a couple of weeks" and wanted to deal only with Reagan or Meese. Meese won the respect of the Democratic negotiators as the administration official who spoke most reliably for the governor. "He's a very intelligent guy with a stick-to-it-iveness that can sometimes drive you up the wall," said Moretti of Meese. "But were I in the governor's seat, I would like to have someone like that on my side."[19]

The California Welfare Reform Act is Reagan's proudest achievement in the eight years of his governorship. By almost any yardstick—liberal, conservative or managerial—the law has been a success. It is easier to administer than the law it replaced, and it pays AFDC recipients more money. However, many who applaud the results of the legislation also believe that Reagan ascribes to it wonder cures which never occurred. The welfare reform bill tightened eligibility in several ways and reduced the number of hours an unemployed father could work and still have his family eligible for aid. Household furnishings were for the first time counted as assets. A complex and confusing "needs standard" was simplified into a uniform statewide schedule which varied only according to family size. A one-year residency requirement, long advocated by Reagan, was written into the law despite warnings that it was probably unconstitutional. Antifraud measures included a state cross-check between county welfare records and employer earnings records and financial incentives to counties to recover support payments from absent fathers. Grants were substantially increased. The family of three which had been getting $172 a month at the beginning of the year received $235 after the cost-of-living increase and passage of the welfare plan. And Reagan's pet demonstration project, the Community Work Experience Program, was introduced in some counties, requiring fathers and AFDC mothers without young children to work at public service jobs.

Both the Reagan administration and the Democratic legislative leadership had pledged to reform the welfare system, and both sides had something to crow about. The welfare rolls started to decline immediately. Within three years the AFDC caseload dropped from a high of 1,608,000 to 1,330,000. The efficacy of Reagan's welfare reform became a national article of faith among conservatives, and even among some who did not rally to the conservative banner. As U.S. commissioner of welfare, Carleson subsequently encouraged other states to follow at least part of California's example. When Reagan ran for President in 1980, he would declare: "When I took office, California was the welfare capital of the nation. Sixteen percent of all those receiving welfare in the country were in California. The caseload was increasing 40,000 a month. We turned that 40,000 a month increase into an 8,000 a month decrease. We returned to the taxpayers $2 billion and we increased grants to the truly needy by forty-three percent."

In many of his speeches Reagan went on to extol the virtues of his Community Work Experience Program and to describe it as a success. It was an inaccurate claim. While the welfare reform bill as a whole was applauded by local government officials, they had little use for the work program. HEW, under Nixon's agreement with Reagan, gave California the waivers it needed to try out the program, limiting the number of participants to 30,000. The actual number of people on community work projects never approached that figure. Most of the AFDC recipients were mothers with young children and those who usually lacked the work experience to make them useful employees. The program was discontinued by Governor Edmund G. (Jerry) Brown, Jr., on July 1, 1975, after assigning only 9,600 persons to jobs.

Except for this provision, the welfare bill was a success. The Democrats, however, quickly learned that voters gave most of the credit for the measure's passage to the Great Communicator, despite the fact that the legislation had been a bipartisan achievement. As a result, the Democrats tried to downplay the impact of the bill, saying that California's rapidly declining caseload was the result of improving national conditions. In rebuttal, Carleson pointed out that the California caseload had increased in several years of economic prosperity and that it was now declining at a rate greater than the national trend. The debate was not susceptible to easy resolution because various administrative and judicial actions also had an impact. The courts struck down the residency requirement. Carleson, as director of welfare, introduced a requirement for monthly reporting of income, which may have restricted caseload as much as any provision of the law. State Senator Anthony Beilenson, writing in the *Pacific Law Journal* of July 1972, said that "expanding use of family planning among AFDC dependents" may have reduced the welfare rolls. Many others thought that this contention was a euphemism for increased use of the abortion option provided by Beilenson's controversial 1967 bill.

Examining these conflicting claims in a report for the Urban Institute, public policy analyst Frank Levy found merit in the argument that an improvement in national economic conditions had reduced the caseload but said this was not the full story.[20] Levy, no fan of Reagan, is convinced that the dynamic increase of welfare caseload in the 1960s was bound to level off anyway, because most of the eligible recipients were on the rolls by 1971. But Levy also estimated that the Reagan reforms, including Carleson's regulations, reduced the welfare rolls by 6 percent more than they would otherwise have declined, a figure (about 21,000 persons) which is hardly inconsequential. "Governor Reagan is a man who works very hard, but he is also blessed with abundant good luck," wrote Levy. "In the case of the CWRA (California Welfare Reform Act), he had the luck to institute a fairly moderate policy just at the time when demographic factors would cause the 'welfare explosion' to end both in California and the rest of the country. . . . At the same time, CWRA is a one-in-a-thousand policy success. The combination of CWRA and associated regulations mandated a large number of changes in a $1 billion program involving thirty-five counties and numerous personnel. . . . The result was a welfare program which, as the governor intended, was reoriented toward fiscal considerations and away from clients— particularly clients with earned income. On balance, however, more recipients appear to have been helped than hurt by this change. . . ."

Levy's "on balance" finding might serve as a judgment for the entire second Reagan administration, which legislatively was far more productive than the first. During his first term, Reagan had declared that his "feet were in concrete" in opposition to any program of state income tax withholding. In 1971, he yielded, saying that "The concrete had cracked," and agreed to this sensible plan. In 1972, a new Reagan-Moretti compromise put together a one-cent increase in the sales tax, federal revenue-sharing funds, and a state surplus to come up with $1 billion for property-tax relief and the financing of local schools. The Reagan budget did even more for elementary and secondary schools than it had done for higher education, increasing spending by 89 percent during Reagan's eight years compared to 71 percent during Brown's two terms. These figures are all the more impressive considering that elementary and secondary enrollment rose 37.6 percent during the Brown years and only 2.6 percent during Reagan's terms. Reagan backed a program for early childhood education and a master plan for special education advocated by Wilson Riles, the progressive state Superintendent of Public Instruction. "We did not go backward under Reagan's regime," said Riles. "We went forward."*[21]

---

* Riles, a liberal Democrat, defeated conservative Republican Max Rafferty for the nonpartisan post in 1970 and became the first black to be elected to a statewide office in California. Reagan had endorsed Rafferty out of a previous commitment, but never men-

Going forward, however, proved to be a more complex business than Reagan had realized when he became governor. In his celebrated "prairie fire" speech that touched off his general election campaign of 1966, Reagan had promised to make California "first in more than size and crime and taxes." The rate of population growth in the state finally slowed after three decades of dynamic growth, but the same could not be said of the other two barometers cited by candidate Reagan. Though Reagan had signed more than forty bills providing stiffer sentences for criminals or other intended improvements in the criminal justice system, California had not become a safer place to live by the time Reagan left office in 1974. In eight years the homicide rate had doubled, and the rate of armed robberies had increased even more. Law enforcement is, of course, primarily a local responsibility. The same cannot be said for taxes, which increased under Reagan as they had never increased in California before. On the campaign trail Reagan boasted of returning $5.7 billion in taxes, including $4 billion in property-tax relief, to Californians. He never said that these taxes came from Reagan-sponsored tax increases that were the largest, up to that time, in California history. Under Reagan the state budget increased from $4.6 billion annually to $10.2 billion. The operations portion of the budget, over which the governor has the most control, went from $2.2 billion to $3.5 billion. State taxes per $100 of personal income, a measure which adjusts both for population and price changes, increased from $6.64 to $7.62.

At the same time Reagan had done much to control the growth of state government. "Reagan was not so much an underachiever as he was an overcommitter," observed Judson Clark of California Research, who served as a top aide to Democratic Speaker Unruh and Republican Speaker Monagan. "He did some important things, but not as much as he said he would do and not as much as he said he did." One of the things Reagan did do was slow the growth of the state work force, which had increased nearly 50 percent during the Brown years. The growth was less than half of this during the Reagan administration, rising from 158,400 to 192,400 positions. If higher education, where Reagan's control was indirect, is excluded, the growth was 7 percent (from 108,090 to 115,090) at a time when government work forces in other states were growing rapidly. If the $4 billion in direct property-tax relief is subtracted from the Reagan budgets, they increased only slightly more than inflation.

---

tioned his name during the campaign unless he was asked a direct question by a reporter. When Riles called on the governor after the 1970 election, he said Reagan told him, "You'd be surprised at how some of us around here voted." The two men became friends who frequently cooperated on education issues despite their differences in philosophy. When Riles appeared to have lost his place on the ballot due to a failure of his office to properly file nomination papers in 1978, Reagan heard about it and called him from New York to cheer him up. The state Supreme Court subsequently put Riles back on the ballot, and he was reelected to a third term.

Ultimately, the judgment of the Reagan administration has to rest on something other than statistics, which can be cited to infinite purpose both by the governor's critics and by his defenders. Reagan came to office an utter novice, proclaiming a conservative gospel which his adversaries confidently predicted was too simpleminded and backward-looking for a modern democratic state. He went through a long learning period at taxpayers' expense during which California's much maligned and highly professional state government bureaucracy did the actual governing. But Reagan did not abandon his ideals or his belief that government had become too little the servant and too much the master. Instead, he learned and accommodated and compromised and found ways of doing things which accomplished parts of his purpose. He found good people to work for him, and by trials and errors learned the limits of what he could delegate and what he could not. In his second term he finally came down out of the announcer's booth and onto the political playing field where men sweat and work and sell judgeships and write laws. He did all right in this world, which was not all that different from the one he had known in Dixon. "He had certain assets," said Moretti. "He had a philosophy he was willing to pursue, to enunciate, that he was willing to attempt to push. Even if you disagreed with that philosophy, the fact that he had one and that he stood up for it was something. And he was a strong personality. . . . He had an enduring desire to leave something behind that was really material which he could point to as a change. He wanted to improve where he had been."[22]

14

Running in Place

Ronald Reagan left office as a popular Republican governor at a time his party had sunk to its lowest public esteem in American history. In the aftermath of President Nixon's resignation in August and President Ford's pardon of Nixon a month later, Republicans lost forty-three seats in the House of Representatives, four U.S. Senate seats and four governorships, including California. Soon after Reagan left office in January 1975, GOP pollster Robert Teeter gave a stark analysis to Republican state chairmen meeting in Chicago. Most Americans thought of the Republican Party as untrustworthy, incompetent and closely allied with big business, Teeter said. Only 18 percent of the American people considered themselves Republicans. Worst yet, Teeter found "unbelievable increases in cynicism toward politics and American institutions in general and toward the Republican Party in particular."[1] Even after the Goldwater debacle of 1964, the GOP was still ahead of the Democrats in voter measurements of integrity. Now this was no longer the case. It was a situation demanding the utmost optimism and faith in the future from party leaders. And it was in this context that Ronald Reagan became an unannounced, uncertain and frequently underestimated candidate for President.

During the decline and fall of Richard Nixon, Reagan rallied to the banner of the Watergate-plagued President of the United States. Against the advice of such aides as Michael K. Deaver, Reagan also defended Nixon's money-grubbing Vice-President Spiro Agnew, perhaps remembering the timely help Agnew had given the Reagan administration during its battle with the federal welfare bureaucracy. Reagan was slow to recognize the implications of the Watergate scandal for the Republican Party and even slower to distance himself from those who were under investigation. On May 1, 1973, he said that the Watergate conspirators "are not criminals at heart."[2] He did not seem to entertain any thoughts that the spreading investigation would bring down the administration, or even cripple it, and he did not for a long time bother to watch the televised hearings of the Senate Judiciary Committee.* Touring the South in November of 1973, Reagan staunchly defended Nixon, saying the President was doing a good job of governing despite Watergate. When it became apparent the following year that Watergate would not go away, Reagan became even stronger in his defense. In private he spoke of "a lynch mob" forming to get the President. In public he counterattacked. Speaking to Republicans at a Lincoln Day dinner in Oklahoma City on February 12, 1974, Reagan urged his listeners to shed any guilt feelings they might have and to go on the offensive. "We in our party have too often been the victims of big city political machines voting tombstones, warehouses and empty lots against us in every election," he declared in a heavily applauded nonsequitur. Throughout the spring and summer of Nixon's discontent, Reagan remained a loyal defender. On June 11, 1974, Reagan was asked about a report by the columnists Rowland Evans and Robert Novak that "the Reagan inner circle flinches over Reagan's refusal to find any fault with the embattled President." Reagan replied that the columnists were "stretching it a little bit" and repeated a frequent statement that Nixon and his advisers should be presumed innocent.[3] Not until August 6, when Nixon's resignation speech was being prepared and all the pro-Nixon Republicans on the House Judiciary Committee had deserted the President, did Reagan acknowledge, "Now, for the first time, it has been revealed that neither the Congress nor the American people had been told the entire truth about Watergate." Even then, he did not demand resignation, but said it was "absolutely imperative" that Nixon go before Congress and make a full disclosure—as if that were any longer an alternative.[4] On August 27, two weeks after Nixon had resigned and two weeks before Ford pardoned him, Reagan said that for the former President, "the punishment of resignation certainly is more than adequate for the crime."[5]

Perhaps alone among prominent Republicans who stuck with the President, Reagan never suffered a moment from his loyalty. Soon after he made his "they are not criminals at heart" statement, I asked Teeter whether this kind of blind defense would hurt Reagan in the public opinion polls. "No, not at all," Teeter replied. "It will just show to everybody that he doesn't know what's going on and isn't involved." Teeter was right. Reagan's popularity increased slightly during this period, even though his administration was in a slump. Perhaps that was because Reagan was so far away from Washington. Perhaps it was because Reagan's loyalty to a sinking President reinforced the idea that the California governor was a man of his convictions. But more than anything, Reagan profited from Watergate because it encouraged voters to look at the human dimension of their leaders, a yardstick by which Reagan is better measured than by, say, an examination of his intimate knowledge of the merits of competing strategic weapons sys-

* At a June 28, 1974, press conference, Reagan was late and was asked whether it was because he was watching the Watergate hearings. "No, I was sound asleep," he said. "As a matter of fact I was having a wonderful dream when they knocked on the door." He denied, jokingly, that it was a dream about being President in 1976.

tems. Watergate, whatever else it did, forced Americans back to first principles, which in the case of the presidency meant examining the character of prospective Presidents. It was an emphasis beneficial to Reagan.

In the last months of Reagan's governorship a respected poll showed that nearly three Californians thought of him as a good governor for every two that regarded him as a poor one.* But Reagan seemed to be marking time as his administration drew to a close. He suffered a stunning defeat, the worst of his second term, when voters in November 1973 rejected Proposition 1, an ahead-of-its-time limitation on government spending that Reagan called "the taxpayers' bill of rights."† Political professionals and several members of the Kitchen Cabinet blamed an inept campaign by the politically inexperienced Deaver, who took a leave of absence from the governor's office to manage the Proposition 1 forces. The critics had a case, but blame for the defeat must be shared by Reagan, the underestimated candidate who this time underestimated the potency of the combined forces opposing him.

The catalyst for the opposition was future gubernatorial candidate Moretti, who saw the measure as potentially harmful to lower-income Californians, and his opposition to it as an opportunity to let voters "see me in some other light than Assembly Speaker." Moretti loaned opponents of Proposition 1 both staff resources and $65,000 from his lobbyist-financed treasure chest for Assembly candidates. He was joined by the California Employees Association, the California Teachers Association and such political figures as Superintendent of Public Instruction Wilson Riles, who told me that Reagan personally appealed for his support. "I didn't want to oppose him, I didn't need a fight, but all our studies showed it would be detrimental," said Riles. "When it became clear it would hurt education, I knew I would have to oppose it. I did, and told him so, at his house."[6]

The final nail in the coffin of the proposition was hammered in by Rea

* The poll, published in the month of Nixon's resignation, also showed that four times as many people thought that Nixon was doing a poor job as a good one. It was taken by Mervin D. Field, the veteran California pollster.

† The major provision of Proposition 1 would have limited expenditures from state tax revenues to the 1973 percentage of state personal income, then estimated at 8.3 percent. It would have lowered this spending ratio one-tenth of 1 percent a year until it reached 7 percent. The measure also would have required a two-thirds vote of the legislature to institute any new tax and would have set tax rate limits for cities and counties that could have been overridden by a vote of the people. Voter turnout was light and the measure received only a 46 percent "yes" vote.

Less than five years later, in June 1978, Californians by a 2–1 margin passed the well-known Proposition 13. In comparison, Proposition 1 would have been a boon to government. Proposition 13 limited local property taxes to 1 percent of a property's value, about two-fifths of the ratio that was in effect at the time. Unlike Proposition 1, the Proposition 13 initiative contained no provision for overriding this limit by popular vote. Confronted with Proposition 13, which provided a huge tax break for business and industry and a severe blow to public spending for education, many foes of Proposition 1 had second thoughts about their opposition. It was then, of course, too late. But it is likely that voter approval of Proposition 1 in 1973 would have headed off the tax revolt which culminated in Proposition 13.

gan himself. Appearing on a question-and-answer session on KTVU in Oakland on October 26, Reagan was asked, "Do you think the average voter really understands the language of the proposition?" Reagan, in a light-hearted mood, answered with a typical quip. "No," he said. "He shouldn't try. I don't, either." The remark caused no particular stir on the show. But Whitaker and Baxter, the pioneering California political management firm hired to oppose Proposition 1, made the most of it in a series of ads which ran in the state's major newspapers during the final days of the campaign. "When a proposition's chief sponsor doesn't understand it, it's time for us to vote no on Proposition 1," the ad concluded.

The rejection of Proposition 1 stung Reagan and seemed to many in Sacramento to signal the last-year decline of his administration. His January 9 state-of-the-state message was uncharacteristically flat and disappointing, even to his supporters. On January 29 the legislature broke Reagan's perfect record of having 797 vetoes sustained by denying the governor the final authority in closing any of the state's eleven mental hospitals. On February 5 a long front-page analysis of Reagan's troubles appeared in the *Los Angeles Times*. Written by George Skelton, who had covered the administration since its early days, the story concluded with an opinion from a "veteran Republican strategist who has been close to Reagan and the administration." Said the strategist: "There's no way a governor is going to lose an override by one vote. There are too many ways to keep legislators happy, too many tradeoffs that can be made. But that takes work, doesn't it? There is a definite sickness in the administration."

Perhaps the better word to describe Reagan's state in this period would have been "malaise," a condition that Jimmy Carter would one day be said to apply to all Americans. In Reagan's life there have been periods of drift and uncertainty when events and the advice of friends tug him in different directions and when he moves first one way, then another, before deciding—or being pushed into—a definite course of action. I traveled with Reagan to the South in the fall of 1973 and interviewed him twice in 1974, once extensively for a review of "The Reagan Years" in *California Journal*. Each time he struck me as a man of conflicting mood and opinion. Should he run for President? Should he simply leave office and resume his place on what he always called "the mashed potato circuit," making millions in the process? Should he retire, with Nancy, to his ranch? At different times he expressed all of these attitudes. Sometimes it seemed to me he wanted to do all three things—and at the same time. Within the Reagan entourage, all aspects of these options were represented. Some were ready for the next political battle. Some needed to make money, far more desperately than Reagan ever did. And some, tired from sixteen-hour days while their leader went home early, just wanted out of government. They had been in Sacramento a long time.

The declining fortunes of Richard Nixon added to Reagan's uncertainty.

Many of those closest to the governor, including Tuttle and Meese, had assumed that Reagan would be a candidate for President in 1976 when Nixon would have completed two terms and been unable to succeed himself. The ascension of Ford as Vice-President disrupted all the smooth and unstated assumptions of Reagan's prospective candidacy in 1976. Some, like Nofziger, were unhappy that Ford's presence had made it easier to force out Nixon and were unhappier still at the likely prospect that Ford would be the Republican presidential nominee. In the month after Nixon abdicated and before Ford pardoned him, the new President was hailed across the nation as the healer of the republic. But the devout Reaganites looked upon him as a usurper.

Long before Nixon became the Republican Party's undetachable albatross, Reagan had made the decision not to risk his own fortunes in the 1974 election. In the spring of 1973 he discussed with his money men and his political aides the possibility of running for the U.S. Senate in 1974 against Democratic incumbent Alan Cranston. Reagan quickly discarded this idea. "There's nothing I can do in the Senate for what I believe in that I won't be able to do anyway," Reagan said to a close supporter. This was the prevailing view of his advisers, and it was strengthened by Nancy Reagan's lack of enthusiasm to live the life of a senator's wife in Washington. Afterward, some Democrats would say that Reagan did not pursue the Senate option because he would have been unsure of beating Cranston, but the discussions never reached this advanced stage of political analysis. Reagan's money men were not interested in a Senate race but in a third term as governor, which would have preserved Reagan's base in California. However, Reagan was tired of being governor, and he pointed out to Tuttle that he had repeatedly promised to serve only two terms. Reagan believed that two terms were enough for anyone, and he had pushed a state constitutional amendment that would have imposed this limitation. When the amendment died in the legislature, Reagan again pledged that he would not run a third time.

Other politicians as undecided about their future as Reagan was in 1974 might talk over their situation with their advisers, retreat to a mountaintop for prayer or take a few extra drinks. Reagan did what he does best, which is to make a speech. The day after Nixon's resignation Reagan was the featured speaker before the National Young Republicans meeting in the casino land of South Lake Tahoe. At a time when most Republicans were more disheartened than a busted gambler, Reagan urged them, in effect, to forget their fallen leader and put their trust in conservative ideology. "You can have faith in the Republican philosophy of fiscal common sense, limited government and individual freedom," Reagan said. "Let me offer the experience of the past seven and one-half years in California to support that assurance." He then recounted his achievements in welfare reform but warned that such struggles are "a never-ending battle." Even while California was cutting welfare costs, food stamps—"intended for a worthy purpose"—had become an "administrative nightmare, a staggering financial burden at the federal level and the newest nesting place for welfare abuse and fraud."

Reagan's speech offered California's policies as a model for the federal government, and many in his true-believer audience considered Reagan a personal model for the presidency. "Government, alone, is the cause of inflation," Reagan concluded. ". . . No government is ever justified in spending a single dollar more than necessary for legitimate functions. And no government should ever tolerate abuses, legal or illegal, that not only defraud the people government is trying to help, but increase the taxes of those working citizens who finance our efforts to help the poor, the aged and the infirm."

It might have been the opening speech of his 1976 presidential campaign, but Reagan was in his own mind a long way from declaring his candidacy. In May 1974, when it still seemed that Nixon would weather the storm, Reagan had talked over his prospects with old and new advisers at a long meeting at his Pacific Palisades home that had many aspects of his early discussions about the governorship with Holmes Tuttle, Cy Rubel and Henry Salvatori. Tuttle was the only one of the original millionaire trio at the May meeting, but Justin Dart, another wealthy contributor, attended. So did Meese, Nofziger, Deaver and the man who would become Deaver's associate in the advertising business, Peter Hannaford. They were joined by other Reagan aides—political strategist Robert Walker, Jim Lake of the governor's Washington office and Jim Jenkins, a shrewd former aide to John B. Connally who had stabilized Reagan's press operation in Sacramento during the second term. There were some outsiders, notably Mississippi state Republican chairman Clarke Reed, whom Reagan knew, and Washington attorney John P. Sears, whom he did not. Sears caught Reagan's attention, however, when he predicted both that Nixon would not survive and that Ford would not be able to lead the country after he was gone. What Sears was suggesting was the heretical notion that loyalist Reagan could run for President in 1976 no matter what happened. If Nixon lasted, there would be an open run for the nomination. If Ford inherited the presidency, then Reagan could seek the Republican nomination against him in the primaries.

This was heady stuff, and the Reagan team was not ready for it. Reagan and Meese were too much the loyalists to concede that Nixon was going down the tubes, and Sears did not have much support for his proposition. But Deaver recalls that everyone was impressed with the bold analysis of this thirty-four-old lawyer, who had skillfully directed Nixon's delegate search in 1968 and appeared to be a rising figure in the Nixon administration until he was forced out by John Mitchell in 1969. Sears had tied his star to Agnew's, believing that the Vice-President would be the candidate in 1976. When Agnew resigned as an alternative to being prosecuted, Sears was left without a candidate. Ford was surrounded by a motley crowd of old congressional pals and aides inherited from the Nixon administration. Sears

knew he had no chance of running a Ford campaign, and he did not want a subordinate role. Walker, his old friend from the Nixon campaign, convinced Sears that he was just the right man for Ronald Reagan.

People in the Reagan camp who later would become sworn enemies of Sears still value the contribution he made in these closing months of the Reagan administration and the period just afterward. The Californians around Reagan were an optimistic and resourceful group, but the Watergate scandal had deprived them of the chart by which they set their compass. All of the grand plans for a 1976 Reagan presidential campaign now seemed worthless, and Reagan himself had no idea of what to do. He was running in place, waiting for something to happen. It was at this moment that Sears arrived.* While many of his ideas were not initially accepted, he planted the seeds for what became the Reagan challenge to President Ford. Reagan was bored by the discussions of political mechanics which fascinated Sears. But the governor accepted the invitation of his new adviser to think the unthinkable. What Sears was telling him and what Reagan eventually came to believe was that he could challenge a President of his own party and get away with it. This idea blossomed slowly but steadily, in the late spring and summer of 1974 as Nixon's troubles deepened. After the resignation, anti-Ford sentiment was kindled in Sacramento by the new President's selection of Nelson Rockefeller as his Vice-President. Conservatives who might otherwise have been tempted to give Ford a chance were infuriated at the prospect that Rockefeller might inherit the presidency. More than any other single act of Ford's, or indeed all of them combined, it was the selection of Rockefeller which fueled national interest among conservatives in a Reagan candidacy. Eventually, Ford would yield to right-wing pressure and allow Rockefeller to take himself off the 1976 ticket. But by this date, November 3, 1975, Reagan's unofficial presidential campaign was already under way.

In 1974 the prevailing view among the Reagan entourage was that the Rockefeller nomination was designed to stop Reagan. As far back as December 1973, Rockefeller's decision to resign as governor of New York had been interpreted in Sacramento as an attempt to gain a head start over Reagan in the race for the 1976 presidential nomination. "It would be great to travel about the country freely and not have to worry about expenses," a Reagan aide told Larry Stammer, then the Sacramento correspondent for

---

* In *Marathon* (p. 73), Jules Witcover, who is close to Sears, described him as a man "with a deceptively shy outer crust that camouflaged a biting humor and political toughness and skepticism. Also, his appreciation of and affinity with members of the Washington press corps set him apart from most of the political operatives around Nixon and Reagan. Where many of the paranoid Nixon types looked upon reporters as the enemy, to be warded off at every turn, Sears saw them as an essential and unavoidable element in the drama of electing a president." Reagan, influenced by Nofziger, did not have Nixon's preoccupation with "enemies" but thought of the Washington press corps as predominantly liberal and distrustful both of Westerners and conservatives. Sears' good relations with Washington correspondents was a major recommendation in his favor with Reagan.

the *San Jose Mercury-News.*[7] Stammer reported that Rockefeller's decision "has renewed interest within the Reagan administration about the California governor's future." After Nixon resigned, that interest was focused on the vice-presidency. On the weekend after Ford became President, Reagan said, "I have always felt that for too long a time we have turned to the legislative branch of our government for our candidates for President and have ignored the fact that those with the most executive experience are governors." Ostensibly, this made a case both for Rockefeller and Reagan. But when Reagan was asked whether Ford might select a liberal or a moderate as his Vice-President, he replied, "I happen to believe that what is termed by many as the conservative philosophy is the basic Republican philosophy. It is a libertarian philosophy, a belief in the individual freedom and the reduction of government. And so, obviously, I would feel that we were more committed to the mandate of 1972, the philosophical mandate, that people handed down in such overwhelming numbers, if the President should choose someone representative of the Republican Party."[8]

Reagan insisted that he was not campaigning for Vice-President. But Gordon Luce, who had left an important cabinet post in the Reagan administration to become California Republican chairman, gave a different signal. Luce telegrammed the forty-nine other Republican state chairmen, urging them to back Ford's selection of Reagan as Vice-President. The telegrams went unacknowledged by the White House. Ford's selection of Rockefeller a week later was regarded in Sacramento as a slap in the face. To true-blue Republican conservatives who recalled the battle of '64, the selection of their old enemy was an unbelievable insult. What concerned Reagan, however, was not that Ford had departed from "the conservative philosophy." He was, instead, disappointed that he had been passed over himself.

As the months went by, Reagan accumulated more grievances against the President. The day before Rockefeller was named Vice-President, Ford had flown to Chicago to address the convention of the Veterans of Foreign Wars. There, he surprised his audience by proposing limited amnesty for Vietnam War draft evaders and deserters, an idea which Reagan sharply opposed. While Reagan said he approved of "compassion based on the individual situation for each individual," he also observed that many of those who refused to fight in Vietnam had no regrets about their conduct. "They didn't feel they did anything wrong in choosing the laws they would break, and they simply want the country to recognize them as somehow being in the moral right," Reagan declared at the same August 27 press conference in which he said that Nixon had been punished enough for his crimes by the mere act of resignation.

When I interviewed Reagan in the fall of 1974, he said nothing positive about Ford and claimed it was too early to judge his administration. But he defended Nixon. "I don't believe the story has come out yet and I sure tried to read those transcripts and I think for myself mistakes were made but at

the same time I think that history [is] probably going to be far more kind to that administration with regard to accomplishments," Reagan said. ". . . When all this is going on our world leadership in times of trouble is far more effective than anything we've had for a great many years." Reagan clearly did not think that Ford was likely to be as effective as his predecessor in dealing with foreign policy. In a November 11 radio commentary that did not mention the President by name, Reagan criticized the United States for abstaining at a meeting of the Organization of American States in the vote on a resolution to lift the trade embargo on Cuba. Reagan insisted that the conditions for any American dealings with Castro should be removal of Soviet bases, a pledge that Cuba would no longer train Communist guerrillas for military action in other countries, and the settling of claims of American citizens whose property was seized after the Castro takeover.

Ford, though still skeptical that Reagan would run, was bothered enough about the Californian's political drawing power among conservatives that he called Reagan in the fall of 1974 to offer him a position in the Ford cabinet. The President and the governor discussed a number of possibilities, including an ambassadorship to the court of St. James's. Ford finally asked Reagan if he would accept an appointment as Secretary of Transportation. Reagan declined. I heard about the possible ambassadorship, though not about the cabinet offer, and asked Reagan about it. "Hell, I can't afford to be an ambassador," said Reagan, who went on to rule out running for the U.S. Senate in 1976.[9] "Now don't automatically assume the other," he went on, though I had not asked him about the presidency. After drawing attention to his own standing with Republican voters in the polls, Reagan then went on to issue an official disclaimer about his own ambitions: "Now, I hope and pray that this administration is successful. And that would take care of '76. Because it's never—in my book—it's never been important who's in the White House, it's what's done. And that's what I mean about the mandate. Whatever may happen, I would like to feel that I can continue to be a voice in the Republican Party insuring that the party pursues the philosophy that I believe should be the Republican philosophy."*

Thus did Reagan, to the dissatisfaction of many of his political supporters and financial backers, preserve his options for 1976. This notion of

---

* These comments of Reagan's are from an interview in his office during the fall of 1974. The interview transcript is undated but apparently occurred in September, since portions of it were used in my evaluation of Reagan's governorship, "The Reagan Years," appearing in the November 1974 *California Journal.* Reagan's comments on the campaign were not quoted in the article, but his view of Edmund G. (Jerry) Brown, Jr., who became Reagan's successor, remains of interest. Said Reagan: "The young man who is running is the cheapest kind of demagogue I ever heard because he is running against me but he is not running against the truth of what we have done. I find no specifics. He generalizes and says 'education' and we are going to pour more money into education. Well, damn his hide! We have poured more money into education, greater increases than have ever been seen in the history of California and the quality of public education continues to go down."

being some sort of ideological watchdog who would carefully eye the Ford administration for signs of ideological defection disappointed political pragmatists like Sears and ideologues like Nofziger, both of whom had already judged Ford and found him wanting. But Reagan, in a mood reminiscent of his reluctance in 1968, could not at this time be pushed further. "I'm not going to make a fool of myself," he told a close adviser, adding that he really did want to see how Ford performed before making any final decision. While Reagan's wait-and-see attitude did not please Sears, Nofziger or Robert Walker, it was accepted by Meese, then leaving the administration for a vice-presidency with the San Diego-based Rohr Corporation. And it was welcomed by Deaver, who had arranged with Reagan to manage the governor's affairs after he left office. In the changing cast of the governor's Sacramento staff, Deaver had remained and earned the confidence of Reagan, who blamed the opposition and not his aide for the defeat of Proposition 1 the year before. Deaver's plan, accepted by Reagan months before he left the governorship, was to open an advertising agency with Hannaford in Sacramento and Los Angeles that would book Reagan's speeches and research and sell his radio commentaries and a syndicated column. Reagan became Deaver and Hannaford's meal ticket. Within three months of leaving office, Reagan was making eight to ten speeches a month at an average fee of $5,000 a speech. His column was appearing in 174 newspapers, and his commentaries on more than 200 radio stations. His income, $49,100 a year in the governorship, was a closely guarded secret but was estimated at more than $800,000 in 1975. Reagan told his friends he was happy to be earning money again. He was in no hurry to give up the column and the radio commentaries, as he would have to do if he became an avowed candidate for President.

Reagan's bearings shifted rightward as his focus moved from the governorship to the conservative banquet circuit. In Sacramento the give-and-take of governance had exposed Reagan to a wide variety of experiences and tempered his ideological proclivities with executive pragmatism. He read the mini-memos, met nearly every week with the press and dealt with legislators of varying persuasion. Meese made certain that Reagan heard from all points of view before he made an important decision. But Reagan was isolated on the lecture circuit, though he saw, and spoke to, many more thousands of people than he met in the governor's office. These audiences wanted the comfort of ideological certainty, and Reagan was accustomed to meeting an audience's demands. As a governor, Reagan had revealed an executive's temperament: He had the ability to go to the heart of the matter and to balance conflicting claims in ways that gave some solace to the losers. As a speaker before right-wing audiences, he succumbed to the simplicities of "A Time For Choosing," rousing his listeners rather than educating them. And away from Sacramento, he had no Meese and no carefully balanced mini-memos to give him all sides of an issue. His favorite reading on the road was *Reader's Digest,* which was full of those amazing statistics he liked to spout, and *Human Events,* which was possessed of more ideological certainty than exists in the world.

For a brief period Reagan considered the possibility of a third-party candidacy in 1976. He was impressed with the thoughtful exposition of this idea by *National Review* publisher William A. Rusher, who wanted to realize the old ideological dream of forming a third party from disgruntled Republican and Democratic conservatives. "There could be one of those moments in time, I don't know," Reagan told reporters in Sacramento on October 15, 1974, soon after he had returned from a speaking tour. "I see the statements of disaffection of people in both parties—the loss of confidence. And you wonder which is the easiest. Do you restore the confidence or do you change the name or something? I don't know. I really don't."[10] But Reagan's money men, who had bankrolled two gubernatorial campaigns and his mini-campaign for the presidency in 1968, knew. "You're a Republican and you're going to stay one," Reagan was told by Tuttle, a party man who had been raising money for Republican candidates since Eisenhower. On this issue the Reagan contributors were on the same wavelength as Sears and Nofziger, who wanted to elect a President, not create a new political party. Reagan, who would rather win an election than charge a windmill, was quickly convinced. When the governor appeared before the state capitol press corps on November 7, a day after Democrats won the California governorship and lopsided margins in the state's congressional and legislative delegations, Reagan punctured the trial balloon he had briefly set aloft. "I am not starting a third party," he said. "I do not believe the Republican Party is dead. I believe the Republican Party represents basically the thinking of the people of this country, if we can get that message across to the people. I'm going to try to do that."

The party was not dead, but many conservatives considered it comatose. Third-party advocates observed the same phenomena that Teeter did—few Americans any longer respected or identified with the Republican Party. And conservatives faced the further practical problem, as they saw it, that Democrats would probably nominate a liberal in 1976 while Republicans would be stuck with Jerry Ford. M. Stanton Evans, the veteran chairman of the American Conservative Union, told a national conservative political action conference meeting in Washington in February 1975 that conservatives should work "to keep the Republican Party as conservative as possible in states, localities and Congress"; but he also declared to loud applause: "At the presidential level, we need a new political party in 1976."[11] But Reagan was not buying it. Speaking to the conference on February 15, he asked rhetorically: "Is it a third party we need or is it a new and revitalized second party, raising a banner of no pale pastels but bold colors which make it unmistakably clear where we stand on all the issues troubling the people?" The phrase "no pale pastels" became a Reagan slogan that some conservatives would hurl back at him the following year when they wanted him to present a more aggressive campaign against President Ford.

Reagan's strength on the speaking circuit was his optimism, a quality of which the Republican Party was then in short supply. He would warm up his audiences with political gallows humor, saying to them, "There are those who will suggest that any mode of optimism expressed at this meeting would be as inappropriate as the captain of the *Titanic* saying, 'Never mind all that ice. Throw a party on Saturday night.' " Then he would tell the old favorite about the pessimistic boy and the optimistic boy, with the punchline in which the manure-shoveling optimist says, "There must be a pony in here someplace." And then still another old joke, this one about the farmer who gets tired of hearing the minister thank the Lord for his many bountiful crops and finally says to him, "Reverend, I wish you could have seen this place when the Lord was doing it by himself." The one-liners were prelude to the Reagan message, which was that Republicans should take the nation's political fate in their own hands and recreate America in a conservative image.

Reagan did not call for ideological warfare within the Republican Party itself. He correctly assumed that the majority of GOP activists who came to hear him speak shared a common faith. He knew that his audiences agreed with him about the evils of government spending, and he knew, too, that many of his listeners were vaguely uncomfortable with the cheerful, inarticulate presidency of Gerald Ford. Reagan almost never mentioned Ford. Instead, he suggested that the "mandate" of 1972 was in danger of being betrayed. "The '72 election gave us a new majority, a long-overdue realignment based not on party labels—but on basic philosophy," Reagan said. "The tragedy of Watergate and the traumatic experience of these past years since then has obscured the meaning of that '72 election. But the mandate registered by the people still remains. The people have not changed in philosophy."

Reagan was as reluctant as ever to make a personal decision before it was absolutely necessary. As always, he drifted in the direction of what he really wanted to do. What Reagan wanted to do in 1975 was run for President, preferably against a Democrat rather than a Republican incumbent. Ford was in the way. Reagan keenly remembered the GOP split of 1964 and his own insistence on party unity as a precondition of victory in 1966. He knew that he risked being cast as the spoiler who would hand over the White House to a Democrat. Still, Reagan wanted to run. He wanted it so much that Ford's lapses became magnified into crises of presidential leadership. Any deficiencies of policy which Ford had inherited from Richard Nixon were viewed as Ford's personal fault. Ford vetoed Democratic spending bills as readily and successfully as Reagan had done in California, but Reagan nonetheless saw the $52 billion federal deficit as a Ford failing. The appointment of Rockefeller rankled, and there were those in the Reagan entourage who repeated and took seriously the conservative scare stories that Ford might decide at the last moment not to run and attempt to hand Rockefeller the prize of the Republican nomination. Ford was not a leader, Reagan told his intimates. In private conversations Reagan referred to him as a "caretaker" who had been in Congress too long. Slowly—far too slowly for Sears and Nofziger—Reagan was selling himself on running for President.

Ford made it easy for Reagan to reach his decision. A traditionalist who accepted the conventional wisdom of Washington, Ford could not really believe that the staid and conservative Republican Party would tear itself to pieces again by ousting an incumbent President. Nor, despite Rockefeller, did he believe that many Republicans would accept a portrait of Jerry Ford as a liberal President. Preoccupied with the problems of the presidency and pulled in different directions by a White House staff divided between old Nixonites and old congressional aides, Ford did not pay consistent attention to the Reagan challenge or treat it seriously enough once he became aware of what was happening. When he acted at all, he did the wrong things. Reagan was especially insulted when Ford had his chief of staff, Donald H. Rumsfeld, offer him another cabinet job, this time Secretary of Commerce. "They're working their way down the scale," a Reagan intimate said incredulously when he heard of this offer.

Rumsfeld had at least acted in private. Worse than this job offer was the muddle-headed approach devised by Ford's former congressional cronies, notably Melvin R. Laird, who told reporters that Reagan would not actually enter the race once he had weighed the options. Ford and his friends, no less than Reagan, were demonstrating that they could talk themselves into believing whatever they wanted to believe. When these stories drifted back to Pacific Palisades, it seemed to Reagan as if he were being described as afraid to take on the President. But there was no way to scare Reagan out of the race through stories circulated to Washington reporters. Ford would have had other options, if he had understood Reagan better. He might have brought Reagan back to the White House for highly visible meetings and given the appearance of taking his guidance. Some Reagan intimates who knew that the governor was susceptible to flattery were worried that Ford would actually try this approach. However, Sears realized that Ford, after a quarter-century in Congress, had a parochial view of national politics and did not grasp the magnitude of the Reagan challenge. He also realized that Secretary of the Army Howard (Bo) Callaway, the wealthy Georgia conservative tapped by Ford to head his election committee, had no standing with the Reaganites and no experience directing a national campaign. Sears remembered how Callaway had bungled as Nixon's southern coordinator in 1968 by inviting George Wallace into the Republican Party and allowing the Nixon campaign to be tagged as racist. Ford, if he ever knew about this incident, did not remember it. To a President of the United States who had spent his entire political life until Agnew's fall in the House of Representatives, Callaway had one sterling quality which commended him as a political manager. Callaway, like Ford, had been a member of the House.

In California not everyone was pleased with Reagan's willingness to take on a President of his own party. One Reagan intimate anonymously expressed his disgust to me late in 1974. "Now is the time for loyalty to a Republican, not when the President is an unindicted co-conspirator," this prominent Republican said. There were some defections in the Reagan ranks. Paul Haerle, a one-time Reagan appointments secretary and now the California Republican chairman, openly supported Ford. Henry Salvatori, one of the original trio of Reagan fund-raisers in the 1966 campaign, recognized that Reagan's challenge was divisive and also backed the President. David Packard, who was thought of highly enough by Reaganites to be invited to their original planning session in the spring of 1974, became Ford's national finance chairman. But Tuttle had by the spring of 1975 swung around to the idea of supporting a Reagan challenge, and Sears and Nofziger were clamoring for the formation of "an exploratory committee." Sears had persuaded congenial Senator Paul Laxalt of Nevada to head such a committee. Laxalt would become Reagan's closest friend in Congress, but he was not at this time that much of an intimate. When Laxalt was running for the Senate in Nevada in 1974, he told me that Reagan was more reserved than other politicians and that he spoke to his friends in private as if he were giving a speech to the multitudes. "Same stories, same one-liners," Laxalt said. But he liked Reagan, shared his ideology and admired him as a governor and national conservative leader. Laxalt had resisted Minority Leader Hugh Scott's efforts to line up Republican senators on behalf of Ford's 1976 candidacy. The Nevadan was shrewd enough to see that Reagan would wind up running for President, and he wanted to be part of the effort. At the time Sears called upon him, Laxalt was one of the few high Republican office-holders willing to identify himself with a Reagan campaign against the President. But he would have been an excellent choice for the job even if Reagan and Sears had been given the entire Senate to choose from.

As a Senate nominee who had been dragged to defeat in the Goldwater debacle, Laxalt realized the dangers of disunity. Instead of an open challenge to Ford, what was required in these early stages was a campaign of quiet subversion in which an organization could be assembled while Reagan presented himself as a superior alternative to Ford without openly knocking the President. As Sears had recognized, Laxalt's low-key and personable style was well suited to this task.

Citizens for Reagan, as the "exploratory committee" was called, came into being on July 15, 1975, one week after Ford had formally announced that he would seek election in his own right. The Reagan committee's precarious mission, reminiscent of 1966, was to determine the extent of public support for a Reagan candidacy. Everyone who counted—Sears, Tuttle,

Nofziger, Laxalt and such rising political aides as Jim Lake—knew that the exploration was only a formality. But it enabled Reagan to keep his radio show and his column, which were important to him and to Deaver. The theme of the committee was that Ford was good but Reagan was better. "We're not saying President Ford is not doing a good job," said Laxalt blandly in making the announcement. "We feel he is. But Governor Reagan could do a better job, because he is totally independent of the federal government scene."

While the committee organized and raised money, the once and future candidate continued to work the banquet circuit with his 1975 version of his 1964 antigovernment speech. The difference, and it was a big one, was that Reagan could now present himself not as some idle conservative theorist preaching about how government could be made to work, but as a successful California governor who had translated his theories into practice. Californian reporters accompanying Reagan on his tours marveled at the former governor's stirring accounts of how fiscal solvency and welfare reform had been achieved in California. There was a mythic quality to the governor's version of his own achievements, which of course made no mention of Moretti's cooperation on welfare reform or the massive Reagan tax increases. It was a selective version of reality, but it was highly effective in convincing Republican audiences that Reagan had the practical experience needed for the presidency.

The speech, however, did not please many of the "movement conservatives" of the American Conservative Union and the Young Americans for Freedom, several of whom privately had grumbled about the performance of their hero at the February political action conference in Washington. They wanted Reagan to challenge Ford directly on détente and the unbalanced federal budget. Above all, they wanted Reagan's speeches to reflect something beyond a general preference for the marketplace and a celebration of his California governorship. Nofziger, a conservative ideologue himself, disputed this view. He realized that Reagan's audiences around the country were as happy with the bromides as they would ever be with new ideas. But Nofziger's view did not prevail. The movement conservatives had unlikely allies among reporters who had covered Reagan for a long time and clamored for "something new" in his speeches. Nofziger resisted them, too, saying that Reagan wasn't trying to make news. Later, Nofziger would quarrel with Sears about the relative blandness of Reagan's approach to Ford. But in the summer of 1975 he was content to let the old Goldwater speech run its course. Sears, and his aides David Keene and Jim Lake, were too busy organizing to pay much attention to Reagan's speeches, one way or the other. If there was one thing Reagan knew how to do, it was speak. Sears and Lake were creating an organization for Reagan in the first primary state of New Hampshire, and Keene was trying to shore up Reagan's southern base. In this context, it was left to others to supply the new ideas. Unfortunately for Reagan, these ideas were not long in coming.

The speech which prevented Reagan from winning the Republican presidential nomination of 1976 was drafted by Jeffrey Bell, a personable conservative on the Reagan committee campaign staff in Washington, and polished by Stan Evans. Bell had heard Reagan's speech in February before the conservative conference and found it devoid of ideas. "Reagan had absolutely nothing to say," Bell told Jules Witcover later, "so I hit on decentralization as his vision of the future. It was anti-Washington; he could talk about it without attacking Ford. People should have more control, and Washington less. You could get out of the old right-wing rut of calling for repeal of everything and saying that spending for things like education was bad."[12] In fact, Bell's idea dovetailed neatly with what Reagan had said for years in California speeches, which was that states and local governments could run programs such as welfare better than the federal government could. The Reagan administration had skirmished in court with the federal government on Medi-Cal and welfare issues, usually losing. Reagan was a delegator and a decentralizer. It is hard to imagine a speech more up his philosophical alley than the one Bell wrote for him and shipped to Hannaford in Los Angeles. Hannaford called Sears to praise the speech and then asked Bell to send him the backup material. Before he sent it, Bell discussed the idea with Sears, Keene and Nofziger. He had never discussed it with Reagan, but the candidate-to-be liked it so much he remarked to an aide that it was in line with what he would hope to accomplish if he became President.

No one remembers the formal title of the luncheon speech Reagan gave to the Executive Club of Chicago at McCormick Place on September 26, 1975. It was called, "Let The People Rule." It will forever be remembered in American political history as "The $90 Billion Speech." Its central premise was that the ills of the nation "all stem from a single source: the belief that government, particularly the federal government, has the answer to our ills and that the proper method of dealing with social problems is to transfer power from the private to the public sector, and within the public sector from state and local governments to the ultimate power center in Washington." With a simplicity and directness that equaled Reagan's own, Bell went on to spell out the consequences of this transfer. "This collectivist, centralizing approach, whatever name or party label it wears, has created our economic problems," he wrote. "By taxing and consuming an ever-greater share of the national wealth, it has imposed an intolerable burden of taxation on American citizens. By spending above and beyond even this level of taxation, it has created the horrendous inflation of the past decade. And by saddling our economy with an ever-greater burden of controls and regulations, it has generated economic problems—from the raising of consumer prices to the destruction of jobs, to choking off vital supplies of energy."

After two more paragraphs about how "the crushing weight of central government has distorted our federal system and altered the relationship between the levels of government," the speech broached the solution that was to sink Reagan politically:

> What I propose is nothing less than a systematic transfer of authority and resources to the states—a program of creative federalism for America's third century.
>
> Federal authority has clearly failed to do the job. Indeed, it has created more problems in welfare, education, housing, food stamps, Medicaid, community and regional development, and revenue sharing, to name a few. The sums involved and the potential savings to the taxpayer are large. Transfer of authority in whole or part in all of these areas would reduce the outlay of the federal government by more than $90 billion, using the spending levels of fiscal 1975. With such a savings it would be possible to balance the federal budget, make an initial $5 billion payment on the national debt and cut the federal personal income burden of every American by an average of 23 percent.

Rarely has so much been promised so sweepingly by a presidential candidate. Reagan did exempt national defense and space programs, Social Security, Medicare, TVA "and some aspects of agriculture, energy transportation and environment" from his transfer proposal. Even so, what he proposed was a mammoth undertaking. Worse yet, the backup material which Hannaford had requested from Bell specified reductions in education and manpower training, community and regional development, commerce and transportation, income security, law enforcement, revenue sharing, Medicaid and health programs.

New speeches by Reagan were rarities in those days, and his top campaign aides flew in from Los Angeles and Washington to hear it. "We thought the speech was an important issue thrust for him," said Hannaford. "The press treated the whole thing with a yawn."[13] Only one Washington-based reporter covered the speech, and he kissed off the proposal in three paragraphs at the end of the story, preferring to write about the then unannounced but long-decided question of whether Reagan would run for President. Joel Weisman, then the midwestern correspondent for the *Washington Post,* filed a story which was buried inside the paper. The chief complaint of Reagan's advisers at the time, as Robert Shogan of the *Los Angeles Times* would later observe, was that the speech didn't receive sufficient attention. But all that changed when Stuart K. Spencer swung into action.

Ford's campaign committee had been an embarrassment ever since its creation. Packard had failed to deliver as finance chairman. Neither the President nor Callaway knew what to do about Reagan. Callaway had repeatedly and clumsily given the impression that he was trying to force Rockefeller off the ticket, at one point describing the Vice-President as "the number one problem." It would have been a better description of Reagan. Finally, in October, Ford reached out to California to bring Spencer into the campaign as his political strategist while keeping Callaway technically in charge of the campaign. Spencer arrived bearing a grudge, an appreciation of Reagan's potency as a candidate, and an irrepressibly candid campaign spokesman named Peter Kaye. The grudge was against the Reagan administration in California, which Spencer had helped bring to power, and, in particular, against Deaver, whom Spencer believed had bad-mouthed him with potential clients and damaged his consulting business.

As Spencer saw it, the crowd around Reagan, except for Sears, was dominated by ingrates who had turned a passive governor against the people who had elected him to office. Spencer was contemptuous of Reagan's relaxed work habits, saying openly that the former governor was "lazy." But he was appalled by the underestimation of Reagan he found in the Ford camp. "Hell, they were asking me if he was going to run at a time Sears had organized New Hampshire and Reagan had set an announcement date," Spencer once told me. He knew that Reagan was a far superior political candidate than the President, particularly on television. Savvy and combative, Spencer realized from the outset that Ford's hope of winning the nomination depended on discrediting Reagan. Spencer is a man without frills, and he and Kaye immediately directed themselves to the task. The $90 Billion Speech seemed like an answer to a prayer. For Spencer, with his painful memories of the 1964 California primary when he had managed Rockefeller's campaign, it was Barry Goldwater revisited. But even Goldwater had never advocated anything this sweeping. Immediately, $90 billion became the No. 1 priority of the Ford election committee. The speech was given to research director Fred Slight for analysis. Kaye, aware that few Washington reporters even knew about the speech, set about correcting their ignorance. He had the advantage of credibility with the press because Kaye was as forthright about Ford's deficiencies as he was about Reagan's, a characteristic rare among spokesmen.*

By early November, $90 billion had become a hot topic of conversation in the press. Then, on November 19, 1975, the day before Reagan formally announced his candidacy, Slight gave Kaye an analysis of the $90 billion plan. Listed among its potential effects were high unemployment because of federal cutbacks, probable bankruptcy for some states and municipalities, and a slump in the recession-ridden housing and construction industries. "Finally, such grand rhetoric is completely out of touch with reality," the

* Eventually, Kaye's candor cost him his job, but his frankness, unappreciated at headquarters except by Spencer, was useful to Ford. At the beginning of the 1976 campaign, reporters were more than normally suspicious of a President who a few months earlier had pardoned Richard Nixon. Kaye won the confidence of the press by consistently telling the truth, even when it hurt. Ironically, he was ultimately fired by Rogers C. B. Morton, whose own loose tongue provided one of the Ford campaign's most embarrassing moments. Morton, who succeeded Callaway, was in the President Ford Committee headquarters in Washington the night of May 4, when Reagan won 131 of 140 delegates in Alabama, Georgia and Indiana. Sitting before a collection of half-empty liquor bottles, Morton said, "I'm not going to rearrange the furniture on the deck of the *Titanic.*"

report concluded. "The question of raising the public's expectations and over-promising on the federal government's ability to deliver smacks of the same faults which Reagan has blamed on other presidents, especially LBJ."

Oblivious to what was about to happen to him, Reagan and Nancy and a few of his top aides were celebrating on the eve of the announcement. Hannaford had brought along a bottle of champagne. Before he opened it, he remarked that Reagan had never actually told them that he was going to run.[14] Everyone laughed. The next day Reagan opened his campaign at the National Press Club, where he talked vaguely about growing Soviet military superiority abroad and declining economic conditions at home. As always, he blamed government, which he said at all levels absorbed more than 44 percent of the national income and "has become more intrusive, more coercive, more meddlesome and less effective." His only slap at Ford was both indirect and unmistakable: "In my opinion, the root of these problems lies right here—in Washington, D.C. Our nation's capital has become the seat of a 'buddy' system that functions for its own benefit—increasingly insensitive to the needs of the American worker who supports it with his taxes." In this opening statement Reagan demonstrated a lack of specific knowledge about defense issues and the New York City fiscal crisis but, on the whole, fielded questions adequately. Immediately after the speech he left on a five-state tour, where he was threatened by a toy pistol in Florida and then gave an ill-informed answer in Charlotte, North Carolina, saying that segregation had ended in the armed forces because of a black mess steward's heroism at Pearl Harbor.[15] But there was as yet no hint of the trouble which was to come with $90 billion. When a question about the proposal came up the night of Reagan's announcement at a "town meeting" rally in Bedford, New Hampshire, he successfully deflected it. Nofziger took a deep breath. Maybe $90 billion would not be such a problem after all.

The following Sunday, on ABC's *Issues and Answers,* the hope of Reagan and his managers that $90 billion might go away was revealed as wishful thinking. Reagan sprang the trap on himself, after he was pressed by Frank Reynolds, who observed that the federal government paid 62 percent of New Hampshire's welfare costs and that New Hampshire would have to either reduce welfare or raise taxes under Reagan's transfer plan. Reagan said that states and local governments could be in a position to pay for these plans if the federal government "stopped pre-empting so much of the tax dollar." It was an unhelpful answer for a candidate waging a primary in a tourist-oriented state that prides itself on the absence of sales and income taxes. When ABC's Bob Clark followed up by asking Reagan whether "in all candor" he wouldn't have to tell New Hampshire voters that either an income or a sales tax would be necessary, Reagan gave a rhetorical answer, saying, "But isn't this a proper decision for the people of the state to make?"

By now, Reagan's managers knew they had at least two problems. The first was the $90 billion plan itself, with its damaging specificity. The second was Reagan, who was winging his answers to questions and not paying attention to the backup material that had been given to him. Like many other candidates before and after him, Reagan had failed to recognize the special scrutiny which the press gives to fledgling presidential candidates. The scrutiny was especially severe in Reagan's case because he was not well known in the East and because the transfer proposal and some of Reagan's wilder statements reminded reporters of Barry Goldwater.

Sears had been hired chiefly on the recommendation that he could help Reagan with the eastern press, and this now became the focus of his activity. He brought in an old Nixon hand, Stanford economics professor Martin Anderson, who constructed a series of elaborate defenses based on Reagan's passing reference in The $90 Billion Speech to transferring back tax resources to the states along with federal programs. Anderson dug up an obscure and unsuccessful proposal made a number of years earlier by former New Hampshire Senator Norris Cotton, who wanted to give states a percentage of federal liquor taxes. He found precedents for decentralization in Dwight Eisenhower, John Kennedy and Hubert Humphrey. When Anderson had finished, the $90 billion tiger had been transformed into a tame tabby-cat of a plan for reexamining federal, state and local government relationships. But Spencer and Kaye had done their work well. Reagan's recitation of the useful generalities constructed for him by Anderson was dogged throughout the campaign by the specifics of his original proposal, which kept being thrown back in his face by the opposition and the press. One survey taken for Reagan by his pollster Richard B. Wirthlin showed that a majority of voters in New Hampshire actually favored the concept enunciated by Reagan. But the poll did not measure—could not measure—the incalculable impact of The $90 Billion Speech on the campaign and confidence of Reagan, who was thrown on the defensive at the very time he had built momentum and was pulling away from Ford. Sears and Lake had built a competent organization in New Hampshire, headed by former Governor Hugh Gregg. They expected to win and almost certainly would have, had Reagan thrown The $90 Billion Speech into the ash can and relied on "A Time For Choosing" instead.

Reagan's own supporters in New Hampshire also damaged his cause. He had the backing of William Loeb, the opinionated publisher of the *Manchester Union Leader,* whom everyone courted in New Hampshire but whose endorsement constituted a mixed blessing.* "When you get Loeb's support, you also get his enemies and there are lots of them around," Lake once observed. The *Union Leader* made its usual outrageous attacks on the candidate Loeb was trying to defeat, routinely describing the President as "Jerry the Jerk." True to his reputation, Loeb extended his attacks to the families of those he opposed, calling Betty Ford "stupid" and "immoral"

---

* Loeb died on September 16, 1981.

after she defended her daughter's right to have an affair. New Hampshire Governor Meldrim Thomson was also a heavy millstone draped around the Reagan campaign despite the best efforts of Sears and Lake to keep him away from the candidate. Thomson, whose positions on many issues made Reagan look like a liberal, wanted to accompany the presidential candidate throughout New Hampshire but was restricted to a single day of travel with Reagan in favorable Manchester. "He killed us on that one day, though,"[16] said Lake in retrospect, remembering how Thomson predicted a 55 percent victory for Reagan on this occasion.

Gregg made no such predictions, wisely declaring that Reagan would do well to win 40 to 45 percent of the vote. But Gregg, whose political perceptions were formed in the organizational trench warfare of New Hampshire, committed a more serious mistake. Gregg believed that the key to victory was election-day mobilization, which was easier to accomplish if the candidate spent the last two days before the primary out of state. What Gregg failed to recognize is that Reagan is his own best campaign asset and that his presence in a close race can make a difference between victory and defeat. Sears and Lake, who are also organization minded, went along with Gregg. They said afterward they yielded to him because Wirthlin's polls showed that Reagan would win.

Wirthlin's four surveys, which Lake had not been shown, gave a far less certain picture of the probable outcome. Reagan led on February 6, but by February 15 Ford had surged ahead on the strength of a two-day visit to New Hampshire which attracted large crowds and favorable coverage from every news outlet except the *Union Leader*. Wirthlin knew that Ford was returning to the state before the February 24 primary, and he wanted Reagan to stay in New Hampshire to combat the President. His polls showed that Reagan's campaigning in his own behalf was highly effective. Wirthlin had not been told of Gregg's intention to export the candidate two days before the election, and he did not realize that Sears had kept to himself the conclusions of the February 15 voter survey. "John believed that knowledge is power," said Deaver later, looking back on what he now regards as the first early warning of the uncommunicative conduct which would cause Sears' downfall four years later.

Wirthlin took his final poll on February 18, six days before the primary. The results were ominous. Reagan was four points ahead in the raw tally, but the undecided vote was high and Ford was returning to the state. The President's previous visit had swung undecided voters to him, and Wirthlin prepared an analysis in which the final assumption was a 2–1 swing of undecided voters to Ford. This assumption gave Ford a tiny lead, 50.7 to 49.3 percent, very close to the actual result. Wirthlin, who on occasion has been accused of putting too rosy a coloration on negative findings, did not pull his punches in the final survey report he sent to Sears. "On February 18 it appears that Ronald Reagan enjoys a whisper of a lead over Gerald Ford,"

Wirthlin wrote in his summary. "Given a confidence interval of plus-or-minus 5.2 percent [the margin of error], it would, nevertheless, be folly to project a winner. Further, at least three important events will intervene between now and next Tuesday. First, Gerald Ford will revisit the state. While research conducted in the past indicates that second visits do not have the potency of the first visit, this event should not be underrated since the foregoing data show that Ford shifted the electorate dramatically through his personal appearance. *Second, Governor Reagan will be in the state between now and the election* [italics mine]. That visit, the issues it raises, and the play received in the press can also impact the rather large bloc of undecideds."*

The Sunday before the election Wirthlin met Deaver at Los Angeles International Airport, believing that the two of them were flying to New Hampshire to meet Reagan. Instead, Deaver informed the pollster that they were catching a Chicago-bound flight with an eventual destination of Peoria. "Why are we going to Illinois?" Wirthlin wanted to know. "To meet the governor," replied Deaver. Wirthlin told me later he had a sinking feeling when he heard this because he recognized that Reagan's presence in New Hampshire until the primary was vital. He did not realize that Reagan himself had not been shown the poll in which he had "a whisper of a lead." The candidate, ever the delegator, subsequently confirmed this. He had not protested when Sears, without mentioning the poll, had told him of Gregg's desires to mobilize the campaign workers. Instead, he had obediently flown off to campaign in Illinois, where the primary would not be held until March 16. After a day of campaigning in the Peoria area, Reagan flew back to New Hampshire on the Monday evening before the primary, still not knowing that his pollster had told his campaign manager that he should never have left the state.

On this return flight Reagan heard the bad news. It came to him from Wirthlin, whom Sears finally had instructed to brief the candidate about what he could expect on Tuesday. Wirthlin uneasily went through the poll with Reagan, trying to put the best face on it but telling him that the race was so close that the break of the undecided voters would determine the outcome. For the first time, as the plane began to descend in the gathering darkness above Manchester, Reagan recognized that he might lose the primary, and with it the presidential nomination. As always, Reagan's customary optimism had been telling him that he would win. But he knew that

* The third factor cited by Wirthlin as important was voter turnout. The pollster wrote that "the conventional wisdom" in New Hampshire was for a 100,000 vote turnout, which would have been beneficial to Reagan. But Wirthlin warned that his survey pointed to a turnout of about 115,000 votes, which favored Ford. "Without question, a large turnout will erode Ronald Reagan's vote margin," Wirthlin reported in his survey. This was because Reagan's supporters, who were ideologically committed, were considered likely to vote under any circumstances. The actual turnout of slightly more than 108,000 votes was midway between these two projections and just enough to give Ford a narrow victory.

Wirthlin was an optimist, too, and that a tie with the President going into election day probably would turn into a defeat. Later he would second-guess the wasted time in Peoria and, later still, come to question why Sears had kept the vital polling information from him. But he did not do that then. As the plane began its final approach for a landing in Manchester, Reagan turned to his pollster and smiled. "I hope someone down there lights a candle for me," he said.

15

Running for President

As it turned out, the path to Kansas City led through the Panama Canal. Two weeks before voters in the New Hampshire primary delivered their judgments, Reagan spoke to restless prep school students at Phillips Exeter Academy in Exeter, New Hampshire, in his first significant foreign policy speech of the campaign. The aim of the forty-minute address was to shift the political dialogue in New Hampshire away from Reagan's $90 billion domestic blunder and onto President Ford's foreign policy. But the speech, though highly critical of the results of this policy, did not mention either Ford or Secretary of State Henry Kissinger by name. Its principal argument was that the United States should not sacrifice development of the Cruise missile for the illusory comfort of a strategic arms agreement with the Soviets. Tucked into the middle of the forty-minute address drafted by Peter Hannaford were two paragraphs which said:

> Our foreign policy in recent years seems to be a matter of placating potential adversaries. Does our government fear that the American people lack willpower? If it does, that may explain its reluctance to assert our interests in international relations.
>
> How else can we explain the government's bowing to the propaganda campaign of the military dictator of Panama and signing a memorandum with his representative signifying our intention to give up control and ownership of the Panama Canal and the Canal Zone?

Had Reagan won the New Hampshire primary, the Panama Canal issue of 1976 might have died with this fleeting passage. But Reagan did not win. Though he was optimistic again on election day after a good night's sleep, and though he led Ford in the early hours of the tallying on primary night, the "whisper of a lead" on election day belonged to Ford. Reagan could hardly believe it. He had been so high about his own prospects that he had flung aside his election-night superstition for the only time in his political career and permitted himself to be photographed with a newspaper headline showing him leading the President. The lead lasted until 1 A.M. the next morning when Ford surged ahead. Reagan lost by only 1,317 votes out of more than 108,000 ballots cast, but he was a loser nevertheless.* The verdict was difficult for Reagan to accept, both because he had become convinced he would be a winner and because he had it in his head that a close defeat would be considered by others as a victory. The next day Reagan pointed out to reporters that the press had counted Eugene McCarthy a winner after he was defeated by President Johnson in 1968, and had reached the same judgment about George McGovern after he was decisively beaten by Senator Edmund Muskie in 1972. But the comparison was misplaced. Neither McCarthy nor McGovern had predicted victory, and neither had expected to win. Reporters might have discounted Governor Thomson's public forecast, but several of them also had been told privately by Sears or Lake that Reagan would carry New Hampshire. This was contrary to a candidate's usual tactic of lowering media expectations by underestimation, but Reagan was not involved in a usual race. Sears had tried to establish the inevitability of Ronald Reagan by diminishing the President's credentials. Ford was portrayed as an accidental President who had no following beyond those who automatically endorsed a White House incumbent. It was difficult for either reporters or politicians to accept this premise, however, without also concluding that Reagan could defeat Ford, particularly in the conservative context of New Hampshire. As a result, Sears did not discourage forecasts of a Reagan victory. And this was fine with the press, which had been justly criticized in the past for deciding the "magic number" which a candidate had to achieve to be declared the winner. In the New Hampshire primary of 1976 the press finally arrived at a useful, and appropriately simple standard: The winner was the candidate who received the most votes.

Sears and Wirthlin did not go to bed the night of the New Hampshire primary. They stayed up, concocting in the dark hours of Reagan's defeat the strategy that would lead to his brightest victories. Immediately they recognized that Reagan needed to go after Ford directly and on the foreign policy issue, where the President was most vulnerable among conservative voters. No matter what the Eleventh Commandment was supposed to dictate, this meant an open attack on Ford by name—and on his Secretary of State.

On its face, the question of whether the United States should turn over

---

* Officially, Ford had 54,824 votes to Reagan's 53,507. However, the actual tally may have been even closer. New Hampshire law at the time allowed delegates who were not on a candidate's official slate to run as pledged to him. Three such unofficial candidates were pledged to Reagan, and could not be persuaded to withdraw. Anyone who carelessly voted for both the official delegates and any of the three unpledged delegates cast an invalid ballot. Governor Thomson and, subsequently, Reagan came to believe that enough such ballots were cast to make the difference between victory and defeat. State election officials at the time disputed this contention. But since the invalidated ballots were destroyed without a count being made of them, no one will ever know for certain.

the jurisdiction of the 51-mile Panama Canal to Panama did not seem a promising issue on which to turn the tide against a sitting President of the United States. Every President since Johnson had tried to renegotiate a treaty with Panama, and only a small percentage of voters were even conscious of the issue. But Wirthlin, in his surveys, had picked up something else. The something was the backlash which had developed in the aftermath of the Vietnam War, a feeling that the United States had allowed itself to be pushed around in the world without doing anything about it. Reagan's denunciation of the Panamanian leader, Omar Torrijos, as a "tinhorn dictator," struck a responsive chord. Most Americans took U.S. control of the Panama Canal for granted. They saw it as an example of American altruism and stability, not colonialism. Even voters who believed that the United States had no business in Vietnam tended to believe that the canal was a legitimate object of American interest. While Reagan slept away his disappointment in the predawn hours of February 25, Sears, Wirthlin and the other members of the Reagan team decided to have a go at foreign policy and the Panama Canal. Their candidate would prove more than willing.

The impact of the New Hampshire defeat on Reagan's campaign imparted urgency to the attack. When the pollsters checked their surveys after New Hampshire, they found that Ford's previously narrow lead in Florida had become a runaway. The President had gained 16 points in his own polls and 14 points in Reagan's on the strength of his eyelash victory. This was staggering news for the Reagan campaign, and this time Sears told the candidate what was happening. Reagan already was hearing speculation that he would drop out of a race which he thought had barely begun. Former Illinois Governor Richard Ogilvie, heading the Ford forces in Illinois, predicted that Reagan's loyalists would desert him if he lost Florida. "One thing about Republicans—they don't like to work for losers," Ogilvie said. Reagan, who quickly talked himself into believing that he had really won in New Hampshire, was at first surprised and then annoyed at the talk that the campaign was over. He told aides and reporters that he was going all the way to the Republican national convention at Kansas City, no matter what happened—and he meant it. But Florida was not promising. In a general election, Florida is "Reagan country" because of the number of conservative Democrats who usually vote for the Republican presidential nominee. However, crossover voting is not permitted in Florida primaries, where the Republican electorate includes many retired Midwesterners and Easterners. Thirty-eight percent of the eligible GOP voters in 1976 were over sixty-five years old. These older voters tend to vote much the way they voted back in Michigan, Ohio and Illinois. As a rule they resist change and favor incumbents, even unelected Presidents. Some of these retirees were susceptible to suggestions that Reagan was "another Goldwater" who would do away with Social Security. Even if Reagan had won in New Hampshire, Florida might have proved a struggle for him. After losing in New Hampshire, his task seemed almost impossible.

Ford, whose reliance on old buddies from the House of Representatives had led to the unfortunate selection of Callaway, made the same mistake in Florida. He chose as his campaign manager Representative Louis Frey, Jr., whose horizons were those of a congressional district candidate, not a state campaign director. Frey and his even less experienced lieutenant, Oscar Juarez, were quickly out-organized by Reagan forces led by David Keene and L. E. (Tommy) Thomas, a Panama City automobile dealer. Unfortunately for Reagan, the ebullient Thomas undermined his own efforts with an extravagant prediction that Reagan would carry the state by a 2–1 margin. Though no one but Thomas believed this, the forecast provided Reagan with an unreachable level of expectation. Still, Thomas and Keene were so effective organizationally that Stu Spencer, back in Washington, became worried that the Ford team would not be able to deliver on election day. Spencer's solution was to bring in Bill Roberts from California to set things right. Several years before Roberts and Spencer had dissolved their partnership, and Roberts had suffered from illness and misfortune since his palmy 1966 days as Reagan's campaign manager. However, he remained an accomplished professional who was keenly aware of Reagan's strengths and weaknesses. Within days of Roberts' arrival in Florida in early February, moribund headquarters all over the state had sprung to life in a busy recruitment of volunteers. A glossy, eight-page mailer was distributed to Republican voters, featuring a full-length color picture of "the President," sitting in front of an American flag and saying, "I'm proud to be an American . . . just like you." Ford was presented as the safe and sure candidate, and a featured issue of the mailer was the President's pledge "to preserve the integrity and solvency of the Social Security system." The none too veiled implication was that Reagan wouldn't. Roberts helped fuel skepticism about the former California governor among Florida reporters by recounting stories about how Reagan had needed naps during the 1966 campaign. When Reagan flew home for a weekend of rest in mid-campaign, this unextraordinary event was depicted in some Florida newspapers as evidence that Reagan lacked the stamina for the presidency.

Against this virtuoso performance and Ford's own effective campaigning in Florida, Reagan fought uphill to establish his foreign policy themes. Five days before the primary, at a televised news conference and rally at Rollins College near Orlando, Reagan said that Ford had shown "neither the vision nor the leadership necessary to halt and reverse the diplomatic and military decline of the United States." After asserting that the Soviet Union had achieved military supremacy over the United States, Reagan said, "Mr. Ford and Dr. Kissinger ask us to trust their leadership. Well, I find that more and more difficult to do. Henry Kissinger's recent stewardship of U.S. foreign policy has coincided precisely with the loss of U.S. military supremacy." But military spending was alive and well in Florida. The day before Reagan accused Ford of presiding over the military decline of the United States, the big news in Orlando was that Martin Marietta, one of the area's largest employers, had been awarded a $33.6 million Air Force contract for an advanced strategic air system.

Ford won the March 9 Florida primary on the strength of the retirement vote, prevailing by a 53 to 47 percent margin. Reagan had indeed made up ground on the foreign policy issue, but it was scant consolation. Encouraged by the White House, Republican office-holders were now beginning to openly urge Reagan to quit the race in the interests of "party unity." Reagan was discouraged, Sears was drinking heavily, the campaign was running out of money and aides were quarreling among themselves. Reagan had by now lost four primaries, including uncontested ones in Massachusetts and Vermont a week after New Hampshire. Illinois, on March 16, took him further down the downhill slope. On the eve of the primary, Reagan said he would be "happy" with 40 percent of the vote, slightly below what Wirthlin's polls had predicted for him. He received almost exactly 40 percent, and he wasn't happy at all. But he again repeated, grimly this time, what he had said before Florida. Brushing aside questions about his mounting campaign deficit, Reagan declared he was going all the way to Kansas City.

North Carolina lay ahead. Many reporters and politicians thought that this primary, on March 23, would be Reagan's last. Without telling his candidate, Sears already was making arrangements for the inevitable. On March 20 Sears met secretly in his Washington office with Rogers Morton, who had been authorized by Ford to talk about conditions under which Reagan might withdraw from the race. Sears knew that the campaign would soon be out of money, both because of Reagan's defeats and because the Federal Elections Commission, which dispensed federal subsidies to presidential candidates, was due to go out of business the day before the North Carolina primary.* Reagan knew that his campaign was financially precarious, but he knew nothing of the Sears-Morton meeting. Afterward, he told me that he would never have withdrawn, no matter what Sears agreed to do. He expressed a similar feeling in even stronger terms to Nofziger and Deaver. Both Californians had much more respect for Reagan than Sears did, and they were struck with Reagan's determination. Until this time, Reagan always had followed the lead of his strategists, whoever they were. Now he was drifting toward the leadership of his own campaign at a time when his chief strategist, perhaps because he knew more about what was going on than Reagan did, was giving up. Reagan was not about to throw in the towel.

* On January 30, 1976, the Supreme Court upheld the constitutionality of much of the Federal Election Campaign Act, passed in 1974 in response to the abuses of Watergate. This law provided public financing for presidential candidates. But the court also found that the constitutional doctrine of the separation of powers was violated by the manner in which commission members were chosen, since four of the six commissioners were named by Congrss to a body which exercised executive powers. Congress was unable to agree on how the commission should be reconstituted, and the FEC temporarily went out of business on March 22, at a time the bankrupt Reagan campaign owed $1 million. By the time the new commission was back in business on May 21, Reagan had lost a vital opportunity to compete in the Wisconsin primary.

Luck, in which Reagan has always believed, then came to his aid in the form of problems for Bo Callaway, the beleaguered Ford campaign manager. Near the end of the Illinois primary, Callaway found himself the focal point of accusations that he had improperly influenced a U.S. Forest Service decision which benefited a Colorado ski resort in which he had an interest. In the long run, nothing came of the charges, but Callaway was eased out of the campaign by White House Chief of Staff Richard B. Cheney. After Spencer, who considered himself a strategist instead of an administrator, turned down the campaign management job, Morton was named to replace Callaway. Ultimately, Callaway's departure was beneficial to the Ford campaign. At that point, however, it was a distraction that for the first time put the White House rather than the Reagan campaign on the defensive.

On the heels of the Callaway affair, Ford advertised his own deficiencies as a presidential candidate. Appearing in Charlotte on March 20, the same day Sears was meeting with Morton, Ford sent his stock plummeting with a speech that ranks as one of the silliest in the annals of presidential campaigning. Speaking to the Future Homemakers of America, Ford said: "I regret that some people in this country have disparaged and demeaned the role of the homemaker. I say—and I say it with emphasis and conviction—that homemaking is good for America. I say that homemaking is not out of date and I reject strongly such accusations." The President did not identify the evil forces that were trying to destroy homemaking. But he made himself the butt of ridicule among reporters who had been told beforehand by White House Press Secretary Ron Nessen that the speech would be Ford's major pronouncement of the day.

Reagan had more controversial themes, and he was presenting them with more conviction that he had in the Florida and Illinois primaries. Responding to a suggestion from Senator Paul Laxalt, Reagan had discarded his five-by-seven cards in favor of a fiery extemporaneous presentation of his foreign policy case against the Ford administration. Reagan's favorite issues were the purported decline of U.S. military power and the "giveaway" of the Panama Canal. "We bought it, we paid for it, it's ours, and we're going to keep it," Reagan would say, to an invariable burst of applause. North Carolina voters proved receptive to this issue, perhaps because it also was a favorite topic of Senator Jesse Helms, who was Reagan's most outspoken advocate in the state. Helms had been sharply critical of Sears in the early stretches of the campaign, blaming him for what the North Carolina senator considered the softness of Reagan's criticisms of administration foreign policy. Reagan's sharpening of the attack, particularly against Kissinger, was highly pleasing to Helms, and he said so to Reagan.* En-

* One of Reagan's central references in his development of the Canal issue was a tract, "Panama Canal: Focus of Power Politics," written by James P. Lucier, the chief legislative assistant to Helms. "If we hand over this territory in response to unreasonable demands in Panama and the clamor of our Marxist enemies, we will pass a watershed in our history," the pamphlet concluded. "One more turning point will mark the decline of a great nation."

couraged both by his audiences and his North Carolina backers, Reagan went full bore after the President. In Lenoir he declared:

> Our party, the Republican Party, has been traditionally the party of fiscal responsibility. For forty years we have opposed the profligate tax and tax, spend and spend, elect and elect policies of our opponents. How will we campaign in November if the Democrats can point to our candidate having presided over the greatest budget deficit in our nation's history?
>
> The Republicans in Congress opposed the Democratic efforts to cut defense spending. . . . How will we respond in the campaign when the Democrats point out that under our candidate we have become second to the Soviet Union in military strength in a world where it is perhaps fatal to be second best?
>
> Mr. Ford and Dr. Kissinger have objected to my criticizing their foreign policy. The Democrats are going to criticize it. How will we defend defending Castro while he exports revolution and makes Cuba a Soviet satellite?
>
> How can we defend the giveaway of the Panama Canal . . .?
>
> How can we criticize the disastrous energy legislation passed by the Democratic Congress but signed by our candidate into law?
>
> How will we defend a candidate who fired Dr. Schlesinger and said he will retain Dr. Kissinger if he is elected President?*

Reagan drew a distinction between these remarks and personal criticism of Ford. When Thomas B. Ellis, Helms' chief aide and Reagan's North Carolina campaign manager, suggested to Reagan that he make Callaway an issue, the candidate refused, saying that the charges had not been proved. And Reagan was even firmer in rejecting a leaflet prepared by Ellis which openly appealed to racial prejudice. The leaflet reproduced a story quoting Ford as saying he would consider Senator Edward W. Brooke of Massachusetts as a running mate and another story quoting Brooke as favoring busing to achieve racial integration. Ford actually had mentioned Brooke on a laundry list of possibly nominees, and everyone in politics, including Reagan, knew the Massachusetts senator was not a serious vice-presidential possibility. Reagan was furious when he heard about the leaflet and directed that it not be distributed. "That wasn't discussed with us," Deaver told me at a rally where the leaflets were supposed to be handed out. "The governor has never campaigned on race or used it as an issue, never will and feels strongly about that," Deaver said. When it was pointed out to Deaver that boxes of the leaflets were present at the rally for distribution, he walked over to the campaign worker who had charge of them and sternly ordered that they be put aboard the Reagan campaign plane so they could not be distrib-

*James Schlesinger was fired as Secretary of Defense on November 2, 1975, and replaced by Donald Rumsfeld in the so-called "Sunday massacre" that shook up the Ford cabinet and caused an adverse reaction to his administration in the press and the polls. But, like the dismissal of Callaway, the change eventually proved beneficial to Ford because Cheney, who worked well with Spencer, became the White House chief of staff.

uted after the candidate had left. Then he saw to it that every leaflet was destroyed.

Ellis, however, was responsible for the most productive tactic of the North Carolina campaign, which was to show a half-hour Reagan television speech on stations throughout the state. Sears doubted whether many people would watch a half-hour speech by anyone, but Ellis pressured Nofziger into coming up with a poor-quality, vintage Reagan speech that the candidate had made during the Florida primary. Nofziger cut out the Florida references and added an appeal for funds. The half-hour shows appeared on fifteen stations and introduced North Carolinians to the old-fashioned Reagan doing what he does best, which is giving his latest version of "A Time For Choosing."

Without recognizing it, Reagan had now reached a moment in his own political career as fully critical as the time he gave his famous speech for Goldwater in 1964. Without that speech, and the subsequent response it produced among millions of Republicans, Reagan never would have been a candidate for governor in 1966. Without his performance in North Carolina, both in person and on television, Reagan would have faded from contention before Kansas City, and it is unlikely that he would have won the presidential nomination four years later. But while Reagan did not fully comprehend the significance of the North Carolina primary, he did sense that something was happening among his audiences. Paul Laxalt, who had flown down from Washington to cheer him up, and who dates their close friendship from this primary, noticed it, too. "He was the old Ron Reagan," said Laxalt, remembering the way Reagan had roused audiences in his gubernatorial campaigns.[1] Talking together, both Reagan and Laxalt realized that they had underestimated the material power of the presidency. In Florida and Illinois, Reagan had sounded resentful of Ford's dispensing of grants and favors, which is standard operating procedure for any White House incumbent. In North Carolina, Reagan began to turn Ford's largesse against him through the potent weapon of ridicule. "I understand Mr. Ford has arrived in the state," Reagan said the Saturday before the primary. "If he comes here with the same list of goodies as he did in Florida, the band won't know whether to play 'Hail to the Chief' or 'Santa Claus Is Coming to Town.' "

Despite his newfound effectiveness, Reagan did not know how to deal with the recurrent question from reporters: "When are you going to drop out?" The Ford campaign was orchestrating appeals from public officials urging Reagan to quit. At a Greensboro television station Reagan reacted to one such statement issued by a group of mayors by saying, "For heavens sakes, fellows, let's not be naive. That pressure is engineered from the same place that they engineered the pressure for me not to run in the first place— the White House. . . . I'm not going to pay any attention to them now they suggest that I should quit. Tell him [Ford] to quit." Reagan's irritation reflected a recognition that marginal voters might be tempted to vote for Ford if they regarded the President as the certain winner. "You have to think that the undecided voters are not necessarily those who are the most committed, and you wonder what the effect will be on them," Reagan told me in an interview two days before the primary.

My most vivid memories of the entire 1976 campaign are of two attempts by Reagan to deal with the question about when he would quit. One was on election day, when Reagan held airport press conferences in four North Carolina cities. "Win, lose or draw, I am continuing in this campaign," he said defiantly. Then, when reporters continued to badger him about what he would do if he lost, Reagan refused to answer again, and said he would respond only to other questions. There was a long moment of silence before someone ended the impasse with a question on another subject. The scene was reminiscent of that other defiant time eight years earlier, when Reagan had refused at a press conference to take any more questions on the homosexual scandal. Both times Reagan had persisted in his tactic, and both times he had prevailed.

My other memory is more personal. It occurred in the same airplane interview in which I asked Reagan whether he was being damaged by the constant questioning about when he would withdraw. Later in the interview, I joined the chorus. "When are you going to quit?" I asked him. "You, too, Lou?" he said, his lips tightening. Then he looked directly at me and said firmly, as if he were on camera: "I'm *not* going to quit."

And in retrospect, it may have been this determination—an echo of the stubbornness Reagan had shown in his second term in Sacramento and a foreshadowing of the determination he would display in New Hampshire four years later—that made Ronald Reagan the President of the United States. Certainly, no one thought so then. "Reagan Virtually Concedes Defeat in North Carolina," said the headline of the *New York Times* story the day before the primary.[2] The headline was based on Reagan's observation that "a close race here would be satisfactory to me," a statement which Reagan did not consider a concession. But neither did he expect to win. By the time the North Carolina vote came in, Reagan was in La Crosse, Wisconsin, speaking to a sportsman's group. The news that he was carrying North Carolina was relayed to him by Nofziger, who was as surprised by the results as anyone else. However, Nofziger proved unsuccessful in trying to persuade Reagan to meet reporters and crow about his upset victory. The final results were not in, and Reagan remembered New Hampshire. He had departed from his superstition then and allowed himself to talk as if he were a winner, and he had lost. This was a lesson Reagan would always remember. He left Wisconsin without making a victory statement.

North Carolina was the turning point of Reagan's political career. It kept him in the race to Kansas City, and it made him the presumptive presidential nominee in 1980. At all times after North Carolina Reagan was a legitimate, full-fledged presidential candidate, even though his campaign was so short of funds he had to abandon efforts to contest Wisconsin, where he won 45 percent of the vote anyway. Reagan was now thrown back on his fundamental resource for raising money, which was to make an emotional ideological speech on national television. When Sears made this proposal, Reagan looked at him and said he had favored doing it all along. This was true enough, but the usually passive candidate had not imposed his view upon his campaign manager. "No one paid any attention when I told them what we could do with television," Reagan told me subsequently. Had he been insistent earlier, it is conceivable that he would have raised enough money to at least have won some delegates in Wisconsin, which he could ill afford to concede to Ford.

The speech which Reagan gave on the NBC network on March 31 was a message for true believers, constructed on the base of the candidate's speeches in North Carolina. Reagan questioned Ford's leadership on economic issues, gave a glowing account of the Reagan governorship in California, and wound up with an attack on Kissinger, whom Reagan depicted as ready to negotiate away American freedoms. Militarily, Reagan asserted again, the United States was now "Number Two in a world where it is dangerous, if not fatal, to be second best." In response to Reagan's attack on his foreign policy, Ford had dropped use of the word "détente" and replaced it with the phrase "peace through strength." Reagan mocked this euphemism as "a slogan with a nice ring to it" which did not reflect the military realities.

Reagan's speech delighted conservatives for its content and pleased Sears because it raised $1.5 million and enabled Reagan to stay in the race. Heading for the Texas primary on May 1, Sears used the prophetic words "new beginning," which would become the Reagan campaign slogan of 1980, to describe the candidate's opportunity. But the new beginning came too late in 1976. By the time of the Texas primary, Sears had already been forced to concede in Pennsylvania and New York, where the delegates were controlled by Nelson Rockefeller and his eastern allies. Sears' own preferred field of battle was the Northeast, as he would demonstrate four years later, but he was in no position to contest the Republican power structure there at this time. Among organizational Republicans in this region, the memories of 1964 were still painful, and there were many who considered Reagan "another Goldwater." The attacks on Kissinger and Ford's foreign policy had rallied conservatives to Reagan's banner while reinforcing regional suspicion in the Northeast. Reagan continued the attacks on friendly ground in Texas, where he hammered away at détente and the giveaway of the Panama Canal. Since Texas was a crossover state, Reagan also openly appealed to the former followers of the crippled and now rejected George Wallace. These Wallace voters had a fierce dislike of the federal government, and both Reagan and Jimmy Carter, then wrapping up the Democratic nomination, exploited these feelings in messages which might have been written by the same speechwriter. "Anything you don't like about Washington, I suggest you blame it on Jerry Ford," said Carter. From Reagan came the same theme song: "I consider it an asset that I am not a member of the Washington establishment."

It was not asset enough. Reagan swept all 96 delegates in the Texas primary May 1 and three days later won 130 of 139 delegates at stake in the Alabama, Georgia and Indiana primaries. He won in Nebraska on May 11 (while Ford was winning West Virginia) and added more delegates at Republican state conventions throughout the West. Then Reagan rolled to a big victory in California, where his margin was swelled by a ferocious Spencer attack.* But Ford won in his home state of Michigan on May 18 and captured a majority of the vote and most of the delegates in Ohio and New Jersey on June 8, the same day as the California primary. This was the last round of primaries. In the subsequent six weeks the Ford and Reagan forces battled for delegates in convention states, with Reagan sweeping some he might have lost (notably, Missouri) and losing one he needed to win (North Dakota). During this period, Ford's steadily improving campaign came up with a new find in James A. Baker III, a wealthy Houston lawyer and undersecretary of commerce who took over the Ford delegate hunt. Baker possessed the Spencer-Kaye virtues of candor, and he also realized the need of establishing credibility with the press and any genuinely uncommitted delegates. Baker recognized that some of Ford's support was soft. A false delegate claim that was exposed by the press might persuade some of the waverers to conclude that the President was going to lose the nomination and precipitate a bolt toward Reagan. So, Baker was conservative in his public pronouncements, claiming only those delegates who were legally bound to Ford or who had proclaimed their support of the President.

Sears could not afford the luxury of such a pristine strategy. Reagan needed more delegates, and Sears claimed, among other things, that they were hidden among the technically uncommitted in Pennsylvania, where the delegates actually had been screened for loyalty to Ford. Interviews with members of the delegation did not disclose any gains in Reagan strength. By mid-July it was clear that Reagan, for all the impressiveness of his comeback, had fallen short of the 1,130 delegate votes needed for nomination.

---

* Answering questions before the Sacramento Press Club, Reagan said he would provide a token contingent of U.S. troops as part of a United Nations command if Rhodesia requested it to fight guerrillas. Spencer and Kaye ran a television commercial with a punchline that said, "When you vote Tuesday, remember: Governor Ronald Reagan couldn't start a war. President Ronald Reagan could." Spencer claimed afterwards that this commercial made Reagan concentrate on California at a time he needed to campaign elsewhere. But Reagan kept to his schedule (which was insufficient in Ohio, anyway), and surveys showed that voters did not believe the commercial. Nofziger, in fact, reran the entire Ford commercial as a Reagan spot, confident that it would be regarded as a smear. Reagan carried California by a 2–1 margin. Long afterward, a Ford aide told me that during the filming of the commercial, they had spoofed Ford in an ad never, of course, shown on television. The anti-Reagan commercial had shown a hand reaching for a red phone in the White House situation room. In the parody, Ford reaches for the phone and knocks it off the desk.

The *Washington Post* count gave Ford 1,093 delegates and Reagan 1,030, with 136 uncommitted. This meant that Ford needed only 37 delegates, slightly more than one-fourth of the uncommitted, to be nominated. The private counts of both sides indicated Ford would do far better than that. One prominent member of the Reagan entourage and two lesser aides talked to me about their plans in the fall, undecided whether they should work for Ford or leave the world of politics. It was a sign that they knew Reagan did not have enough delegates to win. On the flight to Los Angeles after Reagan spoke to a final GOP state convention in Utah, I interviewed the candidate and realized that he also was becoming aware he might lose. "I think my candidacy has been worthwhile," Reagan said. The story based on these interviews ran Monday, July 19, across eight columns at the top of page one in the *Washington Post*. "Reagan's Camp: Air of Resignation," said the banner headline. Underneath was an even more damaging subhead which reflected the story: "He Speaks Not So Much of Victory as of a 'Worthwhile' Bid." Sears and Deaver were furious at this account, and Reagan denied in television interviews the next day that he was resigned to defeat. Nofziger called in reporters and played transcripts of the interview in an effort to demonstrate that Reagan had been quoted out of context. But Nofziger knew, too, that some of his fellow Reaganites were already looking for their next jobs.

The *Post* story came at a time when Sears was preparing a surprise which was to delay recognition of Ford's impending victory. Sears had heard that CBS News would soon be broadcasting a projection which showed that Ford had clinched the nomination. Before this could occur, Reagan introduced a new factor into the calculation. On July 26 he announced that he would choose Senator Richard S. Schweiker of Pennsylvania as his running mate if he were nominated for President. The selection stunned Reagan's conservative supporters in the South, especially in the key delegation of Mississippi. It ultimately gave Clarke Reed, the colorful and power-conscious Mississippi Republican chairman, the excuse he had been seeking to support Ford. It did not gain Reagan any identifiable support in the Northeast, where Schweiker's 100 percent labor-union voting record might have been expected to make a Reagan ticket more palatable. But it did accomplish its immediate purpose of preventing the networks from declaring that Ford had wrapped up the nomination. Before any news organization was willing to go this far, it was necessary to poll the delegates again, especially in Pennsylvania. The Pennsylvania delegates enjoyed their moment in the sun, and several of them delighted in announcing their undecided status to media representatives, even though they planned to, and did, vote for Ford at the convention. But the Schweiker selection had bought time, allowing Sears to maneuver at Kansas City.

Schweiker's selection was a compelling example of Reagan's proclivity for delegation. Unlike some of his actions, however, the delegation in this case was specific and initiated by Reagan, who thought that the last-minute selection of a Vice-President in the hurly-burly of a national convention was both undignified and unnecessary. He had talked to Laxalt about it, who agreed. Two months before the convention he also had discussed the idea with Sears, who saw the advantage of an early selection in terms of constructing a ticket for the general election. Sears and Laxalt agreed to find Reagan a Vice-President. During the first week in July, Sears sounded out William D. Ruckelshaus, the Nixon attorney general who had resigned rather than carry out the President's instructions to fire Special Prosecutor Archibald Cox. Ruckelshaus, a Catholic, believed that he was being offered a place on the ticket to give it balance in the fall. But nothing came of the overture. Ruckelshaus would have been an attractive vice-presidential nominee in the fall campaign, but he did not offer any hope of switching Ford delegates to Reagan.* And there were not many others who held this promise, either. Sears and Laxalt ran through a short list of possibilities. Most were out of the question. Well-known liberals like Senator Jacob Javits of New York were identified with too many positions which differed from Reagan's and would not have met the test of philosophical compatibility. Others, like Representative Jack Kemp of New York, who would have met the test, were not that well known. Schweiker soon emerged as the only likely possibility. Laxalt was enthusiastic about him, which made the selection easier to sell to Reagan.

Reagan told me after the election that he knew "very little" about Schweiker when Sears came to his house on July 23 to make the case for the Pennsylvania senator. My guess is that even this "very little" is an overstatement. Sears told Reagan about Schweiker's liberal record on labor issues but emphasized the senator's opposition to gun control and abortion. Reagan did not know that Sears and Laxalt already had interviewed Schweiker and accepted him. But Reagan's question was direct and political. "Do you think he'd do it?" Reagan asked. Sears assured him that he would. The next day Laxalt and Sears arrived with Schweiker. The two men hit it off. Reagan recalls that Schweiker agreed with most of his positions and said he would support even those he didn't as long as he was first allowed to give his opinion. "I have a strong feeling that I'm looking at myself some years ago," Reagan told Schweiker, referring to his own conversion to conservatism. "I'm not a knee-jerk liberal," Schweiker said. "And I'm not a knee-jerk conservative," Reagan replied.† Afterward, Reagan readily acknowledged that his acceptance of Schweiker as his running mate was an act of political expedience, but also insisted that Schweiker's commitment to conservative

---

* Ruckelshaus subsequently told me he thought that Sears was offering him a spot on the ticket. Jules Witcover in *Marathon* (page 457) quotes Sears as denying that he ever made a firm offer or considered anyone except Schweiker.

† This is Reagan's account in a 1977 interview. A slightly different version of the conversation which makes the same point occurs in Witcover's *Marathon,* page 461, in which Reagan replies to Schweiker, "And I'm not a knee-jerk extremist."

principles during their long discussion on July 24 was genuine. And during the next four years in the Senate, for whatever reason, Schweiker's voting record did take a conservative turn.

The selection of Schweiker, more than any other single action, ratified Sears' reputation for political creativity. Even those Reaganites, and they were the vast majority, who came to believe that Sears was a baneful influence, defend him on the Schweiker strategy. At different times I have asked Reagan, Laxalt, Meese, Nofziger, Hannaford and Deaver about their views, and all say that the choice of Schweiker kept the Republican convention from being a cut-and-dried coronation of Ford. "Sears can be faulted for lots of things, but not for Schweiker," says Deaver, in a typical view. "It kept the whole thing alive."[3]

Sears' subsequent use of the Schweiker selection at the national convention was helpful to the Republican Party, although Sears didn't get much credit for it. What Sears did at Kansas City was force a vote on a rule, which became known as 16–C, that would have required Ford to name his own running mate in advance. Sears reasoned that whoever Ford selected would irritate some faction or region and give Reagan the chance to go after the disaffected delegates. This was a long-shot strategy, but it probably prevented the convention from becoming a donnybrook of the kind which had torn apart the GOP in 1964. A fight on issues which pushed Ford into a corner on foreign policy would have left the convention in shambles and produced a politically ruined nominee. It also would have severely damaged Reagan's 1980 chances. Sears avoided all of this by focusing on a question of process rather than ideological principles. The strategy angered conservatives who argued that Reagan's issue-oriented followers could be rallied only by an appeal to the causes which made them follow Reagan in the first place. But Ford and his managers knew this as well as Sears, and they were prepared to concede almost anything to Senator Helms and his ideological followers in the platform committee. On every issue that the press might have interpreted as a conservative victory, Ford's people simply capitulated. Baker suggested afterward that the Reaganites could have come up with a proposal for firing Secretary of State Kissinger, which the President would have been required to resist. But this was not an option that Reagan seriously considered. "I wouldn't have done something like that," Reagan told me when I asked him much later about Baker's suggestion.[4] Neither Reagan nor Sears wanted to leave Kansas City labeled as party wreckers.

Ford and his strategists believed that Reagan already had played a spoiler's role. When I interviewed Ford in Palm Springs the following year he blamed Reagan for his defeat. "I think he really believed his candidacy wouldn't be divisive, but I knew he was wrong," Ford says in his autobiography in discussing the telephone call Reagan made to him just before he announced. "How can you challenge an incumbent president of your own party and *not* be divisive?"[5]

The might-have-been corollary on the Reagan side was the belief, shared at the time by the candidate and Sears, that Reagan might have beaten Carter while Ford could not. Jim Lake, reflecting on what had happened, said five years later: "So much of Ford's troubles related to Nixon and Watergate and the pardon. He had pardoned Nixon. People were voting against that, and against Washington."[6] The Great Scriptwriter does not allow us to know what would have happened in the world of If, but a persuasive case can be made that both Ford and Reagan were wrong in their speculation. It is true, certainly, that Reagan's challenge drove Ford to the right on foreign policy and exposed some of the clumsier aspects of his candidacy. It is also true that the Reagan challenge forced Ford to expend resources which might have been husbanded for the fall campaign. But this line of reasoning ignores the evidence that Ford improved as a candidate while running against Reagan. Ford had never been a national candidate before, and his initial campaign effort in 1975 was deficient. What became a highly professional Ford campaign was forged in the effort to stop Reagan. Spencer and Baker would not have been involved in any important way except for the Reagan challenge. The campaign cadre consisting of these two men, plus the capable Cheney and Teeter, was formed in the primaries. These four, plus the advertising duo of Doug Bailey and John Deardourff, composed the team which brought Ford from 30 percentage points behind Carter to a 2-percentage point defeat. Without the Reagan challenge the campaign would have been populated with the Callaways and the Freys and the Mortons and the host of present and former House members whose political judgment Ford revered. The President became a better candidate because Reagan had challenged him.

The notion that Reagan would have defeated Carter is even more difficult to accept. Reagan might have won under other circumstances, especially if Ford had decided not to run and Reagan had been handed the nomination through the acclamation of the Republican primaries. Perhaps Reagan might also have won if Ford had proved a paper tiger who was blown away in the New Hampshire and Florida primaries and then withdrew. But Reagan's comeback after those early losses rested on an ideological appeal that advanced his cause in the restricted world of Sun Belt primaries while casting him as a narrow conservative among the electorate as a whole. The Reagan vulnerability was defined by pollster Louis Harris in a survey published May 6 which showed Reagan losing ground among independents and Democrats at the very time he was making the case against the Panama Canal treaty and Kissinger, which was bringing him back in the GOP primaries. The Harris poll found Carter defeating Ford by 4 points and beating Reagan by 19. "It is apparent that Reagan has lost ground among the more affluent, better educated, more independent and less ideological groups in the electorate," Harris reported. "Thus, his strategy in appealing to conservative areas and groups has cut him off from the mainstream of the voting public, which he will need so badly in November if he should be nominated."[7]

Even if Reagan had been able to scramble back to the center, he would have faced the unprecedented political obstacle of campaigning while the President of his own party, whom he had defeated for nomination, occupied the White House. Ford is a generous man, and loyal to his party, but this is asking too much of generosity and loyalty. "It would have been 1964 all over again," said Deaver. "The Republicans would have torn themselves to ribbons."[8] Nor would Reagan's litany about the ills inflicted on the economy by the free-spending federal government have seemed on target against Carter in 1976. The Georgian was, after all, an outsider, too, and one who was then promising an ultimately balanced budget. The Democrats remained the majority party and one did not have to desert them to vote against Washington. "The people wanted an outsider, but they weren't ready for Reagan," Hannaford believes in retrospect.[9]

If Reagan could not have won in 1976, he showed that he knew how to lose. He was counted out at 12:30 A.M. on August 19, when West Virginia's delegates cast their votes for Ford. With all the powers of the presidency and all his early victories and all the delegates locked up by Rockefeller and his allies in the Northeast, Ford's margin was the narrow one of 1,187 delegates to 1,070 for Reagan. Afterwards, in a plan prearranged between Sears and Cheney, the winner called on the loser at Reagan's hotel room in the Alameda Plaza. It was a tense and awkward moment between politicians who had battled each other in too many primaries. Both men were relieved when the meeting and the press conference which followed it were finished and they did not have to pretend to a mutual fondness which they did not feel in their hearts.*

Reagan was weary. But he was up after a few hours' sleep to prepare a speech of consolation for those who had stood by his side. "Don't get cyni-

---

* Ford brought with him to this private meeting a list of six names he was considering for Vice-President. Reagan's name was not on the list because Sears had told Cheney that a condition of the meeting was that Ford not ask Reagan to be on the ticket. Accurately reflecting what Reagan had told him, Sears said that his candidate did not want to be Vice-President, and he would be embarrassed at having to turn Ford down. But there were many in the Reagan entourage who expected Ford to ask anyway, and Justin Dart had urged Reagan to accept the vice-presidential nomination. Reagan said he would consider it, though he told others subsequently that he had not expected Ford to ask him. Would he have accepted it? Reagan has not said, and Ford remarks honestly in his autobiography that he does not know whether he would have asked his beaten foe even if Sears had not laid down the condition. My own view is that Reagan would never have refused such a request from the President of the United States if Ford had said, as Dart had argued, that it was his "patriotic duty" to accept. Instead, Ford said he was considering William Simon, John Connally, Bob Dole, Howard Baker, Elliott Richardson and William Ruckelshaus. Both Ford and Reagan have said that Reagan affirmatively responded to the mention of Dole. A Reagan aide told me afterward that he believed that Reagan also had reacted negatively to the mention of Richardson, Reagan's *bête noire* from Health, Education and Welfare days, but this has never been confirmed for me by either participant in the meeting.

cal," Reagan said to his followers in the crowded ballroom of the hotel late that morning. "Don't get cynical because, look at yourselves and what you were willing to do and recognize that there are millions and millions of Americans out there that want what you want, that want it to be that way, that want it to be a shining city on the hill." It was one of Reagan's most familiar lines, but Nancy Reagan wept when she heard it. Reagan's followers wept, too. They had stood with their candidate from New Hampshire to Kansas City, and now he was here before them, a loser, but a loser who did not engage in apologies or second-guess the efforts which had been made in his behalf. Instead, he thanked the men and women who had carried his bags and put up his campaign signs in scores of towns and airports. As always, he reached back to his movie days for a metaphor, telling of how seventy-five persons had been required to make one scene of a farmer running from his field to tell of an airplane crash. He did not mention Ford.

In his defeat, Reagan looked ahead to other battles, quoting a line from an English ballad he had memorized in childhood. "Lay me down and bleed a while," Reagan said. "Though I am wounded, I am not slain. I shall rise and fight again."*

* The ballad by Dryden, written in 1702, was called *Johnnie Armstrong's Last Goodnight.* It reads: "Fight on, my merry men all/I'm not a little wounded, but I am not slain;/I will lay me down for to bleed a while,/Then I'll rise and fight with you again."

16

A New Beginning

ON a pleasant early summer's day John P. Sears drove the six and one-half miles up a twisting one-lane road from fog-shrouded Refugio State Beach on the Pacific Ocean to a sunlit mountaintop above. His destination was Rancho del Cielo, a 688-acre spread where Ronald and Nancy Reagan retreat from the world to long rides on Arabian and quarter horses and a Spanish-style house heated in winter by manzanita and oak wood which Reagan and a hired hand have cut themselves. Reagan likes to advertise his work habits, knowing that it will prompt others to regard him as vigorous beyond his years. But he wasn't advertising anything this day at his self-named "heavenly ranch," nor was he chopping wood. Instead, the Reagans were deep in discussion with Sears, a man who prefers to spend his own spare time playing poker. There was no poker-playing on this day, either. Sears and the Reagans were talking politics, and the strategy for 1980. Before he left, Sears signed Nancy's ever-present guestbook: "A beautiful place, a nice day and the best of company." It was June 25, 1978, and Ronald Reagan was running for President.

Behind the gracious facade of harmony at Rancho del Cielo, both Reagan and Sears faced uncertain futures. The right-wingers were out in force against Sears, whom they had made a scapegoat of Reagan's narrow defeat in 1976. In the South, the selection of Schweiker still rankled. A few disgruntled conservatives like South Carolina Governor James Edwards had even made Schweiker the reason for deserting Reagan in favor of former Texas Governor John B. Connally. But most of Reagan's ideological followers wanted a new campaign manager rather than another candidate.

Reagan's problem was his age, not lack of loyalty. At speeches throughout the country—he made seventy-five of them in 1977 alone—Reagan still roused the hearts and tapped the pocketbooks of the faithful in behalf of conservative causes and Republican candidates. But even some of the followers were beginning to notice the wrinkles. If they didn't notice, the newspaper stories and columns reminded them. Almost every profile on Reagan,

227

and there were many, pointed out that he would be seventy years old within a month of assuming the presidency. "William Henry Harrison, old Tippecanoe, was the only president to be inaugurated at that age, and he died of pneumonia six weeks later," wrote Marquis Childs in a line typical of those then being written about Reagan.[1] Unlike a number of others, however, Childs did not discount the Californian's chances, saying that Reagan was "more serious than ever" about becoming President.

Reagan's age had been a topic of political conversation since the early 1970s when it was widely assumed he would run for President upon the constitutionally mandated retirement of Nixon in 1976. He usually treated the issue with a one-line quip, his favorite being a comment he supposedly made after viewing a rerun of *Knute Rockne—All American.* "It's like seeing a younger son I never knew I had," Reagan said. On other occasions he would compare himself to Giuseppe Verdi, who composed *Falstaff* when he was eighty, or to Antonius Stradivarius, who made his best violins after he turned sixty and was still making them in the year of his death at ninety-one. Reagan watched his weight, drank infrequently and did not smoke.* He rode or swam at every opportunity and laughed away the rumors that he dyed his hair. Compared to others in their sixties, he looked so young and vigorous that he talked about himself as if he were middle-aged. At a birthday party at the Alexandria, Virginia, home of former Reagan aide Nancy Reynolds, on the night he turned sixty-six, Reagan said, "Middle-age is when you're faced with two temptations and you choose the one that will get you home at 9:30."

There is a famous Sherlock Holmes story in which the detective discovers the identity of an intruder in the night because a dog does not bark and Holmes realizes that the criminal had been a friend of the victim. In the four years between his two presidential campaigns, Reagan's age was the great mystery issue, the dog that didn't bark in the night. Nearly everyone expected Reagan's age to be important. Reagan pollster Richard Wirthlin approached the issue in a dozen different ways, trying to find out if people thought Reagan was too old, too tired, too out of touch or simply not up to the demands of the presidency. He found that people over sixty-five, perhaps conscious of their own infirmities, were concerned about Reagan's age but didn't necessarily reflect this concern in their voting. Pollsters always are bothered by supposedly important issues which they cannot quantify. The depth of racial prejudice against a minority candidate, for instance, is a no-

* After actor William Holden, who had been Reagan's best man at his wedding to Nancy Davis, died in 1981, actor Dana Andrews, a recovered alcoholic, told this story about Reagan's drinking habits: "When Ronald Reagan was president of the Screen Actors Guild, Bill was second vice-president and I was first vice-president and we would go to the Gotham Hotel about half a block from where our meetings were held . . . and we ordered a drink." When they had finished, the waiter asked if they wanted another. "Bill said 'yes' and I said 'yes' and Ronald Reagan said, 'You just had one, why do you want another?' That's the difference between an alcoholic—two potential alcoholics—and one who, I suppose, was not even a potential one because he was worried about not getting high."[2]

toriously tricky issue because there are prejudiced people who do not want to acknowledge their prejudice to a pollster. Was Reagan's age such a hidden issue? No one knew for sure, but the Reagan field workers in the trenches were as worried as Wirthlin. "All of us would like to see him ten years younger," said Reagan's Oklahoma coordinator Clarence Warner to Richard Bergholz of the *Los Angeles Times* in April 1977. Then Warner added what had become the obligatory hope of the loyalists: "If he looks as well in 1980 as he does now, I don't think his chronological age will be important." As it turned out, Warner's hope was realized. The clue for the pollsters, which Wirthlin had observed in 1976 and Reagan had failed to take advantage of in New Hampshire, was that Reagan's presence dispelled any doubts among those otherwise inclined to vote for him. Robert Teeter, polling for George Bush in the primaries, reached a similar conclusion. "I think that age is one of those issues that is not a great issue when he is campaigning and looking like everyone else does," Teeter said. "If there is some way to quantify it, the concern over the age issue is an inverse relationship to his exposure to the voters."[3]

The potential of the age issue did have one effect, and it was a positive one for Reagan. After he lost the nomination in 1976, Reagan quickly realized that many in his own party and the press were likely to presume that his age would disqualify him in 1980. If this happened, his key aides and supporters would be tempted to seek alternative candidates. As a result, Reagan dropped his characteristic coyness about his own intentions and talked no more of becoming a candidate if lightning struck or if his fellow Republicans begged him to run. While privately confessing a continued fatalism about his prospects, Reagan sent out what Wirthlin subsequently called "distinct signals" that he would be a candidate. The first and clearest of these signals came even before the Ford-Carter campaign began in earnest, at a luncheon meeting at Reagan's Pacific Palisades home early in September 1976. Over seafood salad served on avocado wedges and a raspberry dessert, Reagan shared his views with Sears, Wirthlin, Jim Lake, Charles Black, Mike Deaver, Peter Hannaford and Ed Meese. One participant expected the meal to be a farewell and found Reagan talking instead about the issues he would raise in 1977. Another guest remembers that Reagan spoke of the "victory" of the conservative platform which the Ford forces had conceded at Kansas City, and said he would support the GOP ticket in the fall without accommodating Ford on issues where they disagreed. Reagan did campaign in twenty states that autumn, doing more for Ford than the President acknowledged, but he refused to schedule vital, extra appearances in Mississippi and Texas that the Ford committee wanted. Introducing Ford at a fund-raising dinner in Beverly Hills on October 7, Reagan spent his time talking about what the Republican Party had to offer and contrasting its platform with that of the Democrats. He barely mentioned Ford and seemed uncomfortable to be on the same platform with the President.

Any lingering doubts about Reagan's plans were dispelled among the faithful by the creation of a political action committee, Citizens For The Republic (CFTR), financed by $1 million in leftover campaign funds. Reagan had all this extra money because his late surge in the primaries had brought him more contributions than he could spend. The funds were legally his own. When Reagan told the group of intimates who lunched with him in September that he intended to use this money to form a political action committee, he was stating, more clearly than any campaign announcement could, his intention to run again in 1980. "He could have taken that money and bought a palomino ranch if he had wanted to," said one of the inner group. "When he decided to form a political action committee instead, I realized that the country hadn't heard the last of Ronald Reagan." CFTR, publicly announced after the election, was headed by Lyn Nofziger. It became a rallying point and a billboard for Reagan (and Nofziger) to send the kind of messages which make the hearts of true believers go pit-a-pat. Throughout 1977, CFTR newsletters stoked the conservative fires with periodic attacks on the Panama Canal treaty, the Russians, Cuba, government "destruction" of the work ethic and the supposed duplicity of the Carter administration. It was an insufficient platform for winning a national election, but it kept the conservative activists waiting in the wings.

For his part, Nofziger was not waiting. He was fifty-three years old in 1977, and he had spent a dozen years of his life consumed by the notion of electing Ronald Reagan President of the United States. After the Reagan mini-campaign of 1968, he had come to Washington and played the hardball politics of the Nixon era under Murray Chotiner without ever abandoning his dream of a Reagan presidency. Sensitive and abrasive, Nofziger was flawed by an inability or unwillingness to forgive past slights or present heresies. Nonetheless, he remained a valuable link for Reagan to western and southern conservatives, whose certitude about the perfidy of the Panama Canal treaty was exceeded only by their suspicion of the pragmatic course on which Sears seemed to be leading their hero. Nofziger was trusted by these conservatives for his ideology—"I'm much more conservative than Reagan," he told me in 1968—and for his opposition to Sears. Beginning December 3 in Phoenix and continuing over the next six months in western, midwestern and southern states, Nofziger and CFTR promoted a series of regional meetings to discuss the future of Republican conservatism. Ostensibly, these were gatherings of political ideologues unpledged to any candidate. In fact, they served as Reagan rallies which kept alive an organization at the grassroots at a time when John Connally was winning the battle of the boardrooms.

Nofziger had both personal and political reasons to oppose Sears. In 1976 Sears had won the cooperation of Nancy Reagan and Deaver and replaced Nofziger with Jim Lake as Reagan's press secretary. Nofziger wound up directing a California primary campaign where there was never any question whether Reagan would defeat Ford. Perhaps because he is himself an organizational in-fighter who gives little quarter to his opponents, Nofziger recognized before any of the other Californians that Sears meant to pick them off one by one and take solid control of the Reagan organization. But aside from personal feelings, Nofziger genuinely disagreed with the Sears strategy. He thought Sears in 1976 had relied too much on winning over the Washington media and too little on the conservative grassroots organization which was waiting to raise the money and walk the precincts for Reagan. The difference was regional as much as ideological. Nofziger was a western conservative who believed that the best prospects for his party and his candidate lay south of the Mason-Dixon line and west of the 100th meridian. His vision was of a Goldwater approach writ large, a so-called "Sun Belt strategy" that included the frigid climes of the northern Rocky Mountain and Plains states. Because he had been out of favor with Nancy Reagan since the "homosexual scandal" of 1967, Nofziger could not begin to match Sears' influence with the candidate. But Nofziger had a powerful ally in Paul Laxalt, the Nevada senator who in 1976 had been recruited as national chairman by Sears. Since the North Carolina primary, however, Laxalt had been listening to conservative complaints about Sears, and he had come to believe that the campaign manager did not appreciate the ideological and regional roots of Reagan's appeal.

Laxalt had special advantages in his relationship with Reagan not enjoyed by any other member of the entourage. He was a U.S. senator and former governor who approached Reagan as an equal and needed neither his approval nor his largesse. Reagan was addressed as "Governor" by those who worked for him, including Sears and Deaver, but Laxalt always called him "Ron." The Nevada senator's position, courtly manner and good looks made him a favorite of Nancy Reagan. His openness commended him to the press. Like Reagan, he was a conservative Republican who had achieved political success by attracting Democratic votes. But Laxalt's congenial exterior concealed a powerful personal ambition of his own. He had been a lonely Senate supporter of Reagan in 1976, and he did not want to be a figurehead chairman of the campaign in 1980. Later, the depth of Laxalt's ambition would be revealed when he seriously entertained the idea that Reagan would ask him to be his vice-presidential running mate, even though it made no political sense to put another conservative Westerner on the same ticket. Despite this blind spot, Laxalt was a valuable counsellor to Reagan. He was secure with himself, like his candidate, and he believed that it was both possible and necessary to weld the conflicting factions of the Reagan constituency into a cohesive force. Laxalt recognized that Sears was a good idea man but a poor manager. He remembered that Sears in 1976 had refused to accept an office manager in Washington out of fear that he would lose organizational control. Essentially, Laxalt was a Sun Belt strategist like Nofziger. Unlike Nofziger, however, he recognized that Sears was needed in the Northeast, particularly if Ford ran again. The Nevadan's solution, forcefully expressed to Reagan in 1977, was that Sears should become a leading member of the team rather than captain of it, and that he should be focused toward the special constituencies which he knew best—the Northeast delegates and the skeptical Washington press.

Sears, brilliant and brooding, had undergone his own struggles. With discipline and courage he had overcome a drinking problem, giving him more time than ever to plan and plot and maneuver for a candidate with whom he had almost defeated a sitting President. As Sears saw it, Nofziger and his uncompromising western allies were afflicted with the ideological virus of Goldwaterism, a disease known to be fatal to Republican candidates in November. Sears, a pragmatist from the Nixon school of politics, preferred the craft of maneuver to ideological warfare. His frame of reference was thoroughly eastern. A New Yorker by birth, a Notre Dame graduate by choice, a lawyer by training and a politician by inclination, Sears was fascinated by the challenge of making Reagan the political toast of New York and Pennsylvania. He knew that if Reagan could accomplish this and then establish a solid base in the Midwest, his nomination would be assured. But Sears, like Nofziger and Laxalt, was driven by personal as well as private impulses. Moody and tight-lipped, he kept his past triumphs and defeats to himself and focused on the 1980 campaign. Some who knew Sears were convinced that he had never forgotten the aftermath of 1968, when his reward for rounding up vital delegates for Nixon was banishment from the Nixon White House by John Mitchell. In the transition period between the two presidential campaigns, Sears gave the impression of a man who was never going to allow himself to be elbowed aside again.

Reagan, dividing his time between Rancho del Cielo, his Pacific Palisades home and his speaking trips, knew everything and nothing. He did not care at all about the details of Northeast politics which Sears relayed to him, but he was fascinated with the campaign manager's belief that the region was ripe for the taking. Reagan knew of Laxalt's misgivings and Nofziger's distrust, but he, and Nancy Reagan, realized that Sears brought a dimension to the campaign which the others lacked. Ironically, in view of what happened later, Reagan was encouraged in his view by Mike Deaver, then a strong Sears booster.

"We had kind of a western inferiority complex," said Deaver, in looking back on this period from the vantage point of the White House. "We didn't realize that what we had to do was do the things that got us where we were."[4] Reagan, who was present, nodded in agreement, adding that he had valued Sears because of his access to the Washington press corps. And it wasn't just the press. Until 1980, Reagan had always been spooked at what he regarded as a stereotypical reaction to him in the Northeast. I remember one occasion during an eastern swing in the fall of 1968 when Reagan expressed pleasurable surprise at applause he would have regarded as normal anywhere else. Over the years he had developed the theory that his gubernatorial record in California was still unknown to eastern voters who, he once said, thought of him as "some sort of conservative cowboy from the West." Reagan did not realize that his own view of the East as the "liberal" region of the country was also dated and stereotyped in many respects. But he knew that the region remained a mystery to him and that he was dependent on those who understood it. He did indeed have a western inferiority complex, and Sears at the time seemed the best defense.

In addition to this sense of dependence, Reagan had a strong belief in his ability to reconcile differences of approach. He has always been removed from the daily struggles of his staff, and he did not at this time believe that any of the conflicts were irreconcilable. Trying to keep everyone aboard, Reagan adopted a variant of the strategy Laxalt had suggested. He set up a team leadership, which he compared to his California cabinet. Sears, who kept the title of campaign director, was supposed to plot the political strategy while Meese kept Reagan briefed on issues and served as chief of staff. The other members of the collective leadership were Deaver, Hannaford, Lake and Charles Black. Pollster Wirthlin, though not a member of this formal leadership, also played a key role. Laxalt remained a long-distance, but influential, consultant and the national chairman. The structure was not pleasing to Sears, but he was soon once again exercising operational control. He had most of his old team back, except for David Keene, who had elected to have a major role with George Bush rather than a minor one with Reagan. Sears concentrated on New York, where he sent in an energetic young conservative organizer named Roger Stone, and where he also courted Representative Jack Kemp, a favorite with the party's right wing. In Pennsylvania, Sears enlisted first-rate political organizer Drew Lewis, who had held the line for Ford in 1976 against the best efforts of Sears and Schweiker. In the Midwest, Sears resurrected Keith Bulen of Indiana, an old-style Republican professional who had promoted Richard Lugar from obscurity to national fame as "Nixon's favorite mayor" and then to the U.S. Senate. Bulen had lost a step or two by 1980, but he was still among the best of political organizers. The most vital, and the most unsung, cog in this rapidly turning wheel was field operative Black, who served as political director of both the National Conservative Political Action Committee and the Republican National Committee before coming to work for Reagan. Black knew from experience who were the doers and who were the talkers among conservatives and Republican field organizers. His work gave Reagan a long organizational headstart.

As the Reagan organization took shape, Reagan remained above the clouds at Rancho del Cielo. He fully agreed with the counsel of Sears that he should not expose himself as a candidate before it was absolutely necessary. Deaver and Hannaford supported this strategy. They were still marketing the columns and radio shows that would have to be abandoned once Reagan became a declared candidate. These regular commentaries and frequent speeches accomplished the dual purpose of making Reagan rich and keeping him in the public view. After 1976, he was the political standard to which all other prospective Republican presidential candidates compared themselves. Partly, this was because the conservatism of which Reagan had once seemed an unlikely champion increasingly represented the central dogma of the Republican Party and indeed of the nation itself. Even Gerald Ford, a stalward conservative on most issues, had been forced to move right to head off Reagan in 1976.

Beyond his ideological acceptability, Reagan had now reached an elevated status achieved by very few politicians at any given time. He was, as Bob Teeter would observe in retrospect, irrevocably "in the major leagues of presidential candidates," that small group of people of which the public has such high awareness that they accept them as presidential even though they may not vote for them. Hubert H. Humphrey was such a figure in Democratic politics in the 1960s, and Senator Edward M. (Ted) Kennedy is one in the 1980s. "Seniority is how you get into that league," said Teeter. "And the fact that Reagan had been around since 1964 had made him one of those figures." The major league of presidential candidates, Republican division, was short of such men in the post-Nixon era. There was Reagan. There was Rockefeller, but he droped out of politics after Ford discarded him from the ticket in 1976 and died of a heart attack on January 26, 1979. And possibly, just possibly, there was Gerald Ford himself.

Ford was a worrisome and perplexing figure to the Reaganites during this period. Reagan did not believe he would run again, but the public opinion polls gave him scant comfort. Ford led Reagan by 10 percentage points as the preferred presidential candidate of Republican voters in a Gallup Poll of May 1978, and he continued to lead throughout the year, although by declining margins. The hope of the Reagan entourage was that Ford was enjoying his retirement so much that he would not want to abandon it for the rigors of a primary campaign. Up close, Ford gave the impression of a man who would like to be President again but not of someone willing to run. This was not surprising. Ford could literally walk out of his Palm Springs office and be on the golf course for a round of his favorite sport. In the winter there was skiing at his Colorado vacation retreat at Vail. The illness of his wife was also a deterrent.* Still, Ford campaigned for twenty-two Republican candidates in thirty states in the mid-term elections of 1978, and he teased reporters into writing speculative stories about a prospective second presidential race. It was with great relief that the Reaganites read a story by David S. Broder in the *Washington Post* on September 29, 1978, concluding that Ford, despite appearances to the contrary, was unlikely to be a presidential candidate again. "Most of those in his inner circle believe that when the time comes, Ford will say 'no' to another presidential

---

* Mrs. Ford, on April 19, 1978, was admitted to the Long Beach Naval Hospital for treatment of drug and alcohol abuse originally arising from addiction to a medication she had been taking to relieve severe arthritis. Subsequently she was released as cured.

campaign," Broder wrote. "And almost to a man, they hope that is his answer."[5]

Two events in the spring and summer of 1978 foreshadowed important aspects of Reagan's candidacy. One was Reagan's refusal in May, despite the request of Jack Kemp, to endorse the candidacy of Jeffrey Bell in the Republican primary in New Jersey. Bell, author of The $90 Billion Speech which had caused Reagan so much trouble in 1976, was opposing a venerable GOP liberal senator, Clifford Case, and Laxalt warned Reagan it would be unwise of him to get mixed up in a GOP primary. Reagan, who had almost always followed this rule as governor, readily agreed and also prevented any contribution by Citizens For The Republic to the Bell race, although Nofziger donated $50 of his own. As it turned out, Reagan's prudence cost him very little among the right-wingers in his own party, for Bell defeated Case anyway, and Reagan supported him in his losing race against Democrat Bill Bradley in the fall.

But Reagan's refusal to get involved in the Senate primary was an important signal to those looking for such signs. It meant that Reagan intended to present himself as the party's "unity" candidate for President in 1980, as he had done for the governorship of California in 1966. And Laxalt's conduct was a sign that all the pragmatism in the Reagan market hadn't been cornered by Sears. In fact, most of the Reaganites were distinguished more by an affinity for political realism than for ideology. In 1978 both Deaver and Wirthlin were concerned that Reagan had become too much of a Johnny-one-note in his opposition to the Panama Canal treaty, and an effort was made to moderate the tone of his opposition. Without ever actually abandoning the position which had stirred his 1976 comeback, Reagan began talking about making the canal an internationally operated waterway rather than one owned by the United States. This new tack did not attract much attention from the media, but it demonstrated Reagan's political flexibility. Once the treaty was finally approved on April 20, 1978, with Laxalt leading the opposition, Reagan rarely mentioned it. Increasingly, his columns focused upon inconsistencies in the Carter energy policy, the condition of the economy and the President's purported lack of leadership.

The second event which influenced the direction of the Reagan candidacy occurred in June 1978 when California voters overwhelmingly approved Proposition 13 and ushered in the era of the "tax revolution." This draconian measure, with its arbitrary and severe limits on local and state taxation, went so far beyond the spending limits of Reagan's defeated Proposition 1 of 1973 that many opponents of Proposition 13 cited the Reagan plan as a model by comparison. Reagan was never more than a cautious supporter of Proposition 13, often pointing out that his own plan was more moderate and carefully drawn. But when Proposition 13 passed, he expressed satisfaction and gave retroactive credit to his own Proposition 1, which he described as a measure ahead of its time.

Much nonsense has been written about Reagan's subsequent adoption of

"supply-side economics," the theology that tax cuts are desirable even during a period of expanding money supply and inflation because of their supposed stimulus to business activity. Some accounts make it seem as if Reagan were waylaid on the road to Damascus by the blinding economic truth
conveyed by economists Art Laffer and Jude Wanniski. Other accounts have
made it appear that Reagan's conversion was achieved by Sears in an effort
to head off the budding presidential candidacy of Kemp, the leading political apostle of the supply-side faith. Both of these views conveniently ignore
the political context created by Proposition 13 and its offspring in other
states. No one has ever accused Reagan of being an economist, despite his
long-ago major in economics and sociology at Eureka College. But he reads
election returns as well as any politician, and he understood the meaning of
Proposition 13 with perfect clarity. Without needing anyone to draw him a
"Laffer curve" on a napkin,* Reagan was out on the campaign stump for
GOP candidates in 1978 preaching the new gospel of the Kemp-Roth tax
bill. Reagan saw nothing particularly new or radical in what he was doing.
He had been sensitive to tax issues since the end of World War II when his
own rapidly rising income pushed him into high federal income tax
brackets. In fact, it was the tax issue more than any other which signaled
Reagan's drift from Democratic liberalism into Republican conservatism.
The denunciation of "confiscatory" levels of taxation had been a staple of
Reagan speeches in his General Electric days, and he had used the tax issue
against Pat Brown in 1966 during a boom period when California tax rates
were relatively low. Even though Reagan signed a record tax bill in 1967, he
was back preaching "tax relief" in 1969 and in his reelection campaign a
year later. Jack Kemp was knocking on an open door. Over the years there
had been no major political figure in the country who had surpassed Ronald
Reagan in a willingness to advocate tax reduction.

Kemp, a Buffalo congressman who had briefly interned with the Reagan
administration in California during the summer of 1967, had demonstrated
the political appeal of tax reduction in the Northeast. He had consistently
won Democratic votes in his blue-collar, economically depressed congressional district. Sears was not afraid that Kemp, who had little national name
recognition, could stop Reagan. But he wanted Kemp in Reagan's corner in
1980 and believed that he would be politically helpful in New York. What
Kemp saw in "supply-side economics" was its utility for Republicans in
promising increased business activity and new jobs. It gave Republican
candidates the opportunity to advocate something other than a recession as

* The "Laffer curve" was the invention of University of Southern California economics professor Arthur B. Laffer, who one day late in November 1974 was having drinks
with fellow economist Jude Wanniski and White House Chief of Staff Richard B.
Cheney. Laffer was trying to explain his theory that lower tax rates would increase incentives, and with them, taxable income. When Cheney seemed baffled by this unorthodox
contention, Laffer grabbed a napkin and drew a curve intended to show the variable relationship between tax rates and revenues.

a cure for inflation. Reagan has always gone after the blue-collar vote and prides himself on the number of Democrats who voted for him in 1966 and 1970.* He saw readily that blue-collar workers disaffected with Carter were a tempting political target for the 1980 presidential campaign and expressed this view when he lunched with Kemp in Los Angeles early in 1979.

Sears' Northeast strategy was well in place by the autumn of 1979. With Roger Stone's help, he had come up with a moderately impressive list of New York party regulars willing to stand up and be counted as Reaganites. As a further advertisement of Reagan's newfound interest in the Northeast, his formal announcement of candidacy was scheduled for New York City on November 13. By this time, every other Republican candidate had long since entered the race. There was John Connally, who confided to me during a visit to Los Angeles that he was confident he could beat Reagan if he could only get him one-on-one. That was then the hope of almost everyone in a GOP field which included George Bush, Senators Howard H. Baker, Jr., and Robert Dole, and Representatives John B. Anderson and Philip Crane. Connally was far ahead in fund-raising. Sears believed that Baker, who wanted Sears to run his campaign, had the possibility of catching on with the public. Nobody was worried at all about Bush, who had been busy for a year working the political vineyards of New Hampshire and Iowa.

Reagan's most serious problems were internal. The collective leadership had not worked, and Reagan was troubled by constant friction and lack of harmony among his principal lieutenants. The first to leave was Nofziger, who had been given a fund-raising responsibility for which he was temperamentally unsuited. At Sears' behest, Deaver convinced Reagan to let Nofziger go. When Deaver presented this decision to Nofziger, the embittered former press secretary accurately forecast that Deaver would be the next on Sears' hit list. The dismissal of Nofziger did much to fan the conservative fires which ultimately engulfed the power-conscious Sears. On October 26, 1979, Nofziger met with reporters in Los Angeles and said "some of the people around the governor are insensitive to his long-term supporters and to the needs of the media." He didn't identify these people but said that Sears and Deaver were running the campaign. The following day, in *Human Events,* which Reagan usually reads, M. Stanton Evans attacked Sears as "a graduate of the Richard Nixon school of politics . . . a devout pragmatist who has little affinity for issues in general, and even less affinity for conser-

---

* Reagan somewhat exaggerated his support among blue-collar voters, who are more resistant to statistical identification in California than in eastern and midwestern states. He did well in working class constituencies in 1966, and did not seem to recognize that his votes in these areas declined when he ran for reelection in 1970. In the early months of his 1980 presidential campaign, Reagan often remarked that he won the governorship in California by a million votes in 1966 and was reelected "by nearly as many" votes in 1970. In fact, Reagan's 1970 reelection margin was 497,000 votes, half of what it had been four years earlier. Most of the decline was attributable to reduced support in traditional Democratic areas.

vatives."[6] The departure of Nofziger, Evans warned, "removes an important potential counterweight to Sears' influence within the Reagan inner circle."

While these public expressions of displeasure were coming from movement conservatives, Laxalt was privately expressing a similar view directly to Reagan. The Nevada senator had heard of a Sears plan to replace him as national chairman and "broaden" the campaign with a dual chairmanship of Kemp and Iowa Governor Robert Ray. Reagan promised Laxalt that he would remain as chairman and kept his word, leaving Kemp with the undefined and largely meaningless title of "campaign spokesman." But the infighting was beginning to bother Reagan, who confessed to a friend that he was spending too much time on internal problems and "couldn't seem to keep everyone on track." By now, Deaver was trying with little success to take up the slack in fund-raising and was having his own problems with Sears. On November 2, in Boston for a fund-raiser with Frank Sinatra and Dean Martin, Reagan discussed the friction with press secretary Jim Lake, who liked Deaver but distrusted Meese and the other Californians. "Governor, there are two people who are absolutely critical to your campaign," Lake said. "One is John Sears and the other is Mike Deaver, and you need them both."[7] At the time, Reagan thought so, too. But the in-fighting continued and Reagan, at his wife's suggestion, summoned Deaver, Sears, Lake and Charles Black to a meeting at his Pacific Palisades home November 26 in an effort to conciliate the differences.

What followed, instead of conciliation, was a showdown. With Deaver and Nancy alongside him, Reagan found himself faced with a united front of Sears, Lake and Black demanding that he make a decision between keeping Deaver and the three of them. "I can't understand this," Reagan said to Lake. "Three weeks ago you told me that both John and Mike were indispensable to my campaign, and now you're telling me that I have to choose between them." Lake uncomfortably replied that Reagan could no longer keep both men and that Sears was the more valuable to his campaign.* The acrimonious talk wound on, with Sears accusing Deaver of doing a poor job of fund-raising and Deaver insisting that the complaints against him were simply an excuse Sears was using to take total control. After hours of discussion, Sears and his allies remained adamant, unwilling to agree to a compromise that would keep Deaver in the campaign. Seeing what was happening, Nancy Reagan said to her husband: "Yes, honey, you're going to have to make a choice." Before Reagan could respond, Deaver spoke up and said, "No, governor, you don't have to make that choice. I'll resign." And with that he walked to the front door, with Reagan following him in agitation and insisting that he didn't want Deaver to leave.

---

* Lake had long seen himself as the man in the middle. As he recounts it, he would explain Deaver's value to Sears and Sears' importance to Deaver and try to reconcile their differences. "I was just worn out being the broker," Lake said to me in 1981. "I couldn't do it anymore."

Reagan returned to the living room in a fury. "The biggest man here just left the room," he said. "He was willing to accommodate and compromise and you bastards wouldn't." Reagan never talked warmly to Sears again. The confrontation left him depressed and angry with himself about what he had allowed to happen. His mood was not improved when old friends and allies, who had rarely criticized him to his face, bluntly told him that he had made a mistake. Nancy Reynolds, close to the Reagans and to Deaver, protested the decision in a telephone conversation and remembers that it was the only time Reagan was ever testy with her.[8] Meese forcefully told Reagan that he had made a mistake and didn't understand what had been happening in his own campaign. Reagan told me much later that he hadn't needed anyone to tell him that he had done wrong. "But Mike precipitated it," he added. "I really didn't expect him to go."

There are private moments in every election campaign that are special, forever remembered by the participants when memories of more celebrated public occasions have dimmed. The November 26, 1979, meeting in Reagan's home was one of those times. For Sears, it marked the beginning of the end. In insisting on Deaver's resignation, Sears had made an adversary of the one California insider who had defended him to the candidate and Nancy Reagan and who accepted the premise that Sears needed operational control. Others in the inner circle had thought that Deaver was too trusting of Sears, particularly after Nofziger's dismissal. Sears was aware that Deaver had on many occasions spoken well of him, but he seemed unable to restrain his impulse to achieve control by pushing Deaver out of the campaign. Sears was, a friend observed afterward, like a figure in a Greek tragedy whose strength of character is also the flaw which becomes the source of his downfall. Sears wanted to run the campaign his way, or not at all. He could not risk insiders who were closer to Reagan than he was. By eliminating Deaver he insured his own downfall as well.

For Reagan, November 26, 1979, marked the day in which he became a participant rather than an observer in his own campaign. From the moment Deaver walked out on him, Reagan began to question the wisdom of turning over his political future to a man who patronized him and didn't laugh at his old movie jokes. "I look him in the eye, and he looks me in the tie," Reagan said, reverting to a standard used in his midwestern boyhood for evaluating the trustworthiness of a man. Now, at last, the passive candidate was angry enough to say what he really thought and felt about his campaign manager. Once he started doing that, although it took a defeat in Iowa and Nancy Reagan to force him to act, the ultimate decision became inevitable.

It was only when Deaver was gone that the Reagans, both of them, realized how much they had depended on their long-time aide. It was Deaver who performed the role of faithful adjutant and maintained the atmosphere of harmony which Reagan needed, particularly on the road. It was Deaver who intervened when a contributor, or another aide, or a reporter found it necessary to speak to the candidate outside the normal channels. And it was Deaver, not Sears, who had become Reagan's indispensable man. After November 26, though he still needed Sears, Reagan would be guided more by his personal feelings and less by the judgment of outside professionals whom he did not know. He would listen to those he trusted and felt knew him best—Nancy Reagan, Ed Meese, Paul Laxalt, old members of the Kitchen Cabinet like Holmes Tuttle and William French Smith, and old campaign managers like Stu Spencer. After Sears had gone, Reagan would welcome Deaver back like a lost son and keep him at his side throughout the rest of the campaign and into the White House. This was not the way a lot of people would have operated, but it was the best way for Reagan, who does not do well with dissonance around him. Campaigns are won in the hearts of men before they are won at the ballot box. They are won by candidates doing what they do best and knowing themselves and feeling secure about what they are saying. On November 26, 1979, Reagan began to realize that he did not understand what was going on in his own campaign. The struggle to gain that understanding, to speak in his own voice, and to campaign in a way that he felt comfortable made Reagan a better candidate than he would otherwise have been. Because of what happened in his living room after Deaver walked out on him, Reagan became his own candidate for President of the United States.

17

"The O & W"

SHORTLY before Reagan became a formal candidate for President, Sears brought him to New York City to show the flag of his northeastern strategy. Reagan was introduced at one gathering by Barry Gray, a New York radio personality who proclaimed, "The nation cries out for desperate leadership." By the time Reagan announced his candidacy in the ballroom of the New York Hilton the night of November 13, 1979, there were many in both the press and the political community who suspected that was exactly what they were getting. Reagan was the tenth and last Republican candidate to enter the race. Despite his big lead in the polls, many thought he was too old, too unintelligent or too out of touch to be elected. "I think a man approaching seventy is going to have a hard time giving a new speech when he's given the same speech two hundred nights a year for twenty years," the usually astute political consultant John Deardourff told reporters.[1] It was a prevalent opinion. On the night of his announcement, Reagan fueled the worst suspicions about him by stumbling through a formula speech that had reporters groping for a lead.* What little that was new was a Sears-induced proposal for "a North American accord," which as best as anyone could understand was a kind of encounter group among the leaders of Canada, Mexico and the United States. The idea quickly disappeared from public view after serving Sears' purpose of demonstrating that Reagan occasionally could say something original. But the speech was not a politician-pleaser.

* The speech was devoid of a quotable catch phrase or an original theme. Reporters didn't know what the candidate considered important in his own address and were left to their own devices in figuring out what was most significant. The *New York Times* led with the "North American accord" and the *Los Angeles Times* with a statement by Reagan that, "I cannot and will not stand by and see this great country destroy itself." In the *Washington Post* I wrote that Reagan had launched his campaign "with a call for the restoration of American influence abroad and American confidence at home." A similar disparity was reflected in the network television accounts of the Reagan announcement. One result of this, as Paul Laxalt observed, was that Reagan did not take advantage of the opportunity to present a focused message in the first week of his formal campaign.

Sears (and Nofziger, before him) had tried without success for years to get Reagan to say something unkind about big business. Sears came as close to accomplishing this as anyone ever would in this announcement speech with a passage in which Reagan indifferently declared that Americans had not "been given all the information we need to make a judgment" about the magnitude of excess oil company profits. This statement irritated Kemp, who opposed the windfall profits tax and did not like the once-over-lightly treatment Reagan gave the Kemp-Roth tax-cutting plan. Other conservatives were bothered by an almost total lack of specifics from Reagan on defense and foreign policy. Summing up what may have been a consensus among both the press corps and the conservatives, Laxalt told me that he thought the speech was "mostly mush." Whatever it was, it did not seem an auspicious beginning.

Reagan's speech looks better in retrospect. It was uninspiring to many of the conservative faithful and to those of us in the press who had been subjected to the collected works of Ronald Reagan one too many times. But Reagan's target was neither the movement conservatives nor the national press. His audience, as usual, was the millions of Americans watching television, who had learned the hard way not to trust the promises of their Presidents. These Americans had been disappointed by Johnson, disillusioned by Nixon and had not found that much to cheer about in the subsequent performances of Ford and Carter.* Reagan's speech, taped earlier and delivered smoothly, was addressed to these disappointed Americans. If Reagan did not have all the answers, or any answers, he at least was able to establish bonds of association, and of trust, with his audience. Reagan had been doing this for so long many of us had forgotten how important it was. He did it again the night of his announcement, in words that never made it into most of the news stories, and he did it well. Other candidates were telling voters what they could do to save America. Reagan, instead, described what had happened to him in his own life. "I'm sure that each of us has seen our country from a number of different viewpoints depending on where we've lived and what we've done," Reagan said. "For me it has been as a boy growing up in several small towns in Illinois. As a young man in Iowa trying to get a start in the years of the great Depression and later in California for most of my adult life. I've seen America from the stadium press box as a sportscaster, as an actor, officer of my labor union, soldier, office-holder, and as

* President Carter's approval rating, as measured by Gallup, had sunk below the 40 percent level in May 1979, and stayed there throughout the summer and fall. In the November 2–5 period it was 32 percent. After the American hostages were seized in Tehran on November 4, 1979, however, the President's approval rating began to climb rapidly. It was 38 percent in the November 16–19 period right after Reagan announced, and had soared to 61 percent in early December. But this crisis-born confidence in the President did not last long. In February 1980, Carter's approval rating started down again and declined for six consecutive months until it reached a low point of 21 percent in the July 14–25 period when Reagan was nominated for President.

both Democrat and Republican. I've lived in an America where those who often had too little to eat outnumbered those who had enough. There have been four wars in my lifetime and I've seen our country face financial ruin in the Depression. I have also seen the great strength of this nation as it pulled itself up from that ruin to become the dominant force in the world."

Later in his speech, Reagan told the old story of how his father had been fired on Christmas Eve and said, his eyes again moist, "I cannot and will not stand by while inflation and joblessness destroy the dignity of our people." More than anything, his message was: Accept me folks, I'm one of you. With these words of association came the additional reassurance that Reagan was somehow different from other politicians, that he was an ordinary man who would keep his word because he was not really a politician at all. Earlier in the month in Los Angeles he had responded to a question from a reporter about whether he was moving more to the political center, saying: "I am what I always have been and I intend to remain that way."[2]

If we missed the significance of Reagan's message because of our familiarity with it, we certainly caught the impact of his stumbling start. The morning of the announcement speech Reagan appeared on the three network morning news shows, and on NBC's *Today* was caught up in a colloquy about the ages of world leaders. Reagan offered the view that he would be younger than most of the heads of states he would be dealing with if elected President.

"Giscard d'Estaing of France is younger than you," observed interviewer Tom Brokaw.

"Who?" said Reagan, giving the impression he had never heard of the man.

"Giscard d'Estaing of France," repeated Brokaw.

"Yes, possibly," said Reagan, who is fifteen years older than the then French president. "Not an awfully lot more."

Reporters laughed at this exchange, and many of them believed that Reagan in fact did not know, or had forgotten, who was president of France. Press Secretary Lake dampened this concern but raised another. He said that the reason Reagan had responded the way he did was that he had not heard the question from Brokaw, sitting only a few feet away. "We could run a correction in the *Washington Post*," I said to Lake. "We could say that the good news is that Ronald Reagan knows who the president of France is and that the bad news is that he can't hear." Lake, who had done as well as any of the Reaganites in fending off the age issue, laughed and shook his head. "We'd rather have you say he's too ignorant than too old," he said.*

---

* Lake's equanimity did not survive a story I wrote in January which noted that a question had to be repeated five times at an Iowa rally before Reagan could understand it. The story quoted an aide, who upon meeting Reagan for the first time in four years thought he looked vigorous enough but added, "The only difference I have noticed is that his hearing has slipped." Lake told other reporters that this story was a "cheap shot" even

A public reminder of Reagan's age came the day after Reagan's announcement speech from supporter Jack Kemp, who introduced him to a press conference in Washington as "the oldest and wisest candidate." Some members of the Reagan entourage winced. However, the phrase caught on immediately with the campaign press corps, who started referring to Reagan in pool reports for their colleagues as "The Oldest and Wisest," soon shortened to "The O & W." The nickname was taken up by the more irreverent members of the Reagan staff. Nancy Reagan didn't care for it, but the candidate good-naturedly accepted the designation and it stuck.

It was the question of Reagan's wisdom rather than his age which worried Sears and provided the supporting motivation for a late announcement and a front-running strategy. Reagan's knowledge gap showed up immediately. After his Washington press conference, Reagan flew back to New York City and confronted reporters again at the Waldorf-Astoria the following morning. He bobbled an easy question about federal aid to New York City, which he didn't know came with strings attached. In Grand Rapids, Michigan, the next day, Reagan proved even less knowledgeable about pending legislation to bail out the troubled Chrysler Corporation, which was of key importance to the state and community in which he was campaigning. Reporters cornered Reagan after a speech to Kent County Republicans and found him so vague about the issue they couldn't understand what he was saying. The best Reagan could do in talking about bail-out legislation was to say, "I don't believe I'm in agreement with the plan that was presented by the President." Subsequently, Meese came back to reporters on the plane to explain what Reagan "really meant" to have proposed. "What the governor is saying is that Chrysler has not exhausted all of the solutions short of the bail-out," Meese said. He went on to discuss how Chrysler could save itself by reorganization and reduced wages, providing the union was willing to go along. The explanation partially salvaged Reagan for the day, but left Sears furious with Meese, whom he held responsible for failing to prepare Reagan for obvious questions. Reagan's stumblings also reminded Sears of New Hampshire in 1976 and ratified the campaign manager's low opinion of his candidate's intelligence.

My evaluation of Reagan's first trip, written for the *Washington Post* of November 19, was that the candidate had erased questions about his vitality "while raising new doubts about his capacity to serve as President." I had seen Reagan on the ropes before, but couldn't understand why he was so ill-

---

though Reagan's hearing loss was obvious to those who had seen the candidate in other campaigns. Subsequently, on a plane trip from Los Angeles to New Hampshire, Reagan said to me that he had suffered from a minor hearing impairment in his right ear since the late 1930s because of an incident which occurred when he was filming one of the movies in which he played Secret Service agent Brass Bancroft. As Reagan told the story, another actor was supposed to fire a blank .38 cartridge from some distance away. Instead, he fired it next to Reagan's ear.

prepared after starting so late. What wasn't apparent then was the draining effect of the staff struggles, which would culminate a week later with the walkout of Deaver. Reagan needs to focus to do his best. At a time he was supposed to be running for President, he was instead learning the hard way that he was not even running his own campaign. Even so, he showed he had learned something from competing in twenty-five primaries in 1976. Four years earlier he had rationalized his bad days by remembering the good moments in them and failing to be self-critical. Now he looked back at his own opening performance and found it deficient. "What I should have pointed out is that the system is in place and it's working," Reagan said about his muff on New York City aid during an interview en route to the West Coast.[3] He was blunter about his stumbles to his aides, acknowledging to one of them that he had "blown it" in Grand Rapids. This realism would come in handy for Reagan after the Iowa caucuses.

Reagan's schedule was deliberately brisk that first week in an effort to show that he was up to the rigors of a campaign. But Sears slowed him down after that, keeping the candidate on a carefully paced front-running course. Sears' strategy, readily accepted by the candidate despite his personal misgivings about his campaign manager, was to cast Reagan as the presumed nominee of his party. Reagan traveled everywhere by air, avoiding the grubby, ground-level combat in which he might be tripped up by the press or local issues. Hiding behind the rubric of the Eleventh Commandment, which he had frayed so badly in his battle against Gerald Ford, Reagan also ducked debates with other Republicans. This tactic had worked successfully in Richard Nixon's above-the-issues 1968 campaign against Hubert Humphrey, and the same approach was easily transferable to Reagan if one pretended that he had already won the nomination.

Reagan's constant coast-to-coast travel was an expensive form of campaigning under the new campaign spending limitation laws, but Sears was convinced that Reagan could wrap up the nomination early in the Northeast. The campaign manager devoted organizational resources to this target region, concentrating on New York, Connecticut and New Hampshire. Even in the first primary state, however, the candidate's presence was not regarded as essential and New Hampshire Chairman Gerald Carmen's plea for more appearances by Reagan went unheeded. Everyone knew who Ronald Reagan was. He was everywhere, and nowhere. In the final seven weeks of 1979 and the first three of 1980, Reagan became an airborne celebrity candidate, soaring above the earthbound struggles of the mortal contenders for the Republican nomination. By the second week of December the pace was so leisurely that during a swing through South Carolina baggage call was listed on the campaign schedule as an "event."

For a time, this front-running strategy, which really was more like front-walking, seemed to be working. A week before Reagan's announcement, a *New York Times*-CBS poll found him far ahead among Republican voters with 37 percent to John Connally's 15 percent. The following week a *Washington Post* poll showed Reagan gaining among moderate Republican voters. In California, a poll taken the week of his announcement by Mervin Field gave Reagan 61 percent to 12 percent for runner-up Senator Howard H. Baker. On November 17, Reagan defeated all his potential GOP rivals in a raw vote at the Florida Republican Convention, which Connally unwisely had made a test of his organizational ability and political appeal. Reagan won 36 percent of the vote to 27 percent for Connally and 21 percent for George Bush. After this victory, the upcoming caucuses in Iowa seemed a piece of cake. The *Des Moines Register and Tribune*'s respected Iowa Poll, in a survey taken between November 28 and December 1, gave Reagan 50 percent of the vote and 14 percent to Bush in second place.

The Iowa precinct caucuses of January 21, 1980, were one of those wild cards which keep turning up in the American political deck just when it seems that everyone has mastered the game. They were supposed to be important for President Carter, who had parlayed a better-than-expected showing in the 1976 caucuses to victory in New Hampshire and ultimately the presidency. And important they were, delivering a devastating blow to Senator Edward Kennedy in his first campaign test. Initially, the caucuses did not loom as particularly significant to the Republican nominating process. But their importance increased when the *Register and Tribune,* at the suggestion of its enterprising editor James Gannon, decided to sponsor the seasons' first debates between the presidential candidates, a Republican one on January 5, a Saturday, and a Democratic debate two days later. Carter had planned to participate in the latter event because he was trailing Kennedy in the polls. But when Kennedy broke badly from the gate and Democrats rallied in support of their President after seizure of the hostages in Iran, Carter's refusal to leave the White House put the spotlight on the Republican show. Six of the invited GOP candidates—Connally, Baker, Bush, John B. Anderson, Philip Crane and Robert Dole—eagerly accepted the debate invitation. Reagan rejected it, accepting Sears' decision without a murmur. The campaign manager had seen enough of Reagan on the road that he did not want to let his candidate out of the cage. Furthermore, he did not think it was necessary. Both Sears and Black pointedly left open the possibility of a New Hampshire debate, of which Reagan booster William Loeb was an ardent advocate, but they did not think it necessary to expose the candidate in Iowa. In fairness to Sears, it is unlikely that Reagan would have reached a different decision even if he had already changed campaign managers. Reagan had avoided debates with any of his opponents since his disastrous March 1966 joint appearance with George Christopher before the National Negro Republican Assembly. In the intervening years, Gaylord Parkinson's dictum about not speaking ill of fellow Republicans had served Reagan well, and he gave it one last fling in Iowa.

Only 22,000 Republicans had participated in the Iowa caucuses of 1976. The Reagan organizers in the state, who were not among the candidate's best, had no idea of how many would participate in 1980. At least two political professionals, Eddie Mahe, for Connally, and Richard Redman, for Baker, thought that the total could go as high as 100,000, but these forecasts seemed excessively high to almost everyone else. The Reagan forces adopted what they thought seemed a prudent organizational course: They would try to turn out 30,000 certified Reaganites at the caucuses, leaving a hefty margin of error for their candidate in a seven-man field even if the vote was triple that of 1976. Sears and Wirthlin agreed that it would be a waste to poll because of the difficulty of defining the electorate. "Who would you be polling?" Wirthlin said to me a few days before the election. "How do you know who's going to turn out?" But Wirthlin confessed that he was jittery about Iowa, and Charles Black shared his concern. Early in the month an observant fieldman, Kenneth Klinge, had warned about the progress being made by Bush. The signs of trouble were there, but the Reagan campaign did not react to them.

Perhaps both Sears and Reagan would have reacted differently if they had spent more time in Iowa. The candidate made eight appearances in the state, but he flew in and out so quickly that Bush was able to boast he had spent more days in Iowa than Reagan had hours. Wirthlin called these trips "cameo appearances," and they did not fool Iowa Republicans into thinking that Reagan was campaigning. The Reagan visit which attracted the most attention was a fly-in to Davenport two days after the debate. Reagan held a quicky, confused press conference in the lobby of the Black Hawk Hotel, trying to explain why he ducked the debate. One reporter asked about Connally's comment during the debate that he didn't know where Reagan stood on the issues. "He must have been living under a rock," Reagan said of Connally. "I've been saying what I believe for a long, long time, and I spent eight years as governor trying to implement what I believe. I haven't changed these views, and I have been speaking in specifics." However, Reagan had privately changed one important view which he disclosed for the first time at the press conference. The other Republican candidates except for Anderson had criticized President Carter's grain embargo against the Soviet Union. Reagan's own initial reaction had been to support the measure as a proper response to the invasion of Afghanistan, but a strategy session in Los Angeles, in which both Sears and Wirthlin pointed out the importance of grain exports to Iowa farmers, had produced another position. In Davenport, Reagan inaccurately asserted that the embargo punished American farmers without having any impact on the Soviets. Reagan would, as President, keep the promise he made that night to lift the embargo. What he never said was that the promise itself had been made for the most blatant of political reasons.

The Bush organization in Iowa sent a million pieces of mail during the last week of the campaign, a discovery that the Reagan team did not make until after the election. Reagan spent most of the week before the caucuses with Sears at his side, cruising the campaign manager's chosen battleground of the Northeast. While Bush was spending every day in Iowa, Reagan was traveling to New Hampshire, Vermont, Connecticut and New York, wooing politicians in four states which had given Ford 204 delegates and Reagan only 23 at the 1976 convention. By now, Bush's surge was becoming evident to the political desks of the news organizations covering the campaign, and our editors wanted predictive estimates of Iowa from the Sears team. Sears responded as if Iowa were on the moon. Instead of analyzing the upcoming caucuses, he provided me with a highly detailed and generally accurate forecast of where and how Reagan would win delegates in the Northeast. "Reflect on this," said Sears. "This time we don't have the support of Strom Thurmond who was backing Connally and we have the support of half the delegation from New York."[4] True enough, but what about Iowa? Sears gave an expressive shrug.

Reagan made one final appearance in Iowa, delivering a statewide television version of The Speech on the Saturday night before the election. Then he flew home to California. Bush stayed behind, and won. After all of his own work, however, and all of Reagan's neglect, Bush's victory was achieved by the narrow margin of 2,182 votes. The Reagan forces slightly exceeded their original target, winning 31,318 votes. But 110,000 Republicans participated in the caucuses, and Reagan's vote was only 30 percent of the total. Bush received 33,530 votes, 33 percent. The outcome finished off the front-runner strategy, and there were those in Iowa who thought it had taken the front-runner down with it. Wirthlin, the pollster who had not polled, had a sense of *déjà vu.* He remembered 1976 when Reagan had left New Hampshire the Sunday before the election and lost the primary narrowly to Gerald Ford. "It was like sitting through a rerun of a bad old movie you hadn't wanted to see the first time," he said.[5]

Reagan was watching a new movie on this night the returns came in from Iowa. Relaxing while most of his rivals were still campaigning, Reagan had gone to the swank Bel Air home of producer Hal Wallis to see a preview of *Kramer vs. Kramer.* Reagan learned about what was happening in Iowa while the movie was shown, and he was shaken. "It was a jolt," he told me months later, remembering the night the returns came in from Iowa as the low point of the campaign and one of the low points in his life. "There are going to be some changes made," Meese recalls Reagan saying to him grimly that same evening. And changes there were, immediately. Rather than wrecking Reagan, Iowa freed him from the shrouds in which his managers had wrapped him, permitting him to campaign as a natural candidate drawing on the resources of his own personality. "I sensed that weeks before that, psychologically, Ron felt trapped," Laxalt told me afterwards. "He concurred in avoiding the Iowa debate but subconsciously he didn't feel right about it. When he changed, he was liberated and it enabled him to perform in New Hampshire."[6] Ever since Reagan's fiery performance in the 1976 North Carolina primary, Laxalt had believed the candidate was his own best asset. He said this and more to Reagan the next day, speaking bluntly to his friend and recalling the Super Bowl game of the week before where the Pittsburgh Steelers had defeated Reagan's beloved Los Angeles Rams. "The Steelers wouldn't have won if [quarterback] Terry Bradshaw had been sitting on his ass for three quarters, and you were sitting on your ass in Iowa," Laxalt said.[7] Reagan agreed that he had been taking it too easy, and promised that the world would see a different candidate in New Hampshire. And Nofziger, still on the outs, summed up the unanimous attitude of the Californians: "If you're going to follow a Rose Garden strategy, you better be sure you have a Rose Garden."[8]

No one knew better than John Sears the need for change. He was a political professional who understood that the campaign manager takes both the credit and the blame. And he was a tactician who realized that a course of action which doesn't work must be discarded. In a transformation as swift as any ever made at Central Casting, the high-flying and disengaged front-runner became the bus-bound accessible underdog. Weekends were out. During one stretch Reagan campaigned for twenty-one consecutive days, mostly by bus in New Hampshire, with a couple of side trips to the early primary states of South Carolina and Florida. Before Iowa, reporters had swapped jokes about such innovations as the Ronald Reagan doll which, when wound, ran for an hour before it had to take a nap. But the easy duty was gone in New Hampshire, and a sign went up on the press bus saying, "Free the Reagan 44."

Reagan's days were longer, but his life was easier on the ground. He warmed up crowds and was warmed by them. He answered questions bluntly, responding to the predominant conservative strain among New Hampshire Republicans with familiar opposition to budget deficits, the Soviet Union, and permissive abortion laws. He went after Bush, too, raising the issues which were the favorites of his principal New Hampshire supporter, *Manchester Union Leader* publisher William Loeb. In response to a question at the Franklin Rotary Club about differences between himself and Bush, Reagan said that Bush favored a liberalized abortion law, the Equal Rights Amendment and a guaranteed-income welfare plan, while he opposed them. Later in the evening he told the Hookset Men's Club that he had "forgotten" to mention that Bush also favored gun control, an accusation dimly based on Bush's support of a 1968 law restricting mail order sales of rifles and shotguns.

Reagan's greatest success in New Hampshire was in defusing the "age issue," which, after Iowa, had become a prime topic of conversation. Hearing that some of his opponents might "celebrate" Reagan's sixty-ninth birthday on February 6, less than three weeks before the primary, the Reagan team decided to beat them to it. Acting on the suggestion of California Reagan activist Lorelei Kinder, Sears saw to it that birthday parties were organized up and down the eastern seaboard for his candidate. There were balloons and birthday songs and signs and so many mammoth cakes that Reagan finally fell into one of them at a party in Greenville, South Carolina, on February 7. The press scored the birthday parties "Reagan 6, Cakes 1." Taken in their entirety, however, the Reagan parties provided a classic demonstration of how to turn a supposed liability into an asset. After New Hampshire, age never became an issue against Reagan again.

Reagan's big night in New Hampshire was a debate, but not the wonderful theater of Nashua. The celebrated Nashua debate was on February 23, the Saturday before the primary. Reagan's breakthrough came on February 20, three days before, when he joined the six Republican candidates he had eluded in Iowa for a joint appearance in Manchester sponsored by the League of Women Voters. Reagan was nervous at Manchester. He fumbled some questions and at one point offered the startling opinion that it is acceptable for U.S. corporations doing business abroad to bribe foreign governments if that is what is expected of them. But Bush also was uninspiring. He drew few differences with Reagan, and he took mild jabs from the other candidates, who now perceived him as the front-runner possessed of the momentum which Bush liked to call "Big Mo." It was a misperception, shared by many in the press corps. Reagan's stature with Republican voters, and particularly with conservatives, had not been built in a day. He had been their hero since 1964, and he had campaigned for his principles and for himself in two subsequent presidential elections. He stood with them on the gut issues. Most recently, he had fought the good fight against SALT II and against the Panama Canal treaty. To the nation's growing conservative constituency, and especially to the even more conservative electorate of New Hampshire, the concerns about Reagan had nothing to do with his ideology or his steadfastness. All of the doubts were personal ones, centering on his vitality, his capacity and his age. Reagan fueled these doubts by absenting himself from Iowa; he answered them convincingly in New Hampshire with his vigorous campaigning and his appearance on the stump and in debates. Reagan did not have to "win" the debate in Manchester, and a "draw" would not have been good enough for Bush. In a very real sense, Reagan won just by showing up and being himself.

Wirthlin's polls demonstrated the decisiveness of Manchester. Thirty-seven percent of the Republicans intending to vote in the election watched, and most of these picked a winner. Reagan was first choice with 33 percent as the winner, compared to 17 percent who thought that Bush had won. Even viewers who did not think that Reagan had won approved of his response to a question from the audience criticizing him for telling an ethnic joke.* Reagan said he had been "stiffed" by the press and was telling the

---

* The joke went like this: "How do you tell who the Polish fellow is at a cock fight? He's the one with the duck. How do you tell who the Italian is at the cock fight? He's the one who bets on the duck. How do you know the Mafia was there? The duck wins." When news services carried the account of Reagan telling the joke, longtime aide Ed Meese quipped, "There goes Connecticut," a reference to the prominent participation of Italian-Americans in the Republican politics of that state.

joke as an example of jokes which politicians shouldn't tell. This was a lie, as reporters who were covering him at the time were well aware. He got away with it because the joke was not that offensive in itself and because Reagan was sincere in saying that he is not a prejudiced person. And he got away with it, also, because in any contest between Reagan and the national press in New Hampshire, the press is likely to fare even more poorly than George Bush. Wirthlin's polls showed Reagan moving from a point behind Bush to 20 points ahead on the strength of the Manchester debate. But the final tally of the surveys was incomplete when Reagan went to Nashua on Saturday for the face-to-face debate with Bush that would provide the wildest and most memorable moments of the 1980 election campaign.

In a way, what happened in Nashua was a fitting last hurrah for embattled John Sears, the master political tactician. In another way it was a demonstration of the most effective and genuine qualities of Reagan and the most disquieting ones of the man he was to make his Vice-President. Seen without the informing comfort of hindsight, it was a stroke of luck of the sort which has befallen Reagan many times in his life. And it was, even for those in the audience of 2,500 who were not political junkies, a splendid show. The Nashua debate originally was the proposal of Jerry Carmen, who believed after Iowa that the way to cut Bush down to size was to put him one-on-one with Reagan. Bush's managers liked the idea because they believed that such a forum, whatever its outcome, would show voters that the Republican race was now a two-man affair between Bush and Reagan. So, Hugh Gregg, the Reagan campaign manager in New Hampshire in 1976 who was now directing the Bush operation in the state, talked to two old friends, the publisher and editor of the *Nashua Telegraph,* who agreed to sponsor the debate. Then Dole complained to the Federal Elections Commission that this sponsorship would be an illegal contribution to the Reagan and Bush campaigns if the other candidates were excluded. The commission agreed, and Carmen and Sears proposed that Reagan and Bush split the costs of the debate. Had Bush accepted this reasonable offer, the so-called "ambush at Nashua" which Bush and his strategists later blamed on Sears would have been impossible. But Gregg can be stiff-necked when he does not approve of something, and the Bush national strategists were totally deferring to him in New Hampshire, as Sears and Lake had done in 1976. Gregg refused to pay any share, and after further negotiations, Sears agreed that the Reagan campaign would pay the entire cost of the debate. Sears realized, as Reagan was to assert dramatically Saturday night, that this action gave his camp some control of the proceedings despite the *Nashua Telegraph*'s theoretical sponsorship. The campaign manager and Lake then started calling the other candidates, explaining to them that Reagan felt that it was unfair to exclude them. If they came to Nashua, Sears said, there might be an opportunity for them to participate. All of the candidates, except Connally, who was campaigning in South Carolina, agreed to come. Meanwhile, word was passed to reporters that Nashua was not going to be a cut-and-dried affair.*

Reagan didn't know what was happening. He spent the afternoon resting and boning up on debate questions he thought might be raised by Bush. Although he did not know what Sears had arranged for the evening, Reagan had been told that the results of the Manchester debate were positive for him, which meant that he no longer needed to meet Bush in an isolated debate. In the car en route to the debate site at the Nashua High School gymnasium, Lake told Reagan that Anderson, Baker, Dole and Crane would be there as well as Bush. "Fine," said Reagan, who afterward told me that he had never cared much for excluding the other candidates in the first place.

At the gymnasium Reagan met with the four excluded candidates at one end of a long hall while Sears met privately in an adjoining room with Bush campaign manager Jim Baker and told him that Reagan wanted to open up the debate. Baker refused. As Baker left the meeting with Sears, he spotted the other candidates in the room with Reagan and went back to tell Bush that he was about to be "ambushed." Bush persisted in his opposition to an open debate, saying that the rules had been agreed upon in advance. Out in the hall *Nashua Telegraph* editor Jon Breen was telling reporters the same thing, reiterating that he would not change the ground rules. By now, Reagan had agreed with the four excluded candidates that he wouldn't debate if they weren't allowed to participate. Reagan's strategists argued, however, that he couldn't walk out, for that would make it look as if he were afraid to debate Bush. Angrily, without any of his own staff knowing what he was going to do, Reagan stalked to the hall followed by the Nashua Four.† He took his seat at the podium, and the excluded candidates stood behind him

---

* By chance, I happened to be having lunch with John Anderson in a shopping mall when Sears called him on the day of the debate. With us were an aide, two or three reporters from Illinois newspapers, and a like number of youthful Anderson supporters. Anderson, who was scheduled to make an appearance in Concord that night, came back from the telephone call and, with the openness for which he is famed, asked everyone at the table what he should do about it. The aide reminded him of the Concord engagement. The reporters said they were going to the debate. Anderson thought about it a moment and observed that Sears wouldn't have called him unless it was important. "I think I'll go to Nashua and have a look," he said.

† Carmen subsequently told David Nyhan of the *Boston Globe* that he had no idea "until the last minute" whether Reagan was going to go on stage. Carmen quoted Reagan as saying, "If they don't let the others on stage, I'm not going up there," and that he would instead hold a press conference. "Governor, you can't," Carmen replied, and went off to find Senator Gordon Humphrey of New Hampshire and Laxalt to help persuade Reagan to go on. Carmen's concern was that a Reagan walkout would look like he was running out of the debate. "I've thought about it many times," Carmen told Nyhan. "If Bush was thinking he could go on and Reagan would not show, that was not a bad strategy. If that's what he was thinking, it was a gamble that didn't work." This account appeared in a reprise of the Nashua incident in the *Globe* on June 1, 1980. Subsequently, I asked Reagan why he had decided to go out on the stage, and he smiled and said, "It seemed like the thing to do at the time." My own belief is that it was an instinctive reaction rather than a conscious calculation on Reagan's part.

at the back of the stage. Bush, as stiff and unbending, stared straight ahead, looking, as William Loeb wrote afterward, "like a small boy who has been dropped off at the wrong birthday party." The gym was a tumult, and it was clear that even a number of the Bush partisans favored a free-for-all debate. "Get them chairs," some shouted. "Baker can stand on the table," cried a raucous voice, in reference to the senator's diminutive stature. When *Nashua Telegraph* publisher J. Herman Pouliot tried to quiet the crowd, he was booed. Reagan, his face flushed, waited his turn and tried to explain why he wanted the other candidates to participate. "Turn Mr. Reagan's microphone off," said Breen, not knowing that the Reagan camp had seen to it that the sound technician was also a Reagan loyalist. Reagan didn't know it, either, and he didn't need technical help. "I paid for this microphone, Mr. Green," Reagan said with controlled fury, mangling the name of the editor but getting everything else right. Next to me, in a fourth-row seat in the gymnasium, David Broder said quietly, "Reagan is winning this primary right now." And much later, in a retrospective of the tumultuous event, the *Boston Globe* would sum up the entire story in a resonant subhead: "At a high school in Nashua, the Gipper grabbed the brass ring."

Once, in a memo to my editors at the *Washington Post,* I compared Ronald Reagan to a big, lackadaisical tackle I had known on my football team in a high school. The "book" on this player, although it was not a word we used then, was to leave him alone, treat him politely and pick him up if you happened to block him. He was a competent enough player, but of limited range, and no particular menace when he was left alone. If you blocked him from behind or did something he thought was unfair to make him angry, he dominated the field of play. Reagan is like that. He is no menace to his opponents sitting in a plane and working on his five-by-seven cards and taking his naps. But he is a helluva candidate when aroused, and he wiped out Bush in the debate that night. Bush's managers knew it, too, even if Bush didn't. Two days later, Bush's press secretary, Peter Teeley, gave his candidate an irreverent and accurate update: "The bad news is that the media is playing up the confrontation. The good news is that they're ignoring the debate, and you lost that, too."

This time Reagan did not sit on his lead. He did not fly off to Peoria to campaign in another primary. He did not take Sunday off. He did not go home to the warmth and comfort of Los Angeles to watch a movie in Bel-Air. This time Reagan remembered the loss in New Hampshire four years earlier and the defeat in Iowa the previous month. This time Reagan stayed in New Hampshire and campaigned as the story of his big night in Nashua dominated the network coverage and the local news. This time it was Bush who abandoned the field, acting on the same wrong advice that Reagan had been given in 1976—and getting it from the same counsellor. The price Bush paid for obtaining Hugh Gregg to run his campaign in New Hampshire had been turning over total control of his operation in that state to the former governor. Bush's delegation of authority in this instance was as complete as any ever granted by Reagan. Gregg, who had been governor in a day when organizational politics instead of television called the tune, had not learned the lessons of 1976. He sent Bush back to Houston for the same reasons he had rid himself of Reagan four years earlier: To give the campaign workers a chance to mobilize for election day. Tired and distraught, Bush went along with Gregg even though there were those on his staff, like Teeley, who argued he should stay in New Hampshire until the primary was over. Instead, Bush appeared that Sunday on television in the warm, pleasant surroundings of his pleasant Houston home while Reagan was viewed meeting voters in rundown sections of subfreezing New Hampshire. On Tuesday, February 26, Reagan won 51 percent of the seven-candidate vote. He received 54,897 votes to 23,777 (22 percent) for Bush. Baker was a badly beaten third, getting 13 percent of the vote. After his month of hard campaigning and his two debate victories, Reagan was back in the saddle again.

But Sears was not riding along with him. On the afternoon of his big New Hampshire victory, Reagan summoned Sears, Black and Lake to his third-floor hotel room in Manchester and fired the three of them with Nancy Reagan and William J. Casey, the new campaign manager, looking on. It was quickly and unceremoniously done, on a single sheet of paper, which said that Sears was resigning to return to his law practice and that Black and Lake were quitting with him. The only reference in the Reagan statement to the differences which had prompted the action was a declaration that "the campaign requires a sharp reduction in expenses and restructuring of our organization to intensify the people-to-people campaigning I have been doing in New Hampshire." Sears took the news soberly, Black with a quip that he was resigning before he could be fired, and Lake with a blunt denunciation of Meese. "Governor, Ed Meese manipulates you, he manipulates you," Lake said. However, the decision, reached the Sunday before and presented as a fait accompli to Sears and his aides, was more complicated than that. And it was Nancy Reagan, not Meese, who had taken the lead role in it.

Ever since Iowa, Reagan had been under pressure from the far right of his campaign to rid himself of Sears. The candidate was accustomed to resisting these ideological pressures, but he could not adjust to the swirling tensions of his staff under Sears. And in the first weeks of 1980, he had another worry. Campaign treasurer Bay Buchanan, as early as January 5, warned that so much money was being spent that Reagan would be bumping up against the federal spending limit of $17.6 million by the end of April. Publicly, Reagan said the limit was unrealistic because so many states had added primaries. Privately, he prodded Sears without success to explain what was happening. Sears seemed unconcerned, convinced that Reagan would clinch the nomination early. But even some of the staffers loyal to Sears acknowledged that the campaign manager had not focused on the problem and did not realize its dimension. Probably, this was because Sears' frame of reference was the sky's-the-limit campaigns of Richard Nixon, who spent $10 million to be nominated in nine primaries in 1968 and $20 million in the renomination effort of 1972. Reagan was limited to $17.6 million in thirty-three primaries, and he spent two-thirds of his total by the end of New Hampshire. The fiscal condition of the campaign was an important element in the discontent which led to the firing of Sears. Reagan may not have been a candidate who always read his briefing papers, but he was used to keeping an eye on the ledger books.

Early in February, Sears created the context for his inevitable fall. He went to Nancy Reagan with a complaint that, in a washroom in an East Orange, New Jersey, motel, he had overheard Meese in an adjoining staff room telling an aide over the telephone that Sears, Lake and Black would be fired after the New Hampshire primary. It is a call which Meese denies ever having made, but Nancy Reagan at the time expressed some sympathy with the indignant Sears. It gave her the opening she needed to solve the persistent problems of her husband's turmoil-ridden staff. She talked to Sears about the possibility of bringing in an administrator to share the duties of the campaign. Alone among the participants in the staff struggle, Nancy Reagan always acted with the sole interests of her husband in mind. She knew him well, and she knew what it took to get him to make a painful decision. She also knew that he could not operate indefinitely in an atmosphere of worry and tension. "I go out and have these good days and then I get these knots in my stomach when I come back here," Reagan confided one day when he had returned to his hotel in Andover, Massachusetts, where his campaign was headquartered to avoid having lodging costs charged to his New Hampshire spending limit. Nancy Reagan realized that something had to be done and she was not hesitant in doing it.

One of the first things that needed to be done was to reassure the candidate about his campaign finances. This was accomplished by putting Justin Dart, a fund-raiser and friend, in charge of a committee to examine the fiscal condition of the campaign. But the thorniest problem was who should replace Sears in his jack-of-all trades position. Reagan was determined, after losing Deaver, not to give up Meese, the other California aide he trusted for information and advice. His own preferred solution was to keep Sears as a strategist and Meese as chief of staff. But Sears would not accept this division and Reagan ultimately came to realize that he would not accept a diminished role at all. Nancy Reagan recognized this before her husband, and she knew this meant that Sears had to go.

It is doubtful, even if Sears had not been adamant in his position, whether he and Meese could have run a campaign together for very long. Both were really idea men, of vastly different sorts, and neither had displayed a flair for administration. Meese had a gift for defining issues to Reagan in ways he understood and for explaining to others what Reagan's positions were, or were likely to be, without adding the coloration of his own opinion. He was lawyer-like, deceptively affable and thoughtful but inclined to be over-cautious and to rely on others for organization. His greatest value to Reagan, both in government and politics, was that he made sure that his client, whom he liked and respected, heard all possible points of view before he acted. Usually, these were "round-tabled" in the cabinet style preferred by Reagan when he was governor. This approach was anathema to Sears, who played politics close to the vest and liked to reserve tactical decisions for himself. Sears suffered, more than he realized, from a contempt for his own candidate's capacity. He also held a low opinion of Meese, whom he thought prepared Reagan sloppily on issues and poached on political territory reserved for the campaign manager. Meese believed that Sears had become almost totally irrational in his drive for power and regarded anyone who had the ear of Reagan as a personal threat. These were strong perceptions by influential men, and they were not easily reconcilable within the framework of a presidential campaign. Someone else was needed.

The first "someone" was suggested by Sears and pursued by Nancy Reagan. He was William P. Clark, Reagan's onetime executive secretary and later his appointee to the California Supreme Court. Clark has good judgment and Reagan trusts him. Sears said he wanted a buffer whom Reagan could rely on, but the Reagans and most others in the campaign interpreted this as an ill-disguised roundabout strategy for getting rid of Meese. Still, Clark had the needed requirements of management skill and collegiality. Nancy Reagan telephoned him and asked if he would be interested in serving as Reagan's chief of staff.

"Doesn't the governor already have a chief of staff?" Clark asked.

"That's our problem," she replied. "We've got two of them."

So it was that on the second weekend of February, the Reagans' only California interlude of that tumultuous month, Clark came down to Rancho del Cielo to discuss the problems of the campaign. He was loyal to Reagan and told him he would leave the court if asked to do so by the man who had appointed him. But Reagan would not insist upon Clark quitting the court. He respected his ex-aide's insistence that he could not be involved in politics, or take a leave for political purposes, while he was a justice.* The talk turned to other possibilities, and Nancy Reagan brought up the name of Casey, whom the Reagans had met during a successful New York fundraising dinner. Surely someone who had been chairman of the Securities and Exchange Commission could straighten out the finances of a political

---

* The California Supreme Court, which had just survived an aborted investigation into whether some justices had delayed announcement of decisions for political reasons, was a particularly sensitive judicial body at this time. Also, there was a near-balance on the court between judicial liberals and conservatives, of whom Clark was one. Clark believed the balance would be disturbed by his leaving. By the time Clark left for a post in the Reagan administration in 1981, the death of one justice and the resignation of another had changed the court's ideological composition.

campaign, couldn't he? The idea appealed to Reagan and even more to Clark, who neither wanted to disappoint the Reagans nor leave the court. After some talking points were outlined for Reagan on a yellow sheet of paper, they decided to call Casey on the spot at his Long Island home. It was now late in the evening New York time, and Casey was in bed. Still drowsy, he listened to the outline of a proposal by Reagan and Clark which called for him to join the campaign as its chief administrator. Before Casey could respond, Reagan said he didn't need an answer that night but wanted Casey, literally in this case, to sleep on his decision. Next week, Casey met with Meese in New York and agreed to join the campaign, ostensibly to help with the upcoming debates. But the wheels were now in motion for the removal of Sears, who had made it clear to Reagan that he would not accept a subordinate role.

The Reagans announced their decision to the inner circle the Sunday after the candidate's stunning triumph at Nashua. Attending the meeting in the third-floor hotel room were the Reagans, Meese, Casey and Peter Hannaford. Foreign policy adviser Richard V. Allen, a foe of Sears and a friend of Casey's, arrived during the meeting. Reagan also consulted by phone with Deaver, telling him he wanted him back aboard. Midway through the discussion Wirthlin called. "Are you sitting down, governor?" he asked. Wirthlin then told him the good news: The latest survey results showed Reagan leading Bush by 17 points and climbing. A cheer went up, but Wirthlin's confirmation of what the candidate and his staff were already feeling made the timing of the Sears firing even more critical. Everyone agreed that it had to be done on primary day, but before the returns came in. "There was no other choice, really," Hannaford said. "If you won and fired him, you looked like an ingrate. If you lost and did it, you looked like a sore loser."[9]

As it turned out, the timing was politically perfect. The campaign shakeup, momentous as it seemed to some of the political reporters, was overshadowed by Reagan's landslide victory. The big win, the return of Deaver, and the newfound staff harmony relaxed Reagan, who had made his decision to fire Sears with a report before him from Justin Dart telling him that the financial situation was even worse than he thought it was. Straightening out the finances was Casey's responsibility. Though he knew next to nothing about presidential politics and had been a loser in his own congressional campaign, he knew a lot about squeezing the value out of a dollar. Aides were fired by the dozen, sometimes without even so much as a thank you. The cutbacks accomplished the dual purpose of trimming the payroll and purging anyone suspected of loyalty to Sears. Those who weren't fired stayed on, in many cases, for minimum salaries and expenses that often weren't paid on time. Casey also discontinued, in mid-charter, the expensive campaign plane Reagan had used, leaving some reporters stranded in South Carolina. He pared office expenditures to the bone. It wasn't a happy time at the Reagan headquarters in Los Angeles, and even less of one at the campaign office in Washington, but it got the job done. Aided by Verne Orr, a former Reagan state finance director whom Meese had installed in the Los Angeles office, Casey won the battle of the bank account. The Reagan campaign wound up with $500,000 reserved for contingency purposes at the national convention.

This last half million dollars wasn't needed. Baker dropped out of the race after the March 4 round of primaries, won by Bush in Massachusetts and Reagan in Vermont, with Anderson second in both races. Dole, never a factor, was soon gone. Connally, the boardroom barrister with the most experience and the highest negative ratings of any of the candidates, was swamped by Reagan in South Carolina and quit the following day. For all practical purposes, Reagan sewed up the nomination in the March 18 Illinois primary after a debate where his practiced one-liners were as effective as his spontaneous anger had been at Nashua. Only four contestants remained in the race, and one of them, Phil Crane, had never been more than a contingency candidate on the right whose hopes were invested in the collapse of the Reagan campaign. In the Chicago debate on March 13, Reagan tried out the role of statesman while Bush and Crane verbally beat up Anderson, who had made the mistake of saying he would prefer Senator Kennedy as President to Reagan. That remark completed Anderson's uncontested cornering of the limited market of GOP liberalism as he moved toward becoming an independent candidate instead of a Republican one. No one who saw the Chicago debate is likely to forget Reagan turning to Anderson and saying, lightly and in mock astonishment, "John, would you *really* find Teddy Kennedy preferable to me?" At another point Reagan asserted that wage-and-price controls had failed even when the Roman emperor Diocletian had used capital punishment to enforce them. "And I'm one of the few persons old enough to remember that," Reagan said. He won the debate in a walkaway, according to Wirthlin's polls, and he won 48 percent of the primary vote, beating home state Congressman Anderson by more than 11 points and demolishing Crane. It was the first impressive demonstration of Reagan's drawing power among crossover Democratic voters in a major industrial state.

Reagan rolled on, with Bush and the federal campaign spending limit his only opposition. It was tough going for Bush. Nashua had made him the perfect foil for Reagan, casting Bush as the up-tight eastern elitist facing the down-to-earth conservative cowboy from the West, the traditional Republican of wealth and privilege matched against the self-made man. Poor George Bush, one kept wanting to say, as the primary losses piled up during the long spring. On the campaign stump and especially on television, Bush came across as an out-of-focus picture in a vertical frame. His prep school and Ivy League background and senatorial good looks were undermined by a strange, almost boyish, overexuberance which made him seem, at fifty-five, not quite mature. And Bush compounded this impression by his campaign strategy. His comments, and his campaign advertising, stressed his wartime bravery and his athletic interests, especially a daily addiction to jogging. This self-portrait promoted Bush more as a candidate for the Olympics than the presidency and, if anything, distracted voters from the central question about Reagan, which was his intellectual qualifications and not his physical ones. Certainly, on paper, Bush was better prepared than Reagan to be President. He had been an over-achiever at Andover and Yale, a star athlete and certified war hero, a congressman from Texas, ambassador to the United Nations, national Republican chairman, liaison to the People's Republic of China and director of the Central Intelligence Agency. But in some ways the very breadth of this career counted against Bush, for it was seen in party circles as reflecting not only a devotion to public duty but an inability to say no. To many Republicans the whole of Bush was less than the sum of the parts. He was not a focused candidate against Reagan after the New Hampshire debates, and he was never close to winning the nomination. In fact, he won only four of the thirty-three primaries in which he competed with Reagan, who finished first in the other twenty-nine.* However, as the primaries wore on, Bush began to exhibit an unadvertised doggedness which gradually overcame some of the negative aftertaste of Nashua. As a winner, Bush had been enthused, excitable and unimpressive. As a loser, he displayed qualities approaching true grit. "The amazing thing about Bush's candidacy," observed the *Washington Post*'s Bill Peterson, "was not that it failed but that it kept going as long as it did."[10] Battling uphill, Bush improved as a campaigner and as a public speaker. Ultimately, his doggedness did for him what his heritage and glittering resume had been unable to accomplish, making him the widespread party choice, even in the Reagan camp, for the vice-presidency.

During this post-Sears period, the Reagan campaign resumed its California look. Deaver was once more the indispensable adjutant, always on the plane and at Reagan's side. Wirthlin became the strategist, and Meese the actual as well as titled chief of staff. Martin Anderson, a traditional conservative economist who had been exiled to his base at Stanford while Sears pursued the support of Kemp and his supply-siders, returned as Reagan's

* Bush won in Massachusetts, Connecticut, Pennsylvania and Michigan. He also won the Puerto Rico primary, where Reagan did not compete. One salient feature of the Republican primaries in 1980 was that they featured remarkably large turnouts in the early going, when the race was hotly contested, and very small turnouts after Reagan appeared to have clinched the nomination. Compared with 1976, the GOP turnout increased 32 percent in Massachusetts, 46 percent in Illinois and 52 percent in Wisconsin. But by May 20, in the Michigan primary, the turnout was down 49 percent, a key reason that the Republican organization in that state (pro-Bush, because of Governor William G. Milliken) was able to determine the outcome. Reagan won 60 percent of the total vote in the thirty-three primaries in which he participated, a figure that is slightly inflated by his victories in nine final primaries after Bush had withdrawn.

domestic adviser. Eventually, Nofziger came back, too, for still another stint as press secretary. And the Reaganites also brought in new faces who had worked for other Republican presidential candidates, notably Joe Canzeri, a popular long-time travel secretary for Nelson Rockefeller, and James S. Brady, who had gained plaudits from reporters as Connally's press secretary. Brady's mission was to beef up an issues research system which, until then, had failed to bridge the candidate's increasingly visible knowledge gap.

Reagan always has been a better candidate in adversity than when he is running loose in the lead. With no one pressing him after Illinois, he again became the *Reader's Digest* of politics, using old speeches and still older statistics as he coasted to the convention. I wrote during this period that Reagan never met a statistic he didn't like, and it was not much of an exaggeration. He picked up horror stories about federal programs at random, sometimes tearing stray articles out of newspapers as he had done in his General Electric days. He believed what he read in *Human Events* or in Republican newsletters. Working this way, Reagan cited a General Accounting Office report on waste and fraud which never existed, claimed that it cost the Department of Health, Education and Welfare $3 to deliver $1 worth of services (the actual amount was 12 cents), and said that the "finest oil geologists in the world" had told him that U.S. reserves of oil exceeded Saudi Arabia's, a remark which columnist Mark Shields spoofed as representing Reagan's belief that there is "more oil under second base at Yankee Stadium" than exists in the Middle East. One of the problems, Martin Anderson told Douglas E. Kneeland, then of the *New York Times,* was that Reagan used "hundreds of stories for examples" in his campaign speeches. "Ninety-nine times out of a hundred, things checked out," Anderson added, "but sometimes the source is wrong. As all we know, sometimes the written word is wrong."[11] And sometimes the spoken one. Even when Reagan was briefed by his own people, he was apt to get his facts mixed up. In Grand Island, Nebraska, on April 9, Reagan said that Vietnam veterans "are not eligible for GI Bill of Rights benefits with regard to education or anything." Reagan's mind had wandered during a Washington briefing by two high-ranking military officers, who had first discussed with him the problems facing Vietnam veterans. During the same briefing the officers also told him that peacetime veterans of the all-volunteer Army received no educational benefits, and Reagan had confused the two issues. This kind of wool-gathering, when combined with Reagan's proclivity for statistics-spouting and a primitive campaign research system, was a prescription for disaster and an augury of the troubles which would beset Reagan in August.

The candidate blamed the press and not himself for his shortcomings. When a series of reports in *Time,* Knight-Ridder newspapers, the *Washington Post* and CBS News made similar points during the same time frame, Reagan acted as if they were working in collaboration against him. "What I think we're seeing in what's going on is a little journalistic incest," Reagan said. He explained that he was referring to what happens when "one person reads another story and it is accepted as gospel." It is true that so-called "pack journalism" had its place in the Reagan campaign, as in all others. But what Reagan was really experiencing was a magnified version of his experience during the 1976 New Hampshire primary, when reporters began to realize that he could become President of the United States. A case can be made that the added scrutiny was belated in 1980, perhaps because there were many in the media who found it hard to believe that Reagan would actually be nominated. However, when Reagan clinched the nomination early and it was apparent that his opponent would be an unpopular incumbent nominated by a divided party, the prospect of "President Reagan" no longer seemed remote. The scrutiny came all at once, in April, during an anticlimactic period of the primary campaign. Subsequent events would demonstrate that Reagan did not learn as much from this experience as he should have.

If Reagan was unsuccessful in keeping his statistics straight, he remained an effective, practicing politician who understood the need for party unity. In terms of bringing himself up to snuff on issues, Reagan wasted much of the valuable interim between May 26, when Bush finally dropped out, and the Republican convention in Detroit on July 13. But he made good political use of this time, healing some party wounds and preventing an important one from opening while President Carter was still preoccupied with the Kennedy challenge. Defeated Republican candidates would have supported Reagan against Carter in any case. However, they became real enthusiasts after the winner agreed to help the losers pay off nearly $3 million in campaign debts at a series of Republican unity dinners. And Reagan's penchant for unity, at least when he is the nominee, rescued him from endorsing the efforts by Senator Laxalt and Jerry Carmen to replace Republican national chairman William Brock with someone more responsive to the conservative wing of the party. After two weeks of in-fighting and conflicting advice from his own staff, Reagan opted for a course favored by Meese, which was to keep Brock as chairman while installing his own man as chief operational officer at the Republican National Committee. Carmen, who had written a report highly critical of Brock's performance and loyalty, wanted the job, but even Laxalt realized this wouldn't work. So the Reagan man at the committee turned out to be Sears recruit Drew Lewis, who had held the line for Ford in Pennsylvania during the 1976 campaign but was now considered a Reagan loyalist. The compromise gave Reagan the best of both worlds, avoiding a shakeup that would have been seen as a swing to the right, and putting one of the few seasoned politicians in the Reagan camp in the strategic political post at the National Committee.

Reagan's most important unity effort during this period was directed at Ford himself. The former President had been a brief threatening cloud to the Reagan campaign in March when Ford finally realized that no one else in his party was capable of stopping Reagan. A group of Ford's friends had met with him in Washington on March 12, at a time when the deadline for entering sufficient primaries to head off Reagan had passed, and convinced the former President that Reagan had a virtual lock on the nomination. Nonetheless, Reagan recognized that even an abortive Ford candidacy had the potential of reviving party divisions and creating a fight that would certainly extend into the convention and probably into the fall campaign. Reagan appreciated, perhaps more than Ford realized, the ex-President's realistic and helpful decision. And Reagan expressed his gratitude directly to Ford during a June 5 visit to his office adjacent to the Rancho Mirage golf course near Palm Springs. This visit, two days after Reagan had won the last round of now uncontested primaries, was more than a courtesy call. Only a few days earlier Ford had reconfirmed in a private conversation his belief that Reagan's reluctant campaigning had cost him the election in 1976. The substance of this conversation was relayed to Reagan, who came armed with information about the number of campaign speeches he had made for Ford and an appeal for his support against President Carter. More hard-bitten politicans would not have been impressed with the self-serving version of recent history that Reagan presented that day. But no one in politics forgives a grudge as easily as Jerry Ford. Reagan, no grudge-holder himself, is a hard man to dislike, and Ford found himself strangely drawn to this old foe who shared with him a midwestern upbringing and a natural friendliness. Ford also genuinely thought that Carter had been a terrible President and wanted to help defeat him. It was in this atmosphere that Reagan first suggested to Ford a supposed "dream ticket" that would have included the former President as his running mate. Ford's response was negative, but he appreciated the gesture. In ninety minutes of private conversation together at Rancho Mirage, Ford became a supporter of the Reagan candidacy. He also very nearly became vice-president.

The Ford boomlet which crested and broke at the Republican national convention was, more than anything, the product of Reagan's reservations about Bush. When the primaries were over, Bush had won grudging respect in the Reagan camp. He had the quiet but significant backing of fellow ex-Yalie Ed Meese. He also had support from Drew Lewis. Party unity dictated the selection of a prominent Republican from outside the Reagan ranks, and there was never any serious thought in the inner circle to choosing a regional and ideological Reagan soulmate like Laxalt, except by Laxalt himself. Reagan asked a couple of times why he couldn't just pick someone he liked, but the Californians close to the candidate properly considered this a rhetorical expression of Reagan's high opinion of his friend Laxalt rather than a practical political solution. Nor was Senator Howard Baker, whom Reagan and his team recognized would be more valuable to them as Senate leader than Vice-President, seriously considered. The choice of the insiders, except for Laxalt, was Bush. He brought instant unification to the party, and he almost certainly would have been privately selected, though not announced, in June except for the fact that neither of the Reagans liked him at all.

Reagan's disrespect had been born at Nashua. He could not understand Bush just sitting there in his chair and not speaking to Reagan or the other candidates who filed onto the stage. Reagan had told an aide that Bush lacked "spunk," a good midwestern word for a quality which Ford was known to possess in abundance. And Reagan's attitude was ratified after Nashua by a curious little incident during the Texas primary campaign that went almost unnoticed in the national press. The incident was the outgrowth of Bush's increasing irritation with right-wing leaflets that attributed a demonic aspect to his former membership in the Trilateral Commission. To its more than three hundred members in North America, Europe and Japan, the commission is a peaceful private body of distinguished citizens who explore ways to foster international economic cooperation. But to a few activists on the far fringes of the right and left, the Trilateralists are a sinister one-world conspiracy headed by David Rockefeller, the North American regional chairman. Reagan knew better. His former state finance director, Caspar W. Weinberger, had been a member of the commission. But Reagan also realized that some of his more strident supporters shared the conspiracy view about the Trilateralists, and he had done nothing to persuade them otherwise or to stop them from harassing Bush. In Bush's mind this made Reagan responsible for the leaflets, and he called upon his opponent to denounce those who had issued them. "I have never seen any of the literature he's talking about," Reagan replied blandly. "The only person I've seen raise the Trilateral issue is George Bush and maybe he should tell us why he resigned." Instead, Bush continued to blame the Reagan campaign for the leaflets, and the charge began to irritate Reagan. On May 2, in Houston, Reagan was asked during an interview on KTRK about the leaflets and replied, with some force: "I feel that George Bush knows there is nothing true to what he's doing, and I don't know why this desperation gambit which is in violation of everything the Republican candidates have pledged to each other with regard to the campaign." In a resourceful effort to stage its own debate on this issue, KTRK had lined up Bush for an interview at his Houston home immediately following Reagan. Bush was informed that Reagan was on camera at another location and asked to comment on his statement. And then, to the surprise and disgust of the Reagans, Bush backed down! Reagan campaign operatives, not Reagan himself, were "questioning my patriotism because of my association with the Trilateral Commission," Bush told his interviewer. "But it's not a big deal, frankly," he added. Nancy Reagan, not trying to conceal her emotions, hooted. "If it's no big deal, then why does he keep raising it?" she said. Reagan confided later that he was reminded of Bush's performance at Nashua. "He just melts under pressure," Reagan said, a point he would raise again when his aides said to him that Bush was the best choice to unify the party.

It was this low opinion of Bush that kept the Ford option alive. Wirthlin, who took the lead in pushing Ford, had a positive view of Bush but realized that Reagan didn't. The pollster-strategist was convinced that Reagan needed to choose a prominent moderate as his running mate, and a nationwide poll taken by his firm, Decision Making Information, gave him plenty of data to use in his arguments. Bush was actually the first choice in this poll by a wide margin as the person whom voters thought Reagan should put on the ticket with him. Wirthlin made this point to the candidate, knowing that it would have an impact no matter what Reagan thought personally about Bush. Ford led in the characteristics which people wanted to see in a Vice-President, such as "aggressiveness," "independence" and the capacity to take over as President. Bush, however, was a clear second in these categories. What the poll really did was eliminate everyone from consideration except Ford, Bush and Baker. Reagan already had expressed the view, which also was held strongly by Meese, that it would be a mistake to choose someone who was largely unknown to the country and would have to become known during the crucible of campaigning. Wirthlin's poll found that only 12 percent of the voters could identify Kemp and that only 6 percent knew Laxalt's name. Others of the twenty-one potential selections included in the poll were similarly unknown, except for John Connally, who had high negative ratings from the voters. So in practical terms, as the convention neared, Reagan's running mate boiled down to a choice of Ford and Bush. Baker remained a distant deadlock possibility without any strong advocates within the Reagan camp.*

By the time the Republican convention opened Monday night, July 14, most of the Reaganites believed the nominee-to-be would finally, if reluctantly, settle on Bush. Ford's pollster Teeter had told Reagan's pollster Wirthlin that Ford was not interested. Stuart Spencer, then aboard tenuously as a consultant to the Reagan campaign, had sounded out Ford at Deaver's behest and found a similar lack of interest. But Ford, in a fiery speech on the opening night of the convention, denounced Carter and seemed to be sending quite another message. "Elder statesmen are supposed to sit quietly and smile wisely from the sidelines," Ford said. "I've never been much for sitting. I've never spent much time on the sidelines. Betty'll tell you that. This country means too much to me to comfortably park on the bench. So, when this convention fields the team for Governor Reagan, count me in."

* While it wasn't part of his pro-Ford pitch, Wirthlin's poll showed that Bush did best of all with two groups where Reagan was relatively weak—voters with post-graduate educations and voters inclined to support John Anderson. Wirthlin's firm interviewed 1,515 voters in forty-eight states between May 28 and June 10. On the open-ended question, "Whom would you like to see Ronald Reagan choose as his running mate?" Bush led with 20 percent compared to 14 percent for Senator Baker and 13 percent for Ford. Anderson had 4 percent and Kemp and Senator Barry Goldwater 2 percent each. No one else had more than 1 percent. One finding was that a surprisingly large number of voters—as high as 31 percent in New England—acknowledged that the selection of a running mate would influence their voting in November.

Reagan loved Ford's speech, remarking to an aide on what a fine campaigner he would be. He also took Ford's remarks as a sign that he was becoming receptive to the idea of taking second place on the ticket. The two men met privately the next afternoon in Reagan's suite, and Reagan urged Ford to reconsider his earlier rejection of the vice-presidential nomination. Ford said he didn't think he could do it, but didn't firmly shut the door. And that night, Ford's own crowd from the White House—especially Henry Kissinger, Alan Greenspan and Jack Marsh—were at him again. Like Reagan, they noticed that Ford, though negative, stopped just short of firmly saying "no."

What was occurring was an improbable romance whose consummation seemed, from beginning to end, unlikely to political veterans like Teeter and Spencer and remote even to Wirthlin, who had pushed it more ardently than anyone in the Reagan camp. There were many in the Reagan circle who realized, with Teeter, that the "dream ticket" had the potential of turning into a nightmare in which Ford upstaged the presidential nominee and drew unwanted attention to Reagan's lack of experience in foreign policy. It did not take much imagination for loyal supporters of both men to foresee circumstances in which the unique arrangement would have been embarrassing. "The day after the convention Ford would have been 'Mr. President' and Reagan would have been 'Mr. Reagan,'" said Spencer, who was loyal to Ford and would do more than anyone to win the election for Reagan. "How would that play? A Vice-President is supposed to be No. 2." The prospective Ford entourage caused even more obstacles. Conservatives were appalled by the thought that Kissinger would be back in power again, admitted by the conservative champion who had made him an issue in 1976. Some of the supply-siders were equally appalled by the thought of Greenspan, whose presence to them represented an "old economics" which called for tax increases, not reductions, as an answer to inflation. Bush, with his denunciation of their "vodoo economics," was not a supply-side favorite, either, but there was no question as to whether he would be a discreet No. 2 to the President. Of Ford and his group, there were no end of questions.

In the end, these questions sent the "dream ticket" back to the ether where it belonged. Reagan was interested enough to allow Meese, Casey and Wirthlin to draw up ten "talking points" and meet with Kissinger, Greenspan, Marsh and Ford's personal aide Bob Barrett to discuss them. But even Reagan was by then having second thoughts that he might be dealing away some of the constitutional powers of the presidency. Deaver, in the strongest terms, spoke for Reagan in telling Wirthlin that, "Reagan is going to be the President and we do not want to create any constraining conditions on him." Wirthlin agreed, but the talking points included proposals for giving Ford an enhanced role in national security affairs and the federal budget. One of the negotiators said that Ford would become "super director of the executive office of the President," a role never envisioned for the Vice-President by the founders. Nor was such a role actually envisioned by Reagan, who had worked hard for the nomination and did not want to bargain away the prize he had won. The whole idea seemed dubious to many of Reagan's own people and preposterous to the most independent people in the Ford camp—Teeter, Dick Cheney and Ford's old congressional friend, the then Minority Leader John Rhodes. Reagan had allowed himself to be swept away by the idea because he did not want to accept the alternative. More than any other action in the campaign, Reagan's pursuit of the ill-starred dream ticket demonstrated the lengths he would go to avoid doing something he did not want to do, in this case designate Bush as his running mate.

The process which followed exposed a conflict between Reagan's reactive and sometimes hesitant style of decision-making and his usual surefooted political instinct for making the pragmatic choice. But what is often overlooked is that the entire discussion took place within the boundaries of this pragmatism. Other aides working for other nominees might quite sensibly have suggested a compromise course. If you can't get Ford on your own terms and don't want Bush, why not take another GOP moderate like Howard Baker or a conservative you can be comfortable with like William Simon? Such suggestions were not made in the inner circle because the Reaganites knew their man. They knew, among other things, that Reagan is a politician who wanted someone on the ticket who would help him win. Because of his long and dogged campaign and the support he drew from such popular moderate GOP governors as Michigan's William G. Milliken, Bush was this someone. Wirthlin's poll, Meese's opinion and, above all, Reagan's own innate apprecation of political realities led him inexorably toward this conclusion. And, as he almost always does in such circumstances, Reagan accepted the political logic.

In the end, Ford made it easy. By the time the former President appeared for his startling interview with Walter Cronkite Wednesday evening, Reagan already was having second thoughts. The jokes had begun to circulate in both camps, about how Ford would be President before nine, after five and on weekends. Then, when Cronkite asked Ford how he would respond to a draft from the convention floor, the former President gave his own view of the role he wanted to play. Ford said he would not go to Washington as "a figurehead Vice-President." If he accepted, Ford said, "I have to go there with the belief that I will play a meaningful role across the board in the basic and the crucial and the important decisions that have to be made in a four-year period." Reagan was watching this performance on television in his suite at the Detroit Plaza and could not believe what he was seeing. It had not occurred to him that Ford would publicly discuss what Reagan considered to be a private offer. "Is that Ford?" he asked increduously when the unmistakable figure of the former President appeared on the screen. Reagan may not know a lot of things, but he does know what a network television interview can do, particularly when the interviewer is Cronkite. Reagan understood immediately, without anyone telling him, that Ford's remarks would convince the convention and the country that the deal had been struck. Within moments, the unconsummated dream ticket was being promulgated as reality by television commentators who filled in the gaps with their own conclusions. Actually, the negotiators for both sides had bogged down in the talking points, aware that they were skating on thin constitutional ice in trying to define a role for Ford which did not infringe upon the duties and prerogatives of the President. Kissinger asked Meese for more time, extending the informal Wednesday night deadline which the negotiators had agreed upon to Thursday morning. Meese, who was against the extension, talked to Reagan, who was even more strongly opposed to it. The networks had just nominated Ford, an aide remembers Reagan saying, and there would be "a terrible letdown" if he waited a day and then picked someone else. By now Reagan realized that too much would have to be given up to get Ford on the ticket, and the nonprogress of the negotiators confirmed this. Reagan called Ford shortly after nine and said, politely but firmly, that he needed a decision that night. An hour and a half later Ford called on Reagan in his suite and, in an emotional moment, turned down the offer. Then he expressed his affection for Reagan, gave him a hug and promised he would do whatever he could to help him win the fall campaign. Reagan was moved. He had grown to like Ford, and he appreciated that the former President had taken him off the hook. "He was a gentleman," Reagan said afterwards. "I feel we're friends now." Within five minutes of Ford's departure from the suite, Reagan was on the telephone to George Bush. Within an hour and a half, Reagan was back at Joe Louis Arena, smoothly presenting the convention with the ticket that necessity had demanded. He was not hesitant now. Reagan knew what he had to do to cut his losses, and he wanted no stories reflecting on his ability to act decisively. There were a few such stories anyway the next day, but they were overshadowed by the news of Reagan's decision. At the last moment the hero had ridden to the rescue of the girl he had tied to the tracks. It was truly a new beginning.

Reagan further dispelled the doubts he had created about his leadership on Thursday, the final night of the convention. His grace note was an acceptance speech that matched old themes of economy in government with old values of "family, work, neighborhood, peace and freedom." These values were intended to be the basis of a "new consensus" in which traditional Democrats would join with independents and Republicans to replace "the mediocre leadership" of Jimmy Carter with a President who would simultaneously balance the budget and reduce taxes, and who would build up U.S. military capability while pursuing an objective of "lasting world peace." All this was roundly cheered by the convention. But the arena crowd fell quiet when Reagan started quoting from a past President about the need for governmental economy and reform. The words were those of Reagan's first political hero, Franklin Roosevelt, at his 1933 inaugural, and they seemed oddly out of place in the acceptance speech of a Republican nominee who was proposing to undo much of what FDR and his successors had done. Looking down at the silent crowd, David Broder observed, "They're saying, come on, Ronnie, don't give us any of that New Deal guff." But Reagan was speaking to all of his countrymen, not just those Republicans assembled in Joe Louis Arena. His audience was an electorate in which Democrats had remained a majority for two generations because of the political approval of Roosevelt's accomplishments. Reagan knew that this electorate now doubted the leadership ability of its President. To Americans in their living rooms Reagan held up a mirror of the past which told of the days when the White House was the source of the finest leadership in the country. Reagan believed that most Americans yearned for such leadership again. Looking straight into the television cameras, that is what he promised to provide.

18

The Great Deflector

R EAGAN left Detroit with a running mate, a unified party, a commanding lead in the polls, and a campaign plan which correctly anticipated the strategy of President Carter. He faced an opponent who was dogged by the captivity of hostages he could not free, an economy he could not seem to improve, a brother he could not disown, and an opponent he could not shake. Reagan had the luxury of a month in which the Kennedy challenge prevented Carter from focusing on the fall campaign. During two weeks of this month, one of the major stories was the revelation that Carter's brother, Billy, had accepted $220,000 from the Libyan government for lobbying efforts in the United States. The President emerged from the affair depicted as a man who could not even control his brother, much less the country. Reagan had every imaginable advantage going for him. And following a pattern which the Reagan team had established for doing worst when things were going best, the candidate and his staff then went out and almost blew the election before the campaign formally began.

The first sign of trouble came in New York, where Reagan had traveled by way of Mississippi to address the convention of the National Urban League. It was Reagan's only speech to a black organization after his nomination, but his message was addressed to a larger audience not necessarily black. Wirthlin's polls showed that there were many white voters who wanted a President who demonstrated sensitivity to minority problems and urban issues. Few voters of any sort volunteered positive responses about Reagan's social concerns. "At best this implies a neutral image on the social concern dimension of candidate perception," Wirthlin carefully reported to the candidate. "At worst it suggests a negative image for an unsympathetic candidate lacking a personal concern for the people's problems of welfare, aging, health care, etc." Reagan was supposed to correct this impression as much as he could in his speech to the Urban League. Instead he gave the impression that his heart wasn't in it by insisting on an appearance at the Neshoba County Fair, in Philadelphia, Mississippi, where three civil rights workers were slain with the complicity of local police officials in 1964. The symbolism was appalling for a New York bound conservative candidate. Wirthlin knew that scenes from Neshoba would be on television the very day that Reagan was addressing the Urban League. But the pollster-strategist could not convince Reagan, who had been told by Mississippi Representative Trent Lott that a visit to the state, which Carter had carried in 1976, could make the difference between victory and defeat. When the mild-mannered Wirthlin uncharacteristically persisted in his view with Reagan, the candidate became angry. Reagan told Wirthlin that he had learned in show business that an actor should always appear once his billing has been announced. On August 3 Reagan had his way, telling the shirt-sleeved crowd in Neshoba that he "believed in states' rights" and as President would do everything he could to "restore to states and local governments the powers that properly belonged to them." The visual statement on television the next day was a sea of white faces at the Neshoba Fair with Reagan's words floating above them. By then Reagan was at the Urban League comparing himself to President Kennedy attempting to win Protestant votes in 1960. He urged his listeners not to consider him "a caricature conservative" who was "antipoor, antiblack and antidisadvantaged." And he called for creation of inner-city "enterprise zones" where taxes would be reduced as an incentive to employment that would benefit blacks. It was an otherwise uneventful speech, and Reagan escaped to polite applause and sighs of relief from his aides.

The candidate was then whisked off to the South Bronx for one of the more curiously advanced events in the history of presidential politics. The idea was to hold a press conference on a rubble-strewn lot where Carter, on October 5, 1977, had promised a new federally sponsored housing and job training center. Reagan's theme was that Carter made a lot of promises which neither the President nor the government could keep. In case anyone missed the point that the promises hadn't been kept, the word "Decay" had been freshly painted in huge letters on a nearby gutted building. Reagan's advance men had earned an "A" in art while flunking their major. No one seemed to have realized that some local residents might turn up in an area where so many people were unemployed. Soon they formed a shouting crowd which jeered at Reagan and alarmed the Secret Service. Reagan could not hold his press conference because the crowd shouted, "Talk to the people, not to the press." When Reagan tried to talk to the people, he was heckled unmercifully. Finally, in his most effective burst of emotion since Nashua, Reagan shouted back at a heckler, "I can't do a damn thing for you if I don't get elected." The crowd quieted down enough for Reagan to finish his presentation, though a few still jeered when he left. Reagan's command presence had once more dramatically saved the day. The evening television news showed an angry but controlled candidate forcefully putting down a hostile black crowd in a manner which won the respect of the crowd itself. It was the perfect image for a candidate campaigning on the theme that his opponent was a failed leader, but it was a near-run triumph which had narrowly courted disaster. And the disasters were not long in coming.

What Reagan was really doing, although he didn't realize it, was wasting much of the month of August. On paper he had a plan, carefully drafted by Wirthlin, calling upon him to reach out to his core constituencies while also getting out of the way a few appearances before groups, like the Urban League, where he was unlikely to convert any voters. But his campaign lacked focus and cohesion. Wirthlin's poll data and strategic thinking were valued, but the pollster had neither the title of campaign manager nor the necessary clout with the candidate. For all his skills, Wirthlin was not really an instinctive politician, and there were none then associated with the campaign, except the candidate himself. One result was that Reagan was tugged this way and that, making too many speeches when he should have been boning up on issues, and being placed in too many situations where something could go wrong.

In mid-August the candidate launched upon a "defense week" anchored by speeches to the Veterans of Foreign Wars and the American Legion. The idea, as always, related to Carter's supposed broken promises, in this case promises to maintain a strong military establishment and take good care of veterans. Before the VFW in Chicago on August 18, Reagan asserted that Carter had made a "shambles" of the national defense while remaining "totally oblivious" to the Soviet Union's drive toward world domination. These denunciations were a bit on the shrill side for August, but they were overshadowed by Reagan's expressions of his true feelings about the Vietnam War. Reagan had been a supporter of that war since its earliest days. After it was over, he appealed to the frustrations the war had left behind, repeatedly rousing audiences during his 1976 campaign with the line, "Let us tell those who fought in that war that we will never again ask young men to fight and possibly die in a war our government is afraid to win." These words brought the VFW members to their feet that August day in Chicago. Speaking to a convention where neglect of Vietnam veterans was a central issue, Reagan said, "We dishonor the memory of 50,000 young Americans who died in that cause when we give way to feelings of guilt as if we were doing something shameful, and we have been shabby in our treatment of those who returned." Using words he had written into the speech himself, Reagan said, "It is time we recognized that ours, in truth, was a noble cause."

Around the country, these words were taken as an attempt to open wounds that were just beginning to heal. Reagan's comments provoked angry calls to talk shows and letters to the editors from opponents of the war. Vietnam veterans wrote in, too. Some of them supported Reagan. But others bitterly opposed what he had said, and some pointed out that Reagan had never been in combat himself. Writing with conviction and eloquence on the op ed page of the *Los Angeles Times,* former Marine Captain Frank

McAdams recounted the bloody details of a battle on an August day at Cam Le a dozen years before. "A noble cause, Mr. Reagan?" wrote McAdams. "I would call it a horrible experience."[1] Wirthlin's polls, as busily recording Reagan gliches during this period as a seismograph charting a series of small earthquakes, found that "noble cause" hurt Reagan more with the voters than any of his other mistakes.

The voters, if they were paying attention, had plenty of mistakes from which to choose. The most celebrated arose from an orphan brainstorm, which no one is now willing to claim, to send Bush on a fence-building mission to the People's Republic of China, where he had served as U.S. government liaison after President Nixon's historic resumption of relations with the mainland government. The trip was supposed to advertise the competence of the Reagan-Bush ticket in dealing with world issues. Instead, it revealed Reagan's devotion to his old friends in Taiwan. Reagan had twice visited Taipeh, and the Deaver-Hannaford firm in Los Angeles, which represented Reagan before he became a candidate, counted the Taiwanese government as a client at the same time.* In a column drafted for him by Hannaford on May 5, 1978, Reagan had warned that establishing full relations with the mainland government at the expense of Taiwan could "start a chain of events that could prove disastrous, not only for Taiwan, but for the United States itself." When the Carter administration took this action late in 1978, Reagan was one of the loudest critics. And in the early months of 1979, Reagan used the phrase "no more Taiwans, no more Vietnams" as part of his campaign liturgy in calling for a U.S. government that kept its word to its traditional allies.

Reagan foreign policy adviser Richard V. Allen, while sharing his candidate's view that Carter had received nothing in return for the de-recognition of Taiwan, understood that Reagan had no choice but to accept the status quo. He assured reporters at the Republican national convention that Reagan did not intend to "turn the clock back."[2] The Bush mission was seen by reporters as a sign that Reagan did, in fact, recognize that times had changed. Unfortunately for Reagan, his own personal reluctance to abandon Taiwan caused him to say something quite different at a joint press conference when Bush departed from the United States. To the surprise of both Bush and Allen, Reagan said he intended to establish an official liaison office in Taipeh, an act prohibited by the Taiwan Relations Act of 1979. The statement was immediately denounced by the official Chinese newspaper as re-creation of a "two-China policy" and assailed by the U.S. ambassador in Peking, Leonard Woodcock, as a menace to the "carefully crafted relation-

* This relationship was worrisome to Reagan aides, and Meese at one point discussed it in detail with Deaver, who took a leave of absence from his firm for the campaign. The concern was heightened by a page-one story by Don Oberdorfer in the June 6, 1980, *Washington Post*. The firm represented the government of the Republic of China (Taiwan) starting November 18, 1977. Hannaford, who served as a consultant and sometime speech-writer to Reagan during the campaign, took the initiative in signing up the Taiwanese government as a client.

ship" existing between China and the United States.[3] Bush, who understood the requirements of diplomacy, was in a tough spot. A few words from Reagan had turned what promised to be a triumphant trip into a hand-holding mission. Bush tried to reassure the Chinese government that Reagan meant no change in relationships while simultaneously explaining to overseas reporters what Reagan supposedly had meant to say. But the candidate would not be quieted. After Bush returned, Reagan did it again, saying that he regarded the government-funded American Institute on Taiwan as an act of Carter "hypocrisy" because it was really an embassy without a name. By now, however, Allen and negative press clippings had convinced Reagan that he needed to back off. Reluctantly, and in a manner which left little doubt about his true feelings, Reagan said he no longer favored the establishment of an official liaison office with Taiwan.

Reagan was still reeling from the blows dealt him on this issue when he traveled to Dallas on August 22 to address a national rally of fundamentalist Christians which both Carter and independent candidate John B. Anderson had decided to avoid. Once there, he submitted to a press conference in which a reporter for a religious publication asked him his views about creationism. While his aides shifted uneasily, Reagan allowed himself to be drawn into a long-winded answer, finally trying to please his questioner by suggesting that creationism be taught as an alternative theory to Darwinism in schools. The answer never received the national publicity it might ordinarily have been given because Reagan was at the time still debating the Taiwan issue with himself and the national press. "The only good news for us at this time," an aide remarked afterwards, "is that we were making so many blunders that reporters had to pick and choose which ones they would write about. 'Creationism' made Reagan look like an idiot, but he got away with it."

After Reagan's fall campaign formally opened on Labor Day, he was too much the focus of constant media attention to "get away" with blunders. His worst blunder of the campaign came that very day, after an effective opening performance before an ethnic audience in Liberty Park, New Jersey, where the Statue of Liberty provided a television backdrop, and where one of the featured participants was Polish union leader Lech Walesa's father. Reagan, enthused about the rally, saw it as a sign that he could attract the support of blue-collar workers who usually vote Democratic. On the plane from Newark to Detroit, he observed that he was opening his campaign in the "Democratic country" of New Jersey and Michigan, while Carter was protecting his supposed base in the Deep South. Then Nofziger chimed in, saying that Tuscumbia, Alabama, where Carter had addressed his campaign-opening rally, was a center of activity for the Ku Klux Klan. In fact, a score or so of robed KKK members had attended the Carter rally and had been rebuked by the President as people who "do not understand that the South and all America must move forward."

The discussion came back to Reagan with a rush late that afternoon when he spoke to a friendly crowd from a gazebo at the Michigan State Fair. The day was hot and humid, and Reagan was conspicuously tired after a long walk through the fairgrounds. It had begun to rain. In the front row Reagan noticed a woman heckler with a Carter mask. It reminded him of the President at Tuscumbia. "Now I'm happy to be here while he is opening his campaign down there in the city that gave birth to and is the parent body of the Ku Klux Klan," Reagan said. There was a gasp from the crowd. It sounded as if Reagan, who rarely attacked an opponent personally, was somehow linking Carter to the Ku Klux Klan. Reagan knew immediately that he had misspoken. "I blew it," Reagan told his aides afterward. "I should never have said what I said."

Before the night was out, concerned southern Republican leaders were calling Reagan headquarters, and the candidate found it necessary to apologize to the state of Alabama and the community of Tuscumbia, which was not the birthplace of the Klan. By now, the campaign was reeling, and Reagan's own confidence was shaken. Nofziger made matters worse, blaming the press for overplaying the story and declining to tell of his own contribution to Reagan's blunder. The main effect of an acrimonious exchange between Nofziger and reporters on the campaign plane returning to Washington the next evening was to advertise that Reagan was a shaky candidate with a still shakier campaign. Wirthlin's polls confirmed that Reagan, who was supposed to be making Carter's leadership the main issue, was instead rapidly raising questions about his own competence. In a blunder-run of seventeen days, he had forfeited much of his advantage on the issues where Carter was weakest. Fortunately for Reagan, all but one of his errors had been made in the low-pressure period of August before the start of the formal campaign. The "creationism" statement had gone relatively unnoticed, and "Taiwan" was a bigger issue with the press than with the public. But "noble cause" and "Ku Klux Klan" had been big losers, and all of Reagan's stumbles were coming together to create a picture of a candidate in over his head. "We were close, *that* close, to making Reagan rather than Carter the chief issue of the campaign," a Reagan aide said afterwards, holding up a thumb and forefinger less than an inch apart. Stories of Reagan's blunders proliferated. By the end of Reagan's first week on the general election campaign trail, the press was circling the candidate like a hunter whose wounded prey is about to drop. When Stuart Spencer arrived in Washington soon afterward, a reporter asked him what he was doing in town. "I'm here to see old foot-in-the-mouth," Spencer grinned. He didn't have to add that he was talking about Ronald Reagan.

Spencer was not in town by accident. He had been getting distress calls from Wexford, the Virginia hunt country estate near Middleburg where the Reagans lived during the fall. Many of the Reagan senior staff members disliked Wexford, because the rented home was an inconvenient hour's drive from campaign headquarters in Arlington and seemed to forfeit some of the advantage of moving to Washington. But the aides were out in force for meetings at the Reagan home on September 3, the first day back from Detroit, and again for a long sequestered session the following weekend. The top staff included, on a regular basis, Casey, Meese, Wirthlin, Deaver, Nofziger, Bill Timmons and, later, James A. Baker. As the campaign wore on, David Stockman, who impersonated both Carter and John Anderson in preparation for the debates, became a participant. But what the campaign needed in this first week of September, and Nancy Reagan understood it best, was not an impersonator but a genuine politician. Reagan had men of ability and integrity around him, but he lacked someone who knew how to run a high-powered political campaign and deal with the press and make the myriad gut decisions that make the difference between victory and defeat. Casey was not that man. At sixty-seven, he looked a decade older than Reagan and often behaved as if he were. His political experience, before the age of modern media campaigns, was in losing—with Wendell Willkie, with Thomas E. Dewey, with himself as a congressional candidate. He forgot the dates of primaries and the names of politicians, and sometimes the schedule he himself had arranged. One oft-told story had it that Casey had invited two important Republicans from the East Coast to Los Angeles and then left town before they arrived. Behind his back, other senior staffers called him "Spacey." Campaign plane reporters, preparing an irreverent list of mock book titles supposedly appropriate for the Reagan team, invented a biography of Casey called *The Man Who Never Was.** This was an unflattering and in many ways unfair portrait of a man who had held an important role in World War II intelligence and won respect for his performance as chairman of the Securities and Exchange Commission. But Casey was out of his league in national politics. Nor were the others in the Wexford cast able to take over a campaign manager's role. Meese was preoccupied with the headquarters and Deaver with the campaign plane. Timmons, a capable organizer, was not that close to Reagan. Wirthlin, whose polls and campaign plan were the source of many of Reagan's most useful themes and strategies, was not a tactician. "Where's Stu?" Nancy Reagan wanted to know. "Why isn't Stu here?"

Stuart K. Spencer was not the type of man whose presence is ordinarily sought by Nancy Reagan. He is combative, short, rumpled, profane and

---

* Some other mythical books attributed to other campaign figures by the Reagan press corps: *Beyond Reason: The Collected Speeches and Press Conferences of Ronald Reagan; Prospects For Nuclear Disarmament,* by Amy Carter; *The Return of Frankenstein,* by Henry Kissinger; *With All Deliberate Speed, The Memoirs of Edwin Meese; The Case for Chiang Kai-shek,* by Michael Deaver with an introduction on Formosa by Peter Hannaford; *Second Choice: My Years With Reagan,* by Stuart K. Spencer; *Killer Trees,* by James S. Brady, *Lies, Damn Lies and Statistics, An Unauthorized Biography of Richard Wirthlin,* by Pat Caddell; and *Black Like Me,* by Nancy Reagan. The latter was a reference to Mrs. Reagan's quickly corrected reference to the "beautiful white faces" at a Chicago fundraiser.

blunt, kind of a cartoonist's dream of a political operator. Born "Murphy," Spencer took the name of the couple who adopted him. He was a tough, athletic kid, often in trouble, who joined the Navy when he was seventeen. Before he teamed with Bill Roberts to form what became California's best-known political management firm, he was the parks and recreation director in the Los Angeles suburb of Alhambra. Spencer was a natural politician, with a feel for the strengths and weaknesses of other men. Unlike others who have prospered in the media-dominated milieu of California politics, Spencer and Roberts learned organizational skills from the ground up as managers of scores of legislative and congressional candidates for the Los Angeles County Republican organization. Jules Witcover and Jack Germond have written that Spencer is one of those few politicians "who seem to have computers just behind their eyes."[4] It is an accurate observation, but Spencer has something else as well, which is a superb, passionate feeling for politics and politicians. Each campaign, particularly a presidential campaign, is to Spencer a psychological enterprise, a triumph of mind over matter. He believed, from the first, that the key to Reagan's campaign was the restoration of the candidate's own confidence in himself. He knew how to direct Reagan without pushing him. "Remember, Ron, don't talk about China," he would say, making his point in a light way but always making it. Unlike others in the entourage, Spencer wanted no position in the White House and nothing from the administration except an occasional favor for his clients. He did not take himself or his candidate too seriously and said that his own reputation was "based 50 percent on ability and 50 percent on bullshit."[5] But he was deeply combative and believed he could elect Reagan as President. Spencer was a genuine politician, all right, and the Reagans were sorely in need of him.

The question "Where's Stu?" which Nancy Reagan had asked at Wexford had been asked before by the candidate himself and by Mike Deaver. During the period of Deaver's exile from the Sears-led campaign, Spencer and Deaver had buried the hatchet on old grudges extending from the first Reagan administration. At the time, Spencer believed that Deaver was steering clients away from him and with the bluntness for which he is famed said so. He also believed that Deaver had botched the 1973 tax-limitation campaign and did not keep his opinion to himself. In 1976 Spencer had committed the ultimate sin, in the eyes of the Reagan entourage, of working to defeat Reagan with Jerry Ford. Though Spencer's original motivation for this had indeed been anti-Reagan, or anti-Reagan staff, he had developed a deep respect and affection for Ford, whom he believes will be ranked highly in the history books. Before Spencer would serve as a consultant to the Reagan campaign in July, he made a point of checking with Ford, knowing that Ford would approve of it but wanting to demonstrate what had become his first loyalty. Now that the Reagan campaign wanted him back on a full-time basis, Spencer insisted on knowing whether Nancy Reagan also wanted him.

She did, because she always wants whatever will help her husband get elected. Deaver placed the call, and Nancy Reagan told Spencer that he was needed aboard the campaign plane.* On September 4, when "LeaderShip '80" left Dulles International Airport bound for Jacksonville, Florida, Spencer was aboard. He stayed on board for the duration.

On that very first Spencer trip there was a difference in the candidate. Some of the difference came from Spencer's handling. "Ron needed to be shown, very simply, that the level of campaigning he was now in was much greater, much different than anything he'd done in his life," Spencer said afterward. "He needed to know that he was talking to every audience at every stop, that he was talking to the whole nation every time he said something. Everything he said had to be viewed in that light. And everything he said had to be scrutinized ten times more than it ever was before. The rhetoric that brought everybody out of their seat in the primary wasn't going to do it in the general election. . . . Noble cause would have been a good issue in the primaries. . . . And he needed to know that if one of you [reporters] shouted a question at him, he didn't have an obligation to answer that question."[6] All of this advice was heeded by Reagan except the last. Reagan believed in what he was doing, and his natural inclination was to answer any question that was put to him. In those rocky first days of September, Spencer and Deaver concluded that they would just have to keep their lip-shooting candidate away from casual encounters with the press.

Another difference on that first Spencer trip arose because Reagan's issues team at Arlington came up with an accusation that struck an exposed nerve in the Carter administration. On August 22, while Reagan was mired in "defense week," Defense Secretary Harold Brown and Pentagon research director William J. Perry had disclosed at a news conference the plans for the "Stealth" bomber, which was the administration's distant alternative to the then discarded B-1. It was a thinly disguised effort to take the edge off Reagan's charges that Carter had let the nation's defenses slide, but the information given to the press alarmed General Richard B. Ellis, commander of the Strategic Air Command. Ellis and others in the military believed that the administration had disclosed classified information to the Russians for partisan political purposes. In Jacksonville, Reagan called the action "a cynical abuse of power and a clear abuse of the public trust," asserting that Brown and Perry had committed "a serious breach of national security secrets." There were Democrats who agreed with Reagan. Representative Samuel Stratton of New York, heading up a subcommittee which investi-

---

* Casey originally had suggested that Paul Laxalt be Reagan's "man on the plane," and Spencer had proposed the idea to Laxalt in a separate conversation. But Laxalt was up for reelection in Nevada and even more reluctant to neglect his Senate duties and home-state politicking than Spencer was to leave his business. Laxalt had lost a Senate race by 84 votes in 1964 and won his present Senate seat by 624 votes in 1974. "Those are the kind of elections that make you not take anything for granted," he once told me.

gated the disclosure, wanted to know why the two high-ranking officials were "yielding up territory to the enemy."[7] After the election the Democratic-controlled subcommittee would conclude that the Pentagon officials had acted unwisely. At the time the issue was enough to take the spotlight off Reagan and put Carter on the defensive for a few days. Though Stealth did not persist as a major issue, it played a timely role in accomplishing Spencer's No. 1 goal of restoring the candidate's confidence.

For the next ten days, Reagan became a more buttoned-up candidate than he had ever been before. Reporters who had previously enjoyed access to him were kept at a distance, and Reagan was not allowed to stray close enough to the press corps to indulge his habit of giving unrehearsed answers. Within the campaign, the tactic was known as "damage control." Its necessity was demonstrated the following Sunday when Reagan told an audience at St. Joseph's College in Philadelphia that the Department of Education newly created by Carter "is planning all manner of things to limit and restrict institutions of this kind because their faith is totally in public education only." No one in the press or the Reagan entourage had the foggiest idea of what the candidate was talking about. Whether Reagan did, either, was doubtful, but it was late in the day and the candidate was unavailable for questioning. The speech received only secondary coverage and was overshadowed on television by the ejection of a couple of antinuclear demonstrators from the hall.

Details about Carter's supposedly dire intentions against private education were not provided until fifteen hours later, while Reagan was breakfasting with Cardinal John Krol of Philadelphia. As reporters waited outside in the driveway of the cardinal's residence, Nofziger explained that Reagan had been generally anticipating that the department would adopt restrictive regulations, specifically referring to an otherwise unidentified department study that called for the government to take over higher education accreditation. No copy of the supposed study was available. What Reagan apparently had been doing at St. Joseph's was what he had done at the forum of evangelists in Dallas—telling an audience what it wanted to hear without bothering about the evidence. But his remarks were lost in the shuffle of a campaign which each day moved on to other issues. Reporters were angry at this convenient isolation of the candidate, as Spencer had known they would be. Keeping Reagan away from the press was a tactic he used sparingly, knowing that its continuance over a prolonged period would produce a new round of stories questioning the candidate's capability to be President. In the long run Spencer wanted a reasonably happy press corps; in the short run, he needed a confident candidate even more. When a reporter complained to him about Reagan's isolation, Spencer assured him it wouldn't continue and said he was just trying to get Reagan "over the bumps." And, in a short time, that is what he did.

By mid-September, Reagan's optimism had reasserted itself, and the candidate was free to move around naturally again. Spencer brought him back into contact with the press in stages, trying to avoid a bruising news conference from which Reagan emerged as a know-nothing. In accomplishing this purpose Spencer engaged in psychological warfare with the press, no less than with his candidate. One afternoon, on LeaderShip '80, he had Nofziger announce a press conference a half hour before the campaign plane landed at Dulles. His intention was to limit the preparation of reporters and to prevent them from calling their desks ahead of time. The subsequent press conference produced almost no news, which is exactly what Spencer wanted.

But it was a boost for the morale of Reagan, who believed that as governor he had turned most press encounters to his own advantage. He was right about that. What he did not realize in the opening weeks of the 1980 campaign was that the off-the-cuff style of saying whatever came into his head was not acceptable for a presidential nominee. Reagan's struggle was with himself, not with the press. At nearly seventy years of age, he was forced to unlearn some of the habits of a lifetime. This meant refraining from giving casual opinions on arms control or creationism or the myriad other subjects about which Reagan had memorized dangerous scraps of information. It meant running the risk of displeasing his questioners, whether they were campaign supporters or reporters. In a sense far different than Reagan had used the phrase in the primaries it meant "no more Taiwans, no more Vietnams."

Reagan's reemergence as a confident candidate was accompanied by the stabilizing of his position in the polls. A *Washington Post* poll published on September 14, but taken when Reagan was recovering from his case of the staggers from September 3 to September 7, showed him tied with Carter at 37 percent and independent candidate John Anderson far back at 13 percent. A *New York Times* poll a week later put Carter 3 points ahead, and a Gallup Poll taken September 12–14 gave Reagan a 2-point lead. The conventional wisdom was that it was a close race, with the Anderson vote quite possibly holding the key to the outcome. But Wirthlin's surveys in several key states suggested that the appearance of an even race was, in terms of electoral votes, an illusion. Behind the facade of a closely balanced contest, the solid reality of a Reagan electoral vote landslide was taking shape from the time the Reagan campaign stabilized in mid-September. This was because Reagan's base in the West was unassailable by Carter, while Carter's base in the South was not safe from Reagan. And among the "megastates"—the ten most populous and influential states in presidential elections—Reagan had secure leads in California, Texas and Florida, while Carter could not take any state for granted.* The knowledge that Reagan

---

* Only one of the "megastates"—Massachusetts—had been written off by Wirthlin. And even in Massachusetts, it was theoretically conceivable that Anderson would siphon off enough votes for Reagan to win. This, in fact, is what happened. Reagan, without campaigning in Massachusetts, won the state's fourteen electoral votes by a margin of 3,458 votes while Anderson was receiving 382,044 votes.

enjoyed this electoral vote cushion bolstered the returning mood of optimism in the Republican nominee's camp despite a public perception that President Carter had overcome Reagan's early lead and was still climbing. And at this critical moment in the campaign Carter abruptly handed Reagan the initiative.

On September 16, a celebrated anniversary of Mexican independence, Reagan was campaigning in Texas on "a color day" designed entirely for the television cameras. Reagan's short speeches, which featured words of praise for the "undocumented workers" so critical to Texas agriculture, were deliberately overshadowed by the visual images of the candidate wearing a sombrero, riding in a riverboat or attending a mariachi musicale. Other than a brief lapse in Harlingen, where he referred to the Mexican patriot Miguel Hidalgo as "a brave American priest," Reagan kept out of trouble. But Carter, emerging from the Rose Garden where he had conducted his successful campaign against Kennedy, did not. While Reagan was campaigning in Texas, the President spoke to an all-black audience at Ebenezer Baptist Church in Atlanta, which had been warmed up by Representative Parren J. Mitchell of Maryland describing Reagan as someone "who seeks the presidency of the United States with the endorsement of the Ku Klux Klan." Carter, after looking momentarily discomfited, grinned and shook Mitchell's hand. Then the President launched into his own attack on Reagan. Speaking in the church where Martin Luther King, Sr., had preached for years, Carter said that if Reagan were elected, there would probably never be a national holiday for King's murdered son. He criticized Reagan for opposing the 1964 Civil Rights Act. And in an unmistakable reference to his opponent, Carter said: "You've seen in this campaign the stirrings of hate and the rebirth of code words like 'states' rights' in a speech in Mississippi; in a campaign reference to the Ku Klux Klan relating to the South. This is a message that creates a cloud on the political horizon. Hatred has no place in this country."*

The grounds for the attack were particularly ill-chosen. Carter had no record of support for the 1964 Voting Right Act, and Reagan is no bigot. But voters had grave doubts about what Reagan would do in foreign and defense affairs, and Carter's attack in Atlanta deflated the currency of his subsequent comments on those issues. After Atlanta anything that Carter had to say about Reagan and world peace tended to be viewed more as a personal attack rather than as a reflection of a legitimate policy concern. Reagan supporters were quick to recognize the opportunity which Carter had provided them. "Until last Tuesday, Jimmy Carter had contented himself with implying that Ronald Reagan is an equal opportunity warmonger who will

* The race issue originally was injected into the campaign by Patricia Harris, Secretary of Health and Human Services in the Carter administration. In a comment made before Reagan's reference to the KKK on Labor Day, Mrs. Harris said that the Reagan candidacy raised the "specter of white sheets." She was referring to an endorsement of Reagan by a KKK faction. Reagan repudiated the endorsement and denounced the Klan.

incinerate everyone on earth, regardless of race, color or creed," wrote columnist George Will. "But Carter has decided that such moderation in pursuit of power is no virtue. Now he has said that Reagan is a racist."[8] Will recalled Carter's own past campaign record in Georgia, where his supporters in the 1970 primary distributed in segregationist regions a leaflet showing Governor Carl Sanders in the company of a black athlete. He contrasted this tactic to Reagan's opposition to the 1964 Civil Rights Law "on constitutinal grounds." Reagan, meanwhile, said that the 1964 law "had worked" and that he was satisfied with what it had accomplished. He called Carter's accusation that he had injected race hatred into the campaign "shameful." Whether or not one agreed with this assessment, Carter's comments were certainly damaging to the man who had made them. The President did not need to raise the race issue to win black votes. But he desperately needed to maintain among all voters his reputation as a decent, moral man. Wirthlin's polls showed that this perception was widely shared even by many voters who considered Carter incompetent. It was, in fact, Carter's strongest asset, and one he heedlessly threw away.

Reagan's campaign team had been anticipating a personal attack on other issues and was waiting to cry "foul." "Even if Carter and Reagan were running neck and neck early this fall, we could still expect that a strong, negative and highly personal campaign would be directed against Ronald Reagan," Wirthlin had written in the June campaign plan. "Carter's record in office has denied him use of the traditional Democratic theme song of the economy and how Republicans would foul things up. Present issues offer little more help to Carter.... More than ever, the electorate questions Carter's very capacity to lead. So, to beat us in November, Carter's task seems to be clear: Reagan must be demonized." Since Reagan is so difficult to attack on a personal basis, Wirthlin believed this demonizing strategy, if properly answered, would fail. So did one of the best political brains in the Carter campaign, Democratic National Committee Executive Director Les Francis, who knew from his California political experience the difficulty of trying to run Reagan to ground with personal attacks. In a prophetic July 21 memorandum to campaign manager Hamilton Jordan, Francis warned that Carter risked forfeiting his reputation of being "a good and decent person who practiced good Christian charity in his dealings with others." Wrote Francis, in words Carter would have done well to heed: "Quite frankly I hear more and more talk about Jimmy Carter having a 'mean streak' behind his smile; people cite his 'I'll whip his ass' statement vis-à-vis Kennedy last fall, his blast at Cy Vance after the latter's resignation, and our negative media ads during the primaries as grounds for their concern. A *particularly nasty* anti-Reagan campaign—either in our paid media or the President's rhetoric—will serve to play into this developing 'mean streak' concept. ..."

Spencer and the Reagan campaign team had discussed this "meanness factor." Wirthlin's campaign plan had raised some of the same issues as the

Francis memo, including long quotations from the commercials which media adviser Gerald Rafshoon had devoted to the destruction of Kennedy even after Carter had clinched the nomination. Wirthlin concluded: "We can expect Ronald Reagan to be pictured as a simplistic and untried lightweight (dumb), a person who consciously misuses facts to overblow his own record (deceptive) and, if President, one who would be too anxious to engage our country in a nuclear holocaust (dangerous)." It was an accurate forecast, except that Wirthlin expected the attack in the early stages of the campaign to come from surrogates and television commercials rather than from President Carter himself. Spencer, however, was not surprised. He had run a mean campaign of his own for Ford against Reagan in 1976, and he had been through the tough, losing battle against Carter which followed. Spencer knew how nasty presidential politics could get, and he shared Wirthlin's view that Carter had a mean streak. "It's sure to surface someplace," he had predicted accurately to Deaver at the Republican national convention. "And when it comes, it's going to hurt Carter."

Back in March, Republican political analyst Richard J. Whalen had predicted that Reagan would win because of "a secret weapon—the fact that Democrats fail to take him very seriously."[9] The Francis memo which talked of the perception of Carter's "mean streak" was part of a larger effort to deprive Reagan of this advantage. At a June meeting in the Hay-Adams Hotel, across Lafayette Park from the White House, Francis brought in fellow California Democrats Jesse Unruh and Bob Moretti to give "some rough, tough, gruff unvarnished political advice" to the Democratic campaign team. Jordan was impressed by what the Californians had to say and recalled after the election how Unruh had pointed his finger at him, warning him not to underestimate Reagan as a communicator. Moretti, in the course of a profane but respectful evaluation of the Republican nominee, referred to Reagan as "the Great Deflector."[10] By that he was describing Reagan's skill in turning aside the hard question and in making his opponent the issue. In his memo, written right after the Republican convention, Francis tried to reinforce this message, saying: "Although their handling of the Ford situation wouldn't suggest it, most of the people around Reagan are competent and tough. He may not be an intellectual, but he is no dummy; and, the people around him are smart. No matter what doubts may reside in the minds of many American voters about a Reagan presidency, he will always enjoy a public perception that he is a 'nice guy.' To level an attack against a nice guy is certain to result in a backlash which could really hurt us." All of this was a serious effort to deprive Reagan of his "secret weapon." It had some effect upon Jordan, but the inoculation did not take with the campaign as a whole. Rafshoon and White House Press Secretary Jody Powell, who some thought needed to hear the message more than Jordan, did not attend the meeting. White House pollster Pat Cadell attended but continued throughout most of the campaign to describe Reagan as a vulnerable challenger who could be overhauled by Carter. Despite the best efforts of the Californians, Reagan remained underestimated until the end.

The ability of the Great Deflector to make his opponent the issue was vividly demonstrated late in September. Carter, campaigning in Reagan's home state of California,* said in a speech to the California AFL-CIO convention on September 23 that the November election would decide "whether we have peace or war." Even Jody Powell acknowledged that his President had gone too far, characterizing the remark to reporters as an "overstatement." But Carter stayed with the theme the following day, calling upon Reagan to explain his "repeated habit" of calling for the use of military force. As examples of this habit, Powell presented reporters with a number of statements drawn from news clippings. They ranged from a Reagan statement in 1975 that the United States should send destroyers to accompany tuna fishing boats that were being seized by Ecuador, to a suggestion Reagan had made during the 1980 primaries that the blockade of Cuba would be an appropriate response to the Soviet invasion of Afghanistan. Unlike Carter's remarks on the race issue, this portrait of a warmonger had been fully expected, and Reagan was ready to react. Leaving the Marriott Hotel in Miami on September 23, Reagan stopped before the television cameras and was asked about the Carter statement to the AFL-CIO. Using words which had been worked out in discussion that morning with Spencer and Deaver, Reagan said, "I think it is inconceivable that anyone, and particularly a President of the United States, would imply, and this is another incident that he is implying and has several times, that anyone, any person, in this country would want war. And that's what he has been charging and I think it is unforgivable."

This was the prepared response, and it was adequate. But as so often is the case when he is under fire, the issue worked inside Reagan and made him angry. By the time he arrived at the Pensacola Airport an hour and a half later, Reagan had received a full report of Carter's speech the day before and he was steaming. "First of all I think to accuse that anyone would deliberately want a war is beneath decency," Reagan told an airport rally with evident emotion. "I have two sons. I have a grandson. I have known four wars in my lifetime and I think like all of you that world peace has got to be the principal theme of this nation." This was the Great Deflector playing the role of aggrieved candidate and playing it to perfection.

But Carter was just warming up. On October 6 the President started out

* One of the mysteries of the campaign to the Reagan camp and California politicians of both parties was why Carter and his aides took seriously the President's prospects in Reagan's home state. Wirthlin's polls had Reagan far ahead throughout, as did the respected public surveys of California pollster Mervin Field. Carter never carried California against anyone, losing to Governor Jerry Brown in the 1976 primary, to Ford in the general election and to Senator Kennedy in the 1980 primary. He received 35.9 percent of the vote against Reagan, the President's worst showing in any of the highly populous "mega-states."

the day with a detailed criticism of Reagan's old proposal to transfer federal programs to state and local governments. His speech, flat and unemotional, was greeted unenthusiastically by an audience assembled in a technical college in West Allis, a working-class suburb of Milwaukee. Carter then changed styles and themes. In the Republican stronghold of DuPage County, outside Chicago, the President reverted to attacking Reagan's "very dangerous" position on nuclear arms control. "What was striking about the attack was its stridency and directness," wrote Edward Walsh the next day in the *Washington Post.* "Although Carter has made the 'war and peace' theme the centerpiece of his campaign, he has usually done so in a low-keyed manner, often not even mentioning Reagan by name." Carter continued in the strident style that night at a Democratic fund-raising dinner in Chicago, raising his voice as he declared it would be "a catastrophe" if Reagan were elected and then telling his partisan audience: "You'll determine whether or not this America will be unified or, if I lose this election, whether Americans might be separated, black from white, Jew from Christian, North from South, rural from urban." Reagan, campaigning in Pennsylvania, issued a prepared response saying that he was "saddened" by the President's remarks and declaring that Carter owed the country an apology. His real feeling came through when a reporter asked him if Carter "fights dirty." "I think," said Reagan, "he's a badly misinformed and prejudiced man." Carter's comment, said Reagan to an aide, convinced him that the President knew he was losing the election.

Wirthlin's polls gave a more complex picture. They showed that Carter's attacks had, in fact, surfaced latent doubts among significant sections of the electorate about the dangers of putting Reagan in the White House. This was a problem of potentially serious magnitude for Reagan, for it meant that a misstep on the war-and-peace issue in the final weeks of the campaign had the potential for transferring the election from a referendum on Carter's competence to a question of whether Reagan's hand should be allowed on the nuclear trigger. At the same time, Carter had paid a terrible price for his success. The Wirthlin surveys discovered even Carter supporters who were disappointed at the way their President was conducting himself in the campaign. In trying to portray Reagan as both warmonger and bigot, Carter had undermined his valued and carefully cultivated reputation as a decent man who followed a more moral code than other politicians. The gain was not worth the loss. In choosing personally to expose Reagan's political weakness on the issue of war and peace, Carter had forfeited his own strongest asset with an electorate that long since had become disenchanted with his leadership.

Carter also had accomplished something for his opponent which the polls could not measure, and which Reagan may have been unable to accomplish for himself. By his personal attacks, Carter had roused within Reagan those deep competitive fires that had made him such an extraordinary candidate in the North Carolina primary of 1976 and the New Hampshire primary of 1980. That keen competitive edge had been lacking as Reagan approached the fall campaign, and its absence may well have contributed to the series of stumbles with which Reagan began it. He had not been personally distorted by the pursuit of the presidency, but he had not, since New Hampshire, been especially pushed by it, either. His approach combined a self-indulgent fatalism with a traditional patriotic respect for the office of the presidency. Inevitably, although Reagan was no fan of Carter, some of that respect rubbed off on the office-holder and made Reagan a more defensive and quiescent candidate than he should have been. Carter wiped away that respect with his personal attacks, particularly with the suggestion that a Reagan victory would also be a triumph for the forces of racial and religious prejudice. "Ron always thought the President was ten feet tall," said an intimate. "After Jimmy started in on him, the President was cut down to Carter's size. And Ron, of course, is lots taller than Jimmy." Unwittingly, Carter had collaborated with Spencer & Co. in restoring the confidence of a candidate who was shakier than he appeared from the outside. In trying to demonize the Great Deflector, Carter had succeeded only in demonizing himself.

On LeaderShip '80, Spencer and Deaver needed all the help they could get. While Carter floundered and Reagan recovered, the Reagan campaign evolved into a vast, multilayered bureaucracy headquartered in Arlington and beset by the myriad conflicts attendant to such enterprises. The Reagan campaign was particularly susceptible to layering because Casey's title of campaign director was largely a fiction. He knew a good deal about organization but very little about the technical requirements of a political campaign, which meant that he had to rely on others for decisions that could have been quickly made by an experienced political professional.

The daily struggles between the on-plane strategists and Arlington headquarters went beyond the deficiencies of Casey, real and alleged. A presidential campaign is a self-germinating operation involving hundreds of egos and temperaments. There is a natural tendency for participants in the enterprise to equate what often is a rifleman's view of the combat with the entire battlefield. From the vantage point of the campaign plane, Arlington was a behind-the-lines command post given to ponderous decision-making, multiple speech drafts and frequent second-guessing. From the view of Arlington, LeaderShip '80 was a porous three-ring circus in which the press was allowed far too much access to the candidate and his strategists and printed or aired too many "leaks" about campaign strategy. But Spencer saw what was happening on the plane as part of an overall strategy to present Reagan as a better man than Carter. Both at headquarters and on the campaign plane, the Reagan strategists had heard from political sources and from reporters switching campaigns that Carter's aides blamed the "meanness issue" on the press rather than on the President's inferences that Reagan was a warmonger and racist. As Spencer picked it up, the Carter line was that the President had to go out and carry the attack to his opponent because the press was giving Reagan a free ride.* To reporters covering Reagan, this had a hollow ring. They had been rapped by the candidate in the primaries for "journalistic incest" and criticized by Nofziger during Reagan's bad run at the start for concentrating on the Republican nominee's bloopers rather than his advocacies.

The rights and wrongs of such criticisms on either side were of little consequence to Spencer. He is a professional who lauds the press and lashes it, as it serves his purpose. He knows from experience that sinking candidates and their staffs are more apt to blame the messenger than the message. He had benefited from this when Pat Brown was losing in 1966, and he had been damaged by it a decade later when President Ford was losing to Carter. So, to Spencer, what had happened was simply an opportunity that he had not necessarily expected to come his way but of which he was quick to take full advantage. Once "meanness" became established as an issue, the Republican nominee was trotted out for "press availabilities" and interviews, and a relaxed, accessible campaign style was deliberately introduced aboard LeaderShip '80. The on-plane campaign team consciously ran the risk of exposing some additional Reagan lapses in favor of the advantages of drawing a contrast with Carter. Senior staff aides made themselves relentlessly available. Nancy Reagan came back to the press section on every leg of every flight, passing out chocolates and chatting with reporters. When the plane took off, she rolled an orange down the aisle. The takeoffs were accompanied by a tape featuring Willie Nelson singing "On The Road Again" and a fragment of a Carter speech in which the President described glowingly to an interviewer how he and Rosalyn Carter read the Bible to each other in Spanish. The overall effect was less than madcap by the standards of, say, a Kennedy campaign, but it was relaxed enough to keep most of the occupants of LeaderShip '80 reasonably loose and happy. Casey and Timmons objected to this looseness, and to the "leaks." "This isn't Richard Nixon," Spencer would say in response. "This is Ronald Reagan. It gets a little bit trying at times, for me and everyone else, but we're going to reflect the nature of the candidate."

Sometimes, the nature of the candidate got in the way of the candidate's campaign. Neither Spencer nor anyone else could prevent an unleashed Ronald Reagan from telling stories or half-remembering some magazine article which popped into his head when he was trying to make a point. The point that Reagan made most frequently in October, while Carter was fo-

---

* Albert R. Hunt, writing in the *Wall Street Journal,* argued that it was important to hold Reagan accountable for his statements but observed that the only reason Carter was aware of them was because they had been reported in the press. Hunt quoted one Carter operative as saying, "You all don't like Jimmy Carter so you've decided to give Reagan a free ride." This belief, added Hunt, was "a conspiratorial theory that would do Spiro Agnew proud."

cusing on foreign policy, was that the President's domestic policies had failed. Reagan's targets were the working class voters of the nation's industrial heartland, with heavy emphasis on the unemployment-ridden automaking communities of Michigan and the steel towns of Pennsylvania and Ohio. Foreshadowing the theme he would exploit dramatically at the close of the campaign, Reagan invited workers and their families to compare their economic fortunes with the standard of living they had experienced when Carter took office. "I challenge Mr. Carter to defend his record of making Americans worse off economically than they were when he took office," Reagan said in Langhorne, Pennsylvania, on October 7. "And I challenge him to explain to Americans exactly how they could possibly expect a complete turnabout in performance if Mr. Carter is reelected."

The same day Reagan traveled to Steubenville, Ohio, in the economically hard-pressed Ohio Valley, for a rally sponsored by the "Save Our Steel" Committee. The campaign was running loose and a little behind schedule, as usual. Reagan was tired, but happy. He noticed that hundreds of working men were in the crowd at Steubenville, even though the local Steelworkers Union had endorsed Carter and withdrawn from Save Our Steel—an organization of steel and coal company executives and community leaders—because of its sponsorship of the Reagan rally. After Reagan's speech, reporters were herded into a makeshift press room in the lobby of the Ohio Valley Towers while Reagan went to an upper floor of the building to address 150 members of Save Our Steel. Reagan started out by listening. He heard Bill Debkin, a steel company counsel, denounce foreign "dumping" and "environmental regulatory overkill." He heard Bud Ogden, a coal company president, relate his "sickening and discouraging" experience with the "faceless bureaucrats" of the Environmental Protection Agency in trying to work out a compromise that would permit burning of high-sulfur Ohio coal. And he heard other similar complaints which left no doubt in the candidate's mind about the theme on which they wanted him to expound.

Reagan did not disappoint his selective audience. "We are all today environmentalists," he said. "But we've got to realize that people are ecology, too." Some of those in Washington, he said, had gone beyond protecting the environment. "What they believe in is no growth," he said. "What they believe in is a return to a society in which there wouldn't be the need for the industrial concerns or more power plants and so forth. . . . I have flown twice over Mt. St. Helens out on our West Coast. I'm not a scientist and I don't know the figures, but I just have a suspicion that that one little mountain out there in these past several months has probably released more sulphur dioxide into the atmosphere of the world than has been released in the last ten years of automobile driving or things of that kind that people are so concerned about."

By now, Reagan was intent only on his audience of enthusiastic industrialists. He was oblivious to the small press pool which had crowded into the room and didn't know—and in his expansive mood may not even have cared—that the entire speech was being piped by loudspeaker to the press room where reporters, sensing that Reagan was on a roll, had begun to flip on their tape recorders. "Indeed," Reagan continued, "there is a very eminent scientist associated with Texas A & M who has written about nature laughing at us and, according to his research, if we totally eliminated all the man-made sulphur dioxide in the air today, we would still have two-thirds as much as we have because that's how much nature is releasing. I know Teddy Kennedy had fun at the Democratic convention when he said that I had said that trees and vegetation cause 80 percent of the air pollution in this country. Well, now he was a little wrong about what I said. First of all, I didn't say 80 percent, I said 92 percent, 93 percent, pardon me. And I didn't say air pollution, I said oxides of nitrogen. And I am right.* Growing and decaying vegetation in this land are responsible for 93 percent of the oxides of nitrogen."

There was more, too much more. Reagan told his by now enthralled audience that the Great Smoky Mountains are so named because "that haze over those mountains are oxides of nitrogen. I think it's kind of interesting that there are some doctors that are lately investigating and experimenting that they believe that that atmosphere up there in those mountains might be beneficial to tubercular patients." For some reason, this reminded Reagan of a history he had read of Santa Barbara, California, "where we have some oil wells being drilled out in the harbor and a great organization formed to stop that. . . . There have been sixteen permanent oil slicks in the Santa Barbara channel as long as the memory of man and far back beyond any development of oil or drilling of oil any place before we even knew about such things. And an English sea captain back in the 1700s anchored off that shore, woke up in the morning and wrote in his log-book, 'The sea was covered with a viscous material that when the waves moved it gave off iridescent hues.' But around the turn of the century when we did know something about oil, Santa Barbara was a great health spa. . . . And one of their advertisements at that time said in addition to salubrious climate, that the southwesterly prevailing winds blowing across a large oil slick off the coast of Santa Barbara purified the air and prevented the spread of infectious diseases."

A new chapter in Reagan's unusual history of pollution was added the following day in Youngstown, Ohio. While Reagan toured an abandoned steel mill where an advance man had posted a sign, "Carter's Steel Works," the Republican nominee's aides handed out a report on regulatory reform

---

* He was right, but irrelevant. Reagan apparently had confused nitrous oxide, which growing plants emit, with nitrogen dioxide, which is emitted by smokestacks. And he wasn't even close to being right in his guess about the volcanic Mt. St. Helens, which at its peak activity was producing 2,000 tons of sulfur dioxide a day compared to 81,000 tons of sulfer dioxide produced each day by automobiles.

which included the statement that "air pollution has been substantially controlled." By now reporters had transcribed Reagan's rambling discourse at Steubenville. In the manner of many campaign stories, this one slowly gathered force as the transcript circulated and Reagan was questioned about it at subsequent stops. The buildup was helped by the coincidence of a record smog siege in Los Angeles, which was Reagan's destination at the end of the week. When the candidate was asked in St. Louis whether what was happening in Los Angeles didn't contradict his stand in favor of relaxed air pollution controls, Reagan said, "Fellas, I think all of this is, again, a little nitpicky trying to divert us from the real issues." He then went on to recount his support of strict air pollution laws as governor of California. But by the time Reagan reached Birmingham, Alabama, he was denying entirely the Youngstown statement that air pollution was "substantially controlled." A Reagan aide told reporter David Hoffman, covering the campaign for Knight-Ridder newspapers, that this statement may have been issued without ever having been seen by the candidate.

In California, the air was even murkier than Reagan's views of air pollution. Reagan was scheduled to address a triumphant, homecoming Friday night rally in Burbank on October 11 where the musical accompaniment included Roy Rogers and the Sons of the Pioneers playing "Cool Clear Water" and other favorites of their old movie western days. Despite this bit of nostalgia and some extensive advance work, the crowd was relatively small. The smog was so heavy it had driven even pollution-toughened Los Angelenos indoors. And those who did come had a long wait for their candidate. Reagan's plane was supposed to land at nearby Hollywood-Burbank Airport. Instead, it was diverted to Los Angeles International because Hollywood-Burbank had been closed down by smog.

Reagan pushed on. The next day at Claremont College, demonstrators chanted "Smog, smog," and someone tacked a poster to a nearby tree, "Chop Me Down Before I Kill Again." But the smog began to lift as Reagan toured Southern California by helicopter, touching down in four communities and finishing the day with a visit to a Van Nuys synagogue where he donned a white yarmulke and quipped, "In the business I used to be in, the good guys wore the white hats." Reagan's environmental declarations had made him anything but a "white hat" with conservationist groups, but most of them were solidly opposed to him anyway, and the environmental issue was a secondary one to most voters in 1980. Wirthlin's polls showed some slight loss to Reagan in California, where his lead remained commanding, and severer damage in Oregon, where voters take their trees seriously. Briefly, Carter became a competitive candidate for Oregon's electoral votes. Nationally, however, Reagan got away with Mt. St. Helens and the "substantial control" of air pollution, although the issue was a sensitive one at Arlington headquarters for the remainder of the campaign. On one flight of LeaderShip '80, speech-writer Ken Khachigian noticed a forest fire below and said softly, "Killer trees." James Brady, who rarely said anything softly, repeated in a loud voice, "Killer trees." The phrase found its way into the *New York Times,* and Brady was briefly grounded by Casey and his irate operatives at Arlington. Soon, however, Spencer and Deaver brought him back aboard.*

Spencer believes that there comes a time in every campaign, no matter how well it is going, when it plunges into the doldrums and loses the ability to move forward. This had now happened to the Reagan campaign. Early in October, Carter's paid advertisements, rather than the President himself, began to carry the brunt of the attack against Reagan. The President acknowledged in an October 8 interview with Barbara Walters that he had made some mistakes in his comments about his opponent, though he continued to criticize the press coverage of Reagan. It was not quite an apology, but it was close, and Carter began to climb in the polls. On October 14, for the only time in the campaign, Wirthlin's trackings gave Carter a narrow lead. Adjusted for the undecided vote, the percentages were Carter 45.17, Reagan 43.43 and Anderson 11.35. "We were flat, flat, flat," Spencer said afterwards. "We weren't moving and we had to do something." The "something," everyone agreed, should be a new issue—and one that was aimed at a constituency where Reagan needed help.

This was the genesis of Reagan's announcement at a press conference in Los Angeles on October 14 that he would name a woman to "one of the first Supreme Court vacancies in my administration." That promise was to lead to Justice Sandra O'Connor, though at the time Reagan's "one of the first" language seemed so carefully couched that it scarcely looked like a promise at all. Both Spencer and Wirthlin were concerned about reaching out to women voters, who at this point in the campaign were decidedly less favorable to Reagan than were men. On the same day Reagan made his announcement, a poll in the *New York Times* showed the Republican nominee with an 11-point lead among male voters and a 9-point deficit among female voters in the key state of Illinois. In part, this difference related to Reagan's opposition to the "women's issues" of the Equal Rights Amendment and abortion. However, the more significant reason, as reflected in both public and private surveys, was the greater concern among women voters about the war-and-peace issue on which Reagan was most vulnerable. The concern

* Both Khachigian and Brady were valuable members of the campaign team which Spencer and Deaver had assembled on LeaderShip '80. Khachigian, a onetime speechwriter for President Nixon, quickly mastered the far different speaking style of Reagan and was adept at synthesizing sometimes conflicting speech proposals which arrived from Arlington into a single Reaganesque draft. Brady kept his eye out for misplaced statistics of the Mt. St. Helens sort and saved Reagan from several similar errors. His irreverence and sense of humor also kept both staff and the campaign press corps entertained and contributed greatly to the atmosphere Spencer was trying to create on the plane. Brady was immensely popular with reporters, most of whom were pulling for him to become White House press secretary at a time when that seemed an unlikely prospect.

that Reagan might prove too bellicose or too quick to commit U.S. military force was not limited to women voters, either. Reagan had softened his opposition to the defunct strategic arms limitation treaty known as SALT II by saying he would bargain willingly with the Russians for a "SALT III" treaty that would genuinely reduce nuclear armaments instead of merely slowing the pace of the arms race as SALT II would have done. But memories of Reagan's bristling anti-Soviet rhetoric lingered. Spencer knew from long experience that voters were more easily frightened by the repetition of this rhetoric than they were by Reagan personally. The best way to deal with the issue of whether Reagan was warlike, Spencer had come to believe, was to let voters see him side by side with the President and make their own judgment.

Personally, Reagan had always been inclined to debate. I had asked him about it in August at a time when the avowed campaign strategy was to insist that Anderson be involved in any debate format. This position, as well as Carter's insistence on Anderson's exclusion, was based on polling information which showed the independent candidate pulling votes from Carter as long as he stayed above 10 percent. Wirthlin did a series of projections, however, which showed Anderson hurting Reagan if he dropped to the 5 or 6 percent level.* Reagan realized that Anderson would be likely to sink out of sight in the polls if the two major candidates agreed to freeze him out of a debate. Even so, it was clear to me that Reagan had learned both the negative lesson of Iowa and the positive ones of Nashua and Chicago. When I asked Reagan if he looked forward to a one-on-one debate with Carter, he forgot about the strategy and said, "I do look forward to it, not because of any contrast of ability in debating, but because I think the President cannot deny the record. This would be the nature of a debate, these would be the things that would be brought forth in a debate."[11]

Reagan also was aware that challengers Kennedy in 1960 and Carter in 1976 had been declared "winners" by holding their own on the same stage with incumbents. After Carter turned down a three-way debate, Reagan and Anderson agreed to hold their own, under League of Women Voters sponsorship, in Baltimore on September 21. The debate was no barn-burner, but Carter suffered in the public opinion polls and at the hands of editorial writers for avoiding it. The reviews of Reagan were mixed, but the prevailing opinion—again supported by the polls—was that he had held his own

---

* This was because Anderson's core vote contained a disproportionate number of liberal Republicans who were unlikely to vote for Carter under any circumstances. Anderson's presence in the race was a help to Reagan and a hindrance to Carter not because he necessarily drew more voters from the President but because of the states in which he was a factor. Wirthlin's polls showed Anderson taking from Reagan in California and Texas, for instance, where Reagan's cushion was so big it didn't matter. But Anderson drew from Carter in the northeastern states which Reagan would have found it difficult to carry on his own. Anderson's 7.5 percent of the vote in New York probably cost Carter the state and certainly cost the President Massachusetts, where Anderson received 15.2 percent of the vote.

against a knowledgeable and quick-witted opponent. Reagan's showing further bolstered his own growing confidence and contributed to his belief that he would not be overmatched against Carter. This view was encouraged by Laxalt, who was convinced that Reagan's personal charm would override the vast advantage in informational resources available to the President. So, with the campaign in the doldrums, there was no argument from Reagan when Spencer approached him during a flight from Los Angeles to Idaho Falls and proposed that they take the plunge and agree to debate Carter. "I think I'm going to have to debate him," Reagan said, without reluctance. By now, he had plenty of confidence in himself.

Reagan was given an opportunity to test that confidence the following evening in New York City at the annual Alfred E. Smith Memorial Dinner, which was the one occasion on which Reagan and Carter were then scheduled to meet. The dinner is a tradition-hallowed political event where speakers are supposed to blend humor and homage to Smith, the onetime New York governor and 1928 Democratic presidential nominee. It was a made-to-order event for Reagan, and he took full advantage of it, winning the plaudits of the audience with a graceful, self-deprecating speech while Carter tried heavy-handedly to call attention to his Camp David achievements and to Reagan's support by fundamentalist Christian activists.* For Reagan, as well as for close aides like Deaver, this was another demonstration that the challenger's personal qualities could prevail in a debate.

The next morning, in Reagan's Waldorf-Astoria suite, the decision became official. Key aides in the campaign had flown up from Washington for the meeting, and not all of them were enthusiastic about meeting Carter. The organization-minded Timmons believed that Reagan had a superior field force and better media and would turn out his supporters on election day. A debate to him seemed a dubious and high-risk proposition. Wirthlin also opposed the debate. His poll, adjusted for undecided voters, as of that morning of October 17 showed Reagan firmly back out in front, with 48.17 percent to 41.55 percent for Carter. Anderson was holding at 10.28 percent, and Wirthlin was concerned that a debate between Reagan and Carter would cause him to drop off the charts. If so, Wirthlin contended, this could cost Reagan both New York and Massachusetts where "the Anderson difference" indeed made the difference between Reagan and Carter. Wirthlin believed in his data, which had provided a reliable barometer to issues and personalities throughout the year. He considered the 1½-point lead which Carter had taken on October 14 to be something of an aberration.†

---

* Reagan said there wasn't any truth to the rumor that he looked younger "because I keep riding older and older horses."

† Wirthlin's theory about why Carter was ahead in the October 14 survey is that there was a lag between the impact of Carter's attacks on Reagan and the backlash effect these attacks caused on Carter himself. This was particularly true, he believes, with the October 6 speech in Chicago where Carter talked about the election determining "whether

Reagan had otherwise led throughout the campaign and he was leading now. Why take a chance on losing that lead by debating the trailing candidate?

Spencer always trusts his intuitions as much as his polls, and his feelings more than his campaign plans. "Planning is indispensable; plans are worthless," he likes to say, in a quotation he attributes to Dwight Eisenhower. Spencer had found it uncustomarily difficult to reach a settled feeling about the debate. He had learned the hard way in 1976 when Ford had said that the Russians did not dominate Poland how easily a candidate can destroy himself with a chance remark, and Reagan was always a candidate in search of some such calamity. But Spencer kept returning to the idea that the visual impression that could be made in a debate would undermine the portrait of Reagan as a mad bomber. And Spencer was aware, along with everyone else in the Waldorf-Astoria suite, that a "tie" would be recorded as a defeat for the President.

In the end, tactical considerations and Reagan's own inclinations decided the question. All along in the Reagan campaign it was an article of faith that Carter would come up with an "October surprise," which probably meant freeing the American hostages in Iran during the last weeks of the campaign. Wirthlin had raised this possibility in his campaign plan in June, and Casey and Meese had tried to defuse it in advance by bringing it up to reporters at the Republican convention. Though it was a sophisticated political tactic which by inference ascribed the worst sort of motivations to Carter, it was based on a genuine fear which persisted throughout the campaign. Both Spencer and Wirthlin believed until well into October that if Carter were able to bring back the hostages before the election, he could wash away much of the emotion and acrimony of the campaign and the deep concerns about the President's leadership and could rally the voters to his side. Seen in light of this expectation, a 7-point lead didn't seem like much. To Spencer, the debate loomed as a hedge against the October surprise, and as what might be Reagan's only opportunity to regain the attention of voters if the hostages were released. Spencer, remembering the 1976 campaign when Ford had never quite been able to catch up with Carter, read Wirthlin's polls differently in another respect. He reasoned that a late debate would be of immense help to whoever was ahead in the race because it diminished any events which came before it. "It froze the two candidates where they were, which meant it froze Reagan in the lead," Spencer said afterward, repeating a point he had made at the time of decision. These were persuasive arguments, and they carried the day. Deaver, Casey and Nofziger all favored the debate. So did advertising specialist Peter Dailey, originally

---

Americans might be separated, black from white, Jew from Christian," etc. As that statement went the rounds and was repeated, it continued to show up in voter responses well into the final month of the campaign.

a doubter. Meese played his usual collegial role and saw to it that the dissenting views of Wirthlin and Timmons were heard, but in the end, he, too, favored the head-to-head debate. There was another dissenter, who did not speak that morning but who already had made her views known. She was Nancy Reagan, who was skeptical of the idea from the start, apparently out of concern that her husband would make some mistake that would turn the election against him. But she valued Spencer's judgments, and she knew that Ronald Reagan's inclinations were to debate. A participant in that meeting remembers Nancy Reagan sitting and watching in her bathrobe, not saying anything as the decision was ratified. She had been influential in the past, and she would be again. But on this day, on this big decision, Reagan acted without her approval. He followed instead the advice of his most experienced strategist and the sure guide of his own political instincts.

With the skillful assistance of James Baker, events now conspired to transfer the decision into an actual debate. The ticklish point for Reagan was to change positions without appearing to abandon his supposedly principled stand that Anderson deserved to be included. The League of Women Voters, which earlier had set a 15 percent standing in the polls as the magic threshold which entitled a candidate to participation in a presidential debate, gave Reagan a way out when Anderson dropped to 8 percent in the Gallup Poll. The League promptly issued a new invitation for a two-way debate, which Carter was in no position to refuse. Caddell, seeing the mirror image of the advantage perceived by Spencer when a challenger debates a President, had opposed a Carter debate with Reagan. But by mid-October, Carter no longer had a graceful way out. He had consistently turned down the three-way debate, calling Reagan and Anderson "two Republicans," and he had taken a battering in both the press and the polls because of it. Carter campaign strategist Robert Strauss had accepted a number of alternative two-way debates, all of them rejected by Reagan debate-negotiator Baker. A Carter refusal to debate after all that had gone before would have seemed an abject confirmation of the suspicion that he talked out of both sides of his mouth. Also, as Baker reported back to the Reagan campaign team, Carter's strategists were not convinced that Reagan really wanted to debate.

Baker started his negotiations with what seemed like an absurd proposal—an election eve debate designed to give Reagan total protection against a November variant of the "October surprise" and to freeze the lead for the longest possible moment. The Carter counter-offer to debate on October 28, the Tuesday before the election, privately delighted the Reagan camp and was accepted after a bit of play-acting by Baker. The debate was near enough to the election to suit Spencer. If anything happened after that, he reasoned, it could have a backlash effect on Carter because voters would believe the President was deliberately contriving an eleventh-hour event to save the election.* And the idea that Reagan would be frozen into his lead also proved correct. After the debate was agreed to, the press coverage and the candidates' speeches became virtually perfunctory, with everyone waiting for the big event. The beneficiary was Reagan. From October 17 until the day of the debate in Cleveland on October 28, he held a consistent lead in Wirthlin's daily polls, never less than 5 points and never more than 8. Reagan took it easy, boning up for his debate at Wexford with such questioners as Jeane Kirkpatrick and George Will impersonating members of the press panel. David Stockman, who had successfully impersonated his one-time mentor John Anderson in preparation for the earlier debate, played the Carter role. "After Stockman," Reagan said afterward, "both Anderson and Carter were easy."

Easy was too strong a word for it, but it wasn't all that difficult, either. In retrospect, the debate can be summed up in two phrases: Reagan's "There you go again" line and Carter's suggestion that his daughter Amy was a nuclear arms adviser. This summation is unfair to Carter, who had legitimate differences with Reagan over the SALT II treaty, which Carter advocated and Reagan opposed, and over nuclear proliferation, which Reagan accepted as inevitable and Carter had tried to prevent. But Carter's own previous attacks on Reagan made it difficult for the President to strike the right tone. "He had to draw sharp differences without beating up on Reagan or appearing mean," analyzed one Reagan adviser who accurately anticipated the President's line of attack. "As long as Reagan remained pleasant and controlled, this was an almost impossible task." Reagan mentioned "peace" so often it sounded like he had invented the word. "And I'm here to tell you," he said in response to the first question, "that I believe with all my heart that our first priority must be world peace, and that use of force is always and only a last resort when everything else has failed." Concluding his answer to the first question, which called upon him to draw differences between himself and Carter over use of military power, Reagan said, in words similar to those he had used in rebuttal to Carter's attacks: ". . . I have seen four wars in my lifetime. I am a father of sons; I have a grandson. I don't ever want to see another generation of young Americans bleed their lives into sandy beachheads in the Pacific or rice paddies and jungles of Asia or the muddy battlefields of Europe."

It is doubtful if anyone remembers Reagan's citation of his sons and grandson. Yet everyone who watched the debate recalls Carter's rebuttal to an arms control question. "I think to close out this discussion, it would be better to put into perspective what we're talking about," Carter said. "I had a discussion with my daughter Amy the other day before I came here to ask

---

* But the Reagan campaign was not prepared to leave this conclusion to chance. Dailey, working with Casey, Meese and Wirthlin, had prepared $200,000 worth of "just in case" taped commercials criticizing Carter's handling of the hostage issue, which was ready for use on election eve if they were needed.

her what the most important issue was. She said she thought nuclear weaponry and the control of nuclear arms." The remark was greeted by a groan from some members of the politically attuned audience assembled in the Cleveland Public Music Hall. It also was cited derisively by television viewers in some of the post-debate polls. Why? On one level, Carter was clearly trying to do what Reagan had already done, which was to use his parenthood to bolster his credentials as a man of peace. Had he stopped at this and said, "I want my daughter to grow up in a peaceful world," or even if he had expressed his fears that she would not, the remark most likely would have gone unnoticed. But Carter had personalized it (Reagan had not said, "my sons Mike and Ron and my grandson Cameron," which would have been less effective than what he did say), and then given the further damaging impression that he consulted with his daughter on nuclear arms issues. The remark seemed both patronizing of Reagan and of the debate viewers. As Deaver observed afterward, "People may not understand the intricacies of arms control, but they know you don't ask your twelve-year-old for the solution." But Carter had not actually said that he was getting information on weapons issues from Amy. What he appeared to be doing was bringing his daughter's name into the debate to make a point that he was unwilling to express directly. In context, the "Amy" reference came out as weasel-worded, as if Carter wanted to attack Reagan again as likely to lead the nation into nuclear war, but didn't want to say so directly. Whether or not this was intended, post-debate polls found that a number of voters linked the Amy reference to Carter's earlier depiction of Reagan as warmonger. It was another small disaster for the President, coming at the time he needed every break. In the final week of the campaign, "Amy" became a staple for columnists and comedians. "Ask Amy" signs proliferated at Republican rallies.

Self-deprecating humor was not President Carter's strong suit. But Reagan had both spontaneous and rehearsed command of this useful quality. Reagan joked naturally about his age, his movie career and, among aides and intimates, about his own bloopers. Before the debate a memo written by a Democratic strategist advised Carter to let a little humor show. Reagan needed no such memo. The corollary advice to him was, "Make the points you want to make no matter what the question is and stay relaxed." Reagan had difficulty following the last part of his advice at the outset. Maybe it was the natural nervousness of the performer, or perhaps there was, after all, some lingering belief about the ten-foot-tall quality of the presidency which Carter's personal attacks had not totally dispelled. Whatever the reason, Reagan confessed afterwards that he was nervous when he began, and some of his stiffness showed on the screen. But once the first question and his carefully planned "our first priority must be world peace" response was out of the way, Reagan settled down. He paid attention to the questions and answered those he wanted to answer. He also became aware, as a good debater will, that his opponent was pressing, and this relaxed Reagan even more.

The pictures captured by the cameras were of a serious challenger, who was nonetheless not afraid to smile, and an overly intense President who looked daggers at his opponent whenever he disagreed with him. Near the end of the debate, after both Carter and Reagan had bobbled some of their statistics on Social Security and health care, the President said, "Governor Reagan, as a matter of fact, began his political career campaigning around this nation against Medicare." Carter then launched into a defense of national health insurance, pointing out that Reagan opposed this proposal.

Reagan simply ignored Carter's accurate description of his stand on national health insurance. Instead, he jumped at the Medicare remark. "There you go again," Reagan said almost sorrowfully, like an uncle rebuking a none-too-favorite nephew who was known to tell tall tales. Reagan's follow-on rebuttal was that he had supported an alternative to Medicare sponsored by the American Medical Association, an action which at the time would certainly have merited the description of "campaigning against Medicare." But "there you go again" finished off Carter. The reply was the Great Deflector's high point of the debate and perhaps of the campaign itself. It seemed such a wonderful, natural summation of an opponent's excess that overnight it became part of the political language. Long after Reagan was President the phrase lived on in the White House, where people would say to one another in correction of some habitual behavior, "There you go again." A handful of Reagan insiders knew, however, that the famous phrase had all the careful spontaneity of a minuet. During the debate preparation the Reagan issues specialists had tried to fill the candidate's head with facts and figures they thought Carter might bring up. Defense adviser William Van Cleave, especially, wanted Reagan to master the intricacies of strategic weapon deployment. Reagan listened politely to his advisers but spent his time practicing one-liners, believing that the viewing public was more apt to remember a deft phrase than a technical argument. In one rehearsal, Stockman, the Carter impersonator, whaled away at Reagan on nuclear proliferation. After the rehearsal Reagan assembled his closest aides to review what he had done. His answer had not been fully satisfactory, and Reagan, commenting on it, said: "I was about ready to say, 'There you go again.' I may save it for the debate." And so he did.*

The immediate verdict of the press about the debate was not unanimous. When some of us closed a hotel bar that night after filing our various accounts, several reporters thought Carter the winner. Many more agreed with

---

* During a rehearsal for the Anderson debate, Stockman, imitating Anderson, said: "Governor Reagan has no understanding or sensitivity about the environment. If he becomes President, he will throw open the floodgates in Alaska and allow the nineteenth century philosophy of rape and ruin to be reestablished, and our last virgin territories will disappear. He has no understanding of clear air, and if he becomes President, he will tear up the Clean Air Act and allow acid to rain down on our forests and poisons to leach into our streams; he has never heard of the toxic waste disposal problem, he doesn't know that this very day our water is being threatened and our blood veins are being penetrated." Reagan replied: "Well, John, sounds like I better get a gas mask."

the opinion expressed in the subhead of the *Cleveland Plain Dealer* debate story the next day: "Each candidate leaves the ring without errors." But another story on page one of this edition reported that an ABC poll of viewers found Reagan the winner by a 2–1 margin. Other polls were closer but also showed Reagan a winner. CBS put Reagan ahead 44–36, but found that the number of voters who thought Reagan would "lead the country into war" had declined from 43 to 35 percent. This was the statistical expression of a point made in a post-debate analysis by David Broder, who wrote that Carter had "accomplished almost every objective except the most important one: The destruction of Reagan's credibility as a President."

Wirthlin's polls recorded a surge to Reagan that continued unabated until election day. The technique of his poll was to interview five hundred persons a day and compute a three-day rolling average. This gave the pollsters an immediate clue to any significant change in voter sentiment, but it also meant that the full impact of something like the Reagan-Carter debate did not show up until three days afterward. On October 29, the day after the debate, Reagan led by 5½ percentage points. The number increased steadily each day after that as more and more debate viewers were added to the averages. On October 31, when the Reagan data included three post-debate days, the Republican nominee's lead stood at 9 points. It crested on November 2, the Sunday before the election, at nearly 11 points. Adjusted for undecided voters, the figures were Reagan 51.30, Carter 39.33 and Anderson 9.32.

A winner's feeling of exhilaration crept over LeaderShip '80 in the days following the debate. It was difficult to resist, but Reagan resisted it because he is superstitious about claiming victory in advance and because he is mindful of past overconfidences. His superstition was appreciated by comedian Bob Hope, who had joined the campaign in its last days. "He remembers how Dewey fell off the wedding cake," Hope said to me as LeaderShip '80 made its final flight to the West Coast. Nonetheless, the good feeling in the Reagan camp showed through in the candidate's performances on the stump. For the first time since the birth of Carter's attack strategy, Reagan no longer seemed concerned about being cast as the mad bomber. He had taken over the orange-rolling-down-the aisle chores from his wife, and when photographer Michael Evans jokingly warned him about the number of pictures he would have to autograph, Reagan replied, "You know, after you've canceled Social Security and started the war, what else is there for you to do?" On the stump, Reagan had returned to his original theme that Carter was a failed and incompetent President. "In place of competence, he has given us ineptitude," Reagan said at airport rallies in New Orleans and Texarkana two days after the debate. "Instead of steadiness, we have gotten vacillation. While America looks for confidence, he gives us fear. His multitude of promises so richly pledged in 1976 have fallen by the wayside in the shambles of this administration." These were strong words from a candidate who had complained about his opponent's harshness. But Reagan expressed himself with a winner's warmth and conviction that made these words seem less strident than they do on paper. He was not about to claim victory, but he was a happy man.

The happiness was marred only by the news from Iran, where, on the Saturday before the election, the Iranian parliament began debating conditions for release of the Americans held captive for a year. Reagan had been told by Wirthlin of his huge lead, and the consensus view among his strategists was that it was too late for any November version of the October surprise to turn things around. Still, the volatility of the hostage situation introduced an element of risk into what seemed an assured election. By Sunday morning the hostage story dominated the news, sweeping aside all domestic political issues. Every network ran some sort of special commemorating the anniversary of the hostages' capture. The front page of the *Washington Post* that day contained nine stories—eight of them about the hostages and the other an analysis by Broder of the effect on the election.

Reagan and his entourage had spent the night at Neal House in Columbus, Ohio. At 6 A.M. Ed Meese was awakened by a call from Arlington headquarters telling him that the State Department was trying to reach him. At 6:15 A.M. Meese was talking to Harold Saunders, Carter's assistant secretary of state for Near Eastern and South Asian affairs, who informed him that the Iranian special commission on the hostages had issued four conditions for release of the hostages. Later that morning, this briefing became the basis for a final Reagan strategy session on the hostage issue in which the unanimous view was that Reagan should do nothing that could be construed as trying to take political advantage of the situation. Reagan, Meese and Spencer were aware that their own frequent warnings of "an October surprise" had heightened the consciousness of voters to political exploitation of the hostage issue. This could backfire on Reagan if he appeared to be trying to draw political benefit from what literally could be a life-or-death situation for the Americans in Iran. The unanimous view at Neal House was that Reagan should say nothing at all and that his aides should also refrain from comments. "All I can tell you is I think this is too sensitive to make any comment on it at all," Reagan said on the sidewalk outside the hotel. "I won't make any more comment about it."

But Meese did comment, to the surprise of his colleagues in the front compartment of LeaderShip '80. Responding to the requests of reporters, he went back on the plane and had what amounted to a mini-press conference in which he discounted the impact of the news upon the election. Casey discounted it, too, telling Broder in Washington: "The campaign is over. We're just playing it out."[12] From a campaign manager who had complained about the "leaks" on LeaderShip '80 this was a public expression of the private view which had been reached at Neal House. For weeks the Reagan fear had been that some secret deal had been struck to free the fifty-two

American hostages around election day. When the nonexistent "deal" appeared at hand, Carter played it straight, canceling his campaign appearances and flying back to the White House for a day of meetings with his foreign policy advisers. That evening he issued a careful televised statement saying that the Iranian proposals "appear to offer a positive basis" for a solution. "We are within two days of an important national election," the President said. "Let me assure you that my decisions on this crucial matter will not be affected by the calendar." Reagan heard this statement on television en route from Dayton to Cincinnati, and he believed it. But he also believed, as Spencer had said to him, that the voters would remember the convenient timing of past announcements about the hostages which had helped Carter in the crucial Wisconsin primary against Senator Kennedy. As he headed for rallies in his two home states of Illinois and California on the final day of the election, Reagan was, as Casey had said, "just playing it out."*

And then, after all of Reagan's primaries and promises, after all his struggles to find the right themes and the right words and a balance between isolation and accessibility, after Bush and Nashua and "noble cause" and "meanness" and "there you go again"—after all this, the nation's longest political campaign was coming to an end. The crowd in Peoria, where a sprinkling of oldtimers remembered Reagan from his Illinois days, welcomed the finish because they sensed victory. Assembled under a banner of "Reagan Plays Well In Peoria," this happy crowd bantered with reporters and laughed at Bob Hope's warm-up jokes. Amy Carter, said Hope, had developed an interest in nuclear weapons because "Uncle Billy gave her a Raggedy Ann doll with a nuclear warhead." The difference between Jimmy Carter and his brother was that Billy had a foreign policy. And, with Jerry Ford alongside him, Hope said that Ford had told him he would "pardon Carter" if he ever returned to the White House.

Those of us who talked to Ford that day had our doubts. The previous Saturday, Ford had led the Republican campaign triumphantly through his home state of Michigan while Reagan played the role of devoted admirer and said that Carter had failed because of his "total inability to fill Jerry Ford's shoes." On the plane to Oregon and California that Monday, I asked Ford what would happen in the election the next day. "The voters are going to correct a mistake they made four years ago," he said firmly. In their campaigning together Ford had grown fond of Reagan, burying their grievances from the 1976 campaign. But his dislike of Carter, whom Ford considered a failure as a President, still burned brightly.

The last public event of the campaign took place in San Diego, where a

* But while Reagan was "playing it out," the candidate's media campaign was coming on strong. The last week, "Peak Week," in campaign lingo, saw the Reagan campaign spend $5 million of its $15 million media budget for a carefully planned saturation advertising campaign. And the field organization of which Timmons was justly proud also was mobilizing Reagan workers for election day.

carefully crafted patriotic rally awaited Reagan when he arrived late after a stop in Portland. The candidate was jubilant but tired. The motorcade with its phalanx of Secret Service and VIP cars parked nearby the speaker's stand, but Reagan did not get out. Instead, he waited in his limousine, with his wife, as introductory speeches droned on above. He did not seem to be saying anything or going over his notes. What was he doing staying in the car? a reporter wanted to know. "He's scared of crowds," replied Ed Meese, who was pleased that evening to be home in San Diego. And then Reagan was out of the car and up the steps, delivering his collected works of three decades of speech-making to a campaign audience one final time. Curiously, the campaign ended as it had begun, with Reagan responding to a heckler. This time it was not a woman with a Carter mask but a man in a black coat and stovepipe hat who hollered "ERA" and "equality" intermittently throughout the Reagan speech. "Aw, shut up," Reagan finally said. The crowd cheered. The evening ended with a fireworks display and the lighting of a gigantic American flag. The Reagans joined the crowd in singing "God Bless America."

This last event was not seen by most Americans. What they saw instead, interspersed between news programs about the year-long plight of the hostages, was one of the best speeches Reagan has ever given on television. Reagan called it a vision for America, which is what presidential candidates always talk about on election eve, but it really was Reagan's vision, and it had brought tears to Jim Brady's eyes when he watched the taping of the speech earlier that day in Peoria. True to the candidate, the speech was a vision of the past, of Pilgrims landing in New England, of American prisoners of war returning home from Vietnam, of astronauts landing on the moon. "Does history still have a place for America, for her people, for her great ideals?" said Reagan. "There are some who answer 'no,' [who say] that our energy is spent, our days of greatness at an end, that a great national malaise is upon us." Reagan gave his own answer later in the speech, taking issue with a famous speech* that Carter had given in July 1979 without ever mentioning it. "I find no national malaise," Reagan said. "I find nothing wrong with the American people." Foreshadowing what he would say in his inaugural address, Reagan addressed ordinary Americans as "heroes" who had not shirked history's call. "Any nation that sees softness in our prosperity or disunity . . . let them understand that we will put aside in a moment the fruits of our prosperity and the luxury of our disagreements if the cause is a safe and peaceful future for our children."

Concluding his debate with Carter in Cleveland a week earlier, Reagan had asked a series of questions that were intended to make voters measure

---

* Carter never actually used the word "malaise" in this speech. What he did say, in a nationally televised address on July 15, 1979, was that Americans were suffering from "a crisis of confidence . . . that strikes at the very heart and soul and spirit of our national will."

their President against their own expectations of America. He repeated these questions in extended form in this final campaign speech, saying first that President Carter would be reelected "if he instills in you pride for your country and a sense of optimism about our future. . . .

"But consider these questions as well when you finally make your decision:

"Are you more confident that our economy will create productive work for our society or are you less confident? Do you feel you can keep the job you have or gain a job if you don't have one?

"Are you satisfied that inflation at the highest rates in thirty-three years were the best that we could do? Are interest rates at 14½ percent something you are prepared to live with?

"Are you pleased with the ability of young people to buy a home; of the elderly to live their remaining lives in happiness; of our youngsters to take pride in the world we have built for them?

"Is our nation stronger and more capable of leading the world toward peace and freedom or is it weaker?

"Is there more stability in the world or less?

"Are you convinced that we have earned the respect of the world and our allies, or has America's position across the globe diminished?

"Are you personally more secure in your life? Is your family more secure? Is America safer in the world?

"And most importantly—quite simply—the basic question of our lives: Are you happier today than when Mr. Carter became President of the United States?"

Later the next morning, the Reagans voted at the Pacific Palisades home owned by Robert and Sally Gulick. He is a retired Marine Corps officer and a stockbroker. She is a Reagan fan. The table where the voters signed in was decorated with a papier mâché elephant and black licorice jelly beans. The poll workers had brought books and pictures for the Reagans to sign. In their eyes he was already President. The precinct where the Reagans voted is loaded with celebrities, Sylvester Stallone, Lawrence Welk and Vince Scully among them. But Reagan from this day forward was the biggest celebrity of all. He posed for pictures and quipped with reporters and said that he had voted for Nancy. He left to get a haircut. He refused, at the polling place and at the barbershop, to claim victory. When a reporter asked if he had won, Reagan said, "You know me, I'm too superstitious to answer anything like that." Another reporter told him that George Bush had said the ticket was "in like a burglar." Reagan laughed. "I think he was using a figure of speech," he said.

But Reagan was "in" and by a margin as great as Wirthlin's surveys of the last four days had shown. He was showering before dinner in his Pacific Palisades home when network news carried reports of Reagan victories in the South and East, and then, at 5:15 P.M. Pacific time, projected the landslide victory.* "I just can't believe it," Reagan said to Deaver. All that evening, at dinner with his closest friends and aides at the Bel Air home of Earle Jorgenson and later in the top-floor suite of the Century Plaza, Reagan acted like a man who had been happily surprised by unexpected good fortune. Nancy Reagan was visibly excited, hugging Deaver and others who streamed in with their congratulations. Reagan talked patiently on the telephone, thanking politicians who had helped him and congressmen whose support he would need as President. He seemed more contented than excited. When he was told in one call that independent candidate John Anderson had reached the 5 percent threshold he needed to qualify for federal funds, Reagan said, "Good, good," as if it really mattered to him. And soon afterward, Neil Reagan came by and shook his hand and tried to talk to his brother through the din.

"I bet there's a hot time in Dixon tonight," Neil said.

"I'd like to be there off in a corner just listening," said Ronald Reagan, the small-town boy who had just been elected the fortieth President of the United States.

* Reagan won by a plurality of 8,417,992 votes. He received 43,901,812 votes (50.7 percent) to 35,483,820 votes (41 percent) for Carter and 5,719,722 (6.6 percent) for Anderson. The electoral vote margin was even wider—489 for Reagan and 44 for Carter. The President carried his home state of Georgia plus Hawaii, Maryland, Minnesota, Rhode Island, West Virginia and the District of Columbia.

19

The President

H E saw himself as an ordinary man who embodied the hopes and aspirations of the nation. At seventy he could not change the habits of a lifetime, and he did not pretend that becoming President had made him a different person. During the campaign, after an uncommonly early start one morning, Reagan had grumbled to Stu Spencer that the schedule required him to get up too early. "You'd better get used to it, Governor," Spencer had replied jovially. "When you're President, that fellow from the National Security Council will be there to brief you at 7:30 every morning."

"Well," said Reagan, "he's going to have a helluva long wait."

This story told a lot about Ronald Reagan. What told even more was that his closest aides repeated it, knowing that their boss would not mind if they acknowledged his preference for sleeping in and for working regular hours. Reagan was scornful of the idea that a President's worth could be measured by the amount of time he spent in the Oval Office. "Show me an executive who works long overtime hours and I'll show you a bad executive," Reagan had said during the campaign.[1] He did not plan to be an overburdened President.

In office, he was as good as his word. The National Security briefings were moved to 9:30 A.M. and, for a time, simply delivered to him in writing. Reagan had never read *The Twilight of the Presidency,* but he acted as if his operating principles were from the book by former White House Press Secretary George Reedy. He would have agreed with Reedy that "there is far less to the presidency, in terms of essential activity, than meets the eye."[2] And when the *Washington Post* quoted from a passage of Reedy's study of the presidency in an analysis of Reagan's style, he did agree with it. "The concept of the overburdened presidency represents one of the insidious forces which serves to separate the chief executive from the real universe of living, breathing, troubled human beings," Lyndon Johnson's press secretary had written. "It is the basis for encouraging his most outrageous expressions, for pampering his most childish tantrums, for fostering his most arrogant actions. More than anything else, it serves to create an environment in which no man can live for any considered length of time and retain his psychological balance."[3]

Reagan kept his balance. He viewed the presidency as an opportunity for accomplishment rather than a burden. "I think in this age, this time, he was made for the job," says his friend, Nancy Reynolds. "If there was ever a job he felt totally suited for, it's this. He loves the White House, the history of it. There's almost an innocence about him, not a naiveté but an innocence that this Illinois boy is where he is. And yet, I think he feels, in a sense, it was his destiny. I truly think that's a genuine feeling."[4] Reagan also enjoyed being President, and he conveyed this feeling to those who had been intimate with other chief executives. Pierre Salinger, who had been press secretary under President Kennedy, found a similarity between Kennedy and Reagan. "They were at ease in the office of President," Salinger said. "Kennedy, like Reagan, didn't seem to be overburdened by being President and didn't take himself too seriously."[5]

At the same time Reagan tried to demonstrate that he had meant most of what he said on the campaign trail and was determined to carry out the promises he had made. While he and speech-writer Ken Khachigian were working together on the inaugural address, a call came in from his old friend, Senator Paul Laxalt of Nevada. Laxalt told him that word was out in Washington even before Reagan took office that he was prepared to trim his campaign promises. Reagan thanked Laxalt for the warning. "Make sure we get in a paragraph that makes it clear that I am not going to back away from the campaign proposals, and I won't back away from my principles," Reagan told Khachigian.[6] Later, after he became President, Reagan would make the same point to his new Secretary of State, Alexander M. Haig, Jr., when Haig lobbied against lifting the grain embargo which President Carter had imposed on the Soviet Union. "I promised to do it, Al," Reagan said.

He made a point of treating those closest to him the way he had always treated them. It was not a hard thing to do, for Reagan was not puffed up by the presidency. Six months into office, the missing "sense of awesomeness" which Reagan had looked for on inauguration day occurred to him only rarely and "in flashes." Sometimes, he told me, he would be riding in a motorcade and wonder why the people were waving at intersections. "And then I get embarrassed and self-conscious and say, 'Why do they have to do that?' "[7] He did not put on airs with his aides or his old friends or the congressmen who came to see him. Those who had known him best found it hard to stop calling him "Governor," and Reagan never tried to stop them. Once, Lyn Nofziger used the old form of address, then caught himself and apologized. Reagan gently waved away the explanation. "Maybe we should set aside a day each week to call me Governor, so we'll remember where we all came from," he said.

A large part of Reagan's appeal was that he did remember where he came from. Sometimes he made too much of it, sidetracking a discussion by relating an irrelevant story from the Depression or Hollywood or the California governorship. But this was the way Reagan reached out to people, and the way he came to understand what was important to them. He knew he was no intellectual, but he believed that his ability to see the world as other Americans saw it served a useful purpose. On election eve, when a radio reporter asked him what it was that other Americans saw in him, Reagan had replied, hesitantly: "Would you laugh if I told you that I think, maybe, they see themselves and that I'm one of them? I've never been able to detach myself or think that I, somehow, am apart from them."[8]

Unlike many of these other Americans to whom he felt close, Reagan was financially secure. He was a happy man, certain of his place in the world and his role in history. But because of Hollywood, and because of his small-town boyhood during the Depression, his cultural experience was accessible to other Americans. The metaphors and examples he would use on television to explain his programs to other people were the same ones he would use to come to an understanding of the issues himself. Jeane Kirkpatrick, when she first met Reagan, was struck by his manner and style, which she thought more appropriate to a private person than to a public one. "He doesn't," she said, "treat himself like a statue of himself."[9] It is a measure of Reagan's success as a politician that he recognized this quality in himself and sensed its power with other people.

The novice President knew more than the novice governor or the novice presidential campaigner had known. He had learned the hard way that it was crucial to select aides who were suited to his own personality and who were able to run his office without strain. Reagan saw himself as the chairman of the board of a great corporation, but he did not want to abdicate his authority again to a Phil Battaglia or a John Sears. With the experience gained through eight years as a chief executive of the nation's second-biggest government and sixty-two political campaigns, Reagan had come to recognize the limitations of those who had worked for him for a long time. The recognition posed a delicate problem. Though Reagan desired, even needed, to keep close to him the two loyal aides who had been prominently associated with his success, he did not want either of them as his chief of staff. Reagan held an abiding affection for Mike Deaver, but he realized that Deaver was an intensely private person who performed best in a behind-the-scenes troubleshooting role. Reagan valued Ed Meese's advice above all others, believing that Meese would see to it that conflicting points of view were presented to him without coloration. He had fired Sears, rather than get rid of Meese or demote him, and he had never regretted his decision. But Meese was not the man whom Reagan wanted as the chief executive officer of his corporation. Implicitly, he recognized a grain of truth to Sears' sarcastic criticisms of Meese's abilities as an administrator.* While still a candidate, Reagan realized that Meese was more useful to him as an adviser than he would ever be as the administrator of the White House.

Both Spencer, who wanted nothing but a triumphant return to his profitable consulting business in California, and Deaver, whose loyalty to the Reagans and understanding of them fitted him for an adjutant's role, encouraged Reagan in this view. Their preferred candidate for the top administrative post was James Baker, who had earned his spurs as the negotiator on the presidential debates. They talked it over with Nancy Reagan, who agreed with them. But Baker had been a member of the Reagan team for less than six months. Deaver, a Reagan man for nearly sixteen years, proposed to his boss that he make Baker, not Meese, the White House chief of staff. It was a bold suggestion. Baker had been President Ford's delegate hunter, successfully moving to hold wavering delegates in line against the maneuvering of John Sears. In 1980 Baker had worked again to defeat Reagan, managing the primary campaign of his principal opponent George Bush. While Baker had been careful not to divide the party by labeling Reagan an "extremist" or "warmonger," he had approved Bush's description of Reagan's economic proposals as "voodoo economics."† Many conservatives were understandably skeptical about Baker's loyalty to Reagan. And selecting a former opponent's principal strategist as one's own White House chief of staff was unheard of. Would Lyndon Johnson or Richard Nixon or Jimmy Carter have selected as a White House chief of staff the man who had managed the last two campaigns of their principal intra-party opponents? To ask the question is to answer it.

Reagan did not even raise a question about Baker's loyalty. He had been impressed with what he had seen during the campaign, and he did not bear political grudges from the past. The question which Reagan put to Deaver when he made his suggestion was the same one that he had asked of Sears when his then-campaign manager had proposed Richard Schweiker as his running mate in 1976. "Do you think he'd do it?" Reagan asked. Deaver, tipped by Spencer, assured Reagan that he would. On the day after his election, Reagan called Baker in his top floor room at the Century Plaza Hotel in Los Angeles and said, "I want to talk to you before you return to Texas." Baker's wife, Susan, who wanted her husband back after the long campaign and didn't want to lose him to the White House, cried when he told her of the call. "You know," she said, "If he wants to come down here to see you

---

* Sears made fun of what he called "Meese's Briefcase," into which speeches and briefing papers were supposed to disappear never to return. The criticism found its way into press accounts which persisted after Meese was in the White House, giving him a reputation as a disorganized man. Actually, Meese's problem was of a different order than the one described by Sears. Meese was well organized in most respects, but those who worked closely with him said he had difficulty in making decisions.

† After Baker joined the Reagan campaign, reporters on LeaderShip '80 who were inventing mythical book titles for the entourage determined that Baker had written a book called *Third Choice, The Only Campaign in Town.*

before you go back to Texas, it can only mean one thing. And that is that he wants you to be chief of staff in the White House."*[10]

Baker was not the only outsider. Though Reagan valued his loyal cadre of Californians and gave them important jobs on his staff and in his administration, he also brought in others whose first loyalties had been to Ford or Nixon or even suspect liberal Republicans like Elliot Richardson. Richard G. Darman, a Richardson man, became the White House funnel, determining the nature and quantity of briefing material that was passed on to Reagan. David R. Gergen, a veteran of the Nixon and Ford administrations, became a key Baker aide, later emerging as White House spokesman after the tragic wounding of Press Secretary James S. Brady in the March 30 assassination attempt. Brady himself had been a Connally man in the 1980 primaries. Most of his duties in the White House press office, although not his title, were taken over by Larry Speakes, a former aide to Mississippi Senator James Eastland and then to President Ford.

Reagan's most significant link with the Republican past was his selection of Haig, who had been at the center of power during Nixon's fall and had played a significant but shadowy role in that drama. In choosing the former North Atlantic Treaty Organization commander against the advice of his California inner circle, Reagan bypassed Bechtel executives Caspar W. Weinberger, who wanted the job, and George Shultz, veteran of the Nixon and Ford administrations. Reagan had been captivated by Haig in two long preelection discussions, though he did not then share Haig's belief in the necessity of closer ties with the People's Republic of China. It is possible that Reagan also was influenced by Nixon. A Reagan intimate told me late in 1980 that Nixon had spoken well of Haig in a telephone call and a letter to the President-elect. But the clincher came not from the former President but from Senator Robert Byrd of West Virginia, whom the election returns were about to make a former majority leader. When Byrd warned at a press conference that Haig faced confirmation difficulties because of his purported role in the Watergate coverup which led to Nixon's resignation, Reagan correctly interpreted this as an early test of his leadership. He talked to Howard H. Baker, Jr., who would be the new majority leader, and to his old friend, Paul Laxalt. Both GOP senators agreed that Reagan should not shrink from a confirmation test in the newly Republican Senate. Reagan recognized that if he backed down he would be perceived as a President who could easily be bluffed or threatened. "Haig is my choice," he told the Californians. Weinberger was given the important consolation prize of Secretary of Defense.

* Reagan, aware of Susan Baker's feelings, came over to her at the end of the press conference he held in the Century Plaza the day after his election. "Let me tell you something," he said to her, as Baker remembers it. "Your husband's not going to work fourteen hours a day in my White House. I just don't believe in that. I believe in my people spending time with their families." Baker subsequently worked a lot of fourteen-hour days, but his wife was impressed by Reagan's concern. "He won her over there and then," said Baker.

Reagan listened to different advisers in selecting the cabinet members who would become point men for his economics program. Ed Meese lunched with Donald T. Regan at the California Club in Washington and emerged bullish on the abilities of the chairman of the Merrill Lynch brokerage firm, saying afterward that Regan's economic ideas and optimistic outlook were nearly identical to Reagan's. The Regan choice was popular among the Kitchen Cabinet, which liked Regan's millionaire credentials and believed that his selection would help sell the President's program. But Reagan's choice of Michigan congressman David A. Stockman for the Office of Management and Budget was not favored by the Californians. Stockman was the recommendation of New York Representative Jack Kemp, the leading congressional advocate of supply-side economics. Kemp had no trouble convincing Reagan, who believed that Stockman had done much better against him in debate rehearsals than either John Anderson or Jimmy Carter had done in the actual debates. Late in November, Reagan called Stockman and said: "Dave, ever since you battered me in those mock debates I've been looking for some way to get even. Now I think I have the answer. I'm going to send you to OMB."[11]

Overall, the Reagan cabinet provided vital clues to the outlook, character and direction of the new administration. In keeping with Reagan's view of the cabinet as a board of directors, the President-elect had opted for a government that at its highest levels was long on managers and short on experts or ideologues. Even some of those who were experts, as Weinberger could be said to be in budget matters, were installed in posts where they possessed little technical expertise. This was not an accident. Reagan, and Meese under him, took the view in Washington, as they had in Sacramento, that expertise could be hired while management skill and common sense could not. To the dismay of the New Right, the pragmatism in personnel matters which Reagan had demonstrated in Sacramento reasserted itself once he won the election. Reagan is comfortable with self-made, wealthy men who believe that the business of America is business, but he usually has no fondness for zealots. The few genuine politicians in the Reagan administration with cabinet rank—Transportation Secretary Drew Lewis, Health and Human Services Secretary Richard Schweiker and U.S. Trade Representative William Brock—were all pragmatists. Nofziger, the most ideological of the old Reaganites, was isolated in the Executive Office Building in charge of the administration's political arm. He reported to Baker, whose judgment was more inclined to be based on practical political considerations than on ideology.

Overall, bomb-throwers were conspicuous by their absence in the Reagan cabinet. "For attorney general, the new President selected his closest personal and political confidante, a man with little or no courtroom experience," wrote political consultant Alan Baron. "For treasury secretary, he named a New York investment banker with a reputation as a political moderate. For defense secretary, the new President chose a businessman with experience in finance. And for commerce secretary, he selected a man from his vice-president's home region. The President was, of course, John F. Kennedy. . . . But it could also have been Ronald Reagan."*[12]

Like the cabinet team he had brought together in California, the one Reagan formed in the federal government was overwhelmingly white, male, middle class and middle-aged. United Nations Ambassador Kirkpatrick, whom Reagan had come to like and admire during the campaign, was the only woman and the only Democrat. Samuel T. Pierce, at Housing and Urban Development, was the only black. The attorney general was Reagan's crony and long-time personal attorney, William French Smith. Smith headed the original executive search team for Reagan after his election and, as one member of Reagan's transition group put it, "He scoured the country for talent and found himself." But Reagan embraced the appointment, trusting Smith as a safe and cautious lawyer who would not engage in legal activism. In Los Angeles Smith had been known as the political member of his prestigious law firm, building a reputation for accomplishing more outside the courtroom than he did in it. "William French Smith looks like an objet d'art that might be advertised in *The New Yorker* magazine, a sleek figurine called 'The Attorney,' manufactured by one of those companies that produce porcelain owls and bullfinches," columnist George Will wrote nearly a year after his appointment.[13] Counted on to make few waves, the cautious Smith rarely produced even a ripple during his first year at Justice. Unfortunately for Reagan, Smith's caution was not matched by political sensitivity. The attorney general supported an abortive effort to restore federal tax exemptions for racially segregated schools which proved a major embarrassment to the Reagan administration early in 1982.

Even more troublesome for Reagan were his second-choice appointments, which had likewise caused him problems in Sacramento. When Robert H. Finch had left the California lieutenant governorship to serve in the Nixon administration in January 1969, Reagan had wanted to make his executive secretary, William P. Clark, the new lieutenant governor. Clark, who felt himself better suited for the bench, turned him down. But several others who were prominent figures in Reagan's California administration—Weinberger, Tom Reed and Gordon Luce—as well as various legislators, were interested in the job. Reagan believed that the members of his administration who wanted to be lieutenant governor would be less disappointed if all of them were disappointed equally. He instructed Clark to find him an outsider, preferably from the House delegation, who would be compatible with the views of the administration.

Like Reagan, Clark knew little about the Republican members of Con-

* The cabinet officials referred to for Kennedy were Attorney General Robert Kennedy, Treasury Secretary Douglas Dillon, Defense Secretary Robert McNamara and Commerce Secretary Luther Hodges. Their respective counterparts in the Reagan administration were William French Smith, Regan, Weinberger and Malcolm Baldrige.

gress. He sent Deaver, then a junior aide, across the street to the California State Library to pore over congressional biographies. The most promising record was that of Glen Lipscomb, an able and popular Southern California congressman (since deceased) who wasn't interested. The next best bet seemed to be another Southern Californian, a forty-four-year-old sprinkler manufacturer and mechanical engineer named Ed Reinecke who recently had been elected to his third term in the House. Reagan astonished Reinecke by calling him up and offering him the lieutenant governorship, a job which Reinecke had never even considered. His relationship with Reagan, he said afterward, was limited "to a couple of cocktail parties."

The Reinecke appointment stands as a powerful indictment of the wisdom of appointment by resume. After he had traded the anonymity of the House for the spotlight of Sacramento, Reinecke proved a public relations disaster who was forever embarrassing himself and his administration with ill-considered statements. Unfortunately for Reinecke, the worst of these statements turned out to be under oath before a Senate committee investigating the lobbying role of International Telephone and Telegraph Corporation, where Reinecke's statements led to indictment and ultimate conviction for perjury.*

Reagan made two second-choice appointments to his original presidential cabinet. Neither turned out to be another Reinecke, but both, in different ways, proved sources of embarrassment and difficulty to the administration. James B. Edwards, the Secretary of Energy, had the dubious distinction of being Reagan's least qualified cabinet member and the one who most completely owed his appointment to the lowest common denominator of political considerations. Within the Reagan transition team it had been assumed that Michael Halbouty, a millionaire Houston geologist and oilman, would be awarded the energy secretaryship. Like William French Smith, Halbouty was in a position to influence the result, for he was the head of the energy section of the transition team. Halbouty, declining to run the gauntlet of the conflict-of-interest standards which would have required him to divest his holdings to take the position, bowed out. His departure coincided with a mini-revolt against Reagan's cabinet appointments by seven southern conservative senators led by Strom Thurmond of South Carolina. The senators believed that the South had been ignored. They thought cabinet selection was completed, but hoped to raise the Confederate flag in behalf of subcabinet appointments that were yet to be made. Paul Laxalt, however, had been tipped off about the withdrawal of Halbouty from consideration for the energy secretaryship. He called Reagan and said

---

* Reinecke received a suspended sentence and resigned from the lieutenant governorship on October 3, 1974. He was replaced for the brief balance of his term by John L. Harmer. On December 8, 1975, a federal appellate court reversed Reinecke's conviction on grounds that a quorum had not been present at the committee before which he testified.

that the Southerners were steaming about not having one of their own in the cabinet, and that an opportunity had arisen to give them more than they expected. Knowing that it would personally please Thurmond to have someone from his home state in the cabinet, Laxalt suggested Edwards, former South Carolina governor and congenial dentist, whose memorable observation after departing from public life to resume his profession was, "It's so satisfying to have my hands in the saliva again." Edwards knew nothing about energy, but that didn't bother the President-elect, who had promised during the campaign to abolish the department. Mollifying Thurmond with a cabinet post he regarded as worthless made good political sense to Reagan, who two days later, on December 17, 1980, appointed Edwards.

Laxalt also played the key role in Reagan's other "second-choice" appointment of James G. Watt to head the Department of the Interior. White House officials told me subsequently that Laxalt had been given veto power on this appointment, which was the most important cabinet post to a Nevadan.* Laxalt's first choice was Clifford Hansen, a dependable two-term senator from Wyoming who could have been expected to move deliberately, rather than precipitously, toward a policy of opening public lands to development. Given Reagan's and Laxalt's premises, Hansen was a safe choice. But Hansen, like Halbouty, didn't want to submit to financial disclosure requirements. For one thing, he would have had to appraise his family ranch at Jackson Hole at its "highest and best use," which meant housing subdivisions. For another, Hansen owned grazing leases in Grand Teton National Park in the names of his wife and daughter. These leases had been "grandfathered" in when the park was expanded to include this land, but Hansen had been harassed about them when he was a senator and expected even more criticism if he became Interior Secretary. Hansen turned down the job.

Representative John Rhodes of Arizona, the long-time House minority leader, also wanted to be Secretary of Interior and had talked to law school classmate Weinberger about it. However, Rhodes was unacceptable to Laxalt. After the Republican national convention in 1980, Rhodes and Senator Howard Baker had called upon Laxalt in his Senate office. Their mission was to tell Laxalt to lay off Republican National Chairman Bill Brock, whom the Nevada senator was still trying to get rid of even after Reagan had decided to keep him. Rhodes praised Brock, and in blunt, five-letter language, told him that further sniping at the chairman would undermine Republican efforts to gain control of Congress. Brock stayed, but Laxalt did not forget the visit. Instead of giving the nod to Rhodes, the Nevada senator turned to Watt, a forty-three-year-old Denver attorney who had become a hero of the Sagebrush Rebellion for his courtroom battles against the federal

---

* Nevada is the birthplace of the "Sagebrush Rebellion," an attempt to force the federal government to turn over vast amounts of western lands—other than those used for park and defense purposes or reserved for Indians—to state jurisdiction. Eighty-seven percent of the land in Nevada, most of it desert, is owned by the federal government.

government in behalf of the Mountain States Legal Foundation. Patterned in form after the legal advocacy groups pioneered by Ralph Nader, Mountain States had an opposite perspective. Its premise was that the public interest could be equated with a successful and thriving system of private enterprise. Watt wore a $29 digital watch set to Mountain time, which he touched frequently to remind him of his origins and obligations to the West. His critics would come to believe that Watt's inner clock was set considerably further back, to a time in the previous century when the federal government had viewed its reponsibility as developing the land rather than protecting it.

Reagan's most stunning appointment looked not to the past but to the future. On July 7 he nominated Sandra Day O'Connor, a fifty-one-year-old judge on the Arizona State Court of Appeals, to become the first woman justice in the 191-year history of the Supreme Court. Reagan called her "a person for all seasons," and made the appointment with full understanding of both its political and historical significance. At the time Reagan's own record in appointing women to high office was undistinguished. In 1981 only 11 percent of his top executive appointments were women, and only one woman served in the cabinet. Reagan had drawn steady fire from feminist groups for his support of the Human Life Amendment and opposition to the Equal Rights Amendment. Though he had promised on October 14, 1980, to name a woman to "one of the first Supreme Court vacancies in my administration," both the wording and timing of this commitment were suspect. The idea had originated as a political proposal in a discussion with Stu Spencer during a low point in the Reagan campaign. Its timing reflected the obstacles Reagan then faced with women voters both on the peace issue and ERA. The political nature of the promise was underscored by Reagan's record as governor of California, where all three of his appointments to the state Supreme Court had been male.

But Reagan takes campaign promises seriously, for whatever reasons they are made. He would demonstrate this by lifting the grain embargo, by persisting in both tax cuts and defense budget increases in the face of growing deficits and by insisting on creating a cabinet style of government. Deputy Secretary of State William P. Clark, whom Reagan had appointed to the California Supreme Court, discussed the issue with him and came away convinced that Reagan believed "a sense of justice"[14] demanded a woman on the high court. All the political logic pointed to the same conclusion. Reagan was aware that his predecessor, in four years, had not been given the opportunity to make a single appointment to the Supreme Court. So Reagan treated his "one of the first" pledge as if he had promised to name a woman to *the* first vacancy. "I think he liked the idea of being the first President to do it," said Mike Deaver afterwards. "And he also realized that pressure would mount on the second vacancy and that he would get no credit for naming a woman then."[15]

The O'Connor appointment was assisted by the luxury of time and reflection. Sometime in February, Justice Potter Stewart told his old friend George Bush that he intended to leave the court at the end of its 1980 term. White House officials were told that Stewart also had remarked, in passing, that other justices thinking of retirement would be watching to see what kind of appointment the new President made. This was an apparent reference to the two aging liberals on the court, Wiliam Brennan and Thurgood Marshall. The Vice-President passed the information on to Meese. On April 21, while Reagan was recovering from wounds suffered in the March 30 assassination attempt, he was told about Stewart's plans by Attorney General Smith, Meese and Deaver. Reagan's immediate response was to remind them of his campaign promise. "He was saying, in effect, to find a woman who was qualified and come back and discuss it if that wasn't possible," said Deaver.[16] Smith, entrusted with the talent search, understood what Reagan wanted. His first laundry list of a score of candidates, handed to Reagan on June 23, included a dozen women. At this meeting Reagan again reiterated his interest in naming a woman to the court. Smith narrowed the list to four persons—all women.

O'Connor was the clear choice, for a number of reasons. Reagan wanted a Justice who was young enough to serve many years on the court. She was the right age, from the right region, and with the right sponsors in the persons of two former Stanford Law School classmates, Justice William Rehnquist and William Baxter, who headed the Justice Department's antitrust division. Senator Barry Goldwater was an ardent O'Connor fan, and his support brought Paul Laxalt on the O'Connor team. And the Arizona political establishment of both parties was solidly behind O'Connor, who as a member of the state Senate had been the first woman to serve as majority leader in a state legislature. Alone among the women on the final list, O'Connor had political experience.* Democrats and Republicans alike considered her a fair-minded, conciliatory legislator of moderately conservative views. She had a reputation as a meticulous and conscientious judge. "The appointment of O'Connor is a master stroke. . . ." wrote liberal Democratic congressman Morris Udall in the *Washington Post*. "It shows a flexibility, a bigness that the Ronald Reagan stereotype doesn't recognize. It shows a political savvy on the part of the President that I had assumed was not there."[17]

On June 27 Smith sent two aides to Phoenix to interview O'Connor. Two days later he met with her himself at the L'Enfant Plaza Hotel situated midway between the White House and Capitol Hill. Meese, Deaver and Baker interviewed her there, too. On July 1, Clark took time off from his State Department duties for an extended personal discussion with the prospective

---

* The others on the list of four, in addition to O'Connor, were Cornelia Kennedy of Michigan, a judge on the Sixth U.S. Circuit Court of Appeals; Mary Coleman, chief justice of the Michigan Supreme Court; and Amalya L. Kearse, of New York, a judge on New York's Second Circuit Court of Appeals. Kearse is black and was, at 44, the only person on the list younger than O'Connor.

justice. O'Connor told Clark of the time she had sentenced a convicted killer to death, and her feelings about it. It had not been easy for her, though she believed in the principle of the death penalty. Clark, who once had the same experience and held the same view about capital punishment, also had a painful memory of the actual moment of the sentencing. As it turned out, neither condemned man was executed, but the memories of the cases lingered in the minds of the judges. It gave them a common bond. The same day O'Connor went to the White House for a forty-five-minute meeting with Reagan. They broke the ice by talking about their mutual love of horseback riding, but the discussion soon turned to the serious issues of judicial activism and abortion. Deaver, present at the meeting, was struck by how much Reagan and O'Connor liked each other. "He was charmed by her," recalls Deaver. "After talking with her he was convinced he had the right person for the job."[18]

Reagan never interviewed anyone else. He proudly announced the O'Connor appointment six days later, provoking a storm of denunciation from New Right leaders like fund-raiser Richard Viguerie and Moral Majority president Jerry Falwell. The counterattack was viewed by prominent White House aides, none of them New Rightists, as a blessing in disguise. These aides resented and disbelieved the New Right's claim that it had been responsible for Reagan's victory. Wirthlin's polls also disputed this contention. But the coalition of militant conservative organizations, antiabortion groups and politically active religious fundamentalists loosely grouped under the New Right label had been successful in creating a widespread public impression that they were the basic component of Reagan's support. Their ill-timed opposition to the O'Connor appointment isolated the New Rightists and demonstrated that their political clout was far less than they had claimed. When Falwell said that all "good Christians" should be concerned about the O'Connor appointment, Senator Goldwater replied succinctly: "Every good Christian ought to kick Falwell right in the ass." The objections from the right centered on O'Connor's votes in the Arizona legislature, especially her cosponsorship of a bill which made "all medically acceptable family-planning methods and information" available to anyone who wanted it. The National Right to Life Committee equated this vote with support of abortion and urged O'Connor's rejection. The committee pointed to a plank in the 1980 Republican platform calling for appointment of judges "who respect traditional family values and the sanctity of innocent human life." But O'Connor had assured Reagan in their meeting that she was personally opposed to abortion, and that was good enough for him. O'Connor's opponents were unable to find even a single senator willing to stand up against her.

On the O'Connor appointment, more than any other, the antiabortion fervor of the New Right shattered against traditional values of the old right, whose adherents had been complaining for decades that the Supreme Court had been making new law rather than interpreting the laws passed by Congress. In its insistence that judges commit themselves in advance to oppose abortion, the New Right actually was urging judicial activism in behalf of its own causes rather than the judicial restraint which most conservatives desired from the high court. Reagan realized this. He said again and again in his discussions with Smith and Meese and Clark, and also in the statements he allowed his spokesmen to make to the press, that he wanted justices who "would interpret the laws, not make them" and that he would not use a single issue as "a litmus test" for appointment. Without this latter standard he would have been hard put to carry out his campaign promise, for virtually no woman jurist agreed with Falwell and Viguerie on the abortion issue.

Like his first political idol, Franklin Roosevelt, Reagan had proved a master in using the militant fringe of his party when it served his purpose and isolating it when it did not. He had cheerfully accepted support from the New Right during the campaign, though carefully dissociating himself from any manifestations of anti-Semitism or racism. As President, Reagan was careful to extend the appropriate symbolism to the antiabortionists. During his first week in the White House he granted the March for Life the distinction of being the first nongovernmental group to receive a presidential audience, and his aides saw to it that this ceremonial meeting was well photographed and widely announced to the press. The right-to-lifers were ecstatic. Even while this was happening, however, a White House aide who had no use for the prolife militants warned me not to make judgments until I saw what the Moral Majority and its allies were actually given by the administration. "What do you want to give them?" I asked. "Symbolism," he replied. He then offered an analogy drawn from the popular film, *The Godfather,* in which the criminal leader advises, "Hold your friends close, hold your enemies closer." That, the aide said, was the tactic which the administration would follow with its friends on the fringes of the right. "We want to keep the Moral Majority types so close to us they can't move their arms," he concluded.

This technique worked better at the higher rungs of the administration than at the middle and lower ones. Meese, despite the hard line he takes on criminal justice matters, is not an ideologue, and neither is E. Pendleton James, the old school classmate Meese brought in to run the White House personnel office. James' assistant during two vital transition months was the even less ideological and more experienced James Cavanaugh, who had served competently in the Nixon and Ford administrations. Both James and Cavanaugh were loyal Republicans, but they were more interested in the abilities of a prospective appointee than the number of days he had toiled in the political vineyards for Reagan. Before long, Reagan conservatives were complaining that they had been frozen out of jobs in favor of technocrats and careerists who had no commitment to Reagan. Their case was summed up in an "open letter" by John Lofton in the February 1981 *Conservative*

Digest. "Dear Mr. President," it began. "Your mandate for change is being subverted. The very real possibility that this catastrophe could occur is the result of your personnel operation being run by individuals who are politically naive, and, worse still, individuals whose backgrounds reveal a hostility to almost everything for which you have so strongly stood over the years." This was a well-conceived overstatement which helped to mobilize conservative forces. Others made the same point. In the Senate, Jesse Helms of North Carolina, the ambitious self-appointed guardian of conservative political purity, succeeded for months in holding up some of Haig's key State Department appointments. Within the administration, Nofziger took up the ideological cudgel. He had not landed the prestigious White House job he wanted, but Nofziger's political operation did have a checkoff on most prospective appointments. Though Nofziger lasted in the administration for only a year before leaving to go into business for himself, he was instrumental in blocking some pragmatic appointments and in pushing some ideological ones. He made no secret that at all times he valued loyalty to Reagan over the competence of a prospective appointee.* And he was given his due by Viguerie, who said: "Lyn manned the barricades and did the work of the Lord."[19]

The ideological and political pressure for loyalist appointments, joined by some Republican state chairmen and conservative members of Congress, gradually had an impact, especially during a period in mid-1981 when the politically sensitive John Herrington became James' deputy and de facto personnel chief. The result was an anomaly. At the top the Reagan administration installed a pragmatist like Weinberger as Secretary of Defense and under him a deputy, Frank Carlucci, who had served John F. Kennedy and Jimmy Carter as skillfully and unideologically as he now represented Reagan. But in the middle ranges of the administration ideology frequently prevailed. Directing the Office of Personnel Management, for instance, was Donald J. Devine, an ardently right-wing professor from the University of Maryland and a long-time supporter of antiabortion causes. When Devine was trying to find ways to save money on federal health insurance coverage, he opted for a solution which fit his political preconceptions: Abolish coverage for women who had abortions. The government employees' union promptly filed suit against this congressionally unauthorized action, and the decision was set aside, at least temporarily. But the incident demonstrated that an ideological change had, in fact, occurred in the federal government

---

* Nofziger claimed to have these six criteria for prospective appointees to the Reagan administration:
   "1. Are you a Carter appointee? If so, you're rejected.
   "2. Are you a Democrat who didn't work for Ronald Reagan? If so, you're rejected.
   "3. Are you a Republican? Are you the best Republican for the job?
   "4. Are you a Ronald Reagan–George Bush supporter?
   "5. Did you work in the campaign?
   "6. Are you the best qualified person for the job? But that's only No. 6."

because of Reagan's election, even though the change would never be as sweeping as the right-wingers would have liked to make it.

Most of the time, Reagan kept himself securely removed from the appointments struggles.* Once, in a story frequently retold by James, Reagan actually questioned the political loyalty of a Carter holdover and insisted that the job be given to a Reaganite. But this was an exception. Reagan believed that he had "a mandate for change," but he did not interpret this mandate as a requirement to demand an ideological catechism of prospective appointees. He eschewed a single-issue litmus test not only for O'Connor but for most of his other appointments. Nor did he demand this kind of loyalty from his closest subordinates, most of whom knew they could freely disagree with the President on an issue without prejudicing themselves. Usually, Reagan had little comment on the recommendations brought in to him by James. The President knew that his personnel chief had reviewed them beforehand with the dominant staff trio of Meese, Baker and Deaver, and he had confidence in their judgments. Reagan took pride in being a delegator, and he rarely second-guessed those he had entrusted with responsibility.

Nor was Reagan afflicted with a New Right fantasy of fighting a six-front war in behalf of social change. On March 26, Howard Baker said he had an agreement in the Senate to keep controversial "social issues"—including abortion—off the Senate floor for a year. Helms disputed Baker, but the President, in an interview the following day with the *Washington Post,* sided with the Senate majority leader. "I can't quarrel with that," Reagan said. "Right now, we're concentrating on this [economic] package, and I don't think Congress in my memory has ever been faced with anything in quite the dimensions of this. This doesn't mean that we've drawn back from our position on many of these social goals. It just means that these are things that we think must wait. . . ."[20]

Reagan's preoccupation, to the exclusion of everything else during the first year of his presidency, remained the same as it had been in California: reducing the size and growth of government. However, the novice President approached matters differently than the novice governor had done. Governor Reagan's first economies had been symbolic ones that were withdrawn soon after they were offered. He had distrusted the legislators, whom he believed preoccupied with perquisites, reelection and business as usual. President Reagan saved his "citizen-politician" rhetoric for the country and cul-

---

* Reagan did, however, express growing annoyance at the length of time it took the White House Personnel Office to fill vacant jobs. The delays reflected a number of factors: Lengthened conflict-of-interest checks, slower clearances by the FBI, and an overly complex political clearance procedure. But there were also many in the White House, led by Chief of Staff James Baker, who felt that the personnel office under James was poorly organized and badly run. Reagan said in a March 27, 1981, interview with the *Washington Post* that "slowness in filling appointments" was the greatest disappointment of his first two months in office.

tivated opposition congressmen. Before he took office he told Deaver that he could work with Congress, despite the conventional wisdom that the Democratic-controlled House was unwilling to cut the budget and reduce taxes. Reagan was still willing to use his old confrontational style with the legislative branch when the political occasion demanded. But he would not repeat the mistake he had made in Sacramento of speaking solely to the electorate while leaving the legislative branch of government to fend for itself.

Some things had not changed. In his self-written inaugural speech as governor on January 6, 1967, Reagan had taken issue with the idea that government was too complex to be understood by ordinary people and that an elite group was needed to do the governing. He used almost identical words on January 20, 1981, in his presidential inaugural, saying: "From time to time, we have been tempted to believe that society has become too complex to be managed by self-rule, that government by an elite group is superior to government for, by and of the people. But if no one among us is capable of governing himself, then who among us has the capacity to govern someone else?" This was an elongated version of Reagan's favorite California bromide that "there are simple answers, just not easy ones." Reagan viewed the government of which he had been elected chief executive as an overweight adversary that had to be starved and exercised down to size. "It will be my intention to curb the size and influence of the federal establishment and to demand recognition of the distinction between the powers granted to the federal government and those reserved to the states or to the people," Reagan said in his inaugural. "All of us need to be reminded that the federal government did not create the states; the states created the federal government."

Reagan did not recognize the enormity of the task he had set for himself, and no one told him. He had been raised to believe that Americans could accomplish anything they set their minds to, and he believed that the ills which beset the nation could be corrected by an act of will. Reagan is a modest man, but he did not object to the frequent descriptions of him as "the Great Communicator." He approvingly cited Theodore Roosevelt's description of the presidency as "a bully pulpit." With the forum of national television available to the President, Reagan was certain that his own communicative skills were sufficient to persuade Congress and the country to do whatever it was that was asked of them. It did not seem to have occurred to him that Congress in 1981 would do everything he asked, and more, and that this would not be close to doing enough for the nation.

All of Reagan's development as a politician had left unchanged the basic, optimistic simplicity that was the source of his appeal—and that would also prove the source of his administration's most glaring inadequacies. Everything was so simple. Reagan genuinely believed in the easy reassurances of reform without sacrifice he offered to the American people and to the congressmen and to other visitors who trooped through the Oval Office. He thought that most of the nation's problems derived, as he had declared in his inaugural, "from unnecessary and excessive growth of government." President Reagan would display great political skill in his efforts to limit this growth, but the complexity of the task would continue to elude him. Though economic hardships eventually would force him to concede that he had underestimated the difficulty of redirecting a welfare state that had been a half-century in the making, Reagan would continue to believe that most of what he desired to do could be accomplished by an essential act of faith. "What I'd really like to do is go down in history as the President who made Americans believe in themselves again,"[21] Reagan said six months into his presidency. For a man who had always believed in himself, this did not seem an impossible achievement. But nothing would prove as simple as this natural, underburdened President thought that it would be.

President Carter shows President-elect Reagan the White House grounds, November 20, 1980. (© Frank Johnston for the *Washington Post*)

Chief Justice Warren Burger administers oath of office to President Reagan, January 20, 1981. (*White House photo by Bill Fitz-Patrick*)

A tender moment on inaugural day, January 20, 1981. (*White House photo by Michael Evans*)

Reagan phoning congressmen before crucial vote on the tax bill, July 24, 1981. (*White House photo by Bill Fitz-Patrick*)

With Gerald Ford on August 5, 1981. (*White House photo by Jack Kightlinger*)

Jelly-bean time with Richard V. Allen, then the National Security Adviser, and Secretary of State Alexander M. Haig, Jr., on January 26, 1981. (*White House photo by Karl Schumacher*)

With Budget Director David Stockman during the administration's honeymoon, January 30, 1981. (*White House photo by Bill Fitz-Patrick*)

THE WHITE HOUSE
WASHINGTON

Reagan has been an inveterate doodler since boyhood. These sketches were made by the President in a cabinet meeting in March 1981 and autographed by him for the author. The football player at lower right is a recurrent subject of Reagan's doodles, as are cowboys.

Above, Reagan and Supreme Court appointee Sandra O'Connor, July 15, 1981. (*White House photo by Michael Evans*)

Left, Reagan marks his recovery from assassination attempt with a speech to joint session of Congress on April 28, 1981. Vice-President Bush and House Speaker Thomas P. (Tip) O'Neill lead the applause. (*White House photo by Cynthia Johnson*)

Reagan's White House Trio—Michael Deaver, James Baker and Edwin Meese—at the height of their power on April 24, 1981. (*White House photo by Michael Evans*)

Left, Reagan with a favorite horse, August 27, 1981. (*White House photo by Michael Evans*)

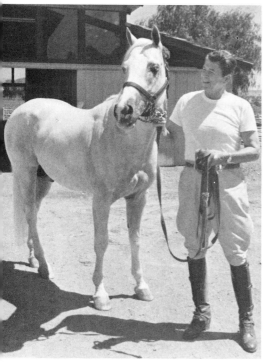

Right, President Reagan passes salad at a working cabinet luncheon with James Watt (far left) and Bill Clark, May 14, 1981. (Washington Post *photo by Frank Johnston*)

George Bush, President Reagan, Secretary of State Haig and White House Counsellor Ed Meese share a laugh during Reagan's first year in office. (Washington Post *photo by Frank Johnston*)

Lou Cannon with President Reagan after the economic summit in Ottawa, Canada, July 22, 1981. The inscription beneath the photo reads "Dear Lou, Are you asking the question or am I? Warm regards, Ron." (*White House photo*)

Dear Lou — Are you asking the question or am I? Warm Regards Ron

Reagan confers with Secretary of Defense Caspar Weinberger in White House on July 18, 1981, at a time when administration faced key decisions on strategic weaponry. (*White House photo by Jack Kightlinger*)

Reagan in working clothes chats with Vice-President Bush, who has just returned from an overseas trip and is stopping off at Rancho del Cielo, July 27, 1981. (*White House photo by Bill Fitz-Patrick*)

20

The Reagan Re-Direction

Its propagandists called it "The Reagan Revolution." Its adversaries, with equal hyperbole, described it as an attempt to repeal the New Deal. Friend and foe alike ultimately settled on "Reaganomics," a nonword which embraced President Reagan's simultaneous attempts to balance the federal budget, increase defense spending, and slash income taxes. Unlike the policies which preceded it, Reaganomics was intended to avoid the hard choices of inflation vs. unemployment. As Reagan saw it, growth of the bloated federal budget would be restrained by targeting "waste, fraud and abuse" and by systematic cutbacks in a wide array of social programs. Only defense, where Reagan wanted to close a "window of vulnerability" he said the Soviets had opened in the arms race, would be sacrosanct. Reagan had convinced himself that the federal deficit could be reduced even while arms spending was increasing. He believed that financial markets would respond to the prospect of lower deficits, and that interest rates would drop as inflation moderated. At the same time, his promised 30 percent personal income tax cut over three years plus special depreciation allowances for business were supposed to trigger a major economic expansion, providing more revenue for the Treasury at lower tax rates and easing unemployment.

"We don't have to choose between inflation and unemployment—they go hand in hand," Reagan said February 5, 1981, in the first televised appeal for his economic program. "It's time to try something different." And try Reagan did. In the months which followed he melded his communicative skills with the budget wizardry of OMB Director David A. Stockman and skillful congressional leadership to divide the Democratic majority in the House and win approval of $35 billion in budget cuts. The administration followed up this triumph by pushing through the largest federal tax reduction in history. "Boll weevil" Democrats like Phil Gramm of Texas became so ecstatic that they claimed Reaganomics had revived not only the American economy but "the American dream."[1] The leading Reaganomician was even more enthusiastic. On July 29, after both houses of Congress had approved his tax program, the President declared that the event would "mark the beginning of a new renaissance in America." Instead, the stock market went into a slide. Five months later the renaissance culminated in recession and Reagan's reluctant admission that the budget was unlikely to be balanced during his administration. Even this acknowledgment did not shake the President's faith in the potential efficacy of Reaganomics. "My program hasn't had a chance to work yet," Reagan told his inner circle on December 4, 1981, after he received forecasts projecting a budget deficit of $109 billion for fiscal 1982 and a $162 billion deficit by 1984, the year the budget was supposed to be balanced. Reagan ignored a warning from Stockman that the deficit was likely to become unmanageable. He brushed aside another warning, this one from White House Chief of Staff James Baker, that mounting unemployment spelled trouble for Republican congressional candidates in 1982. Repeatedly, Reagan assured the inner circle that the tax cuts Congress had enacted would spur business recovery and cause an economic turnaround. Stockman, spared from dismissal after his comments in the December 1981 issue of *Atlantic** revealed the shaky theoretical basis of Reaganomics, tried to persuade the President that he should modify his economic program in order to save it. Reagan listened, but his optimistic nature prevailed over the advice of his aides. "Life is just one grand sweet song, so start the music," Reagan had written as a high school senior in 1928, the year before the great stock market crash. More than half a century later, this pervasive optimism was driving the economic decisions of his administration.

Reaganomics was not born in a classroom. It did not spring full-blown like Athena from the fertile brows of economist Arthur Laffer and writer Jude Wanniski, though it owed much to these high priests of supply-side economics.† It was not the result of Stockman's biting critique of federal handouts, though Reagan owed even more to his budget director than he did to Laffer and Wanniski. Like most Reagan proposals, the President's economic program was a distinctive product of a personal and political evo-

* The article, "The Education of David Stockman," was written by William Greider, an assistant managing editor and columnist for the *Washington Post.* It was based on a long series of Saturday morning taped conversations between Greider and Stockman, who were personal friends.

† Supply-side economics was the creation of a Canadian economist, Robert Mundell, and Laffer, who taught at the University of Southern California. Both favored the gold standard and argued that tax reduction was necessary to stimulate the economy. Their ideas were popularized by Wanniski, who in the mid-1970s was an editorial writer for the *Wall Street Journal.* They contended that reduction of taxes would prompt business expansion and produce an additional supply of goods, hence "supply-side." The word was coined by Herbert Stein, chairman of the Council of Economic Advisers in the Nixon and Ford administrations, who considered the idea ludicrous. But Wanniski liked the term Stein derisively applied to the movement and adopted it as his own.

lution which blended various ideas and dogmas. And like many other of his advocacies, Reaganomics was forged in a political crucible, in this case the 1980 presidential campaign. While its claims were conflicting and its figures never susceptible to normal arithmetic, it was a thoroughly appropriate advocacy for Reagan, the onetime optimistic New Dealer who had become the most optimistic of conservative Presidents. Reagan believed, as his first political hero Franklin Roosevelt had said in his inaugural address, that "the only thing we have to fear is fear itself—nameless, unreasoning, unjustified terror which paralyzes needed efforts to convert retreat into advance." Counsellor Edwin Meese, faithfully echoing Reagan's views, contended that improvement of economic conditions was "50 percent psychological." Others in the Reagan entourage were infected, like Meese, by the contagious optimism of their leader. Seen in this light Reaganomics was less a program than a joyous secular theology not susceptible to examination by statistical data. Reagan believed in Reaganomics and was confident that his untried combination of programs would lead to a new prosperity. The Reagan inner circle believed in Reagan. And the others, whether believers or not, went along.

Reagan had used his inaugural message as an opportunity to express another faith—his belief in the enduring value of American heroism. His own blend of presidential heroes was even more an unusual combination than his economic program. Along with Franklin Roosevelt, he celebrated Calvin Coolidge, whose picture replaced Harry Truman's in the Cabinet Room. Coolidge had been elected President of the United States in 1924, the year that Reagan entered high school in Dixon. He had become the chief executive the year before upon the death of Warren Harding, inheriting with the presidency a cabinet that included Andrew Mellon, a millionaire banker celebrated by his admirers as "the greatest secretary of the treasury since Alexander Hamilton."[2] Mellon remained Secretary of the Treasury after Coolidge's election and, with the President's endorsement, convinced Congress to lower the marginal tax rate (the rate at which the last dollar of income is taxed) from 58 to 25 percent. It was Mellon's theory that this reduction of taxation would spur even greater business activity, and so it did. But that activity ground to a halt in the crushing Depression which came five years later, when Herbert Hoover was in the White House.

In 1930, the year that Reagan was a sophomore at Eureka College with a major in economics and sociology, Congress passed the Hawley-Smoot Tariff Act, imposing the highest duties that the United States had ever enacted on goods imported from other nations. These high tariffs provoked protectionist retaliation from other nations, impeding the normal flow of international commerce and contributing to the worldwide Depression. They remained in place until the Democratic-controlled Congress in 1934 gave President Roosevelt unprecedented authority to reduce, reciprocally, tariffs with other nations.* Reagan, then a dedicated New Dealer, accepted the explanation that high tariffs were a contributing factor to the Depression. It is a view which survived unchanged throughout Reagan's political evolution from liberal Democrat to conservative Republican. Discussing high tariffs in an interview in 1968, he compared them to "high taxes," and said they both discouraged business activity and competition.[4] In Reagan's view, high tariffs and high taxes alike were the impositions of an overly strong and centralized federal government that was unwilling to trust the forces of the marketplace. He described himself in this interview as a lifelong "free trader."[5] Indeed, as President, Reagan has remained so committed to free trade that limitations on Japanese auto imports had to be presented to him as "voluntary restraints" to make them politically palatable. Reagan was no economist, despite his degree from Eureka. He plucked seminal ideas out of his education and experience and, like all of us, embedded them in his world view. That view, even when he was a New Dealer, had been antitariff and antitax. As he evolved into a conservative Republican, he became distinctly probusiness as well. And it was this combination of ideas—the desirability of low rates of taxation and tariffs and the resolute belief in the magic of the marketplace—that was to make Reagan easy prey for the doctrine which came to be known as "supply-side economics."

Reagan's own business experience had made him a burning advocate of income tax reduction. He became a wealthy man in the period after World War II, when marginal tax rates ranged between 82 and 91 percent. As a liberal Democrat, Reagan advocated a "depreciation allowance" on the earnings of actors and athletes, whose periods of productivity Reagan compared unfavorably to the productive period of an oil well. Though Reagan raised income taxes as governor of California and left the state tax system more progressive than he found it, he was able to rationalize his actions as a necessary consequence of an inherited deficit. Reagan's early record as governor was that of a "high taxer," but in outlook he remained committed to the principle of lowering the tax burdens on American individuals and corporations. This commitment was demonstrated by Reagan's 1971 tax-limitation initiative. Though it was rejected by the voters, it established Reagan's credentials as a genuine advocate of tax reduction.

The other principal elements of Reaganomics also have deep political roots. Except for his brief period of youthful pacifism at Eureka, Reagan always has supported a strong military establishment. He held this view as a

* The Reciprocal Trade Agreements Act, the brainchild of Roosevelt's Secretary of State, Cordell Hull, marked the major turn of the United States away from protectionism. It passed both houses of Congress on intensely partisan votes and was denounced by Republican Senator Arthur F. Vandenberg of Michigan as "Fascist in its philosophy, Fascist in its objective." The legislation gave the President authority to enter into commercial agreements with foreign nations, and to lower or raise tariffs by up to 50 percent. "The new bill obviously contemplated a revolution in tariff-making," wrote historian Arthur M. Schlesinger, Jr. "By eliminating the fine old congressional sport of logrolling, it diminished the power of Congress as well as of the lobbyists from protected industries."[3]

liberal Democrat in the late thirties and early forties when Germany and Japan were the U.S. adversaries. Long before he converted to Republicanism, he was warning of the growing military power of the Soviet Union. After a speech to the Chicago Council on Foreign Relations on March 17, 1980, in which he outlined his foreign policy, he said that "in national defense you have to spend whatever is necessary to deter the enemy." He left no doubt that if he had to choose between a balanced budget and a defense he considered sufficient, he would opt for the latter.

Curiously, the element of Reaganomics which the President most readily abandoned—the goal of a balanced budget—was the issue on which he had the best record. The California constitution requires budgets to be balanced. As governor, Reagan freely exercised his line-item veto authority to achieve this result. And he achieved more than the constitution required. While failing in his effort to hold down the rate of increase in state taxes, he succeeded in braking the growth of the state work force. Duplicating this success in Washington was another matter. Despite all his rhetoric about the built-in, escalating costs of government, Reagan failed to recognize the dimensions of that growth. In the early months of his administration he spoke hopefully of achieving his objectives by the elimination of "waste, fraud and abuse," talking about the issue as if it were a separate identifiable budget item. Not until September of 1981 did it become clear even to the optimistic President that his hard-won spending cuts had barely made a dent in the growing federal deficit.

During the 1980 presidential campaign Reagan promised, as Roosevelt had in 1932,* to reduce the level of government spending. Reagan hardly could have pledged otherwise since for years he had been saying that "government spending more than government takes in" was the sole cause of inflation. But Reagan promised more—a balanced budget at least by 1984 even though his administration was cutting federal personal and corporate tax rates by 10 percent a year over a three-year period. The emphasis on the conflicting elements of Reaganomics bounced back and forth, as dictated by political strategy or the changes in Reagan's staff or even the candidate's feel for a particular audience. Reagan emphasized the budget-cutting side of his program before Republican groups, some of whom were aware of George Bush's description of the Reagan plan as "voodoo economics."[7] He stressed tax reduction before blue-collar groups, who wanted to hear how Reagan intended to combat recession and unemployment. But it was not a hard-and-fast division. There were few purists in the Reagan entourage, and even

---

* Roosevelt promised, during a speech in Pittsburgh in the 1932 campaign, to reduce government spending by 25 percent, an act which Rexford Tugwell, a prominent member of his "Brain Trust," afterward called "a piece of unforgivable folly."[6] On September 9, 1980, in the principal economics speech of his campaign, Reagan formulated a goal of reducing government spending levels gradually, starting with 2 percent in fiscal 1981 and extending to 7 percent in fiscal 1985. "Actually, I believe we can do even better," Reagan said in a television speech on October 24. "My goal will be spending reductions of 10 percent by fiscal year 1984."

fewer economists. One of the latter was pollster Richard Wirthlin, a Ph.D. in economics from the University of California. In the campaign, however, Wirthlin's strategic advice was guided not by his economics degree but by extensive survey data which showed public skepticism about federal tax reduction. Wirthlin's polls told him that a significant number of voters doubted any candidate's ability to cut the budget, raise defense spending and reduce taxes simultaneously. Republican voters found John B. Anderson too liberal for their tastes. However, a significant number of Republicans who weren't inclined to vote for Anderson accepted his description of the way Reagan could accomplish his multiple promises. "It's very simple," Anderson said. "You do it with mirrors."[8]

Wirthlin's pragmatism was shared by Reagan's political circle, led by Stuart Spencer, and by his old California aides, led by Meese. These advisers were largely uninterested in economic policy beyond the requirements of the campaign. To a large measure, Wirthlin's skepticism about tax reduction also was shared by Reagan's campaign research director, Martin Anderson, a traditional economist and disciple of Arthur F. Burns, the economic adviser to Presidents Eisenhower and Nixon and later the chairman of the Federal Reserve Board. Both Anderson and his friend and ally, Alan Greenspan, doubted that a huge tax cut would generate unprecedented business expansion. They were concerned that a large tax cut would produce a large federal budget deficit.* At the same time, Anderson recognized that Reagan was committed to tax reduction and intended to carry out his campaign promises. Though Anderson was a useful brake on the excessive claims of the supply-siders, he did not try to turn Reagan around.

Representative Jack Kemp of New York was the countervailing force, even though his direct influence within the Reagan campaign was sharply diminished by the firing of John Sears. While still a professional football quarterback for the Buffalo Bills in 1967, Kemp had worked as a summer intern for the Reagan administration. Reagan was then a novice learning the ropes of government, but he was also an ardent professional football fan who admired athletes. He liked Kemp. The New Yorker was unpopular

---

* This concern was reflected in Reagan's major economics speech of the campaign, which was largely drafted by Greenspan. Addressing the International Business Council in Chicago on September 9, Reagan continued to favor a tax cut but introduced an uncharacteristic note of caution. "I am asked, can we do it immediately?" Reagan said. "My answer is no. It took Mr. Carter three and a half years of hard work to get us into this economic mess. It will take time to get out." A fact sheet handed out with the speech anticipated a 5.7 percent annual increase in deficit spending and a 7 percent annual reduction in overall spending from projected levels for five years. Greenspan observed that federal spending as a percentage of gross national product would remain essentially unchanged and called the program "an exercise in reasonable budget-making." Within the context of what Reagan had been saying, Greenspan was right. But none of the advisers even tried to convince Reagan that he should, as Greenspan and Gerald Ford had suggested, settle for a two-year income tax reduction instead of a three-year plan. Reagan had made it clear repeatedly that he intended to stick with his 30 percent tax cut.

with the Californians who survived in the Reagan entourage in 1980. They considered Kemp brash and ambitious and did not trust him. Kemp, however, had made great strides since 1967, and his success had not gone unnoticed by Reagan. In 1970, at the age of thirty-five, Kemp had capitalized on his athletic fame in Buffalo and won election to the House of Representatives from an industrial district which usually voted Democratic. In 1976, with Buffalo hard hit by recession, Kemp introduced orthodox Republican legislation designed to provide tax relief for business and industry. While this legislation was languishing in the House, Jude Wanniski came along and converted Kemp to the gospel of supply-side economics, which promised relief for both businessmen and workers in Kemp's district.* Kemp became the leading supply-side apostle in Congress. In 1977, he drafted legislation which proposed to reduce federal income taxes by 10 percent a year for three years. Cointroduced by Republican Senator William Roth of Delaware, it became known as the Kemp-Roth Bill.

Reagan followed the progress of Kemp-Roth, endorsing the bill before it became official Republican policy in 1978. He shared Kemp's realization, then rare in Republican ranks, that blue-collar workers were a fruitful field from which to harvest GOP recruits. Because of his own Democratic origins and the practical approach he takes to politics, Reagan knew that the GOP could never become a majority unless it shed what he called the party's "country club-big business image."[9] The conventional wisdom among Republicans was that the way to attract working men and their families was on the basis of what Reagan termed "the so-called social issues—law and order, abortion, busing, quota systems"—which had been so important to Richard Nixon's reelection in 1972.[10] Reagan realized, with Kemp, that social issues were not enough. He knew that Democrats could defuse them simply by adopting the positions of their constituents, as numerous Democratic congressmen had done in 1972 to distance themselves from presidential nominee George McGovern.

Kemp-Roth, opposed by the labor unions which formed the basis of Democratic support in the country's industrial regions, promised more than the social issues. For one thing, it provided Republicans with an issue which the other side was unlikely to embrace. For another, it gave Reagan as a candidate for President an opportunity to make a positive case for tax cuts and industrial expansion that would benefit both business and the working man. The political beauty of supply-side economics was the duality of its appeal. Business was promised tax cuts, investment credits, expansion and higher profits. Labor was promised jobs, tax cuts and a moderation of infla-

* As Rowland Evans and Robert Novak relate it in *The Reagan Revolution* (page 64), Wanniski was walking down the corridor of the Rayburn Building in Washington when he noticed Kemp's office and decided to go in and tell him what was wrong with his original tax package. "The result was a day-long seminar on economics, ending late that night at Kemp's home in the Maryland suburbs," wrote Evans and Novak. "Kemp was converted to the teachings of Mundell and Laffer."

tion. As a former Democrat, Reagan was sensitive to the accusation that Republicans relied solely on "trickle-down economics" to benefit the working man. The charge has been traced by William Safire in his *Political Dictionary* back to Williams Jennings Bryan's "Cross of Gold" speech in 1896 when the Great Commoner declared: "There are those who believe that, if you will only make the well-to-do prosperous, their prosperity will leak through on those below." Hubert Humphrey, the archetypal Democratic liberal, had given a modern definition of "trickle-down" as "feeding the horses so that pretty soon the sparrows will get something to eat, too." On its face, at least, Kemp-Roth looked like more than that. The supply-side approach gave Republicans a long-awaited answer to the Democratic accusation that Republicans sought to balance the budget on the backs of the working man. Kemp-Roth freed Reagan to continue his assault on the evils of government spending and inflation without leaving himself open to the charge that he favored unemployment as a cure. "The Democrats have been running against the specter of Herbert Hoover for forty years,"[11] Reagan once said, in a reflection of his own Depression consciousness. Kemp-Roth offered Republicans an opportunity to exorcise the ghost.

When Reagan finds an idea that serves his purposes, he rarely bothers with details which get in the way of its promotion. One of Kemp's favorite citations, quickly adopted by Reagan, was the beneficial effect of the tax reduction proposed by President Kennedy in 1963 and enacted the year after his death. Reagan brushed aside the differences between 1964 and 1980, including a sixfold growth in the federal budget and a far higher inflation rate. He referred to the Kennedy tax cut inaccurately, too, saying it was a 30 percent reduction when in fact it was 19 percent. But Reagan made good use of Kemp's rhetoric, calling inflation itself a tax, "a penalty imposed on working men and women," because it forced taxpayers into higher and higher brackets. "I do not believe that inflation is caused by too many people working," he said.*

By the time Reagan opened his fall campaign against President Carter, working class voters in the foundry states of Michigan, Ohio and Pennsylvania had become tempting political targets. Wirthlin's polls showed that these voters, many of whom had never cared much for Carter in the first place, were ready to vote Republican and even readier to vote for Reagan. On August 27, 1980, Reagan addressed a Teamsters luncheon in Columbus, Ohio. He said that the lives of working people had "been shattered by a new Depression—the Carter Depression." Unemployment was then 7.6 percent. Reporters hunted up Greenspan, who was traveling with Reagan and had drafted the speech, and asked whether he agreed with the candidate's description. Greenspan said candidly that the language had been inserted after

---

* Kemp used this line frequently. In an interview with Edward Cowan in the *New York Times* of December 23, 1981, he attributed the quotation to Margaret Bush Wilson, president of the NAACP.

he had written the speech. He added that the United States was "in one of the major economic contractions of the last fifty years," but that he would not have used Reagan's language. This disavowal, coming at a time when Reagan was rediscovering the virtues of creationism, Taiwan and the Vietnam War, was treated by some of the traveling press as another Reagan goof. It was not. Reagan had inserted the word "Depression" deliberately, with a good politician's intuitive sense of the most effective phrase. Faced with Greenspan's disavowal, he was forced to issue a correction, but turned this, also, into an effective political statement, saying, "As far as I am concerned, the line between recession and depression cannot be measured in the strict economists' terms but must be measured in human terms. When our working people—including those who are unemployed—must endure the worst misery since the 1930s, then I think we ought to recognize that they consider it a depression. . . ." Later, this evolved into one of Reagan's favorite campaign litanies, one he repeated so often that aides and reporters were tempted to chant it with him in cadenced unison: "If he wants a definition, I'll give him one. A recession is when your neighbor loses his job. A depression is when you lose yours. And recovery is when Jimmy Carter loses his."

Carter lost his job, and Reagan wasted no time embarking on what he thought was the path to recovery. On his first day in office, he kept a campaign pledge and ordered a federal hiring freeze. He did away with the Council on Wage and Price Stability, the Carter administration mechanism for influencing wages and prices. He suspended 199 regulations issued by agencies after the election. He named a task force on regulatory relief, presided over by Vice-President Bush and operated by conservative economist James C. Miller III. Most of these were symbolic measures, with a minimal impact on the budget. A hiring freeze, for instance, had been in force under President Carter. But the announcements demonstrated that the new President intended to carry out his campaign promises. On February 5 Reagan returned to the theme which had been so effective for him during the campaign, declaring in a nationally televised address from the Oval Office that the United States "is in the worst economic mess since the Depression." Promising that his economies would not be timid in nature, Reagan said: "It is time to recognize that we have come to a turning point. We are threatened with an economic calamity of tremendous proportions and the old business-as-usual treatment can't save it."

The point man of the Reagan redirection was Stockman, a two-term Michigan congressman with a staggering command of the complex and disparate elements of the federal budget. At thirty-four, less than half the President's age, he shared with Reagan a disdain for "business as usual" and a fierce desire to curtail the size and scope of the federal government. He knew more about the government than the President did, and he knew it from the frustrated inside perspective of a minority congressman who had been powerless to correct what he considered the abuses of the federal budget process.

Stockman was a conservative and a recent convert to supply-side economics—a lukewarm convert, as events would indicate—but no single label suited him. He had grown up on a farm in western Michigan. At Michigan State University, his familial Republicanism had been shaken by iconoclastic teachers and the backlash of the Vietnam War. Stockman decided to go to Harvard Divinity School, thinking he would become a moral philosopher with a draft deferment rather than a farmer. Instead, he found himself caught up in politics and government, inspired by neo-conservative teachers such as Daniel Patrick Moynihan and James Q. Wilson. One day Moynihan called *Washington Post* columnist David Broder, then teaching a political seminar at Harvard, and asked if a young divinity student who was staying with him could attend. The student was Stockman, who became a semiregular member of Broder's seminar. When Illinois congressman John Anderson, who had been a seminar guest, subsequently asked Broder if any of his students were interested in coming to Washington, the columnist mentioned Stockman. The former Michigan farm boy wound up as issues director for the House Republican Conference, which Anderson then headed. "In three years," wrote one reporter, "Stockman transformed the conference from an intellectual backwater into one of the best research factories on Capitol Hill."[12]

Stockman also attracted the attention of conservative intellectuals, especially with an article in the spring 1975 issue of *The Public Interest*. This article, "The Social Pork Barrel," was a vigorous but thoughtful assault on the federal budget process which contained the seeds of the budget cutbacks that would germinate during the Reagan administration. Implicitly, Stockman accepted the original claims of the New Deal and the need for such welfare state protections as Social Security and unemployment insurance. But he saw the Congress of the 1970s as a body reduced by "conservative duplicity and liberal ideology" to a weak buffer group which lacked either the wisdom or the will to resist special interest pressures. "With revenues fully committed for years in advance, the federal budget process, potentially the basic forum for serious policy choices, has been reduced to a mere annual ritual of accounts juggling," Stockman wrote.

In 1976, when he was twenty-nine, Stockman was elected to the House of Representatives from the western Michigan district where he had been raised. He was now a colleague of the cost-conscious congressmen who had relied on him for issues and budget information, and several of them decided retroactively that they much preferred him as an aide. Stockman was brighter than many of his peers. He worked harder than most of them and gained attention denied those senior in age and experience. Some of his colleagues resented his unwillingness to rise above principle and join his fellow Michigan Republicans in support of legislation to rescue the then failing Chrysler Corporation. But the movement conservatives, reassured that Jack Kemp had at last been listened to, cheered Reagan's selection of Stockman to head the Office of Management and Budget. The supply-side intellectuals were especially gratified. Stockman had read in manuscript the two essential supply-side hymnals, Wanniski's *The Way The World Works,* published in 1978, and George Gilder's *Wealth and Poverty,* which caught the rising tide of Reaganomics in 1981. Stockman helped edit *Wealth and Poverty* and distributed thirty copies of it to his staff at OMB, prompting Gilder to describe the budget director as "an extraordinary man . . . [who] could easily make it as one of America's leading intellectuals, and he's chosen to enter politics."[13] Stockman dazzled Reagan, too. He quickly became a presidential favorite as he brought in budget cut after budget cut during the early weeks of the administration, all of them neatly compiled in a 145-page black binder. Reagan showed his favoritism by teasing Stockman and using him as a foil on which to practice his one-liners. At a cabinet meeting on February 13, the Friday before Reagan's budget cutbacks were formally presented to Congress, the President turned to his budget director and said: "We won't leave you out there alone, Dave. We'll all come to the hanging."[14]

Stockman, pleased by the center-stage opportunity which Reagan had given him, worked day and night to prepare the budget that would carry out the conflicting goals of Reaganomics. His youthful, shock-haired visage stared out at Americans from the vantage point of weekly news magazines and nightly television. In a matter of weeks, Stockman became the best-known member of the Reagan cabinet team—and potentially the most vulnerable. While Stockman was still riding high, a Republican congressman who liked him well enough to defend him after the *Atlantic* article said the budget director spent too many Sunday afternoons on television news shows and too few of them strolling in the park.

The Reagan administration's task in selling its economic program was threefold. First, Reagan was convinced, voters had to be told and retold about the merits of the program. Paul Laxalt called this part of the selling job "continuing the campaign" because Reagan would be saying from the Oval Office essentially what he had been saying on the campaign trail throughout 1980. If the Great Communicator persuaded voters to write, wire or call their congressmen, everyone recognized that the second part of the task—selling Congress—would become easier. Since the Republicans had won control of the Senate in the 1980 election landslide, the administration targeted the House, concentrating on southern and western congressional districts represented by Democrats which Reagan had carried by a large majority. The President and his advisers recognized that House members, up for election again in 1982, would find it difficult to defy this majority. And if the Congress voted for Reagan's budget and tax reductions, the prevailing anticipation within the administration was that the selling of the financial community would take care of itself. Administration spokesmen talked of "a positive psychology" or "the rational expectations" that Wall Street would see lower budget deficits, reduced inflation and an accelerating economy just around the corner and react accordingly. These statements accurately reflected the attitude of a President who, as usual, was brimming with optimism.

When Stockman in January estimated that the deficit would be much larger than expected, Reagan saw this potentially bad news as an opportunity to take even bigger bites out of the budget. When Treasury Secretary Regan and other administration officials in mid-summer expressed concern over the "Christmas tree" effects of some of the benefits for special interest groups which the Democrats were adding to the tax bill, the President accepted the additional reductions without a murmur. Later, Reagan would find it difficult to accept the recommendations of Baker, Stockman and the Senate Republican leadership in favor of a relatively modest tax increase to keep the deficit down. Supply-siders increasingly saw the President as an embattled true believer surrounded by the doubting Thomases of his own staff. The reality, which was simpler, was summed up by Stockman in a November 1981 interview, which came at a time when the supply-siders were arguing for a return to the gold standard which would rescue their policies. "Every time one fantasy doesn't work they try another one," Stockman told me. "Now they say if you restore the gold standard the interest rate will drop to zero overnight, just like they said if you cut taxes 6 percent growth would appear. I don't think he [the President] ever believed that. He was receptive to it because he's an optimist . . . just a fundamental optimist by character and temperament, and he thought with proper policies things would start to change."[15]

The "proper policies"—as seen by both Reagan and Stockman—were contained in the February 18, 1981, economic message which proposed to cut more than $41 billion from the projected Carter budget and make mild to fatal reductions in eighty-three federal programs. The optimism was reflected the following day in a presentation to the Joint Economic Committee of Congress by Treasury Secretary Regan, who asserted that business investment would rise 11 percent a year faster than inflation for at least the next five years. Such an investment would boost spending on new plants and equipment to more than 12 percent of the gross national product by 1983—a level which the U.S. economy had never achieved. The prediction left economic forecasters shaking their heads. One of them, Otto Eckstein of Data Resources, Inc., said the shift of investment "would require a massive restructuring of the American economy . . . far beyond historical experience."[16] Despite such predictions, there were many expressions of enthusiasm on Wall Street for the Reagan program. "I believe the President's program is an important step on a long road to economic rehabilitation," said Willard Butcher, president of the country's third-largest bank, Chase Manhattan. "Perhaps more significantly, the President's speech signaled an important change of direction in national economic policy which I believe now demands the support of the country and the Congress."[17] Similar views were expressed by other Wall Street figures, but the market cast a different ballot. The Dow Jones average declined by more than 13 points, in a harbinger of what was to come throughout the spring and summer of 1981.

Main Street, however, was sold on Reaganomics. A *Washington Post*–ABC News poll taken on February 19 and 20 showed better than 2–1 support for the President's program. Public support helped House Minority Leader Robert H. Michel keep a solid front of Republicans in line for the budget and tax reductions. The White House, led by popular director of congressional relations Max L. Friedersdorf, concentrated on potential defectors among the Democrats. Texas, which Reagan had carried by more than 600,000 votes while Democrats were winning 19 of 24 congressional districts, was the fulcrum. Reagan and his top aides listened respectfully as Texas Democrat Charles W. Stenholm, leader of the Conservative Democratic Forum, presented that group's list of proposed economies, some of which were incorporated into the administration budget. Texas Democrat Phil Gramm became the principal author of the budget bill, requiring the White House to soothe the ruffled feelings of the coauthor, Republican Delbert L. Latta of Ohio. Texas Democrat Kent Hance was designated the principal author of the Reagan tax bill. As a result, Reagan was able to describe both measures as "bipartisan bills" in his televised appeals for voter support.

The President did not rely on television alone. He lobbied House members incessantly, prompting some of them to say that they had seen more of Reagan in four months than they had of Carter in four years. In his first 100 days in office Reagan held 69 meetings with congressmen in which 467 members participated.[18] He went to Capitol Hill for meetings with congressional leaders and twice addressed the nation from the Capitol, including a memorable April 28 speech which marked his recovery from wounds suffered in an assassination attempt less than a month earlier. While the focus of Reagan's personal lobbying was on the southern Democrats known as "boll weevils," he kept his lines of communication open with the House Democratic leadership and developed a personal fondness for Speaker Thomas P. (Tip) O'Neill even as he sought to undermine his leadership. Reagan possessed enormous powers of friendly persuasion and knew how to use them. He realized that a wavering congressman would find it difficult to resist a personal call from the President, particularly when the President had public opinion on his side in the congressman's district. Reagan issued a standing order to his legislative aides: "Tell me who you want me to call and I'll do it." Social invitations and presidential cufflinks and photographs were also widely distributed. The flavor of Reagan's cultivation of Congress was captured in a cartoon by Ben Sargent, in the *Austin American Statesman,* which showed a mythical congressman from "Rendolent, Pa.," dressed as a money-clutching greedy kid and boasting, "I voted for the President's budget and got these cufflinks, a White House tour and tickets to the Kennedy Center. I think the President's program is really neat-o." Congressmen who voted for the President's tax cut were eligible to win a variety of prizes including a "David Stockman pocket knife," a "voodoo economics kit" and a "General Haig decoder ring."

When necessary, the administration provided concessions along with the cufflinks. Few concessions were needed on the original budget bill, which passed the House on May 7 by a vote of 253 to 176. But the Democrats put up a better fight against a followup budget-cutting measure known as "Gramm-Latta II." First, the White House headed off a mini-revolt among moderate Republicans by agreeing to increase budget amounts for Medicare. Then the administration cut deals with southern Democrats. On this bill the focus shifted from Texas to Louisiana where the delegation wanted to revive an expensive sugar support program that had been phased out in 1979. Four Louisiana Democrats agreed to go along with the President's bill, winning in exchange administration support for a program that Stockman considered a scandal. But the consensus view on Gramm-Latta II, which Stockman shared, was that $5 billion of additional budget reductions required making some concessions on principle. "Compromise is part of the political process," White House Press Secretary Larry Speakes blandly told reporters in Los Angeles, where Reagan had gone late in June for a vacation while the House was preparing to vote. Democratic Congressman John B. Breaux, one of the four Louisiana Democrats who went along with the administration, was less euphemistic. "I went with the best deal," he said. When a reporter asked whether this meant that Breaux's vote could be bought, the congressman responded with the most memorable answer of the session: "No. It can be rented."[19]

But the word from Republican congressional leaders on the outcome of the second budget bill was still uncertain. They wanted a single up-or-down vote, knowing that southern Democrats would be reluctant to oppose the President on any package of budget reductions. The Democratic leadership, nominally in control, wanted a series of individual votes. Reagan was informed of the tactical battle on Air Force One en route to Los Angeles with a speech stopover in San Antonio. At first he questioned whether he should risk his prestige in a fight he had been told he would lose. But when Baker and Deaver told him that a head count in the House showed movement in the administration's direction, Reagan agreed to fight. Upon his arrival in Los Angeles he issued a statement denouncing the Democrats for "a divide-and-conquer strategy . . . that would once again allow special interest groups to triumph over the general economic interest of the nation." Then he worked the phones, calling twenty-nine congressmen from his skyroom suite in the Century Plaza Hotel where he had spent election night.* On June 26, the administration won the key parliamentary vote, 217 to 210, and

---

* Columnist Art Buchward caught the essence of the President's telephone pitch in a mythical call to a Congressman Lighter. "I would like you to break from your party and the Democratic leadership, and vote your conscience by passing my budget recommendations without reading them," the President says. Reagan clinches the deal by quoting George Gipp's deathbed appeal for sugar subsidies.

the House the same day passed Gramm-Latta II by six votes. The happy President went off to ride horses and chop wood at Rancho del Cielo.

While the administration had done more than Reagan had expected, it had accomplished less than it believed. Despite all the cutbacks, the administration had failed to produce anything close to its heralded "revolution." The budget deficit and interest rates remained out of control. The supply-side tax cut passed by Congress on July 29 after another effective national television address by Reagan and more presidential calls to congressmen was a pale and confused version of the Kemp nostrum adorned with a clutch of special provisions which had little to do with any economic theory except greed. The measure provided tax relief for the oil industry, for savings and loan associations in the form of "All-Savers Certificates," and for all corporations. The so-called "marriage penalty" on two-income families was reduced. Depreciation schedules for businesses were accelerated and simplified. Beneath this overladen Christmas tree was the remnant of the 10 percent across-the-board tax cut which Reagan had promised during the campaign would be retroactive to January 1, 1981. The date was jettisoned quickly. Even Reagan realized it would cost the government too much in revenues, and he agreed to start the tax cut on July 1. When Congress enacted the bill, however, it became a 5 percent cut, beginning on October 1. Subsequent 10 percent cuts were scheduled for July 1, 1982, and July 1, 1983.

What Reagan had accomplished was not budget balancing or business stimulation but a shift of priorities within the budget. He had kept his promise to increase military spending, providing a $28-billion increase that was the largest in peacetime history. In 1982 Reagan would propose an additional 15 percent growth in the military budget. Stockman wanted to do some paring at the Pentagon as well as on domestic programs, correctly anticipating that the administration was sending "a powerful signal" to the generals and admirals to loosen their belts while everyone else was tightening theirs.[20] Reagan, convinced that the Russians were on the verge of attaining military supremacy, would have none of this argument in his first budget and only a little of it in his second. As a consequence, the military spending boost nearly offset the cuts Stockman was able to make in social programs. Gone entirely were public service jobs under the Comprehensive Employment Training Act and college education benefits provided under Social Security. Drastically reduced were child nutrition programs and trade adjustment assistance, an overlapping unemployment insurance program for workers who had lost their jobs because of foreign competition. Unemployment compensation itself was, in most cases, reduced from 39 weeks to 26 at a time when jobless rolls were growing rapidly. Medicare patients were required to pay a greater share of their health costs. Welfare benefits under the Aid to Families With Dependent Children Program were reduced. Farm state Republican senators like Bob Dole of Kansas stood up for the food stamp program, which survived at a higher level than either Reagan or

Stockman desired. But Congress did cut $1.7 billion from food stamps, eliminating more than a million recipients.

All of these reductions, taken together, did virtually nothing to halt the upward spiral of the federal budget. Partly, this was because of Reagan's insistence on a military buildup. But the more fundamental reason was the built-in nature of federal budget growth. That growth was summed up in the single word "entitlements," all those programs which Americans qualify for by meeting some basic standard of eligibility—being older than sixty-five or out of work or attending a public school. Social Security, which Reagan had pledged to protect, is by far the largest entitlement. Others, mostly products of the Great Society, had started modestly and grown to far greater dimensions than their authors had anticipated. Between 1970 and 1981 spending on entitlements quadrupled from $70 billion to $295 billion during a time when the cost of living was increasing 138 percent. Entitlements accounted for 22 percent of the budget in 1956 and 35 percent in 1970. By 1981, entitlements used up 48 percent of the budget and were still growing. Despite all the cuts, they grew an estimated $50 billion in the first Reagan budget year. The budget squeeze was even greater because Reagan had ruled out any cuts in two Social Security programs and any substantial reduction in five others: Medicare, veterans benefits, school lunches, Head Start and summer youth jobs. These, said Stockman, formed a "social safety net" protecting the "truly needy." The budget director acknowledged that the decision on what belonged within the safety net and what didn't was somewhat arbitrary. Some veterans benefits, for instance, were untouchable for political reasons but meant far less to the "truly needy" than did child nutrition programs which were reduced or eliminated. By and large, the administration took a table knife to the old New Deal programs and a cleaver to the later additions of the Great Society. While most of this operation was performed with considerable skill, the continuing growth of programs which Reagan couldn't touch politically guaranteed that there would be no genuine budget reduction.*

The administration closed 1981 as it began, representing minor and symbolic achievements as major, substantive ones. One of the administration's "major accomplishments," said a year-end review compiled by the White House Office of Public Affairs, was a "new debt collection emphasis" which had discovered that 8,500 dead people on Social Security lists were still being sent checks. The review didn't say how long these deceased recipients had been receiving benefits. But in any case, the figure represented only slightly more than one-fiftieth of 1 percent of those receiving Social Security, which remained financially troubled and politically untouchable at least until after the 1982 elections. Entitlement programs continued to grow. And with them so did the federal deficit.

* The conspicuous exception to this political competence was the bungled handling of the Social Security issue. See Chapter 22, "The Delegated Presidency."

The calculus of Reaganomics never actually made sense. Stockman found this out early in January, when he ran some conventional budget estimates through the OMB computer. They told him what he already sensed, which was that even with the proposed reductions that were accumulating in his black binder of budget cuts, the administration faced an $82-billion deficit in 1982. The figures for the succeeding fiscal years—"out years," in OMB jargon—were even worse. In the symbolic year of 1984, the computer said, the Reagan administration would wind up not with a balanced budget but a deficit of $116 billion.

Stockman did what any optimistic convert to supply-side economics might have done under the circumstances—he reprogrammed the computer. In went rosy estimates of business expansion provided by the benefits of tax reduction. Out came a lower projected deficit. Stockman was hardly the first budget director to change facts to fit assumptions, and he did not hide what he was doing from the President or the White House staff. But Reagan is a President who does not want to be bothered with details, and his top White House trio of advisers had no training in economics. In any event, the source of the administration's absurd early claims for lower deficits and a balanced budget were based less upon the reprogrammed OMB figures than on Reagan's conviction that the program would work—a belief he had expressed repeatedly long before he hired Stockman, and that he reiterated to aides and intimates long after he should have known better. The President's optimism was contagious, and Stockman was infected by it. Like Reagan, he wanted to believe that Reaganomics would work or that a way could be found to make it work. Carried along by temperament and their grand design, Reagan and his budget director were actually following the course sarcastically advocated during the campaign by Stockman's old mentor, John Anderson. The way that Reaganomics worked was by mirrors.

One did not need an expensive computer to determine that the administration's economic forecasts were haywire. *Washington Post* economics writer John M. Berry sat down with "a cheapo pocket calculator" in February 1981 and figured out that OMB was overestimating the gains that would be derived from the tax cuts. Senator Pete Domenici of New Mexico questioned the assumptions, too, without benefit of either computer of calculator. Approaching his first year as chairman of the Senate Budget Committee in December 1980, he told columnist David Broder, "You never heard Pete Domenici make the argument that you could balance the budget, have significant defense increases and multi-year tax cuts simply by eliminating waste and fraud. You have to restructure the entitlement programs, either by adjusting the inflation indexes or redrawing the eligibility rules."[21] Had the Reagan administration engaged in either of these courses, it might have launched a real budget revolution rather than a symbolic one.

Whether by computer or calculator or common sense, Wall Street reached a near unanimous conclusion that Reaganomics couldn't produce the results the President had promised. This opinion was fueled by Stockman's announcement that another $75 billion in "unidentified savings" would have to be achieved to reach balanced-budget-land by 1984 and by the continuation of the tight-money policies of the Federal Reserve Board. In 1979 the Fed had abandoned its attempts to control interest rates directly and had instead tried to regulate the money supply. The result, in the first year of the Reagan administration, was a monetary policy which conflicted with fiscal policy. At the same time that the Reagan tax cuts were supposed to be sponsoring an economic boom, the Fed's tight grip on money and continued government borrowing required by the growing deficit kept interest rates high and put the brakes on expansion. Interest rate levels for consumers hovered near the 20 percent level through much of 1981 before fluttering downward in December under the impact of a deepening recession that sent unemployment to 9 percent—nearly 1½ points above the level which candidate Reagan had termed "a depression." Long-term bond yields reached 17 percent, but few investors proved willing to tie up their money for decades by buying them. Soon after Reagan's election, the Dow Jones average of 30 industrial stocks topped 1,000 for the first time in four years. It reached a 1981 high of 1,024 on April 27 during a brief period of Reaganomics euphoria, then started downward toward the levels of a decade ago. At year's end the Dow average stood at 875, 89 points below its January 1 average and 149 points below its 1981 high. By March 6, 1982, the Dow had dropped to 807, its lowest level in nearly two years.

Economists of almost every variety enjoyed a field day in criticizing the Reagan administration. The Harvard Keynesian economist John Kenneth Galbraith, whom Reagan had sometimes described as "proving that economics is an inexact science," got in his licks: "The administration has promised vigorous expansion through supply-side incentives in combination with monetary policy that works through high interest rates and a powerful contraction of the economy. This contradiction can only be resolved by divine intervention—a task for the Moral Majority."[22] Traditional conservative economists were almost as critical. "I think the administration hurt itself by a series of unbelievable statements, starting with those optimistic forecasts about the growth of the economy," said Martin Feldstein, president of the National Bureau of Economic Affairs.[23] At year's end Feldstein was urging postponement of the 1983 portion of the tax cut.[24] Only the true believers of the supply-side church remained undaunted. Wanniski argued that everything would turn out all right if the administration would adopt a gold standard. "Politically, things could turn around in two or three days," he said.[25]*

* Wanniski understood that the administration was pursuing contradictory policies. "Reagan is still embracing the supply-side tax cuts but at the same time he has been persuaded that he should cling to the monetarist programs," Wanniski said in a December 11, 1981, interview with my research assistant Robin Gradison. "In a supply-side world we argue that monetary policy will be in error whether the Fed is contracting or expanding because the purpose of monetary policy is not to manage the quantity of money but to maintain the quality of money." To Wanniski, that meant tying it to gold or silver.

Stockman had no such illusions. Even before he reprogrammed the OMB computer to a more favorable set of assumptions, Stockman had been aware that Reaganomics was skating on cracked ice. In November 1980, before his appointment as director of OMB, Stockman had drawn up an economic plan of action for Kemp to take to a meeting of Reagan advisers. Called "Avoiding a GOP Economic Dunkirk," the Stockman manifesto warned of a 1981 recession, federal budget and credit hemorrhaging, commodity price shocks and the destruction of monetary policy. From the first, Stockman recognized that the financial community had to be convinced that Reagan's policies would succeed to give them any chance of success. "I thought we could put together an initial plan that would have the tax cut and such a large amount of budget reduction that it would be credibly obvious the deficit was disappearing and that therefore the kind of antiinflation monetary policy which was part of the plan would be supported and facilitated by the fiscal policy," Stockman said.[26] Instead, the financial community perceived the unlikelihood of achieving the unidentified savings and the virtual certainty of higher deficits. "The markets didn't believe that the antiinflation monetary policy could be maintained," Stockman said. "And if markets don't believe that antiinflation monetary policy can be maintained they're not going to have sudden change in attitude about the long-run inflation rate."[27]

The same light had dawned on Capitol Hill, where Republican congressional leaders on October 10, 1981, met with some of Wall Street's leading financiers. This elite group, which included economist Henry Kaufman of Salomon Brothers and investment banker Peter Flanigan of Dillon, Read and Company, bluntly told the GOP congressmen that Wall Street didn't trust the administration's figures and didn't believe in its forecasts. The congressmen were impressed. "They can't flim-flam the smart people in this country with figures as we've been attempting to do here," said House Minority Leader Michel in a subsequent interview,[28] referring to the conflicting budget estimates emanating from OMB and various congressional offices. Whatever the figures said, the "smart people" recognized that huge, continuing deficits were destined to be a fact of life throughout the Reagan administration. They made their decisions accordingly.

The administration's real problems were compounded by symbolic ones. The Reagans had reintroduced conspicuous consumption and elegant living to a Washington surfeited by the straight-laced life style of their predecessors. Designer dresses, personal hairdressers and chauffeured limousines were in. So were real fur coats, which replaced the once environmentally fashionable imitations. Formal wear and ornate evening gowns made a comeback, and tuxedos hung on door hangers at the White House in anticipation of the evening's black tie function. High style had returned, rebuking the informality of the past two decades and reflecting, wrote one art historian, "the taste of older people after all these relentless years of youth."[29]

It was also the taste of the very rich, an entrepreneurial rich whose motto might have been, "If you've got it, flaunt it." The millionaire California friends of the Reagans—the Alfred Bloomingdales, the Justin Darts, the Earle Jorgensens, among others—maintained permanent apartments or hotel suites at Washington's famous Watergate. The millionaire cabinet members exchanged elegant parties with their fellow millionaires. White House menus became elaborate affairs, although the President who had once described himself as "Mr. Norm" still preferred simple food. But he had grown used to comfortable surroundings, and his closest friends were other millionaires. None of them apologized for it. "The preponderance of these people are self-made," said Charles Z. Wick, the millionaire filmmaker and political fund-raiser whom Reagan chose to head the International Communications Agency. "They follow the American dream."[30] Wick told a reporter that he thought that Americans in economic distress enjoyed seeing a luxurious life style in Washington. "During the Depression when people were selling apples and factories were still and guys were jumping out windows because they lost everything, people would go to the movies," Wick said. "They loved those glamour pictures showing people driving beautiful cars and women in beautiful gowns, showing that people were living the glamorous good life."[31]

Nancy Reagan became the national symbol of the New Luxury. To her friends and fellow socialites, she was "pretty Nancy." At sixty, she looked ten years younger than her actual age. She boasted a perfect figure maintained by daily exercise and well-suited to the expensively simple gowns designed for her by Galanos and Adolfo. "I, and many like me, are tired of the 'age of the slob' and delight in the elegance and high ideals of our first lady," wrote an admirer to the *Washington Post*. "She has already changed fashion from dirty jeans and stringy hair to beautiful clothes and good taste. It is like a breath of fresh air and I appreciate it."[32]

Before she came to the White House, Nancy Reagan had often referred to herself as "a frustrated interior decorator." Even her nonadmirers acknowledged that she had good taste. After one look at the White House living quarters she decided to redo them and raised $822,641 toward this end from private contributors, most of them wealthy. Another private donor, the Knapp Foundation of St. Michaels, Maryland, put up $209,508 to pay for a 220-place setting of gilt-edged china embossed with the presidential seal, the first new china since a single anonymous donor provided a 216-place setting during the Johnson administration. Defending his wife, Reagan inaccurately maintained that the purchase cost the taxpayers nothing. He ignored the fact that a top-bracket taxpayer contribution to a foundation could deduct up to 70 percent of the purchase price from his federal income taxes.

There was another view of the New Luxury. It was reflected in one of Washington's best-selling postcards of 1981, "Queen Nancy," which featured the first lady in ermine cape and jeweled crown. The card touched a raw nerve with Nancy Reagan, who had been surprised and upset at press criticism of the china purchase and the executive mansion redecoration. The critical view also showed up in letters to the editor. "Admittedly, Mrs. Reagan's life style is not that different from some first ladies of the past twenty years," wrote one complainant. "What is different is that she pursued clearly hedonistic goals while her husband is asking many Americans to sacrifice and save."[33] This was the nub of the matter. Though Republican politicians were reluctant to criticize the President's wife publicly, a number of them considered her a symbol of what *Time* called "conspicuous prosperity" at a time the nation was sliding into recession. A *Washington Post*–ABC News poll taken late in September 1981 suggested that the combination of budget cutbacks and the New Luxury was having a negative effect on the way Americans viewed Reagan. In February, only 23 percent of his countrymen thought Reagan favored upper-income people. By September, this percentage had climbed to 52 percent.

Nancy Reagan was in many respects a convenient scapegoat for the administration's favoritism of the rich. She was suspicious of the press, and she lacked her husband's practiced gift for dispatching a hostile critic with a well-aimed one-liner. During the campaign she had been reduced to tears by a mean-spirited column which alleged she had "piano legs" and falsely declared that reporters on the plane felt compelled to take the chocolate candies she passed out to them. The column had little circulation, and its only impact was on Nancy Reagan's feelings. Stu Spencer suggested hiding the newspaper from her. She saw the column anyway, and was reduced to tears. Ronald Reagan spent hours comforting her at a crucial time in the campaign. The next day, with the help of Spencer and travel secretary Joe Canzeri, he cajoled her into going to the back of the plane with a hand-lettered sign posted on the box of chocolates: "Take one—or else."

White House aides, encouraged by Mike Deaver, tried the same approach with Queen Nancy. On October 22, 1981, Nancy spoke at the Alfred E. Smith Memorial Dinner in New York City where her husband had shone the year before. She said of the postcard: "Now that's silly. I'd never wear a crown—it messes up your hair." And she also reminded her audience at the Catholic charity fund-raiser of her own project, "the Nancy Reagan Home for Wayward China." The one-liners were well-conceived but delivered awkwardly, for they did not spring naturally to Nancy Reagan's lips. She was a strong-willed woman and Ronald Reagan would not have been President without her, but self-deprecation was not among her abilities. The press criticism continued, and Nancy Reagan did not know how to deal with it.*

---

* She was particularly upset with a column by Judy Mann in the *Washington Post* of November 20, 1981, which declared: "The fundamental problem with Nancy Reagan's image is Nancy Reagan. She is a woman out of her times, a First Lady out of the past. She would have been a smash in the 1950s." Even White House aides who considered Mrs. Reagan a pain in the knee thought the column was unfair because it wanted her to be something she was not and also because Mann said that Mrs. Reagan wasn't involved in anything "substantive" and dismissed her visit to the Howard University Hospital as a publicity stunt. James E. Cheek, president of Howard, wrote the *Post* to say he was "deeply offended" by the column. "It is singularly significant that Mrs. Reagan is the only

"She bleeds pretty good," Reagan had said in Sacramento. She still bled in Washington, and he still defended her, never becoming reconciled to criticism of his wife. "Why do they always pick on Nancy?" Reagan asked an aide one day when he was being pummeled in several columns and she was being mildly criticized in one. The aide, not wanting to say anything that could be construed as critical of the first lady, had no ready reply. But at the prestigious Gridiron Dinner on March 29, 1982, Nancy replied to the critics on her own, making a surprise on-stage appearance in feathered hat, pantaloons and yellow boots to sing her own version of "Second Hand Clothes." One of the lines was, "Even my new trench coat with fur collar/Ronnie bought for ten cents on the dollar." She received two standing ovations from the audience of well-known Washington journalists and their celebrity guests. She did an encore, dropping a china plate which shattered. After this plucky performance, "Queen Nancy" commanded new respect, at least in Washington.

Away from Washington, bread-and-butter issues rather than life style questions dominated the reaction to the Reagan redirection. But the Reagan opulence added to the administration's growing negative image with blue-collar families, especially the unemployed. "I don't think style is something people are directly concerned about," said Republican pollster Robert Teeter. "But I do think it's the kind of thing that could add fuel to the fire if someone's already mad."[34] As joblessness increased, there were plenty of people who fit this description. Returning in December 1981 to Flint, Michigan, a high unemployment area where Reagan had campaigned powerfully against "the Carter Depression," David Hoffman of Knight-Ridder Newspapers talked to Andrea Osborne, a twenty-nine-year-old worker laid off after four and one-half years on the assembly line. "You see them eating $26-an-ounce caviar," she said. "The money is not trickling down."[35] And Carl Hladic, a forty-nine-year-old Chevrolet engine inspector who had voted for Reagan, said of the President: "The recession has been coming on, and he isn't doing a real good job of turning it around."[36]

There were other critical judgments from the victims of Reaganomics. State governments, gasping from the loss of general revenue sharing and pressured by cities to make up for local financial cutbacks, were particularly hard hit. In Olympia, Washington, Republican Governor John Spellman, shaken by the impact of the budget cuts, pleaded for new state taxes. "We must give people what they need or we are buying anarchy," he said.[37] Across the country, New York City Mayor Ed Koch said that federal cuts and the city's fiscal troubles had reduced the police force to its lowest level since 1954—when crime rates had been half the 1981 level.[38] Less than a

---

first lady since Eleanor Roosevelt to visit Howard University and express a personal interest in this institution and the problems and issues Howard was created to resolve," wrote Cheek in a letter published November 23.

week earlier, Koch had addressed the National League of Cities in Detroit
and termed Reagan's domestic policy "a sham and a shame" which threatened the well-being of American cities. "In withdrawing federal involvement from the needs of the people and the cities, President Reagan protests
that he is returning to the states responsibility that is properly a local concern," Koch said. "In truth, he is employing the mask of federalism for a
systematic campaign of abandonment."[39]

The accusation was not without merit, although blame for the "abandonment" must be shared by the Congress of which Koch was once a member. Reagan wanted both to decentralize and cut the budget, but he did not
pursue these goals with equal vigor. Budget decisions wound up driving the
new federalism rather than the other way around. When Reagan took office,
the nation's governors urged a switch from narrow categorical grants to
broad block grants, saying they could readily accept a 10 percent cut in federal aid in return for greater flexibility. The Reagan administration instead
cut programs to states an average of 25 percent. Congress approved the
budget cuts but gave Reagan much less than what he asked in grant consoli-
dation, which in turn was less than the states desired. Reagan sought consol-
idation of eighty-eight categorical programs and received congressional approval for only fifty-seven, some of them with strings attached. More than
four hundred categoricals were left on the books, untouched in their rigidity
but with funding for many of them reduced. By the governors' reckoning,
the states lost more than $11 billion in federal aid while only $2.3 billion in
assistance was freed from federal restraints.[40]

Ever since his controversial $90 Billion Speech in 1976, Reagan had
been promising to turn over various federal programs to state and local governments along with tax sources to pay for them. The truth in Washington,
however, was that the federal government needed every tax source it already
controlled if it were ever to reduce the deficit. This hard reality was brought
home to state and local government officials in October when they met with
Undersecretary of Treasury Norman Ture to discuss financing of federal
programs that were being turned over to them. The meeting was opened by
Richard S. Williamson, the White House assistant for intergovernmental
relations, who advocated additional tax sources for state and local government. Ture quickly threw cold water on the idea. He bluntly told the assembled officials that the federal government "has already substantially accomplished" everything it could do to make new tax sources available by
lowering the federal tax rates.[41] Furthermore, he insisted that "true federalism" required that the unit of government which spends the money should
also be the unit that collects the taxes. The message was clear: If state and
local governments wanted to maintain their previous level of services, they
would have to raise the money to pay for them. Benjamin L. Cardin, the
Democratic speaker of the Maryland House of Delegates, objected that federal tax cuts had been intended to reduce taxation, not shift the burden to

344   R E A G A N

states and cities. He asked Ture what he would do about financing services "in a jurisdiction that has one-fourth the fiscal resources of the neighboring jurisdiction." Ture told him. "You don't do anything," he said. "You determine where you want to live."[42]

If new federalism seemed a sham under the conditions of its imposition, regulatory reform was genuine but slow. Reagan was committed to reducing the volume of federal regulations which poured unceasingly out of every agency in Washington, and his determination was widely shared within the administration. By the end of Reagan's first year in office, most government agencies were issuing fewer regulations.* But the pace of regulation review disappointed would-be reformers. In December more than a dozen economists, some of them members of the Reagan regulatory task force, met under the auspices of the American Enterprise Institute and criticized the administration for not moving far enough or fast enough to cut federal red tape. At this meeting transportation expert Thomas Gale Moore complained that Interstate Commerce Committee Chairman Reese Taylor had "been backwatering" the trucking deregulation legislation enacted in 1980, making it harder for new firms to enter the business.[43] He said that the air traffic controllers strike and their subsequent firing had, in effect, led to re-regulation of the airline industry, with control exercised by the Department of Transportation. While the White House gave itself high marks for regulatory reform, claiming that its actions had saved $2 billion in annual operating costs, Vice-President George Bush was more cautious in his evaluation. Bush, chairman of the Presidential Task Force on Regulatory Relief, said the administration had accomplished only 10 percent of what needed to be done. "We can't say that we've done what we set out to do," Bush said. "But we've started—and made a good start."[44]†

Reagan persevered. His personal popularity remained higher than public support for his economic policies, and his optimism gave ground reluctantly in the face of economic reality. A touch of Reagan luck helped—a world oil glut reduced oil prices and helped moderate the trend of inflation. What also helped, at least on the inflation front, was the old Republican remedy which Reagan had eschewed as a candidate—a recession induced by tight money. The recession reduced the demand for credit, restricted business expansion, increased unemployment and gradually brought down

* One measure of the decline in regulations was the pages of the Federal Register, which totaled 63,353 in 1981, a decline of more than 23,000 pages from the year before. This is less than a perfect yardstick, as T. R. Reid of the *Washington Post* pointed out in a January 1, 1982, article, because the Register takes pages to list discarded regulations as well as new ones. But the trend of new regulations clearly was down in Reagan's first year as President.

† The start was built on a process of deregulation that began under Nixon, continued under Ford and was pursued vigorously under Carter, when trucks, railroads and airlines were substantially freed from government controls. Says the *Washington Post*'s John M. Berry: "Reagan has pushed harder, of course, but he was building on a solid foundation left by his predecessors."

both inflation and interest rates. Much of the credit, or blame, for this policy belonged to the Federal Reserve Board, which, under Chairman Paul Volcker, had tried since 1979 to control inflation by regulating the money supply rather than pegging interest rates. In 1981 inflation as measured by the Consumer Price Index fell three points, the price of every major commodity dropped, and wage increases began to decline. "The cost of breaking inflation is not something Volcker—like so many officials—chooses to ignore," wrote columnist Joseph Kraft after an interview with officials at the Fed. "He considers monetary policy a blunt instrument for managing the economy. He knows very well that high interest rates hit with particularly devastating force certain parts of the economy—especially housing and autos and related industries. He acknowledges that the cost of breaking inflation was recession. Indeed, when an outsider mused last week that Volcker might be Man of the Year, on official said; 'They don't give the Man of the Year award for starting a recession.' "[45]

As the stock market slumped and housing sales sagged, Reagan vacationed in California. He was away from Washington from August 7 to September 3, an unusually long presidential vacation, which the White House press office said cost taxpayers $250,000. When Reagan returned, the news was not good. Treasury Secretary Regan was predicting a recession. Stockman wanted defense cuts to keep the budget under control. The Pentagon, led by Defense Secretary Weinberger, was resisting. Reagan still wanted to keep all his promises at the same time. He made some token cuts in defense, then appealed for significant additional reductions in domestic social spending. The pep talk he made to the cabinet in mid-September echoed with the rhetoric he had used to rouse conservative audiences in the old days. "Can anyone here say that if we can't do it, someone down the road can do it?" Reagan said. "And if no one does it, what happens to the country? All of us here know the economy would face an eventual collapse. I know it's a hell of a challenge, but ask yourselves: If not us, who? If not now, when?"

On September 24, when Reagan made still another national television appeal for his economic program, he believed that a balanced budget was attainable in 1984. But his speech demonstrated the hollowness of that view. At the same time he was requesting $13 billion more in budget cuts, Reagan withdrew his May request for elimination of the Social Security minimum benefit. Without saying so, Reagan was recognizing that Congress had drawn a tight circle around the programs which the administration needed to examine if it were ever to have a hope of balancing the budget while maintaining the other goals of Reaganomics. Inexorably, and without fully realizing it, Reagan was being drawn toward alternatives he did not want to consider, like reducing the defense budget or making reductions in tax loopholes which benefited the corporations he was trying to help. He fought Stockman and Baker on these issues. But as time went by, he could no longer deny the impact of the recession on the deficit. On October 18, before leaving to meet French President François Mitterand in Williamsburg, Reagan stood on the White House lawn and told reporters: "I think there's a slight recession and I hope a short recession. I think everyone agrees on that."

On October 23, the national debt went over the trillion dollar mark, a symbolic landmark which reflected another unpleasant reality of the 1982 budget: $100 billion in interest payments on the national debt.* On October 30, Treasury Secretary Regan said it was "not probable" that the administration could balance the federal budget in 1984. And on November 6, a date when unemployment had reached the highest rate since 1975, the President finally threw in the towel on the balanced budget. "I've never said anything but that it was a goal," Reagan told reporters, ignoring many of his own past statements. In May, he had told the Republican National Committee publication, *First Monday,* that he expected not only a balanced budget but "a small surplus in 1984."

The Stockman bubble burst on November 10, the budget director's thirty-fifth birthday, when Senator Gary Hart of Colorado read an advance copy of the *Atlantic*'s "The Education of David Stockman" into the Congressional Record. Democrats were jubilant at Stockman's admission that he had rejiggered budget figures to make Reaganomics seem more plausible. Republicans facing election in 1982 imagined how the words would sound coming out of the mouths of their Democratic opponents. Supply-siders were incensed by Stockman's vivid metaphors—and even more by his increasingly skeptical judgments of their theories. At one point William Greider quoted Stockman as saying: "It's kind of hard to sell 'trickle-down,' so the supply-side formula was the only way to get a tax policy that was really 'trickle-down.' Supply-side is 'trickle-down' theory."[46] Stockman also said: "The hard part of the supply-side tax cut is dropping the top rate from 70 to 50 percent—the rest of it is secondary matter. The original argument was that the top bracket was too high, and that's having the most devastating effect on the economy. Then, the general argument was that, in order to make this palatable as a political matter, you had to bring down all the brackets. But, I mean, Kemp-Roth was always a Trojan horse to bring down the top rate."[47]

Characteristically, Reagan was unbothered by the first reports of Stockman's exercise in candor. The President did not even get around to reading the *Atlantic* article until the following evening, after the White House had received a series of heated calls from Republican congressmen. Reagan's advisers were split on a course of action. Chief of Staff James Baker said that Stockman was too valuable to let go. His deputy Mike Deaver, who rarely differed with Baker, sided with Counsellor Ed Meese and recommended that

* More than symbolism was involved. In fiscal 1982, for the first time, the national debt became the third largest item in the budget, after entitlement programs and defense.

Stockman be fired. Without telling his aides what he planned to do, Reagan then held a forty-five-minute private lunch with Stockman, who submitted his resignation and apologized for the embarrassment he had caused the President. Reagan, who by now had become concerned about the political implications of the article, rebuked his aide in a manner more kindly than Stockman's subsequent remarks about "woodshedding" would have led anyone to believe. Afterward, in defiance of the long taped quotations from Stockman, the President said he was "more sinned against than sinning." Others in the White House said that Reagan both accepted Baker's reasoning and personally liked Stockman. The budget director, meanwhile, apologized to the world. Armed with an admonition from Deaver that he conduct himself as "one humble sonofabitch," Stockman went out and told the press that he had engaged in "careless rambling to a reporter."

Later, there were other views. Some of the supply-siders viewed Stockman as a traitor, and Senator Bill Roth issued a press release inviting Stockman to a Thanksgiving dinner which included Trojan Horse paté, trickle-down consommé, foot-in-mouth filet, stuffed crow, humble pie with scapegoat cheese and café au Laffer. "Following dinner, Mr. Stockman will be offered a blindfold and a cigarette," the release concluded. Paul W. MacAvoy, a traditional conservative who had been a member of President Ford's Council of Economic Advisers, found that the notion that the article was "a kiss and tell on the secret and devious goals of the Reagan plan" disappeared on second reading. "David Stockman reversed the upward trend in federal expenditures by hitting those domestic programs that most budget examiners and economists had been condemning for at least a decade," MacAvoy wrote. "What went wrong was that the same tactics were not applied to defense expenditures and to the tax cut."[48] The Republican congressional leadership, after second thoughts, accepted the judgment of the President and brought Stockman up to Capitol Hill for a public resurrection. And economics writer Robert J. Samuelson viewed Stockman as something of a hero. "The whole episode of David Stockman's humiliation speaks to the fairyland mentality and rhetoric that surround serious political discussion of the economy," wrote Samuelson. "Stockman's sin was to admit that he no longer believes in fairy tales. It would not have been a sin if the nation's major political leaders—including the President and most prominent members of the Congress—were not themselves such peddlers of economic fantasies."[49]

Reagan still believed in fairy tales, or at least in mirrors. The Stockman episode had demonstrated Reagan's own innocence, as well as the compassion he usually displayed toward valued aides who had transgressed. But neither Stockman's statements nor the growing portents of recession had shaken Reagan's conviction that he could affect wondrous economic reform without inflicting pain. He still believed, deep down, that it was simultaneously possible to balance the budget, increase military spending and reduce taxes. Ultimately, he would have to make some minor concessions, keeping the personal income tax while agreeing to close some business tax loopholes. Ultimately, when unemployment topped 9 percent and stood at the highest level since 1941, he would know that he had at least temporarily flunked the test he had imposed on Carter. Americans were not better off than they had been when Reagan took office. Ultimately, he would retreat, but always grudgingly and always believing that his program would work out in the end. Even those who had known Reagan a long time would be touched by the faith he showed in his policies when there didn't seem to be much hope for them. Deaver would remember the time on December 4, 1981, when Stockman and Baker had tried to win Reagan's support for "revenue enhancements." Reagan stubbornly shook his head. "Revenue enhancements," he said, were by any other name a tax increase. Stockman and Baker left. Deaver lingered behind in the gathering gloom of the Oval Office, talking with the President he both protected and admired about the administration's dwindling economic options. Reagan reviewed what had been said to him, then shook his head. "You know, Mike," he said. "I just don't think that some of my people believe in my program the way I do."

21

The Westerners

HE considers himself a conservationist, an outdoorsman and a lover of
nature. He would rather ride horses than walk. On his first visit to Camp
David as President, Ronald Reagan was appalled to find that Richard
Nixon had paved over the riding trails. As a rancher of varying sorts for
more than four decades, Reagan is a careful steward of his own land. The
trails and woodlands at Rancho del Cielo are well managed. Reagan has rat-
tlesnakes trapped and carted away from the house because he does not want
to kill them. He believes in the value of open space, for himself and his
countrymen. In California the Reagan administration added 145,500 acres
of land and two underwater Pacific Ocean preserves to the state park system.
He signed legislation requiring auto emission controls that were more strin-
gent than the controls required by federal law. Given a choice between al-
ternate measures to protect California's few remaining wild rivers, Reagan
signed the more environmentally protective of the two bills. In 1968 he de-
fied the state's influential dam-building establishment and the Army Corps
of Engineers by saving scenic Round Valley from a high dam which would
have flooded it. Reagan said that the building of a dam would violate a
treaty made long ago with a tiny Indian tribe. "We've broken too damn
many treaties," he said.[1]

But that is only part of the story. As governor, Reagan also fought to
reduce the size of the Redwood National Park which Congress created during his administration. He opposed federal and state land use controls as in-
trusions on private property and sees no contradiction in the taxation benefits his 688-acre ranch receives from a state law favoring agricultural land
use. As President, he has fought to weaken air pollution controls. He has
been unresponsive to the complaints of Canadian officials and domestic
conservationists who warn of the lake-destroying menace of acid rain. Candidate Reagan proudly classified himself as a "Sagebrush Rebel." He appointed a leading light of that rebellion, James G. Watt, as his Secretary of
Interior. And he has brushed aside the substantive criticisms of Watt which

have come even from staunch Reagan supporters as the work of "environmental extremists."

Rarely has a public official so fully exemplified the contradictions of his own region as Reagan does on environmental issues. He is a true Westerner, typifying a region which throughout its tumultuous history has been torn by conflicting claims of development and preservation and has now become the principal national battleground of that struggle. "All regions are conflicted," observed Thornton F. Bradshaw. "But the West is the most conflicted of all."* This conflict reflects the fragility of the West, which is at once the most abundant and optimistic region of the nation and the one in which water and population resources are most precariously balanced. Throughout Reagan's adult lifetime the contradictions between western expectations and western limitations have been especially evident in the region's relationships with the federal government. Westerners always have fancied themselves independent from Washington, which until well into the twentieth century did little to manage or control the expanses of timber, grazing and desert lands technically under its jurisdiction. But Westerners also have always been dependent on the federal government, which drove out the Indians and the Mexicans, laid the telegraph lines, provided the homesteads and subsidized water for agricultural development. The nerve ends of this contradiction between dependence and independence were touched by the Carter administration's decision in 1977 to weigh water projects on a cost-accounting basis. They have been frayed since then by Watt's readiness to open up wilderness areas to energy exploration, a decision supported by President Reagan. "The paradox of the West," says Watt's fellow Westerner, Colorado Governor Richard D. Lamm, "is that people consistently destroy what they come out to seek."[2]

Reagan's mixed environmental record is a product of the timing of his political evolution, of a change in the nation's conservationist values and, most of all, of his proclivity for delegating decisions to trusted subordinates. During the two decades that Reagan was a New Dealer, liberals generally viewed development of water and energy resources as an unmitigated public good. In a 1948 radio broadcast in which he was introduced by Reagan, Democratic Senate candidate Hubert Humphrey said the Tennessee Valley Authority had turned "a poor house into a treasure house" and went on to call for the establishment of other river valley authorities modeled after the TVA. "We must develop every river valley for all of our people," said Humphrey, expressing a familiar liberal sentiment of the time. Today it is James Watt who makes such statements, though he favors private rather than public development of these river valleys.

* Bradshaw, a transplanted New Englander who was then president of the Los Angeles-based Atlantic Richfield Company, made his comment in the *Washington Post* on June 17, 1979, in the first of four articles on "The Embattled West" by the author and Joel Kotkin. Bradshaw later became the chief executive officer of RCA.

The prevailing opinion of Democratic liberalism, especially in the West, has changed profoundly since Reagan's New Deal years. By the time Reagan became a Republican, and especially after his election as governor in 1966, conservationists in the West were trying to preserve river valleys rather than develop them. The Sun Belt population boom and the congestive impact of Los Angeles had produced a new breed of conservationists who were dedicated to saving the remnant of western wild rivers and the formidable reaches of western open space and wilderness from development either by public agency or private enterprise. Often the government, with its sweeping power of eminent domain, was considered as much the adversary as the timber and energy companies. Frequently, a government agency or public utility was a partner with private interests in development. But though the environmental movement in the West had changed its focus, Reagan had not. On most issues, he still expressed the positive view of resource development which he had acquired as a liberal Democrat.

At the same time, environmental issues usually have been secondary ones for Reagan. His speeches of the 1960s yield few references to conservationist concerns of any kind. For a long time he seemed to have thought of conservation as a motherhood issue which everyone favored, and it came as a surprise to him when his prodevelopment positions made him a target for environmental groups in the 1966 gubernatorial campaign.* During that campaign Reagan dealt with organized environmentalists defensively, trying to explain away the ignorance reflected in his famous remark: "You know, a tree is a tree—how many more do you need to look at?"[3] In office, the novice governor displayed an adherence to the development ethic in remarks made about the proposed Redwood National Park at cabinet meetings. "People seem to think that all redwoods that are not protected through a national park will disappear," Reagan said on one occasion. And on another he commented: "I'll be damned if I take away all this privately owned land for no reason. I owe that much to these people in these counties [where the redwood park is being set aside]. I wonder, has anybody ever asked the Sierra Club if they think these trees will grow forever?"

Reagan has a Westerner's sense that "forever" is just around the next bend in the river. The West is so vast, so beautiful, so deceptively rugged that it is difficult even for those less optimistic than Reagan to believe that its fragile ecological system stands at the raw edge of existence. Once, on a flight over Colorado, Reagan turned to me, and with a gesture toward the expanse of mountain wilderness below, remarked on the abundance of un-

* For purposes of simplicity, I have in this chapter used the words "conservationist" and "environmentalist" in their general meanings. Some present-day environmentalists would make a distinction. They would say that a "conservationist" is one who maintains the land for its use by people, i.e., hunters or fishermen. They would say an "environmentalist" is one who preserves the land for future generations. Reagan tends to use the words interchangeably but is more apt to say "environmentalist" if the reference is pejorative.

spoiled land still available to Americans. But the plane, which had taken off through the smog hanging over Los Angeles, landed after passing through another layer of air pollution over Denver.*

Despite his naiveté and personal commitment to development, Reagan dealt with environmental issues successfully as governor of California. He did so primarily because he accepted many of the recommendations of his resources administrator, Ike Livermore, a Lincolnesque lumberman who himself exemplified many of the contradictions of the western experience. Livermore was a member of the Sierra Club and a genuine lover of wilderness. He was tapped as Reagan's natural resources administrator in a conscious attempt by Tom Reed, the governor's politically minded appointments secretary, to defuse the conservationist opposition. Accepted both by environmental groups and by development interests as an honest broker, Livermore sought solutions which respected the claims of conservationists. Though he was inexperienced in government, Livermore had a gift for achieving acceptable political compromises. And unlike some officials to whom Reagan delegated responsibility, Livermore did not keep his knowledge to himself. The cabinet minutes of Reagan's first year in office reflect a step-by-step tutelage of the governor on the needs for setting aside more privately owned land in the proposed Redwood National Park than either Reagan or the lumber companies wanted to yield. Reagan gave ground grudgingly, but ultimately accepted Livermore's compromise for a 53,000-acre park which Congress created out of existing federal land, two state parks and additional land purchased from the lumber companies. On other issues Reagan was more easily educable. In a September 14, 1966, letter, he wrote: "I have long been critical of the Highway Commission for its tendency to go by the rule of the shortest distance between two points, regardless of what scenic wonder must be destroyed, to hold to that rule."[4] As governor, Reagan put this skepticism into practice and helped block a long-sought federal highway through the Minarets region of the high Sierra that would have intersected the John Muir Trail.

Usually, the guiding impulse of Governor Reagan's environmental record was political. While Livermore was inexperienced in government, his bluff, open manner and widespread reputation for integrity won him allies both within the administration and outside of it. Finance Director Caspar Weinberger sided with him on legislation to protect San Francisco Bay and, generally, on the redwoods issue. Livermore received timely assistance from Executive Secretary William Clark in efforts to coordinate the opposition to the Dos Rios Dam which would have flooded Round Valley. There were many sound environmental arguments against the dam, but Livermore and

* The comment was made after an interview on October 15, 1979. I had turned off my tape recorder and did not write down Reagan's exact remarks. My notes and recollection show that he had made some comment about conservationists talking as if the remaining open space in the West was limited when it actually was quite abundant.

Clark emphasized the treaty obligation to the Indians living in the valley because they recognized that Reagan felt strongly about this issue.* Another important environmental force within the Reagan administration was State Parks and Recreation Director William Penn Mott, who had a national reputation in parkland management and acquisition. He deserves much of the credit for the significant expansion of the state park system during Reagan's two terms as governor. But Livermore was the key force for conservationists within the administration, both because of his willingness to take controversial stands and because of his constant efforts to educate Reagan to environmental realities. Under Livermore's prodding, Reagan as governor evolved into a balancer of environmental and development claims and tried to work with moderates in both camps. His rhetoric also began to reflect this balance. "We do not have to choose between the environment and jobs," Reagan said in an April 1973 speech. "We can set a common sense course between those who would cover the whole country with concrete in the name of progress and those who think you should not build a house unless it looks like a bird's nest or a rabbit hole."

Reagan's own five-room, 1,500-square-foot home at Rancho del Cielo is neither a rabbit hole nor a high-rise. Rather it is a century-old Spanish-style adobe ranch house where rustic authenticity has been forced to yield to architectural reality. The tile roof, for instance, is fake. Reagan wanted real tile but found it was too heavy for the existing beams to support. Reagan has done much of the repair and remodeling work on the house himself. He chops and hauls in the oak and madrona wood for the two fireplaces which are the sole source of heating. Reagan calls the ranch his "Shangri-la," and Nancy Reagan, who knows it is important to him, makes a show of liking it as well.

Reagan always has possessed the western impulse for acquiring land and a western penchant for making a tidy profit on the land he buys. He started out in the days of the Wyman marriage with an eight-acre horse ranch in the then pastoral area of Northridge, which since has been overrun by the relentless suburban sprawl of Los Angeles. In 1951, shortly before he married Nancy Davis, Reagan sold his first ranch and bought two parcels of land totaling 290 acres in the rugged Santa Monica Mountains north of Los Angeles. He paid $85,000 for the property, which abutted 2,500 acres owned by 20th Century-Fox. The film company used the land for locations, often in

---

* I felt strongly about it, too, and played a modest role in the efforts of Round Valley rancher Richard Wilson to stop the Dos Rios Dam from being built. My article, "High Dam in the Valley of the Tall Grass," which questioned the project, appeared in the summer 1968 issue of the conservationist publication *Cry California*. Reagan aides who were also skeptical about the dam gave the article to the governor to read on July 4, 1968, during a time when he was waiting to deliver a patriotic speech. He read the piece and, several weeks later, surprised some state water officials who were advocates of the dam by quoting portions of it verbatim—including a section about Indian burial sites in the valley that were important both to archeologists and Indians.

western movies. When Reagan became a candidate for governor in 1966, he decided to sell this land. "I could not have run for office unless I sold the ranch," he told me in 1968. But the sale was not actually consummated until a month after Reagan won the election. He sold the larger of the two parcels, 236 acres, to 20th Century-Fox, which also acquired an option to buy the remaining 54 acres. Reagan received $1,931,000 from the film company, whose executives said they wanted to use the land for location purposes. In 1974, shortly before Reagan left the governorship, the State Parks and Recreation Department purchased all of 20th Century-Fox's land in the area for $4.8 million, paying less than a fourth as much per acre as the film company had paid for the Reagan property. The transactions prompted a spate of investigations by reporters and political opponents, none of whom have ever uncovered any wrongdoing in connection with either Reagan's sale or the state's subsequent purchase of the property.*

Reagan's land dealings had made him a millionaire. 20th Century-Fox never picked up its option on the remaining 54-acre parcel. In 1968 Reagan used these 54 acres as a down-payment on a 778-acre ranch in Riverside County, south of Los Angeles, which he bought for $347,000. Reagan said at the time he intended to develop the Riverside County property, known as Rancho California, as a working ranch. But he couldn't obtain water or power service on the remote property, and acknowledged, in 1973, that he was "getting a little impatient about having a ranch" on the Riverside County land. "The thought has entered my mind that I might have to look for one that is already established instead of starting one from scratch," he said. The Riverside County Board of Supervisors allowed Reagan to subdivide the land, but he found no immediate buyers. Finally, in December 1976, Reagan sold the hilly, undeveloped land to James E. Wilson, a real estate broker and land developer, for $856,000 in a sale that was carefully kept quiet at the time.† By this time Reagan was already comfortably ensconced in Rancho del Cielo.

* The purchase was consistent with the then aggressive policy of the State Parks and Recreation Department in buying available scenic parcels in the Santa Monica Mountains, an open space of great beauty in the midst of one of the nation's most congested metropolitan areas. But the state's purchase price of about $1,800 per acre was so much less than the $8,000 an acre which the company had paid for the Reagan land that it raised questions whether the original transaction was, in effect, a contribution. One reason that the price was so much less, according to state officials, was that the land purchased from 20th Century-Fox included extensive mountain acreage of less commercial value than the Reagan acreage. My own check of comparable sales at the time Reagan sold his land would seem to indicate that he did get a "good deal," but not one that was outlandishly out of line with prevailing market values. The land was strategically located in relation to the property Fox already owned, which may have made it more valuable in the eyes of the buyer.

† The land sale was not disclosed until the *Riverside Press-Enterprise,* a newspaper with a reputation as a diligent chronicler of local affairs, printed a story about it on October 5, 1979—nearly three years after the sale. By that time Wilson had subdivided the parcel into 35 lots, most of them 20-acre parcels, and sold 17 of them for a total price of $1,065,800.

The heavenly ranch nestles on a 2,250-foot-high mountaintop 29.5 miles northwest of Santa Barbara. Often, it is bathed in bright sunlight while fog shrouds the Pacific Ocean below. Access, except by helicopter, is over a tortuous one-lane road which extends 6.5 miles through a brush-covered canyon from Refugio State Beach and the Pacific Coast Highway. The canyon and the Reagan acreage teem with deer, bobcats and foxes, plus occasional bears and mountain lions. In 1955 the devastating Refugio Fire swept through the area, burning 80,000 acres of brush and timber. Such fires are common in the brushy regions of California's coastal areas, and fire-fighters usually are powerless to stop them. The steep slopes of 60 degrees or more on the Reagan ranch and the heavy brush which has built up there in the quarter century since the big Refugio blaze make the fire hazard at Rancho del Cielo especially high. Because there is a small lake next to the Reagan ranch house which serves as a water supply, and because both home and lake are surrounded by clearing, the ranch house would probably survive another fire as it did the one in 1955. "But it is likely," wrote Jerry Rankin after a detailed survey of the fire conditions, "that there wouldn't be much left around it."[5]

Rancho del Cielo, once part of a huge Spanish land grant, was discovered for Reagan by his friend, millionaire investment counsellor William A. Wilson, who owned land nearby as well as property adjacent to Reagan in Riverside County. Wilson is one of the three trustees of The Ronald Reagan Trust,* which manages Reagan's financial affairs, and the owner of a ranch in Mexico where the Reagans have vacationed for many years. Reagan trusts Wilson's judgment, and he also liked the ranch the first time he saw it. He paid $527,000 for the property in 1974, making a down-payment of $90,000.† The property has never been on the market since, but local real estate sources estimated in 1980 that it would sell for two to four times the purchase price—anywhere from $1 million to $2 million. The probable market value of the land is not reflected in the property taxes which Reagan pays. Reagan qualifies for an immense property tax break because his land is zoned "agricultural preserve" under a California law designed to prevent ranchers and farmers from being forced to sell their land to subdividers to pay their taxes. In return for an extremely low rate of taxation the landowner pledges to keep his land in agricultural use. When Reagan bought his Santa Barbara County property, it was a working cattle ranch. The owner, since deceased, had applied for and been granted an "agricultural preserve" designation three years earlier. Without going into business himself, Reagan preserved the tax status of the ranch by grazing only 22 head of cattle. The

* One of the few Catholics in the inner circle of Reagan's millionaire friends, Wilson subsequently was named to the part-time position of the President's personal representative to the Vatican.

† There have been minor discrepancies in the reported purchase price of Rancho del Cielo, ranging from $525,000 to $547,000. The figure used here was confirmed to me by Reagan aides in 1976.

financial benefits of this practice have been enormous. If the ranch were valued at a conservative market price of $1 million, Reagan would have paid $42,000 in taxes in 1979. His actual tax bill under the agricultural preserve designation was $862. Such tax breaks have widespread support in Santa Barbara County, and not only from the ranchowners who benefit from them. By and large, conservationists support the agricultural preserve designations because they insure that large amounts of land—an estimated half-million acres in Santa Barbara County alone—are preserved as open space. However, the special zoning, renewable every ten years by the county board of supervisors, is a huge bonus for Reagan and similar landowners. Other property in the vicinity of Rancho del Cielo, whatever its zoning, has not been subdivided and is unlikely to be. Water is simply too scarce, and the fire hazard too great.

Reagan is a multi-millionaire who does not need the tax break provided by Rancho del Cielo.* But the ranch meets other needs. Reagan is a person who enjoys time spent alone in physical activity. He likes to work with his hands. Assisted only by his long-time employee, Willard Barnett, once the driver of his gubernatorial limousine, Reagan rebuilt the adobe house that he had bought at Rancho del Cielo. He knocked out walls, redesigned the kitchen, tore out a screen porch and replaced it with a sturdy family room. He ripped off the corrugated roof, replaced it with old fence boards and covered the boards with fake tile. He built a fence around his home out of old telephone poles and constructed a rock patio. To build the patio Reagan and Barnett dragged flat rocks into place, put cement in the crevices between them and sprayed the cement with water. Surveying all this in 1976, when Reagan was on the verge of losing the Republican presidential nomination to Gerald Ford, reminded me of that haunting scene in *Death of a Salesman* when Biff Loman talks about how his dead father had enjoyed building a bathroom and a new porch and putting up the garage. "You know, Charley, there's more of him in that front stoop than in all the sales he ever made," Biff says. Watching Reagan describe what he had done with genuine enthusiasm, rather than with the stage polish of his political talks, I thought then

* Reagan has always been reluctant to disclose the extent of his fortune, and, as governor, refused throughout his eight years to issue a statement on his net worth even though there was political pressure on him to do so after it was disclosed that he paid no state income taxes in 1970 because of what he described as "business reverses." Reagan instructed his accountant to make certain he paid a minimum tax every year after that, no matter what his deductions were, but he still refused to issue a net worth statement. In the post-Watergate era, when many politicians made their financial affairs public, Reagan still resisted but finally, during his challenge to President Ford in 1976, issued the only net worth statement of his career. It listed his worth at $1,455,571 and his 1975 earnings at $275,253. During his 1980 campaign, Reagan for the first time made his federal income tax returns public. His earnings by then had nearly doubled (to $515,878 in 1979), most of them from speeches. He paid nearly half this amount in federal income taxes. Reagan did not issue a net worth statement then, or subsequently, but estimates based on examination of the 1980 return and the increase in value of his California property put Reagan's net worth well over $2 million and perhaps as high as $3 million.

that there was more of Reagan in Rancho del Cielo than in most of his speeches. On this one warm Sunday in July he seemed to care more about the way he had carved the tile to fit around a meandering stone fireplace than he had ever cared about the Panama Canal.

The ranch was an extension of Ronald Reagan. After he became President, he took every opportunity to go there, on some occasions ignoring advisers who thought it would have been politically wiser for him to remain in Washington. Reagan was proud of his ranch, and it gave him emotional sustenance. He joked frequently about its isolation, once saying that he could cause consternation among the television cameramen who tried to grab peeks of him with long-lens cameras by suddenly doubling up and falling off his horse. And he declined to turn Rancho del Cielo into a "western White House" like Richard Nixon had created at San Clemente. Reagan has too much of a mystical feeling about the land he owns to turn it into a presidential office complex. In his own eyes he is literally the pioneer who has reached the Pacific, which on clear days is a blue vista of infinite distance that can be glimpsed from a corner of the ranch. Rancho del Cielo is for Reagan a dream come true, a western dream which he talks about as if it were somehow recognizable and realizable for most Americans. When a reporter in 1980 asked Reagan why he would trade the tranquility of his ranch for the turmoil of Washington, he responded: "Well, maybe, because I want to see that it'll continue to be possible to have this kind of life style in our country—namely freedom. I see it endangered more and more every day. This reminds you of how great it is."[6]

Another man who thought he saw freedom endangered was James Watt, the second-choice Secretary of Interior whom Paul Laxalt selected to do battle with the environmentalists. Watt did not grow up in Dixon or Hollywood but in the cattle and wheat high plains country of eastern Wyoming. He enjoys work as much as Reagan does, but he has a less romantic view of the West. "I know the land of the West differently from the way some of you know it," Watt told editors and reporters of the *Washington Post* in 1981. "Some of you know it the first two weeks in August, but I know it with the bitter coldness and the winds and the driving rains. I've fixed the fence, I've pumped water for the cattle. I know the land, and it's important to me because the wealth of the nation springs from the land."[7] This is also a basic western view, the view of those who see the land and the natural elements which formed it as forces to be conquered. Watt set out to conquer them. But first, he believed, he would have to tame the environmental lobbies which had, in his eyes, locked up the mineral riches of the West.

Watt is tall and strong, like Ike Livermore, but the resemblance ends there. Watt is one of those Westerners who believes that the only limits on growth are a man's ability to dream. Watt dreamed of development, not wilderness. Livermore, who was a balancer, knew that his fellow lumbermen had despoiled forests and polluted streams. He recognized that irrational development could properly be called "exploitation." Such a word did not seem to exist in Watt's formidable vocabulary, at least as it applied to development interests. He believed he had a mandate from Reagan and the western conservative senators whom the 1980 election had carried into Washington to make the federal government an active agent of developing the West. As Watt saw it, voters had spoken not only on the question of President Carter's leadership, but on the aspirations of the Sagebrush Rebellion, that emotional and compex movement with roots deep in the history of the West. In its narrowest definition, the Sagebrush Rebellion was a specific attempt to transfer hundreds of millions of acres of federally owned western lands to state control. Actual support for this particular legal challenge, which originated in Nevada, was limited even in the West, where five states declined to endorse Nevada's stand. Watt himself was not particularly interested in the Nevada challenge as such. However, the phrase "Sagebrush Rebellion" also applied to a broader movement, one that took in every antifederal grievance from the 55-mile-an-hour speed limit to President Carter's proposed deployment of the MX missile in multiple shelters in the Utah and Nevada deserts. Watt claimed this broader movement as his constituency, but he seemed to owe his strongest allegiance to a specific faction—that part of the western business community which used the rebellion as a weapon against any restrictions on the booming development of the West. "It was the voice of a regional elite, an economic and political oligarchy, making noises it had made before," wrote western novelist and historian Wallace Stegner. "It was the voice of the united mining industry. It was the voice of the chambers of commerce, the boosters, the real estate operators, the developers. It was not quite so clearly the voice of the energy companies, for those astute and powerful forces, though not friendly to governmental regulation, might have reasonably felt that one federal policy might be easier to deal with than 11 state policies."[8] It was, some said, the voice which spoke through the Mountain States Legal Foundation, of which James Gauis Watt was a founder and the president.

The foundation was a counterforce. Throughout the West during the 1960s and 1980s, ad hoc legal organizations that were conservationist cousins of the public interest law firms inspired by Ralph Nader had blocked nuclear plants, delayed high dams and helped save redwoods, parkland and wild rivers. Eventually, the targets of these lawsuits fought back with foundations of their own. In California they created the Pacific Legal Foundation, with which Ed Meese was associated. In the Rocky Mountain area, there was Mountain States. The purpose of the latter foundation, said Watt while its president, was "to fight in the courts those bureaucrats and no-growth advocates who create a challenge to individual liberty and economic freedoms." Watt made it clear as Secretary of Interior that he intended to continue this fight in the service of Reagan. "If we fail, we won't just see a drift toward socialism," he told an audience of Denver Republicans on September 18, 1981. "We will see the rampant acceleration toward socialism that the liberals will bring to America."

This was Reagan-style rhetoric—but from 1964, not 1981. Reagan had learned during the first year of his governorship the necessity of at least soothing conservationists, and he had made some decisions which pleased them as well. Watt, who acknowledged he spoke "in black-and-white terms without much gray in my life," felt no necessity of appeasing his adversaries by word or deed. Charged with the Secretary of Interior's peculiarly schizophrenic responsibility of conserving and protecting the nation's 750 million acres of federal land while at the same time encouraging the orderly development of its resources, Watt came down on one side of the equation. Departing from the path of his predecessors, Watt saw his role in what he called Reagan's "crusade for America" as shifting the balance in federal policy toward resources development. "We will mine more, drill more, cut more timber to use our resources rather than simply keep them locked up,"[9] Watt vowed when he reached Washington.

From the beginning Watt recognized that he would be a controversial figure, and he seemed to delight in the image he was creating of himself. "God calls each of us to our different missions," Watt said at a Denver press conference after his appointment. "I'm prepared emotionally, spiritually and intellectually to withstand the onslaught, because I'm committed to helping the President-elect make changes in America." He discussed the potential for controversy with everyone who counted—with Laxalt, who had picked him for the job because he had "the gut" to take criticism; with Meese, who respected his legal work at Mountain States; and with Reagan, who had promised to back him against criticisms from the environmental community. "I'm going for the long ball," Watt told an Arizona reporter in March 1981. "I'm Ronald Reagan's high-risk player."[10] Five months later, after he had become the most controversial figure in the Reagan cabinet, Watt tossed aside criticisms of his performance by saying: "You don't come on with business as usual if you're going to bring about the Reagan Revolution."[11]

But the content of that "revolution" was ill-defined. On the one hand, Reagan consistently had favored more energy exploration on public lands and a loosening of grazing restrictions in the West. On the other, Reagan pointed to his record in California as evidence that he would continue to respect the claims of conservationists. It is likely that Clifford Hansen, the Laxalt first choice for Interior, would have at least attempted to give the appearance of balance even while nudging the Department of the Interior into a more pro-development stance. That was not Watt's way. After service in both the legislative and executive branches of the federal government, Watt saw Washington as a liberal and hostile environment where he stood in constant danger of being compromised. He was a serious man, who took himself seriously. Watt had never smoked or drunk alcoholic beverages or coffee. As a schoolboy he had spent Saturday nights studying. His friends called him "James" well into his twenties. Still, Watt had been popular and an achiever—a student body officer, a varsity athlete, a member of the Honor Society and the prince of the prom at his Wheatland, Wyoming, high school. Six years later he graduated from the University of Wyoming with a law degree, intent on a career in politics. But four years in Washington on the staff of Senator Milward Simpson of Wyoming had convinced him, he said later, that "I had an executive and not a legislative mind."[12] He became disillusioned with the compromise and tradeoffs of politics as well as with the then liberal direction of the country. Watt found a source of conviction in fundamentalist Christianity, to which he was converted at a businessman's rally in Washington in 1964. "Jim was impressed by the caliber of the people going up to the altar," said Doug Baldwin, his public affairs director at Interior. "These were Wall Street Christians in three-piece suits, not snake charmers from the South."[13]

The new convert was not impressed, however, with what was going on in Washington. Watt worked briefly as a lobbyist for the U.S. Chamber of Commerce and then eight years for the Department of Interior and the now defunct Federal Power Commission. From 1972 to 1975 he was chairman of Interior's Bureau of Outdoor Recreation, whose successor agency he abolished in 1981. Watt viewed Interior as a citadel in which good men came from the West to be compromised by the forces of environmentalism and politics. He lived in fear of being "Hickelized," which was Watt's reference to the fate of Walter Hickel, the millionaire former governor of Alaska who had served as Nixon's first Secretary of Interior. Hickel expressed anticonservationist sentiments when he came to Washington, including a comment that he did not believe in "conservation for conservation's sake." He backed down from these statements as a price of confirmation and, as Interior Secretary, evolved into a genuine conservationist who advocated strong environmental protections and an expanded park system. Watt believed that Hickel and his successor, Rogers C. B. Morton, had become captives of the system and refused to face up to the necessity for energy development. "The problems I face now I face because Hickel and Morton ducked 'em," said Watt[14] in an interview in his private office, a small, austerely furnished room to the side of the palatial office used by other Secretaries of Interior.

Watt saw himself as an idealist, engaged not in a balancing act but in a moral struggle. He was not a man of wealth like Walter Hickel or Ronald Reagan. Though he had the opportunity and the mental equipment to become a financially successful corporate lawyer, Watt shunned the trappings of wealth and power. He was that rarity of the Reagan administration—an austere zealot in a cabinet of genial millionaires. At the age of forty-three, his net worth of $65,000 was less than anyone else in the Reagan cabinet except for David Stockman, who was nearly nine years his junior. He worked long hours and organized his days productively. Watt spent his free time with his church and family—his son and daughter attended Oral Roberts University, which Watt called "the finest Christian school there is." He detested cocktail parties, an attitude which official Washington is apt to regard as slightly sinister. But Watt does not have much respect for official Washington and its judgments. As he discussed the difficulty of making genuine changes in government policies, he walked with his interviewer from his own cubicle into the formal, majestic office of the Secretary of Interior, gazed at the opulent surroundings and predicted, "It might reach a point where I must be sacrificed, if America won't accept the things I want to do. I'm a team player, and I won't harm the President. There will come a time when I'll be replaced by a congressman who will be confirmed after a half-hour hearing. He'll sit there at this desk and won't do anything the whole time he's there."[15]

Watt wanted to do quite a bit, and do it rapidly. He organized his department more quickly than any other cabinet secretary, an accomplishment which reflected his zeal, intelligence and previous experience in Washington. By moving so swiftly, Watt was able to put the people he wanted in the positions he wanted them. The White House was delighted. The administration's personnel operation was so sluggish and several other departments were organizing so slowly that both the President and his top trio of aides appreciated a cabinet secretary who knew what to do with delegated authority once he was given it. In addition, the administration's entire early focus was on the economic plan. No one outside of Interior wanted to be bothered with the environmental agenda, and Watt was given a free hand. In March some White House aides, including Chief of Staff James Baker, had second thoughts because of the intensity of the environmentalist backlash. This reaction focused on Watt's proposal to lease oil lands off the California coast, which was scheduled for cabinet discussion in early April. The week the item was on the agenda was the same week that President Reagan was wounded by a would-be assassin, and a decision was postponed. Watt continued to chart his own confrontational course. He wanted market forces rather than government policy to set the limits on energy development, a view which accurately reflected the prevailing outlook of the Reagan administration. But Watt leaped from this philosophical premise to a conclusion that 200 million acres of potential off-shore oil lands should be made available for drilling every year for a five-year period. This was a billion acres—more than ten times the amount of off-shore acreage offered for oil-exploration leasing in the entire history of the United States! The wide-open leasing was supposed to be a boon for the oil industry, which could pick and choose its bids and take advantage of a new streamlined leasing process that reduced the attention given to environmental assessments and public comments. Even some oil company executives complained that Watt was giving them more than they could swallow. "Boys, do you want to compete or don't you?" was Watt's response.[16]

The secretary took other initiatives. The one which provoked the loudest congressional and conservationist outcry was his effort to declare a moratorium on national park acquisition and to use the funds appropriated for this purpose to improve deteriorating conditions in existing parks. As Watt saw it, "park barrel politics" in Congress had included in the national park system some properties which were really state or local parks. Actually, this was one of Watt's few undertakings which had support among the affected bureaucrats at Interior, including Park Service Director Russell Dickenson, the only holdover political appointee in the department to keep his job. Dickenson recognized that maintenance of some parks had indeed become slipshod and that a case could be made for a slower pace of acquisition. Watt's attempt to halt the expansion of the park system by shifting land acquisition funds to maintenance struck many of his adversaries as a trumped-up trick to cripple the park system. He was forced to back down from a suggestion he made that some previously approved urban parks be "de-authorized." The impression that Watt was antipark was enhanced by a conversation the secretary held in March 1981 with the National Park concessionaires. A transcript of that conversation quoted the secretary as inviting the private concessionaires "to be involved in areas that you haven't been involved in before."[17] This touched old sensitivities with park lovers. Yellowstone, the first national park, had been created in 1872 for the express purpose of keeping its celebrated geysers from falling into the hands of private resort operators.

Since national parks are uncontroversial assets to most Americans, Watt's choice of the park system as his first target indelibly typed him in the role he had chosen for himself as the "Reagan revolutionary" of the environment. But while Reagan is almost always more personally popular than his policies, Watt proved less popular than his. Watt had hoped to isolate environmentalist critics by driving a wedge between the smaller activist groups and the more broad-based organizations which tended to appeal to hunters and fishermen, the so-called "hook and bullet boys." Reagan's former director of fish and game in California, G. Ray Arnett, came to Washington from his Stockton, California, ranch as assistant interior secretary to oversee his political strategy. Arnett is a woodsy Republican who shoots geese on Chesapeake Bay and drops them by the White House as a present for his former boss, the President of the United States. A plain-spoken and popular conservative who complained that the liberal welfare state had turned people into "park bears" living on handouts, Arnett had twice been president of the National Wildlife Federation, whose 4.5 million members outnumbered the Sierra Club, the Audubon Society, Friends of the Earth and the Wilderness Society combined. But even Arnett could not change the opinion of the federation leadership, which observed that Watt had opposed twelve of the organization's fifteen priorities and ignored the other three. On July 14, after a poll of its membership, the federation joined the militant environmentalist groups in calling for Watt's resignation. The poll showed that more than 60 percent of the group's membership had voted for Reagan.

Other environmental organizations found that mailers with Watt's name and picture served as a potent recruiting poster. The Wilderness Society tripled its fund-raising, and Sierra Club membership grew 25 percent after three nearly no-growth years. "If there hadn't been a James Watt we would have had to invent one," said Doug Scott, director of federal affairs for the Sierra Club.[18] Watt charged that these groups quoted him out of context for their own political and fund-raising purposes. On the park issue, this claim had some merit. But no conservationist hyperbole was necessary when it came to describing the secretary's antiwilderness stand. Though Watt may have been sincere in wanting to improve existing parks, he had no thought of "improving" the wilderness. When he discussed wilderness, Watt did not describe it as wildlife habitat or watershed or a humbling reminder of what came before mankind, but as a playground for backpackers. That was its use. It was a use which Watt saw as carrying little weight against what he considered its higher uses—the economic and strategic importance of finding new mineral or energy sources or even the need of tourists to drive through the back country in recreational vehicles. Watt is not personally a wilderness lover. When he lived in Denver, he drove to the mountains on weekends in a purple Dodge van with swivel seats and a carpeted interior. "I am a symbol of free enterprise," he said. "Many of the problems we have today were caused by secretaries who went flyfishing instead of staying by the office. Now, they provided good photo opportunities and they proved themselves to be virile, tough men who loved to camp, but who chickened out when it came to make the tough decisions."[19]* Watt was no chicken. On May 2, 1981, he met with his staff to draw up a list of goals for the next four years, a vital first step in Watt's management-by-objective system. One of the first five objectives for the solicitor's office was, "Open wilderness areas."

When Ronald Reagan was elected President, he believed, and said many times, that he had a mandate for change. Public opinion surveys on economic issues and on the strengthening of national defense gave some support to this view, though frequently not as much as Reagan claimed. But the "mandate" which Watt believed he was carrying out in Interior did not exist at all, except, perhaps, among the developers and their allies. A Harris Poll taken in June 1981, when the Clean Air Act was coming up for revision, found that 48 percent of Americans wanted to keep the law the way it was,

---

* Watt's speech to park concessionaires on March 9, 1981, included a passage that was widely circulated by his opponents in an effort to show the secretary's low opinion of wilderness. It is an account by Watt about a float trip through the Grand Canyon the previous September: "The first day was spectacular, I'll tell you it was an exciting, thrilling day. The second day started to get a little tedious, but the third day I wanted bigger motors to move that raft out. There is no way you could get me on an oar-powered boat on that river—I'll guarantee you that. On the fourth day we were praying for helicopters and they came."

38 percent wanted to toughen it, and only 12 percent thought it should be less strict. A Gallup Poll taken for *Newsweek* in July found that those willing to pay the extra cost of environmental protection outnumbered the unwilling by 58 to 36 percent. A *New York Times*–CBS Poll in late September found 67 percent of the sample desiring to maintain existing environmental laws even at a cost in economic growth. Private polls by Richard Wirthlin for the Republican National Committee also showed a strong public environmental commitment. But these surveys did not register with Watt, who thought that his opponents were either "environmental extremists" or misinformed. When Watt was told that his friend, Wyoming Congressman Richard B. Cheney, had suggested that he needed "a Sandra O'Connor decision" to improve his image, Watt dismissed the idea out of hand. "I don't think we need a new issue," he said. "What we've done is so eminently sensible that if we explain it to people they'll buy it."[20]

But Congress wasn't buying what Watt was selling. On July 22, only a week before the administration won a smashing victory in the House on its tax program with the help of 48 Democratic votes, Republicans deserted Watt en masse and appropriated $155 million for park expansion in 1982. The House vote was 358–46, a measure both of the popularity of parks and the prevailing congressional view of Watt. A few weeks before this vote, the House Interior Committee had invoked an unusual procedure and declared an "emergency" in an attempt to prevent Watt from allowing oil drilling in the Bob Marshall Wilderness of Montana. Later in the year, Watt received an even more personal rebuke when he tried to allow oil drilling in the Washakie Wilderness, outside Yellowstone Park. The Washakie, like the Bob Marshall, is in the middle of the largely untapped Overthrust Belt, considered one of the great remaining oil sources in the United States. It is also a home for a western Wyoming elk herd and the grizzly bears that roam in and out of Yellowstone. Cheney, the state's lone congressman, had been hearing from the folks back home that they didn't want oil rights in the Washakie, and he came out against it during the Fourth of July recess. Senator Malcolm Wallop soon followed suit. Senator Alan Simpson, the third member of Wyoming's congressional delegation and the son of the senator for whom Watt had worked in Washington nearly twenty years earlier, took a pack trip into the wilderness area to reach his decision. Soon after he returned, he joined his colleagues in opposition, putting all three Republicans from Watt's home state in opposition to opening the wilderness to oil rigs.

Most of what Watt was doing came to the attention of President Reagan only in passing. He was preoccupied, first with his economic program and then with the various turf battles and minor scandals which kept cropping up within his administration. A segment in the comic strip "Doonesbury" suggested that Watt had been appointed while the President was "out riding" one Wednesday. But Reagan, encouraged by Ed Meese, defended his embattled Secretary of Interior at times when a less than enthusiastic defense might well have prompted a resignation. "Jim Watt has been doing what I think is a common sense job in the face of some environmental extremism we've suffered from," Reagan said on August 13, 1981, "and I can assure you Jim Watt does not want to destroy the beauty of America. He just wants to recognize that people are ecology, too. We have some needs, and there has to be provision for us to live."

Predictably, it took a California issue and the protests of influential California Republicans to give the White House a less sanguine view of Jim Watt. Two weeks into his new job, Watt launched his off-shore oil and gas exploration program by announcing that he would allow drilling in four basins off the California coast that had been closed by his predecessor, Cecil Andrus. Taken together the four basins included 80 million acres and stretched from scenic Big Sur to the Oregon border. Watt was aware that the action, known as Lease Sale No. 53, was highly controversial but said he wanted "to give a message to the bureaucracy that we're taking on hard issues." He could scarcely have found a harder one. The entire estimated oil resources in the four basins would provide only an estimated eleven-day supply of petroleum for the nation, but the region supports a multibillion-dollar tourist industry extending along the continent's most scenic coast. California filed suit, with Democratic Governor Edmund G. (Jerry) Brown, Jr., arguing that the law required the federal government to consult states about off-shore leasing plans. Before long, the attempt to stop Lease Sale No. 53 was joined by conservative Republicans, including Senator S. I. Hayakawa, whose Senate seat had been targeted by Brown, and Representative Donald Clausen, whose coastal congressional district was considered politically vulnerable if oil drilling were allowed. On June 1, the California Republican state chairman, long-time Reaganite Tirso del Junco, sent a letter to Watt with copies to the White House which said the oil exploration initiative "comes at a time when Republicans in California are making some genuine headway toward recapturing a majority in the state Senate and Assembly as well as regaining the Governor's office for the first time since President Reagan left office in 1974. But the progress we are making now can be severely hampered should our candidates be forced into supporting the decisions which you have made concerning Lease Sale #53." Bill Roberts, the 1966 Reagan campaign manager, added his voice to the protest in letters to Meese and Lyn Nofziger, which said that the leasing proposal jeopardized chances for Republicans in two congressional districts, one of them Clausen's, "and may hamper the Administration's goal of a majority in the House of Representatives."

These protests were heard in the Reagan administration, especially by the politically minded Nofziger. When the House Appropriations Committee on June 26 voted to ban the oil and gas exploration leases, the White House did not oppose the action. Representative Clair Burgener of La Jolla, who had been a Republican state senator when Reagan was governor, told the committee that California Republicans were firmly against the leasing. On July 27 a federal court ruling in Los Angeles barred leasing on thirty-one tracts off Santa Barbara. The action had no direct bearing on the northern California basins Watt wanted to lease, but gave him an avenue of political retreat. After consultation with Meese and other White House officials, Watt announced he was postponing all leasing off the California coast until at least 1983.

Typically, Watt refused to acknowledge that he was bowing to combined pressure from conservationists and Republican politicians—in the latter case tacitly endorsed by the White House. He said instead that the judge's decision would be appealed all the way to the Supreme Court, that he was confident of reversal and that postponement of the leasing would avoid "long and expensive court battles." Watt's statement, retorted Governor Brown, was "a legal cover for a political decision."[21] However, Meese and Nofziger were more than happy that they had been given a way to cut their losses. Without conceding any poor policy judgment, the administration had postponed the issue until after the 1982 elections. Later, the White House applied the California example to the country and quietly convinced Watt to modify his plan to lease a billion off-shore acres, focusing instead on those off-shore tracts considered to be of high oil and gas potential. The announcement, drawn up a week before, was made on Christmas Eve in a deliberate effort to attract as little attention as possible.

A backdown, under any rationale, was rare for Watt. He called himself "the stalking horse and lightning rod" of the administration and seemed to go out of his way to find dubious and unproductive controversies. One of his first actions as Secretary of Interior was an attempt to undo an eleventh-hour action by Andrus putting into the federal wild river system the five California rivers which Reagan, at Livermore's urging, had given state protection to in 1972.* California officials feared that if the Reagan administra-

---

* Most of the fifty-five rivers in the National Wild and Scenic River system were placed there by acts of Congress, but the Interior Secretary has the power to add to the national system any river that is protected by a state. Andrus had met with California Governor Edmund G. Brown, Jr., the previous summer and agreed to add the five California rivers—the Smith, Klamath, Trinity, Eel and lower American River—to the system. He was opposed by Southern California water interests, aided by the timber industry, who had obtained a federal court injunction which prevented Andrus from acting. In the last days of the Carter administration the White House Personnel Office asked cabinet secretaries to submit their resignations by the close of the business day January 19, which was 5 P.M. Washington time. Every secretary complied except Andrus who said, in a September 23, 1981, letter to Tom Kizzia, that he called President Carter himself and said "the only way I would send in a resignation would be if he personally requested it, then I would take that as his firing of me." Carter, according to Andrus, then told him to handle the matter "in any way I saw fit." Andrus did not, he said, have the wild rivers situation specifically in mind but added that, "My instincts told me I should not resign. . . ." At 6 P.M. on January 19 he was attending a farewell social function at the White House when he received a telephone call from a member of his staff in San Francisco telling him that the court was about to render a decision. Andrus called his chauffeur and returned to the Department of the Interior. At 7:30 P.M. Washington time (4:30 P.M. in San Francisco), he

tion refused to support Andrus' action, the courts might reverse his decision. The Justice Department, which believed that Andrus had acted within his legal rights, wanted to defend the Carter Interior Secretary's action; Watt argued that it should be opposed. The White House, with Meese and Nofziger both supporting Justice, made the decision and Andrus' action was defended and upheld.

Watt was not deterred by such defeats. He continued to go after programs which had on occasion been the target of Mountain States Legal Foundation as well, such as his decision to charge fees for Interior's "adopt-a-horse" program. At Mountain States, Watt had sued Interior for allowing the wild horses to roam on private land. Watt also tried to open ecologically fragile desert lands to motorcycles and trail bikes by quietly proposing the lifting of an executive order restricting their use. And he played hardball politics with the House Interior Committee, threatening to withdraw support of the giant Central Arizona Water Project unless Committee Chairman Morris K. Udall of Arizona reined in hostile questioning. Watt's pole star, in all circumstances, seemed to be the virtue of unrestricted private development. In December 1981 he proposed to open five western national recreation areas to drilling for oil and gas. Andrus also had advocated this initiative, but Watt insisted on going him one better and opening these same areas to "hard rock" mining for copper, gold, silver and other minerals. Watt also tried, unsuccessfully, to dismantle the federal Office of Surface Mining and turn over strip mining controls to the states, in which he expressed great confidence. But Watt wanted to do away with the regional task forces which the Carter administration had created to give states a voice in coal-leasing decisions. Watt nearly doubled the coal-leasing targets in Montana, the Rocky Mountain state most systematically despoiled by past mining operations and the one which in response has become the most conservationist of the region. Observing that Watt had proclaimed a "good neighbor" policy with the states, Montana Governor Ted Schwinden, a Democrat, added: "But the bottom line is his performance, and I don't think it's very neighborly to override our recommendations."[22]

Even by his own standards, Watt was not an especially effective Secretary of Interior. The pendulum was already swinging toward development

---

received word that the Ninth Circuit Court of Appeals had lifted the injunction. In the meantime, said Andrus, a call from "someone at Justice" instructed Interior Solicitor Clyde Martz not to let Andrus sign any of the wild river designations because his resignation was effective at the close of the business day. "I then advised the Solicitor and the other members of my staff that I had never resigned, had no intention of doing so, and was going ahead and make the decisions and designations, which I did," Andrus wrote. "And, if you will look at them, you will see that I dated them and put the time on there as 7:45 Eastern Standard Time. I was in fact Secretary of Interior and I continued to act right up until the last minute."

under Andrus, despite his national reputation for defending a wilderness area from a mining proposal. Watt could have nudged the national consensus further in the development direction if he had convinced the public that esthetic, recreation and wildlife tradeoffs were being made judiciously. But he lacked a political temperament. To Watt, the Audubon Society, which was lobbying for his firing, could be dismissed as "a chanting mob."[23] Speaking to rich farmers in Fresno and foolishly believing that his remarks would not be repeated to the press, Watt divided people into two categories—"liberals and Americans."[24] He had such a proclivity for polarization that he refused—or was unable to—curb his tongue even when his comments undercut his own objectives. He picked needless quarrels with congressmen, ruined the morale in several Interior agencies, and triggered dozens of environmental lawsuits.

"The most striking element of the new leaders at Interior is their almost evangelical confidence in their ideology," said Guy Martin, an Alaskan who had served as assistant secretary for land and water resources under Andrus. "They've out-Reaganed Reagan when it comes to budget cuts, but their effort to impose their own theory about how government should be run is going to end up hurting their efforts to get things done, especially for those resource development constituents whom they most want to assist. The governmental role in evaluating and approving major resource developments is too complicated to be carried out by fiat or by an underfunded and overworked bureaucracy. Watt's administration is frustrated by this complexity. . . ."[25] Watt vowed to avoid "paralysis by analysis," but his efforts to deemphasize and streamline environmental assessments and do away with offices that smacked of planning and delay, like the special projects office in the Bureau of Land Management, actually made it harder to steer complex energy projects through the maze of government.

Watt was not a monster. He was consistent enough in his support for free enterprise to oppose the huge federal subsidies for synthetic fuels, an issue on which he and David Stockman went down to defeat together. On occasion, Watt could display a sense of humor about the self-image he had carefully cultivated. When California Congressman Tom Lantos called Watt "self-righteous" and "dogmatic" during a hearing on the California offshore drilling issue, Watt responded with a smile: "Don't forget 'pious.' " However, Watt seemed to have no concept of the larger role which previous Secretaries of Interior, even those most thoroughly committed to development, had played within the federal system. Udall, a liberal who strove to find a balanced middle ground on development issues, put it this way: "It's quite all right to have a Commerce Secretary who's rah-rah for business, or the Labor Department headed by a man George Meany would help you select, and so on with Transportation and all the others. But with the Interior Department, the country has always wanted somebody there who was the guardian of the land. A man who's going to speak for all Americans and hold the President's feet to the fire on conservation issues. . . . There's a wide mainstream there and there's a consensus that your Interior Secretary ought to be in the mainstream and speak for the environment, for all of us, the seals and coyotes and bald eagles and all the rest. Watt is further out of that conservationist consensus than any secretary in modern times."[26]

Republicans once shared this view of Interior's mission, and some of them do still. Their inspiration is likely to be turn-of-the-century conservationist-reformer Gifford Pinchot, a prominent public official in Theodore Roosevelt's administration, who said, "The noblest task that confronts us all today is to leave this country unspotted in honor and unexhausted in resources, to our descendants who will be, not less than we, the children of the founders of the republic."[27] Ike Livermore, a Pinchot sort of Republican, had taken this view as Reagan's resources administrator in Sacramento and would have brought it with him to Washington. But no one asked Livermore to serve.* Reagan had other issues on his mind, and he had delegated Interior to Laxalt and the western senators, the promoters and products of the Sagebrush Rebellion. Reagan had learned a lot about the environment during his years as governor of California, but he had forgotten, or discarded, most of what he had learned. Part of this attitude reflected the energy shortages of the 1970s, and Reagan's conviction that it was dangerous for the United States to be dependent on foreign sources of energy. Part of it was a reflection of the 1980 election campaign when Reagan was told repeatedly that federal environmental regulations were a chief cause for the shutdown of American factories. The evidence for this is unconvincing, although Reagan didn't know it. But Livermore is convinced that the biggest single reason for Reagan's change in attitude is that he spent seven years isolated from environmental decision-making after he left the California governorship at the end of 1974. "In the seven years since he left Sacramento, he really hasn't had any environmental advisers," Livermore said. "I'd have to agree that the environmental movement has had things its own way for several years, and I think some kind of reaction was inevitable. But Watt is so strident, going after moderate and level-headed groups like the National Wildlife Federation. He's reacting with such excessive zeal, and the moderate voices are not being heard. Reagan has so much on his desk he's not likely to get involved unless someone close to him felt it was important. I think [Mike] Deaver is a duck hunter, but that's about it. So things are left up to [Joe] Coors and people like that, who feel they've been strictured by environmental laws and regulations."[28]

* Livermore, who is Reagan's age, says he was "spoken to" by the transition team about the Environmental Protection Agency but declined because it wasn't his area of expertise. His logical use would have been at Interior where he wasn't even invited to work on the transition because, he says, "the Water Establishment hates my guts." The California leader of that "establishment" during Reagan's days as governor, then State Water Resources Director William R. Gianelli, wound up as assistant secretary of the Army for civil works, the civil agency which oversees his onetime employer, the U.S. Army Corps of Engineers. Gianelli was a principal advocate of the Dos Rios Dam which Reagan blocked as governor.

It was an accurate evaluation of what had happened to President Reagan, the rider of the western range at Rancho del Cielo. In one sense Watt was an accident who might indeed have been appointed Secretary of Interior while Reagan was out riding on a Wednesday. In another respect, the Watt appointment is a perfectly appropriate, if extreme, reflection of a President so ignorant of the realities of pollution that he actually thought that Mt. St. Helens was a greater source of sulfur dioxide than the American automobile. This ignorance is frustrating to those who believe that the Reagan administration has wasted time and opportunities in dealing with such problems as acid rain. "This administration is very pleasant and the people in it say soothing things to you when you tell them that American acid rain is destroying Canadian lakes and will soon be destroying your own," said Canadian Minister of Environment John Roberts. "But they talk and talk, and nothing happens."*

Reagan does not want to be remembered as a despoiler. He does not want his legacy to be that he talked and talked, and did nothing. In private life he is a man who appreciates the beauty of America, and particularly the landscape of the West. He enjoys sunsets and tree-shaded trails and physical work in the out-of-doors, and he recognizes that America has a vital and special environmental heritage. Unfortunately, President Reagan does not realize how precarious that heritage is—how much has been destroyed in the West he loves and how easily its remaining treasures can be ruined. Politically, the environment has held too low a priority for Ronald Reagan. His environmental record, in both Sacramento and Washington, essentially is a product of the men to whom he delegated authority. In California, he was lucky enough to find a true and balanced conservationist in the ranks of industry. In Washington, he wound up with a zealot who sees the land as a source of wealth that must be developed regardless of the environmental cost. The story of Interior under the Reagan administration is, in its way, a typically western one that as yet has no happy western ending. "We will mine more, drill more, cut more timber," Watt had said, and he meant it. It is a far cry from what Livermore had said—and done—in California. And it is further still from what President Reagan could have done, which is to honor Pinchot's unheeded call to leave the country unexhausted in resources for our children who will inherit it.

* Roberts made this comment to me on July 18, 1981, in Ottawa, where President Reagan was attending the Economic Summit. The Canadian minister of the environment, speaking before the American Association for the Advancement of Science on January 4, 1981, observed that the effect of acid rain on Canada's eastern lakes "is simply disastrous." He has repeatedly pressed the Reagan administration to live up to a memorandum of intent signed by the U.S. and Canadian governments in August 1980 announcing that an international air quality agreement would be negotiated that would require vigorous enforcement of antipollution standards, advance notice and consultation on activities, and cooperation in research. In a March 1981 visit to Ottawa, President Reagan pledged to Canadian Prime Minister Pierre Trudeau that he would honor this memorandum, which had been signed by President Carter.

22

The Delegated Presidency

H E had a secure and uncluttered concept of the presidency, inspired by his mythic remembrance of Franklin Roosevelt and molded by his practical experience as public speaker and governor of California. Out of the governorship came a delegative style of decision-making which reflected both impressive strengths and formidable limitations. From his early identification with Roosevelt and his professional training came the Great Communicator. Reagan's idea of a President was of a leader who could rally the country to a cause with the power of his voice and use public opinion as a catalyst for change. His communicative skill was a principal source of his effectiveness as President, but it rested on stronger foundations than mere mastery of television. Like his father, he was a compelling salesman who realized that a salesman must be convinced of the worth of his product before he can persuade others to buy it. Reagan was not a doubter. Even when he was exasperatingly wrong or misinformed, he was so thoroughly convincing and self-assured that others believed him. Believability was the key. Reagan was not believable because he was the Great Communicator; he was the Great Communicator because he was believable. He did not, observed Meg Greenfield, "exude anxiety or defensiveness or duplicity or aggression while he is speaking the most simple pieties."[1] Because he believed in these pieties, he could get away with saying what other politicians were unable to say. He could deliver an improbable Christmas message which simultaneously celebrated a sacred holiday, warned the Russians to keep their hands off Poland and concluded with the words of Tiny Tim, "God bless, us, everyone." He could ask Americans to place lighted candles in darkened windows in support of the people of Poland and know that his countrymen would respond. They responded, even those who did not share Reagan's values or think that lighting candles would do any good, because they trusted him. Above all, they responded because he spoke to them in the ordinary, everyday language which they used among themselves. Reagan's rivals had learned that the hard way. During the 1980 Republican primaries an aide to George

Bush had climbed into a cab and asked the driver what he thought of Reagan. "He's the only politician I can understand," the driver said.

Reagan's skill as a communicator drew upon other assets. He possessed a powerful vision of what he wanted his country to be, a clearly drawn political agenda, and a willingness to use his popularity to accomplish his purposes. "He's the only person I've ever met who doesn't have to weigh things—his ideas seem to come from the depth of the man," said Mike Deaver. "He's resolved something, his being or what he is, a long time ago. He doesn't have to say, on the one hand, on the other. He seems to know what is right."[2] It was a Reagan strength—and sometimes a Reagan weakness. He was better off than Presidents with too many doubts, but Reagan had too few. His mind and his metaphors were locked in the past where energy was abundant, American industrial and military supremacy was axiomatic, and personal charity was the basic channel of social welfare. Along with many other Americans, Reagan yearned to rediscover this lost world. But he lacked an adequate map, if any could be drawn, and he possessed only a rudimentary knowledge of what was needed to conduct the exploration. Intellectually, Reagan was neither a rocket scientist nor a stupid man. Those who dealt with him on a regular basis were impressed with the common sense he displayed in most situations and the uncommonly good judgment he showed at other times. He was a good listener. Though he did not like to be bogged down with briefing papers, he read more than most people realized. What he did read he was likely to retain because he had a photographic mind. However, it was also a mind which throughout Reagan's long lifetime had never been exposed to rigorous challenge. As a young man, he had failed to form the useful habit of subjecting his dearest assumptions to intellectual examination. In some respects, he was a prisoner of his gifts. He remembered what he had read without effort, which tempted him to regurgitate information and anecdotes rather than reflect upon ideas. His intuition was so sound that he relied on it too heavily, letting it lead him down paths where intuition should not go alone. Most of the time, President Reagan was intuitively keen but intellectually lazy. His ignorance was his armor, shielding him from harsh realities which might have discouraged some of his boldest initiatives while gradually weighing down his presidency. He did not know how the federal budget worked or understand the threat to the environment from toxic wastes and acid rain or realize that the Soviets, for all their menace to human freedom, had in fact fulfilled a number of their treaties. He did not understand that a conservative agenda for America could be as costly as a liberal one.* He did not recognize that the "racetrack" method of MX-basing he thought he was rejecting had been discarded long ago by President Carter, not recently by Caspar Weinberger.

---

* This observation was made originally by George F. Will, who points out that new prisons, tuition tax credits, a strong defense and other programs supported by conservatives cost as much money as the social welfare programs advocated by liberals.

He did not know enough. And he did not know how much he didn't know.

Because of Reagan's knowledge gaps, his presidential news conferences became adventures into the uncharted regions of his mind. His advisers prepared the President as carefully as they could and crossed their fingers in hopes that the questioning would coincide with the preparation. Often, however, their well-intentioned concern that Reagan might display his ignorance contributed to the President's problems rather than solving them. Much of the time in Sacramento, Reagan held weekly press conferences, and the brief interval between them enabled his advisers to anticipate most of the questions. In Washington, Reagan met with the press so infrequently* that it was difficult for even the most skillful briefers to anticipate what ground the questions might cover. Unlike Richard Nixon, Reagan was not stiff and fearful with reporters. And unlike Carter, he displayed a cheerful sense of humor which he was willing to employ at his own expense. Reagan liked many of the reporters and they liked him, even though he often could not recall their names. But he found the presidential press conference, with its discomforting demands on both conceptual understanding and detail, a perpetual struggle. Being hard of hearing did not help. Reagan could not catch many of the questions, particularly from the back of the crowded briefing room. This combination of poor hearing and limited knowledge transcended Reagan's communicative skills, dimming the luster of the Great Communicator's triumphant solo performances on national television. Reagan had so much trouble understanding the questions that the White House communications office finally installed a small loudspeaker on the left of the podium just below camera range. From then on he could at least understand the questions, even if he was not always able to answer them.

In both press conferences and private meetings with aides, Reagan was most at sea when the topic turned to foreign affairs. At a June 16, 1981, press conference, Reagan described defensive surface-to-air missiles which the Syrians had placed in Lebanon as "offensive" weapons. He seemed never to have heard of the suggestion that Israel make its nuclear facilities available to international inspection. He fumbled a question about whether a limited war could be contained in Europe or would invariably become a nuclear war between the superpowers. "The President has been skimping on his preparation, neglecting the black book, relying instead on oral give-and-take with his aides for a couple of hours before press conferences," wrote *New York Times* columnist William Safire in a harshly accurate appraisal of this performance. "He thinks he can wing it. Some member of the inner circle with a great sense of security should tell him that this is how a democracy tests its leader's range of comprehension and that he has been flunking the test."[3]

This was advice from a friendly critic familiar with the complexities of

* In 1981, Reagan held six press conferences in Washington and one at Rancho del Cielo. Carter held twenty-one Washington press conferences during his first year in the White House and another one in Warsaw.

preparing a President for news conferences. But Reagan simply has no inclination to cuddle up with a briefing book for any prolonged period of time. Six months later, at Reagan's final 1981 press conference, he was asked about one of the nation's most significant legal cases on affirmative action, an issue on which Reagan has frequently expressed himself. However, Reagan did not know what the "Weber case" was, prompting a reporter to summarize it for him.* The reporter, Isiah Poole of *Black Enterprise* magazine, told Reagan that a union and an employer had "entered into a voluntary agreement to conduct affirmative action programs for training minorities and moving them up in the work force," and that the Supreme Court had upheld the decision. He then explained that William Bradford Reynolds, the assistant attorney general for civil rights, disagreed and was looking for a Supreme Court case which could overturn it. Reagan responded as if he were a man in the street being asked about affirmative action for the first time. "Well," he said, "if this is something that simply allows the training and the bringing up so that there are more opportunities for them in voluntary agreement between the union and management, I can't see any fault with that. I'm for that." It turned out, however, that his administration wasn't. At Justice, overturning the Weber case was seen as one of the principal means for abolishing "quota systems," which Reagan had promised to oppose. The Supreme Court had ruled that the voluntary agreement wasn't a quota, but Reagan didn't know that. Rather than repudiate his Justice Department, he abandoned his man-in-the-street answer. On January 3, 1982, after Reagan had been clued in, the White House released a statement drafted at Justice which declared its opposition to the decision because it protected "a rigid racial quota."

When Reagan arrived in Washington he brought with him a determination to form a "cabinet government" patterned after the management system he had used in California. It was an old dream, valued by Presidents as different as Eisenhower and Carter, and not many in Washington thought much of the idea. George Reedy had pronounced the prevailing judgment on cabinet government when he said that the cabinet as a collective body "was about as useful as the vermiform appendix." But Reagan had promised to utilize the cabinet as a working arm of the government, and he took this commitment as seriously as he did his political promises to lift the grain embargo or to reduce taxes. For a time, in defiance of most presidential experience, he actually used the cabinet and its working subgroups known as cabinet councils as arenas of decision-making. Gradually, the unwieldiness of such forums and the necessity for prompt reactions to events gave way to

* Brian F. Weber, a white employee of the Kaiser Aluminum and Chemical Corporation, challenged an affirmative action plan negotiated by the company and the United Steelworkers of America on grounds it constituted an illegal quota under the 1964 Civil Rights Act. In 1979 the court ruled against Weber, with the majority holding that the plan was not a quota.

a more traditional and centralized style of decision-making.* Nonetheless, Reagan continued to delegate far more to cabinet officers than most of his predecessors had, granting them broad authority and a long leash. Seen on one level, this delegated presidency was a useful mask for Reagan's ignorance of many issues. However, it was just as legitimately a reflection of his belief in the virtues of cabinet government and of his confidence that he could select able managers to carry out his policies. By temperament and training, Reagan simply was not a detail man. Even on issues where he was well informed, Reagan chose consciously to focus on the broad goals of what he intended to accomplish and leave the details to others. He was appalled at the stories that President Carter had become so involved in detail that he took time to determine who used the White House tennis courts. Reagan did not bother with trivia. He saw himself as a leader, a communicator, an executive decision-maker, a chairman of the board. He believed in the efficacy of "roundtabling" issues both in small groups of advisers and in large, full-scale cabinet meetings. A distinctive feature of the Reagan system was that cabinet members and senior advisers were encouraged to comment on areas outside their expertise. As a generalist, Reagan indulged his useful suspicion that energy policy was too important to be left to the Department of Energy and foreign policy too vital to remain the sole property of the Secretary of State. Reagan was right about this, but his method of operation was unnerving to cabinet members who had been weaned in other presidencies.

Al Haig, in particular, found it difficult to understand how a Reagan senior adviser with no foreign policy background felt free to offer opinions on sensitive matters at National Security Council meetings. Haig's frame of reference was Henry Kissinger, who had been the single, dominant foreign policy voice in two Republican administrations. The Reagan system was not conducive to the development of a new Kissinger, whatever his qualifications. It tended to demystify foreign and defense policy, for better and for worse, sometimes harming the administration by pushing aside professionalism, but at other times helping it by allowing a broader, national interest to prevail over a parochial one. In the spring of 1981 the reluctance of domestic White House aides to risk U.S. prestige and Reagan's reputation in an El Salvadoran adventure helped limit direct U.S. involvement in that strife-torn land to a few advisers and a continuation of President Carter's policies. On the other hand, the free-for-all quality of foreign policy formulation delayed Haig's efforts to develop a careful strategy leading to nuclear arms negotiations with the Soviet Union. The result was a proposal so tar-

---

* As time went on, many of the key decisions in the White House were actually made in informal "working groups" whose membership varied but usually included one or more of the dominant White House trio of James Baker, Michael Deaver and Ed Meese, the relevant cabinet member or his deputy, and two relatively little-known but highly influential aides—Baker's Richard G. Darman and Meese's Craig L. Fuller.

dily enunciated by Reagan that it gave the appearance of being a reaction to widespread European antinuclear demonstrations rather than being a genuine initiative.

Whatever its implications, the system suited Reagan. He felt comfortable reaching decisions after back-and-forth discussions between advisers of differing perspectives. Reagan craves discourse, not briefing papers, and troubles arose when that discourse was blocked within the White House staff. While Reagan knows less than most of his predecessors about many policy issues, he has the advantage over Presidents more driven or less secure in that he does not regard policy conflict as an expression of disloyalty. Cabinet officers learned that they did not prejudice themselves in future transactions with the White House by speaking out for the losing side of any given issue. Reagan is not a grudge-nurser, and he welcomes honest differences of opinion. What he does not welcome, and cannot abide, is acrimony and discord. He remembered, without pleasure, the staff maneuvering which dominated the first year of his governorship and the power struggles which marred his early 1980 campaign. Reagan would not let that happen again. Though he could not impose a uniform calmness of disposition on his cabinet, he gathered around him in the White House advisers whom he trusted to work together and to smooth out conflicts among themselves. The fact that they were able to do so for the best part of a year, before the strain of such unnatural peacetime cooperation became unbearable, is in one sense a tribute to the personal qualities of James Baker, Ed Meese and Mike Deaver. More than anything, however, it reflected the certain knowledge by each member of what became known as the Trio that the President expected concord, and the appearance of concord, to prevail among his staff. Reagan had deficiencies as a President, but his great and overriding strength as an executive was that elevation to high office had not distorted his personality or dimmed his perception of the working environment he needed to succeed. Heightened tension would not have made of Ronald Reagan a better President, and Reagan knew it. He did not want his personal harmony disturbed.

Reagan's instrument in achieving the tranquility he sought was Deaver, the least visible member of the White House Trio but the one most personally valuable to the Reagans. Close to the first lady as well as to the President, Deaver understood that the Reagans needed time to themselves and freedom from the pressures of the presidency. As keeper of the schedule and protector, Deaver zealously guarded this time and this freedom. He was not averse to intervention on policy, when he believed he had something to contribute, but his priority was to keep Reagan's routine comfortable and as undistorted as possible. When other aides stacked high the briefing papers for Reagan to take home with him to the White House living quarters, Deaver saw to it that the pile was reduced to manageable size. When Reagan was trying to decide how he should respond to a letter from Soviet leader Leonid Brezhnev after conflicting advice, Deaver once said to him,

"Mr. President, it's *you* who were elected, it's *your* decision. You're the President. Do what *you* want to do."

Because of his understanding of the Reagans and their moods, Deaver was valued within the White House and outside it as a conciliator, a facilitator and a bearer of vital messages to the President—especially if the message contained negative news. Deaver saw his own role in a similar way. "I have a sense about him," he said of Reagan in the spring of 1981. "He and I have been together for so long that I think I almost instinctively know how he will react. And he knows that. And so, he has put confidence and trust in me and others in our structure see that. I am able to cut out an awful lot of time."[4] The reverse side of this coin was that Deaver, at the age of forty-two, was invariably described in the journalistic shorthand of "perfect adjutant" or "loyal aide," almost as if he did not have an existence of his own. His wife Carolyn, whom Deaver had met and married when she was a secretary in Governor Reagan's office, gently reproached her husband for his lack of individual identity. Some of Deaver's friends also thought him too self-effacing. The incident that all of them went back to was Deaver's walkout from the campaign in 1979 when John Sears was trying to force Reagan to fire him. Those close to Deaver knew he had subordinated his own feelings—and his intense resentment of Sears—at great cost to himself. But this same incident had demonstrated Deaver's loyalty in a crucible in which other aides had not been fully tested. The Reagans loved him. Interviewing Reagan for a profile on Deaver, Elisabeth Bumiller of the *Washington Post* asked the President whether it was really true that he thought of Deaver as a son. Reagan beamed fondly at his favorite aide. "Gee, I always thought of him more as a father figure," he said.[5]

Those who had known Reagan from his early days in Hollywood found him little changed by high office. But Deaver had changed. His former classmates at San Jose State College remember him chiefly as an accomplished piano player who performed in bars and bands around the campus. He was a quiet man, with a wry sense of humor and a shyness bordering on the furtive.

Though he had talked about becoming an Episcopal priest, he wound up working at IBM instead. After a year and a half of boredom, Deaver became a youthful drifter, sailing around the world until his money ran out in Australia. Eventually, he drifted back to California and into Republican politics. In Sacramento, as a twenty-eight-year-old aide to William P. Clark, legislators found him too suspicious and uptight. Deaver survived because Nancy Reagan liked him and because he got along well with Clark and the governor. He advanced up the ladder in the governor's office, becoming Reagan's scheduler and time-saver. But after he mishandled Reagan's unsuccessful tax limitation campaign in 1973, his stock sunk to a low point with political professionals. When Reagan left the governorship in 1974, Deaver opened a consulting and public relations firm with Peter Hannaford that boasted Reagan as its chief client and booked his speeches.

Both of the consultants became well-to-do and success in the business world gave Deaver a sense of personal security. In the interim between Reagan's governorship and his campaign for the presidency in 1976, Deaver became a principal adviser. The Reagans and the Deavers socialized. In a short time Deaver found that he had come to value Reagan far beyond the commercial benefit he brought as a client. He had come to believe in him and thought he should be President. And Reagan cared about Deaver in a special way that was limited to a very few aides. Though Reagan is unfailingly courteous to even the most junior aide, his natural reserve usually keeps staff members at arm's length. Deaver, however, had broken through that barrier. The President treated him kindly and seemed to sense that Deaver had never quite gotten over that terrible moment in Pacific Palisades when Reagan had allowed him to walk out. Both men had been miserable in the three months when Deaver was gone. And even before he won the election, Reagan had insisted that Deaver come with him to the White House. Deaver came. He sold his share of the consulting business to Hannaford, who prospered as a consultant influential with the new crowd in Washington.

Deaver had become the protector of Reagan and the Reagan image, and he did not want anyone to embarrass the President. When National Security Adviser Richard V. Allen's poor judgment in accepting gifts from the Japanese became an issue, Deaver urged that Allen be fired. When David Stockman's poor judgment in describing Reagan tax reductions as "a Trojan horse" became public, Deaver favored accepting Stockman's resignation. He liked and admired Stockman and had no use for Allen, but his recommendations did not depend on that. Over the years Deaver had come to think in terms of the Reagans rather than in terms of Mike Deaver. And some of Reagan's own self-effacing perspective had rubbed off on his favorite aide. Soon after inauguration, Deaver was riding in the swanky black limousine that was a symbol of his new power and position when he spotted former White House Press Secretary Jody Powell, alone and unnoticed, walking down Pennsylvania Avenue. "Remember that picture, Deaver," he said to himself, looking at Powell. And telling the story many months later, he wondered how Powell felt that day and how all of those close to Reagan would feel when their President was no longer in office, and he said again, "I'm always going to remember that picture."

In the White House, it was often the things Deaver remembered that made the difference. He remembered to see that Reagan autographed every possible picture, knowing that the President was apt to turn this routine political chore into a triumph by composing some apt one-liner or bit of doggerel.* He kept open the lines of communication with old supporters and

---

* During the 1980 campaign, Associated Press reporter Doug Willis asked Reagan to autograph a reprinted studio picture from *Bedtime for Bonzo* showing Reagan and the chimpanzee in bed. Reagan signed it, "I'm the one with the watch."

contributors and saw to it that politicians who wanted to brag about their personal relationship with the President were invited to concerts or White House dinners or brief chats in the Oval Office. And when Reagan gave a White House lunch for famous baseball players, Deaver made sure that the guest list included Tony Coehlo, a California congressman who is also chairman of the House Democratic Campaign Committee. Coelho is an epileptic whose matter-of-fact radio and television commercials about epilepsy have done much to dispel harmful mythologies about that disorder. Deaver, from long experience, knew that Reagan was certain to tell the ballplayers about famous baseball pitcher Grover Cleveland Alexander, an epileptic whom Reagan had portrayed in the movie *Winning Team.*

The man who profited most from Deaver's knowledge was his nominal superior, former Houston corporate lawyer James Baker. He proved a wise choice for chief of staff, for he was better organized than any of the Californians. Baker, handicapped by personal unfamiliarity with Reagan, used Deaver to bridge the gap. In a short time the two men became friends and allies. Baker trusted Deaver's insights into Reagan. Deaver was impressed with Baker's managerial skills and his ability to make rapid-fire decisions. Baker proved his mettle on his first day as chief of staff when he bluntly refused to approve a far-reaching scheme by Haig that would have given him control of any interagency programs in which the department participated. "This hasn't been done before, and it isn't going to be done now," Baker declared, and he persuaded Meese to join him in opposition. Reagan accepted their recommendation and refused to sign the executive order that would have given Haig his requested mandate. Baker's strength, in addition to his organizational ability, was that he was as personally secure—and wealthy—as the President he served. "He's both strong and compassionate, and that's an unusual combination," observed Margaret Tutwiler, his executive assistant. "He's Mr. Everything in Houston—comes from one of the oldest families, successful lawyer, tons of money. That gives you a type of security that makes you a more powerful person because you don't need the job to be somebody back in your home town."[6]

Because Baker possessed this security and because he saw more clearly than his colleagues the possibility of a backlash in the 1982 elections, he fought some lonely political battles in the White House. He wanted Reagan to take leadership in advocating extension of the Voting Rights Act, but he received no backing from other White House aides and outright opposition from the Justice Department and political aide Lyn Nofziger. Instead of demonstrating leadership, Reagan hung back and gave the appearance, when he did support a modified version of the voting rights law, that he was being dragged kicking and screaming into the twentieth century. Baker also fought to keep Reagan from being entangled in the Social Security issue, knowing that it had no power to help him. Meese was away making a speech when this issue arose, and Stockman, supported by Health and Human Services Secretary Richard S. Schweiker, convinced the President to support proposals that would have raised the retirement age for Social Security and dropped the minimum benefit. It proved to be the administration's most glaring political error of 1981.

The Social Security blunder reflected Stockman's desperation to make further cuts in the fiscal 1982 budget and to convince Wall Street that Reaganomics was sound. A House Ways and Means subcommittee chaired by Democrat J. J. Pickle of Texas, his party's congressional expert on Social Security, was then exploring a plan to extend gradually the retirement age at which recipients received full payment. "The Pickle package was a fairly significant change in the long-run structure of the system, but I didn't like it because it didn't save any money in the next three or four years and we had these huge unidentified savings [in the budget]," Stockman said. "That kind of attracted me immediately to find an alternative that had some immediate budget savings."[7] Stockman's plan called for reduction of $82 billion in Social Security benefits over a five-year period, including elimination of the $122-a-month minimum benefit. The plan's principal feature was a sharp reduction in benefits for workers who retired at sixty-two rather than at sixty-five. The proposal had nothing to recommend it politically, though no one in the administration except Baker seemed to realize this.

"Those who were pushing the policy like Dick Schweiker, myself and [White House policy development director] Marty Anderson were totally negligent in looking at the politics, as we should have done," Stockman said six months later.[8] Baker, unable to head off the proposal, came up with the idea of having Schweiker advocate the plan, hoping to keep it as far away from Reagan as possible. But the Democrats jumped on it anyway, and Tip O'Neill called the proposal "despicable." Recognizing that the Schweiker gambit had failed, Baker urged Reagan to cut his losses and withdraw. Reagan was furious over what he considered Democratic "demagoguery," but he was a good enough politician to know when it was time to retreat. Prodded by his chief of staff, he abandoned the proposal to reduce early retirement and dusted off an old campaign idea of appointing an independent commission to study how Social Security could be made fiscally sound. Ultimately, Reagan retreated further and abandoned the proposal to eliminate the minimum benefit.* Baker breathed a sigh of relief. He guarded against the proposal coming up again by publicly doing a *mea culpa* for the policy he had steadfastly opposed, repeatedly calling it the administration's biggest mistake of 1981. But when Stockman's job was at stake after the December

---

* Three million people received the minimum benefit. Estimates given to Pickle's subcommittee indicated that from 140,000 to 500,000 persons depended on it entirely, and that 1.3 million people would lose some income as a result of its abolishment. The proposal to eliminate the benefit was made May 12 by Schweiker and withdrawn by the President in a nationally televised September 24 speech. The Senate subsequently voted 95–0 against eliminating the benefit.

Atlantic article, it was Baker who argued that the budget director was so valuable to the administration that he should be given another chance. His view prevailed with Reagan against the combined opposition of Meese and Deaver.

Baker won more battles than he lost, but for a long time he took a back seat to Meese on policy recommendations. That was the way the Trio had structured the White House. Baker was the organizer and Deaver the protector of the Reagans. Ed Meese was the policy man. He was the conceptualizer, the synthesizer, the translator of Reagan's ideas to others and the policy funnel into the President. Deceptively affable in appearance, Meese was a strong-minded lawyer who had served as prosecuting attorney in Alameda County across the bay from San Francisco. He was a cool head in a crisis. Those who saw Meese in action during a riot at San Francisco State College in 1969 said that he had prevented a faculty panic. He also locked S. I. Hayakawa, the controversial college president, in a bathroom for safe-keeping. Meese's friends said he would have loved the job of attorney general in the Reagan administration, and he was better qualified for it than William French Smith. But even Meese could not compete against a member of the Kitchen Cabinet. Instead, he went into the White House, where other aides called him "the Prime Minister" and reporters thought of him as "the deputy president" or even "President Meese." Meese knew there was a danger when people began to talk this way, but he could not resist joking about it. He could rarely resist joking about anything, sharing with the President he had represented for so long a penchant both for one-liners and for situational humor. On the stump his jokes were vintage Reagan. ("Today's hardliner is yesterday's liberal who was mugged last night." "An economist is a person with a Phi Beta Kappa key on one end of his watchchain and no watch on the other.") When Haig said he wanted to make a minor change in the draft of the document Reagan was to present at the economic summit at Cancun, Mexico, on October 22, 1981, Meese leaned across the table and said to the grim-visaged Secretary of State, "We don't want to take out the word 'President,' Al." And sometimes Meese would joke about Reagan, too. When I wrote during the campaign that there had been "a struggle for the heart and mind of Ronald Reagan" throughout the governorship and that it was still going on, Meese quipped to another reporter: "We've declared a cease-fire in the battle for Reagan's mind."

If there was, in fact, such an armistice, it didn't last long. Reagan knew what he wanted to accomplish as President, but his skills were in setting goals, not finding the path to them. Meese was Reagan's geographer. He drew maps to accomplish Reagan's purposes rather than his own and knew how to chart a course to reach the President's destination. This was a full-time job, and Meese's weakness was that he didn't realize it. He might have succeeded brilliantly as a minister without portfolio, drawing on the copious staff resources of the White House and living up to his title as counsellor to the President. Instead, Meese created under him a structure that was inherently unworkable, requiring both the Office of Policy Development and the National Security Council to report to the President through him. Even if such concentration of authority had been desirable, this system gave Meese a full-time managerial role and he was not a full-time manager. From the beginning, even when the Trio was riding high, Meese was stretched too thin.

The Trio's unified reign in the White House lasted less than a year, ultimately confirming the initial judgment of skeptics who said that no such equal sharing of power could long prevail. But the collective leadership did hold together in the vital shaping months of the Reagan administration, proving an impregnable center of unity and effectiveness that was difficult for outsiders to circumvent. None of its three members individually possessed the authority of such past presidential strongmen as Eisenhower's Sherman Adams or Nixon's H. R. Haldeman. But in its heyday, the Trio was more than the sum of its parts, exercising presidential authority to a degree previously unknown. The three men began each working day together over a breakfast of fruit and cereal in Baker's office. They ended it together in another such meeting after Reagan had returned to the executive residence. The strength of the Trio lay in a cohesion which astonished even experienced Washington politicians. U.S. Trade Representative Bill Brock, who had worked with six presidential staffs, gave this judgment in May of 1981: "I am constantly amazed at the lack of personal aggrandizement. There are times when I call one [of the Trio] to get a decision that is personally in his area, and I can't reach him because he may be out of town and I'll call the other. . . . I know that once I've gotten that answer that the first person I called will agree with it. Never have I seen one of them come back on the other and try to roll the decision."[9]

From the moment he was designated chief of staff, Baker realized that the key to his success depended on establishing a close working relationship with Meese. It was Baker who suggested the important-sounding title of "counsellor." And it was Baker, the day after the election, who took the initiative in meeting with Meese in a room in the Century Plaza Hotel in Los Angeles where the two men divided up White House responsibilities like conquering generals partitioning a newly captured country. Baker became White House administrator, with responsibility for administration and politics, including personnel, communications, speech-writing, the press office, intergovernmental relations, legislative liaison, the White House counsel, scheduling and advance. Meese directed the two principal policy operations in the White House, the National Security Council and the Office of Policy Development, which other administrations had called the Domestic Council. On its face, Meese's responsibilities insured him the larger policy role in the administration. Baker, however, controlled the staff. And it is a truism in Washington that he who controls the staff ultimately controls the White House.

But this control was slow in coming, and it would never be fully achieved. Meese understood how Reagan approached decision-making, and he knew how to take a half-developed Reagan idea and bring it to fruition. In the first eight months of the administration, Meese exerted enormous impact on presidential policies. His hands were into everything, although he left few fingerprints. It was Meese who engineered and orchestrated the pardons of W. Mark Felt and Edward S. Miller, the former high-ranking FBI agents convicted of illegal break-ins during the Nixon administration's search for radical opponents of the Vietnam War. In was Meese—with enthusiastic support from Baker and Deaver—who kept the White House out of the morass of "social issues" like abortion while the administration concentrated on its economic program. It was Meese who, even while approving of what Jim Watt was doing, quietly saw to it that the Interior Secretary's ambitious off-shore oil leasing plans were pulled back to manageable and less politically damaging scales. And it was Meese who became the behind-the-scenes counsel to Drew Lewis when the Transportation Secretary was trying to limit Japanese auto imports despite Reagan's well-known commitment to free trade.

All of the top economics officials in the administration—Stockman, Regan and Council of Economic Advisers Chairman Murray L. Weidenbaum—were dedicated free traders. But Meese was aware that Reagan had lost his free trade purity when he promised during the campaign to help the hard-pressed auto industry fend off the pressure of Japanese imports.* He knew, too, that protectionist sentiment, some of it orchestrated by Lewis, was growing on Capitol Hill. Meese believed that a pragmatic compromise under which imports would be limited without any public acknowledgment was in the best interest of the administration, the auto industry, and the Japanese. What he then proceeded to do is typical of the way he works. First, Meese persuaded Reagan to name a task force that would prepare recommendations on ways to help the auto industry. Lewis was appointed chairman in a move that Weidenbaum aptly compared to naming "the fox to guard the chicken coop." He used his position to mobilize support for auto import restraints among industry, labor and prominent Republican governors from the Midwest. The task force itself was hopelessly divided on a remedy, with Lewis and Regan clashing in the President's presence over the Treasury Secretary's optimistic prediction that the auto industry stood to make profits of $4 billion in 1982 without the imposition of import quotas. Lewis called this forecast "ridiculous" and the meeting in the Oval Office ended in disagreement. Meese, enlisting the cooperation of Baker and Brock, continued to press for a face-saving solution. The negotiations within

* Speaking in a Chrysler K-Car plant in Detroit on September 2, 1981, Reagan said: "There is a place where government can be legitimately involved—and this is where I think government has a role it has shirked so far—and that is to convince the Japanese, one way or another, and in their own best interest, the deluge of cars into the United States must be slowed while the industry gets back on its feet."

the task force and between the United States government and the Japanese became so involved that Commerce Secretary Malcolm Baldrige, an ally of Lewis, referred to them as "a four-sided Kabuki dance."[10] And the face-saving solution, which bore Meese's imprint though not his name, also had a delicate Japanese quality—negotiations that were described as "nonnegotiations" and import quotas that were called "voluntary restraints."

The negotiators left Reagan undisturbed by details until a March 19 meeting in the Oval Office where Meese and Baker told the President that the task force had agreed to a compromise and was convinced that the Japanese would limit their imports. To satisfy Reagan's concern that a solution was not being imposed on the Japanese, Meese told him that no specific target figures for imports were being used in the discussions. In fact, Haig had told Mike Mansfield, the respected U.S. ambassador in Tokyo, of the number that Lewis (and the auto industry) had in mind.* However, Reagan was comforted at the assurances that anything the Japenese did would be "voluntary." The White House kept the agreement secret. Press Secretary James S. Brady was told only about the uncontroversial part of the task force's action, a proposal to eliminate various government restraints on the auto industry. Brady announced these recommendations. Not until May 1, after a final round of nonnegotiations with Brock in Tokyo, did the Japanese announce their "voluntary" decision to limit exports to the United States. Meese, Lewis and their fellow pragmatists had prevailed. And voluntary restraints gave Reagan a free trade fig leaf behind which to hide a protectionist agreement.†

It might be said that Meese had invented the delegated presidency. He invented it in Sacramento when Reagan was governor and Meese, succeeding William Clark on November 25, 1968, took over as executive secretary. In the six years that followed, Meese learned how to reduce Reagan's unsophisticated advocacies to lawyer-like prose and legislation. His collegial exterior concealed a keen mind and a fierce conservatism that was tempered

---

* The auto industry originally proposed limited Japanese imports, which had reached 1.9 million cars in 1980, to 1.2 million a year. This was never more than a talking point for the industry, and Lewis understood that such a severe limit was unacceptable to both the Reagan administration and the Japanese. The realistic goal of the industry was the 1.6 million limit contained in pending legislation by Senator John C. Danforth of Missouri, a bill which a prominent White House staffer told me enabled Reagan "to cover his free trade ass." The range of figures which Haig gave Mansfield was from 1.6 million to 1.8 million cars, and the final "voluntary" limit was almost at the midpoint—1.68 million cars a year, beginning in April 1981 and ending in March 1982. The agreement included a formula for adjusting the level of imports in 1982. Haig's own role in the negotiations is subject to dispute. He pressed for auto limits in a three and one-half hour meeting in Washington with Masayoshi Ito, then Japan's foreign minister. Some administration officials believe that Japan resented this pressure; others say Haig was a catalyst in achieving the final agreement.

† It turned out to be a useful fig leaf. Since the word "import quotas" had never been used, U.S. negotiators were free to ignore the auto agreement as a precedent when subsequent demands arose from U.S. manufacturers for limits on shoe and textile exports. On these issues, the free traders prevailed.

with, as he put it, the pragmatic recognition that it was "better to get some of what you want than to get nothing." Cabinet officials and legislators learned that Meese could speak for the governor and deliver on his word. They also learned that they could depend on Meese to accurately convey their own messages to Reagan. The trust which Meese enjoyed from so many quarters gave him a latitude possessed by few men in his position. And it was a trust he largely kept. Meese understood that Reagan's governmental inexperience could be a blessing as well as a curse. He observed that Reagan had a gift for "not complicating things" and for finding appointees who agreed with his objectives and then giving them the authority to attain them. "He did not get himself embroiled in the labyrinth of government as some people do by getting all the petty details," Meese said. "But he did, almost from the start, have an instinctive understanding of management in the sense of knowing how to delegate, knowing what to delegate, knowing how to make decisions himself and knowing that he wanted lots of information."[11] Meese provided Reagan with the information and accepted all the delegated responsibility which Reagan gave him. "He gave me basic guidelines as to what he wanted done," said Meese. "I always knew what the limits of my authority were. Within those limits I knew that I could go ahead and handle a riot or disorder or commit state forces or whatever under his basic delegation of authority to do these things."[12]

This was the experience of delegated authority which Meese brought with him to the Reagan White House. Meese's relationship with Reagan was satirized effectively in a song written by Charles McDowell of the *Richmond Times-Dispatch* for the Washington Gridiron dinner on March 28, 1981. It was sung to the tune of "Something Wonderful."

> He will not always say
> What you would have him say,
> But now and then he'll say . . . something *won—*derful!
> Just put it on a card
> He cannot disregard,
> Then ev'ry time he'll say . . . something *won—*derful!
>
> He knows a thousand things that aren't quite true;
> You know that he believes in them
> And that's enough for you.
>
> You'll always go along
> And help him be less wrong,
> And even when he's wrong
> He is—wonderful!
>
> He'll always need Ed Meese,
> He needs to heed Ed Meese,
> And when he heeds Ed Meese . . . he's more *won—*derful!

Meese—like Reagan and many others of the Californians—tended to look upon Washington as if it were a big Sacramento. It was an understandable delusion, since California's budget is larger than all except a handful of countries in the world, and the state is in some respects a microcosm of the nation. Certainly, many of the processes which Reagan mastered as an executive in Sacramento were transferable to Washington, and the lessons learned in dealing with a well-staffed legislature controlled by the opposition party gave him a running start with the Congress. But neither Reagan nor his valued Trio had experience in defense and foreign affairs. Neither, for that matter, did Caspar W. Weinberger, the Harvard-trained lawyer from San Francisco whom Reagan installed as Secretary of Defense. "My personal Disraeli," is the phrase which Reagan once had used to describe Weinberger in California, and Meese did not think this praise extravagant. Meese had a lawyer's appreciation of fellow lawyer Weinberger's fiscal and forensic skills. He supported Weinberger in his efforts to obtain a Defense Department team of his choice against the hard-line opposition of North Carolina Senator Jesse Helms.* Meese and Weinberger had worked well together in Sacramento; they would work well together again. But their performance would show that Washington was in fact quite different from Sacramento. And it would also demonstrate the practical limits to a delegated presidency.

Alone among the cabinet officers, Weinberger faced the options provided by an expanding budget. In some respects they were illusory options. The long-term downward trend of defense spending, when measured either as a percentage of U.S. gross national product or in relation to the Soviet arms buildup, had provided significant gaps in the U.S. military arsenal. Former Defense Secretary James R. Schlesinger estimated that by 1981 the Soviet Union was outspending the United States by 85 percent on military weapons procurement. Candidate Reagan had pledged to reverse this trend, and there was never any doubt that he would try to do it. But this fundamental decision was easier to make than any of the actions which arose from it. Installed in a gigantic third-floor office of the Pentagon, Weinberger faced a complicated array of far-reaching choices, among them the deployment of the neutron bomb, the size and composition of the U.S. Navy, and the training and modernization of the all-volunteer Army. Though he was a quick study and indefatigable reader of briefing papers, Weinberger had no

---

* Weinberger wanted Frank C. Carlucci, a respected career government executive under four Presidents, as his deputy. The two men had been adversaries who had become friends when Weinberger was Health, Education and Welfare Secretary in the Nixon administration and Carlucci was in charge of the Office of Economic Opportunity. During the Carter administration Carlucci was deputy director of the Central Intelligence Agency. Conservatives were promoting William R. Van Cleave of the University of Southern California, who had been a principal Reagan defense adviser during the campaign. Helms was opposed to Carlucci, but he accepted him because Reagan had decided to appoint a Helms favorite, Fred Ikle, to the No. 3 Pentagon job of undersecretary of defense for policy.

background as a strategic thinker. His reputation had been forged as a manager at Nixon's Department of Health, Education and Welfare and as a budget-cutter at Nixon's Office of Management and Budget, where he earned the nickname of "Cap the Knife." Reagan trusted Weinberger, and thought he could do anything. Weinberger returned this trust by showing a keen understanding of Reagan. He prided himself on knowledge of his boss, which meant knowing what Reagan wanted—and giving it to him. Though Weinberger had once been considered rather doveish, his martial anti-Communist rhetoric as defense secretary matched Reagan's own. Weinberger always had responded to the needs of the departmental bureaucracies in the agencies he had managed for Governor Reagan and President Nixon, and he now responded to the desires of the Pentagon, battling with David Stockman for military spending increases which he considered a ratification of what Reagan had promised in the campaign. Weinberger also believed he understood the President's position on the one defense issue where Reagan's bristling rhetoric faded softly into the Nevada sunset—the vital strategic decision of where and how to base the MX intercontinental ballistic missiles that were supposed to deter the Soviet Union from a nuclear first strike.

As a political issue, the MX provoked great passions. Its supporters considered it the only realistic deterrent to a surprise Soviet attack. Its opponents viewed it as wasteful madness that would gobble up billions of dollars and destroy vast stretches of desert and grazing land. But the MX was a submerged issue during the 1980 campaign, when it conflicted with the overall impressions that both candidates were trying to convey. Reagan's campaign stance was that Carter was a weak President who had let America's defenses slide and its prestige crumble. Carter portrayed himself as a man of peace and Reagan as a warmonger. Buried beneath these poster images was the MX issue, on which Carter took the sterner view of Soviet intentions and Reagan the more benign one. Carter proposed to build 200 of the gigantic, super-accurate missiles and shuttle them along 4,600 shelters in the Nevada and Utah desert. In Pentagon nomenclature the system was known as "MX/MPS" for "Missile Experimental—Multiple Protective Shelters." The price tag on this system, estimated at $33 billion by Carter, was by 1981 projected to top $50 billion. Carter, who had entered office talking about ridding the world of nuclear weapons, had accepted the MX with the greatest reluctance. Early in 1977, Carter rescinded funds for MX development and suggested scrapping the system entirely. But in November the President was informed by his respected Pentagon chief, William J. Perry, that the Soviets had staged a breakthrough in their missile guidance system. Perry was convinced that the Soviets could outfit existing missiles with the new system, giving them a capability by the mid-1980s of destroying nearly all of the 1,000 U.S. Minutemen missiles in a surprise attack. Defense Secretary Harold Brown also was convinced that the threat was real. He and Perry persuaded President Carter to respond to it. In 1979, Carter reversed course and proposed funding for the MX/MPS system. The administration decided to base the MX missile launchers in "racetrack" loops that would make them more easily verifiable under the then pending strategic arms limitation treaty known as SALT-II. Essentially, Carter's decision was a negative one. He disliked the MX basing plan, but became convinced that it was superior to the known alternatives. A senior Pentagon official who was no fan of Carter's was impressed at the way the President had done his homework. "Carter was a slave to logic," he said.

No one has ever made that accusation of Reagan. But Reagan was a persuasive critic of SALT-II, which he believed would impose one-sided limitations on the United States without seriously impeding the Soviets. A number of Democratic senators felt the same way. When Carter withdrew the SALT-II treaty in 1980 as an expression of political realism and as a response to the Russian invasion of Afghanistan, Reagan's advisers told him that the rationale for racetrack deployment of the MX had disappeared with the SALT-II treaty. The main purpose of the deployment had been to make the system verifiable, as SALT-II would have required. Reagan's hard-lining chief defense adviser, William Van Cleave, didn't like the racetrack system anyway. He thought it was wasteful to spend billions of dollars on shelters to hide U.S. missiles and then tell the Russians where they were located. Van Cleave's argument impressed Reagan, who criticized the Carter basing plan without ever specifically rejecting the MX. Reagan's opposition to the racetrack idea was sharpened by Senator Paul Laxalt, who was hearing from Nevada ranchers opposed to giving up their land to MX/MPS. With SALT-II withdrawn, Defense Secretary Brown himself abandoned racetrack deployment in favor of a "linear" system intended to cost less money and use less land. "I see no virtue in the closed-loop system," the Defense Secretary told a Senate subcommittee on May 6, 1980. "If you wish to say the racetrack is dead, go ahead."[13] The senators understood what Brown was telling them, but the word never got through to Reagan. "MX" and "racetrack" had been indelibly linked in Reagan's mind. And that linkage would remain after he became President.

Weinberger, sixty-three years old when he took over as Secretary of Defense, has an excellent memory. He didn't need explicit instructions to scrap the MX. He remembered the campaign dialogue. He knew that Laxalt did not support MX/MPS and that the opinions of the Nevada senator carried weight with the President. He believed that the basing proposal faced years of delays from environmental lawsuits. And he had other issues on his mind and did not want to be bothered with MX. When Seymour Zeiberg, who had been Perry's top assistant, briefed Weinberger and his deputy Frank C. Carlucci in February 1981, he was appalled by the technical ignorance of the questions put to him. Zeiberg did not conceal his disdainful opinion, and the briefing alienated the top Defense officials rather than enlightening them. Zeiberg soon left the Pentagon. And Weinberger never afterward wanted to hear about the MX from its proponents, however well informed. This reaction shut out the Air Force, the lead agency in past studies of the MX and a proponent of MX/MPS, from the decision-making process. Air Force attempts to get an audience with the Defense Secretary for a full-scale presentation of the department's views were repeatedly rebuffed, and the Air Force leadership did not insist as forcefully as it should have on a hearing. The Air Force had little influence on the ultimate decision. Instead of consulting Pentagon experts, Weinberger on March 16, 1981, did what his White House ally Meese would have done under similar circumstances—he appointed his own panel of experts to make recommendations on the missile and its basing system. Meese was kept informed. He approved of Weinberger's action, which fit neatly into the early White House strategy of focusing exclusively on the economic program.

The fifteen-member panel appointed by Weinberger elicited no enthusiasm from MX supporters, some of whom believed the committee was stacked against it. More neutral observers had a different worry: they feared that the committee encompassed so many different views it would have difficulty reaching any consensus at all. This also could be fatal to the MX. In any case, there was little doubt about where Weinberger stood on the basing issue. Charles Townes, the Nobel-Prize-winning physicist from the University of California at Berkeley whom Weinberger had named chairman of the panel, began his work with an admonition about lawsuits ringing in his ears. "The one thing that the Secretary was insistent on," Townes recalled, "was his view of the environmental law. As he foresaw it, it would be a very long time getting [the MX] in place in view of the environmental problems."[14]*
While the Townes Committee deliberated, the Church of Jesus Christ of Latter-day Saints (Mormons) declared on May 5, 1981, that the MX/MPS system was "a denial of the very essence" of the church's gospel of "peace to the peoples of the earth."[15] Seventy percent of Utah's population is Mormon as are the state's two senators, Jake Garn and Orrin Hatch. In 1980, Utah was the state in which Reagan won his highest percentage of popular vote. The Mormon opposition was a psychological blow to MX. It ratified Weinberger's belief that the MX/MPS system faced insurmountable obstacles from an unusual coalition of environmentalists, antiwar groups, ranchers and hard-line ideological conservatives. The church's stand also gave Laxalt important allies from neighboring Utah in his effort to limit deployment of the MX missile in multiple protective shelters.

In the summer of 1981 the alternatives to MX/MPS came climbing out of the woodwork at the Pentagon and at think-tanks across the country. Weinberger's initial favorite was an air-mobile MX that had been tested and found wanting in both the Ford and Carter administrations. The proposal

---

* Townes maintained, however, in the November 4, 1981, interview in which he made this statement, that environmental considerations "were not a dominant factor" in the ultimate decision.

Carter rejected called for conversion of C5A transports into MX missile carriers. Air Force tests found many deficiencies in this proposal, one being that the wings of the planes were likely to fall off if the missiles were actually fired. An advanced version of this idea, dubbed Big Bird, made its way to Weinberger's desk. This variation required development of a fleet of new, fuel-efficient, large-winged planes. It was the brainchild of "two little guys from nowhere," according to one of them, Maryland physicist Ira F. Kuhn, Jr., who said he named the proposal Big Bird from the character on television's *Sesame Street*.[16] A story about this plan in the *Washington Post* of July 16 sent MX/MPS supporters on Capitol Hill into full-alert status. Senate Armed Services Committee Chairman John G. Tower warned that adoption of the air-mobile plan would do away with the land-based leg of the U.S. nuclear defense "triad." (The other components of the triad are missile-carrying submarines and conventional bombers.)

Meanwhile, the Townes panel was gradually drifting in the direction that Presidents Ford and Carter had followed, finding that MX/MPS looked best when compared to the alternatives. "It's one of those problems where there are no pretty, pleasing, happy alternatives," said a pro-MX official familiar with the committee's deliberations. "There's a set of alternatives, each of which has undesirable features, and instead of looking for Miss America, you just have to pick the one with the least warts. . . . We never argued that it was pretty, just less homely than those other things." But to Weinberger, MX/MPS was too homely for words. When Townes met with him on June 30 to tell him the direction in which the committee was moving, Weinberger asked him to go back and consider the air-mobile idea. Other cabinet officers disagreed with Weinberger. Haig, Stockman, Central Intelligence Agency Director William Casey and United Nations Ambassador Jeane Kirkpatrick all supported the basing of the MX in deceptive shelters. The Secretary of State pointed out that European countries had agreed to accept 572 new American medium-range, land-based missiles beginning in 1983. If the United States wasn't willing to put the MX on its own soil, Haig said, the Europeans were likely to cancel the agreements. But Weinberger and Meese, not Haig, were guiding the policy. On July 30, in a meeting with the Washington bureau of the *Los Angeles Times,* Meese strongly indicated that the administration would scrap the MX/MPS plan. He called it "a bad idea . . . dictated only because of the Carter administration's slavish adherence to SALT-II, and that was the only reason for 4,600 holes in the ground." Meese had left the technical details, and much more, to Weinberger. The President's counsellor did not know what "MPS" stood for, incorrectly calling it the "multiple positioning system."[17]

The Townes Committee finally reported to Weinberger in late July. He kept the report secret and told Townes not to discuss it with the Air Force, which was still trying to get a hearing to present its case for MX/MPS.

Townes had given Weinberger some of what he wanted, but not enough. The committee observed in an opening section that any land-based system was not survivable if the other side committed sufficient missiles to destroy it. Then, by a "significant majority," it recommended building of 100 MX missiles and putting them into 100 shelters with the option to add additional shelters later.

Weinberger and the other opponents of MX/MPS by now realized that the airborne missile idea would never fly. Without announcing anything, the Defense Secretary and his research specialists now focused on another alternative—a so-called "common missile" which could be employed both in land-based shelters and on missile-carrying submarines. Past Pentagon studies had taken a dim view of this proposal, which in reality was not a "common missile" at all but a plan for converting the D5 Trident II missiles—the next generation of submarine-launched missiles—for use in silos.

Reagan was by now on his month-long vacation in California, and pressure was beginning to build for an MX-basing decision. On August 17, at an expanded National Security Council meeting in Reagan's top floor suite of the Century Plaza Hotel, Air Force Chief of Staff General Lew Allen, Jr., made his case against the airborne missile to Reagan. On August 21, Senate Armed Services Committee Chairman John G. Tower of Texas and Representative William L. Dickinson of Alabama, the ranking Republican on the House Armed Services Committee, followed up with their support of MX/MPS and a critique of the airborne missile. Dickinson came away from the meeting with, he said later, "the distinct impression that one or both [Weinberger and Reagan] were against MPS and they were studying to look for alternatives. Reagan had a deep-seated bias, and Weinberger was affected by Reagan's feelings."[18] Weinberger prudently retreated. When he briefed Reagan at Rancho del Cielo on August 26, he discussed options— including the common missile—but made no recommendation. The briefing disappointed some White House aides who had expected Weinberger to propose a specific course of action.

Weinberger needed time. The alternatives to MX/MPS he had proposed had proved unacceptable to Congress. Haig also was insisting on some sort of land-based missile. The Defense Secretary and Pentagon Research Chief Richard DeLauer came up with a unique solution. The MX would be produced. But the major basing decision would be postponed until 1984, afterward amended by Congress to 1983. In order to enable the President to claim that he had closed the "window of vulnerability" which was supposed to exist in the mid-1980s, Weinberger proposed placing 36 (later changed to 40) MX missiles into existing Minuteman or Titan silos. These silos would be "super-hardened" for protection, even though there was no existing research which supported the idea that any hardening would protect them from a Soviet attack. While the MX missiles were being produced, research would continue on "three promising, long-term basing options for MX," one of them Weinberger's pet proposal for an airborne missile patrol.*

The plan left orthodox nuclear strategists gasping and the Joint Chiefs of Staff in opposition, but it was a stunning political solution, meeting the needs of the western senators and the Mormon Church and enabling Al Haig to tell the Europeans that the United States, after all, was willing to base new missiles on its own soil. It had also made Reagan an unlikely hero of the environmental and antiwar groups who hated MX/MPS. The decision appalled former Pentagon Research Chief William Perry, who told a Senate armed services subcommittee that "the Soviets presently have missiles which are capable of destroying these silos . . . irrespective of how hard we make the silos."[19] It also disgusted Perry's former boss, Harold Brown, who wrote that ". . . in the case of a nuclear war the hardened MX silos will find themselves in the fireball and in the crater left by the nuclear explosion of Soviet warheads. . . ."[20] Even Brown, however, was comforted by the knowledge that the MX missile had not been killed outright. But it was now an unloved missile, an orphan without a home.

The President put his seal of approval on the Weinberger plan at a meeting in the second-floor sitting room of his White House living quarters on the afternoon of September 28. Reagan had just returned from a speaking trip to New Orleans, and he was tired. Weinberger, who had touched base with Meese before the meeting, pushed for his proposal despite the fact it contradicted the recommendations of the Townes panel. Meese supported him. Haig, relieved that Weinberger was at least proposing a land-based missile system, favored the Townes plan but did not push for it. The others in the meeting—Baker, Deaver, National Security Adviser Richard Allen and Vice-President Bush—deferred to Weinberger. Cleverly, the Defense Secretary used what Meese called "the weak recommendation" of the Townes committee against itself, pointing out that the panel had said that no missile was survivable.† Weinberger did not tell Reagan that the Soviets would have to use 9,200 one-megaton missiles to knock out MX/MPS and only 200 to destroy the Reagan administration's option. Instead, Weinberger hauled out a cartoon drawn by Mike Keefe of the *Denver Post* which showed Uncle Sam playing a shell game with a Russian, inviting him to guess which shell concealed the MX missile. The Russian in the cartoon takes out his hammer and destroys all the shells. Reagan chuckled, and approved the Weinberger plan.

When President Reagan announced this decision four days later, on Oc-

* Among the other options for MX on which the Pentagon was to conduct research and development was a ballistic missile defense and deployment in deep underground locations capable of withstanding a nuclear blast.

† The actual contents of the Townes Committee report were unofficially suppressed even after the President had made his recommendations. Some members of the Armed Services Committee who were considering the administration's proposal late in 1981 tried in vain to get a copy of the document.

tober 2, the Great Communicator was nowhere in evidence. Reagan read a statement saying that he had decided "not to deploy the MX in the racetrack shelters proposed by the previous administration," without mentioning that the racetrack shelters also had been discarded by the previous administration. He claimed, ironically, that his decision* came "after one of the most complex, thorough, and carefully conducted processes in memory." What Reagan did not know was that his delegated decision had in fact been made after a one-sided scrutiny which had frustrated and dismayed the administration experts most knowledgeable about the MX. He did not care to know. He tried to leave the podium as quickly as possible, saying, "For all the technical matters, I am going to turn you over to Secretary Cap Weinberger." And then unwisely agreeing to answer a few questions himself, Reagan demonstrated that he knew practically nothing about the decision Weinberger had reached in his name. Asked why the MX would be less vulnerable to Soviet attack in fixed silos, Reagan said haltingly: "I don't know but what maybe you haven't gotten into the area that I'm going to turn over to the Secretary of Defense." Weinberger, standing beside the President, said softly to him that the silos would be hardened. Reagan then repeated Weinberger's words. "I could say this," he said. "The plan also includes the hardening of silos so that they are protected against nuclear attack." A moment later a reporter asked Reagan whether the B-1 bomber, which Weinberger had revived at the same time he was doing away with MX/MPS, could penetrate Soviet defenses. "I think that my few minutes are up and I'm going too turn that question over to Cap," Reagan said. He had turned the decision over to him long ago.†

Afterward, musing on what had happened, Secretary of the Air Force Verne Orr remembered an incident from many years before in California, where he had succeeded Weinberger as Reagan's state finance director. Weinberger, about to leave to join the Nixon administration, gave Orr a thorough briefing and then added a word of caution. Whatever you do, advised Weinberger, don't mention income tax withholding to the governor. He's dead set against it, Weinberger told him, and you'll just be wasting your breath. At the time withholding was an emotional issue in Sacramento.

---

* Reagan's televised statement referred to his entire "strategic plan," which also included development of the B-1 bomber, which Carter had killed in 1977, and development of the Trident II D-5 missile, plus the various research-and-development options for long-term basing of the MX.

† But neither the President nor Weinberger had convinced the Congress that the decision was sound. On December 2, 1981, by a vote of 90–4, the Senate passed an amendment authored by Senators William S. Cohen of Maine and Sam Nunn of Georgia which sent a strong message to the administration and stipulated that money spent for hardened silos should be linked to long-basing solutions that would include mobility and deception. The senators made clear that they had no faith in Weinberger's contention that the silos could be successfully hardened. On March 23, 1982, a Senate Armed Services subcommittee went further and voted to stop the MX missile in its tracks until Reagan decided upon a permanent basing scheme. This was widely interpreted by both friends and foes of the MX as a sign the missile was dead.

Reagan opposed it, saying repeatedly that his "feet were set in concrete" against the plan. Though Weinberger favored withholding as a means of solving a serious state cash-flow problem, he was convinced that Reagan would not accept this solution. Orr, an unassuming and plainspoken businessman, decided there was no harm in asking. He worked up some figures showing the advantages of withholding and cited the widespread support for the change among legislators and fiscal experts. Reagan took Orr's recommendation calmly. After considering what Orr had said to him, he remarked to the finance director, "You mean the emperor has no clothes?" Orr laughed in agreement, and Reagan adopted income tax withholding.

More than a decade later, after President Reagan's opposition to MX/MPS had been assumed into evidence, Air Force Secretary Orr couldn't help wondering what Reagan might have done if someone had said to him: "Mr. President, it turns out that Carter's idea about the MX made sense." No one had done anything like that. Reagan had taken one of the most significant actions of his delegated presidency without realizing that his campaign rhetoric and the political considerations of his western friends had set in motion a decision-making process in which the conclusion was contained within the premise. The premise was that Reagan did not want an MX missile placed in multiple protective shelters in the Nevada and Utah deserts. He got what he wanted—or what Weinberger presumed he wanted. No one had told the President of the United States that he may have left his nation strategically unclothed.

Weinberger was a civilian among warriors at the Pentagon. Alexander Meigs Haig, Jr., at State, was a warrior among diplomats and one who was willing to challenge anyone who crossed his path. Before the Cancun summit in October 1981, Deaver had played devil's advocate, asking why the United States couldn't, in effect, tell the complaining underdeveloped nations to go fly a kite. "That's the most Neanderthal idea I ever heard," Haig said. "It's easy to sit here and take a macho position, but we can't afford that." He then proceeded to lecture the President and Deaver on U.S. responsibilities in the Third World. Haig did a lot of lecturing. He knew far more about foreign affairs than Reagan and his Californians, and he did not wear this knowledge easily. Haig broke the mold of the Reagan cabinet rather than fit it. Reagan likes quiet, easygoing, collegial people who can submerge themselves in a harmonic whole. Haig, who had worked for Henry Kissinger and Richard Nixon, was a workaholic and a battler with a flair for in-fighting. He was never submerged, and rarely quiet or collegial. His life in the Reagan administration was a constant struggle—with Weinberger, with the State Department bureaucracy, with "guerrillas" in the White House. When Reagan, at Meese's urging, put Vice-President Bush in charge of crisis management in March 1981, Haig had a tantrum. Pointing his finger at his deputy, William P. Clark, Haig angrily accused the President of misleading him into thinking that he would be in charge of crisis management. "He lied to me today, not only once but twice," Haig said. "He lied to me.'" Clark pointed his finger back at his superior. "Al, he hasn't lied to me once in fifteen years," he said. "Had he done so, I wouldn't be here."

Later, Clark calmed Haig down and convinced him that Reagan had not lied to him. But the Secretary of State was certain he had been misled by someone, in this case placing the blame on White House chief of staff James Baker. Someone, it seemed, was always trying to do in Al Haig. Sometimes it was Meese. Sometimes it was National Security Adviser Richard V. Allen, who really did undercut him. Sometimes it was Weinberger, who upstaged Haig a lot. Sometimes it was United Nations Ambassador Kirkpatrick, the only Reagan cabinet member besides Haig with a substantive grasp of foreign affairs. Stopping off in New Zealand on June 22, 1981, after a successful visit to the People's Republic of China, Haig became obsessed with the credit Kirkpatrick was getting for successfully steering a compromise resolution through the United Nations that deplored the Israeli bombing of an Iraqi nuclear reactor while avoiding the imposition of sanctions. Reagan considered the resolution a triumph. Haig tried to take long-distance credit for what Kirkpatrick had done and belittled her performance at the United Nations.*

Reagan was furious. He telephoned Kirkpatrick to tell her how much he thought of her, then complained to his aides that Haig kept straying "off the reservation." But by the time Haig's plane had reached Los Angeles, where Reagan was vacationing, the President was in a forgiving mood. He accepted Haig's apology, hoping that such incidents would not happen again. They kept happening, however. Soon after Haig returned to Washington, in an incident that failed to come to press attention, he attended a diplomatic reception where a visiting Japanese dignitary said politely to him, "You've been all over the world like a swallow." Without preliminary, Haig responded, "I've tried to keep out of the way of the buckshot from the White House." An interpreter said that the dignitary did not understand the metaphor. Haig repeated it for him. "I've been going around the world like a swallow to avoid buckshot from the White House," he said.

It is a comment on the value of Al Haig to the Reagan administration that incidents such as these, many times repeated, did not immediately cost him his job. The truth was that Reagan needed Haig, for all his nettlesome ways. And the President was wise enough to realize that he needed him. Reagan may not have done his homework on technical topics, but he was a good judge of people. He recognized that Haig's advice was usually sound.

---

* *Washington Post* reporter Don Oberdorfer, traveling with Haig, inadvertently stumbled across a barroom briefing of two reporters that was being conducted by State Department spokesman Dean Fischer, who arrived with a sheaf of notes. "This and the fact that Fischer is an extraordinarily cautious spokesman suggest he was acting with direction or at least authorization from on high," wrote Oberdorfer.[21]

"Al hasn't steered me wrong yet," Reagan told an intimate during one of Haig's periodic battles with the White House staff. Despite his rough-hewn military manner, the Secretary of State had a far more sophisticated understanding of the world than Reagan did, and he was forceful and effective in transmitting this understanding to the President. Haig never hesitated to express his views. For all his reputation as a bristling Cold Warrior, he was a prudent global politician who preferred skillful diplomacy to military adventure. Repeatedly, he clashed with Richard Allen on the issue of sending more fighter planes to Reagan's beloved Taiwan. Haig believed, and told Reagan, that such actions would damage U.S. relations with the People's Republic of China, which pins down a fourth of the Soviet Union's military divisions. Haig also pushed for talks with the Russians on reduction of European nuclear forces. He was a guiding light behind Reagan's landmark foreign policy speech of November 18, 1981, in which the President offered to cancel American plans to place a new generation of missiles in Europe if the Soviets would dismantle missiles they had already deployed. When the Polish military invoked martial law on December 12, 1981, Haig succeeded in delaying Reagan's retaliatory economic sanctions against the Soviet Union in a successful effort to "insulate" the nuclear reduction talks from the Polish controversy. "I came in looking like I had the talons of a hawk, but you know I have the heart of a dove,"[22] he quipped. Haig was certainly not a "dove" by the standards of such predecessors as Carter's Cyrus Vance.

At times there seemed to be two Al Haigs. A White House adviser, discussing this phenomenon said: "One is the smooth-talking diplomatic machine who represents this country most capably. The other is an angry man who becomes unraveled whenever his mandate is challenged."[23] Haig, a ferocious chainsmoker, had undergone triple bypass heart surgery about a year before he came to the State Department. Some persons who had known him in the Nixon administration thought that Haig was more touchy and irritable than he had been before the operation. Haig was aware of this opinion and tried to make light of it. Speaking at the Washington Heart Association Ball on November 7, 1981, he said: "Some years ago, when one was plagued with a heart problem, the physician told him to slow down life, become shy and retiring. Now they want you to be active and busy. At times they even want you to be notorious and naughty. . . . I want you to know I've been following the orders of my physician. As a matter of fact, I became Secretary of State because my doctor told me to."[24]

If Reagan had needed Haig, he needed Bill Clark even more. Clark's preferred life was the law and his 900-acre central California ranch. But he left the California Supreme Court to which Reagan had appointed him to become Reagan's man at the State Department and, as it turned out, Haig's best advocate at the White House. Clark did not get off to an auspicious start. He knew next to nothing about foreign policy, and his ignorance was evident at his confirmation hearings, where Clark flunked such basic tests as the identity of the prime minister of Zimbabwe.* *Newsweek*'s account of Clark's confirmation performance was headed, "A Truly Open Mind." But Clark knew something more important than the answers to the factual questions thrown at him during the hearings. He knew the heart and mind of Ronald Reagan, and he knew what Reagan expected of others and himself. In many ways Clark combined the strong points of the two California members of the Trio. Like Meese, he knew how to formulate and synthesize Reagan's ideas. Like Deaver, he had sensitivity for the ways in which Reagan operated and the ways in which he could be influenced. "You can't crowd Ronald Reagan," Clark told Haig, during one of his many efforts to keep the Secretary of State from presenting the President with an ultimatum. Somewhat to the surprise of both men, the tall, soft-spoken Clark, whose aides invariably answered the phone, "Judge Clark," got along with the mercurial, hard-driving Haig. Both men were practicing Roman Catholics who shared similar conservative, patriotic sentiments about the world. Haig was pleasantly surprised to find that Clark was loyal to him, as well as to Reagan. Clark was impressed with Haig's dedication and grasp of issues. He argued for Haig's point of view at the White House, talking frequently with Deaver in what amounted to an open back-channel of communication. It took Clark a long time to acquire a substantive grasp of foreign affairs. But in a very short time he was able to make a claim that could not be matched by anyone else in the high councils of the administration. Both Reagan and Haig trusted him. And George P. Schultz would come to trust him, too.

It was this trust of Clark, more than anything, which made possible the major shakeup in the White House staff which occurred in the first week of 1982. The public excuse for the shakeup was the bad judgment of Allen, who had accepted two watches from a Japanese business friend and $1,000 for Nancy Reagan as recompense for an interview she had given a Japanese women's magazine. The actual reason was profound dissatisfaction at both the White House and the State Department with the performance of Allen—and to some degree of Ed Meese. When Reagan became President, he guaranteed Haig that the Secretary of State would be the foreign policy spokesman. Reagan wanted the national security adviser to be a nearly anonymous staff assistant, not the dominant formulator of foreign policy that Henry Kissinger had been for Nixon and Zbigniew Brzezinski for Carter.

Under Richard Allen, the President succeeded beyond his wildest ex-

* When Clark visited Zimbabwe later he met Robert Mugabe, the prime minister whose name he had failed to identify during his confirmation hearings. As Clark tells the story, Mugabe made a mild mistake, referring to the "Byrd amendment" when he meant the "Clark amendment," and then apologized for getting the names wrong. "I've been known to forget names myself," replied Clark, to a burst of laughter from Mugabe.

pectations in diminishing the role of the National Security Council. Allen was an ideological hard-liner, and his briefings of the President tended to be both mechanical and ideological. After a while, Reagan decided that a written briefing, rather than an oral one, was sufficient. The lack of a first-class national security adviser deprived the President of the daily tutelage he needed in foreign affairs, but the problem was by no means entirely the fault of Allen. Meese had created a funnel-like system of organization in which both the national security adviser and the director of the Office of Policy Development, at this time Marty Anderson, reported to the President through him. Since Allen had no regular direct access to the President, except through Meese, there was no need for Haig to deal with the national security adviser except when he wanted to.

Unhappiness with this structural arrangement, as well as with Allen, grew steadily in the White House. Both Baker and Deaver were concerned about the quality of foreign policy information Reagan was receiving and the performance of Meese. The situation came to a climax on August 19, 1981, while Reagan was having a party in his Century Plaza hotel suite with his oldest son, Michael, and other guests. Deaver was away on vacation in New England, and Baker was in Texas. It was 10:20 P.M. California time. Across the world, sixty miles from the Libyan coastline, two American Navy F-14 fighters were attacked by two Russian-built Libyan planes. The F-14s returned the fire and shot down both Libyan jets. Meese and Allen learned of the incident at 11:04 P.M. Los Angeles time. By this time the party in the Reagan suite had broken up and the Reagans had retired for the night. Meese called all the members of the National Security Council and notified Vice-President Bush. But he did not tell Reagan about it until 4:24 A.M. the next morning. The President then went back to sleep. Afterwards, Reagan said Meese had acted appropriately because there was no decision for him to make. But both Baker and Deaver were furious that Meese had not awakened Reagan, knowing that it would be taken as a sign that the President was not in command. Nancy Reagan was angry about it, too, and her confidence in Meese plummeted after the incident. The Libyan affair brought into the open the simmering dissatisfaction with the Meese-Allen arrangement and prompted several articles which portrayed Reagan as a figurehead President.*

The situation did not improve when Reagan returned to the White House in September. By now the vaunted unity of the Trio was shaken, and some subordinates of Baker were suggesting openly to reporters that Meese

* These articles were epitomized by an account in the September 7 issue of *Newsweek* called "The Disengaged Presidency," which portrayed Reagan as "laid back" to the point of laziness and also included this observation: "Jimmy Carter gave hard work and attention to detail a bad name. Ronald Reagan will not make that mistake." And humorist Art Buchwald, in a September 13 column on Reagan's vacation, wrote: "We had a lot of fun. I cut brush, cleared out trees, hiked with my best girl Nancy, and shot down two Libyan planes. I was sleeping when we shot them down and my best friend Ed Meese didn't wake me up in time. But it was fun hearing about it."

was running a shop that was disorganized and out of control. Reagan, for all his public expressions of confidence in both Meese and Allen, realized that the system was not working. He sounded out Weinberger, Haig and Casey and asked their recommendations for a solution. Deaver, meanwhile, talked to Kissinger, who thought that Allen should be removed. Haig and Casey also thought that Meese would have to go on the grounds that he would direct the activities of whoever succeeded Allen, an open question in October 1981. At one point Kirkpatrick, whom Reagan liked, was proposed for the job, but she encountered opposition from both Haig and Deaver. Every suggested replacement had some adversary, except Clark. In the final week of October it was agreed that Clark would come into the White House and replace Allen. Clark was away with his wife in Antigua the last weekend in October. When he returned, he learned that Haig's mercurial reaction to whispered criticism from the White House had upset the carefully laid plans for an orderly change in national security advisers.

The proximate cause of the trouble was an unpublished column by Jack Anderson, who had written that "the secretary of state reportedly has one foot on a banana peel and could skip right out of the Cabinet before summer." White House Communications Director David R. Gergen, queried by Anderson, realized that his boss, James Baker, would be suspected of being the source. Gergen called Haig. Haig hit the roof, telling reporters that a "guerrilla campaign" was being waged against him at the White House, and implying that Allen was the guerrilla. He also called the President. Then he called Anderson, denying the report. Reagan called the columnist, too, with a similar denial. The Secretary of State, with some timely help from the President and Gergen, had taken what would have been another small episode in the ups-and-downs of Al Haig and had blown it up into a full-scale incident. On November 5, 1981, Reagan called both Haig and Allen into his office and ordered them to stop feuding. But he also postponed making any changes in his national security apparatus until the furor had died down.

Had Allen left in October, he might have bowed out with the praise of President Reagan ringing in his ears. His luck was not good. On January 21, the day after the inauguration, Allen had intercepted a $1,000 gratuity for Mrs. Reagan given by a representative of the Japanese magazine *Shufo no Tomo* in exchange for an interview. Allen placed it in a safe and forgot about it, a carelessness which his critics said was illustrative of the way he went about matters in the White House. When the money was discovered in a safe in mid-September, it triggered an investigation. Meese called the Justice Department to ask for an inquiry and followed up with a call to the FBI. Meese's critics, including Nancy Reagan, complained that he was more protective of Allen than of the President. The investigation started in mid-September but did not become public until November 14. By this time Reagan had decided to get rid of Allen, but he let him depart on administrative leave, never to return, until the investigation was over. The investigation cleared Allen of any legal wrongdoing, but it embarrassed the President and exposed the managerial weaknesses of Meese's operation.

Reagan had become convinced, as he told an intimate, that Meese should return to what he did best—being a counsellor—and stop trying to be a rival chief of staff. But he did not want to lose Meese or have him held up to ridicule. He allowed him, in Meese's words, to "get on top of the situation" by telling reporters that he had recommended upgrading of the national security adviser so that he would have direct access to the President. Meese's recommendation was not needed, because the issue already had been decided. On New Year's Day in Palm Springs, Reagan signed a memorandum making Clark his national security adviser and specifying that he have direct access to the President and administrative control of the National Security Council staff. Clark also was designated as the contact man for both Haig and Weinberger, in the hope that he could reduce the inevitable disputes between the two strong-minded cabinet secretaries to manageable proportions. On the first day on the job Clark quietly served notice that he would be an independent power in the White House. When Meese set a chair for him at his morning management meeting and asked him to review the National Security Council briefing, Clark declined. "I'll be reviewing that with the President," he said. Publicly, Clark tried to keep a low profile while he worked on restoring the status and effectiveness of the National Security Council. "I want to be an honest broker,"[25] Clark said. He had no illusions that his job would be an easy one.

Nor was it easy for Reagan. He had gone through a long and difficult learning process in foreign affairs, reminiscent of what had happened to him in California when he was a novice governor. But by the time he reached the White House he was seventy years old. He lacked some of the energy of his earlier years, and his photographic mind was no longer as retentive as it had been in Sacramento. Reagan's agenda on domestic affairs was well formed and had been mastered through repetition over many years. In foreign policy he was starting from scratch. He came into office with a point of view rather than a set of policies—a view that was anti-Soviet, pro-Israel and largely supportive of the Atlantic Alliance. He had no experience in dealing with the substance of foreign policy, and his counsellor Meese, who was well informed on a wide range of domestic issues, was similarly handicapped. Reagan's first Secretary of State was well informed, and highly respected in Europe, but his personal insecurity and his conflicts with White House aides nullified much of his effectiveness.

For a long time Haig had not crowded the President, following the advice of Bill Clark. But after Clark left the State Department for the White House, the angry Al Haig prevailed over the diplomatic Haig. On June 24, 1982, forgetting or ignoring Clark's earlier advice, Haig submitted his resignation at a private meeting at the White House. The next day the President accepted it and replaced Haig with George Shultz. Shultz had earned a reputation for getting along with others and this ability was what Reagan had come to desire most in a Secretary of State.

Postscript—Shultz's appointment did not solve the problems caused by

Reagan's proclivity for delegation nor curb the White House staff's impulse to control both the cabinet and the presidency. Haig's departure, welcomed by both Clark and Baker, became the prelude to a larger struggle within the White House in which the contenders for power gave no verbal quarter and showed little scruple. On one side were Baker and his "pragmatists," Deaver, Darman and Gergen. On the other was Clark, sometimes supported by Meese and usually by Weinberger. As always, the struggle was for the heart and mind of the President.

The battle, which unfolded over many issues, was also a struggle over access. Clark, unlike his predecessors, did not require Deaver's permission to see Reagan. Clark believed that the pragmatists were isolating Reagan and leading him to compromise for the sake of compromising. Baker thought that Clark appealed to both the simplistic and darker side of Reagan, a view ratified in Baker's mind when Clark persuaded the President to approve what turned out to be an inconclusive Justice Department inquiry into the source of purported news leaks of U.S. policy in Lebanon. The Baker faction resolved to get rid of Clark, and Deaver enlisted Nancy Reagan in this cause.

Typically, Reagan resisted becoming involved. He dismissed news stories about the White House feuding as a dispute among "the boys," as he called the middle-aged members of his staff. The solution turned out to be another problem, caused by James Watt, who said during an otherwise routine speech on Sept. 21, 1983, that members of an advisory coal-leasing commission included "a black . . . a woman, two Jews and a cripple." This time Watt's mouth accomplished what his critics could not. He resigned under pressure on Oct. 9 and four days later was replaced by Clark, who had been feeling the strain of his running battle with Baker and asked Reagan for the appointment. Clark was replaced by his deputy, Robert C. McFarlane.

McFarlane, a soft-spoken diplomat and former Marine, was fresh from negotiating a short-lived ceasefire in Lebanon. He agreed with Shultz that the Marines deployed in Lebanon as part of an international peacekeeping force were useful in obtaining a diplomatic solution. On Oct. 23, a week after McFarlane had taken over his new duties, a Moslem fanatic drove a truck loaded with explosives into the Marine compound at the Beirut airport, killing 241 U.S. servicemen. The incident, which a respected investigative body, the Long Commission, subsequently blamed on lax security and an ill-defined mission, was a hammerblow to the Shultz policy and the seminal event in a four-months process that ended with the total withdrawal of U.S. forces from Lebanon.

More than any other event, the Beirut bombing exposed the weakness of the delegated presidency. The Joint Chiefs of Staff had warned against static deployment of the Marines. Weinberger, supported by Clark, had urged their redeployment to ships off shore weeks before the bombing. Shultz, backed by McFarlane, had claimed that progress was being made toward a diplomatic solution, and Reagan accepted the contention without examination and repeated it to the American people. The result was tragic. Once more, Reagan had understood too little and delegated too much.

23

The Hero

H E began the day with a pep talk to 140 enthusiastic sub-cabinet members in the East Room of the White House, giving a speech which emphasized the need for change in economic policy and ending with a favorite quotation from Tom Paine: "We have it in our power to begin the world over again." Later he spoke to 3,500 trade union representatives, many of whom had doubts about his policies. Once more he emphasized his economic program but this time touched also on the social problems which beset America. "Violent crime has surged 10 percent, making neighborhood streets unsafe and families fearful in their homes," he said. It was a routine luncheon speech in the banquet room of a Washington hotel. Afterward, outside the hotel, the speaker paused to catch a reporter's question. It was another routine scene that Ronald Reagan as politician and President had played a thousand times. The reporter shouts a question from the crowd. The obliging President, his press secretary at his side, moves toward the crowd and responds with a wave, a smile and brief answer. Reagan did not see the gunman in this crowd. No one else saw him or knew he was there. The gunman fired. Mike Deaver heard shots whiz by his head and ducked to the ground, assisted by a shove from a Washington policeman.* White House Press Secretary James Brady sprawled forward, a bullet through his brain. Other bullets struck Secret Service agent Timothy J. McCarthy and Washington policeman Thomas K. Delehanty. A woman screamed. A Secret Service agent yelled, "Get back, get back." Reagan stood frozen for a split second. "The smile just sort of washed off his face," said Michael Putzel of Associated Press, the reporter who had sought to ask him a question about

---

* On April 2, in an interview with the author for the *Washington Post*, Deaver described the sequence of events: "The President and I were walking out together. The press started asking their usual questions. I turned and moved Brady up because he was the press secretary. I took three steps, then the first shot went over my right shoulder. I knew what it was. I ducked down, with the help of a shove from a Washington policeman, who was also falling to the ground. I never saw the policeman."[1] Deaver was a last-minute substitute at the speech for White House Chief of Staff James A. Baker, who was so busy that day that Deaver volunteered to go in his place.

developments in Poland.[2] Agent Jerry Parr, an eighteen-year veteran of the Secret Service, pushed Reagan into the waiting presidential limousine while other agents rushed toward the gunman.* Parr shoved him so hard that Reagan's head struck the doorway of the car and he landed on the transmission hump in front of the rear seat with the agent on top of him, trying to protect the President with his body. "Take off," Parr said to driver Drew Unrue, "just take off." Pain poured over Reagan.[3] He felt a paralyzing blow, as if he had been struck with a hammer. "You sonofabitch, you broke my ribs,"[4] he said to Parr as the limousine sped away. Brady lay behind on the sidewalk, blood from his head trickling across an iron grate and down the walk to the entrance of the Washington Hilton hotel.

The gunman had fired six shots within the space of two seconds, wounding four persons. One of the wounded was President Reagan who, for all his pain, did not know that he had been shot. Parr did not know it either. The bullet that struck the President had bounced off the limousine and richocheted through the space between the body of the car and the open car door. It was an explosive "Devastator" bullet with a small aluminum canister designed to fly apart inside the body of its target. The canister collapsed as the bullet hit the limousine. The collision flattened the bullet into the shape and size of a dime, sending it careening into Reagan like a Skilsaw that had flown off its axle. Inside the limousine en route to the White House, Parr searched the President for gunshot wounds and found none. The bullet had made a slit like a knife wound under Reagan's left arm. The wound was not visible, but Parr realized that Reagan had been hurt. The agent saw bright red blood coming from the President's mouth and knew from his medical training that this was oxygenated blood passed up through the lungs. Parr thought that the shove he gave Reagan might have cracked a rib which in turn had punctured a lung. In a quick decision that may have saved Reagan's life,† Parr directed Unrue to drive the limousine to George Washington Hospital instead of to the White House. "Rawhide is going to George Washington," Parr advised his command post over the radio, using the Secret Service code name for the President.

At the hospital Reagan walked into the emergency room with the assistance of Secret Service agents, then fell to one knee. "I can't breathe," he said. Agents helped him onto a table and members of the hospital's trauma team rushed over to him. Later, doctors found that a bullet had lodged to within an inch of Reagan's heart, missing the vital aorta by about the same distance. And as television played and replayed its filmed tape of the shoot-

* The accused assassin was John Warnock Hinckley, Jr., a 25-year-old drifter who had been undergoing psychiatric treatment.

† "If the President had been taken to the White House after he was shot instead of to George Washington Hospital or taken to a more distant or lesser hospital, I think he would have been in big trouble," said Dr. Benjamin Aaron, the surgeon who operated on him. Aaron said that Reagan was never in real danger of death at the hospital "because he got first-class care from the first minute. But he needed it. He was right on the margin when he got here."[5]

ing, Americans heard echoes of past gunshots that had felled American leaders and heroes in Dallas, in Memphis and in Los Angeles. The sounds of these shots foreshadowed others that would be heard the same year in Rome and in Cairo.* In a world of violence, the assassin's bullet had also become routine.

President Reagan, wounded on March 30, 1981, after two months and ten days in office, did not die. He survived to show the nation the wit and grace that was on daily display before his friends and family. "Honey, I forgot to duck," he told Nancy Reagan, who rushed to the hospital at the first word of the shooting.† "Please tell me you're Republicans," he said to the doctors who were preparing him for operation soon thereafter. One-liners were the way that Reagan dealt with the mysteries of life and death. He used them to soften up audiences and to entertain his aides and to bring smiles to the faces of those he loved. One-liners were Reagan's badge of courage when he was deeply frightened. He used them to wash away the fear, and White House spokesmen repeated them to the American public, knowing they would serve as reassuring signals to the country that the President was unimpaired. They were the best of signals, and Reagan kept sending them. "All in all I'd rather be in Philadelphia," he wrote on a notepad that night in the recovery room, paraphrasing comedian W. C. Fields. The nurses laughed, and the nation laughed with them. The one-liners were the testimony of the man.

The White House spokesmen did not repeat all of Reagan's words and messages from the hospital. In a time of crisis they did not wish to talk of fear, and Reagan had been afraid like other men. When a member of the trauma team attending him exclaimed, "This is it!", Reagan reached for a notepad and wrote to a nurse: "What does he mean—'this is it'?" The nurse stood by him and held his hand. Her name was Marisa Mize, and she had seen many patients similarly afraid. Soon after Reagan entered the emergency room, an endotracheal tube had been inserted down his throat to help him breathe. Reagan felt that the tube was choking him. "You know, I can't breathe," he said to Nancy and their son Ron when he emerged from the anesthesia after the operation. And Reagan's son leaned over to him and said gently in reference to the tube: "Dad, don't worry. It's like scuba diving."[6] The words reassured Reagan, who later wrote another note to those attending him. Quoting Winston Churchill, Reagan wrote: "There's no more exhilarating feeling than being shot at without result."

---

* Pope Paul II was shot and wounded in St. Peter's Square on May 13. Egyptian President Anwar Sadat was shot and killed during a military parade in Cairo on October 6. Both of these shootings were harsh reminders to the President—and to Nancy Reagan— of the personal dangers facing world leaders. Reagan decided for security reasons not to attend the Sadat funeral or to send Vice-President Bush in his place. Instead, he sent a unique assemblage of former Presidents—Jimmy Carter, Gerald Ford and Richard Nixon.

† The line, like many of Reagan's best, was an old one. Jack Dempsey reportedly said it to his wife after losing the heavyweight boxing title to Gene Tunney in 1926.

But the attempt on Reagan's life had, in fact, many results. In the short run it produced a wave of popular sympathy which assisted the passage of Reagan's economic legislation. In the middle distance it slowed Reagan's learning curve on foreign policy and encouraged his inclination to over-delegate. And in the long run, Reagan's grace under pressure destroyed forever any lingering doubts that the President was a cardboard man whose aspirations and emotions were as synthetic as a celluloid screen. The heroism reflected in Reagan's humor was genuine, and everyone knew it. Forever afterward, criticisms of Reagan's policies would be separated from an evaluation of the man. During sixty-nine days in the presidency Reagan had shown an abundance of personal ease and charm. "When he displayed that same wit and grace in the hours after his own life was threatened, he elevated those appealing human qualities to the level of legend," wrote David Broder.[7] Reagan had become a mythic figure, reminding those of his own generation of the courage displayed by President-elect Franklin D. Roosevelt when he was the target of an assassination attempt that killed Chicago Mayor Anton Cermak.* "I have never seen anything more magnificent than Roosevelt's calm that night. . . ," wrote an associate afterwards.[9] It was a description that could have been applied with even greater force to the wounded Reagan.

Those attending Reagan at George Washington Hospital came to love and admire him. They appreciated the one-liners and Reagan's uncomplaining acknowledgment that he had been afraid. Reagan may not have known much about the MX missile, but he realized that bravery was more than the absence of fear. In the hours after the shooting and the operation, Reagan feared that he would not be able to resume the physically active life he had always led. "What does my future hold for me?" he asked in a note written in the middle of the night after his surgery. "Will I be able to ride my horses again? Will I be able to cut brush?"[10] When doctors told Reagan that he would be riding again in two months, Reagan held up one finger to say that he would be back in the saddle in half the time. He was a resilient man, whose optimistic nature rallied at any sign of encouragement. He knew how fortunate he had been to dodge what he called "the awful awful," and it changed him subtly. After the shooting he sometimes wondered if assassins lurked in crowds, and he accepted a Secret Service suggestion to wear a bulletproof vest in potentially dangerous situations. The shooting had provided Reagan with an appreciation of his own mortality that was soon reflected in his jokes and memories of the incident. When the President was asked later in the year what he would have done differently in the first six months of his

---

* The attempt on Roosevelt's life occurred February 5, 1933, in Miami. Roosevelt was still the President-elect because Presidents were then not inaugurated until March. Wrote Arthur Schlesinger of the attempt on Roosevelt's life: "If the thin chance which had saved the people their President-elect was sobering, his own response was more than that—it was heartening and exhilarating. For Roosevelt, it was clear, really lacked physical fear, and an impulse of courage now flowed out to the nation against the backdrop of gunfire at Miami."[8]

administration, he replied: "I wouldn't have gone to the Hilton Hotel."[11]

Reagan's consideration for others in the hospital was as impressive as his courage, though less advertised. He was saddened by the grievous wounding of Brady, whose survival he regarded as miraculous. Reagan was troubled, he told aides afterward, that others had been exposed to mortal danger because of him.* He had always been a considerate man, but he was even more considerate after the shooting. For several days in the hospital Reagan ran a fever, and doctors refused him permission to shower or bathe. One night, drenched with perspiration, Reagan decided to clean himself anyway. He went into the bathroom, filled the basin with water and gave himself a sponge bath. When he had finished, he noticed that the bathroom floor was covered with water. Reagan went down on his hands and knees to mop it up. "What did you do that for?" George Bush wanted to know when he visited Reagan at the hospital. Reagan told the Vice-President that he knew the nurse on duty would be blamed if the doctors found out that he had bathed. "I didn't want her to get in trouble," he said.

The action was typical of Ronald Reagan, who cared for ordinary people when he dealt with them directly even if his economic policies were far from a model of compassion. After the 1980 election Richard Nixon met for dinner with a group of jubilant Republican congressmen. Nixon lauded Reagan's leadership abilities and predicted to the group that he would make a good President. One of the congressmen pressed Nixon, however, wanting to know what he regarded as Reagan's liabilities. The former President thought for a moment, then replied: "He may be too nice to be President."[12] Instead, this "niceness" has been a mainstay of Reagan's popularity in the face of policy shortcomings. "He's cutting the heart out of the American dream to own a home and have a good job and still he's popular," observed House Speaker Tip O'Neill, an old-style personality politician who has become symbol and scapegoat for Democratic defeats. "He's always got a disarming story. . . . I don't know where he gets them but he's always got them, stories about the World Series, football games, everything. 'Tip, you and I are political enemies only until 6 o'clock. It's 4 o'clock now. Can we pretend it's 6 o'clock?' "[13] O'Neill believes that Reagan will continue to be more popular than his programs. Speaking to Haynes Johnson of the *Washington Post* in November 1981, at a time when the cracks in Reaganomics were

* Reagan's one-liners were delivered before he learned what had happened to Brady, the popular White House secretary, whose death had been prematurely reported on television the day of the shooting. Doctors shared Reagan's view that Brady's recovery was miraculous. "I expected him to die," said Brady's physician, Arthur Kobrine, when Brady was released from the hospital on November 23, 1981, after four operations, to continue his long, painful recovery at home. Reagan promised Brady in a visit to the hospital that he would hold the press secretary's position open for him, a pledge that resulted in the creation of a truncated White House press operation in which responsibility was divided between principal deputy Larry Speakes and Assistant for Communications David R. Gergen. Whenever the question of making a permanent change came up, Reagan reminded aides of the promise he had made to Brady.

widening, O'Neill said of Reagan: "People like him as an individual, and he handles the media better than anybody since Franklin Roosevelt, even including Jack Kennedy. There's just something about the guy that people like. They want him to be a success. They're rooting for him, and of course they're rooting for him because we haven't had any presidential successes for years—Kennedy killed, Johnson with Vietnam, Nixon with Watergate, Ford, Carter, and all the rest."[14]

Will Reagan be considered a presidential success? No heroism may be sufficient to rescue Reaganomics, which has always required a suspended disbelief from its adherents. The bond market passed a negative judgment in 1981 and the stock market another in early 1982 as growing budget deficits prompted fears of renewed high interest rates. Other judgments will be given in other years in the markets and at the polls, a prospect which offers little consolation to Republicans. Reagan adherents remember only too well how the "misery index" (inflation rate plus unemployment rate) which candidate Carter invented in 1976 came back to haunt President Carter in 1980. The "are-you-better-off?" test which Reagan employed against Carter has now become a test by which to measure the Reagan presidency.

But the ultimate determination of Reagan's success will not be based on any simple calculus of domestic economics. It will depend in part on foreign policy events which Reagan cannot control and on the success of nuclear arms negotiations with the Soviets. It also will depend on how well other Presidents do after him. "On the day he leaves office, a President's place in history depends heavily on some history that hasn't happened yet," wrote Hedley Donovan, observing that the reputations of "both Harry Truman and Dwight Eisenhower stand significantly higher today then when they left the White House."[15] Reagan's vote for Truman in 1948 was the last he cast for a Democratic President. His vote for Eisenhower was the first he gave to a Republican presidential candidate. Truman left office with an unpopularity not matched until the "smoking gun" of Watergate drove Nixon to the helicopters. Today the "mess in Washington" that Truman supposedly left behind provokes nostalgia, and the man from Missouri is remembered chiefly for his wise and resolute foreign policy in Europe after World War II. Eisenhower was always personally popular but was viewed in Washington as vapid and ineffectual. Seen through the prism of the Vietnam War, Watergate, the double-digit inflation of the Carter presidency and the double-digit unemployment of the Reagan recovery, the eight Eisenhower years take on the luminescence of a golden age. Will Reaganomics look better after President Bush or President Mondale (or President Rockefeller or President Kennedy or President Hart or President Glenn) have a go at reindustrializing America or trimming back the welfare state? Will Reagan's rhetorical belligerence against the Soviets be seen as a necessary precondition to international negotiation leading to genuine arms reduction? We shall see.

We do not have to await the judgments of history to discover repetitive patterns in the Reagan presidency. Reagan is a man of integrity and conviction, and the presidential office is a measure of the man who holds it. Personal presidential decisions rather than the abstract actions of an institutionalized presidency involved the United States in Vietnam and Richard Nixon in the Watergate coverup. President Johnson's decision to declare a "war on poverty" and President Reagan's decision to end this combat were executive expressions of deep personal commitment, even though both actions required ratification by Congress. Reagan's views are well known, and his pattern of behavior when he is technically well informed is usually predictable. No union leader who had taken the trouble to find out that Governor Reagan had replaced striking workers on the California Water Project would have thought that President Reagan was bluffing when he vowed to fire air controllers who refused to honor their no-strike pledge in 1981. No one who examined Reagan's long personal antipathy to high federal income tax rates should be surprised to find that the President clung stubbornly to the view that the rates must be reduced.

We can say confidently about Reagan that he will usually try to carry out his promises whenever he can.* He lifted the grain embargo against the prophetic warning of Al Haig. He stuck with the personal income tax cut at a time when many of his top aides were willing to abandon or to modify the proposal. He appointed a woman to the Supreme Court. He proposed reduction of nuclear missiles in Europe. He seeks a realistic arms control treaty with the Soviet Union. When Reagan pledged during the 1980 campaign a willingness to sit down with the Soviets "for as long as it takes" and negotiate an arms control treaty, he was doing more than defusing Jimmy Carter. Like Nixon in his overture to the People's Republic of China, Reagan recognizes that he has a credibility and an opportunity on arms control that might not be accorded a Democratic President. He knows that any treaty he is willing to sign is likely to be ratified by the Senate, and he understands that the Russians recognize this, too.

George Reedy wrote in *The Twilight of the Presidency* that the essential activities of the presidency can be reduced to two fundamentals: "He must resolve the policy questions that will not yield to a quantitative, empirical analysis; and he must persuade enough of his countrymen of the rightness of his decisions so that he can carry them out without destroying the fabric of society."[16] Reagan measures up to the second of these fundamentals better than anyone since Roosevelt, but he has some trouble with the first. On various key defense and foreign policy issues, Reagan has simply failed to do his

---

* The conspicuous exception is President Reagan's decision to continue draft registration despite his campaign promise to end it. Reagan changed his mind on the urging of Secretary of Defense Caspar W. Weinberger, who in turn had been told by a variety of military leaders that both the quantity and quality of the all-volunteer Army was inadequate.

homework. This failing could have grave consequences. On the issue of arms control, for instance, Reagan's ignorance and his unwillingness to make himself conversant with the complex issues of strategic nuclear weaponry has substantially undermined his own campaign position of negotiating from a position of strength. Because of rapidly rising Pentagon costs and the delegation of strategic decisions to Weinberger, Reagan has reduced the U.S. fleet of missile-carrying submarines while simultaneously escalating the retirement of U.S. land-based missiles. "If a Democrat were in the White House today," wrote Walter Pincus in January 1982, "conservative Republicans almost certainly would be accusing him of unilateral disarmament."[17]

Some politicians seek to conserve their popularity; others invest it in the policies and programs they seek to accomplish. Reagan is the latter sort of President, and he has paid a price for it in the public opinion polls. After reaching a 68 percent approval rating early in May 1981, Reagan's public support slid steadily downward throughout the last half of that year. He finished the first year with an approval rating of 49 percent, slightly less than Carter at the same point and well below the comparable approval ratings given Presidents Eisenhower, Kennedy and Nixon.* Reagan's policies are not derived from any polls. He wants to be remembered as the chief executive who reined in the welfare state and slowed the growth of government, and he came into office with a sense that time was running out. If anything, the assassination attempt enhanced this attitude. Mike Deaver, who has a keen understanding of Reagan, believes that the shooting left the President with a great sense of mission and a recognition that he had a finite time available in which to accomplish his goals.

Even before the shooting, Reagan's track record suggested that he would not quit in the stretch. His geniality masks a stubborn streak and a doggedness which leads him to keep coming back for bits and pieces of his programs. Reagan has not dismantled the New Deal, and he has not really altered the fundamental structure of the welfare society his administration inherited. What he has done is make a start in the direction he intends government to go. "Cut, cap and block," is the way that Republican Senator David F. Durenberger of Minnesota sums up the first session of the 97th Congress. "The strategy was to reduce the increase—to achieve a stalemate with the thousands of overextended good intentions of the last decade."[18]

Some thoughtful Democrats realized that Reagan was doing what needed to be done, even if the medicine he prescribed left a bad taste in their mouths. "I've told many disgruntled Democrats and special interest groups that if you look at the positive side of this, we can go after the waste which is part of the structure and better serve the programs and, quite frankly, the needs of the Democratic constituency."[19] says Leon Panetta, a Democratic

* Kennedy had a 71 percent approval rating at the end of his first year in office, while Eisenhower stood at 61 percent and Nixon at 56 percent. All the cited surveys were taken by the Gallup Poll.

congressman from California who voted with Reagan half the time during the first session of the 97th Congress. Another Democrat, speaking even more bluntly behind the cover of anonymity, said to me in March of 1981: "Some of our programs are out of hand and we can't cut them. Reagan can and it will save us, and him." This congressman voted against the Reagan budget cuts, and denounced them as "heartless" or "inhumane." It is what some congressmen do. At the same time the congressman recognized that Reagan's actions might ultimately serve to preserve the welfare state rather than to destroy it. If one takes as a premise the notion that a public reaction against the costs of federal social programs was inevitable, Reagan may turn out to be the salvation of the New Deal much as his idol Franklin Roosevelt proved the savior of capitalism. The survival of democracy in the United States during the Depression required government intervention and some restrictions on the predatory practices of the marketplace. After a half-century the pendulum had swung so far the other way that corrective action was needed beyond anything the Congress could provide. Reagan tried to halt the swing of that pendulum and push it back along the arc of individual freedom. He was a conservative, but one who was conserving the New Deal. Like Roosevelt, he saw himself as a force of history. Like Roosevelt, he was anathema to those whom his policies ultimately benefited most.

No one who knew Reagan was surprised to find that he proved a dedicated President who was seriously committed to his political agenda. Despite the easy grace and the one-liners, he had always been an over-achiever. He mastered his crafts. He was serious about his labor union. He tried to carry out his campaign promises. Comparing him to the last elected Republican President, the *Boston Globe*'s Marty Nolan observed that one difference is "that Reagan sought to be President in order to do something and Nixon sought to be President in order to be something."[20] There is a lot of truth to that. Everyone saw the flair and friendliness in Reagan. Everyone saw the optimism and the easy manner and the sense of country. These attributes were there, and they were important, but it was the commitment which made the diifference. The commitment came from his boyhood. Ronald Reagan had grown up in a time and place where it was literally possible for a young American to think that he could be whatever he wanted to be. He grew up with the democratic dream. His father told him that he could go as far as his talent would take him, even though his father, who had talent, had not gone far. His mother encouraged his dreams of glory and urged him to persevere. "Perseverance" seems an odd word to use in describing Reagan, who valued his free time and his family and who did not always work as hard as he should have worked. But persevere he did. He was too slow to make the first-string football team, even at a small college, but he made it. He did not read commercials well, but he became one of the best sports announcers in the Middle West. He struggled in B films until the role of George Gipp came along to give him a lifetime nickname he deserved. Reagan was "the Gipper," all right. If anyone had ever asked the real Ronald Reagan whether he could run with the football, he probably would have said, "How far?" just like the movie Gipper did. It turned out that he could run a long way.

Reagan did not lose the knack of perseverance as he grew older. He began his public career as a novice, ineffective governor and ended up a good one. He was too old and too out of touch as a presidential candidate, and ended up a winner. "We have every right to dream heroic dreams," he said, and his heroes were always other people who persevered. He admired people who had come up the hard way, a category which included opposition politicians like Tip O'Neill as well as a surprising number of his wealthy friends.

In the White House Rose Garden on June 5, 1981, Reagan did what his predecessor had refused to do, awarding Ethel Kennedy the special congressional medal struck in honor of her husband who had been killed thirteen years ago that day. "The facts of Robert Kennedy's public career stand alone," Reagan said. "He aroused the comfortable. He exposed the corrupt, remembered the forgotten, inspired his countrymen and renewed and enriched the American conscience." Reagan did not have much in common with Robert Kennedy, but both men were authentic American heroes who dared to follow their dreams. What was heroic about Reagan was that he dared and that he never stopped striving. I liked him best in the North Carolina primary of 1976, when he entered as a loser who was out of campaign funds and down on his luck. "When are you going to drop out?" he was asked, over and over again. "I'm not going to drop out," Reagan said, and he didn't. He stayed in the race and won North Carolina, and though he eventually lost the nomination he became a hero in the process. He won the next time because, in his world, heroes are supposed to win. He had come a long way from Tampico, a very long way, and the dreams of Tampico and Dixon and Eureka had carried him far beyond even his most distant imagined destination. He had persevered in defeat. He had been gracious in victory. He belonged in the White House. He had every right to dream heroic dreams.

Epilogue

On February 8, after lunch at the White House with all-star players from the National Hockey League, Ronald Reagan flew to Minneapolis for his first political fund-raiser of 1982. Outside the Carleton Dinner Theater hundreds of demonstrators waited for him in sub-zero cold, one of them bearing a banner which proclaimed, "Welcome President Hoover." Inside, at a reception and dinner for Senator David Durenberger, Reagan praised the spirit and works of voluntarism. He took as his text an account in the Minnesota weekly newspaper, the *Kirkhoven Banner,* about how sixteen farmers had "donated their time, their calluses and their equipment" to help a fellow farmer who had been seriously injured in an automobile accident. Afterward, he gave a rambling interview to WCCO television and radio correspondents during which the President said "1941" when he meant "1981" and described the 1970 recession as a "depression." When interviewer Dave Moore asked Reagan how he expected to win congressional support for his economic program in the face of opposition from Republican congressional leaders, the President replied: "I don't think they fully understand yet."[1]

By early spring of 1982, Republican congressmen and Reagan's closest advisers came to believe that it was the President himself who did not understand. As economic recovery failed to meet his rosy predictions and discontent grew over administration foreign and defense policies, Reagan became noticeably more stubborn and isolated. His optimism rescued him from the bitterness which had afflicted several of his predecessors, and he remained gently tolerant of staff members who made no secret that they hoped Reagan would modify his policies. But he did not follow their advice. On January 22, two days after the *New York Times* had reported the confident assertions of the White House staff that Reagan would accept excise taxes on liquor, cigarettes and gasoline to lower the federal deficit, Reagan told Mike Deaver he had awakened in the middle of the night and decided he couldn't agree to any tax increases. "I learned something from the process," Deaver told me afterward. "Never try to talk any man who holds deep convictions out of them for reasons of political expediency because it would destroy him. We almost destroyed Ronald Reagan, and I was one of the people arguing for this."[2]

What was really damaging Reagan was his failure to understand the increasingly precarious nature of his mandate and the fundamental structural obstacles to the long-term economic recovery. When my assistant Robin Gradison asked an economically knowledgeable Republican congressman whether Reagan was a good listener, he replied: "Well, he's a good listener but he doesn't seem to really hear."

In some cases, this was literally true. Though his health was otherwise remarkable for a seventy-one-year-old man, Reagan's hearing noticeably declined in 1982. In the White House residence, the television was kept at a level intolerably loud for those with normal hearing. In the Oval Office, where the acoustics are difficult at best, Reagan strained to hear what was being said, and aides spoke at the top of their voices. Reagan's poor hearing made it easy for him to tune out of conversations which didn't interest him.

Reagan worked harder and read more than most outsiders realized. He responded quickly when presidential decision memos were presented to him for his acceptance or rejection. But Reagan was resistant to information which challenged his preconceptions. Sometimes he nodded off in important meetings. And he was more unyielding than he had been before the assassination attempt, which had left a subtle but significant imprint on the man and his presidency. Deaver, for one, believed that the shooting had reinforced Reagan's sense of mission in his presidency and made him mindful that he had a limited time in which to carry out his objectives.*

What worried Reagan's advisers was that his growing rigidity would make him appear so unreasonable that it would undermine his opportunities for leadership and give him less, not more, time in which to carry out his policies. In March, Senator Paul Laxalt told reporters—and Reagan—that Republicans faced the prospect of losing more than 30 congressional seats in the 1982 elections if the budget deadlock weren't broken quickly. A loss of such magnitude would make Reagan "virtually a lame duck" in 1983, an adviser told me, preventing him from gaining congressional cooperation for his programs. When I asked the adviser if Reagan realized this, he sadly shook his head.

Distanced from many of the controversies which engulfed his administration, Reagan kept his own counsel and followed his own timing. The same adviser who had worried about Reagan becoming a lame duck fretted

* While Reagan was still recuperating from his wounds, he was visited in the White House on Good Friday (April 17), 1981, by Terence Cardinal Cooke, the Roman Catholic archbishop of New York. "The hand of God was upon you," Cooke said to the President in reference to the shooting. "I know," Reagan replied. "And whatever time He's left for me is His."[3]

in mid-March about the growing nuclear freeze campaign, saying, "It's the fuel of the nuclear freeze that's going to burn us on the defense budget." A few days later Reagan used a prime-time televised news conference to announce his support of a bipartisan Senate resolution calling for negotiations with the Soviet Union to reduce the nuclear arsenals of the two superpowers.

Then, on May 9, Reagan tried simultaneously to defuse the domestic nuclear freeze campaign and to capture the international political offensive by proposing an arms reduction plan that had as its centerpiece the reduction of U.S. and Soviet nuclear ballistic missile warheads by one-third. "The monumental task of reducing and reshaping our strategic forces to enhance stability will take many years of concentrated effort," the President said in a commencement address at his alma mater, Eureka College. "But I believe that it will be possible to reduce the risks of war by removing the instabilities that now exist and by dismantling the nuclear menace."

Reagan had not changed his views about the Soviets. In the speech at Eureka the President reminded his audience of the lack of freedom in the Soviet Union, which he described as clinging to a faltering empire through fear because its rigid, centralized control "has destroyed incentives for innovation, efficiency and central achievement." He also accused the Russians of violating treaties, trampling on the freedom of Poland, supplying toxins in Southeast Asia and "employing chemical weapons on the freedom fighters in Afghanistan." But Reagan had been persuaded, largely by Haig and Clark, that the troubled Russian economy was in decline and that the Soviets were willing to talk seriously about arms reductions. Though ailing Soviet President Leonid Brezhnev quickly rejected Reagan's specific proposal, the Soviets did agree to open talks on nuclear arms reductions in Geneva on June 29. Reagan considered this a ratification of the advice which had been given him that the Russians, whatever their motives, were willing to deal. Almost imperceptibly, and without acknowledging that it was happening, Reagan was becoming more sophisticated and less primitive in his attitudes toward the Soviet adversary.

Only one accusation deeply bothered Reagan. That was the charge that his programs were unfair to poor people and to minorities. Blacks, never a pro-Reagan constituency, were stung by a series of insensitive appointments and an abortive effort to reverse the Nixon administration's denial of tax exemptions to segregated academies. Reagan's crony at Justice, Attorney General William French Smith, showed even less sensitivity on these issues than did his boss and damaged the administration's reputation by his handling of civil rights issues. But Smith was more sophisticated than Reagan in his response to criticism. The President, a kind man in his personal relationships, could not seem to understand that many of his critics were evaluating the results of his policies rather than his motivations.

Economic unfairness was the Achilles' heel of the Reagan presidency.

"It is fundamentally unfair for the administration to concentrate almost exclusively on cutting assistance to the poor while simultaneously providing an excessive array of tax breaks to affluent persons and corporations," Norman C. Miller wrote in the *Wall Street Journal* on February 8. Wirthlin's polls showed a growing majority of Americans agreeing with this view. "Fairness is the major problem," Wirthlin told me in mid-March.[4]

Reagan believed that the judgment of the press and public about his programs was in itself unfair. Overlooking his own campaign promises of a speedy economic rejuvenation, the President rationalized that he was being blamed for the failures of past policies. Speaking to the National Conference of Christians and Jews on March 23 an hour after thousands of demonstrators had massed outside the New York Hilton to protest his policies, Reagan compared himself to Franklin Roosevelt and confessed his frustrations. "Today I'm accused by some of trying to destroy government's commitment to compassion and to the needy," Reagan said. "Does this bother me? Yes. Like FDR, may I say I'm not trying to destroy what is best in our system of humane, free government—I'm doing everything I can to save it: to slow down the destructive rate of growth in taxes and spending; to prune nonessential programs so that enough resources will be left to meet the requirements of the truly needy."

Reagan was, for all his optimism, running out of time. His reach had exceeded his grasp. His knowledge had proved unequal to his courage. Age and events had dimmed a sense of leadership that was among the best of modern Presidents. By 1982, it was an axiom in the White House that Reagan, like so many of his modern predecessors, would be a one-term President.

But this axiom, like so many in politics was wholly wrong. Reagan's fortunes soared in 1983 with the arrival of the economic recovery that he had been predicting since his inauguration. In early 1983, the president's approval rating stood at 35 percent in the Gallup poll. A year later it had increased 22 percentage points, a gain unprecedented in Gallup's fifty years of polling for an incumbent president seeking re-election.

I was convinced when I completed this book at the end of 1981 that Reagan would step down if he could find a way to leave the White House gracefully. Wrong again. By July 1983 I was informing readers of *The Washington Post* about the reformation of the campaign organization and the confident predictions of the President's advisers that he would be a candidate for re-election. Among other things, I had reckoned without the compelling impact that the White House exerts on its inhabitants or on Reagan's commitment to what he regards as an unfinished agenda. Deaver, after observing that Reagan didn't think any successor would perform as well as he was doing, asked rhetorically, "Why should he leave? Where would he go from here? This is a chance for him to do what he's been talking about for twenty years. He would be bored at the ranch."

Whatever happens to Reagan in a second term, I believe that the impact of his presidency will resonate for many years. Despite his failings, Reagan was a presence in the American political system from the moment he made his historic speech for Goldwater on October 27, 1964. He had a vision of what America had been and what it should be again, and he tried to translate this vision into reality. The government of California was not the same after Reagan left it, and the government of the United States will not be either. Today, the economic alternatives to the New Luxury are alternative reductions in social programs, not a return to the cornucopia of the Great Society. Today, many thoughtful liberal critics of the President's policies accept as a premise the desirability of some decentralization of federal responsibilities.

It is Reagan's achievement that he defined the ground of political discourse of both his governorship and his presidency. He has set the agenda and, on most issues, outlined the priorities. Although he has failed to accomplish much of what he set out to do, he has set the nation on a course of change. Some see these changes as divisive and even dangerous, undermining the social gains of half a century. Others view them as the salvation of American incentives and economic freedom. Whatever the judgment of future historians, Reagan has made a difference. Like his hero Roosevelt, he has tried to lead the nation in the direction he thinks it should go rather than follow it in the direction he believes it to be going. Ronald Wilson Reagan has been a leader. He has not left the world the way he found it.

Notes

Confidential sources are a Washington reporter's stock in trade, and they are both valuable and dangerous. People given the protection of anonymity may be willing to tell a reporter—or a biographer—what they would be unwilling to say on the record or what they have been forbidden to disclose. At the same time such confidences impose an enormous burden on the confidant, as well as on the reader. The reporter or historian who is privy to confidential material must, to the best of his ability, examine every available source or record of the information being given him, holding anonymous information to a higher standard of verification than that which is given to him for attribution. The reader, too, is entitled to a higher standard of skepticism and should properly demand of the author a fullness of account that goes beyond single-source journalism.

In *Reagan* I have tried to steer a middle ground between those who make the impractical demand of insisting on a source for every quotation about a sitting President and those content to let the reader take the author's anonymous assertions on faith. Whenever possible, I have quoted sources. When this is not possible, I have tried to identify whoever was responsible for an important action, advocacy or assertion. In a few cases, most notably the tracing of the decision made by the Reagan administration regarding the MX missile, the demands of confidentiality have prevailed. Even in such instances, however, I have endeavored to identify the principal advocates of a course of action and the role they played in a decision. In all cases I have measured comments made to me about Reagan's role in a particular matter against my own knowledge of the man formed over seventeen years of reporting and writing about him.

By and large, I have relied on original interviews conducted by me or my assistant, Robin Gradison, with two significant exceptions. Interviews about the Interior Department section of Chapter 21, "The Westerners," were conducted by Tom Kizzia for exclusive use in this biography. Some interviews, notably those involving Reagan's first campaign in 1966 and the first year of his governorship in 1967, were conducted for my 1969 book, *Ronnie and Jesse: A Political Odyssey*. I have referred to the original interview where different material is quoted or when the information appears in a different context. In other cases reference has been made to the earlier book.

I have also followed the practice of not identifying the source of material in the chapter notes if it is clearly indicated in the text.

1. *The Worlds of Ronald Reagan*

1. Interview with Michael K. Deaver, July 30, 1981.
2. Interview with Ronald Reagan, July 30, 1981.
3. Interview with Ken Khachigian, April 9, 1981.

4. Ibid.

5. Reply to O. Dallas Baillio, director of the Public Library of Mobile, Alabama, 1977. Cited in "Young Reagan's Reading," by Jerry Griswold, *New York Times Book Review,* August 30, 1981.

6. *Coming up for Air,* by George Orwell, London, 1939, pp. 130–131.

7. "Young Reagan's Reading," op. cit.

8. Reagan made these comments about the end of segregation during a news conference in Charlotte, North Carolina, on November 21, 1975, during the first week of his campaign to win the Republican presidential nomination. The remark to the author was made during a subsequent airplane interview that same week.

2. *The Optimist*

1. Reagan press conference, June 16, 1981.

2. He has said this on a number of occasions. I am quoting it here from a 1976 interview during his campaign against President Ford.

3. *Where's the Rest of Me?* (hereafter cited as WTROM), p. 16.

4. Interview with Neil Reagan, 1968.

5. This story was passed down to the Reagan brothers, apparently by their father. It is also recounted in what I consider to be the best magazine account of Reagan's boyhood—"Growing up in the Midwest," by Myron S. Waldman, which appeared in the January 18, 1981, issue of *LI,* the *Newsday Sunday Magazine.*

6. Interview with Ronald Reagan, 1968.

7. Interview with Ronald Reagan, July 30, 1981.

8. Again, this is a story familiar to most people who knew Reagan in the 1960s. It is recounted in WTROM, p. 15.

9. Interview with Neil Reagan, 1968.

10. WTROM, page 12.

11. Associated Press, November 1, 1980.

12. Interview with Neil Reagan, 1968.

13. *Ronnie and Jesse,* page 5.

14. "President Reagan's Wide World of Sports," by Mark Shields, *Inside Sports,* March 31, 1981.

15. Ibid.

16. "Growing Up in the Midwest," op. cit.

17. "Reagan's Roots," by James M. Perry, *Wall Street Journal,* October 8, 1980.

18. Interview with Balz, March 1981.

19. "Reagan's Roots," op. cit.

20. Interview with Ronald Reagan, 1968.

3. *The Shape of Things to Come*

1. Reagan speech, October 17, 1980.

2. Reagan interview, 1968.

3. Ibid.

4. WTROM, page 37.

5. Ibid.

6. Reagan interview, July 31, 1981.

7. "Ralph McKinzie—A Living Legend at Eureka," a hand-out issued by Eureka College in 1981.

8. Garrard Camp in "Reagan's College Years Recalled by Fellow Students," by Harold Adams, *Woodford County Journal,* October 16, 1980.

9. "The Saga of Burky and Dutch," by Henry Allen, *Washington Post,* March 7, 1981.

I talked to Burkhardt by phone soon afterward and also discussed this story with Mark Shields, who had interviewed Burkhardt for an article in *Inside Sports.* Most of the quotes are from the Allen story.

10. *Ronnie and Jesse,* page 8.
11. Ibid.
12. Quoted by Myron Waldman, "Ronald Reagan's America," *Newsday,* January 18, 1981.
13. *Peoria Journal-Star,* October 17, 1980, page A-4.

4. *The Announcer*

1. *Employment and Earnings,* Bureau of Labor Statistics, 1981.
2. *The Crisis of the Old Order,* by Arthur M. Schlesinger, Jr., 1957, page 250.
3. Ibid., page 267.
4. *Dixon Evening Telegraph,* February 28, 1981.
5. Ibid. This story also has been recounted by Reagan.
6. WTROM, page 54.
7. Interview with Reagan, 1968. Also recounted in WTROM, pages 55–57.
8. Interview with Neil Reagan, October 14, 1981.
9. Interview with Suzanne Hanney, November 19, 1981.
10. WTROM, pages 57–65.
11. *Time,* January 5, 1981. "Out of the Past, Fresh Choices for the Future," by Roger Roseblatt, with Laurence I. Barrett, pages 13–14.
12. Interview with Myrtle Moon, August 25, 1981.
13. *Ronnie and Jesse,* p. 5.
14. Ibid., pages 67–68.
15. Myrtle Moon interview, op cit.
16. Interview with Harold Rissler, August 23, 1981.
17. *Newsday,* January 18, 1981. "Growing up in the Midwest," by Myron Waldman.
18. Rissler interview, op cit.
19. Waldman, op. cit.
20. Interview with Reagan, 1968.
21. These stories of Myrtle Moon's come from the August 25 interview of her, from Waldman's piece and from portions of his own interview that were not published and which he graciously let me use.
22. Waldman, op, cit.
23. Interview with Reagan, July 31, 1981.
24. *Des Moines Register and Tribune,* June 13, 1937, "Dutch Reagan's Own Story," by Ronald (Dutch) Reagan.
25. *Ronnie and Jesse,* page 30.

5. *The Actor*

1. Interview with Reagan, 1968.
2. Ibid.
3. Myron S. Waldman, "Ronald Reagan's America," July 18, 1981, *Newsday.*
4. This is another of those Reagan stories he has told over and over. I first heard it in 1966, but there is a version in identical form at least as early as January 1, 1949, when it was quoted in the *Saturday Evening Post.*
5. Reagan's series in the *Register,* titled by the newspaper "The Making of a Star," began June 13, 1937, and continued through October 28. He wrote under the byline of "Ronald (Dutch) Reagan."

6. Interview with Pat O'Brien, June 29, 1981.

7. Ibid.

8. Reagan commencement speech to Notre Dame, May 17, 1981.

9. Reagan interview, 1968.

10. Ibid.

6. *The First Time Around*

1. *Photoplay,* August 1942. "How to Make Yourself Important," by Ronald Reagan.

2. Ibid.

3. *Southern California: An Island on the Land,* by Carey McWilliams, Peregrine Smith, Inc., 1946, page 343.

4. Quoted in *The Forties Gals,* by James Robert Parish and Don E. Stanke, Arlington House, 1980, page 374.

5. Ibid.

6. *Silver Screen,* August 1941. "Making a Double Go of It," by Mary Jane Manners.

7. Quoted in *The Films of Ronald Reagan,* by Tony Thomas, 1980, Citadel Press, page 20.

8. WTROM, page 223.

9. *Photoplay,* April 1948. "Last Call for Happiness," by Louella O. Parsons.

10. Ibid.

11. This is a familiar Reagan line. It was recalled by him in a 1968 interview.

12. *People,* August 10, 1981.

13. This is a personal comment from a not-for-attribution interview by the author with a Reagan friend.

14. *People,* December 29, 1980.

15. *Ronnie and Jesse,* page 39.

16. Interview with Reagan, July 31, 1981.

17. Interview with Pat O'Brien, June 29, 1981.

18. Interview with Reagan, 1968.

19. Interview with Reagan, 1974. He has made the same point in various interviews and in his autobiography.

20. Interview with Reagan, 1968.

7. *The Politician*

1. *Washington Post,* May 31, 1981.

2. WTROM, page 154.

3. Ibid.

4. *Hollywood Citizen News,* January 14, 1954.

5. Interview with Reagan, 1968.

6. WTROM, page 173.

7. *Los Angeles Examiner,* January 14, 1954. The lawsuit was a $200,000 action filed by Michael Jeffers against the Screen Actors Guild.

8. Carey McWilliams, *Southern California: An Island on the Land,* page 335.

9. *Ronnie and Jesse,* page 36.

10. Interview with Reagan, 1974.

11. *Ronnie and Jesse,* page 37.

12. Testimony before House Un-American Activities Committee, April 10, 1951.

13. For a detailed account of this incident see *The Inquisition in Hollywood,* by Larry Ceplair and Steven Englund, Anchor Press, 1980, pages 225–239.

14. Testimony before House Un-American Activities Committee, October 23, 1947.

15. *Time,* November 3, 1947.

16. Testimony before HUAC by Reagan, op. cit.
17. Ibid.
18. *Take Two,* by Philip Dunne, McGraw-Hill, 1980, page 206.
19. Testimony before House Un-American Activities Committee, October 30, 1947.
20. *The Committee,* by Walter Goodman, Farrar, Straus & Giroux, New York 1964, page 300.
21. Interview with Reagan, July 31, 1981.

8. *The Conservative*

1. Column by Hedda Hopper, 1950.
2. *Variety,* March 12, 1951.
3. Interview with Reagan, July 30, 1981.
4. *College: A Smith Mosaic,* by Jacqueline Van Voris, page 5.
5. *Ronnie and Jesse,* page 41.
6. Interview with Reagan, July 30, 1981.
7. *Nancy,* by Nancy Reagan and Bill Libby, page 125.
8. WTROM, page 285.
9. Interview with Reagan, July 30, 1981.
10. Ibid.
11. Interview with Edward Langley, July 8, 1981.
12. Ibid.
13. *Ronnie and Jesse,* page 68.
14. Interview with Reagan, July 30, 1981.
15. Ibid.
16. Ibid.
17. Ibid.
18. Ibid.

9. *The Candidate*

1. Interview with Maureen Reagan, August 31, 1981.
2. Ibid.
3. *Ronnie and Jesse,* page 72.
4. *What Happened to Goldwater?,* by Stephen Shadegg, New York, 1965, pages 252–54.
5. *Ronnie and Jesse,* page 72.
6. Ibid.
7. Ibid.
8. Ibid.
9. Ibid.
10. Ibid.
11. *Ronnie and Jesse,* page 74.
12. Ibid.
13. *The Republican Establishment,* by David S. Broder and Stephen Hess, New York, 1967, page 274.
14. *Ronnie and Jesse,* page 78.
15. Ibid., page 82.
16. Interview with Reagan, 1974.
17. Interview with Lyn Nofziger, April 15, 1981.
18. Interview with Frederick Dutton, September 2, 1981.
19. Ibid.
20. *Ronnie and Jesse,* page 86.

10. *The Novice*

1. *Ronnie and Jesse,* page 131.
2. Reagan news conference, March 14, 1967.
3. "Phil Battaglia, Chief of Staff," feature report by Tom Woods, Pacific Coast News Service, February 2, 1967.
4. Ibid.
5. *Ronnie and Jesse,* page 134. While Champion gave a slightly different account of this conversation in a 1968 conversation with the author, he confirmed the gist of it and said that it would have been necessary for any administration to raise taxes in 1967.
6. "The Transition from Pat Brown to Ronald Reagan," a thesis by the late F. Alex Crowley of Princeton University.
7. *Ronnie and Jesse,* page 138.
8. Ibid.
9. Reagan news conference, March 21, 1967.
10. *Ronnie and Jesse,* page 180.
11. Interview with Reagan, October 1968.
12. Ibid.
13. Ibid.
14. General Report, State of California, Department of Health Services, Center for Health Statistics *Abortion Report,* 1967–1980.
15. WTROM, page 118.
16. Interview with Reagan, July 30, 1981.
17. *Ronnie and Jesse,* page 184.
18. Interview with Reagan, October 1968.
19. "Sir Ronald Meets the Pearson-Person," by Art Hoppe, *San Francisco Chronicle,* page 43, November 20, 1964.

11. *The Reagans*

1. "A Reagan at Large," by Camilla Snyder, *Washington Star,* November 9, 1975.
2. *Nancy,* page 25.
3. Ibid.
4. *Ronnie and Jesse,* page 158.
5. "Pretty Nancy," by Joan Didion and John Gregory Dunne, *Saturday Evening Post,* June 1, 1968.
6. Interview with Nancy Skelton, August 11, 1981.
7. Skelton article, 1974.
8. "Nancy Reagan, 'Behind the Mask': Street Smarts and Sweet Certainty," by Wanda McDaniel, *Washington Post,* November 11, 1980.
9. *Ronnie and Jesse,* page 161.
10. Interview with Reagan, October 1968.
11. Ibid.
12. "What is Nancy Reagan Really, Really Like?" by Eleanor Harris in *Look,* October 31, 1967.
13. Skelton article, 1974.
14. Interview with Michael K. Deaver, April 18, 1981.

12. *The Governor*

1. *California: The Great Exception,* by Carey McWilliams, New York, 1949, page 25.
2. This proposal was first made in Reagan's campaign opening speech of September 7, 1966, and repeated at intervals during the campaign.

3. *Ronnie and Jesse,* page 232.
4. Reagan interview, October 1968.
5. Speech by Alex C. Sheriffs to Commonwealth Club of San Francisco, May 19, 1967.
6. Ibid.
7. Interview with Paul Beck, October 1968. Quoted in *Ronnie and Jesse,* page 257.
8. Reagan speech to Commonwealth Club, July 13, 1969.
9. *Ronnie and Jesse,* page 241.
10. Ibid., page 151.
11. *Here's the Rest of Him,* by Kent H. Steffgen, Reno, Nevada, 1967.
12. Reagan interview, October 1968.
13. This was quoted to me by a Reagan presidential campaign organizer in September 1968.
14. From a column written by Baxter Omohundro of the Washington bureau of Ridder Publications (now Knight-Ridder) in September 1967.
15. Reagan interview, July 30, 1981.
16. *Ronnie and Jesse,* page 269.
17. Reagan interview, October 1968.
18. Interview with Nancy Reagan, November 1968.
19. Quoted in *Ronnie and Jesse,* pages 274–75.
20. Reagan interview, July 30, 1981.

13. *The Reformer*

1. Reagan collection of state papers, Hoover Institution on War, Revolution and Peace, Stanford University.
2. Ibid.
3. *California Journal,* December 1970, page 341.
4. Interview with Bob Wells. Quoted in *Ronnie and Jesse,* page 108.
5. This account of Unruh's visit to Salvatori's home is drawn from stories by Leroy Arrons in the *Washington Post* and Richard Bergholz in the *Los Angeles Times* of September 8, 1970, and from a conversation with Katharine Macdonald, who was then on the Unruh staff, about the incident.
6. "Both Unruh, Reagan Glad of Slug Out," by Lou Cannon, *Pasadena Star-News,* November 2, 1970.
7. Ibid.
8. Ibid.
9. Ibid.
10. Cited in "Welfare Reform: California Meets the Challenge," *Pacific Law Journal,* July 1973, page 781, by Ronald A. Zumbrun, Raymond H. Momboisse and John H. Findley.
11. Interview with Bob Moretti, August 5, 1981.
12. Interview with William Hauck, August 5, 1981.
13. Ibid.
14. Moretti interview, op. cit.
15. Interview with Reagan, 1974.
16. Moretti interview, op. cit.
17. Meese papers in Hoover Collection.
18. Ibid.
19. Moretti interview, op. cit.
20. "What Ronald Reagan Can Teach the U.S. About Welfare Reform," by Frank Levy, The Urban Institute, 1977.

21. Interview with Wilson Riles, September 25, 1981.
22. Moretti interview, op. cit.

14. *Running in Place*

1. "GOP Image Fares Badly in New Poll," by Lou Cannon, *Washington Post,* January 26, 1975.
2. United Press International dispatch, May 1, 1973.
3. Reagan press conference transcript, June 11, 1974.
4. Reagan press conference, August 6, 1974.
5. Reagan press conference, August 27, 1974.
6. Interview with Wilson Riles, September 25, 1981.
7. "Reagan Checks His Options for '76 White House Drive," by Larry Stammer, *San Jose Mercury News,* December 16, 1973.
8. "Reagan Future: Which Office to Aim For?", by Richard Bergholz, *Los Angeles Times,* August 13, 1974.
9. Interview with Reagan, October 1974.
10. Reagan press conference, October 15, 1974.
11. "Conservatives Eye Third-Party Option," by David Broder, *Washington Post,* February 15, 1975.
12. *Marathon,* by Jules Witcover, New York, 1977, page 373.
13. Interview with Peter Hannaford, October 14, 1981.
14. Ibid.
15. See Chapter One, note 8.
16. Interview with James Lake, October 13, 1981.

15. *Running for President*

1. Interview with Paul Laxalt, 1976.
2. "Reagan Virtually Concedes Defeat in North Carolina," by James M. Naughton, *New York Times,* March 22, 1976.
3. Interview with Michael Deaver, October 13, 1981.
4. Reagan interview, 1977.
5. *A Time To Heal: The Autobiography of Gerald R. Ford,* Harper & Row, New York, 1979, pages 333–334.
6. Interview with James Lake, October 13, 1981.
7. *The Harris Survey,* May 6, 1976.
8. Deaver interview, op. cit.
9. Interview with Peter Hannaford, October 14, 1981.

16. *A New Beginning*

1. "Reagan: More Serious Than Ever," by Marquis Childs, *Washington Post,* May 16, 1978.
2. "Personalities," by Michael Goldfarb, *Washington Post,* December 5, 1981.
3. Interview with Robert Teeter, October 14, 1981.
4. Interview with Michael Deaver, July 21, 1981.
5. "Intimates Doubt Ford Will Run," by David S. Broder, *Washington Post,* September 29, 1978.
6. " 'Sears Factor' Is Troubling Conservatives," by M. Stanton Evans, *Human Events,* October 27, 1979.
7. Interview with James Lake, October 12, 1981.
8. Interview with Nancy Reynolds, July 14, 1981.

17. *"The O & W"*

1. "Reagan's Latest Campaign Brings Same Message, but New Audience," by Martin Smith, *Sacramento Bee,* November 18, 1979.

2. "Reagan Declares He's Not Moving Toward Center," by Richard Bergholz, *Los Angeles Times,* September 30, 1979.

3. "Reagan Displays Vitality but Bobbles a Few on Opening Tour," by Lou Cannon, *Washington Post,* November 19, 1979.

4. "Reagan Woos Northeast, the Key to His Nomination Strategy," by Lou Cannon, *Washington Post,* January 20, 1980.

5. Interview with Richard Wirthlin, May 1980.

6. Interview with Paul Laxalt, May 27, 1980.

7. Ibid.

8. This was a frequent quip of Nofziger, then not a member of the Reagan staff, after the Iowa caucuses. It is jotted down in my notes from an undated conversation, apparently in February 1980.

9. Interview with Peter Hannaford, October 14, 1981.

10. *The Pursuit of the Presidency,* by Richard Harwood, New York, 1980, page 152.

11. "Challenges to Statements Putting Reagan on the Defensive," by Douglas E. Kneeland, *New York Times,* April 13, 1980.

18. *The Great Deflector*

1. "What Price Glory, Captain Reagan?", Frank McAdams, *Los Angeles Times,* August 27, 1980.

2. "Reagan to Keep Status Quo on China, Aide Says," Larry Green, *Los Angeles Times,* July 11, 1980.

3. "Woodcock Warns Reagan Stand Perils Ties to China," Linda Mathews, *Los Angeles Times,* August 27, 1980.

4. *Blue Smoke and Mirrors,* Jack W. Germond and Jules Witcover, New York, 1981, page 221.

5. "The Campaign Chieftans," by Myra MacPherson, *Washington Post,* January 18, 1976.

6. Interview with Stuart K. Spencer, November 18, 1980.

7. "Brown Denies Politicking," by George C. Wilson, *Washington Post,* September 5, 1980.

8. "The Smear," by George F. Will, *Washington Post,* September 21, 1980.

9. "Why Ronald Reagan Will Be the Next President," by Richard J. Whalen, *Washington Post,* March 23, 1981.

10. "The Campaign Carter Couldn't Win," by Hamilton Jordan, *Life* magazine, January 1981.

11. Interview with Ronald Reagan, August 19, 1980.

12. "The Unfolding Hostage Drama Adds New Volatility to Election," by David S. Broder, *Washington Post,* November 3, 1980.

19. *The President*

1. "Charley Rose Show," KXAS, Fort Worth, Texas, May 1, 1980.

2. George Reedy, *The Twilight of the Presidency,* page 21.

3. Ibid., pages 22–23.

4. Nancy Reynolds interview, April 9, 1980.

5. "Live from Paris, Pierre Reports on President's Power," by Paul Wilner, *Los Angeles Herald Examiner,* November 23, 1981.

6. Interview with Ken Khachigian, April 9, 1981.

7. Reagan interview, July 30, 1981.

8. Interview of Reagan by Dan Blackburn, NBC Radio, October 31, 1980.

9. Interview with Jeane Kirkpatrick, July 18, 1981.

10. Interview with James Baker, March 31, 1981.

11. Interview with David Stockman, November 14, 1981.

12. "The Reagan Cabinet: Sharp Conflict Ahead," by Alan Baron, *Los Angeles Times,* December 14, 1980.

13. "A Good Idea Concealed in a Bad Speech," by George F. Will, *Washington Post,* November 8, 1981.

14. Interview with William P. Clark, July 3, 1981.

15. Interview with Michael K. Deaver, December 3, 1981.

16. Ibid.

17. " 'A Master Stroke,' " by Morris Udall, *Washington Post,* July 13, 1981.

18. Deaver, op. cit.

19. "Appointments by White House Take Right Turn," by Lou Cannon, *Washington Post,* June 18, 1981.

20. Reagan interview with *Washington Post,* March 27, 1981.

21. Reagan interview, July 30, 1981.

20. *The Reagan Re-Direction*

1. "A Democrat Sticks with Reaganomics," by Phil Gramm, *Los Angeles Times,* October 9, 1981.

2. *This Was Normalcy,* by Karl Schriftgiesser, Boston, 1948, page 84.

3. *The Coming of the New Deal,* by Arthur M. Schlesinger, Jr., Boston, 1957, page 433.

4. Interview with Reagan, October 1968.

5. Ibid.

6. *The Crisis of the Old Order,* by Arthur M. Schlesinger, Jr., Boston, 1957, page 433.

7. "Bush Ends His Waiting Game," by Robert Shogan, *Los Angeles Times,* April 14, 1980.

8. John B. Anderson in the Iowa forum of six Republican presidential candidates, Des Moines, January 6, 1980.

9. Speech before the Conservative Political Action Conference, Washington, D.C., February 6, 1977.

10. Ibid.

11. Interview wth Reagan, 1973.

12. "The Stockman Express," by Walter Shapiro, *The Washington Post Magazine,* February 8, 1981.

13. "An Interview with George Gilder," by Martin Levine, *Book Digest,* August 1981, page 25.

14. "Now the Real St. Ronald vs. the Rhetorical Dragon," by Lou Cannon, *Washington Post,* February 18, 1981.

15. Interview with David Stockman, November 14, 1981.

16. "Plan Keyed to a Boom in Spending," by John M. Berry, *Washington Post,* February 20, 1981.

17. "Financial Leaders Enthusiastic Over Reagan Plan, Concern Over Chances of Passage," by James L. Rowe, Jr., *Washington Post,* February 20, 1981.

18. Figures supplied in an interview with Annie Hughes, December 28, 1981.

19. "Reagan Triumphs in House Budget Vote, Horse Trading," by Ward Sinclair and Peter Behr, *Washington Post,* June 27, 1981.

20. Interview with David Stockman, op. cit.

21. "Domenici: The Virtues of Being Consistent," by David S. Broder, *Washington Post,* December 20, 1981.

22. "Making It Work," by Charles Alexander and David Beckwith, *Time* magazine, September 21, 1981.

23. Ibid.

24. "Economist Urges '83 Tax Cut Delay," by Jonathan Fuerbringer, *New York Times,* December 30, 1981.

25. Interview with Jude Wanniski, December 11, 1981.

26. Interview with David Stockman, op. cit.

27. Ibid.

28. Interview with Robert H. Michel, December 7, 1981.

29. "The Reagan Style—What Is It?," by Anne Hollander, *Washington Post,* February 2, 1981.

30. "Reagan Aides Show Capital Luxury Style," by Lynn Rosellini, *New York Times,* August 16, 1981.

31. Ibid.

32. "Should We Give First Ladies a Break," Letter to the Editor by P. Nuhn, Arlington, Virginia, *Washington Post,* December 2, 1981.

33. Ibid., Letter from Joseph Cowart, Washington, D.C.

34. "The Reagans Try to Soften Their Millionaire Image," *U.S. News and World Report,* October 19, 1981.

35. In an article from David Hoffman filed from Flint, Michigan, Knight-Ridder Newspapers, December 13, 1981.

36. Ibid.

37. "Washington State Reeling as Both Its Tax Revenues and Federal Aid Drop," by John Herbers, *New York Times,* October 17, 1981.

38. "Number of Police in New York Force Is Lowest in Years," by Leonard Buder, *New York Times,* December 6, 1981.

39. "Reagan's Policies Labeled by Koch 'Sham and Shame,' " by Clyde Haberman, *New York Times,* December 2, 1981.

40. "The Governors Have Their Fingers Crossed," by David S. Broder, *Washington Post,* August 16, 1981.

41. "Tax Turnback to States Is Done, Aide Says," by David S. Broder, *Washington Post,* October 23, 1981.

42. Ibid.

43. "Economists Call Regulatory Reform Too Slow, Narrow," by Caroline E. Mayer, *Washington Post,* December 9, 1981.

44. "Bush: Rules Reform Has Long Way to Go," by Caroline E. Mayer, *Washington Post,* December 31, 1981.

45. "The Way Volcker Sees It," by Joseph Kraft, *Washington Post,* December 29, 1981.

46. "The Education of David Stockman," by William Greider, *The Atlantic,* December 1981.

47. Ibid.

48. "David Stockman's Secret," by Paul MacAvoy, *New York Times,* November 22, 1981.

49. "The Supply Side Revisited," by Robert J. Samuelson, *National Journal,* November 21, 1981.

21. *The Westerners*

1. *Ronnie and Jesse,* page 226.

2. "Old Frontier Sees Bright New Frontier," by Lou Cannon and Joel Kotkin, *Washington Post,* June 17, 1979.

3. Speech to the Western Wood Products Association in San Francisco, March 12, 1966.

4. Letter to Jane Ashman, September 14, 1966.

5. "Reagan Ranch: Next Western White House?" by Jerry Rankin, *Santa Barbara News-Press,* June 22, 1980.

6. "Reagan's Ranch a Retreat, Tax Shelter—and Security Risk," by Lou Cannon, *Washington Post,* July 5, 1980.

7. Interview of James Watt by *Washington Post* editors and reporters, May 20, 1981.

8. "If the Sagebrush Rebels Win, Everybody Loses," by Wallace Stegner, *The Living Wilderness,* summer 1981.

9. "It Takes a Lot of Energy to Keep up with Interior's Jim Watt," by Bill Hosokawa, *Denver Post,* March 1, 1981.

10. "Jim Watt: Interior Secretary Echoes Values of America's Frontier," by J. J. Casserly, *Arizona Republic,* March 3, 1981.

11. Interview of James Watt by Tom Kizzia, July 29, 1981.

12. Ibid.

13. Interview of Doug Baldwin by Kizzia, August 6, 1981.

14. Watt Interview with Kizzia, op. cit.

15. Ibid.

16. Watt interview with *Washington Post,* op. cit.

17. Watt address to National Park concessionaires, Washington, D.C., March 9, 1981.

18. Doug Scott interview with Tom Kizzia, July 16, 1981.

19. "Watt Plans Campaign to Change His Image," by Ann McFeatters, *Ft. Smith Southwest-Times Record,* June 9, 1981.

20. Watt interview with Kizzia, op. cit.

21. "Off-shore Drilling Shelved by Watt," Michael Harris, *San Francisco Chronicle,* August 8, 1981.

22. "Watt Gaining the Approval of Most Western Governors," William E. Schmidt, *New York Times,* September 13, 1981.

23. Quoted in Joe Scott's *The Political Animal,* October 23, 1981.

24. Political Notes, *Washington Post,* James R. Dickenson and David S. Broder, November 30, 1980.

25. Interview of Guy Martin by Kizzia, September 25, 1981.

26. Interview of Morris K. Udall by Kizzia, July 27, 1981.

27. Quoted in *How to Kill a Golden State,* William Bronson (New York, 1968), from a 1913 book, long out of print, called *Conservation of Public Resources.* It was compiled by Edward Hyatt, then the state's superintendent of public instruction, for use in the California public schools.

28. Interview of Norman Livermore by Kizzia, September 16, 1981.

22. *The Delegated Presidency*

1. "Our Unfashionable President," by Meg Greenfield, *Newsweek,* July 27, 1981.

2. Interview with Michael Deaver, August 20, 1980.

3. " 'Those Upraised Hands,' " by William Safire, *New York Times,* June 16, 1981.

4. Interview with Michael Deaver, April 18, 1981.

5. "Mike Deaver, The Man Who Looks After the Man," by Elisabeth Bumiller, *Washington Post,* March 8, 1981.

6. "The Big 3: Meese, Baker and Deaver: The Triangle of Power," by Lou Cannon and Lee Lescaze, *Washington Post,* May 24, 1981.

7. Interview with David Stockman, November 14, 1981.

8. Ibid.

9. "The Big 3: Auto-Import Compromise Bore Meese's Subtle Mark," by Lou Cannon and Lee Lescaze, *Washington Post,* May 26, 1981.

10. Ibid.

11. Interview with Edwin Meese III, April 9, 1980.

12. Ibid.

13. "Less Costly MX System Adopted by Defense Department," UPI, *Los Angeles Times,* May 7, 1980.

14. Interview with Charlie Townes, November 4, 1981.

15. "Mormon Church Joins Opposition to MX Program," by Bill Prochnau, *Washington Post,* May 6, 1981.

16. " '2 Little Guys' with a Big Idea," by Walter Pincus, *Washington Post,* August 13, 1981.

17. "Administration to Scrap Original MX Land-Basing Plan, Says Meese," by Robert C. Toth, *L. A. Times/WP* News Service, *Boston Globe,* July 31, 1981.

18. Interview with William Dickinson, November 3, 1981.

19. Dr. William J. Perry, Testimony before the Subcommittee on Strategic and Theater Nuclear Forces of the Senate Committee on Armed Services, November 13, 1981.

20. "Wrong on the B-1, Wrong on the MX," by Harold Brown, *Washington Post,* November 13, 1981.

21. "Haig's Asian Venture: From Diplomatic Heights to a Political Downer," by Don Oberdorfer, *Washington Post,* June 27, 1981.

22. "Role Reversal in the Reagan Cabinet," by Hedrick Smith, *New York Times,* September 14, 1981.

23. " 'The Haig Problem,' " by Lou Cannon, *Washington Post,* July 7, 1981.

24. "Heart to Heart with Haig and Weinberger," by Ann L. Trebbe, *Washington Post,* November 9, 1981.

25. Interview with Bill Clark, January 9, 1982.

23. *The Hero*

1. "The Day of the Jackal in Washington," by Lou Cannon, *Washington Post,* April 5, 1981.

2. "The Shooting," by Lou Cannon, *Washington Post,* March 31, 1981.

3. "The Day of the Jackal in Washington," op. cit.

4. Ibid.

5. "Bullet Lodged an Inch from Reagan's Heart," by Victor Cohn, *Washington Post,* April 16, 1981.

6. Interview with Michael Deaver, April 18, 1981.

7. "End of a Dream," by David S. Broder, *Washington Post,* April 1, 1981.

8. *The Crisis of the Old Order,* by Arthur M. Schlesinger, Jr., Boston, 1957, page 465.

9. Ibid., page 466. The comment is by Raymond Moley.

10. "Despite Fortitude, Reagan Had Fears," by Marlene Cimons, *Los Angeles Times,* April 3, 1981.

11. *Washington Star* interview of Reagan, August 4, 1981.

12. " 'High-Risk' President Reassessed," by Haynes Johnson, *Washington Post,* November 8, 1981.

13. Ibid.

14. Ibid.

15. "Fluctuations on the Presidential Exchange," by Hedley Donovan, *Time,* November 9, 1981.

16. *The Twilight of the Presidency,* by George E. Reedy, New York, 1970, page 29.

17. "Behind Reagan's Tough Talk, a Unilateral Arms Reduction," by Walter Pincus, *Washington Post,* January 10, 1982.

18. "Reagan's Broom Sweeps Uneasily," by Robert Shogan and Gaylord Shaw, *Los Angeles Times,* January 17, 1982.

19. "Reagan as the Savior of American Liberalism," by Lou Cannon, *Washington Post,* March 8, 1981.

20. "Chairman Reagan," editorial in *Boston Sunday Globe,* June 14, 1981.

Epilogue

1. President Reagan in an interview by Curtis Beckmann and Dave Moore, February 8, 1982, Bloomington, Minnesota.

2. "A Decision from a Wakeful Night," Lou Cannon, *Washington Post,* February 1, 1982.

3. "A Year Later, Subtle Imprint Left by Attack on President," Lou Cannon, *Washington Post,* March 30, 1982.

4. "Flunking the Fairness Test," Norman C. Miller, *Wall Street Journal,* February 8, 1982.

Bibliography

Books and Manuscripts

Boyarsky, Bill. *The Rise of Ronald Reagan.* New York: Random House, 1968.

Broder, David S., and Stephen Hess. *The Republican Establishment.* New York: Harper & Row, 1967.

Bronson, William. *How to Kill a Golden State.* Garden City, New York: Doubleday, 1968.

Cannon, Lou. *Ronnie and Jesse: A Political Odyssey.* Garden City, New York: Doubleday, 1969.

Ceplair, Larry, and Steven Englund. *The Inquisition in Hollywood.* New York: Anchor Press, 1980.

Cresap, Dean R. *Party Politics in the Golden State.* Los Angeles: The Haynes Foundation, 1954.

Crowley, F. Alex. "The Transition from Pat Brown to Ronald Reagan." Unpublished Thesis, Princeton University, 1968.

Dunne, Philip. *Take Two.* New York: McGraw-Hill, 1980.

Edwards, Lee. *Reagan: A Political Biography.* San Diego, California: Viewpoint Books, 1967.

Evans, Rowland, and Robert Novak. *The Reagan Revolution.* New York: E. P. Dutton, 1980.

Ford, Gerald R. *A Time to Heal: The Autobiography of Gerald R. Ford.* New York: Harper & Row, 1979.

Germond, Jack W., and Jules Witcover. *Blue Smoke and Mirrors.* New York: Viking Press, 1981.

Gilder, George. *Wealth and Poverty.* New York: Basic Books, 1981.

Goodman, Walter. *The Committee.* New York: Farrar, Straus & Giroux, 1964.

Heritage Foundation. *A Mandate for Leadership Report: The First Year.* Richard N. Holwill, ed. Washington, D.C., 1981.

Levy, Frank. "What Ronald Reagan Can Teach the U.S. About Welfare Reform." Washington, D.C.: Urban Institute, 1977.

Lewis, Joseph. *What Makes Reagan Run.* New York: McGraw-Hill, 1968.

Lewis, Sinclair. *Main Street.* New York: Grosset & Dunlap, 1921.

McWilliams, Carey. *California; The Great Exception.* New York: A. A. Wyn, 1949.

————. *The Education of Carey McWilliams.* New York: Simon and Schuster, 1978.

————. *Southern California: An Island on the Land.* Peregrine Smith, 1946.

Neustadt, Richard E. *Presidential Power: The Politics of Leadership.* New York: John Wiley & Sons, 1976.

Orwell, George. *Coming Up for Air.* London: Victor Gollancz, 1937.

Parish, James Robert, and Don E. Stanke. *The Forties Gals.* Westport, Conn.: Arlington House, 1980.

Perrella, Robert. *They Call Me the Showbiz Priest.* New York: Trident Press, 1973.

Phillips, Herbert L. *Big Wayward Girl.* Garden City, New York: Doubleday, 1968.

Reagan, Nancy, and Bill Libby. *Nancy.* New York: William Morrow, 1980.

Reagan, Ronald. *The Creative Society.* New York: The Devin-Adair Co., 1968.

Reagan, Ronald, with Richard G. Hubler. *Where's the Rest of Me?* New York: Duell, Sloan, Pearce, 1965.

Reedy, George. *The Twilight of the Presidency.* New York: World Publishing Co., 1970.

Safire, William. *Safire's Political Dictionary.* New York: Ballantine Books, 1978.

Schlesinger, Arthur M., Jr. *The Coming of the New Deal.* Boston: Houghton Mifflin, 1958.

————. *Crisis of the Old Order.* Boston: Houghton Mifflin, 1957.

Schriftgiesser, Karl. *This Was Normalcy.* Boston: Little, Brown, 1948.

Shadegg, Stephen. *What Happened to Goldwater.* New York: Holt, Rinehart and Winston, 1965.

Steffgen, Kent H. *Here's the Rest of Him.* Reno, Nevada: Foresight Books, 1968.

Thomas, Tony. *The Films of Ronald Reagan.* Secaucus, N.J: Citadel Press, 1980.

Thompson, Warren S. *Growth and Changes in California's Population.* Los Angeles: The Haynes Foundation, 1955.

Van Voris, Jacqueline. *College: A Smith Mosaic.* West Springfield, Mass.: Smith College, 1975.

Wanniski, Jude. *The Way the World Works.* New York: Simon and Schuster, 1978.

Washington Post, National staff of. *The Pursuit of the Presidency.* New York: Berkley Books, 1980.

White House, Office of Public Affairs. *The Reagan Presidency: A Review of the First Year.* Washington D.C., 1981.

Witcover, Jules. *Marathon.* New York: Viking Press, 1977.

Wright, Harold Bell. *That Printer of Udell's.* Chicago: The Book Supply Company, 1903.

Articles and Documents

Aarons, Leroy F. "Unruh Tackles Reagan Dreadnought," *Washington Post,* 8 September 1970.

Adams, Harold. "Reagan's College Years Recalled by Fellow Students," *Woodford County Journal,* 16 October 1980.

Allen, Henry. "The Saga of Burgie and Dutch," *Washington Post,* 7 March 1981.

Balz, Daniel J. " 'Reagan,' The Citizen's Guide to the 1976 Presidential Candidates," Capitol Hill News Service, 1976.

Baron, Alan, "The Reagan Cabinet: Sharp Conflict Ahead." *Los Angeles Times,* 14 December 1980.

Beilenson, Anthony, and Larry Agran. "The Welfare Reform Act of 1971." *Pacific Law Journal,* July 1972.

Bergholz, Richard. "Camp Intact," *Los Angeles Times,* 9 April 1977.

———. "Reagan Declares He's Not Moving Toward Center," *Los Angeles Times,* 30 September 1974.

———. "Reagan Future: Which Office to Aim for." *Los Angeles Times,* 13 August 1974.

———. "Unruh, Salvatori Meet in Angry Confrontation," *Los Angeles Times,* 8 September 1970.

Berry, John M. "Plan Keyed to a Boom in Spending," *Washington Post,* 20 February 1981.

Blubaugh, Ronald. "Evidence of a Double Standard for Education," *Sacramento Bee,* 2 March 1969.

Boston Sunday Globe, Editorial. "Chairman Reagan," 14 June 1981.

Boyarsky, Bill. "Another Democrat Contributor, Foe of Unruh, to Back Reagan," *Los Angeles Times,* 11 August 1970.

———. "Reagan, Unruh: The Final Week," *Los Angeles Times,* 28 October 1970.

Broder, David S. "Conservatives Eye Third-Party Option." *Washington Post,* 15 February 1975.

———. "Domenici: The Virtues of Being Consistent," *Washington Post,* 20 December 1981.

———. "End of a Dream," *Washington Post,* 1 April 1981.

———. "The Governors Have Their Fingers Crossed," *Washington Post,* 16 August 1981.

———. "Intimates Doubt Ford Will Run," *Washington Post,* 29 September 1978.

———. "Reagan Banks Prairie Fire," *Washington Post,* 14 January 1968.

———. "Tax Turnback to States Is Done, Aide Says," *Washington Post,* 23 October 1981.

———. "The Unfolding Hostage Drama Adds New Volatility to Election," *Washington Post,* 3 November 1980.

Brown, Harold, "Wrong on the B-1, Wrong on the MX," *Washington Post,* 13 November 1981.

Buchwald, Art. "Ronnie's Retreat," *Washington Post,* 13 September 1981.

———. "Winning One for the, Uh, Gipper," *Washington Post,* 24 September 1981.

Buckley, William F., Jr. "Reagan: A Relaxing View," *West,* 1 October 1967.

Buder, Leonard. "Number of Police in New York Force Is Lowest in Years," *New York Times,* 6 December 1981.

Bumiller, Elisabeth. "Michael Deaver, The Man Who Looks After the Man," *Washington Post,* 8 March 1981.

Bureau of Labor Statistics, Employment and Earnings, 1981.

California Cabinet Minutes, 1967–1968.

California Journal. December 1970.

California Journal. "The Reagan Tax Initiative." September 1973.

California Migration: 1955-1960. California Department of Finance, Sacramento, 1964.

California Population, 1967. Department of Finance, Sacramento, October 1967.

California Statement of Vote: 1950-1976. Secretary of State, Sacramento.

California, State of. General Report. Department of Health Services, Abortion Report, 1967-1979.

Cannon, Lou. "Appointments by White House Take Right Turn," *Washington Post,* 18 June 1981.

————. "Both Unruh, Reagan Glad of Slug Out," *Pasadena Star-News,* 2 November 1970.

————. "The Day of the Jackal in Washington," *Washington Post,* 5 April 1981.

————. "GOP Fares Badly in New Poll," *Washington Post,* 26 January 1975.

————. " 'The Haig Problem,' " *Washington Post,* 7 July 1981.

————. "High Dam in the Valley of the Tall Grass," *Cry California,* Summer, 1968.

————. "High-Risk Presidency at Crossroads," *Washington Post,* 21 January 1982.

————. "How Reagan Said No to Advisers and Taxes," *Washington Post,* 1 February 1982.

————. "Now the Real St. Ronald vs. the Rhetorical Dragon," *Washington Post,* 18 February 1981.

————. "Reagan as the Savior of American Liberalism," *Washington Post,* 8 March 1981.

————. "Reagan's Camp: Air of Resignation." *Washington Post,* 19 July 1976.

————. "Reagan Displays Vitality but Bobbles a Few on Opening Tour," *Washington Post,* 19 November 1979.

————. "Reagan's Ranch a Retreat, Tax Shelter—and Security Risk," *Washington Post,* 5 July 1980.

————. "Reagan Woos Northeast, the Key to His Nomination Strategy," *Washington Post,* 20 January 1980.

————. "The Reagan Years," *California Journal,* November 1974.

————. "Ronald Reagan," *Political Profiles,* 1980.

————. "The Shooting," *Washington Post,* 31 March 1981.

Cannon, Lou, and Joel Kotkin. "The Embattled West," *Washington Post,* 17 June 1979.

Cannon, Lou, and Lee Lescaze. "White House Decisions," *Washington Post,* 24, 25, 26, and 27 May 1981.

Casserly, J. J. "Jim Watt: Interior Secretary Echoes Values of America's Frontier," *Arizona Republic,* 3 March 1981.

Champion, Hale. "The First 100 Days: A Democratic Appraisal," *West,* 23 April 1967.

Childs, Marquis, "Reagan: More Serious Than Ever," *Washington Post,* 16 March 1978.

Cimons, Marlene. "Despite Fortitude, Reagan Had Fears," *Los Angeles Times,* 3 April 1981.

————. "Reagan Pursues Vision of a Dark-Haired Nurse Who Held His Hand," *Los Angeles Times,* 9 June 1981.

Cohn, Victor. "Bullet Lodged an Inch From Reagan's Heart," *Washington Post,* 16 April 1981.

Congressional Quarterly Almanac. Washington, D.C., 1960–1982.

Cowan, Edward. "View From the Supply Side," *New York Times,* 25 December 1981.

Crowther, Bosley. Film reviews: "The Hasty Heart," January 21, 1950; "Kings Row," February 3, 1942; "Knute Rockne—All American," October 19, 1940. *New York Times.*

Didion, Joan, and John Gregory Dunne. "Pretty Nancy," *Saturday Evening Post,* 1 June 1968.

Donovan, Hedley, "Fluctuations on the Presidential Exchange," *Time,* 9 November 1981.

Evans, M. Stanton, "Sears Factor Is Troubling Conservatives," *Human Events,* 27 October 1979.

Farrell, Harry. "Reagan Blasts Unruh Tactics," *San Jose Mercury News,* 14 September 1970.

Fuerbringer, Jonathan. "Economist Urges '83 Tax Cut Delay," *New York Times,* 30 December 1981.

Getler, Michael. "President Scrapping 2nd MX Idea," *Washington Post,* 11 February 1982.

Glaser, Vera. "Nancy," *Washingtonian,* July 1981.

Goff, Tom. "Looking Back: His Bark Has Exceeded His Bite," *Los Angeles Times,* 20 July 1970.

Gold, Mike. *The Daily Worker,* February 12, February 23, March 2 and March 16, 1946.

Goldfarb, Michael. "Personalities," *Washington Post,* 5 December 1981.

Gramm, Phil. "A Democrat Sticks With Reaganomics," *Los Angeles Times,* 9 October 1981.

Green, Larry. "Reagan to Keep Status Quo on China, Aide Says," *Los Angeles Times,* 11 July 1980.

Greenfield, Meg. "Our Unfashionable President," *Newsweek,* 27 July 1981.

Gregg, James E. "Educator Probes Causes of State College Crisis," *Sacramento Bee,* 19 January 1969.

Greider, William. "The Education of David Stockman," *Atlantic,* December 1981.

Griswold, Jerry. "Young Reagan's Reading," *New York Times Book Review,* 30 August 1981.

Haberman, Clyde. "Reagan's Policies Labeled by Koch 'Sham and Shame,' " *New York Times,* 2 December 1981.

Harris, Eleanor. "What Is Nancy Reagan Really, Really Like," *Look,* 31 October 1967.

Harris, Michael. "Off-shore Drilling Shelved by Watt," *San Francisco Chronicle,* 8 August 1981.

Heller, Walter. "Politics and the U.S. Economy in 1982," *Wall Street Journal,* 6 November 1981.

Herbers, John. "Washington State Reeling as Both Its Tax Revenues and Federal Aid Drop," *New York Times,* 17 October 1981.

Hoffman, David. Article filed on unemployment. Flint, Michigan. Knight-Ridder Publications, 13 December 1981.

Hollander, Anne. "The Reagan Style—What Is It?" *Washington Post,* 2 February 1981.

Hoppe, Art, "Sir Ronald Meets the Pearson-Person, *San Francisco Chronicle,* 20 November 1967.

Hornblower, Margot. "Reagan: 'Though I Am Wounded, I Am Not Slain,' " *Washington Post,* 22 August 1976.

Hosokawa, Bill. "It Takes a Lot of Energy to Keep up With Interior's Jim Watt," *Denver Post,* 1 March 1981.

House Committee on Un-American Activities testimony, October 23, 1947, October 30, 1947 and April 10, 1951.

Hunt, Albert R. "The Inner Reagan," *Wall Street Journal,* 22 May 1980.

———. "Shaky Start," *Wall Street Journal,* 4 September 1980.

Johnson, Haynes. " 'High-Risk' President Reassessed," *Washington Post,* 8 November 1981.

Joint Committee on Higher Education of the California Legislature. *The Academic State,* 1968.

———. *The Challenge of Achievement,* 1968.

Jordan, Hamilton. "The Campaign Carter Couldn't Win," *Life,* January 1981.

Keppel, Bruce. "An Offer Californians Did Refuse," *California Journal,* December 1973.

Klurfeld, Jan. "The MX Debate: U.S. Rethinking the Unthinkable," *Newsday,* 3, 4 and 5 February 1980.

Kneeland, Douglas E. "Challenges to Statements Putting Reagan on the Defensive," *New York Times,* 13 April 1980.

Lescaze, Lee. "Reagan Returns to the White House but Work Schedule Still Limited," *Washington Post,* 12 April 1981.

Letters to the Editor, *Washington Post,* 2 December 1981.

Levine, Martin. "An Interview With George Gilder," *Book Digest,* August 1981.

Lofton, John. "Open Letter," *Conservative Digest,* February 1981.

Lucier, James P. "Panama Canal: Focus of Power Politics," *Strategic Review,* Spring 1974.

MacAvoy, Paul. "David Stockman's Secret," *New York Times,* 22 November 1981.

MacPherson, Myra. "The Campaign Chieftans," *Washington Post,* Potomac Magazine, 5 September 1980.

Maltz, Albert. "Moving Forward," *New Masses,* 9 April 1946.

———. "What Shall We Ask of Writers," *New Masses,* 12 February 1946.

Mann, Judy. "Bad Image," *Washington Post,* 20 November 1981.

Manners, Mary Jane. "Making a Double Go of It," *Silver Screen,* August 1941.

Matthews, Linda. "Woodcock Warns Reagan Stand Perils Ties to China," *Los Angeles Times,* 27 August 1980.

Mayer, Caroline E., "Bush: Rules Reform Has Long Way to Go," *Washington Post,* 31 December 1981.

———. "Economists Call Regulatory Reform Too Slow, Narrow," *Washington Post,* 9 December 1981.

McAdams, Frank. "What Price Glory, Capt. Reagan?" *Los Angeles Times,* 27 August 1980.

McDaniel, Wanda. "Nancy Reagan, Behind the Mask," *Washington Post,* 11 November 1980.

McFeatters, Ann. "Watt Plans Campaign to Change His Image," *Ft. Smith Southwest-Times Record,* 9 June 1981.

Miller, Norman C. "Perspective on Politics," *Wall Street Journal,* 8 February 1982.

Naughton, James M. "Reagan Virtually Concedes Defeat in North Carolina," *New York Times,* 22 March 1976.

Newsweek. "A Disengaged Presidency," 7 September 1981.

———. "The First Lady's World," 21 December 1981.

———. "A Grand Old Man of Parts," 14 March 1980.

———. "Reagan Is Back in the Saddle," 10 March 1980.

———. "Reds: Star Witnesses," 3 November 1947.

———. "Ronald Reagan Up Close," 21 July 1980.

Nugent, Frank S. " 'Brother Rat,' " *New York Times,* 5 November 1938.

Nyhan, David. "A Golden Night for Reagan," *Boston Globe,* 1 June 1980.

———. "Yessir, He's Quite a Guy," *Boston Globe,* 7 August 1980.

Oberdorfer, Don. "Haig's Asian Venture: From Diplomatic Heights to a Political Downer," *Washington Post,* 27 June 1981.

Parsons, Louella O. "Last Call for Happiness," *Photoplay,* April 1948.

People magazine. "Five Former Co-Stars Rate Reagan as a Leading—and Sometimes Misleading—Man," 10 August 1981.

———. "The President-Elect Talks About His Health, His Children and His Divorce," 29 December 1981.

Peoria Journal-Star, 17 October 1980.

Perry, James M. "Reagan's Roots," *Wall Street Journal,* 8 October 1980.

Perry, William J. Testimony Before Senate Sub-Committee on Strategic and Theater Nuclear Forces, 13 November 1981.

Pincus, Walter. "Behind Reagan's Tough Talk, A Unilateral Arms Reduction," *Washington Post,* 10 January 1982.

———. " '2 Little Guys' With a Big Idea," *Washington Post,* 13 August 1981.

Prochnau, William. "Mormon Church Joins Opposition to MX Program," *Washington Post,* 6 May 1981.

Quinn, Sally. "A One-Man Woman, A One-Woman Man," *Washington Post,* 10 June 1976.

Radcliffe, Donnie. "The Texas Mission," *Washington Post,* 17 February 1982.

Rankin, Jerry. "Reagan Ranch: Next Western White House?" *Santa Barbara News Press,* 22 June 1980.

Reagan Campaign Plan, Decision Making Information. Santa Ana, California, June 1980.

Reagan, Collection of State Papers, Hoover Institute, Stanford University.

Reagan, Ronald (Dutch). "Dutch Reagan's Own Story," *Des Moines Register and Tribune,* 13 June 1937, with occasional articles until 28 October 1937.

Reagan, Ronald. "How Do You Fight Communism," *Fortnight,* 22 January 1951.

———. How to Make Yourself Important," *Photoplay,* August 1942.

Reid, T. R. "Reagan's Register Totals 25 Percent Less," *Washington Post,* 1 January 1982.

Rosellini, Lynn. "Reagan Aides Show Capital Luxury Style," *New York Times,* 16 August 1981.

Rowe, James L., Jr. "Financial Leaders Enthusiastic Over Reagan Plan," *Washington Post,* 20 February 1981.

Safire, William. "Those Upraised Hands," *New York Times,* 16 June 1981.

Salditch, Martin. "Style Triumphs Over Knowledge When Reagan Meets the Press," *Riverside-Press Enterprise,* 19 March 1967.

Samuelson, Robert J. "The Supply Side Revisited," *National Journal,* 21 November 1981.

Schmidt, William E., "Watt Gaining Approval of Most Western Governors," *New York Times,* 13 September 1981.

Scott, Joe. *The Political Animal,* Torrance, Ca.

Shapiro, Walter. "The Stockman Express," *Washington Post Magazine,* 8 February 1981.

Sherwood, John. "The Real Life, Inside, Movie Mag Scoops About Ronnie and Jane," *Washington Post,* 23 November 1980.

Shields, Mark. "President Reagan's Wide World of Sports," *Inside Sports,* 31 March 1981.

———. "The Reagan Difference," *Washington Post,* 11 November 1981.

Shogan, Robert. "Bush Ends His Waiting Game," *Los Angeles Times,* 14 April 1980.

Shogan, Robert, and Gaylord Shaw. "Reagan's Broom Sweeps Uneasily," *Los Angeles Times,* 17 January 1982.

Sinclair, Ward, and Peter Behr. "Horse Trading," *Washington Post,* 27 June 1981.

Skelton, George. "Reagan Calls CHP to Protect UC Campus," *Sacramento Union,* 6 February 1969.

———. "Reagan Setbacks: Is Political Grip Failing," *Los Angeles Times,* 5 February 1974.

Skelton, Nancy. "An Hour With Nancy," *Sacramento Bee,* 5 May 1974.

———. "Nancy Reagan—Does She Run the State or the Home," *Sacramento Bee,* 10 July 1968.

Smith, Hedrick. "Role Reversal in the Reagan Cabinet," *New York Times,* 14 September 1981.

Smith, Martin. "Reagan's Latest Campaign Brings Same Message, But New Audience," *Sacramento Bee,* 18 November 1979.

Snyder, Camilla. "A Reagan at Large," *Washington Star,* 9 November 1975.

Stammer, Larry. "Reagan Checks His Options for '76 White House Drive," *San Jose Mercury News,* 16 December 1973.

Stegner, Wallace. "If the Sagebrush Rebels Win, Everybody Loses," *Living Wilderness,* Summer 1981.

Stockman, David A. "The Social Pork Barrel," *Public Interest,* Spring 1975.

Time. "Backing Down on Benefits," 12 October 1981.

———. "Making It Work," 21 September 1981.

———. "Out of the Past, Fresh Choices for the Future," 5 January 1981.

———. "The President's Men," 14 December 1981.

———. "Reagan's Rousing Return," 10 March 1980.

———. 6 October 1947.

————. 7 October 1966.

————. 16 August 1968; 6 September 1968.

Toth, Robert. "Administration to Scrap Original MX Land-Basing Plan, Says Meese," *Los Angeles Times, Boston Globe,* 31 July 1981.

Trebbe, Ann L. "Heart to Heart With Haig and Weinberger," *Washington Post,* November 1981.

Udall, Morris. "A Master Stroke," *Washington Post,* 13 July 1981.

U.S. News and World Report. "The Reagans Try to Soften Their Millionaire Image," 19 October 1981.

Waldman, Myron S. "Growing up in the Midwest," *Newsday Sunday Magazine,* 18 January 1981.

Walsh, Edward. "Carter Criticizes Reagan on Arms Control," *Washington Post,* 7 October 1980.

Weisman, Steven R. "Reagan's Style: Focusing on 'The Big Picture,' " *New York Times,* 7 August 1981.

Whalen, Richard J. "Why Ronald Reagan Will Be the Next President," *Washington Post,* 23 March 1980.

Wicker, Tom. " 'Working On' Blacks," *New York Times,* 16 February 1982.

Will, George F. "A Good Idea Concealed in a Bad Speech," *Washington Post,* 8 November 1981.

————. "The Smear," *Washington Post,* 5 September 1980.

Wilner, Paul. "Live From Paris," *Los Angeles Herald-Examiner,* 23 November 1981.

Wilson, George C. "Brown Denies Politicking," *Washington Post,* 5 September 1980.

Woods, Tom. "Phil Battaglia, Chief of Staff," Pacific Coast News Service, 2 February 1967.

Zumbrun, Ronald A., Raymond H. Momboisse, and John H. Findley. "Welfare Reform: California Meets the Challenge," *Pacific Law Journal,* July 1973.

Index